Almost a Crime

Also by Penny Vincenzi

Old Sins
Wicked Pleasures
An Outrageous Affair
Another Woman
Forbidden Places
The Dilemma
The Glimpses (short stories)
Windfall

Almost a Crime

Penny Vincenzi

First published in Great Britain in 1999 by
Orion
An imprint of Orion Books Ltd
Orion House, 5 Upper St Martin's Lane, London WC2H 9EA

A CIP catalogue record for this book is available from the British Library

ISBN 0 75281 448 6 (hardcover)
0 75282 506 2 (trade paperback)

Typeset by Deltatype Ltd, Birkenhead, Merseyside

Printed in Great Britain by
Clays Ltd, St Ives plc

For my family. Almost a dynasty . . .
With lots of love.

ACKNOWLEDGEMENTS

Almost a Crime has been even more of a learning curve than usual; even more than usual therefore, I owe a great deal to my teachers, who have been required to be even more patient and long-suffering than usual. I would like to thank the following people who gave of their time, expertise and seemingly bottomless well of knowledge: the roll call in no particular order, alphabetical or otherwise, includes Lorraine Lindsay-Gale, Frances Sparkes, Diana de Grunwald, Roger Freeman, Pete Frost, Chris Phillipsborn, Penny Rossi, Julia Kaufmann, Virginia Fisher, Martin Le Jeune, Jane Reed, Alison Clark, Fraser Kemp MP and Carol Reay. I would like to thank Nicola Foulston for allowing me such full access to Brands Hatch and its environs, and also Tim Jones of Brands Hatch for his kindness; Henry Talbot for an absolutely marvellous tour of the House of Commons; Sue Stapely (yet again) for a specially wide-ranging contribution and set of contacts, and Georgina and Christopher Bailey for their hospitality and generosity in Barbados.

I have to thank, as always, Orion for yet more brilliant publishing, most notably Rosie de Courcy for her editing which is tactful, patient and inspired in equal and equally important measures. Other Orion luminaries include Dallas Manderson who sells the books with such determination and skill, Lucie Stericker who made *Almost a Crime* look beautiful, Susan Lamb for her own particular brand of clear-sighted input and Camilla Stoddart who put the nuts and bolts in place. Others who should certainly not go unthanked are Kati Nicholl who worked such a miracle in cutting out thousands of words from the book without me ever noticing it, Emma Draude from Midas PR who has seen that the entire world knows about it, and Trevor Leighton who took yet another dazzling cover photograph. And of course Desmond Elliott, my agent, who not only does all the usual agent-like things, but makes me laugh and tells me wonderful stories I can incorporate in the books. And on the home front, I'd like to thank dear Carol Osborne who so tirelessly sees that the front of the home does indeed remain orderly, makes the best puddings in the world and even walks the dogs when the deadlines don't permit me to do it.

A large and heartfelt thank you to my four daughters, Polly, Sophie, Emily and Claudia, so frequently, inescapably and patiently on the receiving end of my wails of panic that the book will never be finished/ get published/be read by anyone at all; and most of all and once again my husband, Paul, who continues to soothe my anguish, steady my nerves, even at three in the morning, pour me endless glasses of Chardonnay when all else fails and most importantly never proffers advice or opinion until I absolutely drag them out of him (when both are invariably of five star quality). As always, looking back, it was the best fun . . .

CHAPTER I

The first time Octavia Fleming was asked if she and her husband would appear in a feature in a glossy magazine about power marriages she had laughed aloud; of course she and Tom weren't powerful, she said, they were just two rather overworked professional people and what was a power marriage anyway? It was a marriage, the editor had said carefully, that was mutually supportive professionally as well as personally: 'and, we feel, one of the major sociological icons of the 'nineties'. Octavia had said that neither she nor Tom had any idea they were sociologically interesting.

'Well,' the editor had said, 'there you are, you in the charity business, your husband in public affairs; there must be so many occasions when your paths cross, when you can help one another with contacts, or by discussing things together, by being aware of the same sort of situations. One of our other interviewees,' she finished, 'defined it as a marriage whose sum was greater than its parts.'

'You mean the opposite of divide and rule?' said Octavia, and the editor said yes, she supposed she did and that would be a good quote too.

Octavia had said she'd think about and discuss it with Tom; rather to her surprise he agreed, providing he could approve the text. He said his consultancy could do with the publicity; Octavia had supposed that rather proved the editor's point.

The article about five such marriages as theirs appeared three months later and was entitled 'Combine and Rule'. The feature was illustrated with some rather nice photographs – Octavia with her intense dark beauty, Tom with his slightly gaunt elegance, both of them inevitably over-glamorised. That, together with what had then been a new and rather attractive concept – the power marriage – had raised their profiles considerably.

Other articles followed: in glossy magazines or the women's pages in national and Sunday newspapers. Tom and Octavia became used to being recognised in the sort of places where the chattering classes gathered; people would pause with their forkfuls of rocket salad raised to their lips in smart restaurants and point them out to one another, would hurry across the room at receptions to claim a greater acquaintance with them than they actually had. And they would receive invitations to parties to launch products or meet people whom they had never heard of or hardly knew, their very presence, vaguely famous, helping to lend the right connotations of gloss and glamour to a gathering.

They didn't mind, rather the reverse (although the quote from one 'friend', that she would practically pay them to have them at a dinner party, had made Octavia squirm), and there was no doubt that both their professional lives benefited.

What it did for the marriage itself, Octavia was rather less sure . . .

CHAPTER 2

June 1997

'Octavia, I've got Tom on the line. He says can you possibly fit in drinks with him this evening? Six in the American Bar at the Savoy. He says it won't take more than an hour because then he's got to go on to a dinner. I said I didn't think you could, but—'

Octavia sometimes thought that Sarah Jane Carstairs, her awesomely efficient secretary, would make a much better job of being Mrs Tom Fleming. She would never double book herself, over-extend her energies, spread herself too thin. If Sarah Jane thought she couldn't be at the Savoy by six this evening, then she couldn't.

'I don't think I can either. I've got the meeting with a possible sponsor for Cultivate coming in at four thirty, haven't I?'

Sarah Jane smiled at her approvingly. 'I'll tell him. Now you'd better start winding up for lunch, Octavia. The cab's just phoned, be here in five minutes.'

'Yes, okay. Where am I going?'

'Daphne's.'

'Fine. Have you got the notes?'

'Yes. I'll just get them . . .'

She reappeared with a thick, rather battered file. 'Tom's rung again. He says if he makes it six thirty could you manage it? He'd really like you there.'

'Can I do that?'

'I should think so. Yes. Yes, I'll tell him. Now, I've put *everything* in here. Mrs Piper is always impressed by volume. The fact half the things in there are years old doesn't really matter. Oh, by the way, Tom also wants to know when Gideon's sports day is. I did tell him, but he's obviously forgotten.'

'July tenth.'

'Fine. I'll fax it, I think.'

And that conversation, thought Octavia, really did sum up her whole life. And how absurd a life it was, where she and Tom communicated through their secretaries, tried (and failed) to make appointments with one another, struggled to find the time to have a conversation together about quite ordinary things.

We must have a talk about the holiday, he would say, or we really should discuss Gideon's extra coaching, she would suggest, and they would both agree that yes they should, but there would be no time that day – he with a late dinner, she with a meeting out of town involving an overnight stay – nor the next – separate drinks parties, then a dinner, much too tired after that – maybe the weekend, except they were going to the country, taking the children but not the nanny, might be a bit tricky, but Sunday morning should be all right, yes, they'd try to talk then.

Time to spend together on their own had become a luxury, traded in for money, success. Most of the time, they had agreed, it was worth it, and even if one of them had thought it wasn't, there had been neither the time nor the opportunity to discuss that either.

Just the same, their marriage, in all its frantic singularity, seemed to work.

As Octavia walked out of her office, bracing herself for what was undoubtedly going to be a difficult lunchtime meeting, a loud shout of 'Shit!' came from the next office.

'What did you do this time?' she said, putting her head round the door.

'Wiped a whole report. Fuck, I hate these bloody things!'

Melanie Faulks, her business partner, was technophobic, and shrieked obscenities filled the air throughout the day, as she deleted her voice mail, wiped crucial information from reports and saved things under file names which no one could ever find.

'Mel, Lucy will have saved it.'

'I don't know that she has. And I need it for lunch. Oh, God—'

'Who are you having lunch with?'

'Some bimbo from the *Express*. Dear God, Lucy, where are you, please, please come and help me . . .'

As Octavia pushed through the swing doors on to the landing, she heard Lucy, Melanie's wonderfully serene secretary, saying, 'Melanie, of course I've got it, and I've run it off already, here, look . . .'

Octavia and Melanie ran a charity consultancy, Capital C, its claim being that it put client charities 'into capital letters' by advising on the raising of both funds and profile.

It was not a large company – there were two partners, and a handful of executive and administrative staff – but it was one of the top ten in the country; the turnover had run at over two million for the past three years, and looked like hitting two point five before the millennium.

Octavia had joined Capital C five years earlier. She had a degree in law, but she had disliked private practice, finding it at once tedious and stressful, and moved with relief into the corporate legal world, and thence into corporate consultancy, where one of her clients had been a large Third World charity, and another a chain of pharmacists. Five years later the pharmacy had been running at number three to Boots; Octavia's advice, shrewd and creative, was seen as a considerable factor.

She had met Melanie Faulks at a lunch; Melanie, then on the staff of a large charity herself, had phoned Octavia later that day; she was in the process of forming her own company and wondered if Octavia would like to discuss a possible involvement. It was love at first sight, Octavia often said, laughing; two meetings later she and Melanie were engaged, and three months after that married.

Octavia brought to her clients a book of contacts that was breathtaking in its range, and she networked tirelessly ('Octavia does all her best work in the ladies',' one of her rivals had been heard to say rather bitterly). One of the stronger arms that Capital C had developed as a result of her input was that of broker, persuading individuals and institutions to sponsor clients with considerable amounts of money.

Octavia's profile was high and she was smoothly skilful at her job, at handling the odd blend of cynicism and sentimentality that characterises the charity business. 'And it is a business, however much people dislike the fact,' she would say at every presentation, every client pitch.

The offices were in a mansion block at the South Kensington end of the Old Brompton Road; she and Melanie had chosen them with great care. Not a shiny, modern ritzy job (bad for the image), not too expensive an area (same reason, although the consultancy could easily have sustained a higher rent), sleekly streamlined in design inside (to avoid any possible connotations of ladies working at home, playing at business). Octavia and Melanie had small self-contained offices, the rest was open plan divided by furniture, smoked-glass screens, and – the only gesture towards femininity – a great many plants and flowers. There were white roman blinds at the windows, bleached faux-parquet on the floor, and the furniture was starkly functional, in black and white.

The charity field was tough and very competitive. Octavia, also competitive and fairly tough, loved it.

Margaret Piper was already at the table when Octavia arrived, sipping at a glass of tomato juice and flicking through a very battered diary.

'We did say one, didn't we?' she asked.

'We did,' said Octavia, looking at her watch, managing to smile at her. 'So we're both early. Which is very good, as we have so much to talk about. I'll have a mineral water,' she said to the wine waiter, 'and shall we order straight away, Margaret, so we can concentrate on business after that?'

'Yes, very well.'

Octavia ordered a green salad and some steamed sole for herself, listened enviously as Margaret Piper asked for deep-fried mozzarella and rack of lamb, and pulled out some papers.

'Now then. I've prepared a report on progress so far this year—'

'But there hasn't been very much, has there, Mrs Fleming?' said Margaret Piper. 'Our profile has hardly been raised at all, and we are very disappointed in your failure to find us a sponsor.'

'Well, I can understand that,' said Octavia, 'but these things do take time. You're competing for a share in a very overcrowded market.'

'Overcrowded perhaps, but certain charities continue to get a great deal of publicity. Every time I pick up the paper I seem to read about the Macmillan nurses. And Dr Barnardo's. And Action Aid—'

'Yes, of course you do, Mrs Piper, but you have picked three charities out of the really big league. All those have incomes of over twenty-five million pounds. They're extremely well established, terribly popular, household words.'

'All the more reason, surely, for getting some publicity for Cultivate,' said Margaret Piper.

'It isn't quite that straightforward . . .'

'Obviously not. That is why we came to you. Now there's some other new charity, what is it called, oh yes, Network, which is getting a great deal of publicity. How do you explain that?'

'Oh, well now—' Careful, Octavia, not to start justifying yourself, it won't help, especially as Network was also one of Capital C's charities. 'Network is in exactly the field I told you about at the very beginning, that gains high visibility very quickly. It's a support organisation for bereaved parents and therefore attracts great sympathy. Everyone can imagine themselves in that situation, most people know someone in it. Cultivate is outside most people's immediate realm of experience. And there are so many big charities in its field, like Oxfam, Action Aid . . . you really are facing some very stiff competition. And you may remember I said, at our first meeting, public sympathy, and therefore interest, does go primarily to children, anything to do with children, particularly sick children and little children. Now Cultivate is a marvellous charity, encouraging communities in the Third World to help themselves, but it isn't something that gains instant memorability or appeal. It's a slow process, do believe me. But we will get there.'

'Well,' said Margaret Piper, buttering her second roll rather viciously,

'I suppose we have to believe we are in the hands of experts—' her tone and expression making it clear she believed nothing of the sort – 'but our finance director has said that we really cannot commit ourselves to another year of expenditure on your services without considerable results.'

'Fair enough. And you shall have them,' said Octavia, sending up a fervent prayer to the Almighty, who she hoped was hovering in the area of Draycott Avenue at the time. 'I really think I might have a sponsor for you at last, and we have an excellent chance of a big article in the *Guardian* next month. They're doing a supplement on overseas charities and—'

'I would have hoped for something more exclusive.'

'Yes, but this would still be very good.' Octavia raised her arm, waved at the waiter. 'Mrs Piper, are you sure you wouldn't like a drink while we wait for our food?'

'Well, perhaps just a small gin and tonic.'

That was good. Octavia remembered her mellowing very swiftly under the influence of alcohol at their last lunch. 'Now, if I could just take you through these figures I think you'll see that things are much improved on this time last year, and I have to tell you I'm still wondering about the name . . .'

Tom was already in the American Bar at the Savoy when Octavia rushed in, almost fifteen minutes late, but he was not looking alternately at his watch and the entrance as she would have done, he was at one of the prized corner tables – of *course* he was at a corner table – reading the *Financial Times*, apparently perfectly relaxed. Only a handful of people, Octavia included, would have known that Tom was never relaxed, any more than she was, but he was masterly at appearing so. It was a great part of his charm, making people feel comfortable and at ease in his company.

He was already in his dinner jacket – he had two, one kept at the office. He loved clothes and spent a lot of money on them. His suits were all hand tailored, and his shoes were handmade; his shirts he bought mostly from Thomas Pink and other such establishments in Jermyn Street, or from Brooks Brothers on trips to the States, his leisure clothes mostly from Ralph Lauren. He often said that in another life he would like to have been a fashion editor. Octavia was the reverse. She would spend hours trying and retrying things on and still often go back to change or return them. She was thinking of turning the whole thing over to a style consultant to do her shopping for her; apart from ridding her of a great deal of indecisive misery, it would save her time. Precious time . . .

Tom stood up, kissed her. 'Hallo, darling, it's very good of you to come, I know it was difficult.'

'Oh, anything for you, Tom,' said Octavia, returning the kiss. She sat down opposite him. 'Anyway, it's nice to stop for a bit.'

'You look tired. Bad day?'

'Terrible actually.'

'Have a drink. Can I tempt you, just for once?'

'No, I'll just have a mineral water. With lots of ice.'

She hardly ever drank; she hated any loss of control, any blurring of her clear cool mind.

'What was so bad about your day?'

'Oh, the usual. Disgruntled client at lunchtime, useless sponsor over tea – now where is it you're going after this, Tom? I've forgotten.'

'City dinner.'

'With?'

'Oh, a couple of captains of industry. Look, I haven't got time to discuss that now, Octavia. Luckily the client is late so I can brief you.'

'I'm all ears. Who is it?'

'It's Michael Carlton. Property developer.'

'Oh, that one. Opera. Last autumn.'

'Yes, that one. Anyway, he wants to build on a greenfield site. Local people don't like the idea, big protest group formed. We've done all the right things, courted the planners and councillors, gone to endless meetings with terrible Nimbys. And it might have just about gone through, but today there's a horribly nasty piece in the local paper, and I fear it'll make the nationals in no time.'

'Well, I'm very sorry for you and your Mr Carlton, Tom,' she said briskly, 'but what can I do about it?'

'I'll tell— Oh, shit, here he is now. Michael! Hallo, do come and sit down. You remember my wife, Octavia, don't you?'

'Of course I do. Very nice to see you again.'

Octavia's hand was pumped over-vigorously. She remembered Michael Carlton now. He was very large, not just overweight, but extremely tall, about six foot five. He had a shock of white hair, rather alarmingly brilliant-green eyes, and was surprisingly well dressed, in a dark grey three-piece suit, an old-fashioned gold watch chain slung across his large belly. Sitting beside Tom, he should have looked gross and vulgar, but for some reason he didn't.

His voice was booming, his accent neutral, his laugh loud; she remembered now enjoying his rather determined vulgarity. The opera had been one of Tom's rare pieces of bad judgment; Carlton had confided to her in a very loud stage whisper as the lights went down, that when it came to operas, *Phantom* was more his style. She remembered his constantly dropping off to sleep and fighting it, and liking him for that.

'Nice to see you too, Mr Carlton. How is your wife?'

Betty Carlton had been cheerfully plump, badly dressed, eager to please.

'Oh, not so bad. She's a bit low at the moment. Empty nest, all the kids gone. I'll have a large vodka martini, please,' he said to the waiter, 'and a very big bowl of peanuts.' He scooped the remaining nuts from the bowl on the table into his fist, ate them at one go.

'Terrible things, these,' he said to Octavia, 'thousands of calories each. But you know what? I don't care.'

Octavia, who would have given a great deal at that moment for even one peanut, forced herself to smile.

'Don't mention calories to Octavia,' said Tom, 'she's obsessed with the things. Virtually anorexic, aren't you, darling?'

'How absurd,' said Michael Carlton, 'with a wonderul figure like yours.'

People always said that, Octavia thought, smiling more determinedly still, people who could never connect the obsession with calories with the wonderful figure, assuming it came of its own accord.

'I asked Octavia along tonight,' said Tom, 'because what you're proposing is very much in her field.'

'Really?' said Octavia, staring at him. 'What *are* you proposing, Mr Carlton?'

'Michael is proposing, as well as the usual planning gain—'

'I'm sorry. Remind me about planning gain . . .'

'It's something a developer offers the local community along with the rest of his plans,' said Tom, irritation skimming briefly across his face. 'Might be a park, a swimming pool, something like that. Michael is offering a community centre. You know, social hall, sports club, all that sort of thing. And he wants to include some facilities for the handicapped.'

This was obviously an extremely sensitive site, thought Octavia.

'Where is it?'

'Oh, Somerset/Avon borders. Not so far from our cottage actually. Anyway, I told him about your work, particularly with Foothold—'

Foothold was one of the charities Capital C advised. It funded research into juvenile arthritis, equipment for the children, and perhaps most crucially, respite weekends for the parents.

'Oh, yes?'

'And we thought you might have a local group down there who would be interested . . .'

'Oh, I see,' said Octavia.

'It could help us a lot. Get some of the locals on to our side, make the others see this development isn't all bad. Which it isn't.'

'No, I – suppose not.'

Octavia suddenly felt rather upset. Foothold was particularly dear to her heart, she had worked very hard on it, seen it move from a really small time charity into the five-million-a-year level with quite a high profile. She didn't really want it used in this way.

'Well, I could look into it, I suppose. People are always interested in improved facilities.'

'Of course,' Michael Carlton said. 'That's why I want to help.'

Yes, thought Octavia, and cut a swathe through yet another lovely forest or meadow, rape a bit more of the countryside. She felt very strongly about these things, hated it when Tom was on the side of the rapists. They fought about it endlessly. But she ought to give Carlton the benefit of the doubt.

'How marvellous of you,' she said. 'To think of the disabled, I mean. Well, I can certainly ask.'

'And I thought perhaps see what you could do to help in the way of local publicity?' said Tom.

'Well, possibly. Yes.'

'Now, talking of publicity, Tom, what are you going to do about stopping this stuff getting into the nationals?' said Michael Carlton. 'We can't afford it at this stage. I hope you're on top of that one.'

'We're doing all we can,' said Tom. 'I did get a couple of calls today, one from the *Express*, one from the *Mirror*. I played it very low-key, made it sound like a non-story.'

'You didn't talk about the community project? I'd have thought that would—'

'Michael, trust me. That could have been counterproductive. Journalists are very cynical. Far better tell them, as I did, it's yet another Swampy story. They're getting bored with those. So I think I've diverted them for now. But that's why I thought it might be a good idea to talk to Octavia. Get her to come in with some positive support at the local end. Don't you think, darling?'

'I'm not sure,' said Octavia, aware that she should be sounding more enthusiastic.

'Octavia—'

'You mustn't make your wife compromise herself if she doesn't want to, Tom,' said Michael Carlton suddenly.

'What I meant,' she said quickly, 'was that I really couldn't commit my clients – and therefore myself – to anything at all.'

'No, of course not. I appreciate that.' His martini had arrived, been drunk and reordered. The peanut bowl was empty again. 'Tell me, what other charities are you involved in, Octavia?'

'Oh, dozens,' she said lightly.

'She's a great star in that world,' said Tom. 'Aren't you, darling?'

'Well, you know,' she said, 'maybe a medium-size one.'

'My wife's a great charity worker,' said Michael Carlton. 'Always standing outside the local supermarket, shaking a tin, organising ladies' lunches, that sort of thing. Takes up a lot of her time though.'

'It would,' said Octavia, 'but without field workers like your wife, all charities would be quite lost.'

'Is that so? Tell me, do you get involved with those big bashes? Royalty coming along and all that sort of thing?'

'Sometimes . . .'

'I imagine people will do anything to get in on one of those things. Pressing the flesh and so on.'

'To an extent. It's still not easy.'

'Oh, go on. I bet you can think of a number and double it. Supposing it was someone like Di?'

'Well, yes. Obviously. But she's virtually impossible to get.'

'That is the holy grail though, isn't it, darling? The honeypot number,' said Tom. 'Get your charity associated with someone really charismatic, and the money just flows in. How was your meeting this evening, by the way? With your would-be sponsor? Any good?'

Octavia stared at him. He knew it hadn't been. Why should he ask her again? Then she realised.

'Octavia is looking for a sponsor for one of her charities,' said Tom to Michael Carlton.

'Really? Which one would that be?'

'Oh, it's confidential, I'm afraid,' said Octavia.

'Why on earth should it be?' said Tom. 'Tell us about it, darling, we'd like to hear.'

'It's a Third World charity,' she said quickly, confident Michael Carlton wouldn't be interested in such a thing, 'one of the God-helps-those-who-help-themselves sort, called Cultivate. We supply tools, grain, pumps, know-how, and then they farm and feed themselves.'

'Jolly good,' said Michael Carlton unexpectedly. 'That's exactly what they should be doing. My son works out in one of those places, you know – he's a man of the cloth – and he says Ethiopia is only just beginning to recover from what he calls the Geldof effect.'

'What on earth's that?' said Tom.

'The whole country was flooded with free food, right?' said Carlton. 'After that concert of his.'

'Yes. So?'

'So anyone who was farming just starved to death themselves. Who would pay for food if they didn't need to?'

'Yes, it was a terrible piece of misplaced benefaction,' said Octavia.

'It was indeed. Counterproductive. And your Cultivate is doing exactly the opposite?'

'Yes. Yes, it is.'

'And what sort of a sponsor are you looking for?'

'Someone who'll put X thousand pounds into the fund in the coming year.'

'And what do they get in return?'

'A high profile. Their name and logo on all promotional material – programmes, advertising material and press releases. Maximum visibility at fundraising bashes and so on.'

'And you can't get it?'

'Well,' she said carefully, 'it's very very hard to get sponsorship. Products are easy, people can always come up with a car or a holiday to auction. But sponsorship means parting with money. *Real* money.'

'Yes, I can see that. Well, you tell me how much you're looking for and I'll tell you how much I'm prepared to find. How's that?'

She stared at him. 'Well, I . . .'

'Oh, come on,' Carlton said impatiently, 'this is a no-strings offer. Or don't you trust me?'

'Of course I do. It's not that, I just—'

'You just think I'm doing this for my own ends. Well, I am. But all good publicity is good publicity. And I can hardly start pumping money into your other charity, can I? That really would be a bit transparent. Besides, I like the sound of this . . . Cultivate. Terrible name, that. They ought to change it. Well, there's the offer. Yes or no?'

Octavia stared at him, her mind totally engaged suddenly. Margaret Piper had made it very clear that if no sponsor was forthcoming, she would sack Capital C at the end of the year. That would mean not just the loss of income, but loss of face. It was always bad to lose an account. And there was no one else she could think of to approach for money. On the other hand, if she accepted Carlton's offer, it would put her in a very difficult position with the local branch of Foothold – always supposing there was one. She would be obliged virtually to drag it into his fight for local approval, and that would be very unethical. Better in the long run to lose Cultivate.

'I really feel I should refuse,' she said, genuinely reluctant. 'It might compromise all of us. If we were seen to be in each other's pockets. Don't you, Tom?'

'I don't think so, no,' Tom said, and she could tell he was annoyed. 'I certainly feel you should think about it carefully. It's a very generous offer, Michael.'

'Balls,' said Carlton cheerfully. 'Not generous at all. It could help me. And to that end, what's – shall we say fifty grand, Octavia? Or would a hundred be more like it?'

Octavia felt suddenly dizzy. 'I haven't really thought about exact figures,' she said.

'Well, that doesn't impress me too much,' said Carlton. 'I thought you were a businesswoman.'

She was stung; he had hit her where it hurt. Probably as he intended. 'Fifty is around what we're looking for actually. The bottom end, that is.'

'Good. I'll make it seventy-five. All right?'

'Well,' she said, feeling slightly panicked by the pressure, 'of course I must talk to my partner. Perhaps we could all meet.'

Tom looked at his watch, stood up. 'I must leave you, I'm afraid,' he said. 'Have to be at the Mansion House in ten minutes. My driver's waiting. Octavia, darling, I shouldn't be too late. Home about eleven thirty.'

'Fine,' she said. 'I'll probably still be up, I've got loads of paperwork to do. Only thing is, I've got an early start, breakfast meeting.' She lifted her face to his, he bent and kissed her cheek. 'Bye, Tom. Have a good evening.'

She watched Tom as he left, then turned back to Carlton. He was leaning against his seat, looking at her, his own eyes amused.

'Ah, the joys of – what is it you and Tom share? Oh, yes, a "power marriage"? I was reading about you only the other week, Betty showed me the article.'

'You shouldn't believe everything you read in the papers, Mr Carlton.'

'Michael, Octavia, please. I don't. Another drink?'

'No, thank you. I have to get home, to my children.'

'The twins? And a baby. Is that right?'

'Yes,' she said, surprised he should remember.

'I seem to recall you'd only just had the baby. I was impressed you stayed awake. Ours have all gone. I miss them, not as much as Betty does, of course, but I still do. You want to make the most of them while they're little.'

'Yes,' she said, 'I try to.'

'You're missing a lot, you know,' he said, looking at her thoughtfully, 'working all the time. Pity, really. It's over so quickly.'

Irritation and resentment suddenly filled Octavia. 'Mr Carlton – sorry, Michael – I don't really think it's anything to do with you,' she said, smiling at him with a great effort, 'how I run my family. Of course I miss them, but—'

'It *is* something to do with me,' he said, 'because I like you. And I can see you're not nearly as tough as you make out. You'll regret it when they're grown up. You'll wonder where the time went. Anyway – sorry. You must do things your own way of course. And I've got to go as well. Let me know about the sponsorship deal. I really mean it.'

'Thank you,' she said. She felt close to tears. 'And of course I will get back to you, but I don't really think . . .' As they both stood up, he towered over her and she felt oddly swamped by him, not just his size, but the strength of his personality. He would be a dangerous opponent, she thought.

He handed her her briefcase, smiled at her. It was a genuinely warm, fatherly smile. 'I've enjoyed our conversation,' he said. 'Honestly. Can I get you a cab?'

'No, the doorman will do it. Thank you. Goodbye – Michael.'

He grinned again, his huge hand surrounding hers. 'Goodbye, Octavia. And I think you should cut out the power breakfasts at least.'

She managed to smile again and left.

The twins were in their pyjamas watching the nursery TV when she got back, and greeted her rather desultorily. Minty was asleep, her bedclothes thrown off, nesting amongst a mound of toys in her cot, small bottom thrust into the air, dark curls stuck damply to the nape of her neck. Octavia looked at her, in all her small sweet rosy perfection, tried to imagine her one day noisy, restlessly argumentative like the twins, and failed, or rather quailed from it, heard Carlton's voice again – 'You want to make the most of them when they're little.'

She pulled the quilt tenderly up over the small body, and as she turned and left the room, she found her eyes full of tears.

She knew why: and it wasn't just because of what Michael Carlton had said.

Caroline, the nanny, was in the kitchen when Octavia went down, and greeted her rather coolly. 'Ah, Mrs Fleming. What happened?'

'What do you mean, what happened?' said Octavia sharply. She felt unable to cope with any more conflict.

'I thought you were getting home by seven at the latest, this evening. At least, that's what you said.'

'Oh, God!' She had told Caroline she could have the evening off.

'I'm so sorry, Caroline. You were going out, weren't you? Well, it's only—'

'Eight. Too late, I'm afraid. We were going to the cinema.'

'Caroline, I am sorry. My husband suddenly needed me to meet one of his clients and – oh, dear, what can I say? I forgot. How dreadful of me. Are you sure it's too late?'

'Yes, I'm afraid so. I'd arranged to meet my boyfriend at seven.'

'You should have rung me. On my mobile.'

'I did try.'

Yes, and of course she had switched it off, for the Savoy. She looked at Caroline rather helplessly. 'Well, look, you must have – oh, dear, not this weekend off, we've got people over from the States. Maybe next—'

'The next one would be nice, Mrs Fleming. As actually we did agree – perhaps you've forgotten.' Her voice was polite, but her expression was very hard. 'I've arranged to go away, and—'

'No, of course I haven't forgotten,' said Octavia quickly.

Caroline was supposed to have three weekends a month off; lately it had dwindled to more like the other way round. She was quite good natured beneath her daunting manner, and she was very fond of all three children, Minty in particular, but reneging on what was, after all, a written contract, clearly made her angry. She did not smile now at Octavia, merely turned towards the door.

Octavia, reading her body language, sensing danger (for she had seen four nannies off already in her eight years of motherhood), said, 'No, of course you must have that weekend. Why don't you take the Monday as well, make it a really long one? Friday would be more difficult, we've got some do, I think, but—'

'Oh, that would be marvellous, Mrs Fleming. Thank you. If you can manage it . . .'

'Yes, of course I can. We certainly owe it to you. And Caroline, I'm sorry about this evening. Again.'

'Thank you, Mrs Fleming. Right, well, I think I'll go up to my room now, I'm very tired. Oh, by the way, your father phoned. No message, but he'll ring again.'

He certainly will, thought Octavia; she might leave the answering machine to deal with him. 'Fine,' she said, 'thank you.'

Caroline turned and ran up the stairs. Octavia watched her, thinking distractedly what good legs she had, how pretty she was altogether, tall, fair haired, athletic looking, wondering why she had chosen to be a nanny of all things. Her father was a prosperous solicitor and she'd gone to a good school; she had A-levels, she could have done anything, anything at all, and yet she'd opted to take care of other people's children. Very odd: even if the rewards (£200 a week clear, own flat, sole use of car) were so good. No status, no freedom . . . Well, better not waste time meditating on that one, thought Octavia, pouring boiling water on to her peppermint teabag – she could save on a lot of calories if she cut out supper – and went back to the playroom, concentrating her thoughts and the necessary willpower on her children. They deserved some of her, quite a lot of her; they really didn't get enough.

The twins had wearied of their video and were engaged in their favourite occupation of arguing. People who disapproved of Octavia – or who, more precisely, were envious of her, resented her success, her charmed life, her gilded lifestyle – often said it was irritatingly predictable that she would have had twins, would have instantly acquired a family, rather than just a child, would have got pregnancy and breastfeeding and postnatal exhaustion and the inevitable career break over and done with all at once. No wondering when or indeed whether to embark on the next pregnancy for Octavia; there it was, her family (and even a boy and a girl, for heaven's sake), readymade, with the least possible inconvenience not only to herself but her colleagues and her clients as well.

Octavia herself, delighted by the charm, the distinction of twins, was at first unaware of the professional benefits they brought her, and was surprised and hurt the first time she heard these expressed by an outside source; later on, she was amused – and faintly shocked – to find herself recognising its wisdom.

The first occupant of a professional woman's womb is a novelty, interesting both to herself and to others – not least in the challenge it represents to her lifestyle and working systems; the second is an also ran, recognised for what it is, a necessary adjunct to the first, at once easier and more difficult to accommodate, the absence from the desk so much less acceptable, the non-availability to clients and colleagues so much more tedious. All Octavia's professional friends had taken less time off with the second baby (while needing it more), most of them back within two months: all pale, thin, manically over-conscientious. In contrast, Octavia's progress through the maze of working motherhood was, if not smooth, at least steady, and she was most gratefully aware of the fact. Until, of course, the arrival of Minty . . .

But she thought now, climbing the stairs on legs that were suddenly heavily and weakly weary, the twins, however convenient, were immensely exhausting. She could hear them arguing about what they were going to watch or do next; they argued all the time, it was to them like breathing, a constant background to everything they did. She had hoped that when they had been separated, sent to different schools – or rather when Poppy had been sent to Bute House, as part of her inevitable progression to St Paul's Girls' School, leaving Gideon at Hill House, on his own inevitable one to Winchester – that they would meet at the end of each day more peacefully. But they did not. It wasn't that they didn't like each other, rather the reverse, but simply that they possessed a tumultuous energy, which fuelled in its turn an intense need to pursue any disagreement, any difference of opinion, to its logical end. Peaceable settlement of any matter was out of the question.

Even asleep they were restless, tossing and turning, talking, even giggling. They had wild, unruly dark hair, brilliantly deep-blue eyes, ceaselessly watchful expressions. They were almost nine now, and very alike; perhaps more so in their middle childhood, resolutely asexual, than they ever would be again. They were incredibly exhausting: that was another thing people said about twins, that they were easier, once the first year was over, than ordinary siblings, but nobody could have said that of Gideon and Poppy.

Octavia took a deep breath now, braced herself, went into the playroom. 'Hallo again. Had a good day?'

'Gross,' said Gideon.

'Brilliant,' said Poppy.

'Okay, one at a time! Why gross, Gideon?'

'Got gated.'

'What for?'

'Talking. In Latin.'

'What a surprise.'

'Yeah, and I didn't get into the soccer team. That pig Johnson did instead, he's so—'

'Much better than you?' said Poppy sweetly.

'Shut up, Poppy! Of course he's not. He's been practising on the sly, that's why, and sucking up to—'

'You can't practise on the sly,' said Poppy, who was a stickler for syntax. 'You can only do things on the sly that aren't allowed. Practising soccer is obviously allowed, there's nothing wrong with it.'

'There might be,' said Gideon darkly.

'How could there be?'

'Look,' said Octavia, 'Johnson wouldn't have been chosen for the team unless he was good enough. Bad luck, Gideon, but there's always next time.'

'It's all right for you,' said Gideon. 'You don't care about games, you wouldn't want to be in a team.'

This was so unarguable that Octavia was silent for a moment; then she rallied.

'No, but I know about getting in other things. Like companies I want to work for and can't, it's like that really. I know about being disappointed.'

'Work!' said Gideon. 'That's all you think about. How could work be as important as playing for your school?'

'I think it's about the same actually,' said Octavia firmly. 'Now then, Poppy. What was so good about your day?'

'Lots! I came top in French *and* got asked to Camilla Bartlett's party.'

'Did you, darling? How lovely.'

'More than lovely,' said Poppy. 'Her dad's renting a plane and flying twelve of us to France. I've got a letter here.'

'Good heavens,' said Octavia, her eyes scanning the letter ('. . . love you to join us . . . 19 June . . . Le Touquet . . . day by the French seaside . . . bring swimmers and something a bit more formal to wear for lunch . . . ask your mother to phone me . . . Lauren Bartlett . . .'), 'whatever happened to musical bumps?'

'It might be bumpy,' said Gideon, 'on the plane. They often are, those little ones. Then you'd be sick. Then you might not be so pleased.'

'Oh, shut up, Gideon. Why do you have to spoil everything?'

'That's not spoiling it. That's just being truthful.'

'Of course it's spoiling it, it's saying it won't be nice, when it will.'

'You don't know that.'

'Yes, I do.'

'Twins, please!' said Octavia wearily. 'Listen, shall we play something before you go to bed?'

'Like what? Murder Mystery?'

'No, there isn't time for that. You know those games take hours.'

'So what, then?' Poppy's voice was heavy with sarcasm. 'Something like Scrabble? Pelmanism?'

'Something like that, yes.'

'Bor-ing,' they said in unison. 'No thanks.'

At least she had stopped them arguing.

They watched the first twenty minutes of *A Hundred and One Dalmations*, and then went to bed. The last thing Octavia heard as she went back down the stairs was them arguing (from their different rooms) about whether the landing light should be on or off.

Octavia went into her bedroom and changed into some leggings and a sweatshirt and then walked very slowly along the corridor to her study. She always spent her rare solitary evenings there, working, writing letters, making phone calls. It was where she felt happiest, most at home, most safe.

The day's post was on her desk, placed there by Mrs Donaldson. She put Poppy's invitation on the top of the pile, and sat looking at it, oddly unsettled by the events of her day; by the difficult lunch with Margaret Piper, by the contretemps with Caroline, by the near confrontation with Michael Carlton.

He was right, in a way, about the children. They did grow up so quickly, and you did miss so much. She hadn't been there when the twins had taken their first steps, or when Poppy had said her first joined-up sentence (although it was engraved on her heart and her conscience: 'Mummy gone work'), but could she really have spent all that time in all those years with them, long, long tedious days with nothing to think about but the house and the supper and whether they were going to get chickenpox this time round?

It was very shocking, but she feared she could not; the restless, questing, ambitious Octavia would have become bored, depressed, and therefore, and inevitably, a bad mother. Far better that she was fun, adoring, interesting for them. Only – that was what all working mothers argued. And it wasn't quite true. She knew it. She quite often wasn't interesting or fun; she was too tired, if she was there at all. The whole concept of quality time was a dreadful con. The quality was frequently very poor. And children wanted you when they wanted you; they didn't save things up to tell you, to talk to you about, cry over.

She sighed. She had always promised herself that one day, when the business could stand it, she would work less, a four- or three-day week, spend more time at home with the children. Only clients were rather like children, they also wanted you on demand. Most of their lives belonged to clients, Tom's as well as hers; no moment was sacred, no corner safe from them. She sometimes thought, in her wilder, more distressed moments, that if she woke up and found one of them lying between her and Tom in bed, and an earnest discussion going on about budgets or tactics, she would not be in the least surprised.

And sometimes, when she was really tired, really low, she had thought that whatever happened to their marriage, neither of them could possibly afford to leave it, so inextricably entwined was it in their professional as well as their personal lives.

CHAPTER 3

Octavia had sometimes been tempted to make up an interesting story about how she and Tom had met; it had been so extraordinarily dull, not good copy at all. Other people always seemed to have been blind dates, or met in operating theatres or on aeroplanes. Lauren and Drew Bartlett, the neighbours who were hosting the children's party in France, had met through a shared divorce lawyer. Louise, Octavia's best friend, had had a flirtatious letter sent over to her table by her husband at a ball. Melanie Faulks had met her one time husband doing a charity bungee jump.

Octavia and Tom had met at a lunch party, nowhere more original, more prophetic than that. She had seen him across the room and thought how absurdly good looking he was, and how well dressed (blue Oxford shirt, chinos and very nice shoes, brown brogues, Octavia always noticed shoes), and thought also that with looks like that he must be vain and immensely conceited. But later, when she was introduced to him ('Octavia, this is Tom Fleming, he's something to do with politics') and he was shaking her hand and smiling at her almost diffidently, assessing her with wonderfully dark grey eyes, and they began to talk, she realised she was wrong, that he was very far from either vanity or conceit, seemed actually slightly unsure of himself. It was very slight, the unsureness, and he had a tendency to play upon it, but he was certainly far more likeable than she would have imagined. He also possessed that particular genre of charm that persuades people they are much more amusing and agreeable than they had realised; in Tom's company silent people talked, dull ones made jokes, nervous ones relaxed. Octavia did not make jokes, but she relaxed and she found it easy to talk.

She told him she had never met a politician before, and he told her she still hadn't, he was far from being anything of the sort, thank God: 'No, I work for one of those new inventions, a public affairs consultancy. Which means we dabble in politics a bit: try to influence politicians and civil servants on behalf of our clients, that sort of thing. It's actually much more fun than politics, I think. What about you?'

'I'm a lawyer,' Octavia said, 'a corporate lawyer.'

'That sounds very grand,' he said, smiling. 'Let me get you some food while you tell me about it.'

'Only if you tell me about public affairs,' she said. Afterwards she thought how prophetic it had been that even their very first conversation should have been so workbased. And how genuinely enthralling each of them had found it. He asked her if she would like to have dinner with him, took her phone number.

Flattered, but never expecting to hear from him, she was amazed when three days later she came home to a charmingly diffident message on her machine: 'Octavia, I hope you remember me. This is Tom Fleming. I wondered if you were free one night next week. Give me a ring.'

They had dinner, enjoyed the evening enormously, did it again, and then again; a month after the party, they were in bed, Octavia having been seduced as much by Tom's interest in her and admiration for what went on in her head as his initially tentative physical advances.

She was sexually inexperienced; had only had three lovers in her twenty-four years (a one-night affair after a drunken May Ball not included), indeed, had begun to fear she must be frigid, so generally uninterested did she feel in the whole business. She would read articles in *Cosmopolitan* about young women's sex drives and wonder what was the matter with her, that she didn't seem to have one – or that if she did, it was certainly rather weak. Lying in Tom's arms, after what was really a very happy if not earth-shattering event, she told him so.

'One man I went out with told me I was rather forbidding. You don't think that's right?'

'Not in the least. Rather the reverse. I think you are lovely, extremely sexy and clearly not in the least frigid. But then, I am clearly in love with you, and probably prejudiced.'

He had, even in his everyday speech, a very elegant turn of phrase.

Tom was extremely clever; he had gone to Oxford from a good grammar school and got a First in history. This should have freed him, but didn't, from the entirely illogical sense of inferiority he had from not having gone to public school; he was, he told Octavia, going to be proving himself for the rest of his life. She found this touching and baffling, not least because he had done so well, and said so. He had smiled and said that no one who had not been put down by an Old Etonian in the nicest possible way on their first night dining in College – 'Which school? Ah. Don't think I know that one' – could understand how much it mattered. 'I know it's silly, but I am silly. I can't bear being second best.'

His background was modest; his father had been an insurance salesman, and his mother had devoted her entire life to him. 'I came a very poor second. I don't think they ever wanted children, certainly they never had any more.'

They had died within a year of each other of heart disease: 'Not a good prognosis for me, I'm afraid.'

Octavia was then twenty-four years old. Her own background (adored only child of very rich man, Wycombe Abbey and Cambridge) initially worried Tom, and he was so nervous the first time she took him home to meet her father, he was physically shaking as he did up his jacket. No one would have known, of course. Watching him chatting easily in the dark, heavy Hampstead drawing room, carefully respectful, he seemed the embodiment of self-confidence and charm. It wasn't until she was able to reassure him, truthfully, that Felix Miller had pronounced him 'interesting and impressive' that he relaxed, said he felt himself able to continue their relationship.

As they grew closer, as it became clear Tom was extremely important to her, his relationship with her father darkened. Octavia, who had seen this happen before, was terrified of the eventual outcome.

She was not just an only child, her mother had died when she was two, giving birth to a brother, who had died also, after three agonising days. She and her father had been all the world to one another from that day; she adored him, saw him as the source of all wisdom. Early boyfriends he tolerated, or, rather, dismissed as unimportant. 'He's a child, darling,' he would say. 'Very sweet, and of course you must go to the party with him, you'll have fun. But he's not nearly clever enough for you.' Or 'I suppose he's all right. I don't exactly admire his manners. I think you deserve better.'

She would say, immediately, that if he wasn't happy about whoever it was, she wouldn't go to the pictures or whatever, at which he would laugh and say, 'My darling, it's not important. You're not going to marry him, are you? Just have fun. You're young, you must have a good time. Go.' She would, with at least half her mind fixed on her father's judgment, and very often the first outing would be the last. She accepted her father's judgment in all things.

But Tom had taken Felix Miller on, in all his powerful, manipulative jealousy, and if he didn't exactly win him over, developed a *modus operandi* with him at least. There had been one period – after the honeymoon of her father's relationship with Tom, before he had come finally to realise that he must accept him – when Octavia had despaired.

The atmosphere whenever Tom came to the house was appalling; her father aggressively, bullyingly brusque; Tom acerbic, icily polite.

When Tom had left, Felix would tear the occasion apart, criticising every move Tom made, every sentence he uttered. 'Darling, you know what you're doing of course, but do you really think a man who interrupts you seven times during lunch has any real respect for what you say?' or 'I can see he's very witty, Octavia, but are you sure he has a sense of humour? That's rather different, you know, and a marriage can't possibly work without it.' And of course she was affected by it, by the criticism, she couldn't help it, would analyse the interruptions, the lack of humour.

Somehow, Tom won through, the darkest hour a confrontation when Felix questioned Tom's ability to support her, to make his way in the world. Tom lost his temper. He told Felix his attitude was intolerable and left in the middle of dinner. It preceded the dawn of a grudging acceptance. Like all bullies, Felix Miller respected, even feared, courage. Tom had turned up the following morning with a set of bank accounts, a client list, and a couple of editorials in the *Financial Times* outlining the success and rapid growth of the company he worked for over the previous three years. I want you to know this sticks in my craw,' he had said, glaring at Felix Miller. 'I cannot stand self-promotion.' (This was not strictly true, Octavia thought, hearing about it afterwards, but wisely kept her counsel.) 'But if you won't accept my own assurances, then I am driven to presenting you with other people's.'

Miller never apologised, but from then on he stopped fighting the marriage. There had been an unhappy exchange with Octavia two nights before the wedding, which Octavia had never told Tom about, and had sworn she never would, when Felix had, in a last ditch stand, asked her if she was really sure if she knew what she was doing, and when she said she was, told her she was mistaken. 'In six months' time,' he said, pouring a brandy, looking at her across the drawing room, 'you'll wish you were dead. And don't come running to me when it happens.'

Octavia stared at him for a moment, then went straight up to her room, locked the door and lay on her bed, staring out at the darkness, afraid, in spite of being so much in love with Tom, such was her father's power over her.

Later, when Felix Miller came and knocked on her door she told him to go away, and when he ordered her to open it, for the first time in her entire life she disobeyed him. A note was pushed under it, in Miller's copperplate hand, saying he hadn't meant to upset her, he'd been upset himself, loving, caring about her so much. She still didn't go to him, but in the morning, recognising the enormity of the gesture, she kissed him and said she hoped they were still friends.

'Friends! My darling Octavia, you are everything to me, you know that, surely.'

'I know,' she had said. 'I do know.' But the whole incident had frightened and disturbed her more than she would have believed. And haunted her for the rest of her life.

The wedding, of course, was wonderful; she came down the aisle on the arm of a Felix Miller beaming with pride and love, although many people remarked that his expression as they left the church, walking behind her now up the aisle, was markedly less happy. And he made a very sentimental speech, probably all he could have done in the circumstances, Octavia thought, saying how much he loved her and all he wanted was her happiness. Tom's speech had a slightly sharper edge to it, and there was an awkward moment when the best man referred to Octavia as moving from the centre of one man's life to another, but on the whole, as Tom remarked as they drove literally weak with relief, towards the airport, en route to Felix's cottage in Barbados, it could have been enormously worse.

Their troubles were far from over even then; Felix Miller's determination to move in on his son-in law's professional life, pushing clients his way, advising him on business strategy, offering him backing, was a constant crucifixion to both Tom and Octavia, and there had been endless conflict between the three of them. Octavia was particularly anguished, veering between love and gratitude to her father, and a desire to reassure him that she wanted him still to be a major part of her life, and loyalty to Tom and a passionate desire to see him prove himself.

It was an ongoing problem, still unresolved. Felix, genuinely baffled by what he read as an entirely irrational pride, genuinely hurt by the continual rejection, took vengeance in a kind of truculent interference in his daughter's personal and family life, and indeed her own professional conduct, for she, too, had refused to take money from him, had raised the money for shares in Capital C from her own bank. Octavia was able to endure it because she loved Felix so dearly, but it was an endurance, and getting no easier . . .

'Octavia,' said Felix Miller's voice now. 'I really do want to speak to you. Ring me back, please, whenever you get in.'

Octavia jumped. She had been so lost in the contemplation of her life that she had not even heard the phone on her desk ring. She was surprised at herself; she must have been very disturbed by Michael

Carlton's words. By the whole complex Carlton issue; the development, her charity . . .

She sighed, waited for a while, wishing she could ignore the instruction, but she knew she couldn't. The habit of obedience to her father was impossible to break. She pressed the button that automatically dialled him. It was picked up immediately.

'Felix Miller.'

'Hi, Dad. Sorry, I was in the loo.'

'How long have you been home?'

As always, she felt nervy at the inquisition. 'Not long,' she said. 'Why?'

'Because I left a message with that nanny of yours to ring me. Didn't she give it to you?'

'Yes, Dad, she gave it to me. But I did have a few things to do. I've only been in just over an hour. I wanted to see my children, make myself a cup of tea—'

'Yes, all right.' He didn't like those sorts of excuses. 'Well, as long as you got the message. It was important. Are you all right? You sound a bit – odd.'

'I'm fine,' she said quickly. 'I'm tired, obviously—'

'You work too hard,' he said. 'It's ridiculous. Your job's all right, I suppose, but not all these out-of-hours things you do with Tom. He asks too much of you.'

'Daddy, it's no more than any wife would do.'

'Yes, but any wife doesn't work all the hours God sends as well.'

'But that's my choice. I can't help it, I seem to need to work. No prizes for guessing who I get that from.'

'No, maybe not. Well, how about a good holiday? That might help. Give you a bit of time with the children. Maybe you should go alone, without Tom. You could come and stay with me at the cottage.' The cottage was an exquisite small house in Barbados, right on the beach.

'Daddy, honestly. You're not exactly subtle.'

'I don't pretend to be subtle. It would still do you good. Think about it.'

'Honestly, I can't. Much too busy.'

'You really ought to look after yourself. Shortsighted not to. You're no good to anyone if you're exhausted. Anyway, I want you to get Tom to ring me urgently. Got a possible project for him.'

'What's that?' she said, knowing she had to ask, otherwise he would upbraid her for taking no interest in him, in what he could do for Tom and his company.

'Oh, colleague of mine. Involved in a big takeover. Someone's after his company. He'd like some advice, wonders whether he can get the

Monopolies boys involved. Name's Cadogan, nice chap, you'd like him. So anyway, I suggested he talked to Tom.'

'Oh, Dad, why don't you ring Tom yourself, if it's urgent?' she said, exasperation raw in her voice.

'You know why. He's so damn touchy, probably tell me once again I was trying to muscle in on his business.'

'Don't be silly,' said Octavia wearily.

'I'm not being silly. You know perfectly well that's quite likely.'

'In that case, what difference will it make if I mention it?'

'Give him a chance to turn it down right away. But ask him to ring me about it, would you? It could be very big.'

God, he was enraging, thought Octavia. Year after year this went on, Felix making the simplest, most straightforward matter tortuously complex. There was no earthly reason why he shouldn't have suggested to his friend that he phoned Tom direct – except that he would have missed yet another opportunity to let her know that Tom resented any help he might have given him, and that Felix resented that in turn.

'I'm sure Tom would be glad to help if he can. And I will certainly ask him to ring you. I might not see him tonight though.'

'Where is he?'

'Oh, having dinner with some businessmen. In the City.' She sighed. Usually she enjoyed her rare evenings alone, they gave her a chance to catch up on things, but tonight she wished Tom was there. He was so good at allaying her anxieties, dismissing her fears.

'Darling, you do sound down. What's the matter?'

Suddenly she wanted to tell him about Michael Carlton, get his reaction, his advice. 'You've got time?'

'Octavia, of course I've got time.'

She told him: about the lack of a sponsor for Cultivate, about the development, about Carlton's offer, about the possible involvement with Foothold.

'Well, the sponsorship side of things doesn't sound too serious. Solves the situation at a stroke, doesn't it?' Felix said, half surprising her. One of the things she loved best about him was that he was always on the side of absolute pragmatism – she could trust him to be honest.

'Yes, but, Dad, it puts me in his pocket. Makes me feel I'll have to go along with his horrible development.'

'Well, it shouldn't. Make it clear you won't. If that's what he's after, it's his problem not yours. As for the other charity, let them make their own minds up. They'll probably hate the idea of his development if it's on their own doorstep, but they might not. You don't have to get any more involved than that. What does Tom think about it?'

'I don't know. He went straight off to this dinner.'

'Rather unfair of him, I'd have said,' said Felix Miller. 'He shouldn't expose you to that sort of pressure. He relies far too much on you. And your good nature. Anyway, is he beastly, this Carlton man? I think I recognise the name.'

'Yes, he's very well known,' said Octavia, 'and no, he's not beastly, not really. Although obviously ruthless. And tactless.'

'Well, you don't get to be a big property developer by being oversensitive. You sound so tired, Octavia. Have an early night at least. You never relax, don't see enough of those children.'

'Don't you start,' said Octavia and put the phone down. It rang again immediately. 'Sorry,' she said and burst into tears.

'Octavia, has someone been getting at you? Is Tom—'

'No,' she said firmly, 'no, it's nothing. I keep telling you.'

'All right, we'll leave it for now. Look, I must go. Work to do.'

'And you criticise me for working too hard. How old are you, Dad?'

'I'm a very young fifty-nine,' he said, and she could hear him smiling. 'Take care of yourself. Will I see you at the weekend?'

Octavia hesitated. 'I'm not sure,' she said. 'We've got some Americans here, needing entertainment.'

'Pity. Got some tickets for the ballet. You'd have enjoyed it. Although you've probably seen it already. *Manon*, superb production, I'm told.'

'We have,' said Octavia, 'but thank you for thinking of us. And it *is* a superb production. We saw Sylvie Guillem in it.'

'Good. Well, I'm taking Marianne anyway. Maybe her children will be able to come.'

'I hope so.' Marianne was her father's mistress of a great many years: she and Octavia enjoyed a rather taut friendship. 'Is – is she there now?'

'No, no, I'm here on my own,' said Felix. A notional sigh hung in the air.

There was a silence. Then, 'Well, good night, Dad,' she said. 'I'll get Tom to ring you.'

'Now why did you say that?' said Marianne Muirhead, lifting her head from the magazine she was reading, and looking at Felix with cool green eyes. 'As if I needed to ask.'

'Say what?' said Felix.

'That you were on your own. Felix, you are a nightmare. It's a miracle poor Octavia isn't even more of a neurotic mess with you for a father.'

'She's not a neurotic mess!'

'Of course she is. Well, maybe not a mess, but certainly neurotic.'

'I would call it highly strung. And it's the life she leads that contributes to that, nothing I do.'

'I would beg to differ. She was obviously upset about something and the last thing she needed was all that loaded stuff about her husband. Or to be told you were all alone in the house, after she'd turned down your invitation to the ballet. The words "lonely" and "neglected" hanging heavy in the air. Really, Felix!'

'Look, I don't interfere with the way you manage your children,' said Felix irritably, pouring himself a large scotch, 'so perhaps you'd be kind enough to allow me to handle my own.'

Marianne didn't answer, returned to her magazine. Felix turned up the stereo; Bruch's violin concerto filled the room.

'Felix, not quite so loud, please. It was perfectly all right before.'

'I thought you liked this. You always say it's one of your Desert Island Discs.'

'I do, but not when it precludes all thought.'

'You're only reading *Vogue*, for Christ's sake. That doesn't require much thought.'

Marianne closed her magazine, stood up. 'I think perhaps I might go home tonight after all,' she said. 'I'm rather tired.'

'Oh, don't be so ridiculous,' he said irritably. 'Now who's playing games?'

'Felix, I'm not playing games. I don't play games. I am tired, and I don't find your mood very restful.'

It was true: Marianne didn't play games. She was an extraordinarily straightforward woman, coolly intelligent and self-assured. She was thirty-nine years old, with a pale blonde beauty, slender, elegant, always perfectly dressed. It had once been famously said of Marianne Muirhead in an article in *Vogue* that she did not follow style, her own particular version followed her. Neither ultra-fashionably nor classically dressed, she had evolved a look of her own over the years that she simply adapted as she felt required to; a long lean silhouette, a splash of primary colour added fairly sparingly to black, always high heels, almost always hats, skirts just above the knee, and a wardrobe that contained at any one time (also famously) at least thirty white T-shirts, in every possible fabric and style. She looked as good on the golf course, which she claimed was her natural habitat, as she did lunching at Caprice, or on the floor at a charity ball. Any slight tendency to severity in her appearance and manner was counteracted by her laugh, which was loud and exuberant.

She had married Alec Muirhead, a London-based American lawyer, in 1975 when she was only eighteen. Her own father had been in the diplomatic service, based for much of his life in Washington, and she was herself half American – and, her only brother was entirely American-based – so she settled happily into what most Englishwomen would have found a difficult life. But she had discovered after the birth of their third child in 1982 that Alec had been unfaithful to her for years; since he spent at least half his time in New York, and she had anyway grown to dislike him considerably, this did not greatly distress her. She had agreed to a divorce, on the basis of a hugely generous settlement and an agreement that she should have full custody of the children. Having obtained both, she surprised everyone by granting him full access to them, and conducting their separate lives with good temper and generosity, insisting that they spent Christmas, Thanksgiving and at least one family holiday together. Alec, settled now permanently in New York, had never married again, merely had a long series of ever-younger mistresses, and the Muirhead children had grown up with a view of marriage that was unconventional but well balanced. Marianne and the two younger children, both girls, lived in London; the oldest, Marc, was at the University of Harvard reading Classics with a view to following his father into law.

Marianne had met Felix Miller at a fundraising dinner at the Royal Opera House, of which they were both patrons. Five years into her divorce, she was ready, if not for love, for a new relationship, and Felix was the only man she had met who seemed to her to have the same power and magnetism as her ex-husband, and, it had to be said, the same potential for unpleasantness.

Seven years on, she was very happy with him; in spite of his considerable complexities (most notably his appallingly dangerous and difficult relationship with his daughter) she continued to love him and to greatly enjoy his company and his bed.

Marianne was one of those seemingly unemotional women who are actually extremely passionate, and she would look sometimes at Felix Miller across a room or a table, with his thick silvering hair, his unreadably dark eyes, his large frame with its almost visible pent-up energy, and feel a rush of pure sexual desire for him. It was not unknown for the pair of them to leave parties or restaurants rather swiftly, and even for them to enjoy rather rampant sex on some isolated beach or remote piece of countryside. Their children, had they known, would have been appalled.

They spent two or three nights a week together in London, always at his house, never at hers, and holidayed together at his cottage in Barbados, hers in Portugal. She had no career, but found herself extremely fully occupied (apart from her golf) with a serious involvement in funding and profile raising for both the arts and various charities, and in caring for her two daughters, who were still young enough – Zoë at eighteen, Romilly at fifteen – to need a great deal of her attention.

They lived, the three of them, in a large triplex apartment on the north side of Eaton Square; exquisitely furnished and decorated in a style as determinedly light as Marianne's personal one was dark, it was very much a home. The girls had the top floor to themselves, with a bedroom each, a sitting room and a bathroom, which gave them an illusion at least of independence and freedom.

Marianne's children were not exactly fond of Felix Miller, but they liked him, and accepted his position in their mother's life with tolerable grace; he was very fond of Romilly but found Zoë, with her spirit and a beauty and sexuality eerily like her mother's, difficult to cope with. He also found Marianne's attitude towards them – tolerant, easy, almost detached – impossible to understand.

He watched her now as she came across the room to kiss him, and said, 'You sure you don't want to stay?'

'I'm quite sure. I'm tired and I've got a big match tomorrow.'

'Well, you certainly mustn't let me keep you from something as important as that.'

The amount of time and energy she spent on her golf irritated him, particularly when he was displeased with her; it baffled him that a woman so intelligent, so culturally sophisticated, should devote herself to such a thing.

'You could be running a company easily,' he had said to her more than once, and she had laughed and said she had no desire to run a company; she saw life as something to be enjoyed, experienced, rather than worked through, and if there was no need for her to work, and there clearly was none, then why should she? The girls needed her at home, she enjoyed being at home, and she also wanted to be available to Marc whenever he was in London. Felix, whose entire life had been dedicated to the pursuit and acquisition of success, struggled and failed to understand her; it constantly amazed him that he should find himself compatible with such a creature.

And maybe he wasn't, he thought now, listening to her car driving down Well Walk, maybe they should consider parting; and then knew that he couldn't possibly, that, compatible or not, what he felt for Marianne was as near to love as he had ever felt for any woman. Any woman apart from Octavia, of course.

Tom was still not home by eleven thirty. Octavia decided to go to bed in the spare room so that Tom wouldn't wake her when he did get in. She turned out the light and tried to sleep, but the insomnia that always haunted her was very powerful tonight. She was tempted to take a sleeping pill, but she had to get up early, perform well; the pill would make her fuzzy headed, less competent. So would being exhausted; it was always a conflict, that, trying to decide which evil was the lesser. And so she lay in bed, staring into the darkness, doing one of the relaxation exercises her yoga instructor had given her – absolutely useless but they were at least something to do – willing herself to stay calm . . .

She had just turned the light on again to read when she heard the chugging of a taxi in the street below, and Tom coming in and up the stairs very quietly. She knew what would happen next: he would find her not in their bedroom, and then he would come looking for her. He didn't mind her moving out of their room, he was sympathetic about her insomnia, but he hated to go to bed without saying good night to her. She found it at once touching and irritating that she must be awoken from her precious sleep to be kissed and told to sleep well.

She smiled at him as he came and sat down on the bed, kissed her.

'Sorry I'm late. Bob Macintosh was at the dinner, got into a rather long conversation with him.'

'What about?'

Bob Macintosh was one of Tom's longest-standing and most important clients; he owned a small but very successful chain of supermarkets in the Midlands and North of England. He was outspoken, rather rotund, prematurely grey haired, with brilliant dark eyes. Octavia was very fond of him.

'Oh, he's not very happy.'

'Really? How's Maureen?'

'Maureen's the reason. She's been playing around. Again.'

Maureen was a flashy redhead, ten years younger than Bob, loud, funny, extremely extrovert. She was fond of Bob and fonder of his money, but she was serially unfaithful.

'Oh, dear. Poor old Bob. I don't know how he puts up with it.'

'Usual thing. Can't live with her, can't live without her,' said Tom. 'Anyway, it's rather complex this time. She's been sleeping with an MP.'

'An MP! Heavens, Tom, who?'

'Well, that's the trouble. Or rather what makes it complex. He's a junior minister. Quite high profile. And Mr Blair's squeaky-clean new government can't be tainted with any Tory-style sleaze. Not yet anyway. They want it hushed up, but the press are on to it, and so they need Bob's co-operation.'

'What on earth do you mean?'

'Alistair Campbell, or rather one of his merry men, is looking for a garden-gate job. You know, David Mellor-style, whole family looking wonderfully happy.'

'Both families?'

'Yes. And Bob's just not sure if he can go through with it. He says it turns him up.'

'It would me,' said Octavia, 'and it would you, surely. I hope,' she added, leaning forward and kissing him.

'Yes, of course it would,' he said. He sounded irritable.

She looked at him thoughtfully. 'So what's it got to do with you? Apart from the fact he's your friend. And your client of course.'

Tom sighed. 'He wanted to know what I thought about it. About the whole thing.'

'And?'

'I said it all came down to how he felt about Maureen. Whether he can forgive her yet again.'

'And?'

'Well, he says he can, he wants her back, still loves her. Poor sod. But on his own terms. And that certainly doesn't include making everything fine and dandy for her lover.'

'He should turn it to his own advantage,' said Octavia briskly.

Tom stared at her. 'What do you mean?'

'I mean he should get something in return if he does agree to play ball with them. As well as Maureen, I mean. I presume she wants to stay with him.'

'Of course she does. Faced with the prospect of losing Bob and the money and that monstrous house and everything, she suddenly finds him the only man in the world—'

'You don't like Maureen, do you?' she said.

'No, I don't. I can't bear those money-grubbing, kept women.'

'You like Lauren Bartlett though,' she said suddenly.

'No, I don't. I can't stand her, actually.'

'You don't behave as if you can't stand her. I seem to remember some rather tactile dancing, the other night.'

'Oh, Octavia, don't start,' he said wearily.

'I'm not starting anything. Just making an observation—' She stopped. This could get nasty. She was horribly, painfully jealous, couldn't bear Tom flirting even, had never learned to laugh it off, to accept it didn't mean anything. And he flirted a great deal; it was part of his charm, as natural to him as breathing.

'Anyway, that's the advice I'd give Bob,' she said quickly now, anxious to backtrack. 'If he really wants Maureen back, that is. He doesn't have to do anything, it seems to me. He holds all the cards. He should play a few of them. Only don't ask me which ones and how,' she added, slithering down on the pillows, 'I'm much too tired to think. I just feel dreadfuly sorry for poor Bob.'

Tom sat looking at her very intently for a moment or two, then leaned forward and kissed her. 'You're a clever girl,' he said, 'and I love you. Having trouble sleeping?'

She nodded.

'How would you like me to help you relax? I swear I'll go back to our room later.' His dark grey eyes were very intense, very serious.

She looked back at him, equally so.

'I think I'd like that a lot,' she said. Against all logic, all common sense, the fact it was late, that she had an early meeting, that she would be exhausted, she wanted him. Quite badly suddenly; she could feel her body stirring, feel it reaching out into desire. She moved lower in the bed, held her arms up to him, like a child. His eyes fixed on hers, he pulled off his clothes, climbed in beside her, started to kiss her. They were both in a hurry, strangely, almost guiltily so; she reached to put the light out.

'Don't,' he said. 'I want to be able to see you.'

He liked studying her, stroking her, kissing her small breasts, her flat stomach, her neat, taut thighs, liked her to look at him, to learn about him and what pleased him. She had found that difficult at first; it had been part of her insecurity, her nervousness. She preferred darkness. He had teased her about it, told her she was an anal retentive, that it was all part of her father-complex; that had upset her, she had cried, been angry, pulled away from him. It had taken her a long time to learn to relax in bed; and she had known in her innermost heart that Tom was right, that her father did haunt her sexuality, that even as she welcomed Tom into her, felt him exploring her, felt her own sensations growing in violence and pleasure, she knew that a small part of her still held back, watching herself anxiously, afraid of losing herself entirely, of doing something she could not quite allow herself.

But he taught her to trust herself and him; taught her to enjoy herself, literally. In a relationship that was often taut, pressured, over-demanding, what happened in bed was an important, easeful thing for them both, an exploration of one another on every level, still careful, still looked forward to and savoured, and still, to Octavia at least, a most vital element in her self-esteem.

But tonight, there was no holding back. He was in her quickly, and they came quickly too, both of them. It was as if they were somehow in a hurry, rushing towards pleasure, grasping for it, as if there was something beyond it that they both had to reach, that would not wait long for them. She felt herself climbing into her orgasm, felt it break, sweetly fierce, felt him follow almost at once; afterwards they lay, holding each other, breathing hard still, smiling but slightly surprised by the violence, the urgency that had overcome them both.

'I'll go now,' he said, as she drifted into sleep, but, 'No,' she said. 'No, don't, stay with me, I want you here.'

The last thing she heard was his voice saying he loved her; the last thing she thought was how much she needed him . . .

She had not expected to see him in the morning, slipped out of bed, showered and dressed and got the notes for her meeting, thinking him still fast asleep. But he appeared in the nursery, very wide awake, as she kissed Minty goodbye, followed her downstairs.

'I'll see you tonight,' he said. 'It's the Savoy again, I'm afraid.'

'I know. Drapers, regional newspapers, right? I'll be there.'

'How did you get on with Carlton?' he asked. 'After I'd gone?'

'Oh, all right. I have to say it's a bit of a minefield, Tom.'

'I know. I can see that. But good about the sponsorship, surely?'

'Ye-es. Hope so. Bit loaded. And then he gave me a lecture about neglecting my children.'

'I'm sorry about that. I'm sure you were very patient.'

'I was. Of course. 'Bye, Tom. Oh, and by the way,' she added, turning back into the room, 'my father wants you to ring him. He's got some prospect or other for you.'

'Oh, Christ,' said Tom.

Octavia's breakfast meeting was at the Connaught; she was early, but Melanie was already there, drinking orange juice and coffee like one possessed, glass in one hand, cup in the other. As always when she suddenly saw her away from the familiarity of the office setting, Octavia was struck with great force by Melanie's rather strange beauty: she was tall, almost six feet – 'I look down on most men' she was fond of saying – with a strong, fit body, and long powerful legs. Her streaky brown hair fell below her shoulders in a waving mass, and her eyes, peering through an over-long fringe, were a fierce, deep blue. Her nose was rather large, but it suited her, and her mouth wide and generous. Her voice was most singular, slightly gravelly in tone, with a South London accent half worn away by years of contact with the middle- and upper-class tones of her clients and associates. She wore clothes with the slightly ethnic look of the 'seventies, long skirts and elaborately embroidered shirts and a mass of silver bracelets on her strong brown wrists – against Octavia's classic chic she looked like some large exotic bird. Tom Fleming, who tended to like his women conventional, was surprisingly fond of Melanie, and frequently proclaimed her 'dauntingly sexy'.

Octavia slid into the seat beside her, nodded gratefully at the waiter who was advancing on her with the coffee pot.

'You look rotten,' said Melanie, looking at her critically. 'You all right? Not pregnant again, are you? Octavia, please, please don't say that.'

'No, I'm not pregnant,' said Octavia slightly defensively.

'Good. Just usual domestic trauma, is it? Wearing you out?'

'You could say that.'

'Surely the divinely handsome Mr Fleming isn't giving trouble?'

'Not as far as I know,' said Octavia lightly. 'Honestly, Mells, I'm fine. Just tired.'

'Well, that's all right then. Now let me tell you quickly, before she gets here, that Mrs B is dead set on a ball this Christmas. We have to talk her out of it. Those things are no good at all without a really high-profile patron, and we ain't got one.'

'Any good trying Kensington Palace? She was very keen we did that, said she was sure Diana would respond.'

'They *all* think Diana will respond. No, I did put a call in to the Palace, but never got past the outside office. Anyway, it's no good just saying no ball, we have to come up with an alternative, something she can latch on to. Any ideas?'

'I did meet Neil Balcon the other night,' said Octavia, 'you know, the thinking woman's Michael Ball?'

'Oh, him. Yes. And?'

'And he's just done one of those Sunday night benefit things. They made forty grand for Deafaid. He said it was always worth asking him, he liked doing things like that. As long as he was sympathetic to the cause.'

'Did he? What was he like? You do manage to meet the most glamorous people, Octavia.'

'Oh, it was at one of those fundraising bashes for the Labour Party,' said Octavia. 'You know Tom gets invited to them sometimes.'

'What, at Ken and Barbie's little place?'

'No, not Follett Towers this time. Brian Tweedie, same difference. Anyway, he was very nice, and extremely handsome. So we could try that.'

'Sounds good. Ah, here's Kate now. Come and sit down, Kate. Coffee?'

There was a message for Octavia when she got into the office, from Lauren Bartlett. Octavia asked Sarah Jane for a glass of mineral water, took two Nurofen for a thickly growing headache, and dialled the number.

'Lauren Bartlett.' Just hearing her voice put Octavia's teeth on edge: slightly braying, aggressively well bred.

'Oh, Lauren, hi. This is Octavia Fleming.'

'Oh, Octavia, yes.'

'You called me. Incidentally, if it was about the party, Poppy would love to come, thank you. Sounds wonderful.'

'Fine. I'll tick her off the list. She has got her own passport, has she? Last year we had a nightmare because some child didn't. I forgot to put that in the invitation.'

'Yes, of course.'

'Right. No need to worry about safety, by the way. George's pilot has ten thousand miles' experience. Never so much as a bumpy landing.'

'I wasn't,' said Octavia, wondering if she should have done.

'Good. Some people were. Now, Octavia, I'm on the fundraising committee of Next Generation. As you know.'

Octavia did know; it would have been hard not to. Next Generation was very high profile indeed – at one point it had been strongly rumoured that Princess Diana was to become its patron. Capital C had done a presentation to them two years earlier and failed to get the business; as a flagship it would be superb. It ran a privately funded hospice for children with AIDS, and two refuge houses for abused children. ('Very fashionable, very Diana,' Melanie had observed tartly after the first meeting with them.) Diana's patronage had not yet materialised, but the charity continued to win a great deal of attention and publicity.

'We're planning a fundraising day in September, at Brands Hatch. We thought of getting professional help and your name came up. Now, we do know you're awfully expensive, so it could be we'd be better managing without you. I just wondered if you'd consider meeting us halfway on the cost, as we're friends and so on.'

'Unlikely, I have to say,' said Octavia coolly, 'this is a business, you know. But we could talk. It sounds a wonderful idea, your fun day, and you'll find it very productive. We did something similar at Brooklands a year or so ago. Raised over a hundred thousand for Foothold, one of our charities. Children with arthritis. I got one of the big drug companies to come in with lots of lovely sponsorship money.'

'Oh, really?' Interest flashed briefly into the drawling voice.

'Yes. So if you did think it might be worth talking—'

'But you wouldn't do it for free? For old times' sake?'

'Lauren, I couldn't. Sorry.'

'Well, we'll think about it. I must say it seems a bit – wrong – for a business to be making money out of charities.'

Octavia had had this argument so many times before, she moved smoothly into her automatic defence of it. 'Lauren, you know as well as I do a charity's books have to balance. It's an expensive business running a charity. We do, in the long run, make it more cost effective.'

'Yes, yes, I know that's the argument,' said Lauren dismissively. 'Anyway, as I say, we may ring you. I must go now, Octavia. Off to the Harbour Club. Bye.'

'Bitch,' said Octavia aloud as she put the phone down.

Tom Fleming forgot about telephoning his father-in-law until he was in the middle of a very complicated conversation over lunch. Most of his meals were accompanied by complicated conversations, indeed every meal he ate during the week was a working occasion. His day began over breakfast, either at a hotel or in a boardroom, proceeded to lunch, almost always at the Connaught or the Savoy or the Ritz, and thence to dinner, often after the theatre or the opera, at some other high-profile eaterie, Bibendum, Quaglino's, the Mirabelle. He was never relaxed, always watchful, platefuls of perfectly prepared, immensely expensive food being placed before him and then removed again, sometimes half eaten, sometimes still less; endless glasses of fine clarets, perfectly chilled champagnes poured and not consumed while he and his colleagues and his guests or his hosts stalked one another in their ceaseless and complex battle for influence.

Tom ran a public affairs consultancy, known in the trade as a lobby shop. People he met at parties, outside the business, were always asking him exactly what did, and it always surprised him how hard it was to explain to them.

'It's not quite politics and much more fun,' he would say. 'It's all about persuading people, simple as that. Persuading the clients what to do, and how to do it, insofar as it affects, and is affected by, politics. And persuading others my clients are right.' He would then give them his famously charming and engaging smile, and refuse to say any more. 'Otherwise I shall become boring. And then Octavia will be cross.'

The presentation folder of Fleming Cotterill (glossy, fat, expensive) went a little further, describing itself as above all 'seeking to get a company's case across to people, whether in Westminster, Whitehall or out there on the Clapham Omnibus'.

Fleming Cotterill was seven years old, hugely successful, high profile. Tom and his co-director Aubrey Cotterill had founded it six years earlier, having formed a splinter group from another very well-established consultancy; they were the senior directors and biggest shareholders and there were now three other directors. The early days had been – as Tom described it when he had had a few glasses of wine too many – 'good for the bowels: we'd both taken out enormous second mortgages and bank loans. It had to work.'

For the first few months it looked as if it wouldn't; they had a couple of clients but not nearly enough to meet their overheads (small but glossy office in Westminster, much expensive entertaining, and the high interest rates of the early 'nineties). Tom and Aubrey were financially stretched to the hilt; large personal overdrafts, houses remortgaged. They always said they couldn't decide which were the worst in those early days; the days when the phone didn't ring at all, or the ones when it rang and a smooth voice on the other end would tell them how impressed it had been by their operation, but nevertheless how sorry it was that it had been decided to take the business elsewhere this time . . .

Then in the space of three days they won two key accounts: a radio station in search of further franchises; and a small grocery chain, both classically demanding in public affairs terms. They proved their mettle immediately; the radio station picked up an enormous amount of publicity by fighting off a takeover, Fleming Cotterill advising them with great success both to capitalise on the inevitable redundancies if it happened and to hire a highly controversial disc jockey, and the grocery chain by playing devil's advocate and speaking against the Sunday trading lobby. The radio station won, and the grocery chain lost the battle but won their own personal war, emerging with their image enhanced as one of the good guys who cared about Sundays.

After that Fleming Cotterill became well known very swiftly; they picked up a lot of new business and launched a campaign, through a cross-party group of MPs, to improve food labelling. Perhaps most importantly, not one of their original clients had left them; nothing could have provided a better testimony to their skills.

In the heady post-election air of May 1997, when the whole country seemed to be celebrating, and a new age truly dawning, everything to do with politics was thrown into the air. Those lobby shops that had grown up in the long years of undisputed Tory rule were furiously hiring new young Turks who were in with the new in-crowd, and presenting themselves as politically non-partisan. It was not an entirely edifying spectacle.

Fleming Cotterill was not among them; two of its five directors had held posts in the offices of Socialist cabinet ministers, and a third had worked famously on the Nolan Committee, with all its whiter-than-white associations of a new, less corrupt age. Tom Fleming had several longterm friends in the new government; his star and that of his company was very much in the ascendant.

*

Today Tom was lunching with Bob Macintosh, and the problems under discussion were at least fifty per cent personal.

The non-personal conversation had been about the interminable new regulations coming in from Brussels governing the food industry. 'They're going to drive us mad, Tom,' said Bob, 'and costs are going to soar. I really want to fight at least some of them, but a small voice like mine won't be heard, will it?'

'You need to get the big boys on board, form a coalition, which might be difficult initially. They can absorb these things much more easily. But if you can start making waves . . .'

'Well, that's your department. What do you suggest we do?'

'The ideal thing would be an agreement to look at them very closely at government level. A parliamentary committee, even. That's easier said than done, though, especially at the moment. There's so much business for them to get through in this first few months, and whatever Blair says, he's passionately pro-Europe, so no one's going to give it very high prority. We can do some lobbying, of course, and I can try and set up a meeting between you and the appropriate minister, but that won't be easy either. I agree with you, these regulations are a nightmare. And the trouble is, being British, we will play by the rules. Places like Italy and Spain, they ignore half of them. Much more sensible.'

The personal conversation, which had been much longer and more difficult, concerned Bob Macintosh's marital difficulties, and his reluctance to go along with the spin doctors within the new, rollercoasting Labour Party and be photographed playing happy families with his adulterous wife.

'I just don't see why I should, Tom,' he said, draining his claret glass, nodding gratefuly as Tom refilled it. 'I'm prepared to take Maureen back because I love her and I know she's sorry—' 'Tom doubted this very much, but didn't say so – 'but I don't give a monkey's about the wonderful new government being tainted with sleaze, as that little shit who called me put it. Why should I? As far as I'm concerned, the bloody minister can drown in his own excrement. It's so undignified, and hard on the kids. They're not daft, they know why the press suddenly want to photograph us. The lad doesn't know what's been going on, too young, but the girls have a pretty shrewd idea, and I don't like the signals we'll be sending them.'

'Like what?' said Tom.

'Well, like, it's all right if you don't get caught, and then it's still all right as long as you keep on lying.'

'Presumably the other chap's got to put on the same performance?'

'Oh, yes, and he's more than willing. There he is, only about a month into his grand new job. His wife's agreeable too; she's enjoying her new life as well. And their kids are younger.'

'I'm amazed they want you to do it,' said Tom. 'I'd have thought they'd be into a new form of damage limitation by now. Everyone knew that picture did Mellor more harm than good. No, of course you shouldn't do it if you don't want to.'

'I bloody don't,' said Macintosh. His jaw set in a way that Tom recognised, and had come to dread himself.

'The only thing I would say is that there might be something you could get out of it.'

'Oh, yeah? What? I've got Maureen back, that's all I care about. On my terms too, this time, no more of that lingerie party nonsense.'

'But is that really all you care about?' said Tom.

'Well, yes. That and the kids. I mean, what did you have in mind, Tom?'

'I'm not quite sure. It was something Octavia said, she—'

And then he remembered Felix and the missed phone call and its inevitable consequences – thinly veiled implications that he hadn't wanted to call at all, truculent questioning as to whether he could cope with the project anyway if he was so busy, Octavia's resentment at his negligence, when she heard about it from her father – none of these things was helping his concentration. He'd have to ring Felix straight away.

'Look,' he said. 'Look, Bob, can you excuse me a minute? I have got an idea, but I've got to ring my secretary. She was getting some information for me that I need before I go on to the House.'

It always worked, that one; sounded as if he was going to the House of Commons to speak on the floor, rather than hang about in the committee corridor for an hour or so, or in the main lobby, waiting for someone to arrive.

'Sure. Can I order another coffee?'

'Of course. Brandy?'

'No, thank you. Got work to do this afternoon.'

Tom ran down the wide steps to the men's cloakroom, pulling out his mobile phone, and punched out Miller's private number.

Felix Miller's secretary said she was sorry, but Mr Miller had left the office for the day and couldn't be contacted until that night, when he would be in Edinburgh. Could she ask Mr Miller to phone Mr Fleming from there? She couldn't give Mr Fleming the number as it was a private house, and she had specific instructions not to.

Tom said that would be very kind of her and would she give Mr Miller his good wishes and tell him that he had been unable to call any earlier, as he had been in back-to-back meetings since eight thirty that morning.

He went back to the table, sat down again, drained his coffee cup.

Macintosh was leafing through some papers. 'You'll get back to me then on this regulation business? Very soon.'

'Yup. Early next week. I'll have a chat with an old chum of mine in Whitehall. Meanwhile, sit tight, don't do anything rash.'

'You sure about that? I did meet someone at a dinner last week, someone quite high up in the government, who said any time I wanted help, I had only to lift the phone. We could shortcut the whole—'

'Bob, please don't do that. Let me put it more strongly. On no account do that. Half the time these guys you meet at dinners don't mean it, or don't have the clout and then you've ruffled feathers in Whitehall which in the long run are more important. Okay?'

'Yes, okay,' said Macintosh. But he didn't sound convinced. 'And you don't think I should do this ruddy photo shoot?'

'No, I don't. Not if you don't want to. Unless—' Tom stopped. He felt rather cold suddenly, as he always did when he had a brainwave. 'Unless we did something really very clever. Made everybody happy.'

'Does that include me?'

'Oh, it does, Bob. It most certainly does. Pass me the water, would you, there's a good chap. Now listen . . .'

'Fleming!' Melanie's head apeared round Octavia's door. 'Look, if it wouldn't be too much to ask, could you possibly come into my office? We do have a meeting scheduled and it's already ten minutes late.'

'Sorry. I was on a complicated call.' Octavia was never sure if it was Melanie's personality, or her own innate sense of hierarchy, bred from her rigid childhood and education, that made her so constantly nervous of annoying her.

'That's okay. Now listen,' she said, leading Octavia back into her own office, pushing a large tortoisehsell comb into her wild hair, 'any progress on Cultivate yet, and a sponsor? Margaret Piper's written me a letter, saying she's very dissatisfied.'

'Evil old bat,' said Octavia. 'She's my client, what's she doing complaining to you? Honestly, she's getting more of my time proportionately than any of my other clients. I watched her feeding her chins for over two hours, and she didn't even thank me.'

'I think she sees me as headmistress here,' said Melanie. 'Now calm down, Octavia, I'm not blaming you, obviously, and I know how hard it is to get sponsorship at the moment, and specially for a charity like that one. But I don't want to lose her, and if we're not careful, we will. And if, as you say, Lloyds Bank aren't going to come up with the goods, then we do have a problem and maybe I should throw some names into the ring.'

It was pride as much as anything else that made Octavia say she had actually, she thought, now got a sponsor for Cultivate. Foolish, dangerous pride, as she saw very clearly afterwards . . .

Marianne Muirhead had had a very good day. She had won her golf match, on a course she was particularly fond of, the Royal Surrey in Richmond. It had been the first course ever to be designed for women players, and was extremely pretty, studded with trees and ornamental shrubs and set on the edge of the Old Deer Park, in that lovely area between the Thames and Kew Gardens.

She had then stopped off to shop in Sloane Street on her way home and bought herself an extremely chic black crêpe trouser suit from Prada, some perilously high-heeled boots to wear with it, and an exquisitely beaded evening bag in Valentino, and had then reached home to find a spur-of-the-moment dinner invitation with one of her more interesting women friends, a barrister, waiting for her on the answering machine. She phoned to accept and to agree on a restaurant – Mon Plaisir in Monmouth Street, 'so pretty *and* the best frites in London' – and then went down to greet Romilly, who was calling her from the hall, flushed with excitement at being chosen to play a saxophone solo at the concert her school was putting on at the end of term.

'Very well done, darling! That is just so exciting. What are you going to play?'

'"Summertime." From *Porgy and Bess*. It's really really hard but—'

'But you'll be wonderful. Darling, I'm really pleased for you. And proud. We must make sure Daddy is here – let me have the date straight away, so I can brief him.' It was one of Marianne's strengths as a divorced parent that she did not just pay lip service to involving her ex-husband in their children's lives – she worked extremely hard and succesfully at it.

'Sure. Thanks.'

Romilly kissed her mother. She was very tall for her age, as tall as her sister Zoë, and still growing. She was very thin, and she had braces on her teeth, but she was clearly going to be lovely, with a sheet of fair hair falling down her back, perfect clear skin, and her mother's large green eyes and full mouth. She was shy and rather serious, hard working and dutiful.

Zoë, who was none of those things, found her sister's goodness trying and teased her constantly about it, not always kindly, while using her remorselessly as slave, banker – Romilly always had money in her account while Zoë's allowance was spent long before she got it – and source of alibi. Nevertheless, Zoë adored her and was fiercely protective of her, more so than Marianne, constantly watchful for what she felt might be unsuitable friends and influences, critical of any clothes that seemed to her remotely sexy – 'Mum, you *can't* let her go out in that dress! It's disgusting, you can see her knickers' – and volubly anxious at Romilly's naiveté and gullibility. 'Honestly, Romilly, you'll end up in a brothel one of these days. If some old perv came up to you in the street and told you he needed you to come home with him, and make him a nice cup of tea, you'd believe him.'

It annoyed Romilly, this protectiveness, and amused Marianne, who was inclined to be liberal and argued that Zoë would never have submitted to such censure. Zoë, however, responded with some truth that she had been born streetwise and could see trouble before it actually hit her in the face.

'You've got to be more careful with her, Mum; she's okay translating Chaucer, but she's a complete spastic when it comes to real life.'

Marianne said humbly that she would try to be more careful.

But it was Zoë who was occupying her attention that day: she needed to talk to Alec about her. Zoë planned to take a gap year when she left school and spend it working with some youth volunteer scheme in Zimbabwe. It sounded rather worrying to Marianne, and, she couldn't help feeling, owed less to Zoë's highmindedness and social conscience than to an attachment to a boy she had met and fancied who was joining the scheme himself. Marianne didn't dislike the boyfriend, he was extremely nice and considerably more highminded than Zoë, but she felt he was better equipped to survive the rigours of the scheme than her daughter, and that he might become disillusioned with her and thus prove a disappointment over the time they spent out there: with potentially disastrous results.

It was, of course, out of the question to suggest any of this to Zoë; the only hope was to distract her with a more attractive and suitable plan for her gap year. Alec had suggested he spoke to his sister in Sydney who ran a fashion PR business, to see if she could employ Zoë in some capacity. Zoë had long wanted to go to Australia, and from Sydney would be able to join the teenage travel trail round the rest of the country; Marianne had heard no more from Alec about it, though, and Zoë was pressing her to sign papers and make large deposits on the volunteer scheme.

Zoë was going to be late home that evening, so Marianne went up to her room, picked up the phone next to her rather beautiful French roll-top bed, and dialled her ex-husband at his Washington office.

Mr Muirhead was in a meeting, his secretary said, but she would have him call. Less than half an hour later, Alec Muirhead's voice – drawly, gravelly, the voice that Marianne had so foolishly fallen in love with – was on the line.

'Good morning, dear. How are you?'

'I'm fine, Alec. It's late afternoon here, of course, it's a perfect English summer day, and I've won a golf match. And bought a very expensive outfit. What more could a woman ask?'

'Very little, I'm sure. And the girls?'

'Fine. I'm ringing about—'

'Zoë, yes. I'm sorry I didn't get back to you. I've talked to my sister; she's delighted to have her, says she can be genuinely useful to her, not just be hanging around, folding up T-shirts.'

'Marvellous. I think it would be best if the invitation came from Bella, don't you? Otherwise she'll suspect us of (a) collusion and (b) be much less likely to want to go.'

'Sure. I'll tell Bella to call.'

'There's something else. Romilly is playing an important solo in the school concert second week in July. Can you be sure to be available?'

'Of course. Well, crises permitting. I'm writing it down right now. Give her a big hug from me.'

'I will. If only Marc could come too,' she said and sighed. But, Marc was lost somewhere – not literally, as she prayed earnestly every night – with several friends on a vacational expedition to Nepal and the Himalayas, and would not return to civilisation until the summer was over and he went back to Harvard.

'Well, there it is. He's having a marvellous time.'

'I know, but—'

'Cut the apron strings, Marianne. I'm always telling you that.'

He was, but it was easy for him. He saw a lot of Marc anyway; she hardly ever did these days. And she found that hard. She and Marc had been so close once; now she came a poor second in his life, to the long string of leggy blondes whom he seemed to attract so easily.

'Anyway, he's done extraordinarily well in his exams. Second highest marks in his year. He'll be heading up this firm in a couple of decades, no doubt about that.'

'No doubt,' said Marianne, hearing an edge in her voice, hating herself for it. Of course Marc should inherit Muirhead Templeman, and he was clearly going to be a brilliant lawyer in his own right. It was just that she nurtured a dream of having him move to London to take up a career there. Unlikely, but . . . Well, you couldn't have everything. And she certainly had pretty close to it.

Sandy Trelawny, unlike Marianne Muirhead, had had a bad day. An order he had been banking on had fallen through, his rather elderly Volvo had been most uncharacteristically overheating all the way home from Birmingham, which would no doubt mean an expensive trip to the garage, and he had had a rather heavy letter from the bank, expressing the usual pained surprise that his account had gone over its agreed limit. He had a throbbing headache, and he had been looking forward to getting home to Louise and Dickon, his wife and small son and relaxing in front of the television. They had been away, visiting Louise's parents for a couple of days.

Only, as he walked into the house, raising his nose hopefully for one of the delicious garlicky smells that meant supper was well on its way, he realised the day was going to continue on its inexorably unpleasant way. For Louise was not upstairs bathing four-year-old Dickon, and nor was she reading to him, as she did on the very good days – in fact, Dickon was nowhere to be seen. Nor was she in the kitchen, creating the delicious garlicky smell that would be supper as she did on the fair to middling days. She was sitting in front of the television, watching *Neighbours*. *Neighbours* days were the worst – no, not quite the worst; Oprah Winfrey and Ricki Lake days were the very worst. If he found Louise sitting gazing mesmerised into the riff-raffish evangelism of those programmes, he knew things were going to be very terrible. Not that there had been many of those days lately, or even a *Neighbours* one. But there was one now.

Sandy braced himself physically, a reflex reaction from his army days, took a deep breath and forced a cheerfulness into his voice. 'Darling! Hallo! Lovely to have you home. How was your mum? I've missed you.'

Louise turned her face to him; it was white, her eyes swollen with crying. Sandy was shocked, almost fearful. She hadn't looked as bad as that for a long time.

'Darling, whatever's the matter?'

'It's Mummy,' she said, her voice shaky, raw with grief, totally devoid of its lovely musical huskiness. 'She's got cancer, Sandy. She's probably going to – to die.'

And Sandy, staring at her in horror, felt a pang of absolute panic, not only at the thought of losing Anna Madison, so lovely, so young still, a source of such wisdom and strength and so very dear to him, but at what the dealing of this new blow would do to Louise. And how he was going to be able to endure it.

'Have you talked to Octavia?' was all he could think of to say.

CHAPTER 4

'You look lovely,' said Tom, 'and I owe you a big thank you. You're wonderful.'

'What for?'

'Well, you've solved poor Bob's problem for him. About the photo shoot, remember?'

'Of course. What did I say?'

'That he should use it for a bargaining point.'

'What, with Maureen?'

'No, darling, not with Maureen. Something much more important. You see – ah, Jim. And Susan. How nice. Come in and sit down. How are you both? Lovely to see you again. You remember my wife, Octavia, don't you?'

'Yes, of course.' Jim Draper shook Octavia's hand vigorously. 'Very good to see you here, Octavia. Susan was hoping you'd be able to make it. She wants to talk to you about your charity work, don't you, love? Wondered if you could help her with something, as a matter of fact.'

Octavia's heart began to sink. The evening was going to be even longer than she had thought.

The Drapers owned a chain of local freesheet newspapers and were in the process of acquiring a local radio station. They were successful and ambitious, and tediously self-congratulating. Susan Draper, Jim told them proudly over their first drink, had absolute editorial control over all the papers. 'She used to be woman's editor of the *Eastern Morning News*, a very big job. She was about to come up here to Fleet Street, only she had the misfortune to meet me.'

'Well, Fleet Street's loss was your gain,' said Tom.

'Yes, but the loss of her career really hurt her,' said Jim Draper, 'so it's marvellous she's been able to pick it up again now. You're lucky, Octavia – that never happened to you, I suppose. Although, as I understand it, you and your husband work very closely together, rather like ourselves.'

'Well, not exactly,' said Octavia carefully, 'but our paths do cross quite a bit.'

'And how does that work exactly?' said Susan Draper.

'Oh, it's a bit complicated.'

'No, do tell me. It would make a feature for our papers.'

'That's a very good idea, love,' said Jim Draper, beaming proudly at her, 'and Susan would do the interview herself – she does that when it's a really big project. Would help your business as well, I expect, Octavia, bit of publicity. What do you think?'

'That would be a – a very interesting idea,' said Octavia, trying to sound enthusiastic.

It was a long evening; the Drapers ate their way through the menu, insisting on the cheese board as well as the fruit trolley, and drank a great deal as well. It must be costing hundreds, thought Octavia, smiling sweetly at Jim Draper over her iced water and fresh raspberries as he told her how lucky she was not to put on weight. 'I have a terrific battle, don't I, love?' he said, crunching into a biscuit ladled with both butter and Brie.

'You do, yes. Octavia, you must go to a lot of charity functions. Have you ever met Princess Diana?'

'No,' said Octavia, 'I never have. Other big names of course . . .'

'Like?'

'Well, the Duchess of Gloucester is a great favourite of ours. Princess Anne is wonderful, and—'

'What I would really like,' said Susan Draper, leaning forward and blowing a fog of smoke into Octavia's face – 'God, I must give this up – what I would really like is to write an article about a big charity bash. Now I wonder if you could ever see your way to arranging for me to attend one? And meeting one of those ladies?'

'It really is rather unlikely,' said Octavia. There was a point beyond which she was not prepared to compromise herself. 'It's an unwritten part of the deal that the royals particularly are given privacy inside the functions. Otherwise, they just won't do it. Naturally.'

'Yes, well, of course I can see that. But I do assure you I would be extremely discreet. Could you at least think about it for me?'

'I will think about it,' said Octavia, 'but—'

'Susan, leave off,' said Jim Draper unexpectedly. 'You mustn't force Octavia's hand if she doesn't want it. She and Tom have been very co-operative over the feature, and given us a wonderful evening, and I found all what she had to tell us about those charity auctions absolutely fascinating. Privileged information, I'd say, Octavia! Now, Tom, I've been looking at all the stuff you've given me about your company and I must say I'm very impressed. I liked your partner too, and the executive you say we'd be working with. All very pleasant people. Now your charges are high, no doubt about it, but we do need some advice, all this legislation is very complex, and I'm prepared to go so far as to say that I would like to see us doing business with you – maybe in three to six months' time. Can't be fairer than that, can I? Just have to dot the t's and cross the i's with the rest of my board – that's the mother-in-law and the cat – no, only joking. Oh, now yes, I could force down another of those brandies, if you twisted my arm . . .'

'My darling you were magnificent,' said Tom, returning to the table with a sigh of exhaustion, picking up his brandy glass swirling it round. 'It was you who did it really, you know. Tipped the balance. How can I thank you?'

'By getting me off the hook with that woman's interview,' said Octavia.

'Of course I will. No problem. Promise.'

'And telling me about Bob's solution. I couldn't think of anything else all evening.'

'Like several others, I hope,' said Tom. 'Listen . . .'

Octavia listened. When he had finished she looked at him and smiled. 'And I thought of that? How brilliant.'

'*We* thought of it. And we are brilliant. A brilliant team. Why don't you have a drink just for once?'

'Oh, all right,' said Octavia. 'A glass of champagne would be very nice. And I forgot to tell you, I've decided to go with Michael Carlton's sponsorship offer. Providing we can make it work, and I don't have to compromise myself with my client too much. I'm still a bit unhappy about that.'

'Don't be. It'll be fine.'

'I hope so. And I have to tell you, I do worry about his development.'

'But why? I don't understand.'

'Because you know how much I hate the wrecking of the countryside.'

'Octavia! It's only a few houses. People have to live somewhere.'

'Yes, I know, but not in little brick boxes, set down on the graves of trees. I hate it, and I hate the thought of being, however slightly, part of it.'

'Maybe you won't be,' he said.

'You mean he might not get his planning permission?'

'Well – yes.'

'I bet he will,' she said soberly, 'they always do.'

*

'Think we're going to get that account?' said Aubrey Cotterill casually. He and Tom were sitting in the boardroom, having breakfasted with a couple of fairly senior civil servants, in order to discuss the possibility of any real likelihood of a differential in car taxation levels. They were considering launching a campaign on the subject, pulling together any of their clients with a vested interest in the subject; it was the fun side of lobbying, as Tom often said.

'Oh, yes. I'm pretty confident,' said Tom. 'I had dinner with the Drapers last night and they more or less committed theselves. Just a matter of talking the board round, as Jim Draper put it. I think that mostly means the Drapers themselves.'

'Good. We've put a lot of money into getting it. Was Octavia there?'

'Yes. She was great. I'd say she tipped the balance.'

'Great. You're a lucky man, Tom, having her.'

'I know it,' said Tom soberly.

'Apart from her innate instincts for pulling them in, prospective clients are always so charmed by her and her own success. Well, I have to say that's something of a relief. Or will be when they've signed. I'm a cautious old biddy, as you know.' He reached for the cigarette box that was on the table, pulled one out, lit it, inhaled hard.

Tom looked at him thoughtfully. Aubrey was usually the more relaxed of the two of them, despite a ferocious intellect. He was a Winchester Scholar, with a First in Greats, divorced, after a brief, unhappy marriage, rotund, balding, slightly baby faced, but with immense charm and a rather surprising success with women; Octavia was very fond of him.

'We really do need that account, Tom,' he said suddenly, as if he had taken a decision to unburden himself. 'We need it rather badly. We're sailing very close to the wind once again, very close indeed. I know we've got more accounts than we can handle, but they're all costing a hell of a lot.'

'They've always cost a hell of a lot,' said Tom. 'It's a costly business. They pay a lot as well.'

'I know that, but salaries have shot up recently, and so have the rates on this building, not to mention running costs. And then there's the back interest and penalties to our friends in the Revenue; that's really hit us this half year.'

Eighteen months earlier they had appointed a new young, brash accountant who had said he could get their tax liability down: he had suggested that part of their vast entertaining budget – 'not tax allowable, should be, it's a disgrace, when you think what you boys are doing for the economy' – could be put down as new equipment. 'It's entirely reasonable, you've spent a fortune on this new system of yours. I've just bumped it up a bit, you pay enough to the buggers anyway. Down to you, of course, but that's what I'd suggest.'

Confronted by an urgent need – as always – for cash, and presented with a way to find at least some of it, they had agreed to turn a blind eye to that section of their tax return. The Inland Revenue had taken a hard look at their accounts the following year, and discovered the discrepancy. The amounts had not been large enough to incur serious penalties, and they had fired the accountant, but there had been a hefty slug of back tax and interest which had hurt their cashflow.

'Even the Drapers don't solve our immediate problem,' said Cotterill, 'not until they've signed. I think we may have to increase our charges again.'

'We can't, not on the new business, and there's a lot of it. We've won – what? – four new accounts this year. They're all in for fifteen grand a month, except for Carlton, and I'm charging him twenty. And on the ongoing stuff, we only put the standard rate up in September. They all took it on the chin. We can't do it again.'

'The simple fact is we need to. Or get a couple more accounts without incurring any extra costs whatsoever. Make do with the resources and people we've already got. Otherwise—' he shrugged – 'otherwise, we could be in a bit of trouble. In the short term. Long term our position and our prospects are superb. It's the old cashflow problem.'

'So?'

'So we need the Drapers and their Pro-Media. Or another account. Or to cut costs.'

'I don't see how we can cut costs any further,' said Tom. 'We're down on staff as it is – everyone's working an eight-day week. Look, my father-in-law's got some new prospect for me apparently – if he ever deigns to ring me about it. That could save our bacon.'

'We don't just need it saved,' said Cotterill, 'we need it fried into really nice, tasty, crispy pieces. Think you can do that?'

'Oh, I expect so,' said Tom.

'Got a minute?' Melanie Faulks looked over her half-moon spectacles at Octavia. She was probably the only woman in London who looked good in half-moons, Octavia thought; they suited her rather zany, wild-haired charm.

'Yes, of course.'

'Now look, about this sponsor you've found for Cultivate. Clever girl.'

'Yes. Melanie, I've been meaning to – that is, I'm a bit worried—'

Octavia's direct line rang sharply. 'Excuse me.' Only three people had that number: Tom, Caroline and her father. She couldn't ignore any of them.

It was Tom.

'Hi. Look, I'm really sorry about this, but I've had Michael Carlton on the phone. He says he hasn't heard from you about his sponsorship suggestion. Or your local lot, down in Somerset.'

'Good timing. I'm just going to talk to Melanie about it.'

'Oh, fine. Look, I don't want to pressurise you, Octavia, really, but—'

'Tom, just leave it with me. It's complicated. For lots of reasons. But I'll do my best. Sorry, Melanie,' she said, putting the phone down.

'That's okay. But I do hope the sponsorship isn't going to to fall through. I'd like Margaret Piper to know about it as soon as possible, she's been on the phone again. You said you were worried?'

'No, I don't think it's going to fall through. Although I must phone him. But, Melanie, I did tell you he was a client of Tom's, didn't I? The guy who's offered to put up the money?'

'No, I don't think you did tell me,' said Melanie slowly, 'not that he was an actual client. You said you'd met him through Tom. Well, I don't suppose it matters. It can't, it's too important. We'll have to do the usual window dressing, of course, make out his wasn't the only hat in the ring.'

'Yes, of course.'

'So what was the worry?'

'Oh, nothing really. It can wait.' This was not the time to air her further anxieties about Carlton's development; she certainly shouldn't discuss it until she had done her homework, checked out any local branches of Foothold.

'Good. Like I said, clever girl.'

'Well, let's hope he doesn't change his mind. I'll fix a meeting, shall I?'

'Yes, sure. Soon as poss. And let me have the details, would you? The amount he's prepared to put up, when we could have it, what he would be looking for in return, all the usual stuff. And does he want to come in, have a meeting here? He'd better, I think.'

'Yes, of course. Although . . .' It should be avoided for as long as possible; he was sure to start talking about his development and the centre.

'Fine. Just fix it.'

Michael Carlton was out when Octavia phoned, wouldn't be back until after five, his secretary said. She left her number, mentally crossed her fingers, crushing her unease about the whole venture, and reached for her file on Foothold. Please, please God, don't let there be a branch in – where was the actual town? Oh, yes, Felthamstone.

There was. A big one.

Octavia suddenly felt rather sick.

Bob Macintosh, who had done as Tom told him and played a waiting game, was finally phoned after lunch that day by the press officer who had suggested the photocall. Had he made his decision yet and if so when would it be convenient for the photocall to be set up? 'The minister and his own family are more than happy about this.'

Bob Macintosh said that he was still very unhappy about it, but that he was prepared to consider it, and that he would, in any case, prefer any future discussions to be held not with him, but with his advisers at Fleming Cotterill.

The press officer said that sounded unnecessarily complicated, that it would be far better just to arrange things between the two of them. Bob Macintosh said that in that case there was nothing to arrange, and that he felt it should be known that a journalist had approached him direct about the affair, very anxious to hear his version of the story.

Five minutes later he phoned Fleming Cotterill. 'He said he'd be in touch with you, Tom. I do hope this is going to work.'

Tom said he was very confident that it would and settled down to wait for a call from Westminster.

The first call Tom received came not from Westminster, but Felix Miller, disproportionately irritated at Tom's failure to return his call. Most of his emotions with regard to Tom were disproportionate, certainly the less pleasant ones. It was something they both recognised, but were totally unable to do anything about. Felix, because his hostility to Tom was so deeply rooted, an intrinsic part of the passionate emotion he felt for Octavia; Tom, because short of lying down and dying, as he had been heard to remark, nothing he could do would endear him to Felix. All they could do was dissemble, struggle for courtesy.

'Hallo, Felix. Good of you to ring. Sorry about yesterday. Got terribly tied up.'

'Yes, yes. Pity though. Probably too late now.' It wasn't of course, but he wanted to make his point. Tom should return phone calls promptly; it was not only discourteous, but inefficient not to.

'Well, in case it's not, maybe we should meet? With your man.'

'I'll have to speak to him, Tom. He may not actually want to pursue it. All other things being equal, though, you'd be able to take it on, would you? Got the capacity and so on?'

'Yes, Felix, we have the capacity.'

'Because better not get involved at all if you can't cope with the workload.'

'We can cope.'

'So you say, but if you're too busy to return a phone call . . .'

'That was not an indication of our overall capacity, I do assure you. I didn't personally have the time to phone you yesterday morning. An assistant would not have done, I imagine? I was in one long complex meeting after another and—'

'Yes, yes, all right. You've made your point. Well, I'll endeavour to set up a meeting. With my contact. Cadogan's his name, Nico Cadogan – his company's Cadogan Hotels, as I expect you know.'

'I certainly do. Very interesting company. Although not doing terribly well just at the moment.'

'You hadn't heard any rumours? About a bid?'

'No,' said Tom, 'but—'

'I'd have thought your ear was closer to the ground than that. Anyway, it's no secret. Or won't be much longer. Western Provincial are after him.'

'That would be an interesting marriage.'

'One that naturally Cadogan wants to prevent.'

'Naturally,' said Tom. 'Difficult, though. Can't always be done, in my experience.'

He had picked up on the analogy about marriage, thought Felix, regretting he had used it. Tom didn't often get to score points off him, but when he did, he enjoyed it.

'Well, it would be up to you to prevent it,' he said shortly. 'Anyway, I'll set up a meeting. I've done quite a hard sell on you, Tom, but from now it's entirely up to you. Now, while you're on the phone, is Octavia all right?'

'Yes, I think so. Why?'

'She sounded terribly tired the other night. She does too much – you should try and make her rest more.'

'Felix—'

'She's not physically very strong, you know. She never has been.'

'Felix, I hate to argue with you, but I think Octavia is quite physically strong. Actually. And if she's tired—'

'Of course she is. Surely you've noticed it?'

'Not especially, no, I hadn't. I agree with you she does too much, but that is largely of her own volition.'

'Is it? I don't know that that's true. She puts in a lot of hours for you, all the entertaining—'

'I don't—' Tom stopped suddenly. 'Yes, she does do a lot. Of course. But she is quite driven herself.'

'Driven? I wouldn't have put it quite like that. She drives herself.'

'Felix, I take your point. And I'm sorry if she's particularly tired. I'll – talk to her, make sure she's all right.'

He shouldn't have to be asked to talk to his wife, thought Felix. It wasn't fair.

'Right. I'll get Cadogan to ring you. And make sure you return any calls promptly this time, won't you, Tom?'

'Felix, of course I will. I'm sorry again. And thanks for thinking of us.'

Felix sat looking at the phone after Tom had rung off. The warmth in his tone, the wholeheartedness of his apology had sounded genuine. He clearly wanted this account. And if he got it he would handle it well. Felix had no doubts whatsoever as to Tom's business ability; if he had, there would have been no question of his recommending him. And he also recognised the power of Tom's brain, which was first class. It was indeed one of the problems, as Marianne had once rather courageously proposed, of his relationship with his son-in-law; had he had an inferior intellect to his own, been less well read, with less capacity for original thought, Felix could have despised him. As it was, he was forced into a fiercely uneasy admiration for him. This, combined with an emotional distaste and a ferocious jealousy, made for a dangerously powerful mix. He had never, he had once admitted to Marianne, had any reasoned grounds for his dislike of Tom. But he also knew, and had also said to her, that if Tom did anything that really hurt, truly damaged Octavia, he would have no compunction whatsoever in killing him. 'In fact,' he had said, with an icily regretful smile, 'I would be unable not to.'

He had made this statement on the back of a bottle and a half of claret; but Marianne had always felt that it was actually terrifyingly true.

It was almost the end of the day when Tom phoned Bob Macintosh. 'Progress, I think,' he said. 'Just had a very interesting conversation with your friend at the House. He does seem very concerned that you should co-operate with them over this. I said you weren't quite so keen, but there was another matter I would like to discuss with him. He was fairly unhelpful initially, but I did tell him I was already hearing talks of Toshigate being bandied about among my contacts down at Canary Wharf.'

'Toshigate?'

'Yes. Tosh as in Macintosh, gate as in Watergate.'

'Oh, I see. Yes, that's very funny, Tom, I must say.'

'Yes, I thought so. I made it up,' said Tom modestly. 'Anyway, an hour or so later, I got another call; I think we'll find that any lobbying we do on Euro regs *vis-à-vis* the retail food industry will receive a sympathetic ear, and there's a good possibility of a parliamentary question on the subject, or even an Early Day Motion, particularly if they are persuaded of a broad span of interest. So I think, under the circumstances, a quick photo session might be at least worth considering, don't you?'

'Oh, I do,' said Bob Macintosh. 'Under the circumstances. Certainly worth considering.'

Octavia arrived home at nine, after a rather tedious committee meeting with the regional representatives of a new client, a sponsor-a-child charity looking to raise their profile – they all wanted to raise their profiles and they all didn't want it to cost anything, she thought despairingly. She finally managed to persuade them into a series of 'fasting' lunches. 'People pay to come and then eat bread and cheese and drink water; it raises a lot of money, and at grass root level does a very good PR job. It's what the charity's about, earns it respect, and it still gives the ladies who lunch a reason to dress up and gossip.'

Tom was out at a dinner when she got home; the children were all asleep. She had been hungry, but it had worn off by now and that was good. Calories in hand, as she thought of them. She made herself a large mug of peppermint tea and went to check the answering machine.

There was only one message, left at ten that morning: 'Hallo, Boot. Only me. Give me a ring if you have a minute over the next few days. I'm not doing anything. As usual. Seems ages since we talked properly. And there's something I have to tell you.'

Louise. She'd been thinking about her a lot lately, missing her. They met far too seldom, separated by their lifestyles, but they managed to remain close by phone, picking up a conversation almost where it had been left off, often after weeks of silence.

She dialled Louise's Cheltenham number: it rang for a while, then Louise's husky, musical voice, breathless, slightly fraught, said, 'Hallo?'

'Louise, it's me. Octavia.'

'Oh, Octavia. How *lovely*. Listen, can I ring you back in ten minutes? No, make that half an hour. I'm just putting Dickon to bed, he's not very well, and there's also a very nasty case of outraged hungry male here, demanding its food. Let me feed the beast and then I'll get back to you. Or are you going out?'

'No,' said Octavia, 'no, I'm not going out.'

'I'll ring you nine at the latest. 'Bye, Boot.'

That silly nickname; a diminution of Old Boot, which was what Louise had called her whenever she was being bossy, or humourless. Which had been a great deal of the time, thought Octavia, putting down the phone, staring into space, seeing Louise suddenly, vividly, as she had been then, this person who had been the most important thing in her life for all her growing-up years. She remembered watching her on almost her first day at Wycombe Abbey, running across the lacrosse pitch at the end of a game, chasing after two girls, laughing, and then catching them up, walking between them, talking animatedly, her arms round their shoulders, tall and graceful and golden haired, wondering who she was, hearing someone say, 'Louise Madison gets prettier every term,' and envying her, from her lonely, frightened, friendless state, finding it impossible to imagine what it must be like to be her.

For the first half term, she watched her from afar, fascinated by her; they were in different houses, and different forms, in spite of being in the same year, and their paths hardly crossed. Louise would smile at her sometimes, even say 'hi', and Octavia would nod at her, and say 'hallo' awkwardly back, but that was all; Louise was gloriously popular, the star of the games circuit and settled comfortably near the bottom of every academic subject; Octavia was on a full academic scholarship, got top marks for everything and couldn't hold a ball if it was dropped into her hands. Louise had already been at the school for a year, having been been kept down because of her poor scholastic performance; Octavia was still unsettled after two months, wretchedly homesick, an only child, over-protected, young for her age, while intellectually precocious and trailing the glory of her scholarship.

It had been a strange friendship then, formed one evening after supper as they met in one of the cloakrooms, each emerging from a lavatory where they had been crying silently, or as silently as they could manage – Octavia because nobody liked her and her entire table had gone off giggling without her, Louise because she had just come from an interview with the headmistress and been threatened with unspeakably nameless horrors if her marks didn't improve. They had looked at each other shamefaced, both sniffing, smiling embarrassedly through their tears.

'You all right?' Louise had said.

'No, not really,' Octavia had said, too wretched to pretend any longer. 'What about you?'

'Not at all,' said Louise. 'Should we go and talk about it, do you think?' and she pulled a great length of paper towel from the wall unit, handed Octavia half of it, and then took her arm, blowing her nose as she did so. And from then on they had been inseparable. Had actually mingled their blood, drawn with their compasses, to the accompaniment of much giggling and squeaks of 'ouch' and sworn eternal friendship, 'For ever and ever. Amen.'

A strange alliance it had been, between the awkwardly difficult little girl nobody liked, and the charmingly easy one everyone did, but for some reason it had worked; Octavia had dinned her Latin verbs and her mathematical tables into Louise, Louise had insisted that Octavia be allowed to join the large gang of giggling, gossiping insiders that she led, and mutual gratitude and need had grown quite quickly into a lot of other things, not least affection and a very real respect. They stayed with one another in the holidays, at the lovely sprawling manor house in Gloucestershire where Louise lived with her doting parents and her two younger brothers, and the darker splendour of Felix Miller's Victorian Gothic mansion in Hampstead. From those weeks came Octavia's first experience of the happy, easy, noisy family life that Louise so carelessly enjoyed, Louise's of the tension and discipline and fierce possessiveness that drove Octavia; their very differences drew them closer, taught them tolerance and respect for one another.

When they had left Wycombe Abbey – Louise to do a secretarial training amidst the most dire prognostications of a life wasted and ruined, Octavia to Cambridge to study law – they drifted apart for a while; back in London at law school, studying for her final exams, Octavia had seen Louise's lovely face in the *Daily Mail* one morning (not greatly changed, even if the golden hair had been bleached and teased into a shape that defied gravity and the brown eyes had apparently doubled in size, with the addition of several layers of dark brown eye shadow and three pairs of false eyelashes). She was tipped as the hottest thing on the catwalk since Twiggy, the *Mail* informed its readers.

Octavia had contacted Louise through her agency and they became close again, Louise taking Octavia shopping ('You look awful, you'll never get a job wearing clothes like that'), and Octavia dragging Louise to theatres and art galleries ('No need to be pig ignorant and empty headed just because you're a model'). Octavia went to supper parties in Louise's big sunny studio flat near Primrose Hill, and met her friends – other models, photographers, dress designers, fashion editors, rather alarming they seemed to her, with their wild clothes and outrageous gossip. Louise was invited to slightly intense evenings in the rather grand flat Octavia's father had bought her in the Old Brompton Road, formal three-course dinner parties with Octavia's fellow lawyers and old friends from Cambridge.

Louise, by then, had a string of lovers, Octavia one fairly serious one; they shared appallingly intimate details of their sex lives, saw one another through pregnancy scares, heartbreak, career crises – Louise was fired by her agency for turning up late once too often; Octavia decided, just into her first big case, that she hated law, could stay in it no longer –

and then Louise took off for America for five years to work and Octavia met and became engaged to Tom.

Louise had approved of Tom: ecstatically. 'Heaven!' she had said happily, over supper with Octavia the night after the engagement party Felix had insisted on giving, and which she had flown over for. 'Too good looking and charming for words, of course, but you can handle that, can't you, my darling?'

Octavia had said she was sure she could, but quite what had Louise meant? Louise had got a bit flustered and said nothing, nothing at all, it was just that terribly good looking and charming men did tend to be a bit of handful, she should know, and Octavia had said if Louise meant she thought Tom was going to play around, then she was wrong, they had both agreed that fidelity was of paramount importance, or perhaps she'd meant that she, Octavia, was less good looking and charming than Tom, in which case she would rather Louise came out and said so.

Louise had become very upset and said she hadn't meant anything at all, and anyway it had been the champagne talking and Octavia had obviously forgotten what a lot of nonsense she did talk, champagne or no. Octavia had forgiven her, of course, but it had cast a shadow over the evening.

Louise had come over again, for the wedding, had been chief bridesmaid, and in his speech thanking her, Tom had said he half expected her to join them on honeymoon, so integral a part of his bride's life did she seem; Louise had stood up laughing and said was it an invitation because she'd adore to accept; Octavia and Tom went to Barbados without Louise, and when they got back to London she had gone.

For a while they had lost contact; then the phone rang one morning in Octavia's office and the lovely voice said, 'Boot? I'm getting married. He's called Sandy and he's divine, and utterly right for me. Come and meet him and approve – and keep quiet if you don't.'

She hadn't approved and she didn't keep quiet: she felt she couldn't, felt it was her duty as Louise's friend to be truthful.

'He is – marvellous of course,' she had said carefully, 'but I don't think quite right for you.'

'But he is,' said Louise, her blue eyes shining with earnestness. 'Almost everyone says he's not right, even Mummy says it, just because he's in the army, and not a photographer or something, but he's what I want, he's so stable and utterly reliable and – and English.'

'But your lives are so different, Louise. You'll have so little in common and—'

'We do, but I've had enough of that life, Boot. It's so ridiculous, so excessive, and everyone treats you like shit in the end. Sandy is so wonderfully old fashioned. And romantic. He's like – well, he's like Daddy. Daddy's the one person who's very happy about it. Now do stop fussing, I know we're going to be utterly, perfectly happy.'

And she had married him in a cloud of euphoria and wild silk on a glorious spring day in the village church in Gloucestershire, emerging to a guard of honour formed by Sandy's fellow officers, a cloud that broke up fairly soon into a series of storms before changing heavily and permanently into a grey mass, overhanging what clearly was, to Louise, an endlessly disappointing landscape.

Octavia, saddened by the disappointment (unacknowledged by Louise), had formed her own theory about the alliance. Despite (or perhaps because of) more than half a decade in the fashion industry, with its careless morality, its shifting emotional sands, its frenetic concern with style and appearance, Louise was extremely romantic. It was a joke about her that her sexual fantasies were not of multiple lovers, of night-long orgasms, of outrageous practices, but were set in a time warp, Hollywood style; Louise dreamed of eyes locking across a crowded room, meetings in slow motion along a deserted beach, passionate embraces against a storm-tossed sky. Sex to her only worked in the context of such things – as a pleasure in itself it was a devalued currency. And Sandy, when she met him, came from that segment of society that was – on the surface at least – courteous and considerate to women and well behaved, in a rather old-style way: totally different from most of the men she met in her coolly fashionable world. His dark looks were best described by that old-fashioned adjective 'handsome', he was flamboyantly well mannered, rode superbly, played polo for his regiment, had been mentioned several times for his courage and resourcefulness during an horrific tour of duty in Bosnia; but he was a man's man, not quite at ease with women, at once protective and very slightly patronising. Louise had been charmed by the protectiveness and did not discover the tendency to patronise until it was too late.

He had dined and wined her, insisted on paying for everything, told her repeatedly she was the most beautiful girl in the world, sent her a great many bunches of flowers and didn't even suggest they went to bed together for quite a long time. For Louise, moving in a world where sex was seriously devalued except as a rather transient pleasure, as much taken for granted in the briefest relationship as food and drink, this was in itself rather romantic. When they finally did go to bed, it was in a country house hotel that Sandy had booked; the bed was a four poster, there were white roses on the dressing table, and champagne on ice beside the bed. Louise was so overwhelmed by all this that she managed to ignore the fact that the sex itself was rather run-of-the-mill; the fact that after it Sandy had toasted her in what was left of the champagne, told her he was in love with her and had never before felt quite as he did, had been to her ineffably more important.

Sandy had left the army a year after they were married and set himself up with a fellow officer in the wine business. A small local chain, it ran a wine club for its customers, offering tastings, masterclasses in wine and even trips to vineyards. Having developed a strong brand loyalty, Sandy intended to move it from its purely Cotswold base to London and the home counties.

Louise, released at least from the crippling boredom (as she had found it) of being an army wife, had found herself happily pregnant; Dickon was born, and two and a half years later, a little girl, Juliet. She threw herself wholeheartedly into motherhood and being a good wife to Sandy.

Octavia had seen very little of her at this time. Their husbands had not been greatly impressed with one another: the fact that Sandy was an Old Etonian with an extremely patrician background did nothing to endear him to Tom, and Tom's ceaseless pursuit of success and money seemed to Sandy a rather severe case of bad form. Meetings between the two families were awkward, and after a few attempts, both Octavia and Louise agreed they should be avoided.

And then one day, nine months after the birth of Juliet, Octavia's phone rang. It was Louise, her voice leaden, strange, panic underlying it.

'Octavia,' she had said. 'Octavia, Juliet's dead. Please come.'

It had been a cot death; she had gone in to pick the baby up for her morning feed and found her. 'White, cold, quite quite still. And dead.'

Octavia had gone at once. Louise was calm, deathly calm, enduring the dreadful ritual demanded by the law, the police visit, the registration of the death, the taking of her baby to hospital for an autopsy, the planning of the funeral. Louise's mother, Anna Madison, was there, gently, sweetly efficient; Sandy was there, ghastly pale, pacing the house. Octavia had felt like an intruder. But she had found a role for herself, caring for Dickon, who was stumbling about looking terrified and lost. She had taken him out for much of the day, brought him back when the worst of it was over, suggested he came to stay with her for a couple of days.

Louise had accepted the offer, in her new flat, still voice. 'It would be such a help. He loves the twins. And you will come to the funeral, won't you? It would help me so much if you were there.'

Octavia had promised she would, shrinking from the very thought of witnessing such pain; she drove Dickon back to London, where the twins, only half-comprehending what had happened, drew him into their rather rough kindliness; he finally fell asleep that first night in Poppy's plump little arms.

He woke in the night, screaming from a nightmare; and then said he wanted to phone his mother.

'Dickon, darling, it's three in the morning.'

'She might be dead, though,' he said. 'She might! Please ring, please . . .'

Octavia had given in and phoned, and a clearly wide-awake Louise had answered the phone, reassured him, fetched Sandy to do the same. Dickon had spent the rest of the night in her bed, tossing and turning restlessly; after a second, identical night, she had been deeply grateful when Anna Madison phoned and said she thought it would be better if Dickon came home, Louise was missing him, and she drove him down to Cheltenham with some relief.

Louise had greeted her strangely, almost detachedly, still with the same deathly calm.

'Louise, are you sure you're all right?'

'I'm fine. Really. Sandy isn't too good,' she added, almost matter-of-factly. 'He was in tears last night. I told him he had to be brave, for Dickon and me.'

It had seemed a curiously harsh reaction, but Octavia supposed she could hardly expect rational behaviour from her.

Later, as she walked to the car, Anna Madison had come running out of the house. 'Thank you for everything, Octavia. I'm so pleased you're coming on Friday.'

'Of course I'm coming,' Octavia had said, and then added, 'Louise seems – odd.'

'Yes, she's in shock. God knows when it will break. But actually, it's getting her through this dreadful time. Things like choosing a coffin, the flowers . . .' Her large blue eyes, so like Louise's, had filled with tears.

Octavia put her arms round her; she adored Anna. 'Thank goodness she's got you. Look, I have to go. Please ring if there's anything else I can do.'

'I will, Octavia darling. Thank you.'

Louise had still seemed in shock at the funeral, icy calm and composed, watching Sandy carry the tiny coffin into the church, with dull, expressionless eyes; she had sung a hymn, listened to the agonisingly touching address with courteous attention. Even at the graveside, she had not broken down, had knelt and placed a note and a flower on top of the coffin, had then gone back to the house with her family and Octavia and Tom – the only non-family present – and although quiet, had managed to offer them tea, and thank them politely for coming.

'I'll come and see you soon,' she had said, kissing Octavia goodbye. Octavia had put her arms round her, tried to hug her, but she was rigid, unyielding. The last they saw of Louise was her waving them off down the road, holding Dickon's hand, Sandy standing behind her.

'How brave,' said Tom, 'how terribly brave she is.'

'Too brave, I think,' said Octavia.

That night Louise had cracked, had cried for three days and nights, had finally been heavily sedated – and when she came round, began her slow and painful journey out of grief and back to normality.

'I worry about them all so much,' Anna had told Octavia one night when she phoned to see how Louise was. 'It's dreadful for Louise, of course, so dreadful, and she is quite fragile, you know, emotionally, and little Dickon is terribly upset, but Sandy has had a terrible time too, and Louise doesn't seem to recognise it.'

Octavia had gone down to see them quite frequently during that time; she felt helpless and useless, and Louise had been strange with her, oddly distant and almost hostile, but she always thanked her effusively for coming, told her she felt better afterwards, and Sandy was always deeply grateful too and told her so. He had changed visibly, more than Louise, through the experience, looked older, seemed less confident.

'Oh, doesn't matter about me,' he had said one night as Octavia was leaving and she had managed to ask him if he was all right, 'it's Lulu we have to worry about.'

'Well, she was your baby too,' Octavia had said quietly, and he had said, yes, of course, but he hadn't given birth to her, it was different for men. He sounded as if he had rehearsed the small speech; in a way no doubt he had, she thought, he must have made it dozens of times, poor man.

There was a time after that, over much of the following eighteen months in fact, when they hardly saw one another. Louise withdrawn further into herself, discouraged visits, was almost taciturn on the phone. Octavia had several worried conversations with Anna Madison, who had been equally ostracised from her daughter's life, and a few with Sandy who clearly felt quite out of his depth and embarrassed by any attempt to discuss the matter. 'She'll be fine,' he'd say, determinedly cheerful, 'just a matter of time.'

To her shame, Octavia had given up. She was, in any case, pregnant – unbearably poignant, she felt, for Louise. And then, struggling to cope with the new baby and her professional life it seemed easier, better indeed, to stay away. She hoped she wasn't making excuses for herself, opting out; she was rather afraid she was. She had written of course to let Louise know about Minty's birth, had been almost shocked – while telling herself that of course she understood – to receive only a card in return.

Then, at Christmastime, she had felt things were getting out of hand. She missed Louise, she was concerned for her; she herself was strong, her own life so good, how could she possibly not present broad and loving shoulders to her friend? She had written a long letter, saying how much she missed her, and inviting her and Sandy to the Christmas party, which Louise had always loved: 'So many glamorous people, you're so clever, Octavia.'

Louise had phoned, full of fun and charm, and said how marvellous, they'd adore to come to the party, and she was buying a new frock. She had turned up looking luminously beautiful. 'I'm quite quite all right now,' she had said, hugging Octavia, 'and I'm sorry I was – difficult. Now where is darling Tom? I want to give him the biggest Christmas kiss. And to meet dear little Minty – I have a present for her. Don't look at me like that, Octavia, I'm quite all right. Honestly.'

Octavia had felt a huge sense of relief – not only on Louise's behalf, but from her own guilt.

After Christmas, the Trelawnys had visited them in Somerset, although only for a day. It had been, as always, difficult, the men uneasy together; after lunch Octavia had proposed a walk, hoping that Tom and Sandy would decline, but they had both said it was exactly what they needed. She had found herself, rather than having a long, healing conversation with Louise, chatting over-brightly to Sandy while Louise walked ahead with Tom. Afterwards, when they had gone, she had asked Tom what they had talked about.

'Nothing much,' he had said. 'She just prattled. As she does.'

'She didn't mention the baby?' she had said.

'No, rather the reverse. When I told her I was – sorry, you know, she just said she hated talking about it.'

'She ought to talk about it,' Octavia had said. 'It would do her good.'

'Octavia,' said Tom rather shortly, 'everyone's different. You can't make rules about these things.'

He had been in a difficult mood altogether: Sandy always affected him like that. Octavia had changed the subject.

They had met a couple of times since then, talked on the phone a lot; as far as Octavia could tell Louise was much better. She was very cheerful, and apart from being thinner than she had ever been, and rather restless, she was as much herself as could be reasonably expected. But she refused to talk about Juliet's death. 'I know it's meant to be therapeutic, but it just hurts me,' she had said, and was wary of any suggestion that she might have another baby. 'People keep suggesting I do that, as if – Juliet—' she hesitated over the word – 'could be replaced. I don't want to. Ever. She's gone and it's quite over. That's what I want. Now let's talk about other things. I'm just so glad we're together again.'

Octavia, still faintly concerned, had telephoned Anna Madison to ask her if Louise was really as recovered as she insisted, but she had been airily cheerful, rather like Louise herself, and had said she was very proud of her and the way she had coped.

'You've been such a good friend to her Octavia, thank you. We're all so grateful.'

'Darling Boot, it's me. Sorry I couldn't talk before.'

'Is Dickon all right?'

'What? Oh, yes. He's fine. Too many Mr Men yoghurts, I think. He has a passion for them.'

'And Sandy?'

'Oh, he's all right,' said Louse dismissively. 'Just hungry. Feed the brute, that's what Mummy always says . . .' Her voice tailed off and there was a long silence.

Octavia frowned. 'Louise, is something the matter?'

Another silence. Then, 'Yes,' she said, finally, in the same odd voice, 'yes, there is, I'm afraid. It's why I rang you tonight. I've had some rather bad news. It's – it's Mummy. She's ill. Quite ill.'

'Oh, Louise, no. What, how . . .'

'Big C, I'm afraid.' Louise's voice was suddenly harsh.

'Oh, Louise, I'm so *so* sorry.' The thought of lovely, golden Anna, ill, in pain, was horrible. 'What, I mean where . . .'

'Breast,' said Louise briefly, 'so there may be some hope. Daddy told me late yesterday. She'd gone in for what I thought was a check-up, but she'd had a biopsy done. Oh, God. Octavia, it's so unfair, she's only fifty-seven.'

'It's ghastly. Horrible. But they can do a lot these days. All those treatments—'

'All those horrible, hideous treatments. Yes. Well, we'll learn more this weekend.'

'Louise, you should have phoned me earlier, at the office.'

'I didn't want to talk to you there. When you might be rushed.'

Guilt ripped through Octavia; was she really so fraught at the office she couldn't talk to her best friend about such a thing? Maybe she was.

'I'm sorry,' she said again, for that as much as Anna's illness. 'And, Louise, please give her my love, my best love. And to your dad.'

She felt very upset after that, incapable of doing all the things she had planned. She sat in the television room watching a very bad film, waiting for Tom, who had promised not to be late. He would be upset, he was so fond of Anna too.

He was: very upset. She was surprised how much. He went very white, sat down heavily on the sofa beside her.

'Christ, how awful,' he said. 'How absolutely bloody awful! Poor woman. How bad is it?'

'I don't think they're sure yet. She has to have more tests. They'll know better at the weekend apparently.'

'And Louise told you, did she?'

'Yes. This evening.'

'How did she seem?'

'Oh, you know. Not very good.'

'But not – well, you know, not how she was after the baby?'

'No.'

'Thank God for that.'

'Yes. But it's early days, Tom. If Anna does – die, it will be very dreadful for her. She adores her so.'

'Well, we must hope. When did she hear?'

'Oh, a few days ago, I believe. Why?'

'I just wondered why she hadn't told you sooner, that's all.'

'She said she didn't want to ring me in the office. Where I was so busy, as she put it. That made me feel bad. Oh, dear . . .' She started to cry herself.

Tom put his arms round her.

'Darling, don't. No guilt trips. Louise is lucky to have you at all. Such a good friend.'

'I suppose so, but I'm lucky to have her too. She's just as good as me.'

'Yes, maybe.' His voice was heavy.

It seemed a slightly odd thing to say. She knew he considered the relationship one sided, had found it hard to be patient with her acute anxiety over Louise's nervous breakdown. Male jealousy, she supposed. She looked up at him, but he was smiling down at her, very tenderly.

'Look, let's get you to bed. How would you like me to bring you some warm milk?'

He must be feeling very sorry for her. Her hot milk habit, as he called it, enraged him normally – it was a hangover from her childhood when her father would put her to bed with warm milk, laced with honey if she was unwell or upset. 'Warm milk and love,' Felix would say, smiling at her, 'just what the doctor ordered.' And then he would sit and cuddle her to sleep. As soon as she was old enough, she would do the same for him; he was plagued by migraine and he said the sweet drink helped him.

'You go up to bed,' Tom said now, 'and I'll bring it up to you. Go on, pretend I'm your father.'

'Don't be silly,' she said, smiling through her tears, but she was very surprised. Her relationship with her father was usually much too serious a subject for him to be able to joke about.

CHAPTER 5

Nico Cadogan had proposed that he and Tom meet without Felix: 'It would delay things by at least forty-eight hours, and I daresay you and I could manage a brief chat on our own.'

Tom agreed that they could and asked Nico to meet him for a drink at the Ritz.

He was intensely excited at the prospect of getting this account. Cadogan was a chain of medium-range hotels, with a few jewels in its crown, most notably the three Cadogan Royals, immensely expensive hotels in Edinburgh, Bath and London. Western Provincial, who had made the bid, were also a hotel chain, most of them motels. George Egerton of Western had long had his sights on the Cadogan chain: mostly because he was an arriviste of huge personal as well as corporate wealth, and longed for the cachet of some five-star hotels.

Tom's first impression of Cadogan was that he would find him extremely tricky to work with. He was tall, dark, patrician looking, surprisingly young – he'd put him at about forty-five – with an exaggeratedly public school accent, and a bombastic manner.

'I know all about your consultancy from your father-in-law,' he said, interrupting Tom as he began to outline what Fleming Cotterill might do for him. 'Obviously it's very sound. And anyone recommended by Felix Miller can command my attention. What I need is swift action. And an assurance that you can deliver it.'

'What stage are things at?'

'Egerton has told me he's going to be making a bid. That's all the information I have at this time. I've been expecting it: we're a very tempting proposition, and the last two sets of results haven't been too good. The shareholders would look very carefully at any offer.'

'Why haven't the results been good?'

'Largely because of heavy investment. Getting the Cadogan Royals off the ground has cost a great deal. But actually, it's the Cadogans that have been costing the money. They've been over-resourced in terms of staff, and I've spent a fortune on installing a computer system to sort that out.'

'So you'll be able to make some savings now?'

'Oh, without doubt. But it'll take time to turn round, and meanwhile there's not a lot of profit in it. So Egerton thinks it's going to be easy.'

'And why shouldn't it be?' said Tom. 'Sorry to play devil's advocate, but it doesn't sound too good.'

'Well, I've hired a new MD. Bright young chap, setting the whole place on fire, lots of ideas. And I think we could take it to the Monopolies Commission. His mid-range hotels and mine are in direct competition. I don't need to tell you what that means in terms of keeping prices down. What do you think? I want advice on how to approach them. Can you help or not?'

'It's not simple at all, I'm afraid.' Tom's voice was at its easiest, his smile its most professionally engaging. 'There's a bit more to do than just talk to the MMC, and they wouldn't even get involved at this stage. Cases have to be referred to them by the Office of Fair Trading. And there's no guarantee it would be. If we are to act for you, the first thing we need is an immediate and very full working knowledge of your company, its assets, its history, its future plans. Then I can give you some indication of whether this is a likely one for referral or not.'

'Yes, of course. I realise that. I'm perfectly prepared to take you right through it, make anything and anyone available to you that you need.'

'Yes, and I'd certainly need it fast,' said Tom. 'We're talking if not the eleventh hour here, then certainly the tenth.'

'I realise that as well. But that's why I would be hiring you – to short-circuit things. Can you do that?'

'I don't know. Honestly. Until I have the information. And short-circuiting is not what we're about, so much as moving swiftly and efficiently through. You can't ignore legislation, dance round it. Or indeed Whitehall.'

'Well,' Cadogon said, draining his glass (a double whisky sour – obviously a strong head, thought Tom), 'I'm a bit disappointed. Miller said you would be able to fix it for me, get on to the big boys straight away.'

'Unfortunately,' said Tom, 'he doesn't understand my business, any more than I understand his. And I can't walk on water.'

'I see.' Cadogan looked at him. 'In that case, may I say I admire your honesty. I never managed to walk on water either. Maybe between us we could construct a lifeboat?' He grinned at Tom. 'When can you come in?'

'Monday morning,' said Tom. 'First thing. As I said, we can't afford to waste any time.'

'Good man! I thought Miller couldn't have got you wrong. How is he as a father-in-law, by the way?'

'Oh – fine,' said Tom. 'Great.'

'If we're going to work together,' said Cadogan thoughtfully, 'you mustn't lie to me. I'm extremely discreet.'

Tom was to remember those words a great deal in the months to come.

'Fleming, this won't do. Crying in office hours is not allowed.'

Octavia wiped her eyes, blew her nose, tried to smile. 'Sorry, Mells.'

'I wasn't serious, you know.' Melanie's face softened. 'Anyway, it's after office hours, so you can blub away. What's the matter?'

'Oh, friend of mine. Louise, you know? Well, she phoned last night. Her mother's got cancer. I'm just really fond of her. And it was a shock.'

'Of course. Poor woman.'

'Yes. She's only fifty-seven. And now Tom's going to be away tonight and I thought we were going to have an evening on our own. Just for once. Oh, it sounds silly, but I feel so down, and—'

'Want to have a meal with me? I'm not doing anything.'

'No, I don't think so. Thanks all the same. Nanny's night off and all that.'

'Where's Tom going?'

'Oh, Birmingham way. He's got a client there who's in trouble, and then some sales conference he decided he ought to go to at Leamington Spa. And then we've got a gruelling weekend with some Americans. I could do without that, I tell you. They want to see *Les Mis*. That'll be the fourth time. And it's so long . . .' She blew her nose again, smiled weakly at Melanie.

'Poor old thing. Well, you'd better go on home, and have an early night. Sorry about your friend.'

'Thanks, Melanie.'

'Look at this,' said Tom. He waved the *Mail on Sunday* at her. 'You did that.'

She looked; a picture of Bob Macintosh, sitting on the sofa in his drawing room, one arm round Maureen, the other round his elder daughter's shoulders. The younger children were on the floor in front of them, together with the yellow Labrador.

'The millionaire's wife, the MP, and the lies that make Maureen Macintosh see red,' screamed the headline across the top of the page, followed by a long interview with Maureen, headed 'The value I put on my marriage . . .'

'Yes, about three million,' said Octavia. 'Excuse me while I throw up. And what do you mean I did it?'

'This is the result of your brilliant idea. The bargain, you remember?'

'Ye-es. What did he get in return?'

'Some realistic discussion in the corridors of power about the bloody Euroregs,' said Tom.

'I don't remember suggesting that.'

'No, the small print is down to me. Broad canvas sketched in by you. What a team!' said Tom. 'And it's even made the broadsheets.'

'Very clever,' said Octavia, smiling at him. He was stretched out on the sofa in the drawing room, his long legs encased in jeans, a cashmere sweater draped over his shoulders. He looked like a picture in an upmarket leisurewear catalogue, she thought, rather than a machiavellian schemer. It occurred to her, quite suddenly, that she wouldn't like to be on the wrong side of that scheming. And then wondered why she'd thought it, as if it was even remotely likely.

She sighed. Her head ached, and she had promised to take the twins to the adventure playground in Holland Park when the Americans had gone. And now they had.

'That was a very good weekend,' said Tom, 'with the Bryants. They've gone home very impressed.'

'I'm glad it wasn't all in vain,' she said. 'It certainly was hard work.'

'Darling! Hardly hard work. Theatre, dinner at Langan's, a shopping trip with Mrs Bryant, brunch at the Connaught . . .'

'Yes, and hearing about every possible complex relationship in the Bryant family from Mrs B, a minute-by-minute history of the early days of Bryant and Co from Mr B . . .'

'Well, you were magnificent. And next time I go to New York to see them, you can come. Promise.'

'Wow! What a lucky little woman I am. No thanks.'

'All right,' he grinned at her. 'Don't say I don't try. By the way, I've asked this new prospect of mine, Nico Cadogan, the one your father put my way, to come to Ascot with us next week. Now that you will enjoy. He's a nice chap, very good looking, oozes charm.'

'I can hardly wait.'

'And darling, that reminds me, what news of Michael Carlton, and the sponsorship deal?'

'Ah, yes. That one. Meeting pencilled in for Friday. And before you ask me, I still haven't spoken to the Foothold people. But I will. All right? Now, Tom, if you really wanted to show your gratitude for the weekend, you'd take the twins to Holland Park for me. Or at least come with us.'

'Darling, I can't. I have a speech to write for a dinner on Tuesday. I swear next weekend I'll take them out all day on Sunday. How's that? Incidentally, I was hoping to get back on Tuesday night, after the dinner, but I really don't think I can, I'll have to dash back at dawn. I must spend a couple of hours at my desk before we go to Ascot, so I'll meet you there. Up in the box. Is that okay?'

'It's fine. Where's the dinner?'

'Bath. It's—'

The phone rang: it was her father.

'Octavia, hallo. Just rang to see if you were all right.'

'I'm fine, Daddy. How would you like to come with your grandchildren and me to the adventure playground in Holland Park?'

'Can't Tom go with you?'

'No, he's – working,' she said, gritting her teeth, looking at Tom who had now closed his eyes, put *The Sunday Times* over his face.

'I see. It seems a pity he doesn't have more time for his family. I think, yes, that sounds rather nice. Nice to have you to myself for a bit.'

'You'll have to share me with the twins.'

'Well, that will be a pleasure.'

'We'll meet you there in an hour.'

She put the phone down, sighed. Now why had she done that? It would actually have been easier if she'd taken the twins on their own. They got very frustrated with their grandfather, who would talk to them for a very few minutes and then switch his attention straight back to her. She knew why of course; it had been to annoy Tom, to get back at him.

Felix drove across London, contemplating happily the prospect of having Octavia to himself for a couple of hours. It was a rare treat these days. That had been the greatest shock of her falling in love: of finding her no longer automatically available to him. Until she met Tom, he had come first; if he wanted to see her, if he was feeling unwell or even lonely, needed her to hostess an evening for him as she grew older and socially competent, he had only to ask her. She would give up anything, more or less, for him.

She had once when she was only about ten, forgone a very special treat for him, a birthday outing with friends to the ballet at Covent Garden. Fonteyn and Nureyev were dancing *Giselle* and she had talked of nothing else for weeks, had planned what to wear, the present had been bought and wrapped up days before the event. She didn't get asked to very many parties, was not popular at school – too clever and altogether too grown up for the other children, he felt, not interested in the sort of nonsense they liked, those dreadful Barbie dolls and pop singers.

He had become faintly irritated by the ballet outing as it drew nearer; he liked to provide her with the really big treats of her life himself. And this was something very special for her. The night before, when they had supper, she had eaten very little; he had asked her if she felt all right.

'Absolutely all right,' she had said seriously, 'just terribly, terribly excited about tomorrow. The best day of my life, it's going to be.'

He hadn't said anything, simply smiled and patted her hand, but jealousy quite literally twisted his guts.

Next morning he had woken with a bad throat. By lunchtime he realised he felt really unwell, had a headache, a foreboding that this might be going to be a really nasty flu.

Octavia had sat at lunch, chattering excitedly about the ballet, saying she couldn't believe she was really really going; it had begun to irritate Felix. He excused himself from the table, went to lie down on his bed. His headache was definitely worse.

After a while, he had heard the door open softly. 'Daddy?' Are you all right? Why are the curtains pulled?'

'Well, my head aches. But not too badly.'

'Poor Daddy. Can I get you an aspirin?'

'Oh, darling, I've already taken something much stronger than an aspirin. This is a real headache, I'm afraid.'

'Not a migraine?'

He got them sometimes: when he was upset. She worried about them, hated the whole process, the pain he was so clearly in, the vomiting. She knew he got them when he was overworking or upset about something, took a pride in trying to ward them off, making him leave his desk on Saturdays or Sundays to go for a walk: 'Come on, time to get some fresh air,' she would say, holding out her hand as if she was the parent, he the child.

He had smiled at her, at her worried little face, had said no, no, not a migraine. 'More like flu, I think. Got a bit of a temperature. Don't you worry about me, poppet. Look, hadn't you better be getting ready to go?'

'I don't want to leave you,' she had said, with enormous reluctance. 'Not if you're ill.'

'My darling,' he had said, struggling to sit up, 'my darling sweetheart, you're not missing that ballet for me. For your old daddy.'

'I'd miss anything for you,' she had said, 'if you wanted me to.'

By a quarter to six, when she had put her head round the door again, all dressed up by then in a dark plaid taffeta frock, and a ribbon in her hair, tied by Mrs Harrington, the housekeeper, he had realised he was feeling much worse.

'Oh, Daddy . . .' She had come over to the bed, put a small hand on his forehead. 'Daddy, you're hot!'

'A bit. Yes.' Of course it had been silly, under the circumstances, to shut the window, turn up the central heating; but when he'd gone up to the room, he'd felt rather cold. 'But no one ever died of a temperature. Or flu. Did they?'

'I don't know. I suppose Mrs Harrington will be here, to look after you.'

'Well, not, actually. It's her evening off, remember? She's taking it instead of tomorrow. But she'll leave me something. Not that I feel like eating.'

'So you'll be on your own.'

'Yes. Poor old me.' Then he had smiled at her again. 'But for heaven's sake, Octavia, I am a grown-up. Going on forty. I'll be all right for a few hours.'

'I think I should stay with you,' she had said in a small voice. 'Daddy, I can't leave you alone. Not with a temperature and maybe a migraine.'

'Darling, I'll be fine—' an imperceptible pause, he heard it himself – 'of course I will.'

'No,' she said slowly, pulling the ribbon out of her dark curls, 'no, you won't. I wouldn't enjoy it, worrying about you. I really wouldn't.'

'Oh, darling, you're so sweet. So good to your old dad. I feel so mean—'

'Daddy! Stop it. I'll just go and phone Flora's mummy quickly, and then I'll come and sit with you. Make you a milky cure.'

'That would be wonderful.' He heard her voice indistinctly on the phone in his study next door, then her footsteps running downstairs. She came back after ten minutes, with a drink on a tray, and a book.

'I'm going to read to you,' she said. 'Robinson Crusoe, your favourite.'

Her voice sounded slightly funny: he looked at her. She had been crying.

'My darling,' he said, 'I can never thank you enough for this. I feel so bad. I tell you what, as soon as I'm better, I'll take you to that ballet. We'll go together. How about that?'

'It's all sold out,' she said brightly. 'Never mind. Next time perhaps. Now be quiet, and rest your poor voice. I'll read to you.'

She did, and he fell asleep, watching her, listening to her, thinking how beautiful she was, and how sweet, how much he loved her, how much she must love him.

In the morning he felt extraordinarily better. Just a twenty-four-hour bug obviously.

She was right about the tickets, but he managed to pull some strings and hire a box. They sat in it together, just the two of them, and he ordered a bottle of champagne and gave her a small amount, mixed with orange juice, and she smiled at him as she sipped it, and told him she loved him and this was much much better than going with lots of girls from school.

'Is it really?' he said. 'Are you sure? That would surely have been more fun.'

'No, this is more fun. Honestly.'

'I still feel guilty.'

'You mustn't.'

So he didn't.

CHAPTER 6

'Right, then. I've had a look at all the background, the figures and so on. More coffee?'

Nico Cadogan shook his head. George Egerton had offered two pounds fifty a share for the Cadogan Group, and Cadogan had had an emergency meeting with his bankers. 'I'm awash with the stuff. What do you think?'

'Well, this offer's going to tempt your shareholders, with the shares at two pounds at the moment. What can you offer them to stay with you?'

'Precious little. I thought you were going to find a political process to stamp on it.'

'Cadogan, it isn't as easy as that. We can do quite a bit of stirring, yes. We can write to the MP in Romford – where your head office is – stir things up, say Provincial are ruthless, half the staff are going to be made redundant, we can table a few questions, try to put down an EDM – an Early Day Motion. It's a sort of petition. You find an interested MP—'

'How?'

'This is why you're hiring us,' said Tom, grinning at him. 'Anyway, you write something for him, saying something like "This house notes with concern the proposed merger, blah blah blah," and the person who puts it down goes round the House, trying to get likeminded people to sign it. Then it gets printed in the order paper for that day, and hopefully gets signed some more. You can use it for support, it has strong moral authority. Nothing much more than that, though. And then we can write to Margaret Beckett, point out that hotel prices will almost certainly go up. Write to the papers – you're very good copy – say you've got a family company, have a personal holding of fifty-one per cent, look after your staff well, all that stuff.'

'Sounds good to me.'

'Yes, but there's a catch, isn't there?'

Cadogan looked at him, sighed. 'Yeah. I know what you're going to say. Our duty to the shareholders.'

'Precisely. They're not going to like the idea of losing out fifty pence a share, simply to keep a few people in their jobs. I wouldn't.'

'So what do we do?'

I like that we, thought Tom; *we* is good. He felt a surge of confidence.

'You have to win the shareholders round. Present your overhauled company, your aggressive plans for expansion, your new MD; tell them you're planning to trim the sails a bit more, tell them two pounds fifty is not good enough, that within a year, if they stick with you, the shares will be worth three fifty. We can still plant the stories about loss of competition, speculate about rising costs. If it goes to referral—'

'What, to the Monopolies people?'

'Yes. If the Office of Fair Trading don't clear it, say it should be referred to the MMC – Monopolies and Mergers Commission – then we can start beavering away quietly about jobs being at risk, all that sort of thing. This is a PR job as much as a political one. It boils down to that: are you game?'

There was a long silence. Cadogan got up, went over to the window. Tom studied his back view, the black and silver hair, the broad shoulders, the perfectly cut suit, the exceptionally long legs; if you sent to central casting for A City Executive, they'd come back with someone who looked exactly like Nico Cadogan. And sounded like him.

'Okay,' said Cadogan turning back to him. 'You're on. Now, what sort of fee are we talking here?'

Tom took a deep breath. 'Twenty grand a month,' he said.

There was a silence, for at least five seconds. 'That your standard fee?'

'Yup. For a case like this.'

'It's extortionate.'

'It's realistic.'

Another silence. Then, 'Okay, I pride myself on being realistic. But you'd better deliver.'

Tom experienced the adrenalin rush very physically.

She couldn't put it off any longer, Octavia thought: she must phone the chair of the Felthamstone branch of Foothold, see what reaction, if any, she got to Michael Carlton's development. Someone she presumed was the cleaner answered the phone, said Mrs David was out 'at the physio's with Megan, but she'll be back any minute. Do you want to leave a message?'

Octavia remembered Mrs David now from the AGM, a tall, slim, exhausted-looking woman, pretty in a faded-blonde way, whose ten-year-old child was in a wheelchair.

'No, it's all right,' said Octavia. 'I'll call back.'

'Not even a name?'

'Oh, well, could you say Octavia Fleming—'

Octavia could hear a washing machine spinning, a dog barking, and then the front door opening, and a voice calling for Mrs Jackson.

'Just coming, Mrs David. There's a lady on the phone for you.'

'Well, I can't talk to her now, I have to get the shopping in. It's piled on top of poor Megan. And it's just starting to rain. Tell her – oh, look, you go and start on the shopping, would you, Mrs Jackson? I'll deal with the call. Yes, hallo, Patricia David speaking.'

Not the best moment, thought Octavia, very inauspicious.

'Mrs David, I'm sorry, bad moment, I can tell. I'll call back. It's Octavia Fleming here from Capital C, the consultancy, you know, that helps with Foothold.'

'What? Oh, yes, of course. No, that's quite all right, anything for that charity, it's done such wonders for us.'

'I'm glad. How is your little girl?'

'Not too bad. She's just been for her physiotherapy in the local pool. She loves that, but of course it's not very often we can get a booking, it's very overloaded with people.'

That's promising, thought Octavia; maybe a new, custom-built one . . .

'It won't be terribly quick, I'm afraid. I wanted to see what you thought about the new development proposed down your way, near Bartles Wood.'

'Oh, we're all marshalling ourselves for that one. Hoping Swampy will be down to help us. Seriously, it's an appalling prospect. How much have you heard about it?'

'Not much,' said Octavia.

'Well, what the developers have bought is Bartles House, a rather odd old place, currently being used as a nursing home. That and the grounds. They're going to rack and ruin – a tragedy in itself – and Bartles Wood sits just on the edge of the grounds, near the lane. There's a right of way cutting through it, fenced off from the rest of the land, but it does still belong to the same people. It's always been regarded as public property and there's a lot of wildlife there, dragonflies and so on, and wonderful water plants. Children have collected tadpoles there for generations: it really is a tragedy.'

'Is the house coming down?'

'Oh, yes, but that's no great loss.'

'And the old people, what about them?'

'They're being rehoused in some modern place the other side of the town apparently. I expect the developers are one and the same.'

'Maybe . . .'

'Anyway, how did you hear about that? Nothing to do with you, I hope.'

'Not directly, but I did hear that the developer might be going to open a community centre. With facilities for the disabled. I wondered if you were aware of that, whether Foothold might welcome it.'

A snort came down the line. 'Bribery. Nothing more. I tell you what'll happen, Mrs Fleming; the house will come down, the wood will be torn up, the houses and shopping mall will be built, and somehow, mysteriously, the community centre won't materialise. It's always the way. Something similar happened near my mother. It's an absolute outrage, all this development, and I have every intention of lying down under that bulldozer when it arrives.'

'Yes, I see. Right. Well, I can see I'm wasting my breath and your time.' Octavia managed to laugh. 'I'm sorry. Go and get your little girl in, please. It was only an enquiry. I just heard, as I say, that this was on the cards, and I thought you might welcome it.'

'Sorry, Octavia – you don't mind if I call you Octavia, do you? And do call me Pattie – but welcome is the last thing I'd give it. We've a very big protest committee being drawn up, and a great deal of support. Including, hopefully, our new MP, a very nice young man, although he *is* Labour. But he told me privately, at one of the meetings, that he would be very sad to see Bartles Wood go. Although he was playing devil's advocate, saying there was a need for more housing round here. Anyway, if you want to discuss this further, just phone. Any time. Perhaps you could help us with publicity . . .'

'It's rather unlikely, I'm afraid, since it's nothing to do with Foothold, but we'll certainly keep in close touch about it,' said Octavia carefully, and put the phone down.

'Oh, God,' said Tom.

'What's the matter?' His secretary, Barbara Dawson, had just brought the morning's mail and the papers.

'Look at this.' He pushed the *Daily Mail* at her: there was a photograph of a group of women with small children in pushchairs on page three, holding banners which read, 'Save our countryside' and 'Save Bartles Wood'. It was captioned 'England's New Army'.

> The women of Felthamstone are drawing up contingents and preparing to fight a long hard battle to save their local beauty spot, Bartles Wood. It is under threat from a developer, who plans to

build a large complex of houses, shops and a multi-storey car park. 'The whole of our country will be under concrete soon,' said one of the young mothers who have spearheaded the campaign. 'We have to save what is left for our children and grandchildren. We owe it to them.'

'If the men won't help, we'll fight them alone,' said another woman, whose daughter is in a wheelchair suffering from juvenile arthritis. 'We'll lie down under the bulldozers if we have to.'

The property developer in question, Michael Carlton of Carlton Homes, was not available for comment.

'Oh dear,' said Barbara.

'I thought you said we could keep this out of the nationals, Tom.' Carlton's voice was raw with irritation. 'What went wrong?'

Tom sighed. 'I didn't say I could keep it out. I said the best thing was to play it down. Usually it is. Look, I really don't think the rest of the press are going to pick up on it.'

'Is that right? Well, perhaps you could tell that to the chap at the *Express*. He's been on to me.'

'Oh, God,' said Tom. 'Leave it to me, I'll talk to him.'

'I keep leaving it with you. Fat lot of good it seems to be doing me. All right, see if you can sort this one out. I'll hang on a bit longer. And let me know what the *Express* say. I'm available for comment any time.'

'Sure.' Tom put the phone down, noticing with irritation that his hand was slightly shaky. Get a grip, Fleming. This is serious stuff.

'Octavia? This is Michael Carlton.'

'Oh, hallo.' Octavia tried to sound welcoming.

'I expect you've seen the paper.'

'The story about the protest? Yes, I have.'

'Monstrous regiment of women. Now, I rang to see if you'd been able to sound out your contacts down there. Put in a good word for us, tell them about the community centre, the facilities for the—'

'Michael, I'm afraid they're naturally very against the development. Well, not the development, as such, of course, but the destruction of Bartles Wood.'

'Rather an emotive word, Octavia, that. I don't think Tom would like you to go round using it.'

Her hackles rose; how dare he imply that Tom had any control over what she said?

'I don't know how else you'd describe it, Michael. You're going to cut down the trees, aren't you? Bulldoze the site? Some people would call that destruction. Whatever the pros and cons of the development, of course.'

There was a silence; then he said, 'So you won't help?'

'I can't. I'm sorry.'

'I see. Oh, well, I'll see you tomorrow, at Ascot. We can perhaps talk about it more then.'

Octavia hesitated. 'Michael, look – if you feel differently about that now, if you'd rather pull out of the sponsorship . . .'

Go on, Michael Carlton, say you would. It would make life so much simpler and cleaner.

'Oh, no, Octavia.' He sounded quite amused. 'No, I do want to work with your company very much. And with you. I think all this mutual involvement is extremely – beneficial. See you tomorrow.'

Bastard! He was very clever. He knew he'd got her over a barrel. It was quite a small barrel at the moment, but it could get bigger.

Octavia wondered if she should mention any of this to Melanie, and decided not. The whole thing would die down of its own accord. She probably should have mentioned the possible Foothold connection, but . . . for God's sake, everything was connected with everything else, if you looked far enough. And Melanie was in a filthy mood this morning.

'Darling, we're going to have to work very hard on Michael Carlton tomorrow. At Ascot. He's raging about that piece in the *Mail.* I don't give a fuck about the countryside, or whether Bartles Wood gets blown up or bulldozed down. All I care about is keeping Carlton sweet. I'm relying on you.'

'Tom, I told you, the meeting's been fixed. For Friday.'

'This Friday? That's great. And Melanie's not worried about the connection?'

'No.'

'Good. Because it will help us a lot, your liaising with him. A lot. As of course you realise. You're such a star. What would I do without you?'

'I have no idea. Look, I have to go now. I'll see you tomorrow. Hope the speech goes well.'

'So do I,' said Tom. 'Thanks, darling. Lots of love. And I meant it. I really couldn't manage without you.'

'And just possibly, I couldn't manage without you,' she said, smiling into the phone.

'Of course you could.'

Those words came back to her in a piece of hideous and total recall next morning when she discovered that Tom was having an affair.

CHAPTER 7

Zoë Muirhead was standing on the rush-hour Tube trying very hard not to scream out loud. This was it: the day when it was going to become extremely apparent that she had done no work, or hardly any work. Why had she been so stupid? Why hadn't she spent all those evenings studying instead of reading magazines and watching TV in her room? Because studying was miserable and boring. She might, just might, pass English, get a D or even a C; but French and history, no way. She had never even finished reading two of the French literature texts. So she'd fail her A-levels, and have to do retakes at a crammer and miss her year out in Australia.

Zoë sighed, and to distract herself from her misery began reading a magazine over the shoulder of the girl standing next to her. An ordinary, lucky girl, Zoë thought, with nothing more to worry about than what to spend her next pay-packet on, and obviously (from the way she was reading an article on the subject so intently) whether or not to have her hair cut very short. And then she saw something that was rather more interesting – the accouncement of a model competition. Zoë thought she would make a rather good model: other people had told her so, she was tall and quite thin, and she did look pretty good in photographs. She wondered if she might go in for it. Now that really would solve all her problems: it wouldn't matter in the least if she failed all her exams if she got some modelling contract for thousands of megabucks. It would show her parents she had some thoughts about her own life, apart from theirs; and they'd have to get off her back anyway, because she'd be independent. It was worth a try, anyway.

The girl got off the Tube at the same place, stuffed the magazine into a rubbish bin outside. Zoë pulled it out again to study later in the unimaginably far off moment when the exam was over. If it seemed even half worth doing, she'd send off the form that very day . . .

★

Octavia was sitting on the bed, reading a quote of hers in the *Express* about how brilliantly she managed her marriage, when she noticed the handkerchief. It didn't mean very much straight away. Well, it didn't mean anything at all, but she did notice it, sitting right on the top of the pile of ironing just brought in by Mrs Donaldson, because it didn't belong there. It wasn't hers, she never used handkerchiefs, and it obviously wasn't Tom's and it wasn't Poppy's. And it didn't look like the sort of handkerchief that Caroline would have. It was a very pretty, lacy, embroidered thing – Caroline always had rather plain hemmed, boarding-school-type handkerchiefs. But maybe this was the exception. She could ask her. Anyway, she should get on, not sit here wasting time thinking about handkerchiefs – she had to go to the office before she went to Ascot.

She ran downstairs to the kitchen. Caroline was just clearing up the twins' breakfast things. 'Caroline, is this by any chance your handkerchief? It's got caught up in the family washing, and it's much too pretty to lose.'

Caroline looked at the handkerchief briefly, and said no it certainly wasn't hers.

Octavia turned to her daughter. 'Poppy, you didn't bring this hanky home from somewhere by mistake, did you?'

'Never seen it before. Maybe it's Gideon's.'

'Don't be silly, Poppy. Off you go, darling. I won't see you till tomorrow, I'm afraid.'

''Bye, Mum.'

Octavia went back upstairs, switched on her hairstyler, and then looked at the handkerchief again. Why was it bothering her so much? Why? It was only a handkerchief. But – well, handkerchiefs didn't get into the house by magic. Someone brought them.

There was a knock at the bedroom door. Mrs Donaldson looked in. 'All right if I do the beds tomorrow, Mrs Fleming?'

'Yes, of course. Mrs Donaldson, this hanky, I just wondered – it's not yours, is it? You didn't leave it with the rest of our stuff?'

'I should be so lucky,' said Mrs Donaldson, 'to have a lovely thing like that. No, I did notice it in the linen basket and thought it was rather nice. I didn't put it in with the whites,' she added slightly defensively.

'It was in the basket, was it?' said Octavia. What was she doing? Why, why did she care so much about it?

'Yes. On Monday morning, caught up with all the rest of yours and Mr Fleming's stuff. He'd obviously just emptied his bag into it the way he always does when he's been away. I found a biro and a fifty pence piece as well, lucky they didn't go into the machine!'

'Yes,' said Octavia, 'yes, that was very lucky.'

She suddenly felt slightly sick.

It was ridiculous, of course. Absolutely ridiculous. To be so upset. But the handkerchief had been in Tom's bag. From Friday night, when he had been away. With a client and then at a sales conference. Working. As always.

Even so. It was strange. Intriguing. Maybe it had belonged to one of the reps at the sales conference. Tom could easily have picked it up and brought it home by mistake. Well, fairly easily.

Maybe it was his secretary's. She couldn't quite imagine the rather terrifyingly tough Barbara Dawson using antique lace handkerchiefs, but you couldn't assume anything. You *shouldn't* assume anything.

She started tonging her hair, trying to ignore the persistent stirrings of panic. In between staring at the handkerchief and her own face and obediently neatened hair in the mirror, she also kept looking at the article in the *Express*, and her comments on her own marriage. They suddenly seemed rather smug.

'It's a bit of a tightrope, a working marriage . . . don't look down, and everything will be all right . . .'

And while you weren't looking down, what might be going on? Down there, just under your nose?

Oh, this was ridiculous. There was such an easy way to settle it. Ask Tom. Just casually. Lightly. As if it was a sort of joke.

'And just whose handkerchief was that in your bag, Mr Fleming?'

That sort of thing. Only she wasn't very good at asking questions like that, lightly and casually. It would come out sounding neurotic and probing. Another manifestation of her jealousy. It would probably lead to a row.

Like the near-one they'd had over Lauren Bartlett. After the party and the dancing.

She put on the red silk dress and jacket she'd bought for Ascot. It had been a mistake. She'd bought it in too much of a hurry, and it didn't suit her. The jacket made her look short rather than small. Damn. And the hat didn't help, it was too big. Too big for the shape of the suit. Well, there was nothing she could do about it now. Tom had said he liked it. And he never lied to her. Never.

She had to pass the handkerchief to get her shoes; she had managed not to look at it for a bit. It looked more innocuous now. She'd just been over-reacting. As usual. She took the suit and hat off again, put the suit back on its hanger under a nylon cover, the hat into its hat box, carried them downstairs with her shoes and bag to take to the office, still feeling oddly wretched. Maybe she should ring Tom. But he wasn't there. He'd been away last night. Again.

Twice in a week.

Bath last night. Leamington Spa on Friday. Friday when he'd picked up the handkerchief. Where had he stayed? Oh, yes, the Regency. He had stayed there before, said it was awfully good. She'd phoned him there, so he'd definitely been there. No, he hadn't. She'd phoned him on his mobile. Of course. Maybe . . .

Octavia, this is dreadful. Go to the office, get some work done.

She put the *Express* into her briefcase to show Melanie, and then on an impulse, she picked up the handkerchief, stuffed it into her underwear drawer. When she found out who it belonged to, she'd give it back.

The traffic was bad, going down to the Old Brompton Road. She switched on the radio; she felt jittery, strung up. Well, anyone would, going to Ascot, looking terrible.

The radio offered her nothing to calm her nerves, so she switched it off again. She phoned Sarah Jane, said she was on her way in. And then heard herself asking Directory Enquiries for the number of the Regency Hotel, in Leamington Spa.

Obviously she wouldn't ring it. Wouldn't check up on Tom. Obviously. That would be an awful thing to do. Awful. She just wanted the number, in case. She hadn't got it and it was a nice hotel. She had a huge bank of hotel numbers, but not that one.

When the girl gave it to her, she scribbled it down on the back of her *A to Z*. She could transfer it to her Psion when she got to the office.

She definitely wouldn't ring it. It would be a terrible thing to do.

'Oh, good morning. This is Mrs Fleming. Mrs Tom Fleming. Yes. My husband stayed there the other night, Friday. Yes. Yes, definitely. Well, anyway, he thinks he might have left a book behind. What? Yes, this Friday just gone. The thirteenth.'

Friday the thirteenth: how hideously, horribly significant. She hadn't even registered it till now.

'I'm sorry? Are you quite sure? Yes. Oh, I see.'

Octavia put the phone down.

She felt quite different now: driven by a white hot need to know. Clear headed, almost excited. She asked Sarah Jane for some coffee, told her not to put any calls through for half an hour. The sales conference had definitely been in Leamington Spa. She'd seen the folder he'd brought back.

She phoned the Regency again. She was so sorry, she'd made a stupid mistake, could they give her the name of any other comparable hotels in the area? Yes. Yes, that would be very kind. She wrote them down. Six.

She dialled Directory Enquiries, got the numbers.

And started. She said she was Tom Fleming's secretary. Not his wife. It was easier that way. If she got to the second question. So far she hadn't.

With each one, each time she was told no, Mr Fleming hadn't been there, she felt more ashamed of herself, somehow dirty. Like some seedy private detective. It was awful of her, a dreadful obscene demonstration of her jealousy. But she had to know. She had to.

She looked at her watch. God, nearly ten thirty. The car would be here in less than an hour, and she had things to do first. Just one more. The others would have to wait.

'Good morning. Carlton Hotel, Leamington Spa.'

'Good morning. This is Tom Fleming's secretary. From Fleming Cotterill Public Affairs. Mr Fleming has asked me to ring you. I believe he and Mrs Fleming stayed there last Friday. Friday the thirteenth.'

'Yes?' The voice was politely bland.

'Anyway, I'm trying to track down a book Mrs Fleming thinks she might have left there. On antiques.' How was she doing this, how was she managing to sound so calm, so efficient?

'Just let me have a look . . .' The inevitable endless computer clicking. 'Hallo? Yes, that's right. Last Friday. Mr and Mrs Tom Fleming. Just the one night. But I don't think we have any books—'

'Thank you,' said Octavia automatically. 'That's perfectly all right, don't worry.'

She felt hot. Very hot. And was finding it terribly difficult to breathe.

She put the phone down carefully and sat looking at it for a moment. And then she had to rush to the lavatory where she was violently sick.

'You all right, Octavia?' Sarah Jane looked up at her as she walked past her, smiling carefully, back into her office.

'Yes, I'm fine. Why shouldn't I be?'

'Oh, you look a bit pale. That's all. Hair looks nice.'

'Thank you. Yes. Jonathan fitted me in at seven last night.'

She had thought it so important at the time, had been so relieved. Relieved: about her hair. How extraordinary.

Sarah Jane's phone rang. 'Hallo. Octavia Fleming's— Oh, hallo, Barbara. Yes, she's here, I'll ask her. Octavia, can you possibly get there for eleven forty-five, instead of twelve?'

'No,' said Octavia, suddenly brisk. 'I can't possibly.' It was a revenge of sorts on that dreadful day: small, but important.

Barbara Dawson, thought Octavia: did she know about the affair? Did she book them hotel rooms, put through bills, order presents, lace handkerchiefs even, from shops, and did half the staff know, did Aubrey Cotterill? Probably they all did. A wave of misery swept over her, misery and humiliation, and she sat down suddenly on the edge of Sarah Jane's desk.

'Octavia, are you sure you're all right? You look rotten.'

'Yes, I'm fine. Honestly. Just a bit tired. I'll be all right.'

'Good. You always enjoy Ascot so much. Oh, this phone – yes? Oh, Mrs Piper, can you hold on a minute? Octavia, can you . . . ?'

'Yes, of course. Put her through.'

It all seemed so normal, so absolutely the same: as if nothing had changed at all.

'God, you're a handsome man, Cadogan.' Nico Cadogan picked up the glass of champagne he had been sipping while he got ready, raised it to his reflection in the mirror.

He was looking forward to the day: he loved race meetings, or at least the social, flashier variety. He liked the spectacle, he liked the atmosphere, he liked the heady blend of well-bred people and horses looking glossy and well presented: and he very much liked winning money on the horses. Which he always did.

He was also looking forward to meeting Octavia Fleming. There was a picture of her and Tom in the paper that morning – she was extremely pretty – with a silly quote about how she managed her life. In Nico's experience women who thought they knew how to manage their lives were heading for a fall. It would be amusing to observe this model liaison in action.

And exactly how did you face your husband, Octavia wondered, as her car carried her quite fast down the M3, how did you do that, having made the discovery since you last met that he was committing adultery? Did you smile, kiss him, ask him how he was, pretend that all was as it had been? Or did you go up to him, hit him, throw something at him, scream at him? And if you did none of those things, would he know, would he realise that you were pretending, would he know that you had discovered what he was doing, doing without you, would he sense a change in you, would he breathe in the anger, smell the hostility, feel the fear? And how could he not know, when he had lived with you, been married to you for so long, when he had shared every intimacy, had conceived children with you and watched them born? All that morning the vision of Tom in bed with someone else had surfaced, obscenely, in her head, had been buried again with a furious, dark determination.

She had thought for a while she could not possibly face the day, face everyone; that she would phone to say she was ill, but that seemed suddenly more difficult than going through with it. Simpler and indeed easier to go; there would be so many people there – cheerful, happy, ordinary people having a good time – her misery would be well camouflaged. She felt in any case totally removed from reality, rather as if she was watching herself in a bad film. Ascot, with its well-worn rituals, its requirement to behave to a well-known, well-rehearsed script, would fit well into that.

She was actually very glad she was to meet Tom in public, protected from him, from domestic intimacy, from close scrutiny, from her own emotions even. She walked into the courtyard, stood by the bandstand, looked up to the top floor where their box was, and just for a moment she quite savoured the challenge of the role she would be playing, that of loyal, perfect wife, marvelled at her own self-control and professionalism in being able even to contemplate it. And then in the next moment she wanted to run away. She was to become very familiar with this emotional switchback over the next few months.

'That's an extremely nice hat,' said Nico Cadogan. He held out his hand to her. 'Nico Cadogan. And you must be Octavia.'

'Yes, I am. How do you do?'

In spite of – or because of – her misery she absorbed a great deal about him: this was a very attractive man. Dark, very dark hair, with wings of grey at the temples, that looked as if they had been painted there, very dark grey eyes, a long, perfectly straight nose, and an expression of great good humour. He was very tall, a good two inches more than Tom, very slim, and superbly dressed.

He took her hand at once, and shook it, while looking at her intently with his grey eyes, and his hand was very warm, very smooth – elegant hands, he had, with fine long fingers, and he wore a signet ring on his little finger, and a superb classic Piaget watch on his wrist. He smiled at her, a rather thoughtful smile, and said, 'You don't look in the least like your father, you know.' His voice was light and quick, almost impatient; everything about him spoke of a desire, indeed an expectation, for instant gratification.

I wouldn't like to work for this man, Octavia thought – and hoped he would give Tom a very hard time.

Nico Cadogan had arrived in the box last and been introduced to what seemed like a large number of people he couldn't imagine ever wanting to meet again: a huge man called Carlton, and his wife Betty, a stocky Brummie called Bob Macintosh and his rather tarty redhead of a wife, Maureen. Aubrey Cotterill was charming of course, but Cadogan wasn't too keen on his companion; finding Octavia out on the balcony had been a very pleasant relief.

'You don't seem to have any champagne. Let me get you some.'

'No, really, I'm staying with orange juice for now. I'm pacing myself, it's a long day.'

She was very attractive, he thought, but in a nervy, oddly watchful way; she was over-vivacious, laughing too much, and her rather extraordinary brown eyes, large and very heavily lashed, had a wary look to them. This was not a woman comfortable to be with. She was in great contrast to Tom's easy, languid style.

Felix appeared on the balcony, put his arm round her. 'Here you are. Morning, Nico. I see you've met my daughter. Octavia, you don't have any champagne. Hasn't Tom offered you any?'

'Daddy, of course he has. I've already refused several glasses. Mr Cadogan has offered me some too.'

'That's all right, then. You look lovely, my darling. Doesn't she look marvellous, Nico?' The dark eyes, so like Octavia's own, were fixed on her, thoughtful, tender with love. 'Red's always been her colour. Even when she was quite small. Lights her up. I used to give her a red dress every Christmas.'

God, thought Cadogan, he really is in love with her. The day was going to be even more interesting than he had expected.

Marianne and Tom came out on to the balcony.

'What a wonderful day,' said Marianne, smiling. 'Aren't we lucky?'

'We are indeed,' said Tom, 'and the going is perfect. Got any tips, Felix?'

'No,' said Felix Miller shortly. 'You know I never bet on anything.'

Cadogan, watching them both intently, could see this annoyed Tom intensely; hence, no doubt, the apparently innocent question. Well, it did amount almost to rudeness, to take up space in a box at Ascot and then refuse to take any part in the proceedings.

'There's one horse I'd mortgage my house for,' Cadogan said, his natural good manners troubled. 'Filly. Belongs to the Maktoum brothers. Running in the Queen Elizabeth Stakes. Can't fail.'

'That's quite an endorsement. Where *is* your house, Nico?' said Marianne, smiling at him.

'Belgrave Mews. A poor thing, but my own.'

'Well,' she said lightly, 'quite a lot to lose if the horse doesn't win. I shall put some of my money on your filly as well. Although I don't plan to take out any mortgages.'

'Excellent. I like decisiveness in a woman. Shall we go and do it now?'

'Why not?'

She smiled at him. He smiled back; now *she* was lovely, he thought, coolly sexy, with her long legs and her lean body, and her dress, a slip of black crêpe, extremely stylish. Her hat, wide-brimmed scarlet straw with a huge black bow, was stylish too, rather more so than Octavia's tiered confection. Octavia looked just slightly overdone altogether, in a red silk dress and red and black spotted jacket, which was a pity, he thought; not quite chic. Marianne's quiet beauty was more agreeable. He had thought a mild flirtation with Mrs Fleming might be fun; he was rapidly changing his mind.

He followed Marianne now out of the box, down to the mezzanine floor below, to the Tote; the area was filling up fast, with well-dressed, well-heeled and for the most part well-spoken people, although the occasional twang of London or North Country cut through the braying. This was a marvellous opportunity for making contacts. He had already seen three separate people who had wished him well in his battle with Egerton. Yes, he would enjoy today, very much: especially in the company of Mrs Marianne Muirhead. That should prove an unexpected bonus.

'Darling, are you all right?' Tom's face was mildly concerned as he came over to Octavia.

'Yes, I'm absolutely fine,' she said, marvelling at the complex process of smiling when it was something every instinct fought against.

He was looking wonderful, almost unbearably handsome and stylish: and would *she* have seen him in those clothes? Octavia wondered. Had *she* admired him in them, done up his cufflinks for him, told him how nice he looked? Rage filled her physically, rising in her throat. She felt like ripping the tie off, tearing at the shirt: until she remembered that he had changed at the office, had taken his morning suit in with him the day before, and with a huge effort she smiled at him again.

'Now, darling, I do want you to look after Betty Carlton. She's a bit nervous, apparently, and—'

'Tom, I don't need to be told how to be a hostess, thank you. Please don't insult me,' said Octavia. As she turned away, she drew a shred of satisfaction from the expression on his face. It was an interesting mixture of embarrassment and alarm.

'So how are you getting on with Tom?' said Marianne, as she and Nico made their way back to the box.

'Professionally? Or personally?'

'Both. He's hard not to like, though. Don't you find?'

'Yes, I like him very much. I get the impression Felix is rather less keen.'

'Only because he's so obsessed with Octavia. He thinks Tom isn't nearly good enough for her, doesn't treat her properly.'

'And does Tom treat her properly?'

'What?' She turned to look at him. 'That's a very personal question.'

'Well, I want an answer,' he said, smiling at her. 'That's why I asked it.'

'I don't know. That's the only answer I can give you. Who does know, outside a marriage, what goes on inside it? I think so, yes. He seems very sweet to me.'

'But Felix isn't satisfied with him?'

'I don't know. It's so complex. I sometimes think he'd welcome a real problem, so that he could use it as an excuse to tell her to come home. Oh, dear, how very indiscreet of me. It's the champagne talking – so early!'

'You know, Tom said much the same thing to me,' said Nico.

'He did? Oh, dear, he must hate Felix so.'

'Not hate. I do get the impression he finds him difficult.'

'Well, we're all difficult,' said Marianne lightly.

'You don't strike me as being in the least difficult.'

'You'd be surprised,' she said.

'I would, yes. In my experience women are only difficult because they are not being taken care of properly.'

'I see. Well, I shall have to tell Felix that.'

'Probably better not.'

He stood back to let her pass into the box, was borne down upon by a large woman in yellow patterned silk.

'Nico, how marvellous to see you. All well with you?'

'Oh, yes, wonderful. Thank you. And you?'

'Splendid. You must come round for a drink very soon, I'll give you a ring.' The woman passed on.

He met Marianne's eyes and grinned slightly shamefacedly. 'Sorry I couldn't introduce you, but—'

'You hadn't the faintest idea who she was. Don't worry. Happens to me all the time. Come along, Tom wants to get lunch going, well before the royals arrive.'

Octavia had been watching Tom; he had been standing just outside the box, smiling, chatting to people as they passed, shaking hands, kissing the women. How did he do it, Octavia thought, how could he do it, with everything seething beneath the surface of his life?

Was *She* one of these perhaps? Was it possible that *She* was someone she knew, that they both knew? Octavia had assumed until that moment that *She* must be some stranger to her, someone Tom had met from right outside their circle; now, watching him with all these pretty women, it occurred to her that *She* might actually be someone quite familiar, somone here, someone who might be enjoying the private knowledge, the shared secret, and she felt so sharply and freshly hurt, so violently jealous she could have pushed him backward off the balcony, down to the courtyard below.

And then as she stood there, she heard Lauren Bartlett's voice: that dangerous sexy voice. 'Tom! Hello!' it said, and then she saw her, looking stunning, horribly stunning, in a pale blue silk suit and a large cream straw hat. Her blue eyes were brilliant as she reached up to kiss Tom, and Octavia watched, miserable, as she whispered something in his ear. God, she hated women who did that. Hated them, *hated* them. How dared she stand there, behaving as if she and Tom had something exciting and private to share. Maybe they did. Maybe *She* was Lauren. Oh, God, thought Octavia, I can't stand this, I really really can't, and she felt dizzy suddenly and sick again: and then Lauren saw her, over Tom's shoulder, and smiled, waved a cream-gloved hand.

'Octavia, hallo. What a marvellous hat. I was hoping I'd see you. I want to talk to you about Next Generation – maybe we could meet after lunch.'

'Of course,' said Octavia, smiling at her with enormous difficulty, 'lovely idea.'

And for want of anywhere else to hide, made her way along to the ladies' and stood there, staring at herself in the mirror, realising this was how it was going to be from now on, everyone under suspicion: the world lopsided, weighed down with this new ugly presence in it.

Half an hour later Octavia felt worse. They were sitting at lunch. Tom had put her in between Aubrey and Michael Carlton and misery was making her clumsy; she had already knocked over her glass of wine, and every time Carlton spoke to her she felt herself physically jump. Her discovery felt like an obscene growth somewhere on her body. Had it really only been this morning, only a few hours ago, she had made her discovery? The end of life as she knew it, her successful, carefully controlled life? And what could she possibly have found to worry about within it? What trivial obsessions, like her weight, not being able to sleep, the twins' arguing?

'Are you all right, Octavia?' said Aubrey, refilling her glass with quiet courtesy; and 'Are you all right, Octavia?' said Michael Carlton at almost exactly the same moment.

'Yes, yes, thank you,' she said, smiling at Aubrey, and 'Yes, I'm fine,' she said slightly less graciously to Carlton.

'Good,' Carlton said. 'You look wonderful, and this is a marvellous day out. Very good of Tom to invite us. Betty was over the moon.'

'I'm so glad you were able to come,' she said, adding, carefully dutiful, 'Betty looks lovely.'

'Oh, now come on. Not lovely. A bit much, really, those colours on her. But bless her, she just went out and bought it all, so what could I do but admire it?'

He was actually, underneath the bluster and the scheming, she thought, a perfectly nice man, and without doubt a very nice husband, loyal and supportive. She had to like him for that.

'Still upset about that business in the paper yesterday,' he said conversationally, loading a roll with butter. 'Bit disappointed in Tom – I thought he had the press wrapped up on this one.'

'There are some things even Tom can't do,' she said coolly. Like wrap up the press. Like cover up an affair indefinitely.

'Yes, well, I pay him to be able to do anything I need. Anyway, I'm looking forward to our meeting on Friday,' said Carlton and turned his attention to Nico Cadogan.

She looked at Tom, sitting between Marianne and (most dutifully) Betty Carlton, a citrus nightmare in lime-green dress, orange jacket and shoes and a brilliant lemon-yellow hat. He was laughing heartily at something Betty had said, refilling her glass: the model host. Bastard! Absolute bastard. She wanted to smash her own glass, drag the broken pieces down his smiling, handsome, treacherous face, she wanted to—

'Good gracious, Octavia,' said Betty Carlton, smiling. 'You looked very fierce then for a moment. Whatever were you thinking about?'

'Oh, whether I'd told my secretary something,' said Octavia. 'Sorry!'

'Well, I'm glad it wasn't more serious than that. I do hope you're enjoying today as much as I am. It really is wonderful.'

'I'm glad,' said Octavia. Betty was so nice: she had made a great effort to chat to her before lunch, ask her about her charity work. Betty, who had not appeared to be nervous at all in spite of Tom's warning, had said stuff charity, she was having the time of her life today, didn't want to think about anything dreary at all.

'It doesn't have to be dreary,' said Octavia laughing.

'It does if you're down to collecting-tins and bring-and-buys,' said Betty. 'Which I do gladly, don't get me wrong, but fun it isn't.'

Octavia resolved to ask her up to London for lunch with the chair of one of her charities. Field workers got so little appreciation, and it wasn't fair.

There were fourteen of them in the small room, and it was very hot, in spite of the french windows opening out on to the balcony.

'You look rather pale,' said Carlton thoughtfully, turning his attention back to her. 'You sure you're all right?'

'Yes, I'm fine,' she said, trying to sound relaxed, 'but it is very hot.'

She caught her father's eye across the table; he was looking at her thoughtfully, his eyes anxious. She smiled quickly, carefully back; the last thing she wanted just now was an interrogation from him.

Before the pudding, they saw the royal procession starting on the television. 'Come on,' said Aubrey, holding out his hand to her, 'let's get out quickly, get the best view. I always love this bit, don't you?'

She took his hand, finding it strangely comforting. 'Yes, I do, but I'm surprised you do.'

'Oh, I'm a great royalist,' he said. 'The day they replace the Queen with a President is the day I leave the country.'

The carriages were in view now, quite near: the Queen in yellow, smiling – 'God, she loves this,' said Aubrey, 'you can see that smile from up here' – the Queen Mother in lavender, Margaret, Charles, Philip, the Gloucesters, the Kents.

'What a shower,' said Carlton, in her ear. 'Only one I've got any time for isn't here.'

'Diana?'

'Yeah. I think she's great. So does Betty, don't you, love?'

'I think she's lovely,' said Betty Carlton. 'And the way she's been treated – well! Quite dreadful. Not that I blame the Queen, she's a wonderful woman – it's the rest of them. Charles should be ashamed of himself, while they were still on their honeymoon too, she was such a baby . . .'

And she was off on the well-rehearsed Diana Worshipper's Litany; Octavia, who took a slightly dimmer view of Diana herself, listened with half an ear, wishing she was anyone, anyone at all except herself, any of those pretty, well-dressed, happy people who had nothing to worry about except the racing and their hats. And then saw a woman in the next box looking at her, smiling at her, and thought probably that was what people saw in her; a pretty, well-dressed woman with nothing to worry about either.

It was the second race; Nico Cadogan shouted, 'My God, look at that horse, did you ever see anything like it?'

He's going to fall over the balcony in a minute, Octavia thought; he suddenly seemed quite unlike the smooth, rather controlled creature she had imagined, was more like a small boy. She smiled and then realised his hand was resting on Marianne's back, and felt absurdly like crying, felt unattractive, undesirable . . . The horse was indeed remarkable, pulling ahead as if endowed with some sudden hidden power – horsepower, thought Octavia through her misery, how appropriate.

'Well, that's Fleming Cotterill safe,' said Aubrey, grinning. 'I put next year's profits on that horse.'

As if he would, thought Octavia, so careful, so cautious.

'So is my house,' said Nico Cadogan. 'God, what an animal.'

'Let's go down to the paddock,' said Marianne. 'I love it down there. Octavia, you coming?'

Octavia nodded. Anything would be preferable to sitting here, looking down on a thousand women and wondering if any of them was *Her*. Tom had disappeared; so had her father. Nico and Carlton and two other men were now engrossed in business talk. She looked at Betty Carlton, who was sitting fanning herself with her race card.

'Would you like to come, Betty?' she asked.

'No, love, if you don't mind. I'm a bit warm. I'll just sit here and have a cup of tea.'

Nobody else wanted to come; Marianne slipped her arm through Octavia's and they walked to the lift. 'You all right?' she said suddenly.

'Yes,' said Octavia, trying not to sound defensive. 'Why?'

'You seem – subdued.'

'I'm a bit tired. You know. Life and all that.'

'I do know,' said Marianne, smiling at her. God, she's nice, thought Octavia; I hope my father appreciates her.

They walked in silence through the darkness of the tunnel, out into the brilliance of the paddock, wandered about, watching the horses being led down for the next race, watching the people.

'At last,' said Marianne, smiling happily, 'I feel I'm actually at the races now. It's marvellous up there, but you feel very apart from the action, don't you?'

A line formed suddenly, a corridor of people, and the royal party walked through it, smiling graciously, on their way back to the Royal Enclosure, the Queen Mother, walking slowly, bravely spurning her motorised buggy; there was a ripple of very polite applause.

They walked over to the Royal Enclosure themselves, looked in: the atmosphere in there was less frenetic, more languid, the clothes more monotone, a lot of creams and beiges and very pale pastels. 'All thoroughbreds in there,' said Marianne, laughing. 'Come on, we'd better get back to our own paddock.'

They started back. And then Octavia saw Tom: standing at the entrance to the tunnel, talking very intently to a woman she had never seen before, very pretty, quite young, thirty-something, dressed in pale pink silk, with a tall, pink hat; she was staring up at Tom, and reached up suddenly and kissed his cheek.

The sick dizziness started again, the panic: she stood there staring at them, wondering, fearing, tears stinging her eyes.

'Octavia,' said Marianne, gently, 'Octavia, what is it, what's the matter?'

'Nothing,' she said fiercely. 'Nothing, honestly.'

'But you're crying – it can't be nothing!'

'No,' she said with a deep sigh, trying to calm herself, 'it isn't nothing. It's quite a lot actually. But I don't want to talk about it. Sorry, Marianne. I'm very sorry.'

'It's all right,' said Marianne, taking her arm again, walking slowly, patently trying to calm her, 'don't apologise to me. I'm just sorry you're unhappy. I won't press you. But – well, if you want to talk. At any time. I'm there. And I won't tell your father, if you'd rather I didn't.'

'Oh,' said Octavia, 'yes, thank you, but it really is nothing.'

'I'm pleased to hear it. Oh, Nico, hallo.'

'I thought I'd like to get a bit nearer some horseflesh,' he said, smiling at her, removing his hat, bowing slightly. 'Care to take a turn with me? And you, Octavia?'

'No, really, I think I should be getting back,' she said. 'Do my wifely duty. But thank you all the same.'

'We'll see you later, then,' said Marianne and smiled at her slightly anxiously.

Octavia managed to smile back. She had not really seen this aspect of Marianne before, this gentle, careful aspect; she supposed because she had never before let her guard fall in her presence, had presented her most brittle, confident self. Possibly – probably, indeed – because of repressed jealousy of Marianne. She had no recollection of having a mother; but she thought, in that moment, that if she had, she would have liked her to be exactly like Marianne. Even more than Anna Madison.

Anna was watching Ascot on the television with Charles, and Louise and Dickon, who had come over for the day. They had set up a racing party in the morning room, where Anna spent most of her time these days, lying on the chaise longue. She and Charles had always gone to Ascot; today she took up what she called a Royal Enclosure seat at home, and became as excited when the camera panned over the paddock as when a race was being run. 'Look,' she would say, 'there's Bunty Harewood, she's aged a lot, shouldn't have had that eye job,' or 'Doesn't Sarah Wadham-Brown look marvellous, and that husband of hers, just heavenly!'

Charles looked at her thoughtfully; she was a very bad colour, almost jaundiced, and the hand that held her glass was skeleton thin. He feared for the ravages of chemotherapy, what that would do to her frail body.

He looked over at Louise; she was sitting, ostensibly watching the television, but actually staring beyond it, into some distant thought. She didn't look very well either, he thought: pale and drawn, and very thin. She was taking her mother's illness hard.

Louise seemed to come back to them suddenly, smiled at her mother. 'I was just thinking Octavia would be there. Tom's company takes a box every year.'

'Yes, of course they do. It's very much a working day for these businessmen.'

'Tom never stops working, as far as I can make out,' said Louise. 'Octavia says she's always surprised the clients don't go on holiday or spend Christmas with them. It must be very hard, that.'

'Well, my darling, you're very good to Sandy's clients, and under rather less favourable circumstances than Octavia. I'm sure she doesn't have to do her own cooking. I'm always full of admiration for you, managing without any help.'

'Well, I don't have to work all day as well as entertain at night. I certainly wouldn't like to be Octavia, I do know that. Very tough.'

'I thought you were very fond of Tom. I certainly am. He's such a sweet, kind man.'

'I didn't say I wasn't fond of him, and yes, he is very sweet and charming. I said I wouldn't like to be Octavia.'

'I don't quite see, but . . . Charlie!' Anna's voice was uncharacteristically irritable. It was the cancer, the doctor had said; an unpleasant side-effect. 'Charlie, I said I'd like some more champagne. Please. And I think I'd like a couple of my painkillers as well.'

'Darling, should you? The two don't really mix.'

'Of course they do. Look, I know what I can and can't cope with. I don't need lecturing about it. I'm in pain and it isn't necessary for me to be in pain. Now please get them for me, Charlie, or shall I do it myself?'

Charles and Louise exchanged glances; after a moment's hesitation, Charles poured a second glass of champagne for Anna and went up to her bedroom to get her painkillers. What was the point of fretting over something so unimportant, what did it matter?

And then he realised that for the first time he had thought the unthinkable, and downed his own glass of champagne in one go.

'Shall I go in for this, do you think?' said Zoë. She was sitting at a pavement café just by the Royal Court in Sloane Square with one of her best friends, Emilia; Emilia had agreed the exam had been impossible, although Zoë knew she didn't quite mean it; Emilia had done marginally less work even than she had, but was clever enough to get away with it.

'What? Let me see? Oh, God, another of those. Yes, why not? If you really want to. I think they're a bit daggy myself.'

Zoë knew why she'd said that; Emilia had gone in for a model contest herself the year before and not even reached the final selection. Well, much as Zoë loved her, Emilia did have very dodgy legs.

'I think I will. You never know. In fact I'm going to do it right now. Before I go home and get too depressed about the exams.'

'You'll need to,' said Emilia. 'This is last month's magazine – look, closing date's tomorrow.'

'Oh, shit. Never mind, I can still do it. I've got some pictures Mum took of me and Romilly the other day, here, look, when we were sitting in the garden. It says just a snap will do, as long as it's full length and they can see your legs. I thought this one, and maybe that. Nice?'

'Very nice,' said Emilia. 'I think that's the best, that one with Romilly, on the swingseat. You look very sexy.'

'Okay, I'll send that as well. I'll cross her out, scribble on the back which is me. Well, maybe if I win this thing, I won't ever have to worry about exams again.'

CHAPTER 8

Tom had gone: to dinner at Langan's with the Carltons and the Macintoshes and Aubrey and his girlfriend. His expression was hostile as he said goodbye to her, feigned concern at her terrible headache; he was angry with her, she knew, for her behaviour that day, for her patent hostility to him, for refusing to join them for dinner. When he got home, he would be in an appalling, silent rage that would go on quite possibly, for days. The only thing that brought him out of such moods was a tireless onslaught of apology; he wouldn't be getting that this time, Octavia thought.

She couldn't possibly have gone out with them this evening, continued to drink, to eat, to smile, to talk. She felt as if a layer of skin had been flayed off her; she was acutely sore all over her body, her muscles ached, her head was excruciating.

Mercifully, when she got home Minty was in bed and the twins were watching television in a state of happy exhaustion; they had been to a swimming party, and were too tired even to argue. When she asked them about the party, they both said shush, and returned their attention to *Back to the Future*. Octavia went gratefully into her study with a very strong cup of coffee, and wondered what she could do next; and then realised that what she wanted to do, and what would undoubtedly make her feel better, was to talk to Louise. Louise would understand; Louise would make her feel better.

Louise's first reaction was to burst into tears. Helpless, painful tears: Octavia listened, half touched, then mildly irritated.

'Sorry, Octavia,' she said, through sobs, 'sorry. I'll have to ring you back. Just give me a few minutes.'

Octavia sat drinking her coffee and waiting. She understood; she had felt equally at a loss when Juliet had died, a complete loss to know what to say or do.

Five minutes later, the phone rang again. Louise sounded calmer. 'I'm sorry, Octavia, I just couldn't bear anything else awful happening to the people I care about. It's terrible, I shouldn't be crying, I should be rushing up to London, to dry your tears.'

'I wish you could, but it probably wouldn't be the best idea. Just at the moment.'

'No. Maybe not. I can't believe it, Octavia, I really can't. How could he do that to you, you of all people, such a loyal, perfect wife?'

'Hardly,' said Octavia, surprised at the bitterness in her voice. 'If he's done this. I must have failed badly somewhere along the line.'

'You mustn't say that. Of course you haven't failed him. It's him that's failed. Does he know you know?'

'No. I could hardly confront him at Ascot, could I?'

'Are you going to tell him tonight? When he gets back?'

'I – I suppose so,' she said. 'Yes. Yes, I'll have to, I think. I can't not really, can I?'

'Well – I don't know. No, you can't. Poor Boot. I'm so sorry.'

'I feel so awful,' she said. 'Angry. Hurt. Humiliated. Maybe humiliated most of all. It was so terrible today, at Ascot, seeing him flirting with all those women, kissing them, hugging them, wondering if any of them were – well, you know, were *her*. I felt so – so degraded.'

'Of course you did. Of course. Oh, God. What a bastard. What an absolute bastard. Did he – did he realise, do you think, there was something wrong?'

'He must have done. I wasn't exactly warm and friendly. Oh, I feel so absolutely – stupid,' she said suddenly and burst into tears herself.

'Oh, darling Octavia – oh, dear . . .' Louise sounded distraught again. 'I'm so so sorry. I just wish I could help. And you don't have any idea at all who – who it might be?'

'None whatsoever. I mean, I keep thinking of people, obviously, but—'

'And – well, are you quite quite sure there couldn't possibly be another explanation?'

'What? How could there be?'

'Well – oh, I don't know. I mean, does the handkerchief *really* have to belong to a mistress? Someone might have lent it to him at this conference or whatever it was.'

'Louise, he was staying at a hotel, in a double room, booked for Mr and Mrs Fleming.'

'Oh.' Her voice was very bleak again. 'Sorry. Oh, God. What a shit. I just can't believe it – I mean he adores you so.'

'Oh, really? You could have fooled me.'

There was a silence.

'And you really don't have any idea at all who – well, who it is?' said Louise.

'No, of course not. I told you. It's one of the reasons I feel so terrible, being so trusting, so stupid . . .'

'Oh, darling Boot, don't cry. I feel so helpless. Are you sure you don't want me to come up and see you?'

'No,' said Octavia, blowing her nose, 'not just now, anyway. I have to decide what I'm going to do. Maybe this weekend I'll come down. I'll phone you.'

'Yes. Do that. Whenever you want to. I'll be here. Or at Rookston. I'm there quite a lot at the moment. Daddy's finding it so hard.'

'Oh, God. Yes, of course. I forgot about your mother for a moment. I'm sorry, I must come and see her. 'Bye, Louise. Thanks for listening.'

'Goodbye, darling Octavia. I'll be thinking of you so much.'

'Thank you,' said Octavia. 'Louise, don't tell Sandy yet, will you? I can't face everybody knowing.'

'Of course I won't. Good night. Lots and lots of love.'

Octavia poured herself a very large and very strong gin and tonic. She drank so seldom, she knew it would practically knock her out, but she didn't care. That was what she wanted. Then she ran herself a bath. The conversation with Louise had made her feel worse, not better.

She climbed into the water, and lay there, sipping her drink and contemplating her life as it was to be from now on, and how she was going to manage it. And for the first time that day she slowly began to feel something other than helpless and defeated.

It was largely the gin, of course, but there was something else as well, and it had come to her as she undressed and looked almost fearfully at herself in the bathroom mirror. She had never felt confident about her body, had never considered it sexy; and like all deceived wives, she had felt that day not only hurt and wretchedly unhappy, but plain, dull, unattractive. She was only five foot five tall, and had an ongoing struggle with her weight; left to itself it would have been plump, her body, with a rounded stomach and full breasts. A stringent diet, a twice-weekly appointment with a trainer at the gym, and a workout on her own when she had the time, had earned for her something rather different, but it meant very little to her, in terms of self-esteem. It was her former body that she carried about with her, that haunted her, that threatened her, what she forced herself to confront in the mirror that night was, by any standards, pleasing; small, firm breasts, a flat stomach, legs that were undeniably good, with tiny ankles and narrow thighs and hips.

She lay thinking about her body, about what she had been able to do to it by sheer force of will and diligence; and that led in turn to a contemplation of her personality and what she had been able to do to that. Naturally shy, unsure of her opinions and over-eager to please – largely due to her father's influence – she had learned to present to the world a confident, articulate and coolly independent woman, a woman other people admired, whose opinion they sought, a woman who – in that ubiquitous phrase of the 'eighties – had it all.

Now what would they say? That she was a fool, that she had lost her husband, that she had very little, certainly not all; her friends would sympathise with her, but her enemies, and indeed most of the people she came across, would quite possibly say she had been complacent, foolish, would smile at the irony of it, at all the nonsense about her perfect power marriage.

But – and at this thought Octavia sat bolt upright in the bath, so forcibly did it strike her – supposing they didn't need to know? Supposing she kept quiet about it, supposing she told Tom she had no desire to know any details of his squalid affair, that he could do what he liked, for all she cared: would that not be a far more dignified – and controlled and controlling – solution?

Life was not the same now as it had been for earlier generations of women, dependent upon their husbands, with no way of retaliating; women of today – for whom she had somehow become a kind of role model – were independent creatures, financially, professionally, emotionally. Even sexually: should she so wish, she could retaliate in kind to Tom. That thought in itself was exciting. Sexually exciting.

And that way there need be no humiliation, no loss of esteem, indeed she would rather gain in it, by her courage, her cool, her tolerance. Much of her misery that day had been caused by a sense of her own naïveté; by the fact that she had wrongly assumed that Tom loved her and needed her as much as he had always done. That he clearly did not was painful, very painful, but she could possibly learn to live with that. And there was more to a marriage, surely, than sexual fidelity. There were other things that mattered as much the stability of the family unit – financial security, social standing, professional success.

The more she thought about it, about this approach, the more her spirits lifted. Of course it would not be easy, but it would be easier than the other way. She would tell Tom that night, tell him what she had discovered and what she had decided, and he would be bound to do what she said. Or find himself caught up in a very expensive divorce. He was so sure of her, of her emotional dependence on him, it would be quite amusing, pleasing even, to show him she was not.

She felt odd, almost excited, pain and humiliation gone. She wasn't even sure what she felt for Tom any more: it seemed to be very little.

Well, that was good. The less the better. As for The Woman, whoever *She* was – well, this way she could deal with *Her*. This way she would win.

She got out of the bath, pulled on her robe and went downstairs again, made herself a cup of herb tea – her head was spinning quite badly – and went into the family room, to wait for Tom.

It was after one when Tom came home; Octavia woke from her slightly drunken, confusing sleep to hear the taxi chugging in the street. She sat up, pulled her robe round her, and sat waiting, dry mouthed, for the door to open, for the confrontation with him and what he had done: she felt very frightened.

She heard him go up to their room, then along to the guest room, up to the top floor, and then his footsteps on the stairs, coming down again, and still she didn't move. She couldn't.

Finally the door opened, and he looked in, saw her; he was clearly exhausted. 'What on earth are you doing here?'

'I didn't want to see you,' she said with simple truth, sitting up, staring at him, breathing rather hard.

'Why not?' he said. 'Why the hell not? And what the hell were you doing today? Behaving as you did, letting me down?'

'Me letting you down! Oh, Tom, I like that. I like that very much.'

'And what is that supposed to mean?' he said, and she had just opened her mouth in a rush of courage to tell him, when he suddenly said, 'Whatever it is, I'm too exhausted. I'm going to bed. You sleep wherever you please. Safe in the knowledge you have done great harm today. I hope you're well pleased with yourself.'

'I've done harm! What harm am I supposed to have done?'

'Oh, I thought you'd be gloating over it. Being difficult with Michael Carlton, practically ignoring the Macintoshes, refusing to come out to dinner, embarrassing Aubrey and me: how much more do I have to spell out? Well, if Fleming Cotterill go down the pan, which is not impossible, you might be interested to know, you can be quite confident you contributed to it in your own inimitable way.'

'That is ridiculous! Of course I didn't do anything that would inflict that sort of damage. I wouldn't, I—'

'Oh, just stop it,' he said. 'Good night, Octavia. I'm going to bed.'

He walked out, shut the door after him. She sat there, staring at it, marvelling that even then her courage had failed her, wondering why she was so afraid to confront openly what he had done; it was as if it was she who was the guilty one. She sat for a while, cold now, huddled in her robe, and then decided she would go to bed herself. She felt too frail, too confused to talk to him now.

She went up to the guest room very quietly, got into bed. She had been there for a few hours when Tom slipped into the bed beside her. She had been thickly asleep, did not remember just for a moment everything that had happened, turned to him, relaxed and warm. And then it came back, ugly, violent, and with it the memory of how she hated him; but in that moment, he had pressed himself against her, taken her in his arms, moved his mouth to hers. She pulled back, outraged, horrified, but 'Don't,' he said, 'please don't. I'm sorry, sorry about what I said, come here, come to me please . . .'

'I won't,' she said, sitting up, feeling breathless, her heart pounding. The early dawn of high summer was just beginning to break, she could see him looking at her; could see him, unbelievably, smile at her, the rueful, sweet smile of proposed intimacy, that she had always loved and now must mistrust.

'No,' she said, again, 'no, Tom,' but he ignored her, reached up his hand and began to outline her nipple very gently with his fingers.

'I want you most when you're angry,' he said, and she sat there, wanting to hate him, wanting to be repelled by him, but something extraordinary happened. Quite without warning she looked at him, and through the violence of her misery and shock and rage came a desire to have him. Afterwards she was absolutely unable to explain it, was ashamed even, that sexual hunger could be so strong, so treacherous, but in that moment she only knew she wanted him furiously, frantically.

How can I be doing this, she wondered, even as she felt the familiar sweet sensations begin, how can I be lying here, submitting myself to this, and not just submitting, savouring it? How can I let him do this, how can I allow him to use his hands, his mouth, how can I want him in me, how can I feel myself growing round him, how can I, it's terrible, horrible, don't, Octavia, don't, don't come! But it wasn't terrible and nor was it horrible, it was wonderful, unwelcomely wonderful, as she rose and rose, higher and sweeter and fiercer than she could remember for a long long time, and then the sharp bright fragments broke around her and within her; and she lay there afterwards, turned away from him, shocked and wondering what sort of a creature was she, that she could not just endure but enjoy, and enjoy acutely, a sexual experience with a man she knew to be in love with someone else, betraying trust, vows, love.

She woke two hours later; Tom was still asleep. She eased herself out of bed, went and stood in the shower for a long time, trying to explain it, to justify it. The nearest, she supposed, was that she had wanted to feel desirable herself still, not dull, not sexless, not someone to be set aside in favour of another lovelier, more joyful body. Or perhaps – far worse –

that she had found the thought of his sexual treachery in some way exciting, arousing. That really brought her to self-distaste, a sense of self-betrayal; this had not been the behaviour of the sort of woman she had decided to become.

Well, too late: much too late. She had done it, put herself much further into Tom's thrall. Too late now to say that she knew, that she was shocked and disgusted by him, that she wanted nothing more of him than the trappings of their marriage; he would know it was not true. Despair filled her: despair at her situation, at her marriage, most of all at herself.

Her father phoned her as she was driving the twins to school; trying to hear him, while negotiating the traffic and at the same time trying to stop Gideon shouting at Poppy, was impossible. She said she would ring him back and did so, sitting outside Hill House; he had been worried about her, he said; was there anything wrong? No, she said firmly, nothing, and was then not too surprised to be asked why, in that case, she had been crying at Ascot the day before.

'Who on earth told you that?' she said irritably, giving herself away rather neatly.

'Marianne saw you,' he said shortly, 'she was concerned about you. Now, you would tell me if there was really a problem, wouldn't you?'

'Yes,' she said, thinking with something approaching terror of his reaction if he had known what the problem really was. 'You know I would. I was tired and – well . . .' Inspiration came to her. Her father was always deeply embarrassed by anything of a gynaecological nature. 'It was, you know, hormonal problems. Bad time of the month.'

'Oh,' he said, and she could hear him digesting this, wondering whether to pursue it, deciding without too much difficulty not to. 'I see. Well, I hadn't thought of – something like that.'

It wasn't until she had rung off that she realised in a moment of brilliant, piercing relief, that it was actually all right, that Tom need not know – yet – that she knew, that she could actually bide her time, reassemble her self-respect, and then still move safely into her new persona.

CHAPTER 9

'I'll be honest with you, Mr Madison. I know you'd prefer that.'

Duncan Fry had been a cancer specialist for almost thirty years; he still found it as painful to inform patients and their relatives about their prospects, or rather their lack of prospects, as he had the very first time. And now here he was telling a middle-aged husband that his wife of nearly forty years had a tumour in her liver, a secondary from the one he had removed from her breast, and in a very few weeks she could be dead. Charles tried and failed not to cry. Duncan Fry stood up and turned and looked out of the window while Charles blew his nose and hauled himself back under control, knowing that Charles would be embarrassed by his own tears, that he was that kind of old-style Englishman.

'Octavia, I feel absolutely terrible. I must have eaten something last night, went to a sushi bar, can't believe how stupid of me . . . I just have to get home before I start throwing up. I'm sorry, with this meeting with Michael Carlton, but—'

Octavia looked at Melanie; she did look genuinely ghastly, her large blue eyes shadowed and sunk somehow deeper in her head, her whole face set with a greenish pallor. 'Melanie, it's fine. Honestly. Just go home and don't worry about a thing. As they say.'

'Please explain to Carlton that we have to do the usual window dressing, as he's linked with Tom, announce he's been chosen as sponsor from a shortlist of three, okay? And could you ring Patricia David, she phoned for you this morning, sounding very waspish, that's an important account, Octavia, we mustn't—'

'Melanie, go! We can cope.' Octavia was rather meanly relieved. At least she wouldn't have to go through the difficult process of explaining to Melanie about the awkwardness of the Bartles Wood connection. Yet . . .

*

Michael Carlton was clearly annoyed that Melanie wasn't going to be there, but in the end it was a fairly satisfactory meeting; Margaret Piper was clearly very taken with Michael Carlton, graciously delighted with the sponsorship deal, agreed all his terms – the Carlton logo to be on all stationery, promotional literature, to be prominently displayed at any events.

When Mrs Piper left, Michael Carlton looked at Octavia and grinned. 'Charming woman. Well, it seemed to go very well to me. How about lunch? We can talk about the other business then.'

Octavia said briskly there was still nothing to talk about, and that unfortunately she already had a lunch; she offered him a drink, which he refused.

'Never drink in the middle of the day. Well, thank you for a good meeting, Octavia. Excuse me.'

His mobile had rung shrilly. He listened, barking out yeses and nos, finally turned his phone off, turned to her, his tone triumphant. 'Well, that was interesting news. Apropos of my earlier question. We come up before the planning committee next week. With the Bartles House development. There's a strong rumour that we're going to get it. But I'm still going to need your help, Octavia, to win the locals round.'

'Michael, I really don't think there's anything I can do in that direction. And they'll appeal if you do get planning permission.'

'Why do I get the impression you're not entirely on my side in this?' he said, his voice hard edged suddenly.

'It would be wrong of me to pretend I was entirely. I feel rather emotional about the countryside. I can't help it. But of course I have to be pleased that Tom's been able to help you. Anyway, I shall wait to hear. Good morning, Michael. Thank you for coming today. I'm sure this is going to be a very fruitful liaison.'

She sat and stared out of the window when he had gone, thinking about the undoubted beauty of Bartles Wood, under threat of being bulldozed away, thinking that Tom had helped to bring that about, thinking of Carlton's absolute confidence that he would be able to force her to help him, and felt suddenly furiously angry.

And picked up the phone, as instructed, after all, by Melanie Faulks, to a distraught Patricia David, who had also heard a rumour that the development was to be given planning permission, and heard herself saying that if there was any *small* and unofficial way she could help, she would certainly try.

'I've done everything I can for now,' said Nico Cadogan to Tom Fleming. 'Drafted a letter to the shareholders, I'd like you to look at first—'

'Yes, of course,' said Tom. They were sitting in Cadogan's office in the penthouse of the Knightsbridge Cadogan Royal, the always surprising stretch of green that was Hyde Park below them. It was mid-morning; the Horseguards in all their gleaming splendour were making their way back to the barracks. 'Good site, this. The tourists must love it.'

'Yes, they do. And I'm not letting Egerton get hold of it. Now I've agreed your first press release, quite good that, I thought, liked the touch about my grandfather being a great benefactor, and I've got a letter on hold to the MP for Romford North, Matthews his name is. I'd like your opinion on that one, too. You know him personally, do you?'

'Yes,' said Tom, 'although only slightly. Good chap. I thought I'd go the House and see him at the end of the week. Give him time to digest your letter.'

'You know,' said Cadogan suddenly, 'I can't quite adjust to the idea we're a Socialist country, you know. After all that time.'

'We're not really,' said Tom lightly. 'Blair's more right wing than Major ever was. The word in the corridors is that he's Thatcher reborn. You know he's had two meetings with her already? Extraordinary. The man's a genius at public relations.'

'I'm not too keen on this love affair with Clinton,' said Cadogan.

'Blair's, or the bimbos in the White House?' said Tom laughing.

'Blair's. I think the man's got his eye on being president here.'

'Oh, I don't think that's very likely,' said Tom easily. 'Everyone still loves the monarchy.'

'I'm not too sure. Everyone loves Diana, not the rest of them. And she's not the monarchy.'

'Well, she's about to blot her copybook, if you ask me,' said Tom. 'I hear she's getting mixed up with the Al Fayeds. The British won't like that. A foreigner, and a dodgy one at that. Anyway, nothing to worry about with Blair's policies, there's no way he's going to squeeze the rich. Now I've also written to Margaret Beckett and a couple of civil servants whom she might consult on this; early days for that, but we can be absolutely ready if it does go to referral. And I've approached someone about putting down the EDM I mentioned to you. I found a real keenie, woman who made her maiden speech on the dangers to the leisure industry if the big boys get too much of a grip. So if I could just have your approval on those—'

'Felix Miller's a devious bastard, isn't he?' said Cadogan suddenly, looking up from the letters. 'I was watching him, never misses an opportunity to try and trip you up, does he?'

'No,' said Tom briefly, 'he hates me.'

'But why?'

'I broke up the great love affair of his life. The one he had with his daughter. And he remains a pretty ferocious rival.' He grinned at Cadogan. 'He's just waiting for her to see the folly of her ways and go home to him again.'

'You can't be serious?' said Cadogan.

'I'm absolutely serious,' said Tom.

In the offices of *Alive!*, the fashion and beauty editors and the senior director of Choice, the model agency, were leafing through the final selection of twenty girls that had been whittled down from the nine thousand who had entered the model competition. This was the third year they had run the competition, and they agreed it wasn't a good one. Even the final twenty had no real star-quality winners.

'Shit,' said Annabel Brown, the fashion editor, 'there isn't anyone here I'd want on my cover.'

Ritz Franklyn, of Choice, sighed. 'Well, maybe they'll be better in the flesh. They're coming in here next week, right?'

'Yup.'

'Excuse me.' It was Annabel's secretary. 'This one just came in. Late entry. She looks quite good to me. Worth showing you anyway.'

'Let me see. Oh, yeah. Hey! This one is – look, Ritz. Could be.'

Ritz looked. And experienced the flesh-crawling sensation that only came about once a year, when she saw a girl who she knew, just knew, had real one hundred and one per cent potential. Not looks, not shape, just – well, *it*.

'I agree. She could be. Susie, get her on the phone, will you? Explain the situation. And let's get her in on Wednesday anyway. Well done, Suze!'

'Thanks,' said Susie and went back to her office to make the phone call. She felt rather pleased with herself. She had thought, the minute she looked at the girl's face – and her figure – that she was pretty remarkable.

'Oh, hi,' she said, into the answering machine, 'this is Susie Bowman from *Alive!* magazine. You sent your picture in for our model contest. Could you give me a ring about it, please? Before six? The number is . . .'

Well, I'm doing all right, thought Octavia, after Carlton had gone: still functioning, running meetings, running a business, running the house. I'm not giving in. He isn't winning yet. And the longer he didn't win, the longer she could. It was a sort of self-fulfilling prophecy. Of course she had yet to do it, to make the confontation; but she would. When she felt strong enough. She had to be feeling pretty strong. It was hard to explain, even to herself; but the thought of coming to that scene, that conversation, was like approaching some vast obstacle, some huge, terrifyingly vast obstacle, a sort of Beecher's Brook. She had to make a start on it, gather speed, gain confidence; once she was on her way, perhaps, the momentum itself would carry her over. But not yet; not just yet.

Octavia's phone rang: it was Louise sounding sad and tired.

'Octavia, hallo. I'm sorry I didn't phone yesterday, we've been having a – well, Mummy's much worse. It's in her liver. We have only weeks now. No hope at all. Not any more.'

'Oh, Louise.' God, what did you say to someone in this situation, someone whose adored mother was going to die? 'I'm so, so sorry.' Suddenly Bartles Wood, Michael Carlton, even Tom, seemed unimportant. 'What can I do?'

'Just keep listening to me. And she'd love to see you. Really love it. I told her you'd offered. Can you come? Quite soon?'

Octavia looked at her diary. 'How about Sunday? Tom's promised to look after the children. Caroline's got the weekend off. I'd much rather leave him to it. I can't stand being alone with him.'

'Have you – said anything to him yet?'

'No,' said Octavia briefly, 'I haven't.'

'I'll see you on Sunday, then. Thank you so much. And – are you feeling *any* better?'

'No, worse,' said Octavia briefly.

'Poor angel. I wish I could help. Well, I can at least give you a hug. Goodbye, darling Octavia.'

Life was so boring at the moment, Romilly thought. She didn't have a boyfriend, she'd never even been to a proper club, she wasn't part of the cool lot at school. When Zoë had been fifteen, she had been having a really wild time, and she'd had loads of boyfriends, some of them really amazing looking. She had some new one now whom Romilly hadn't met, Zoë said she was sure Marianne would disapprove of him – Ian was a builder, as far as Romilly could make out.

She'd asked Zoë to take her to a club, once or twice, but Zoë always said she was too young, she'd never get in without an ID. When Zoë had been fifteen she'd had a faked ID, and Romilly had asked her about that, but Zoë just said she'd never get away with it. Romilly had to admit she was probably right, but that didn't stop her feeling dreary and as if she was missing out on life generally.

The house was very quiet; her mother was out, playing golf, and Zoë was presumably celebrating finishing the first week of her A-levels in some shop. It was all a bit dismal; Romilly sighed and went to phone Fenella Thomas, one of her best friends.

The answering machine was blinking: no doubt for Zoë. And her mother.

The first one was for Marianne, the second for Zoë, and the third was for Zoë too. Very much for Zoë; the sort of phone call people dreamed about. And they wanted to hear from her by six. Romilly looked at her watch. It was already half past five. It would be awful if it all fell through because Zoë hadn't phoned back. And goodness only knew when she would be in. She took a deep breath, picked up the phone and started dialling the number.

Tom phoned Octavia towards the end of the day and said shortly that he'd be very late back that night. 'In fact I might stay in a motel, come back in the morning. I'll let you know. Got to do a presentation to the Drapers. Very unexpected. Just came up.'

'Oh, really?' said Octavia.

There was no way she was going to give him the satisfaction of letting him think she cared how late he came back, or who he was with.

'You all right?' said Tom.

'Yes. I'm fine. Oh, you know you said you'd look after the children on Sunday? I'm going down to see Anna Madison. She's terribly ill. Much worse than they thought. So it seemed a good day to go. All right?'

'Oh, yes. Fine,' he said. He sounded rather taken aback.

Good, thought Octavia. The further he was taken aback, the better. She was beginning almost to enjoy this.

Octavia was shocked at the sight of Anna Madison. She seemed to have grown much smaller and her colour was appalling. But she had clearly made an effort; her hair was freshly brushed, and she was sitting up in bed on a pile of lace-trimmed pillows, wearing a white lawn bedjacket, 'And Louise has done my nails, look, in your honour,' she said. 'It's so terribly sweet of you to come, Octavia, darling. You're always here when we need you.'

Octavia laid down the flowers she had brought by Anna's bed.

'Oh, how lovely. All my favourites. Louise, can you fetch a vase, darling, and how about some tea?'

'Yes, I'll get some. Octavia, do you want anything to eat, a biscuit or something?'

Octavia shook her head; she found the sight of Anna almost unbearable. And thought suddenly back to the first time she had met her, the first time she had stayed with Louise.

Anna's car had failed to start and they had had to get a taxi to the village of Rookston from Stroud; she had greeted Octavia on the doorstep of the lovely house, a tall, dazzling figure, wearing a long, floaty dress in wonderful bright colours, all shades of blues and greens, and bright blue suede boots, her fair hair a riot of waves and curls tumbling on to her shoulders, her large blue eyes, Louise's eyes, heavily ringed in kohl. She had hugged Octavia and told her it was so lovely to be meeting her at last, she had heard so much about her, and she was so grateful for all her help to Louise – me help Louise! Octavia had thought, how ridiculous when it had been so utterly the other way round. Anna had then put her arm through each of theirs and led them inside, into a warm, untidy, sunlit kitchen, with a great many jugs and pots filled with dried flowers and grasses, and three dogs, golden cocker spaniels, and several cats, and told them to sit down and talk to her while she made lunch, and had giggled at all Louise's funny stories and threw in a few of her own, irreverent anecdotes about her neighbours. Octavia had tried to imagine her father talking in such away about his fellow grown-ups, and had failed totally.

That night, Anna had sat next to Octavia at supper and had her talking about her own life, which suddenly seemed to Octavia particularly dull and bleak, and had told her it sounded wonderfully interesting and intellectual to her; after supper she had asked them if they would help her top and tail gooseberries for a fool she was making for a dinner party next day, and then took them up to her room to help her decide what she was going to wear. She had a huge wardrobe, crammed with clothes: Octavia had particularly admired a patchwork waistcoat; Anna had told her to try it on, and then said she should have it. 'Honestly, it's too small for me and it suits your wonderful dark colouring much better than it does me.'

By the end of the day, Octavia was in love.

'It's so lovely to see you,' Anna said now, 'and, darling, I do want to know everything. Your important, exciting life, and how is your lovely husband, and those wonderful twins of yours and the darling baby, come along, sit down here, darling, tell me everything . . .'

Octavia dutifully chatted for a while, telling her things, trying to make her laugh, afraid of tiring her. Louise came back with tea and a plate of biscuits, and they all talked for a while about the old days, when the girls had been together at Rookston Manor for long, golden weeks in the summer holidays, running wild.

'Oh, dear, what lovely memories, how lucky I am,' said Anna. 'Louise, darling, would you go and find some of the photo albums? I'd so love to look at them all with Octavia.'

'Well – yes, if you like,' said Louise, looking at her doubtfully, 'but aren't you tired?'

'No, angel, I'm not tired, it's given me a new lease of life, seeing Octavia. Now I want all of them, the early ones. They're up in the old playroom – see what you can find anyway.'

Louise left the room, smiling at them both as she went.

'No secrets now,' she said, 'without me.'

'Of course not.'

Anna looked at Octavia as the door closed behind her, and smiled, sweetly, but slightly warily. 'It's about our – secret – that I wanted to talk to you,' she said.

'Of course she can't go. It's ridiculous. Mum, you can't let her.'

Zoë was horribly upset; Romilly could understand it. Her main thought, after she had finally come down from her high, wild excitement, had been how upset and jealous Zoë would be. Just the same, it was so wonderful to be the one, just for once, who was the star.

She still couldn't quite believe it. Couldn't believe hearing that girl's voice saying no, look, that's the whole point, we don't want your sister, we want you, she's great of course, but we think you're the one with the right look.

It had taken her ages to pluck up the courage to tell Zoë; she'd decided to wait till Saturday morning, as Zoë had come in in a foul mood from her exam and from meeting a friend – presumably – and then had been getting ready for about two hours. She'd wanted to talk to her mother, but Marianne had also been distracted – was going to some charity dinner with Felix – so she'd waited till they were all out and then phoned Fenella who'd said oh my God Romilly at least ten times.

In the morning she had told her mother; Marianne had been pleased for her, but said she really didn't think she could go, she was much too young, and what about school. Romilly had burst into tears of rage and disappointment, and said what harm would it do, just to go along to the semi-final, she probably wouldn't even make the photo and make-over session, which was for the last six, she was really totally unlikely to win, and even if she did, it didn't mean the end of her education as her mother seemed to think, she could do a bit of modelling in the holidays or something.

'Please, Mummy. You can't not let me at least try, you're always going on about how you wasted opportunities.'

That seemed to swing Marianne round, and she said all right, just the semi-final. 'And now you must tell Zoë,' she said.

Zoë had taken it badly; so badly that Marianne finally told her she was ashamed of her.

Zoë had left the room and slammed the door; but half an hour later (as Romilly had half expected she would, she was nothing if not generous) she came down again and said she was sorry, it was cool, she was pleased for Romilly, but she still didn't think Marianne ought to let her do it.

'I mean it, Mum, it's such a terrible, evil world, that. All those girls sleep with the photographers and do drugs and smoke and go anorexic and—'

Her anxiety was undoubtedly genuine; Marianne looked at her. It was typical of Zoë; underneath the bluster and the moods and the strop, she was kind, caring, and generous.

'Zoë, I really appreciate your concern for Romilly, and I can see it's genuine. But I think it would be fun for her, even if it gets no further than this session next Wednesday. I'm not a complete innocent, Zoë, and I shall be with Romilly if and when she meets the people from the agency. And I have no intention of her being exposed to any of the horrors you've mentioned—'

'Okay Okay,' said Zoë. 'Just don't say I didn't warn you, when she comes home weighing five stone with a heroin habit. I'm going to do some work.'

They looked after her as she left the room.

'Thanks, Mummy,' said Romilly, giving her a hug.

'I'm so sorry,' said Anna, 'but she saw your note to me when she was helping me sort some things out, a few weeks ago. It just fell out of my bedside table drawer. And she wanted to know what it was you were thanking me for. I said I didn't want to tell her, but she got very upset and said it wasn't fair to have secrets from her, you were her friend, and if I wouldn't tell her, she'd ask you. Well, I thought that would be worse, darling, so I told her.'

'Oh,' said Octavia. 'And what did she say?'

'She hardly took any notice. She just said how sensible of you, that I'd given you absolutely the right advice, and how lovely it had all turned out right for you in the end. She might have been a bit upset that you hadn't talked to her, but—'

'But you explained why I couldn't? Why I felt I couldn't?'

'Yes, of course. And she said how sweet and how typical of you, and I honestly don't think she thought any more about it.'

'I wonder why she never said anything to me about it,' said Octavia.

'Well, darling, she's very sensitive about such things. About people's feelings, Too sensitive, I often think.'

'Yes, I know. I might speak to her about it. Now I know, it feels as if it's sort of there between us.'

'I hope it isn't going to cause any trouble between you,' said Anna, her drawn face anxious, 'I'd feel so bad. But I didn't want to lie to her.'

'What's done's done,' said Octavia, leaning over her, giving her a kiss. 'And I'm sure it doesn't matter.'

'I hope so. I feel better for telling you anyway. I wish I had before. Now look, I'm awfully tired suddenly. I might like a little sleep. Come again, darling, won't you?'

'Yes, of course I will.'

'I haven't got awfully long,' said Anna suddenly, 'I know that. They don't know that I know, but I'm not stupid. They'd have started the chemotherapy by now if there'd been any point.'

'Oh, Anna,' said Octavia, tears welling up unbidden. 'Anna,—'

'No,' said Anna, quite fiercely, 'no, Octavia, you are not to cry. If I can be brave, then so can all of you. Listen, there's Louise coming back now. Louise darling, I was just saying I'm rather tired suddenly. I'd love to look at those, but another time. Now take Octavia off for a chat. I'm sure you must be dying for some time on your own. Your father's arriving any minute, so I'll be fine for the rest of the day, I really will.'

Downstairs, Octavia looked at Louise.

'If she doesn't need you for a bit, would you like to come for a drive for an hour or two? I've promised to look at something, and I'd love to have you with me.'

'So where are we going?' said Louise, settling into Octavia's BMW with a smile of pleasure as they struck the main road. She had left Dickon with Janet, Anna Madison's night and daily as she called her.

'Place called Bartles Wood. Just south of Bath. Have you read anything about it?'

'No. Should I have?'

'It's been in the papers quite a bit.' Octavia looked at Louise and grinned. 'I forgot you never read them. It's another Newbury bypass. I presume you read about that?'

'Yes. Well, saw it on the news. Why are you so interested in it?'

'Because I care about England,' said Octavia briefly. 'I care it's being deluged with concrete. Losing its woods and lanes and meadows. Just for the greater convenience of the motor car.'

'I hadn't noticed you travelling about on a bike very often,' said Louise mildly.

Octavia grinned at her. 'I know. But if push came to shove, I would drive less.'

'And not get to your cottage at the weekends?'

'We could come by train.'

'With the children and the luggage and the nanny and the food and—'

'Yes, all right,' said Octavia irritably.

'Sorry.' Louise looked at her thoughtfully. 'You're very thin, Octavia.'

'You'd be thin, if your husband was playing around, you didn't know who with, who knew about it—'

'Yes, I'm sorry. Of course. Have you told him yet?'

'Louise, I can't. Something keeps stopping me. While he doesn't know I know, I feel safe, in some perverse way. Does that sound crazy?'

'No, not really. I think I can understand that. Has he ever done it before, do you think?'

'I don't know,' said Octavia slowly. 'God, that is the worst thing. I feel I don't know anything about him any more. I can't believe anything he says – it's horrible.'

'Octavia, is he still . . .' Her voice trailed away. 'Well, are you . . .'

'If you mean is he sleeping with me, yes, he is.' She could hear her own voice angry and raw.

'Sorry,' said Louise, gently, 'it seemed a bit – well, relevant. I'm really sorry, Boot. It's nothing to do with me.'

'No, you're right, I suppose. It is relevant. And I don't quite know how I can. I've only done it once. Since I knew. I found it rather – can you believe this, Lulu – rather exciting. Almost as if it was me having the affair. Does that sound crazy? God, I really think I am going mad. I find myself going down these false trails, suspecting the most ridiculous people.'

'Like?'

'Well, like Lauren Bartlett, a friend – well, associate – of ours. Like some woman at Ascot in a pink hat. I can't look at anyone, actually, any more without thinking it might be *Her*. It's horrible, I feel like I'm walking through a minefield. All the time.'

Louise was silent; then she said, very gently, 'Octavia, I'm so so sorry. I do feel so sad for you. I wish there was something I could do.'

'There is. Just keep listening to me. That's all I ask.'

It was almost seven when Louise and Octavia reached Bartles Wood; a golden, gleaming evening.

It was quite a small wood, sunk into one of the small valleys between Bath and Frome, and from the top of the hill its shape, rather like a comma, was clearly defined. Bartles House itself was hidden from the road by another small sward of trees, but the grounds below it were grassland, and nothing remarkable until they met the wood. Octavia could see why Carlton would wish to build there; it was spectacularly beautiful countryside, the hills forming a natural fortress for the whole area, a river running through the valley, cutting through the edge of the wood, the sloping meadows studded with trees. Horses grazed in those meadows, and sheep and rather grown-up-looking lambs, and in the dark golden sunlight, small, still, black splodges that were rabbits cropped at the grass.

They drove down the hill, winding into the lengthening shadows, over a stone bridge, began to climb again the other side.

'We can walk down there, look, through that field, follow the river to the wood,' said Octavia, pointing.

They parked near a gate; it had a crude notice nailed to it, covered in polythene, which said, 'Save Bartles Wood'.

'There was one of those by the bridge as well,' said Louise. 'Did you see it?'

'No, I didn't. Oh, dear, they'll have to do better than that.'

They climbed over the gate. Some cows looked at them curiously, found them uninteresting, returned to their supper. Everything was lush, the grass tall by the river, the cow parsley almost waist high. There was a path, one-person-wide, leading along the riverbank, hung over with willows; flies danced in clouds above the water, two dragonflies in a sudden glitter of blue, and 'Look!' said Louise suddenly. 'Look, a kingfisher.'

They reached a stile that actually led into the wood; they climbed over it, stopped after a few hundred yards and looked back. The river, little more than a wide deep stream, curved behind them, the long shafting sunlight slowly losing brilliance. A fish surfaced, then another, breaking the calm of the water, and two ducks made a rather stately progress from the bank, followed by an unruly gaggle of ducklings.

'And they're going to do what here?' said Louise, her voice quiet in the stillness.

'Build executive homes and a shopping mall,' said Octavia briefly. 'Oh, and a community centre.'

'They can't. How can that be allowed?'

'It's called progress,' said Octavia.

'And you know the man who's going to do it?'

'I know the man who *wants* to do it. He's a client of Tom's. And I've got involved with him professionally too. As a sponsor. And Foothold, one of my charities, has a branch down here. They're fighting it, have asked me to help with publicity and so on.'

'Difficult.'

There was a long silence. Then Octavia said, 'No, Louise, do you know, suddenly not difficult at all.'

CHAPTER 10

'Darling? You there? I'm home.'

Sandy had been half asleep in front of the television; it was, he often said, his main hobby these days. He fought his way back to reality through a fog of the best part of a bottle of Beaujolais.

'Yes,' he said, standing up, switching the TV off. 'Yes, in here, in the breakfast room. Want a cup of tea?'

'Yes, please,' she said, coming in and sinking on to the old sofa. 'That would be lovely. I'm awfully tired. Dickon's asleep in the car.'

'I'll get him in. How's your mum?'

'Dying in front of our eyes. The hardest thing is not to let her see it herself. Being brave and cheerful and pretending—'

'She's not stupid,' said Sandy carefully. 'Don't you think she knows?'

'Sandy, if she knows, she's pretending too. It's her way of coping.' Her voice was sharp; she was clearly struggling to be patient, not reproachful.

Sandy felt instantly clumsy and insensitive: as he did most of the time with Louise. 'Sorry. Sorry, darling.'

'They're talking about getting further nursing help now. Daddy and Janet and the District just aren't enough any more.'

'So – how long? Do they think?'

'Oh, weeks. Possibly less. I hope less, in an awful way. It's so terrible to see her like this. She can hardly eat now, and what she does often comes up again. Oh, dear.'

She started to cry; Sandy sat down beside her, put his arm round her. She was very thin; thinner than he could ever remember, even after – well, after *then*. That.

'This is an awful lot for you to cope with,' he said, suddenly. 'And coming back here all the time, to look after me. It adds to the strain. Why don't you just stay there? Until – well . . .'

'Oh, Sandy, no. I can't abandon you. You've got a lot on your plate at the moment as well, it's not fair.'

'It's fine,' he said, 'as long as you have Dickon with you. I obviously can't cope with him.'

'I know you can't. Of course I'd take him. Oh, Sandy, it's so sweet of you. I really don't deserve you.'

'Yes, you do,' he said, 'and it's nice to be able to do something for you for a change. Now look, drink this tea and I'll go and get Dickon from the car.'

He undressed Dickon, and tucked him up in bed.

''Night night, old man.'

'Daddy, Granny's very ill, you know,' Dickon said, his dark eyes very large. 'I'm frightened she'll die. Like Juliet.'

Sandy couldn't think what to say. Dickon's terror of death completely defeated him. 'Granny's very strong,' he said finally. 'And doctors are very clever these days.'

That was wrong, he supposed; Louise and the child psychiatrist had both insisted Dickon should be always told the truth, said he must confront and be helped through his fears, not led away from them. Sandy, who found any emotional confrontation difficult, felt uneasy with that. Anna was almost certainly going to die, but Dickon should be spared from that knowledge for as long as possible in his view; he wasn't yet five years old. Equally he disliked the insistence that Dickon must realise what death actually meant; Sandy was not religious himself, but when his own grandparents had died, he had been told they had moved on from earth to heaven, where they were having a very pleasant time indeed, up above the clouds, sitting among flocks of angels. The thought of them being up there together and probably with their two smelly old Jack Russells and his grandmother's hunter had comforted him a lot. By the time he had grown out of that vision, he had grown out of his grief at losing them; he couldn't see why Dickon couldn't be fed with the same harmless nonsense.

'So she probably might get better, then?' he said now, looking up at his father, his voice more hopeful.

'She probably might.' That wasn't actually a lie; extraordinary things happened to cancer patients. You heard about them all the time. 'So don't you worry about her, old chap. Just be nice and brave and cheerful for her and Mummy, and that'll help a lot.'

'I will.' Dickon's eyes were closing. ''Night, Daddy. You go and look after Mummy. She hasn't been very well on the way home. She told me not to tell you.'

'Really?' said Sandy. 'What sort of not very well?'

'She was sick. She—'

'Dickon—' it was Louise's voice, speaking from the door – 'you promised, I didn't want to tell Daddy, make him more worried. Sandy, I'm fine. Honestly. Good night, darling one, give Mummy a kiss . . .'

'What sort of not very well?' said Sandy again, as they went downstairs.

'Oh, hideous sore throat. Had it all day. Nothing to worry about, honestly. But they make you feel rotten all over, those things.'

'Poor old you. I'll find you the Lemsip.'

'Would you, darling? Thank you.'

She did look rotten, he thought; it undoubtedly added to the exhaustion. The familiar old raw panic gripped him; then he pulled himself together. She absolutely could not be pregnant. It still haunted him, that – despite everything he had done, despite her passionate avowals that she would never, ever even consider it. He thanked God, or the power that he imagined to be God, not to mention medical science, every day, every week, every month, most fervently every month, that she couldn't be pregnant, that they weren't ever going to have to go through that again.

When Octavia was getting dressed next day, she pulled the handkerchief out of her drawer by mistake. It made her feel very odd; she threw it down on the bed as if it was something obscene, something she couldn't bear to touch, and stood staring at it for quite a long time, her eyes boring into it, as if it could tell her something, trying to summon up some kind of image from it: almost as if, she thought, and had to laugh at herself, it was a latterday Turin Shroud. It stopped seeming funny quite quickly.

She folded it up again and wrapped it very carefully in some tissues and put it in her briefcase to take to the office. She didn't want it at home, but she felt she had to keep it; it was important, central to her strange new life. Then she went and washed her hands, several times. Like Lady Macbeth, she thought distractedly.

She felt very tired that day; she had slept badly the night before. Tom had been very late, and, until she heard his car, she'd tortured herself with visions of him in *Her* bed, wondering what *She* was like in bed and how *She* behaved, and in the end began to feel she was watching some porn movie. She had finally taken a sleeping pill at three, had found waking up almost impossible, struggling out of a thick, dry-mouthed fog, had taken a taxi to work early, not daring to drive.

She was drinking a strong coffee when her phone went. It was Tom,

Tom sounding slightly distant, and she heard her voice, not tearful at all, saying, 'Yes?'

'Just to let you know,' he said, 'that I've just had a call from Michael Carlton. He said the meeting with you went well. He seemed pleased. I just thought I should thank you.'

'That's all right,' she said, and put the phone down quite gently. Only the thought of what she was going to do for Patricia David and Bartles Wood kept her from slamming it viciously enough for him to hear.

'I saw Michael Matthews last night,' said Tom, 'MP for Romford North. He's very interested in this takeover of yours, going to table a few questions for us.'

'Good. I've balloted the shareholders,' said Nico Cadogan, 'and presented the streamlined new company to them, as you said. All we can do now is pray, I suppose.'

'I think you're paying me to do a bit more than that,' said Tom, laughing.

'Maybe. Very good day at Ascot, by the way. I enjoyed it. Thank you. You must let me take you and Octavia to dinner one evening soon.'

'That would be very nice,' said Tom, 'thank you.'

'She's very bright, your wife, as well as beautiful. You're a lucky man.'

'I hope so,' said Tom.

It seemed to Cadogan an intriguing reply.

'This is marvellous, Octavia!' Patricia David's voice was breathless with pleasure. 'We could never have done anything as good as this. Thank you so much.'

'That's all right,' said Octavia. 'It was quite easy, really. I went there, you know, to the wood, and it can't be allowed. But you really will have to do much more than issue that press release, and put up a few of those notices. Now, as long as it's turned down at local level, you've got time on your side. They'll appeal, it'll take months, with luck. But if it's true, the rumour, that it's going to be passed – well, that's more difficult.'

'What should we do?'

'I'll try and find out for you. I'm better informed on getting planning permission than fighting it. But let's see. You should hear this week, I understand.'

'Yes. After the planning meeting. Two days' time. Anyway, I'm going to whack this release of yours out to the local papers right now.'

'Yes, do. And no reason why you shouldn't try the nationals. The

Guardian would be a good idea, and the *Independent*. They're the greenest papers.'

'Thank you. Octavia, we're so lucky to have you on our side.'

'Yes, well, remember, just keep quiet about it,' said Octavia. 'I really mean it, Patricia. It would do you, never mind me, huge harm if it got out I was involved in all this.'

God, she thought, putting the phone down. This really was playing with fire. The funny thing was, it was making her feel so much better.

Melanie came in. 'Hi. Everything okay? Look, we've had a call from your friend Lauren Bartlett. She wants us to call her. Next Generation, I presume. Do you think we've got a chance there after all? It would be marvellous to get it, such high profile, a real honeypot account, and Diana's rumoured to be very interested.'

'I really don't know,' said Octavia.

Lauren Bartlett was in a hurry. 'Big dinner party for Drew. I'm frantic. I've got to get the flowers and my hair done before the cook arrives. Now look. We've decided we might like your firm to help us with our day at Brands Hatch. We really are just slightly out of our depth, so providing we can meet on the fee—'

'Lauren,' said Octavia firmly, 'our fee is fixed. We don't work for less, for anyone.'

'Not even friends?'

'Well—' She knew Melanie could bend the rules to get this one. 'Well, we could talk about it.'

'Oh, I see. I have to say, if it's not possible, there could be a problem. Anyway, there's something else. There's a children's hospice we make a grant to each year, which is under threat. Basically it needs rehousing, and a lot more money than we can possibly supply. We've applied for lottery money, of course, but we're not hopeful. Needless to say, our old friends the cuts are to blame. Tom knows all those MPs, do you think he could help?'

'I really don't know,' said Octavia.

'This is what I thought. We'd like to come in to your company and have a meeting; if we made it towards the end of the working day, I thought Tom could join us, you and me, that is, afterwards. Discuss what he might be able to do.'

The arrogance was breathtaking. 'I will ask,' she said, 'see if he has any ideas.'

That was usually enough; people felt soothed into a sense of security, usually false, by the notion that Tom Fleming, who famously spent half of his working life at the House – or so he encouraged people think – would address his brain and contacts to their problems.

Lauren was not most people.

'No, I'm afraid that's not good enough, Octavia. I want to discuss it with him personally. Could you put it to him?'

'Yes, of course, but I can't promise—'

'No, I realise that. Now how about next week for the meeting, Tuesday, say? Tuesday afternoon. That would suit me very well. I've another dinner party on Monday and the theatre on Wednesday, so – yes, Tuesday. We could come in at four thirty?'

Octavia looked at her diary; it was enragingly empty. 'All right by me. Let me just check with my partner, Melanie Faulks.' Melanie was also free; Octavia gritted her teeth, went back to the phone. 'Yes, that's fine.'

'Good. And you'll speak to Tom?'

I try not to these days, Octavia thought, a sudden sadness sweeping over her, but, 'Yes, I will ask him of course.'

Tom said he couldn't possibly meet anyone anywhere next Tuesday; he had to attend a meeting with Nico Cadogan and his bankers in London, and then had a late meeting in Oxford. 'I probably won't be back that night.'

'Any other day next week?' said Octavia. She hated this, but Lauren Bartlett's account probably hung on Tom's association with it.

'No, sorry,' he said shortly.

'Well,' she said with an enormous effort, 'could I suggest dinner with the Bartletts? Or drinks? Another time?'

'If you really want to, but God knows when I could make it. And I would feel bound to make it clear to Lauren there wasn't much I could do. Look, talk to Barbara about it, I've got to go.' He put the phone down.

Octavia sat staring at it. Her power marriage seemed to be becoming rather impotent.

'How was today, then? The all-important exams?' Ian Edwards grinned at Zoë. They were sitting in a pub just off the Fulham Road. 'I don't know why you're bothering. Gorgeous girl like you. You could make a fortune modelling, you don't need to bother with all that rubbish.'

This was a sore point; so sore it even pervaded the week-kneed light-headedness that Ian Edwards' company reduced.

'Oh, no thanks,' she said. 'Seriously boring, modelling is. I've got loads of friends who do it, I'd really hate it.'

'Anyway, you don't have to worry about getting a job, do you? Daddy and Mummy'll see you all right.'

'In your dreams! They spend their life telling me I've got to make my own way, stand on my own feet,' said Zoë gloomily.

'Yeah? Well, I've been standing on mine for four years. Can't see there's a lot to be said for it, personally.'

'You're not sorry you left school when you did, though, are you?' said Zoë casually. She was fascinated by everything to do with Ian. He could have come from another planet, so alien was he to all the boys she had grown up with. She had met working-class boys before, but never got close to one. They were so much more attractive than the public school wallies she knew; sexier, sharper, funnier, more glamorous.

'You kidding?' 'Course not. Here, come over here, Zo . . .'

He leaned forward, started kissing her. Zoë responded enthusiastically. She liked the way he did it anywhere, in the pub, on the Tube, not caring about anyone seeing.

'What you doing tonight, then?' he said when he had finally released her.

'Revising. And I've promised to help my little sister do her hair. She's going somewhere important tomorrow.'

'That's nice, Zoë. You're a really nice girl, you know. Not how I thought you'd be at all.'

'How did you think that I might be?' said Zoë.

'Oh, you know. Spoilt, up yourself. But you're not. You're a bit like my sister.'

'Really?' She couldn't have had a nicer compliment. 'How old is your sister? What's her name?'

'Jade. She's twenty. She's a hairdresser. She wanted to stay on at college, do some A-levels, but my dad wouldn't let her.'

'Why not?' said Zoë, and then wished she hadn't. Ian was looking at her with a mixture of amusement and disdain.

'It's called money. He didn't want to keep her no longer. You know? No, you probably wouldn't. Nobody in your house would be told they couldn't do anything, would they? Not because of money. What is it your dad does?'

'He's a lawyer. He doesn't live in London. I told you. He's in New York. They're divorced.'

'Yeah, I remember that. Well, I'd better be getting off. If you won't come out tonight, what about tomorrow?'

'No, I can't, Ian, I'm really sorry. Not till Friday. More than my life's worth.'

'Dear, oh dear.' He shook his head at her sorrowfully. 'What a good little girl you are. Here, let's have another kiss.'

They walked down the road together; his arm round her shoulders, his hand occasionally moving down on to her breast. Zoë looked at him. He was incredibly sexy she thought; he was very dark, with close-cropped hair and thick black eyebrows, quite tall and very muscular and tanned from working out of doors; he was wearing a black sleeveless T-shirt and black jeans, and she wondered how he'd look without anything on, and felt quite weak.

He grinned at her, nibbled at her ear. 'What you thinking about, Zo?'

'Oh, what we might do on Friday.'

'Want to go clubbing? And after that – who knows?'

He had already hinted at that; that they might have sex. She couldn't wait. Zoë hadn't had a lot of sex, but what she had, she had enjoyed, and she was sure she would enjoy it with Ian Edwards. The only thing was, where? All the opportunities that life in her circle usually provided – parties, parents away, weekend cottages – were hardly going to apply to Ian.

Ritz Franklyn didn't often get the thud in her guts that told her this was a big one, but she had it now, looking at Romilly Muirhead, standing there with her mother, politely nervous, huge green eyes looking round the magazine offices, great mass of gleaming, silver-blonde hair falling from a high forehead, tiny heart-shaped face, wide lovely smile, its radiance quite undimmed by the thick braces on her teeth. God, it was all eyes and mouth, that face, virginal sex incarnate, she was, and she had no idea, no idea at all . . .

'Hi,' she said, carefully casual, 'you must be Romilly. And Mrs Muirhead, how do you do. I'm Ritz Franklyn. We're so glad you're here. Now what we're going to do today is take some polaroids of you, see how you move, have a bit of a chat, and then we'll let you go. If you're lucky, we'll want you back next week, for a real photo session, and then the judging. Now here's Annabel Brown, she's the fashion editor, and this is Frannie Spencer, the beauty editor. They're the other judges, together with Jonty Jacobson, the photographer. Want a drink, Coke or something? And Mrs Muirhead, would you like a cup of tea?'

'It was wonderful,' said Romilly to Fenella, 'honestly, I can't tell you. They were so nice, all of them, really down to earth, not a bit stuck up, just really kind and encouraging. I had to walk up and down a bit, pretend I was on a catwalk, I felt a bit silly, but they said just relax, they'd put on some music, so that helped, and then they did this picture and—'

'What were the others like?'

'Oh, fantastic,' said Romilly, her voice drooping slightly. 'Much older than me, more Zoë's age. One of them had already done some modelling and another had been in a commercial with her mum when she was small, so they knew what they were doing. And there was another, she was gorgeous, she looked just like Naomi Campbell. So there's no way I'll win. Or even get in the last six probably. But it was a fantastic afternoon, and I get to keep some of the pictures.'

'Well, that's an easy one,' said Ritz.

'Yeah. Absolutely no contest. It's a farce going through the final selection, really. She's gorgeous. And the legs! My God, those legs.'

'Only thing about her is,' said Ritz, 'how much we'll get out of her. Mum's no fool. She'll keep a very tight watch on things.'

'Yes, but she'll be sixteen by then. She'll learn to look out for herself, fight back. And once she's done her GCSEs, the mother'll probably give in as well. I mean, I reckon Christie's might well want her. For their new young line. They're desperate for a face – and what a story for a cosmetic house. Made for each other, the new girl and the new line. I mean think about it, Ritz, that is half a million smackeroonies. Not many people could resist that. Not even mothers with attitude.'

Michael Carlton phoned Fleming Cotterill later that afternoon; Tom was in a meeting, his secretary said, and she didn't think—

'I don't want you to think,' said Carlton, 'I want you to put me through. It's urgent.'

Tom called from the meeting, listened to what he had to say with a sinking heart. The council had turned down his application to develop at Bartles Park. It would mean an appeal, a long delay and considerable expense. Carlton clearly felt Tom was largely to blame.

'You said this was unlikely. That the council wouldn't risk the cost of an appeal, in case they got lumbered with costs. What went wrong?'

'I don't know, Michael,' said Tom carefully, 'it happens sometimes. Obviously there is strong local opposition. Look, you'll get it in the end. I know you will. It's just a question of time and—'

'It was all those bloody editorials, wasn't it? Those wretched women and their placards. Put them up all over the place, they have, all over the countryside down there, I went to have another look last week.'

'Did you?' said Tom, surprised.

'Yes, I did. You might have found the time to do that yourself, if I might say so. Know your enemy, it's the first rule of war. And that piece in the *Mail*. I spoke to some woman on the local paper, asked her if no one was interested in the community centre. She said she didn't know anything about it. That doesn't say a great deal for your public relations, Tom.'

'People hear what they want to hear, Michael.'

'They do indeed. And I want them to hear about the community centre. I'm fed up. Octavia hasn't been much help down there either, has she? So what happens next?'

'I told you, we'll appeal. We can do it in writing or at a public hearing. Or go for a full public inquiry. I would advise the public hearing. Quickest and cheapest.'

Carlton glared at him. 'You just do what you think's going to work,' said Carlton. 'That's what I'm paying you for. Rather a lot, I seem to remember. Right now it doesn't seem entirely worth it. Afternoon, Tom.'

CHAPTER 11

'Oh, God,' said Romilly and burst into tears.

'Darling, what is it?'

'This!' said Romilly, holding out a letter. '*Alive!* want me for the final! For the last six. Oh, Mummy! I can't believe it. I must phone Fen!'

'Romilly, darling, you'll see her in half an hour—' But Romilly had gone.

Zoë came in. 'What was that all about?'

'She got into the final of this model competition,' said Marianne, trying to sound cool and relaxed and, to her own ears, failing.

'Oh, Mum. Told you. Well, it's too late now. See you!'

'Yes. Good luck today, darling. What is it?'

'French Lit.'

'You'll be fine. Are you in tonight?'

'No. 'Bye.'

She was up to something, Marianne could tell; going out with someone unsuitable. She knew the signs: a greater than normal cloak of mystery thrown over her movements; a reluctance to talk at all. Last time it had been the older brother of a schoolfriend: much older. Twenty-four to be precise. Zoë looked and seemed older than she was, with her rather sultry beauty, her rich, sulky mouth, her heavily lidded green eyes, her ultra-cool manner; but she had been completely out of her depth. Marianne had literally offered a prayer of gratitude when she had found Zoë sobbing over the affair's demise. This couldn't be worse. Could it? Maybe it could. She sighed.

Romilly reappeared. ''Bye, Mummy. I'm so excited!'

'Me too, darling, but you really must practise your saxophone tonight – you haven't got to grips with that piece.'

'Oh, there's plenty of time. I can't think about that now. 'Bye!'

It was only a tiny thing; but it was a change. A change if not for the worse, then certainly not the better. Marianne sighed.

The phone rang: it was Felix. 'Good morning. Are you well?'

'Yes, thank you. Nice dinner last night. I enjoyed it.'

'Me too. Now look, I've been thinking. I want you to speak to Octavia.'

'What about?'

'About whatever it is that's troubling her. I did ask her what the matter was, and she gave me some cock and bull story about it being hormonal. I really would like you to talk to her. See what you can get out of her.'

'Felix,' said Marianne, 'I have enough problems with my own family at the moment. Romilly seems to be in danger of winning this wretched model competition, Zoë's up to something or other, and I haven't heard from Marc for literally weeks.'

'Well, I'm sorry to hear that,' he said, 'but you do know, don't you, it's largely your own fault? You've spoilt those children, over-indulged them, and now—'

'Felix,' said Marianne, 'I'm sorry, but I don't need this. I really don't. And I have absolutely no intention of speaking to Octavia about her quite possibly nonexistent traumas. The whole idea is absurd. Good morning.'

She put the phone down on him and sat, shaking slightly. It rang again, sharply. She picked it up, said 'Yes?' furiously, thinking it would be Felix.

'Marianne? You don't sound very pleased to hear from me.'

It was Nico Cadogan.

'I'm *terribly* pleased to hear from you,' she said and meant it. 'More pleased than you could possibly imagine.'

'Octavia, isn't it wonderful? We've won!' Patricia David's voice was ecstatic.

Octavia smiled down the phone. 'It is wonderful news. Yes. But you do realise—'

'Yes, of course. He's already said he's going to appeal. But that gives us time. Lots of time. Our MP says it could take two years.'

'What's his name? Your MP? I might know him.'

'Oh, rather romantic. Gabriel Bingham. Straight out of Thomas Hardy. I must say, for a Labour man, he's a bit of a surprise.'

No doubt he speaks nicely, thought Octavia, and has good manners.

'He's very well spoken and extremely polite,' said Patricia David. 'Quite young and good looking in a wild sort of way. He's been to a couple of the meetings. Very noncommittal of course, but I'm hopeful of his support. Now, the *Daily Mail* want to interview me, about the latest development. Is that a good idea?'

'Yes, but make some really solid noises, Patricia. Don't just waffle on about the wood and how lovely it is. Say you're starting an appeal fund, that you plan to brief a barrister, take it to the European Courts if necessary. Sound as if you really are going to be tough opponents. Not just an emotional band of mothers.'

'Hang on, I'm just writing that down. Marvellous. I know I've said it before, but we really are lucky to have you on our side, Octavia. I wish you could meet our Mr Bingham – you'd like him such a lot and maybe you could persuade him to come in on our side.'

'Now that really would be dangerous,' said Octavia, laughing. 'For me to meet him.'

Marianne looked at Nico Cadogan across the table and wondered quite what she was doing here. At Le Caprice, where half the clientele would know either her or him and wonder what they were doing together.

'Well, this is fun,' he said, as if he read her thoughts. 'Good to do something just for fun, don't you think?'

'Yes,' she said, slightly doubtfully.

'Come along. Drink your champagne. I want to hear all about these terrible problems you're having with your family.'

When he had phoned that morning, ostensibly in search of Felix, she had told him she was the last person Felix would be with at that moment, and he had asked why, and rather rashly she had told him.

'You sound as if you are feeling neglected,' he said. 'Come and have lunch with me, and let me treat you rather better for a bit.'

She had said no, of course she couldn't, and he had said yes, of course she could, and she had suddenly looked over her life and thought that yes, he was right, of course she could. And here she was, sitting opposite him, feeling absurdly nervous and more than a little confused, both emotionally and sexually, by the rather fearsome force of his attentions.

'I'm finding it rather insulting,' he said, looking at her over his glass of champagne, 'that you're not enjoying this more.'

'Oh, I am,' she said, taking another sip of the champagne – not the house champagne either, but Veuve Cliquot. Clearly, Nico was not over-concerned about his personal financial stability.

'No, you're not. You're worrying about whether someone you know will see us; you're worrying about what Felix might say if he knew – or does he know?'

'No,' she said, half amused, half indignant at the question, 'I don't have to tell Felix everything I do – we're not married.'

'Why not? You've been together a long time, you're obviously very fond of him, you're both free . . .'

'We choose not to be,' said Marianne firmly. 'And, Nico, I'd rather not talk about it. It really is nothing to do with you.'

'Yes, it is,' he said.

'Why?'

'I think you should use your imagination on that one.'

'I'm afraid, Tom, we may have to look for an extra injection of capital,' said Aubrey.

'Christ. Is it that bad?'

'Not yet. But if we lost an account, even a small one, we'd be done for.'

'Well, we're not going to,' said Tom lightly. 'Everything's going well.'

'Including Michael Carlton?'

'Oh, I can steady him. He'll get his permission. It's just going to take a bit longer. You could argue it's a good thing; we'll get his fee for longer as well.'

'Okay,' said Aubrey with a sigh, 'we'll hang on. I'm having dinner with an old City chum on Tuesday night. You're not free, are you? You and Octavia? I know he'd like to meet you. *Both* of you,' he added, stressing the point.

'No, sorry,' said Tom. 'I'm out of town. Got a meeting in Oxford with a group of environmentalists, interested in forming a parliamentary committee. I won't be back, I'm afraid.' He was thumbing through some papers, just a bit too intently.

Aubrey looked at him for a moment. 'I see,' was all he said.

'Where have you been?'

Marianne jumped; she had thought the house was empty.

Zoë was sitting in the kitchen watching TV. 'You look nice. A bit flushed, but really nice. Cool dress.'

'Thank you,' said Marianne with some difficulty. She felt flushed all over. Her body, always sexually responsive, was in shock with desire: she wanted only to get upstairs, and into the shower, to try and drown the acute reaction she was experiencing after two hours of Nico Cadogan and his intense sexual attentions. It wasn't that he had even touched her – well, apart from a kiss goodbye, utterly casual, at the door of Le Caprice. And the occasional covering of her hand with his. And the smile – that dangerous, intent smile. He had put her into a taxi, apologised for not being able to escort her in it back to Eaton Square – he had an urgent meeting. Thank God for that, thought Marianne. Her mother had talked laughingly about men in her youth who were labelled NSIT – Not Safe In Taxis. She wouldn't be at all safe in a taxi herself, with Nico Cadogan, the state she was in; she would have been hard pressed not to make the first move and start kissing him. It was an event that must not be repeated. Much too dangerous.

She smiled at Zoë carefully, pushed her hand through her hair, and even that was disturbing. Nico had done the same, pushed his hand through it, said I do like a woman's hair that isn't all fussed to bits. And where had they been when he had done that? In the lobby of Le Caprice. Well, most people had gone by then, it had been ten to four. Only the manager and the hat-check girl and the barman and the doorman and about a dozen other people could have noticed. Oh, God.

'I must go and have a shower,' she said to Zoë quickly. 'I really am very hot.'

'Okay. Cool,' said Zoë. She grinned at her, rather conspiratorially. Marianne felt like a teenager in the presence of her mother, rather than the other way round.

'I'd like to invite Louise over on Sunday,' said Octavia. 'And Sandy, obviously.'

They were going to the cottage, had been invited to a big fortieth birthday party on the Saturday night; but that still left Sunday to be alone with Tom. The prospect frightened her.

They were in bed. He had been late the last three nights and she had been able to pretend to be asleep when he came in; tonight they had been out together, and she was inescapably in bed with him.

Tom was looking at some papers, annotating them. 'I'd really rather not,' he said. He sounded distracted.

'Why?'

'I've got a lot of reading to do. Bloody Sandy'll want to play tennis, and—'

'Tom, they're having an awful time at the moment. Louise's mother is dying!'

'Well, if her mother's dying, surely she won't want to drive an hour in the opposite direction. Suppose something happened while she was with us?'

'I think she needs the break,' said Octavia firmly. 'In fact, I've already asked her.'

'Well, you must un-ask her. Or I'll go back to London on the train. I really can't face an afternoon of Sandy talking about his days in Bosnia. He really gets up my nose.'

'Tom, he's not that bad.'

'I find him very bad.'

'You wouldn't find him bad if he was a client, would you? We'd all have to hang on his every word about Bosnia, if he had a nice fat fee to wave at you!'

'Oh, shut up,' he said wearily. 'Look, I think I'll go and sleep in the guest room. I really do have to work on this thing. All right by you?'

She shrugged.

He got out of bed and gathered up his things. 'Good night, Octavia.'

'Good night, Tom.'

It was frightening how swiftly the relationship had deteriorated since she had made her discovery. What scared her was what would have happened if she hadn't made it. Would she still have been living with him perfectly happily, sitting at the same table as him without feeling sick, discussing things with him without wanting to scream, getting into bed with him without shrinking away? Would he have been making love to her still – it hadn't happened since that first night – would she have been enjoying it, responding to him? And would he, all the time, through the meals and the discussions and the lovemaking, have been thinking of *Her*, wishing he was with *Her*, comparing her to *Her*? How long had it been going on, and why, why had it started in the first place? What had she done or not done, that he had felt the need to turn from her, seek comfort, fun, sex or whatever it was he wanted, from someone else?

For the thousandth time she wondered how much longer she could go on like this, saying nothing, pretending she didn't care, getting on with her own life.

Why, why in God's name didn't she have it out with him?

But she knew the answer to that one. She was afraid.

'How about it, then?' Ian's eyes were very confident as he looked at Zoë; they had just left the Garage in Brixton, and had been standing outside kissing for a while.

Zoë, as she always was when she had been clubbing, was in a feverishly over-excited state. She was desperate for sex now: desperate for him. She hoped he didn't know it.

'I've got somewhere. Quite near here. Few streets away. One of the houses I'm working on. It's empty. I got a key.'

'But what if we get caught?'

'Zo, we won't. The owner's in the Maldives. It's really nice, got good beds and everything. Come on, Zoë, otherwise I'll think you don't want to.'

'Okay,' she said. 'Sounds cool.'

The house was what estate agents used to call bijou; a Victorian cottage in one of the smarter squares in Brixton. Zoë found herself walking on thick carpets, then saw in the dim dawn light a half-done, patently expensive new kitchen.

'Nice, innit? I put most of this in. Come on upstairs, there's a great bed up there, just been delivered.'

'Ian, I don't think we ought to—'

'Oh, for God's sake. 'Course we ought. Come on, Zoë, life's too short for worrying.'

'Where's the loo?' she said. She was shivering, partly from cooled sweat, partly from nerves.

'In there. Go on, then, I'll turn the bed down.'

Zoë used the loo then went on upstairs. She had lost all desire for sex: only her fear of being called a wimp or worse by Ian kept her from running away.

Ian called her from the front bedroom: 'Come on, Zoë, what you doing, for Christ's sake?'

She went in nervously. He was sitting naked in a large, brass-headed bed, under a very expensive-looking white duvet cover. He grinned at her. 'Come on, I'm all ready and waiting for you. Look, got something to warm you up. Or cool you down.' It was a bottle of champagne.

'Ian! How gorgeous. When did you buy that?'

'It was in the fridge. Very nice brand of bubbly indeed. None of your rubbish.'

'Ian! You can't take things out of their fridge.'

'I'll be putting it back, won't I? And they don't exactly need it out there in the Maldives, do they? It's a loan, Zoë. I'll replace it Monday, when I come to work. Here, out the way, I'm going to pop it.'

He pulled the cork; there was a loud bang. Zoë was terrified, half expecting the neighbours to hear, start knocking on the wall.

He held out the bottle, let her drink from it, then dribbled it slowly down on to his cock. Zoë looked at the cock in awe. It was extremely large.

'Try sipping from there now,' he said, and laughed. 'Go on, it won't bite yer. And don't you go biting it, either.'

Zoë took a deep breath and slithered down the bed.

The cab dropped her on the corner of Eaton Square; it was almost six and completely light. She often got home at four from clubs, but that was with friends, who came in with her and then slept the clock round on her floor. She wondered what they would think if they knew what she had been doing, having sex in a bed and in a house where she had had no business to be, where she could be arrested for breaking and entering or whatever it was called. With a boyfriend who had stolen some champagne and some cigarettes from the house. And it had, actually, been exciting. Given the whole thing an edge. And Ian was very very clever in bed. Definitely the best sex she'd ever had.

Tom had suggested they left the cottage very soon after breakfast on the Sunday. 'I really need to get back. If you and the children want to stay, you can drive me over to Warminster. That's fine by me.'

Louise had phoned and said they wouldn't come in that case: Sandy had been reluctant to spend the day with just the two of them. 'Giggling, as he puts it. Sorry, Boot. You know how awkward he can be.'

'Well, if that's okay. How's Anna?'

The lovely voice became heavier. 'She's very bad. I can't believe how fast it's happening.'

'I'd like to see her again. When could I come?'

'Oh, I don't know. You say. You're the busy one.'

She sounded slightly hostile; Octavia was stung. 'Not that busy. How about—' she looked at her diary – 'Thursday afternoon? I could easily do that.'

'If it's easy.' Again the note of hostility in the voice; Octavia struggled not to mind. It was understandable.

'It is. I'll see you then. 'Bye, Lulu.'

The children did want to stay; she drove Tom to Warminster, in silence. He got out and kissed her briefly. She wondered suddenly if he was going to see *Her*. She hadn't thought of that. She turned her head away from him, and drove off ignoring his wave.

After lunch, eaten in the garden, she said brightly to the children, 'I want to show you something.'

'What? A bird's nest or something?' said Poppy, her voice heavy with sarcasm.

'It's about half an hour away, and it's something very important to me.'

'It *will* be a bird's nest,' said Gideon to Poppy.

She had been afraid there would lots of people at Bartles Wood, picnicking, tramping through it, but it was almost deserted. One small happy-looking little family was standing on the small stone bridge, playing pooh sticks, and as they walked into the wood itself, Octavia carrying Minty, for it was too bumpy to push the buggy, a young couple came out, holding hands. Her dress was very creased.

'They've been snogging,' said Gideon, with all the worldly wisdom of the nearly nine. 'Come on, Mum, where's this exciting thing, then?'

'This is it,' said Octavia, smiling into the dim sunlight. 'This is Bartles

Wood. Look, did you see that dragonfly? And there's a whole duck family, look.'

'Great,' said Poppy. 'Oh my God. Wow. Ducks.'

'Poppy, don't be silly. It is a lovely place and what's exciting is that they were trying to build shops and houses on it and now they're not. Well, hopefully not.'

'What, here?' Even Gideon sounded shocked.

'Yes. Here. Cut the wood down, knock a big house down that's just up the hill, divert the stream, build a housing estate.'

'That's awful,' said Poppy.

'Let's go in a bit further. There's a little clearing there, look, we can sit down and Minty can crawl about. She's getting very heavy.'

They walked under the trees, out into the clearing. The news that the wood might have disappeared endowed it with interest, and the twins began looking around them, arguing about where the houses might be and where the shops.

The sun was very hot; Octavia put suncream on Minty, argued briefly with the twins about whether they should have some too, then watched them disappear towards the stream and the shade with some relief. They wouldn't get burned there. Minty crawled towards some bracken fronds, pulled at their curls tentatively, smiling with pleasure as they curled back again.

Tall foxgloves grew amongst the bracken; a large bee buzzed lazily in and out of the bells. Octavia suddenly felt very happy and at peace.

The twins were building a dam on a small tributary of the stream, arguing about techniques; Minty sat looking round with large dark eyes, then reached up and stuffed a piece of bracken into her face.

'I wouldn't eat that if I were you,' said a voice, and a young man came into the clearing. He smiled at Octavia and she smiled back. He was rather attractive, in an untidy way, with wild brown curls and large hazel eyes. His mouth was wide, and his teeth slightly crooked; it was somehow engaging, a welcome change from rigid orthodontic perfection. He was tall and thin, and was wearing corduroy trousers and a check shirt and heavy black farmers' Wellingtons: obviously a local.

'It's lovely here, isn't it?' she said, smiling at him.

'Very lovely.'

'Let's hope it stays this way.'

'Ah! You mean the development. You've read about it in the papers, I suppose,' he said, studying her (horribly townie-looking, she thought, in her Armani jeans, her Cutler & Gross sunglasses, Minty in her Baby Gap dungarees).

'Yes. And I saw the signs,' she said quickly. 'Back by the bridge and the entrance.'

'And did you see what had been written on them? Saved!'
'Which it has been, I believe?'
'For now. We shall have to see what happens.'
'I presume you're in favour of keeping it. Not developing it.'
'Well – yes and no,' he said carefully. 'It would be a shame to build on it, but we do need housing round here, quite badly.'
'Of course you don't,' said Octavia briskly. 'There's far too much housing already, empty buildings everywhere in the city centres.'
'I hadn't noticed many of those in Bath,' he said.
'Well, maybe not Bath. But Bristol and Frome and Warminster. The town centres are dying.'
'And you'd like to live in one of those empty buildings, would you?' he said. 'In the town centres?'
'Well . . .' She hesitated.
'Where do you live?'
'London.'
'And we've got a cottage, near Bath,' said Poppy, who had come over to view this stranger, 'where we come for wekeends.'
'How very nice for you,' he said, and the hazel eyes were just slightly contemptuous as he looked at Octavia. 'You must know all about the area, then. And its needs.'
'Look,' she said, longing to tell him, not daring, of her involvement in the fight, 'I'm not really like that.'
'No?'
'No. Of course I think people should be be decently housed. But why can't the brownfield sites be developed, why can't the city centres be improved, the houses that are already there refurbished? It would cost no more. Probably less.'
'You sound rather well informed. And there may be some truth in what you say. But people want to live in the countryside, want to bring up their children in the countryside. And I think they should have a choice. Not be told where they've got to live. And they can't all afford country cottages,' he added heavily.
'But there won't be any country left soon,' she said heatedly. 'Surely it's better for there to be some left, so people can visit it, than every inch covered in – in executive homes.'
'And what's wrong with executive homes?' he said, sitting down beside her, looking at her intently.
'Well, they're pretentious. And hideous.'
'According to you'
She felt herself beginning to lose her temper, then suddenly smiled. 'This is silly. We only met because we both like it here'
'True.' He held out his hand. 'Gabriel Bingham.'

'Oh, my goodness,' said Octavia. 'Now I understand. You're the MP here, aren't you?'

'I am indeed. How do you know that?'

'Oh, local friends. Anyway, I'm Octavia Fleming.'

'Nice name. And do you work for your living, Octavia Fleming?'

The question was just faintly patronising. Clearly he saw her as spending her life and her husband's money in idle self-indulgence.

'Yes. I run my own company,' she said firmly.

'Do you?' He was clearly surprised. 'And what does it do, your company?'

'Er, marketing,' she said hastily. This was getting rather close to home.

'Marketing! Very trendy. Well, it's been very nice meeting you. I'd like to continue our discussion, but I have to get back.' He gently removed Minty, who was trying to climb on to his legs, and stood up, towering above her.

Octavia looked up at him, then stood up herself. 'To your own family?'

'No, no. Nearest to that is a putative fiancée.'

'Only putative?'

'Yes, she's not quite sure about me yet. Well, not quite sure enough. But I do have work to do. Good day to you.'

He smiled, held out his hand again. Octavia looked down at it: a strong, brown, very large hand. She took it, and it folded round her own. For some reason she felt quite literally weak at the knees.

CHAPTER 12

Anna was being sedated now, needed stronger painkillers; but for most of the time she was blithely brave, pretending for them all that she would soon be better.

Charles looked at her over his teacup, smiled at her. 'Shall I tell you something? Something nice? I think Louise might be pregnant again.'

Anna's eyes were puzzled, watchful suddenly. 'Why do you say that?'

'Oh, call it masculine intuition. When she was here last week she had that pale, dark-eyed look. And Dickon told me they had to stop for her to be sick coming over. I just think she might be, and it would be the best possible thing,'

'I'm not sure that it would,' said Anna slowly. 'And anyway, she – well, it's very unlikely. Very. Darling, I'm hurting a bit, is it time for me to have a pill yet?'

'Of course it is. More than time. You're doing well.'

She took the pill, sat looking at him, smiling. 'I love you, Charlie.'

'I love you, too. Now, why do you think it's so unlikely? About Louise being pregnant?'

But she was asleep again, drifting off into her drug-induced peace.

Tom was at home for breakfast on Tuesday morning. He seemed edgy, nervous, making a great performance of reading and opening letters.

'You do know I've got a late meeting tonight?' he said finally, looking up.

'I'd forgotten,' Octavia said coolly. 'What is it you're doing? Exactly?'

'Oh, meeting a group of environmentalists who are trying to form an all-party committee. Asked me to join them.'

'It doesn't sound quite your style,' she said, briskly. 'Tom, have you seen Bartles Wood?'

'Yes, of course I have. But Carlton's development – as you would see if you took the trouble to look at the plans – will blend in extremely well with the surrounding countryside.'

'Tom, don't talk such total garbage!' said Octavia, and then, after a pause, 'I suppose you met the local MP down there?'

'Gabriel Bingham? Yes. He came to one of Carlton's meetings. Bit of a Bollinger Socialist.'

'You mean he went to public school? Dear oh dear, Tom, are we ever going to see that particular chip fall off your shoulder? Terrible sign of insecurity, you know.'

He flushed, but didn't respond. 'So what are you doing today?' he asked, making a clear effort to keep the conversation on a positive level.

'Oh, endless meetings. Including one with Lauren Bartlett. Look, I must go, I have to take the twins to school.'

'By the way, if you want to fix that drink with the Bartletts, if it would help, that's fine by me. Thursday would be okay, or Tuesday next week.'

'Right. Thank you.' He must be feeling guilty. Very guilty. 'And will you be back tonight?'

A pause, then, 'Possibly. I'll see how the day goes. I'll let you know.'

'Fine,' she said, keeping her voice carefully level. 'Goodbye, Tom.'

'Goodbye, Octavia.'

'Good news, Pattie.' Meg Browning, one of the Save Bartles Wood committee, put the down the telephone and looked across her kitchen at Patricia David. 'That was Gabriel Bingham. He says he'll come tonight. To our follow-up meeting.'

'Really? Marvellous.' Patricia's thin face flushed with pleasure. 'I never thought he would.'

'He says he doesn't want us to think he's automatically on our side, merely that he wants to be as well informed as possible on all the issues, and to inform us on party policy in the light of Mr Carlton's determination to appeal.'

'I see. Well, that's terrific. Golly, I don't suppose Octavia would come to this meeting, would she?'

'You could ask her.'

Patricia David phoned, and Octavia said that, much as she'd love to, it would be very unwise.

Lauren had brought her sidekick to the meeting at Capital C, an appalling woman called Fiona Mills who argued with every point Octavia and Melanie made. She was wearing her husband's money on every inch of her, including, Octavia decided, her very tautly lifted jawline.

'We are fairly confident of a certain person's involvement, aren't we, Lauren?' she said. 'If not officially, then unofficially. You know who I mean?'

Melanie said she presumed she meant Princess Diana and Fiona Mills said possibly, discretion was everything in these matters.

'Well, that's marvellous,' said Melanie. 'Simply marvellous.'

'Now, on the question of your fee,' said Lauren. 'I'm afraid we can't see our way to paying the quoted rate. It's really very high. What would you suggest on that?'

'I told Lauren we couldn't—' said Octavia.

Melanie flashed a brilliant, warning look at her and said, 'Lauren, we can meet you on the fee, of course. We want to help and you are a friend of Octavia's. Tell us your budget and we'll work something out.'

Octavia felt a flash of anger and humiliation; Melanie's concession had diminished her in Lauren's eyes at a stroke. I'm the boss round here, that statement had said, *I* make the crucial decisions, it's my word that counts.

'Marvellous,' said Lauren, smiling briefly in her direction. 'I had hoped Octavia might be wrong on that one. Now, as to the details of the day, what would you suggest?'

After they left, Octavia walked back into her own office and shut the door. Melanie followed her in without knocking.

'Well done, bringing that one in, Octavia.'

'Melanie, why did you do that? Agree that she could pay whatever she liked, really, without consulting me at all? I'd already told her we couldn't do anything about our fee, I felt extremely silly.'

'Octavia, I'd do that job for absolutely nothing, just to get Next Generation. It's one of the highest-profile charities there is, a huge notch in our gun. I'm going to do a release to the papers right now.'

'Melanie, I don't need a lecture on our position in the league table. We're partners, or so I understood. I'm not some pathetic little assistant, however much you like to give that impression.'

Melanie's face became very hard suddenly. 'Don't be so fucking stupid, Octavia. And don't let your personal insecurities colour your professional ones.'

Octavia stared at her. 'What's that supposed to mean?'

'I would have thought it was perfectly clear.'

'Well, it's not. Clearly I am fucking stupid, as you put it so attractively.'

'Octavia, you've been in a highly neurotic state for days now. Impossible to work with. I don't know what's the matter with you, but—'

'Nothing's the matter,' said Octavia and burst into tears.

Melanie was silent for a moment, then she said, quietly, 'Is it Tom?'
'What do you mean? Why should it be Tom?'
'Octavia, I'm not a complete idiot. Something's happened to you. Most likely explanation is it's Tom. Come on, you'll feel better if you talk about it.'
'Yes,' said Octavia, after a long silence. 'It's Tom. He's – well, having an affair.'
'I thought he might be,' said Melanie.
Octavia stared at her. 'Why did you think that?' she said, trying not to betray her panic. This was what she had most feared: people knowing, talking about it, laughing at her. 'How long have you been thinking it, does anyone else know?'
'Octavia, calm down. Of course I thought it. It was inevitable that—'
'Oh, was it really? Inevitable he should have an affair? Why, because I'm so unattractive, so unsexy, so fucking naive?'
'No! None of those things. Oh, God – excuse me a moment.'
She went out of the room, came back with her cigarettes and a bottle of whisky.
'Here, have a drop of this,' she said, pouring some of it into Octavia's water glass.
'Melanie, I don't need alcohol. I don't need nicotine. Come on, tell me for fuck's sake. What did you mean?' Tears of fright stood in her eyes; she had shocked herself, she never swore.
Melanie looked at her, blew out a cloud of smoke. 'I meant that when a woman is as upset as you are, it's almost always because of a man. In your case your husband. That's all, for Christ's sake. That's all I meant.'
Octavia stared at her in silence, then she reached out for her glass. 'But you didn't suspect before?'
'No, of course not.'
'Oh, I see.' It was strangely comforting.
'When did you find out?' said Melanie.
'Last Tuesday. The day we went to Ascot.'
'And there's no doubt? You couldn't be mistaken?'
'No. No doubt at all.'
'Have you confronted him with it?'
'Not yet.'
'Why the hell not?'
'Melanie,' said Octavia, a stab of violent irritation over-riding her misery, 'just leave me to run my own . . .' Marriage, she had been going to say, then realised it was the last thing she could be trusted to run and her voice tailed off. She sipped at the whisky.
'Bastard,' said Melanie. 'Bastard. Do you know who it is?'

'No. I've no idea.'

'God, I hate men,' said Melanie savagely, blowing out a great cloud of smoke. 'They're all the fucking same.'

'All fucking the same,' said Octavia and giggled. Then she couldn't stop giggling, and then she was laughing hysterically, and then she was crying again, wailing almost, really quite loudly.

In the middle of the noise, her direct line rang; Melanie picked it up. 'Yes? Oh, hi, Mr Miller, it's Melanie Faulks. Sorry, she can't talk to you now. She's a bit upset. No, nothing serious. Yes, sure, I'll get her to call you.'

'Oh, God,' said Octavia. Her tears stopped abruptly, her father's name as effective as the traditional hard slap. 'Did he hear me? Crying, I mean?'

'Shouldn't think so,' said Melanie cheerfully, who had actually had some trouble hearing Felix Miller herself above the noise. 'Anyway, what if he did? So what are you going to do? Divorce the bugger, I hope.'

'I don't know. I don't know anything any more. I'm just trying to get by. For the moment.'

'I'm very sorry,' said Melanie. 'Sorry I said what I did. About you being insecure and neurotic. It was unforgivable.'

'It wasn't, but thank you, Melanie,' said Octavia. She sat there, sipping her whisky, wondering what she would feel next. There didn't seem very much left. But the conversation had done one thing for her; had made her decide it was time to talk to Tom.

Octavia was surprised at the calm of her voice. 'Tom?' she said.

'Yes?' His voice was wary, cautious.

'Tom, will you be back tonight?'

'I'm afraid not. I've just spoken to the chap, he's booked me into a hotel.'

'Which one?'

'He didn't say. You can get me on my mobile if you—'

'Oxford isn't so terribly far. I'd appreciate it if you did get back. However late. There's something I really want to discuss with you.'

A long, long silence. Then he said, rather heavily, 'No, I'm sorry. I really can't get back tonight. We can talk tomorrow maybe. I'll be back quite early, nothing on in the evening.'

'Sure,' she said and put the phone down. And picked it up again almost immediately.

Patricia David was massaging Megan's legs when the telephone rang. She went to answer it, and came back smiling.

'That was Mrs Fleming. You know, you met her once, she helps us run Foothold. And now she's helping us to save the wood. She's coming to a rather important meeting down here tonight. I'm so pleased.'

'From London?' said Megan. 'That's a long way to come for a meeting.'

'Yes, all the way from London. She says it'll only take her about two hours. I expect she's got a very powerful car.'

'Is she rich?' said Megan.

'Yes, I'm sure she is,' said Patricia. 'I don't think there's very much that Octavia Fleming hasn't got.'

After the meeting, Octavia thought, she might go and see Louise.

The thought of Bartles Wood and the havoc that her future and very public outward involvement in it would cause at Fleming Cotterill was cheering her up considerably. She felt only a little sorry for Aubrey – he must have known what was going on, must have. Every time she thought about the people who must have known about Tom, who would have known about other, earlier liaisons, and kept it from her, people she saw and dealt with almost every day – Aubrey, Barbara, everyone probably at Fleming Cotterill – she felt like screaming very loudly and shrilly, for a very long time. The conversation with Tom, his refusal to come home even when she specifically requested it, had had a very odd effect on her. Something had closed down in her heart, and for the moment at least she felt no pain: merely a fierce, clear rage. She knew it would come back, the pain, but the respite was very sweet.

Her father had phoned three times; she had not spoken to him, couldn't risk herself, simply let him leave messages on her voice mail.

Each one was the same. 'Octavia darling? It's Daddy. I know you're upset. Let me know what I can do to help.'

She knew if she spoke to him today, she'd have to tell him. And she couldn't cope with that. Not today.

'Tom? This is Barbara. Is it okay to talk?'

'Yeah, sure. Go ahead.'

'Have you got time to speak to Felix Miller? He phoned in a state of great agitation, said it was terribly important.'

'Oh, Christ,' said Tom. 'It'll be some bloody nonsense about Cadogan. I can't face it. You'd better say you couldn't contact me.'

'He's got your mobile number, hasn't he?'

'Yes. Look, I'll put it on to Divert. Get the calls put back to the office. That okay?'

'Ye-es. Until I go home at seven.'

'I'll switch it back then,' said Tom.

*

Octavia started calling the Madison number as soon as she was clear of Heathrow; it was engaged. After the third try, she gave up. Probably some crisis with Anna, and they were trying to get hold of the doctor. She hoped it wasn't anything too serious. Every time she thought of Anna dying, she felt a great slick of fear. She was so brave, Louise, but she was vulnerable too: how would she cope with this second, awful loss? She would ring her later: after the meeting. Plenty of time.

'Oh, dear,' said Barbara.

She was listening to Tom's voice mail.

'Tom, this is Felix Miller. I need to talk to you urgently, about Octavia. I phoned her at the office today and she was hysterical. I could hear her screaming down the phone. There's obviously something very wrong, and if you don't know what it is, you ought to. Would you ring me, please, most urgently.'

Barbara decided she should pass this message on to Tom, but she couldn't contact him. His mobile appeared to be switched off.

'Tom Fleming,' she said aloud, 'you really are an absolute bloody idiot.'

CHAPTER 13

Gabriel Bingham was beginning to wish he hadn't said he'd come to this meeting. The women who were organising it clearly saw it as an indication of his support. He felt genuinely torn about the whole issue; he had moved to the area five years earlier, when he had been adopted as Labour candidate for the constituency, and had fallen in love with its beauty. He had been born and brought up in Suffolk, and had studied estate management at university. While there, he had become involved in the political scene, first, and ironically, rather actively with the Conservative Party, and then, after some impressively fierce debates with them, the Socialists. By the end of his three years, driven as much by a conviction that Socialism was the only way forward for the country as by a genuine passion for social change and a strong distate for unearned privilege, he was president of the university Labour Party, and a committed party member. After ten years' hard graft in local politics he began to apply for seats. Two turned him down, then Somerset North became vacant. He won the nomination by one vote. At the '92 election he was hopelessly beaten, but that magical Tony Blair's May, he turned an 8,000 Tory majority into a 2,000 Labour one. His philosophy, like Blair's, was totally pragmatic. 'We've got to get in,' he would say, at meeting after meeting, in the face of opposition from the old-school Socialists. 'Once we're in, we can do something. Trust us.'

They trusted him; he was popular, despite being young, having no wife, no family, a public school accent, a posh name, was seen as genuine, thoughtfully idealistic. He worked tirelessly, his surgeries often continuing until late into the night, had a reputation for getting things done, for cutting through officialdom; and he was not predictable, outspoken against the worst excesses of the Welfare State, the workshy, the black economy. For this reason he was popular with some of the old-guard Tories as well as the new-style Socialists; for this reason also,

Patricia David and her cohorts felt at least hopeful in looking to him for support.

'Mr Bingham, a cup of tea?'

'Oh, thank you, Mrs David. That would be very nice.'

'Please call me Pattie.'

Gabriel looked at Pattie David, looked at her rather faded face, at her faded fair hair, her middle-cass uniform of neat skirt, white shirt, navy blazer, absorbed the slightly high-pitched braying voice, thought that she must have been quite pretty once, that really she was his least favourite sort of person. Snobbish, prejudiced, foolishly worthy: then he remembered the small Megan, sitting in her wheelchair at a previous meeting, handing out stickers at the door, her large eyes fixed trustingly on her mother's face as she spoke, and felt ashamed of himself.

The hall – attached to a Methodist church – was only about a third full; mainly with middle-class women, a handful of husbands, and a small group of the local green contingent – young men with beards and sandals, young women with trailing hair and skirts and a lot of silver jewellery.

Gabriel was suddenly jolted, with a force that he felt physically, into a state of acute and pleasurable awareness, half sexual in character, half cerebral, by the appearance of a woman in the doorway of the hall: the woman he had met three days earlier in the sunlit heart of Bartles Wood; the woman he had at once so disapproved of and enjoyed; the woman who had occupied a sufficient area of his consciousness for him to know scarcely without looking at her that her hair was dark and heavy, and swung just short of her narrow shoulders, her eyes were large and very deep brown, her jawline exceptionally well defined and set in what seemed permanent determination; that she was small and more than averagely slim, that she had very beautiful hands; that her breasts were small – had he really noticed them? Yes, it seemed he had – and her legs extremely good; that—

'Mr Bingham, could I introduce Octavia Fleming? She's involved with Foothold, a charity I am very close to, and has become interested in our attempts to save Bartles Wood. Octavia, this is Gabriel Bingham, our local MP.'

And 'Yes,' they said, at the same time and then she laughed and he smiled. 'We've met before.'

'Where in God's name do you think she's gone, Marianne? I really am terribly worried. If you could have heard her this morning . . .'

'Felix, I have no idea. I'm sorry. Doesn't the nanny know?'

'Apparently not. Just said she'd gone out, that she was going to be back very late.'

'Well,' said Marianne, 'if Octavia is able to go out, there can't be anything very wrong with her. Now could I suggest—'

'That's a rather naive assumption, I think. She could be anywhere, anywhere at all, driving round, feeling desperate . . .'

'Had she been home?'

'No.'

'And Tom's not there?'

'He's in Oxford. He's always away, never at home when he's really needed . . .'

'Felix, that's hardly fair. Tom works terribly hard, he has a very demanding business to run.'

'I also have a demanding business to run. Even more so in the past. And if Octavia needed me, I made sure I was there.'

'But that was when she was a child, for heaven's sake, she's—' Marianne managed with great difficulty not to finish her sentence.

'That's not the point. Anyway, as you reminded me recently, she is now Tom's responsibility. One he seems to be totally neglecting. I have called him three times today, told him how upset Octavia was, he's ignored all my calls. What's going on?'

Marianne's resolve snapped totally. 'Felix, please stop this. Octavia is Tom's wife. When are you going to realise that? So she's upset. I get upset sometimes, you do, everybody does. Just leave her alone, leave them both alone. And while you're about it, leave me alone as well. I'm trying to have a peaceful evening.'

She put the phone down, finding herself enragingly near to tears for the third time that day. It wasn't like her, she thought, blowing her nose, it wasn't like her at all. Her cool self-control seemed to have deserted her. She tried not to think why.

'Well,' said Octavia briskly, as she and Gabriel stood rather awkwardly outside together, 'I suppose I'd better get back to London.'

'Where's your car?'

'There,' she said, slightly shamefaced.

'The Range Rover?'

She looked at him. He was smiling – just – but his eyes were quite hard. Irritation sawed at her. 'Look,' she said, 'I think you've got me a bit wrong. I really do.'

'And how do you think I've got you?'

'A a rich, spoilt townie wife, playing Lady Bountiful, taking up a rather attractive, trendy cause, and then roaring back up to my London house and getting on with my own expensive life.'

'Well, that's how it looks. I must admit.'

'It's so unfair,' she said, trying to keep her voice calm. 'I really care about the wood. And I actually work very hard, you know.'

'Very commendable,' he said, heavily polite.

'Oh, stop it!' she said, the strain and misery of the day breaking over her. 'It just might interest you to know, in your pompous self-satisfaction, that my husband referred to you as a Bollinger Socialist. Which on the surface sounds actually quite fair to me. You went to Winchester and then Durham. Hardly bastions of underprivilege.'

'How do you know that?' he said, genuinely astonished.

'I looked you up. I was – interested,' she said, irritated with herself now, 'having met you.'

'And why on earth should your husband have a view on me? What does he actually do, this husband of yours?'

'Oh, he's in – in marketing. What are you doing here anyway?' she said suddenly. 'It's the middle of the week, you should be at Westminster.'

'I had to come down to see a hospital consultant. Nothing interesting, I'm afraid, old sports injury, and I'm safely paired. I shall be back in the morning, and—'

'Octavia! Good night, and thank you so much for coming. And for everything. Your little speech was wonderful, we thought. Really wonderful. Such passion. And – and would it be all right now to tell people you're involved?'

Octavia looked at Pattie David, and then up at Gabriel Bingham's politely cynical face. Until that moment her courage had been wavering. Even then she might have held back; but behind the cynicism, which she devoutly wished to confound, she recognised something else: recognised it and greeted it with the same from herself.

'Yes,' she said firmly, 'it would be perfectly all right. Good night, Pattie. Good night, Mr Bingham. I'm sorry we can't talk more.'

She half ran forward, climbed into her car, revved it up, drove rather fast out of the car park. She wanted to get away: quickly. She pulled out into the road, turned sharply left – she had come in from the right, she was sure – drove down the road to a crossroads, went straight over it and found herself looking at sign that read 'Felthamstone Industrial Estate'.

'Damn,' she said, going into reverse, yanking on the steering wheel to turn the car, and then finding the road blocked by a rather elderly Golf. Gabriel Bingham was getting out of it.

'Good thing you've got power steering,' he said, and started laughing. 'No, no, don't look like that. I came after you to say I was sorry, and also to put you on the right road. I was extremely rude, and it was unforgivable. And Mrs David was right, your speech was wonderful. It even affected me, and God knows I should be immune to the things.

Now, could I buy you a glass of orange juice or something before you set out for London? I'd make it Bollinger, but of course you have to drive . . .'

'It is a loathsome phrase,' he said, setting a glass of tomato juice in front of Octavia, settling himself beside her. There wasn't a lot of room on the bench; his long body was rather close to hers.

'Sorry. Bit of a squash. Shall I sit opposite you instead?'

'No, it's fine,' she said, and meant it. 'What's a loathsome phrase?'

'Bollinger Socialist. We all hate it. And it *is* unfair. I can't help my background, any more than you can. All I've done is see sense, moved away from it.'

'And you never utilised it? You've never utilised your education, your accent, your – your self-confidence, your ability to express yourself?'

'Yes, of course I have,' he said, looking at her in genuine astonishment. 'I use them to get things done for the people who haven't got those things. That's the whole point.'

'And where do you live?' she said. 'Down here, I mean? In a high-rise flat in Bristol city centre? In a squat in Warminster?'

'A squat in Westminster. During the week. But no actually, I have a small house in Bath.'

'Oh, really? In Bath? So not a high-rise, then. A Georgian cottage is it, perhaps? Or a little terrace house?'

'It's a terrace, yes. You are a funny lot,' he added, shaking his head, smiling at her, 'you Tories.'

'Why do you think I'm a Tory?'

'Well, aren't you? What did you vote?'

'I'm a Socialist. I voted for Blair, of course.'

'That's not—' he said and stopped himself.

'Not Socialism?' she said, laughing, 'Oh, dear, Mr Bingham. I hope that was the bitter talking. What a terrible thing to say. I must tell my husband.'

'That is not what I was going to say at all,' he said, his untidy face slightly pompous suddenly. 'The fact is that probably half the people who voted us in are Tories at heart. Next time round they'll go back to the fold. You will, I daresay. Where do you live?'

'Kensington,' she said. 'And don't start again. Let's talk about Bartles Wood. How do you really feel about it? Off the record?'

'Off the record, I'm undecided. It's a bit like the grammar schools. Marvellous if you can enjoy them, worse than nothing if you can't. And this chap, Carlton, who's put in the application, you know, he's talking about a community centre with—'

'Facilities for the disabled.'

He stared at her. 'You have gone into it very thoroughly.'

'Well,' she said quickly, 'I'm interested.'

'And?'

'I'll believe in those facilities when they're there and being used – and what use are they anyway, so far from a town centre? Anyway, what about you? What's the official party line on it?'

'The rule of thumb is, permission gets granted where there's a need. There usually is.'

'Oh, really? What about the Newbury bypass? Everyone said a much smaller scheme would have done, they could have saved the water meadows. What about Bath?'

'The Tories were in then,' he said. 'Absolutely not guilty.'

'Okay. What about Manchester airport?'

He smiled at her. 'You really do mind about all this, don't you?'

'Yes. I told you, I told you all in my speech, I love England, I love the countryside, I love lanes and woods and streams and hedgerows. Soon they'll all be gone. Buried in concrete boots. With lorries thundering over them. This is such a tiny country. We have to do what we can to save it. And you, Gabriel Bingham, you could do so much. If you wanted to.' She stopped and looked at him. 'Do you want to?'

'I'm not sure. Politics isn't about emotion, it's about facts.'

'There should be emotion as well. Emotion and passion.'

'Emotion gets in the way of truth. Politics is a science, not a humanity.'

'So you're not going to let your heart rule your head? Not even to a small degree? Over so important a matter?'

'Now why do you think my heart believes in saving Bartles Wood?' said Gabriel Bingham, smiling at her.

'I know it does,' said Octavia simply. 'I met you there, remember?'

'Yes, actually, I do,' he said and the hazel eyes on hers were thoughtful, thoughtful and very serious suddenly. 'I remember it very well . . .'

In the finest suite of the Buchan Hotel (slightly flashy, very luxurious, on the edge of the Cotswolds), champagne on ice, Tiffany necklace in its turquoise box by the bed, Tom Fleming was waiting for the phone call that would tell him his guest had arrived, unable to decide if he was in heaven or hell. He looked longingly at the vast round bath, with its jacuzzi jets. That would relax him. But she would arrive any moment, and he wanted to be totally ready for her, totally in control from the moment she arrived. It was difficult to be in control if you were naked and wet. Unless, of course, you were both naked and wet. Later they would undoubtedly both be in the bath, and that would be glorious. It would all be glorious – for a while. Meanwhile he would have to wait.

He looked at the Tiffany box, with its white ribbon; he was a little worried about that, about so incriminating a present, but it seemed an occasion for grand gestures. He had paid cash for it, as he always did. As he did for the hotels and the restaurants. And under the circumstances, perhaps, worth the risk. Christ, he hoped it was going to be all right . . .

The room phone rang fiercely through the silence.

'Yes?'

'Your guest is here, Mr Fleming.'

'Thank you,' he said. 'Please ask her to come up to the room.'

He was not a religious man; but as he waited, in those last few minutes at the door, he did find his brain forming what in some ways resembled a prayer.

Octavia didn't after all phone Louise. By the time she left the pub and Gabriel Bingham it was already nearly ten thirty. Much too late to disturb a stricken household. Somehow it had been quite hard to finish the conversation with Gabriel Bingham.

He had, she decided, a rather sexy mind: disturbing and distracting. He was rather sexy altogether. Not good looking, not conventionally charming, not her type at all: but still sexy. She had enjoyed their conversation. He had enjoyed it too; he had said so. She had been extremely surprised, he had seemed to disapprove so strongly of her and all she stood for; but, 'I find you interesting,' he had said, as they stood by their cars.

'As a social curiosity?' she had said, and he had said yes, that too, but he actually found her mind interesting and talking to her an interesting experience.

It had seemed a rather surprising thing for him to say, after making it so plain he disapproved of her, but she had found the words pleasing; they warmed and comforted her after the earlier horrors of the day. She was not entirely stupid, it seemed, not entirely worthless; a man, a hugely intelligent man – he had been a Winchester scholar, she had discovered, as the conversation slithered away from intellectual challenge and into social exploration – had told her he actually found her mind interesting.

'In fact,' he had said, looking at her rather solemnly, 'I find you interesting altogether.'

As she had pulled out of the car park, looked into her driving mirror, she saw that he was watching her still, not moving. And although he could not see her, she had smiled into the mirror and felt, foolishly, that he would have known.

Of the putative fiancée, there had been no word at all.

CHAPTER 14

'Now I want you to go easy on the sex in these pictures, Jonty,' said Ritz Franklyn. 'I know she's the ultimate in sensuous virginity, and you'll know it too when you see her, but I don't want the mother frightened off. She's rather sharp. Quite capable of pulling the plug on us if she thinks we're going to corrupt her little baby.'

'Yeah, okay. That's fine. I wasn't actually going to have her lying on the bed, playing with her pubes, Ritz. I do have some sensitivity.'

'You could have fooled me. The other thing is that I'm going to try to get Christie's along to the session. I want them to see her before we go public with her. Get their mouths watering, put her price up. So just act dumb if they turn up, okay?'

'Okay, but not Fido.'

'No, definitely not Fido. He really would put the mother off.' Fido was their codename for George Smythe, managing director of Christie's; overweight, sweaty and famous for his propensity for trying to mount, as Ritz put it, any young and half-attractive woman who entered his orbit. 'No, I've put in a call to Serena Fox. She has a lot of clout there.'

'Charles? Hallo, it's Octavia Fleming here. Could I possibly speak to Louise? Oh, I see. Nothing serious, I— Oh, well, I'm so sorry. Give her my love. Look, I was just wondering. Would it be all right if I came down tomorrow? To see Anna? Yes? Well, tell Louise to ring me if not. Oh, and tell her I've gone public on Bartles Wood. Made a speech down there. Yes, she'll know what I mean. And give Anna my love as well, won't you? My best love.'

Octavia put the phone down, dialled Tom's direct line.

'Tom? Hallo. It's me. I just wanted to make sure you would be home tonight. We do have to talk. It's very important.'

'Yes,' he said, 'I'll be there. Maybe not till about eight thirty but—'

'That's fine. Oh, and tomorrow, I won't be home till very late. I'm going down to see Anna Madison.'

'Oh really? Is that a good idea? When she's so ill?'

'Tom, it's precisely because she's so ill that I'm going. She's very special, very important to me.'

'Well, if you think that's best. Will Louise be there?'

'I expect so, yes. She's virtually living there at the moment. Although she's not well today herself, apparently. I just spoke to her father. So, I'll see you tonight, then?'

'Yes. I won't be late.'

'Please don't be.'

She felt, shockingly, almost excited at the prospect of the conversation.

Serena Fox was just putting the final seal on her brilliantly red mouth when Ritz Franklyn phoned. Serena was the creative director of Christie's Cosmetics. She was forty, darkly and dramatically beautiful, chic, brilliant and worth every one of the hundred and fifty thousand pounds Christie's paid her each year. She was also a lesbian.

She liked Ritz; she had hoped for a while she too might be a lesbian, or at least a bi; but a tentative, carefully coded approach to her after an award dinner revealed that she was wrong.

'Serena, hi. You're still on for tonight, aren't you? Our final?'

'Yes, of course. I'm looking forward to it.'

'Look, you don't have a window in your diary at around four this afternoon, do you?'

'No, I don't. Why?'

'We have got this incredible babe as a finalist. I mean *gorgeous*. She is going to win. No doubt about it.'

'Yes?'

'Serena, I think she could be your girl. She's so – perfect. Untouched. Skin like you haven't seen. Sheets of pale blonde hair. And – wait for it – huge green eyes.'

'Green!'

A girl with green eyes: that had been their ideal. So far they had auditioned over a hundred girls; with blue, brown, grey, hazel eyes. Not one pair of green.

'Yup. Now look, I shouldn't be doing this, and Jonty will freak, but if you just happened to be around his studio at four, you could get a preview. Revlon are coming tonight. And Arden. They're both looking too. You could get in just that bit sooner . . .'

Serena put the phone down and told her secretary that she would be going out for an hour that afternoon and to move everything in her diary along to accommodate it.

Tom had only just reached the office when Octavia had rung. When he switched on his voice mail and listened to his father-in-law's message, he knew his fears about Octavia and her reasons for wanting to talk to him were very well founded.

Felix Miller was contemplating calling his son-in-law yet again when Octavia phoned. She sounded absolutely fine, he thought: quite breezy and cheerful.

'Daddy, hi. How are you?'

'Octavia. Where on earth have you been? Why didn't you ring me yesterday? I was so worried about you.'

'Why?'

'Why? Because I heard you crying on the phone, that's why, hysterically. And because then you wouldn't phone me back, and because you were out last night. Are you all right?'

'Yes, I'm fine. Truly. I'm sorry you were worried. I had a bit of a bad morning. Very bad. Then I had to go down near Bath, to a meeting.'

'So why were you in that state?'

'Oh, I've probably lost a client, an important one, and—'

'Octavia, you don't get hysterical because you lose a client.'

'I did. Yesterday. Look, I really can't go into it all now, but I will. I promise. Maybe we can have dinner one night. I'd like to talk to you about it.'

'Darling, of course we can. Any night. Tonight?'

'No, tonight I have to be home. And tomorrow I'm going down to see Anna. She's very ill.'

'Yes, I remember. What about Friday?'

'Friday'd be good. Do you want to come to the house, then you can see the children?'

'Will Tom be there? I phoned him about you yesterday, told him how worried I was, but he didn't phone me back.'

'Tom won't be there, no,' said Octavia. 'Definitely he won't be there.'

She really had sounded all right, thought Felix, putting the phone down; quite cheerful in fact, and very positive. Maybe she had just been having a bad day. Still unforgivable of Tom not to have phoned him.

'Felix? Tom.'

'Good morning.'

'I'm sorry I didn't ring you yesterday. I simply didn't get the message. I was out of town and my mobile was up the spout.'

'Not very impressive,' said Felix heavily. 'Suppose I'd been a client?'

'If you'd been a client, Aubrey could have talked to you,' said Tom, his voice on the edge of rage. 'Anyway, Octavia's perfectly all right. I've just spoken to her.'

'As have I. Well, she sounded far from all right yesterday. And if it was really about losing a client, she's obviously at the end of her tether, she shouldn't be reacting like that.'

'A client? She didn't mention losing a client to me. But it happens all the time. Part of life's rich pattern, isn't it? If I had hysterics every time we lost a client, there'd be a world shortage of Kleenex. Anyway, no doubt I shall hear in due course. I must go now, Felix. Good morning to you.'

'Bastard,' said Tom said heavily as he put the phone down; interfering, sanctimonious bastard. What was it the Princess of Wales had said about her marriage? That there were three of them in it, and it was a bit crowded. He could commiserate with her there. Only his was even more crowded. There'd been three in his, from the very beginning. And then four. Not for the first time, he reflected that being forced to accommodate the third had led him, almost inevitably, to allowing in the fourth.

Felix had forgotten, when he made the arrangement to have dinner with Octavia, that he had promised to take Marianne away for the weekend. She needed a break, she had told him, her family was wearing her out, and if he cared for her at all, he would think of some nice way of distracting her. He had accordingly booked them on Eurostar to Paris on Friday night, and into a suite at the Crillon, her favourite hotel. Now he had either to cancel Octavia, or postpone the trip to Paris. Postponing it would be easier; they could leave early on Saturday morning instead. Octavia might think she was all right, but she clearly wasn't. Losing a client was unfortunate, serious even, but not grounds for having lengthy and noisy hysterics. No, it was too important, their dinner, to cancel; she would be relying on him.

He phoned Marianne to ask her if she would mind postponing their departure until Saturday morning, and explained why; and was extremely surprised and irritated when she told him she would mind very much, so much indeed that she would prefer to postpone the whole weekend, and that not for the first time she was beginning to find the role of understudy to his daughter very tedious indeed. Then she put the phone down.

*

Marianne sat in the studio, watching her daughter being made love to. She felt rather sick. The fact that it was only a camera lens working on her, arousing her, making her aware of her sexuality, didn't help very much. They were being very careful of course; she was not so stupid that she couldn't see that. Ritz Franklyn had been courtesy itself, assuring her that nothing would be done to Romilly in the way of hair and make-up that Marianne would not be entirely happy with, that she could have a say in the clothes she wore for the pictures, that anyway all the girls were being photographed first in jeans and white T-shirts, before changing into a dress – 'Most of them are long, and the short ones really young looking.'

Marianne wouldn't have said that the dress Romilly was wearing was particularly young looking, although it was very short; it was pale pink crêpe, covered almost entirely in overlapping pink and silver sequins, and Romilly's make-up was rather extreme, huge pink and silver arcs painted above each eye, right up to her brows, and a large silver tear added to one cheek. She had looked so lovely though, that when Ritz had asked if Marianne was happy with it, she had felt she couldn't possibly object; and then the straight fall of hair had looked unhappy with the stylised make-up, and the thick plait they had done and then wound up on top of her head had clearly been so exactly right. They were very clever, there was no doubt about that.

But the change in Romilly's appearance was affecting the photographer's reaction to her, and indeed hers to him; he had been gentleness itself on the first shot, in the jeans and T-shirt, asking her about school, teasing her about her exams, but as she had walked in from the dressing room, taken up her position in front of the camera – and was she imagining it, thought Marianne, or was she walking differently, more slowly, languidly almost, surely not, not already – she had seen Jonty Jacobson study her in silence, and then, as he bent over his camera, looking at her through the lens, saw him smile, a small, intent smile into it, then saw him look up again, meet Romilly's eyes, saw her smiling back, less hesitantly than before, and then he told her to lower her head, just a bit, and stand with her legs just slightly further apart, 'Just a tiny bit, Romilly, yes, that's right, now still look at the camera, yes, that's lovely, and again, yes, great, turn your head sideways just a fraction, yes, still keep your eyes on the lens, good, very good, yes, yes, now a bit further, yes, that's lovely, now just a bit of a little smile, not too much, yes, yes . . .'

Marianne couldn't bear it any longer. She got up and went out to the lavatory.

'Yes, I have been having an affair.'

Tom's eyes meeting Octavia's were very steady.

'I'm sorry,' he said then. 'Terribly, terribly sorry.'

She had expected denials, justifications, accusations even, of her own bad behaviour, of selfishness, lack of understanding, even; was taken aback totally by his reaction.

'But it's over. Quite, quite over.'

'Over? But you were with her last night?'

'Yes. In order to finish it.'

'Which you did?'

'Yes, I did.' The tone was strange; unfair to call it complacent, but there was a tinge of satisfaction in it.

'Well,' she said, slightly nonplussed, 'you always were very good at keeping to an agenda.'

'That's why I insisted on – on being away last night. Not coming home. Because I had to do it. Get it over.'

'I see. It was an ordeal, was it, something you were dreading?'

'Well – yes. In a way, inevitably it was.'

'And how was it, as an ordeal, Tom? As ordeals go?'

'I'm sorry?'

'How bad was the ordeal?'

'Well, it was – that is, I knew that it would be – difficult.'

'You bastard,' she said quietly. 'You fucking bastard. You're so devious, aren't you? Christ, you call my father manipulative. What do you think you are?'

'Octavia, I—'

'You thought that would make it much much better, didn't you? All right, even. Combining telling me with telling me it was over. Like one of the twins, "I did break the glass, but I've brought you a cup of tea."'

'Look,' he said, taking a slug of whisky, 'you're taking this absolutely the wrong way. Of course I didn't think it would make it all right. Nothing can ever do that. I was just hoping against hope I wouldn't have to tell you at all. That you wouldn't find out.'

'Bad luck, Tom.'

'No, Octavia, you misunderstand. I was hoping that you wouldn't have to be hurt.'

'Oh, really!' she said. 'You didn't want me to be hurt? Well, why did you bloody well start it, then? Did it not occur to you that it was just possible that I'd be hurt, when you first arranged the first meeting? When was that, by the way?'

He was silent.

'Well, what did you think that day? Or night? That you'd get away with it? That there was no danger? Or did you want her so much it was worth the risk?'

He was silent.

'Who was it?' she said, and the words were like a whiplash.

'I won't tell you. I am not going to tell you. Ever. It wouldn't help.'

Ritz and Annabel had stepped out on to the catwalk, raised their hands. The music had stopped, the talking stopped. There were a lot of people there, Romilly thought, far more than she had expected.

'Thank you all for coming this evening,' Annabel was saying. 'I hope you've enjoyed it. We certainly have. And I think you'll agree the girls – *our* girls, as we think of them – are an incredibly high standard. As always. *Alive!* will be dedicating at least four pages to tonight, in our October issue – which of course is the biggie, as far as advertising is concerned – book your space now, if you haven't already—' much laughter – 'so you can see all of them again then. That's one of the prizes: along with an outfit, and the pictures from today's session. The first prize, of course, is five thousand pounds, and the biggest, as far as the girls are concerned, I hope, is being on the cover of *Alive!* in the November issue.'

'Enough of *Alive!*,' said Ritz, cutting in. 'The real biggie is a contract with us, Choice Agency, for a year, and the chance to get into the modelling world from the best possible position. As well as representation, of course, Choice offers financial and legal advice, and a tie-up with our agencies in Milan and New York. Now then, I won't keep you in suspense any longer; you or the girls. In reverse order, the third place goes to . . .'

I might get this, thought Romilly, crossing her figners, I might get third, that's just possible.

'The third place goes to Jade Morgan. Jade, can we have you out here, please?'

Well, that was that. Jade's disappointment cut into her rather mean prettiness just for a second, then she rallied, smiled brilliantly, sashayed out on to the catwalk.

Romilly felt suddenly violently sick.

'Second place goes to . . . Tiffany. Tiffany, can we have you, please?'

'This is agony,' hissed Zoë in Marianne's ear. 'Poor little Rom.'

Tiffany was gliding down the catwalk, her great brown eyes roaming the room; Marianne looked up at her, thinking how sexy she was, wondering how Romilly could possibly have even been asked to compete with this lot.

'Well done, Tiffany. I'm sure this won't be the last time you're seen on a catwalk,' Annabel was saying, smiling, kissing her.

A long silence then: a roll of drums.

'And the winner, the outright winner is – Romilly Muirhead. The baby of the class, only fifteen, but an absolutely unanimous decision.'

'Oh, my God,' said Marianne. 'Oh, Zoë, what have I done?'

'Tom, I have to know. You've got to tell me. Who was it?'

'I meant it, Octavia. I'm not going to tell you.'

'You make me feel sick,' she said. 'So sick, I can't even stand being in the same room as you. Ever again. I want you out of here, out of this house. I suppose you'll say that it didn't mean anything. That's what men always say, the lie they always tell. I was drunk, it didn't mean anything.'

'No,' he said, very quietly. 'I wasn't going to say that.'

'Have you ever done it before?'

He stared at her, clearly shocked himself by the question. She felt comforted, however faintly, by that shock.

'No. Never. I swear.'

'I'm not terribly impressed by your swearing, Tom. You swore to be faithful to me until death did us part. Forsaking all others. I remember it very well. It's sort of stuck in my head. For some reason.'

There was another long silence. He got up, poured himself another whisky. 'I have never, ever done it before,' he said. 'You have got to believe that.'

'Even if I did,' she said, 'how do think I feel? Knowing other people must have known, were watching me, laughing at me, sorry for me. And all the time, all that garbage in the papers, about our bloody perfect, successful marriage. What do you think that does to me? Word gets around, doesn't it? Barbara knew, I suppose, and—'

'How did you find out?' he said abruptly. 'Did anyone tell you? Because if—'

'Nobody told me. It was quite a sweet story, actually. It would have done well in a book. It was all because of a handkerchief, Tom. Like Desdemona's. It got caught up in your things, and tipped into the laundry. And I started putting two and two together. It was a very pretty handkerchief. But you'd know that of course. You'd have seen it.'

'Oh, my God, Octavia, I – when was that, how long have you known?'

'It doesn't matter how long. Tom, who was it? Who did the handkerchief belong to?'

'I'm not going to tell you,' he said. 'I can't and I won't.' His eyes were very steady, very determined.

'I shall find out,' she said. 'Be sure of that.'

'I hope you never will,' he said.

It seemed to her, even then, an odd thing to say.

*

'Mrs Muirhead, more champagne?'

They were having dinner in Langan's, Ritz, Annabel and the Muirheads: nobody else. Just a quiet, family evening, Ritz had said, after all the excitement.

'I still can't believe it. I made so many mistakes, like smiling at Zoë when you said not to.'

'Oh, yes,' said Ritz, remembering that moment, that wonderful, radiant moment when the sun had come up, so unexpectedly, so sweetly: when the whole room had smiled back. 'Well, it didn't really matter. As it turned out.'

'What am I going to do about my braces?' said Romilly suddenly.

'Nothing,' said Marianne quickly. 'Nothing whatsoever. They stay.' She saw Ritz turn to look at her quickly, half open her mouth, then shut it again. Good. Let the ground rules be laid down now. She was in charge; Romilly was a minor.

'When's your birthday, Romilly?' said Annabel, right on cue.

'So what do you want to do?' said Tom quietly.

'I want a divorce,' she said.

'Are you sure?'

'I'm quite sure.'

'Well,' he said, his voice heavy, 'if you're sure, then you must have it. I certainly can't stop you. I wouldn't try.'

'Don't you want one?'

'No,' he said.

She was astonished. 'Why not?'

He looked at her levelly for a long time, then said, 'I can hardly bear to say it. Knowing how you'll react. But I still – love you.'

Octavia felt disgust, physical disgust, rising in her throat, sharply acid. 'Oh, please,' she said, 'spare me that.'

'I can't spare you. I have to say it. It's true. You shouldn't ask questions if you don't want the answers.'

'How can you say such a thing?' she said, her voice shaking violently with anger. 'How can you even think such a thing? It degrades you. It degrades me. Love me! Of course you don't love me. If you loved me you wouldn't have fucked someone else. Don't talk about loving. You don't know what it is.'

'I do know what it is for me,' he said, 'but I won't insult you by spelling it out. Octavia, I know I'm a shit. A feeble, frightful shit. I do realise that.'

She was crying harder now, sobbing, wiping her eyes and her nose on the back of her hand; he got up, went out of the room, came back with a box of Kleenex.

'Don't talk about loving me,' she said. 'Please. I can't bear it.'

'Why not?'

'Because you can't possibly love me. Having affairs, sleeping with other people, lying to me, deceiving me, making me a laughing stock—'

'You really are obsessed with with people laughing at you, aren't you?' It really matters to you.'

'Of course it does. For God's sake, Tom, think about it. Put yourself in my place; imagine walking into rooms, restaurants, people saying look, there's poor old Tom, his wife's having an affair, he has no idea, isn't it pathetic . . . Are you trying to tell me it wouldn't matter?'

'Of course it would matter. But—'

'Tom, you've got to tell me who it is! I need to know. I need a – a face. A person. Who is it Tom, who?'

'Octavia, you don't need to know. You're not going to know.'

She got up then, went over to him, started hitting him round the head with her fists, sobbing, shouting at him. 'Tell me! Tell me who it is. You've no right not to, you owe me that at least!'

He caught her wrists, held her from him, his face such a terrible study in remorse and something else – what? fear, yes, it was fear, raw, pitiless fear – that she stopped abruptly, stopped crying, stared at him.

'Don't,' he said, 'please don't. It won't help.'

'I don't understand,' she said. 'Why is it so important that I don't know?'

He said nothing; just stood up, picked up his glass and walked out of the room.

CHAPTER 15

'Tom. Everything all right?'

'Morning, Aubrey. Sorry I'm late. Bit of a tough night.'

'You look like that, I must say. Anyway, I'm afraid we've got a serious problem on our hands.'

'Oh, God, what?'

'You haven't seen the *Mail*, then?'

'No. Why?'

Aubrey ignored the question. 'I'm afraid we've lost Michael Carlton.'

'What? Why? What the fuck's happened?'

'Read this.'

Tom read it. 'Oh, God,' he said. 'Dear God in heaven.'

'Pattie, how did they get all this stuff? How could you have done this to me? I know I said I'd support you openly now, but that didn't extend to talking about my husband.'

'Octavia, I didn't! I had no idea about that, anyway. And I talked to the *Mail* before the meeting, I didn't even mention you.'

'Well, who did? My God, it must have been Bingham. The bastard! I wonder if I can get hold of him. Where's his card?'

'Of course I haven't talked to the *Mail*,' said Gabriel Bingham. 'I have my principles. And, no, I haven't seen it. And I haven't talked to a single journalist since we last met.'

'Oh. Well, I'm sorry I misjudged you, but who else would have talked about my speech?'

'Anyone who was at the meeting – a local stringer who knew about the interview with Pattie David, I suppose.'

'Yes, maybe!'

'I'm about to go to the House. I shall go to the press gallery and study this article which has caused you such distress. I can't imagine what it might say. I'll phone you if I can throw some light on the matter, having read it.'

'Octavia, if this is some kind of revenge, it's extremely destructive. To us all.'

'Tom, it's not supposed to be anything. It's simply an attempt to stop something terrible from happening.'

'Well, you might well have dealt a body blow to Fleming Cotterill in the process. I'd call that fairly terrible in its own way. I've got to go, I'll speak to you later.'

'I won't be—' she said, but he had put the phone down.

It was not even mid-morning when Gabriel Bingham walked up to the press gallery at the House of Commons. There was nobody there; it looked, he thought, rather like a stage set before the actors arrived, the long row of phone boxes empty, the desks bare, the whole place utterly silent. He went over to the newspapers, found the *Daily Mail*, flicked over the first few pages, and then found it. And read it. Twice.

'Well,' he said aloud and finally, 'well, well, well.'

> There has been a reprieve (one Jeni Thomas informed him) for North Somerset beauty spot, Bartles Wood, first reported in the *Mail* three weeks ago. The local council has refused planning permission for a housing development complete with shopping mall and community centre, thanks to the efforts of local protestors.
>
> 'We will not be resting on our laurels, though,' said Patricia David (photographed right, with other supporters). 'The battle isn't over yet. We understand the developer is going to appeal, so we are establishing a fund to fight this and will take it to the European courts if need be. Nothing can be allowed to steal our precious countryside from us.'
>
> The developer, Michael Carlton, who is behind the project, has already announced his intention to appeal.
>
> A surprise intervention came from charity consultant Octavia Fleming. She has pledged her support to the protestors and attended a meeting where she made an impassioned speech, declaring that England and what she called its 'tender beauty' must be saved from the rapist tendencies of developers. Her consultancy, Capital C, advises the charity Foothold, of which Mrs David is the local chair. Ironically, Octavia Fleming's husband, Tom, has a public affairs consultancy, of which Michael Carlton is a client.
>
> The newly elected MP for North Somerset, Gabriel Bingham,

was also at the meeting. 'I am not necessarily on the side of the protestors,' he said, 'but they invited me to this meeting and I wanted to hear their views.'

Octavia phoned the *Mail*, and asked to speak to Jeni Thomas. 'She doesn't actually work here,' said the girl on the newsdesk. 'She's a stringer from the West Country, works at a news agency in Bristol.'

Jeni Thomas was friendly. She hadn't been at the meeting herself, had sent someone to cover it. 'I was furious he didn't get a quote from you. I'm against the development myself,' she said. 'I live near there.'

'And who gave you the information about my husband, and Michael Carlton being a client? Slightly embarrassing, to put it mildly.'

'That didn't come from me. Apparently it was an anonymous tip-off, direct to the *Mail*.'

Octavia suddenly felt rather sick.

'My word,' said Nico Cadogan, putting down his copy of the *Daily Mail*. 'Silly girl.' His observation, at Ascot, that Octavia was dangerously overwrought, seemed to have been correct. But he wouldn't have expected her to be quite this reckless. Not to mention professionally destructive, both to her husband and herself. Slightly worrying altogether. He wondered what Marianne thought of Octavia Fleming . . .

'Well,' said Gabriel Bingham, 'I've read the piece now. Carlton's your husband's client, is he? No wonder you were careful to conceal your connections with the project. Public affairs consultant, eh? Not just – how did you describe your husband to me? oh, yes – interested in politics. He can't be very pleased.'

'He isn't,' said Octavia. 'Not that I care.'

'I think it's very brave, what you're doing,' he said suddenly. 'I wanted to tell you that.'

She felt absurdly pleased that he should say such a thing. He hadn't seemed to her the sort of man to dole out compliments in any form.

'Thank you.'

'Do you want to come and have a steadying glass of bitter at the House at lunchtime? Or even a thimbleful of Bollinger?'

'No,' she said, although the temptation was considerable. 'I'm off to see a friend. In the country. But thank you anyway.'

'Oh, well. Another time, maybe.'

'Yes, maybe. Thank you.'

'You think I'm crazy, don't you?' said Octavia to Melanie.

'Fairly crazy, yes. And we've lost a patron too, which is a pity. We'd better talk about that. You haven't heard from Mr Carlton?'

'Not yet, no. I'm sorry, Melanie.'

'That's okay. I must say I think it's very clever.'

'Clever?'

'Yes. Don't get mad, get even, that's what the lady said. You've certainly got pretty even today.'

'It wasn't actually to get even,' said Octavia. 'I know it looks like it, but it wasn't, though I suppose Tom's behaviour made it easier. I just suddenly felt I wanted to do what I thought was right, and that I was, well, free to do it. I do care about the countryside so much and—'

'Honey,' said Melanie, 'I don't think you're going to find many people who'll believe that. If they do, they'll probably be members of the Flat Earth Society.'

'Octavia,' Sarah Jane's face was concerned as she looked round the door, 'I've got *The Times*' features pages on the phone. They want to do an interview with you, round the theme of conflicting loyalties. I told them you probably wouldn't, but—'

'You were right,' said Octavia. 'Thanks.'

'And the *Express* phoned earlier, before you came in. They wanted to interview you on much the same thing. Shall I say no to that as well?'

'Just tell 'em all no,' said Melanie. 'Octavia, why don't you get out of London, go and see your friend now? I'll see you in the morning. I'll just tell our friend Mr Carlton, and everyone else, you're unavailable. You can pick up the baton tomorrow.'

'Thanks, Melanie. For everything.'

Melanie seemed to be proving a more reliable friend than she would ever have expected. Better in some ways than Louise . . .

She was just leaving when Tom phoned.

'Octavia, I beg of you, please phone Michael Carlton. It might help. And it's so important to me.'

'I'm really sorry, Tom,' she said, 'but I don't see why I should. Or what good it would do. There's nothing I could tell him that would reassure him. Now you must excuse me. I'm going to see Anna Madison.'

'Octavia, I cannot tell you how much I feel that's a mistake. To go there today. You should stay in London. For the next few days. It's very important.'

'Tom, Anna Madison is dying. Now that really is important. Rather more than some client account.'

'Octavia, I really don't want you to—'

'Goodbye, Tom. I may be late. I'll sleep in the guest room. In fact,

I've moved all my things in there. Until we can work out something permanent. Oh, and Tom—'

'Yes?'

'My father's coming to dinner tomorrow night. You will be out, won't you?'

'Yes, I'll be out,' he said. 'You can rely on that. You'll be telling him, I expect. About what has happened.'

'No,' she said, contemplating and then rejecting the horror of that conversation, 'not yet. Don't worry, Tom. Your guilty secret is safe with me. Pity it wasn't safer with you.'

He sighed so heavily she could hear it down the line. And then he said, 'Be careful, Octavia. Please.'

It seemed a strange thing to say, she thought as she put the phone down.

Marianne was sitting at the kitchen table, reading the article in the *Mail* and trying to imagine what kind of madness could have led Octavia into such a thing, when Zoë came in.

'Hi, Mum. I'm just off. Last exam. You reading the story too?'

'Yes. You know about it, then?'

'Yeah. Nice one, Octavia.'

'Zoë,' said Marianne, 'it's a little hard on Tom, I think.'

'Well, there are serious principles at stake here.' Zoë grinned at her. 'I'm on her side. Someone has to stop all this wrecking of the countryside.'

'Yes, maybe. But she's actually going a fair way towards wrecking Tom's business. Or at least that bit of it. Wives ought to be supportive to their husbands,' said Marianne. She felt rather uneasy as she said it; she was playing the opposite of a supportive role herself to Felix at the moment, increasingly impatient with his concerns over Octavia. Felix couldn't help his neurotic worries about his daughter, he certainly wasn't going to abandon them now, and in a way they exemplified his two greatest virtues; his capacity for love and his intense loyalty. The two things she had never had from Alec, and that she valued so highly. And then she was fecklessly encouraging the attentions of another man – a dangerously conscienceless man – to hurt Felix. Having dinner with him, for God's sake. And he was also Felix's friend. She should cancel it. She would cancel it. It wasn't too late.

'So how do you feel today?' said Zoë. 'About Romilly?'

'Oh, you know. Everything you might expect.'

'What, chuffed, proud?' Zoë was laughing.

She smiled reluctantly back. 'A bit, I suppose. But much more worried. Terrified, even. I don't like that woman. Not one bit.'

'Who, Ritz? Me neither.'

'Really? I'm so glad. It makes me feel less neurotic.'

'I don't think Romilly's too sure about her either.'

The phone rang sharply. Zoë picked it up. 'Hallo. Oh, yes, hi. Sure. Yes, she's here. Hold on.' She covered the phone, looked at Marianne. 'Speaking of the devil . . . Ritz Franklyn.'

Marianne took a deep breath. 'Ritz. Good morning. Thank you for a delicious dinner. What? Oh, she's fine. Yes, she loved it. I know, she was very excited. But – I'm sorry? Oh. Oh, I see. Heavens. Already? Well – well, I really don't know. I'd better come and see you about it. No, Romilly most certainly will not be there. She's still at school fulltime, you know, Ritz. I did make that very clear. Oh, yes. Possibly tomorrow? I shall have to speak to Romilly's father as well about it. Yes, I'll get back to you.'

She put the phone down and stared at Zoë.

'Mum, what's the matter?'

'A cosmetic company, Christie's, have offered Romilly a contract. Or rather are about to. Some Americans are coming over on Monday, want to meet her, but it's a formality, Ritz says. It's for half a million dollars. They'd want to shoot the campaign in New York. Zoë, this is appalling. What am I going to do?'

Octavia was actually in her car when Louise phoned. She sounded very tired.

'Octavia, I'm so sorry. I'm going to have to put you off. Some specialist's coming to see Mummy, and I just think a visitor on top of that, even you, would be too much for her. Will you forgive?'

'Of course I will. Don't be silly. Maybe one day next week?'

'Yes, of course. I'll let you know.'

'Are you all rght? You sound terrible.'

'I feel pretty terrible. Still, how are you? I saw the piece in the *Mail*.' The husky voice was almost amused. 'That can't have helped things. Or did it?'

'No. To put it mildly. Tom lost that account. The man who was building the development, you know.'

'Good,' said Louise. She sounded more cheerful suddenly. 'He deserves it, wouldn't you say?'

'I suppose so,' said Octavia slowly. Just for a second she felt a stab of discomfort, a sense of disloyalty; then she realised Louise was perfectly right. Of course he did.

'This is very awkward,' said Aubrey. 'We're going to need some cash very quickly. Carlton's fee was just about holding us together. If I fix a meeting with the bank, are there any times you can't manage?'

'No,' said Tom, 'absolutely any time. Middle of the night, if you like.'

'Unlikely. Hopefully he'll see us early tomorrow. If he says no, we'll have to go out with a begging bowl. Bad publicity, though.'

'It's all bloody bad,' said Tom. 'The other clients won't like it either. I've already had Cadogan on the phone, asking me if Octavia's got any Western Provincial shares. Meant to be funny of course, but still . . .'

'Oh, to hell with it,' said Aubrey. 'It'll pass. And I'm sure the bank'll play ball.' He sounded more confident than he looked.

'I'm so sorry,' said Tom.

'Tom, it was hardly your fault.'

But it was: in a way. And they both knew it.

Marianne was in the middle of an argument with Zoë when Nico Cadogan phoned.

'Hallo, Marianne. I've been missing you.'

'Oh. Yes. Hallo.'

'I'm just ringing to confirm the arrangements for tonight. I've booked a table at the Waterside Inn.'

The Waterside Inn, at Bray. One of the loveliest, most romantic, most expensive restaurants she knew. Taking her there spelt out Nico Cadogan's intentions very clearly indeed. She couldn't go. She wouldn't go.

'Look, Nico—'

'Yes?'

'You see, the thing is . . .' said Marianne rather helplessly and to her rage felt herself blushing. Zoë was watching her interestedly.

'Yes?'

'Well, I've been thinking, and—' She realised Zoë had recognised an opportunity and was sliding out of the door with a distinctly shrewd expression in her green eyes. She waved, grinned and disappeared; the front door slammed.

Marianne felt foolish and ruffled. A dinner. One dinner. What harm would it do? And it would be easier to explain then, to say it must be the last occasion, than on the telephone.

'Sorry, Nico. Bit of domestic admin. No, I was only going to say could we go slightly later? Yes, seven thirty here would be fine. I'll be ready.'

She'd be very ready. Outside the front door. The last thing she wanted was Romilly realising she was going out with a man who wasn't Felix.

Meanwhile she had to do something really very unpleasant and tell Alec about Romilly.

'She is going to be big trouble,' said Ritz Franklyn, putting the phone down on Marianne, looking across her desk at Serena Fox. 'We have to find some way of working round her. Otherwise we're going to lose that girl.'

'What did she say, then?'

'Oh, that she'd phoned her husband, that he was very unhappy about it, that Romilly was far too young, that there was no question of her going over to New York, she was going to have to rethink the whole thing. And she hasn't actually signed anything, has she? Shit, Serena, what can we do?'

'We could shoot the campaign over here. I think I could swing that. It would look like a huge concession to her fears, it might calm the bitch down.'

'She's coming in to see me tomorrow. Could I put that to her?'

'I'll come along,' said Serena, 'float it as an idea. No point getting everyone worked up about it if she doesn't bite.'

'Yeah,' said Ritz, 'or if Daddy changes his mind. They often do, once the first shock is over. It's a lot of money. And Romilly has to hear about it yet. Fifteen-year-olds can be pretty voluble. Even little angels like Romilly.'

'I suspect she may not be allowed to hear about it.'

'Well, we can fix that one . . .' said Ritz.

'Outrageous,' said Nico Cadogan, 'but I'm glad you told me.'

'Why?'

'Well, now I feel impelled – or is it compelled? – to take you away for the weekend instead.'

'Nico, of course I can't come away with you.'

'Why not? You're not married to Felix Miller. Most fortunately for you, I'd say. You're not married to anyone. Therefore if you would like to come away with me, you are absolutely able to do so. And I know you would like to.'

'You know no such thing.'

'Oh, but I do,' he said, 'I really do.'

He took her hand, which was lying on the table, and began to massage her palm very insistently with his thumb. Marianne looked down at her hand, under siege from his, hoped he could not see or feel the fronds of desire uncurling from it, moving slowly, insidiously, deep within herself, stirring, disturbing her.

'Look at me,' said Nico. 'Look at me, Marianne, and tell me you don't want to come away with me this weekend.'

'I don't want to come away with you this weekend,' she said. Not looking at him.

'You're a terrible liar. Really terrible.'

'If I did – which I don't,' she said, with a huge effort, 'I wouldn't.'

'Why not?'

'For reasons of loyalty.'

'Loyalty? To a man who puts his daughter's needs before your own? Fails to support you when you need it?'

'Nico,' she said, laughing, 'you're exaggerating terribly.'

'Yes,' he said unexpectedly, 'I know. I'm prone to exaggeration. I always think sex is a rather exaggerating thing, don't you think? The pleasure it gives is quite out of proportion to logic. I mean, who would think that – oh, yes, thank you. Put it there.'

The waiter had arrived with a great bowl of wild strawberries. Marianne was so grateful to him she almost kissed him.

She pulled her hand away, leaned back in her chair, stared out over the water. It was a perfect evening, the sky brilliant turquoise still, with the purple rising into it, and in the blue, the moon, virginal white, a star trailing beneath it.

'"Softly she was going up,"' said Nico, following her gaze, '"and a star or two beside." Two of the most beautiful lines in the English language. Do you like poetry, Marianne?'

'I do, but I'm rather illiterate, I'm afraid,' she said. 'Music is my great love. Do you like music?'

'Sadly, tone deaf. Is that very bad?'

'Very bad. There can be no relationship between a tone-deaf person and a musical one, I'm afraid.'

'Then I shall take music lessons. Immediately. Perhaps you could teach me. The only music I like is opera. Very orgasmic.'

There was a pause, then he said, 'Such a good word, orgasm, isn't it? So onomatopoeic. First the drawing together, then the tightening, then the wonderful explosion of release. The climb and then the fall . . .' He stopped, smiled at her, picked up her hand again, kissed it gently. 'Come away with me, Marianne. You know you want to.'

'No,' she said, and made her fatal mistake. 'I might want to, but I really can't.'

He looked at her and smiled. 'I can be very patient, you know,' he said. 'I'll wait.'

CHAPTER 16

'He's not going to do it, is he?' said Tom gloomily, as they walked out of the bank into Lombard Street after a preliminary discussion.

'He might,' said Aubrey. 'Don't start sinking the ship before its time. And you mustn't see this as entirely down to the Carlton débâcle. We were in trouble months ago. Bastard's right, our expenditure is huge, but the real problem was that we were under-capitalised from the beginning.'

'It's very good of you to be so magnanimous,' said Tom, 'but the fact remains if this bloody business with the wood hadn't cropped up now, we'd still be flying along. However close to the wind. And I feel above average responsible, I'm afraid. Christ—'

He stopped, wondering if he should come clean, talk the whole filthy mess over with Aubrey; Octavia had said he must have known something had been going on, she was probably right. And a bit of self-flagellation might ease his misery.

'Look,' said Aubrey, cutting in on him smoothly, making it plain he wanted nothing of the sort, 'we all make mistakes. Even me. "He who never made a mistake never made a discovery,"' he added. 'Samuel Smiles, *Self Help*. Now let's go and have a drink, even if we can't really afford it, and have a look at our other options. Just in case the bank doesn't come good.'

'What a shit,' said Melanie cheerfully. She tossed *The Times* at Octavia. A large photograph of Terence and Caroline Conran was on the front page, above a report on the £10 million divorce settlement he had been ordered to pay.

'Can you believe it? He actually said, "She cooked a few meals now and again." That's how he summed up their marriage, her contribution to it. Arrogant so-and-so.'

Octavia wondered how Tom would sum up her contribution to their marriage. Maybe, 'She came to a few client dinners now and again.' And how she would sum up his? 'He paid a few bills now and again'? She sighed.

'Sighing not allowed,' said Melanie, grinning at her. 'Not in office hours. Or regrets.'

'Sorry. It's just so sad. We had such a lot going for us, once. And things don't go wrong for no reason, do they? I mean, *I* must have done something wrong.'

'Octavia! Of course you didn't. You married an ace shit.'

Octavia's phone rang.

'Octavia Fleming.'

'Mrs Fleming! I didn't expect to get straight through. This is Gabriel Bingham here.'

'Oh,' she said, 'Oh, hallo, Mr Bingham.'

'I just wondered how the little local difficulty might have been working out for you. And to see if you might be at your charming cottage this weekend.'

'It's not working out too well,' said Octavia, briskly. 'And I don't know about the weekend yet. And I didn't know you were familiar with our cottage.'

'I'm not.'

'Well then, I don't quite see how you can describe it as charming.'

'Oh, but of course it must be. All weekend cottages are. Otherwise what would be the point? Anyway, I have some stuff on the Bartles Wood project that might interest you. I could send it there, or even drop it over, if you like, or I could send it to your other residence. Which I'm sure is charming too.'

'I'll have to get back to you,' said Octavia, carefully putting some frost into her voice. Gabriel Bingham clearly became over-confident very easily.

'Fine. I'm sorry to have disturbed you. Goodbye, Mrs Fleming.'

'Goodbye, Mr Bingham.'

In spite of everything, as she put the phone down she smiled. It was soothing, in the middle of her hurt and confusion, to know that someone found her if not actually attractive, then at least interesting enough to pursue. However irritating and over-confident they might be.

'Romilly! What a lovely surprise. What are you doing here?' said Ritz.

'This is where I go to school. Just over there, look.'

'I had no idea there was a school here. I thought it was just doctors in Harley Street. Well, I mustn't keep you. You're with your friends, I expect.'

'No, it's cool. We were just walking down to the Tube. That was a great night on Wednesday. I enjoyed it so much.' Romilly smiled at her. The Smile. The literally almost-million-dollar smile.

'Me too. So how are you feeling about it all now?'

'Oh, trying to come down to earth. You know. It was wonderful, but I can't see anyone actually wanting to book me, photograph me or anything. Not for a while, anyway. What with the braces and being so skinny and everything. I mean I know models have to be thin, but, well . . .'

'Romilly,' said Ritz, and she sounded genuinely shocked, 'hasn't your mother said anything to you about the contract with Christie's?'

'So where is your husband this evening?' said Felix.

'Out with clients. As usual.' Octavia smiled at him: a bright, careful smile. He was going to have to know, sooner or later. And probably sooner; living under the same roof as Tom was clearly going to be intolerable. She could scarcely bear to look at him, never mind sit at the same table, share a conversation. It was odd, how the lancing of the boil had released such vicious poisons; she felt far more fiercely hostile to him now than at any time since she had made her discovery. She wanted to hit him, kick him, wanted to scrape her nails across his face, that hideously perfect, sculpted face, wanted to punch him in the balls.

The twins had not yet picked up on the hostility; during the week she and Tom were seldom together with them, so it had been easy. But now, with a weekend ahead, something had to be done; she had suggested Tom went to the cottage, but he said no, he had to be available to Aubrey all weekend, suggested she went there instead. She would have liked that, but it was Camilla Bartlett's party on the Saturday, and Poppy clearly could not miss that, and Gideon had a cricket match and coaching, which was crucial; and so they would both be in London, in the emotionally foul-aired prison that the house had become, and they must get through the weekend somehow. It would be no time, with the children watching them, listening to them, to discuss such things as who would do what and when, who would live where, who would pay for what, all the ugly, immediate essentials of the ending of a marriage. They had earmarked Monday morning for that, with the children safely at school, and Caroline and Minty at swimming.

'I think you're so very good about it,' her father was saying now. 'These endless absences. Of course some are inevitable, but in Tom's case it seems to be extreme, always—'

'Daddy,' she said, 'please. Not now. Let's have a nice evening. I've bought the entire meal from Marks and Spencer: honey-baked salmon, rocket salad, Pavlova, all your favourites.'

'How sweet you are, darling, to remember,' he said, unpacking two bottles of wine from a coolbag, 'and I've brought some wine, I hope you'll have a glass at least. I chilled them before I left.'

He followed her into the kitchen, opened one of the bottles, poured two glasses.

'To us, sweetheart,' he said, coming over to her, handing her a glass, giving her a kiss. 'Isn't this lovely, just the two of us, like old times?'

'To us,' said Octavia, carefully ignoring the second half of his speech; 'Thank you, Daddy. It's lovely to see you. Lovely. Look, sit down, and I'll serve the salad. Parmesan?'

'Thank you. You do look tired, Octavia. Very tired. I wish you'd take me up on my offer of a holiday.'

'Well, I might. A bit later on.'

'Good. Now, then, tell me about this client you've lost.'

'It isn't exactly my client,' she said, and started on the saga of Bartles Wood.

'Mummy, how could you? How could you?'

'How could I what, darling?' said Marianne. She was tired and slightly fractious; she had slept badly, having come in very late from her dinner, had somehow managed not to allow Nico to do more than kiss her once in the car on the way home, had sat determinedly far from him, discomfited by his patent amusement; even so, when they reached Eaton Square she was in a state of such suppressed sexual arousal that when he did kiss her goodnight, lightly, gently on the mouth at first, then slowly, deliberately sinking his lips on to hers, moving his tongue with appalling confidence into her mouth, she had found herself responding with rather distressing enthusiasm, had finally pulled away and hurried out of the car, praying the children would all be in bed. Another absurd piece of role reversal, she had thought, half shocked, half amused at herself.

Earlier, before her meeting with Choice, she had phoned Felix, enquired after Octavia, and made it plain that should he wish at least to see her over the weekend, she would be available. When he said he had made other plans now, she had put the phone down, annoyed again, so that now she was in no mood for teenage hostility.

'I just think it was so mean, not telling me about the offer of the contract with the cosmetic company. You had no right to keep it from me!'

'Romilly, you are only fifteen years old. Of course I was going to tell you about it. But I had to discuss it with Daddy first, decide what would be best.'

'Without discussing it with me? You always say *we* should discuss everything. That it's the only way to run a family. Everything: holidays, exams, where we all might want to go to college. Suddenly it's different. Why? Well, I think I know,' said Romilly and the expression in her green eyes was contemptuous. 'You never wanted me to hear about this because it wouldn't be good for me or something. You thought you could decide, without ever telling me about it. Because of course I'd want to do it. Of course I do. Who wouldn't?'

'Romilly, you haven't even got the contract yet! There are some Americans coming over on Tuesday to talk about it.'

'Yes. With *me*. Not just you. Mummy, I am not a child, you know. In three months I'll be sixteen. I've won this competition on my own. You had nothing to do with it. Sorry. So you really have to let me follow it through. And if you don't want me to go on Tuesday, that's tough. Because I'm going. I know where it is and when, and unless you shut me in my room, which of course you wouldn't, you can't stop me. Good night. Sweet dreams,' she added, purely out of habit. But she didn't lean forward to give her mother the usual bedtime kiss. It was the first time ever. And it hurt Marianne more than anything she could ever remember.

'So,' Octavia said, finally, sipping at her virtually untouched chardonnay. 'That's it. What's your reaction?'

'I'm not sure,' said Felix. 'It was a little foolish. Reckless even. Very bad for Tom's business.'

She looked at him, startled. If *he* thought that, showed even a sign of criticising her, what she had done was clearly very bad indeed. Alarm lurched in her guts.

'It will do you no good either, in your own business, if you're seen to be acting without proper consideration.'

'But, Daddy, I was. I was putting my money where my mouth is. If you like.'

'Where Tom's mouth is, I would venture to suggest. How did he take it?'

'He was pretty cross.'

'I'm not surprised. Not businesslike, Octavia, not businesslike at all.'

She wondered what his reaction would have been, had he known part at least of her reason for doing what she had. Briefly, momentarily, she was tempted to tell him, but with all her fierce hatred of Tom, she still shrank from the thought of how her father might react, what he would do.

'Well,' he said, swift to forgive her as always, 'I admire you at least for having the courage to stand up and be counted. You've lost Carlton as a patron, presumably?'

''Fraid so,' she said, flinching even in retrospect from the cold fury in Michael Carlton's voice earlier that day as he informed her their agreement was terminated, that he had no desire to have any dealings with her in any way, professionally or otherwise, from now on. 'Although it seems you have absolutely no concept of what the word professional means,' he had said and put the phone down.

'And how did Melanie feel about that?'

'She was great. She even said she admired me for what I'd done. I don't think she was entirely happy to have Carlton as a sponsor anyway. Given that he was a client of Tom's. Bit too incestuous.'

'She certainly seemed to be taking care of you very competently the other day. When you were so upset.'

'Yes,' said Octavia quickly. 'Yes, she was great.'

'So, another client. Two in a week. She must be very – how did you once describe her? Tough.'

'Two? I haven't lost another client,' she said, forgetting briefly that had been her explanation for her hysteria.

'You told me you had,' he said, and his brilliant dark eyes on her were very fierce, very probing. 'You told me that's why you were crying. Was that not the real reason, Octavia, because—'

'Oh, Daddy, of course it was.' Panic filled her. 'Sorry, I wasn't thinking. No, that was exactly what was upsetting me, the Carlton thing. I felt so stupid, so ashamed, Tom had been so angry, I just – freaked out. Now look, let's forget all that, I've got something else to tell you. Anna Madison is terribly ill. She has cancer of the liver, no hope at all. She has only a few weeks to live apparently. I feel so upset about it and poor Louise is distraught . . .'

'We've only got this place for another week,' said Ian, 'then we'll have to move on. But I got another one for us. Very nice indeed. Up Kennington way, in a square. They've gone away, like the other two. Very considerate of them. Lovely big bed. And a very good cellar. We'll be very happy there.'

'Oh, good,' said Zoë.

She was tired; it was already four, and they'd not got home till after two the night before. She'd found it quite hard to respond tonight to the sex, brilliant as it had been; she'd actually had to fake an orgasm, just to get a bit of peace. She was surprised how easy it had been; he had been completely deceived.

'Right. Well, look, I'll just have a quick fag, and then we'll go. Okay?'

'Sure.'

He smoked a lot, and she didn't mind that, she did herself whenever she could; but she didn't like the way he smoked the Maldives' cigarettes. He had stopped even pretending to put them back; said they'd never miss them.

'Don't do that, Ian,' she said sharply, as he flicked the ash straight down on to the carpet.

'Oh, for fuck's sake, Zo. What's the matter with you? Is this your house? Your carpet?'

'No, but—'

'Well, fucking leave off, then.'

'Sorry,' said Zoë.

'There was something else,' said Octavia to Tom at breakfast, as they sat with their children, fighting to be pleasant, courteous, even to smile occasionally.

'Yes?' He looked exhausted, had clearly not slept. Good.

'I shall be seeing Lauren Bartlett this morning,' she said, 'when I take Poppy over. She'll want to know about next week, our dinner. What do you want me to say?'

She had expected him to tell her to cancel it, but he said, 'Do whatever you like. I don't care. I'll be there, if you want me to. It's a business arrangement. No point both of us going down. If you want me to join you and the Bartletts, I will. Now I have to go. I'll drop Gideon off at cricket. As I said.' He got up, kissed her briefly on the top of her head.

Feeling the children's eyes on them both she struggled to smile at him. 'Good luck today.'

'Thanks. Come on, Gideon, get your stuff, I need to go. And Poppy, you have fun. Don't try and fly the plane quite by yourself, will you?'

'Thanks, Daddy. See you tonight?'

'Of course. Although I might be late.'

'So might I!'

When they had gone, and Poppy had gone upstairs to change, Octavia phoned Louise at Rookston; she wasn't there, Janet said, had gone home to Cheltenham for a few days.

Sandy answered the phone. 'Hallo, Octavia. How are you?' His voice was hearty, cheerful as always.

'Fine, Sandy, thanks. Is Louise there?'

'She certainly is. I'll go and find her.'

'Thanks, Sandy.'

Louise sounded very tired. 'Hallo, Boot.'

'I just rang to see how your mother was.'

'Oh, pretty bad.' Louise sighed. 'The doctor says she's going down very fast. I'm going back there tomorrow, when I've sorted poor Sandy out. He's been so wonderful.'

'When can I come, Louise? To see her again? I don't want to – you know, to . . .'

'Miss saying goodbye, you mean? No, of course not. Well, sooner rather than later. If you can manage it.'

Octavia felt the same stab of hurt and injustice as she had the week before. It hadn't been her putting the visit off. She said so.

'I know, Boot, I'm sorry. Look, how about Wednesday, Thursday?'

'Thursday,' said Octavia. 'I'll come about lunchtime. If that's all right?'

'Of course. Wonderful. Thank you. She'll be so pleased.'

'We'd like to help,' David Jackson was saying. 'We do like to support our customers through both the good times and the bad.' Not true, thought Aubrey, only the good. 'But we really have pushed the boat out as far as we can, in this instance. Frankly, your record and your prospects simply do not justify extensive further borrowing. And to be honest with you, I don't think you would thank us in the long run for enabling you to increase your debts to any significant extent. At this moment in time . . .' He paused, looked at them almost hopefully, as if expecting gratitude.

'What about insignificantly?' said Tom. 'Are you prepared to make any concessions at all?'

'Ah. Well, we are prepared to increase your borrowing for the foreseeable future by ten thousand pounds. That is to say, the further loan that I agreed last Friday. But no more, I'm afraid. That should help you with your immediate problems.'

'Yes, of course, but longterm, it won't be nearly sufficient.'

'I realise that.' A long silence.

'Any suggestions?' said Tom.

David Jackson looked uncomfortable. 'Well, could I suggest you take out second mortgages on your houses? In that instance, the bank would—'

'We've already done that,' said Tom.

'Ah. Yes, I see.' David Jackson gave him a look; Tom realized he had never known quite what the phrase 'naked pity' meant before that moment. 'Another option would be to take in a third partner, who would make an advance of, say, the hundred thousand you are looking for, in return for a third share in the equity. If these projections of yours are correct, the company has huge potential. I'm sure you would have no difficulty finding an investor on that basis.'

Bastard, thought Tom. Fucking bastard. 'What about the investment arm of this bank?' he said, forcing an element of courtesy into his voice. 'Or any investment bank? Any possibility there?'

'Unlikely. They're really not interested in investing anything less than a million. Not worth it to them, you see. There is just one other avenue you might find it worth exploring.'

'Yes?'

'There are – private investors. Known in the trade as business angels. I expect you've come across them.'

'Not personally,' said Aubrey, 'but I know what you mean.'

'Indeed. They bridge the gap between the high street and the investment banks. Advance comparatively small amounts of money, the fifty thousand you are looking for being typical, in exchange for a share of the profits. Or a share in the company, of course, which he might agree to sell back to you at some future date. When Fleming Cotterill are flying high again, as I am personally convinced they will be.'

So convinced, you're not prepared to help us, you bugger, thought Aubrey. He smiled, leaned forward. 'Well, short of the more traditional type of angel, and we have explored that avenue—'

'I'm sorry?' David Jackson looked puzzled.

'You know. The ones up there. With God. White robes, wings, that sort of thing?'

'Oh, yes.' He smiled uncertainly.

'They didn't seem to be willing to do much. So the other sort does sound more interesting. Is there a list of such people?'

'Well, yes. Rather amusingly known as dating agencies. They advertise in the *FT*, that sort of thing. Your accountant would be able to advise you. Have a word with him.'

As they reached the sunlit street, Tom said, 'Aubrey, what are we going to do?'

'Christ knows. We can try his idea of a private investor.'

'He'd need his brains examined,' said Tom gloomily.

'Now, Tom, don't get downhearted. It's all true, what's in our projection. We will be back on our feet, given just one, maybe two new clients. More than on our feet, flying. Nothing's changed. We'll find someone. Maybe we'll have to do what you always swore you wouldn't, and approach your father-in-law. He's always trying to muscle in on the company, isn't he?'

'Over my dead body,' said Tom grimly. 'Or his.'

'Steady on, dear boy. Only joking. Octavia coming to this do tonight, by the way? The dinner at the House?'

'No,' said Tom sharply. 'No, she's not.'

'Pity,' said Aubrey.

*

He had guessed the reason of course; she had looked wretchedly unhappy at the last party. What was besetting him more even than a harrowingly deep sympathy for her and Tom in their patent difficulties, was the already visible effect. The Flemings had always been a team, working together, drawing strength professionally from one another; each a stronger force than they would have been individually. Both their companies recognised it, traded on it. Octavia lent Tom humanity; he gave her substance. To have Octavia, albeit notionally, at a business pitch, was hugely helpful; her high profile not only as a hugely successful businesswoman, but also in a field of apparent moral probity.

By the same token, he knew, Capital C used references to Tom's contacts at Westminster, his working knowledge of various parliamentary procedures, to impress their own clients, giving the impression (while saying, of course, no such thing) that where governmental intervention might be necessary to promote a cause, fight an injustice, Tom Fleming could instigate it.

Their relationship was dazzlingly productive – 'A rolling stone,' Aubrey had once said, 'gathering an inordinate amount of moss.' And for years it had worked beautifully. But the whole structure was none the less fragile, based on a mutual regard, a professional trust, a desire in each to see the other succeed; if the foundations began to decay, the walls would follow with terrifying speed.

Aubrey was, with great sadness, seeing the beginning of that process; and the timing, both from a professional as well as a personal point of view, was catastrophic.

CHAPTER 17

It was only a small thing, the hand sliding into hers, but it made Marianne feel much better. She squeezed it, very gently. Romilly's eyes met hers, large and tremulous. Neither of them said anything; just got out of the lift and walked into Christie's reception. By then they were both smiling.

'Good morning, Mrs Muirhead. And Romilly. You look very grown up. And young-ladylike!'

'Yes. Sorry!' said Romilly. It had been the bargaining point; either she wore her school clothes and went straight on to school, Marianne said, or she didn't go. Romilly had worn her school clothes.

'Well, come on in. Everybody's here. Mrs Muirhead, Romilly, this is Donna Hanson and John Bridges, both from New York, and this is George Smythe, from the UK division. Coffee, everyone?'

George Smythe, she really didn't like, Marianne decided; nasty, sweaty, lechy little man. But the Americans were fine; especially Donna Hanson.

Donna was about her own age, and told her she had two teenage daughters herself. 'So I can see this is a little troubling for you.'

'Just a little,' said Marianne.

The talk was general; they asked Romilly about herself, her ambitions, her schooling, looked at her photographs, asked her how she'd feel about coming to New York.

'Fine,' she said, smiling at them. 'I know New York because my dad lives there. I love it.'

'Oh, good!' said Donna Hanson. 'So you could stay with him.'

'Possibly,' said Marianne. 'But I would come over with Romilly in any case.'

'Yes, of course. Fine. Well, that's one problem out of the way. Now there's another small one: if we do decide we'd like to use you,

Romilly, and if everyone is happy, then there are the braces . . .' Her voice tailed off tactfully.

'I'm afraid there's nothing to be done about them,' said Marianne. 'They have to stay on. I can't have Romilly's teeth ruined. However much we may all want her to do this thing.'

'Mummy, I'm having a check-up next week,' said Romilly. 'He might say they can come off then.'

'I'm sure he won't,' said Marianne. 'They've only been on six months.'

She sounded harsher than she meant; she could see that from Romilly's eyes.

'Her teeth do look beautifully straight,' said Serena. It was the wrong thing for her to say; Marianne felt a stab of violent irritation.

'I agree with you. They look like that precisely because she has been wearing the braces. Anyway, as Romilly says, we are going to the dentist. We could let you know. Always assuming—'

'Of course. Well, I think we would want to know anyway. It might have a bearing on the final decision.'

So they haven't actually decided, thought Marianne. Maybe they won't want her. She looked at Romilly; her expression was strained. She had been very upset that morning; she'd got a spot, her period was due, she said, had cried, tried to squeeze the spot, made it worse. Only Zoë's calm intervention with some lotion and cover-up had calmed her down. God, she was cursing this whole thing already.

'Well, thank you for coming in, both of you. You have to get back to school, Romilly, I believe.' John Bridges smiled at her. 'Your mother's a very sensible woman, you're lucky.'

Romilly smiled at him, a rather wobbly smile; no glimpse of its usual radiance.

She said nothing.

In the car, driving up to Harley Street, she was silent, picking at her skirt.

Marianne looked at her. 'Darling, don't be upset.'

'Of course I'm upset. They didn't like me. It was the spot and these stupid clothes. And you weren't exactly helpful about the braces.'

'Darling, I am not sacrificing your teeth to some stupid contract.'

'Well, what's the point of having perfect teeth if no one ever sees them?' said Romilly. 'Look, we're here. 'Bye.'

She got out of the car and slammed the door; she was near to tears again.

'Damn,' said Marianne under her breath. 'Damn damn damn.'

*

'Glorious,' said Donna Hanson, 'quite glorious. Perfect face, perfect skin – well, except for that one little pimple. Inevitable at her age. Hormones, I expect; we may have to work round her cycle. We must definitely have her. Mother's a bit difficult, I can see that. And those braces are a problem.'

'We can get round both,' said Ritz Franklyn. 'Don't worry.'

'Good,' said John Bridges. 'I'll leave you and Serena to draw up the paperwork. I agree she's simply beautiful. Wonderful eyes. Very, very virginal. There can't be many like that any more. Not at her age.'

'No,' said Serena. 'No, sadly not.'

Ritz looked at her sharply; but Serena's eyes, meeting hers, were devoid of any expression but steely professional satisfaction.

'So, it's looking good, wouldn't you say?' said Nico Cadogan.

He and Tom were lunching together at the Ritz.

'I would,' said Tom: the shareholders had turned down Egerton's offer by a comfortable majority.

Nico signalled to the waiter to refill Tom's glass. 'And is referral a foregone conclusion now? Or is there still a chance the MMC will nod it through?'

'It's a bit more complex than that. The Office of Fair Trading will now look at it, and if they do say it's okay and there's no real danger of a monopoly, then politicians are not allowed to question that. But we'll continue to lobby hard to have it referred. And I think it will be. We've got a very good case, what with the support from your MP – who's put down a question, incidentally.'

'What does that mean exactly?'

'It means he's put in a request to ask a question. He's waiting now to be given parliamentary time to ask it, by the speaker.'

'And what will he ask, exactly?'

'Oh, something like – does the Secretary of State for Tourism realise the consequences of the proposed merger, blah blah. He'll say he doesn't of course, but it will open the case up, help to air it.'

'Good.'

'Then there's the Early Day Motion, the petition I mentioned to you – she's got at least thirty signatures apparently. And I've got a couple of journalists interested in the story, one of them will be ringing you in a day or two, so it's all looking as good as it could be.'

'Excellent! And if you were a betting man, Fleming, would you put money on this one?'

'Which way?'

'That I'll win. Obviously.'

Tom sighed. 'I've personally nothing left to gamble with. And it's not in my interest to raise your hopes.'

'That's not an answer to my question. Anyway, betting men aren't inhibited by a small matter like a lack of funds. Come on now, off the record. I won't hold it against you.'

'Oh, all right. Off the record.' Tom hesitated, then grinned at him. 'Off the record, I'd put at least half my shirt on it.'

'Good man! That's what I like to hear.'

It was a conversation neither of them ever forgot.

All Octavia's own grief and anxieties left her at the sight of Louise. She looked appalling: ashen pale, with heavy dark rings under her eyes, her hair uncared for, her skin dull. Always slim, today she looked almost macerated, drowning in a big sweater, her jeans hanging on her hips. 'Hi,' she said. 'Hi, Boot,' and gave her a hug; her body felt oddly insubstantial.

'Louise, you look—' She stopped herself. Not helpful to be told you looked terrible. 'You look awfully tired.'

'Yes, I am tired. It's hard. But we have to battle on.' She smiled, but her lips trembled. 'How's things? With Tom?'

'Oh, pretty terrible. We had another huge row the other night, he was flirting with this woman at dinner, and—'

'What woman?' said Louise sharply.

Octavia stared at her. 'A new client of mine, Lauren Bartlett.' She stopped; she felt suddenly and absurdly disloyal. Tom had only agreed to dinner with the Bartletts to help her, and she had done nothing but bitch about it ever since. Then she shook herself, remembering why she had come. 'God, Louise, what does that matter? Compared to what you've had to cope with? Sorry. I'm so sorry. How is your mother?'

'Not good. We're down to days now, the doctor says. It's so frightening. Four weeks, Boot, that's all it's been. Maybe five. Since they diagnosed the liver.' She stopped, tears welling up. 'But she's not in pain. And she knows you're coming. She is confused, though, so don't be hurt if she doesn't seem to know you. Or worry about anything she says.'

Octavia was shocked at the sight of Anna. Shocked and distressed. Her face had grown skull-like, her eyes vacant and dull. The once lovely hair was spread back from her face on the pillow, and when she turned her head, she pushed at it fretfully, with a clawlike hand. The cancerous liver was huge, looked like a five-month foetus, under her nightdress, and her skin and even the whites of her eyes were jaundiced. For one awful moment, Octavia thought she would be sick; then she took a deep breath, smiled, went forward, took Anna's hand. Or what had been her hand; it had changed in texture, in form, become weightless and heavy at the same time, a dead hand already.

'Anna, hallo. It's Octavia.'

The blue eyes struggled to focus, looked puzzled, then, very slowly, she smiled; a strange drawing back of the mouth, a tightening of the skull-like jaw. 'Lovely to see you, darling.'

'It's lovely to see you, Anna.'

There was a long silence. Then Anna said, 'The – children?'

'Very well, Anna. The twins, so naughty and noisy, but such fun. And the baby, Minty, she's lovely. I wish you could see her again.'

'I shan't now, darling.' Again, the awful smile. 'Does she look like you?'

'No, not really. She's just like – just like Tom.'

'Darling Tom. Louise was – talking about him – the other day.'

'She was?' Surely she couldn't have told Anna?

'Yes. Very very fond of him.'

The voice stopped; the eyes closed. Octavia was puzzled by Anna's words. It was hard to imagine Louise sitting by her mother's bed, saying how fond of Tom she was. Especially at the moment. Obviously the drugs. Obviously confusion. A past conversation.

There was a very long silence; Anna appeared to have gone to sleep.

Louise came into the room, very quietly. 'Mummy, we're just going to go and have a bit of lunch. See you later.'

'Back – again, Octavia.' Anna's voice was very slurred.

'Yes, of course,' said Octavia. She stood up, smiled down at the bed. 'I'll come back. Very soon.'

'Oh, Louise. Before you go, darling. Something's been worrying me, I keep forgetting these wretched – wretched – Something I need your help with . . .'

'Of course, Mummy. Excuse me, Octavia, I'll be with you in a minute.'

As she closed the door, she heard Anna say, her voice suddenly clear and lucid, 'Daddy mustn't know about this, he'd be so cross!'

As if Charles would be cross with Anna about anything ever again.

She felt very drained. And she had only been with Anna for ten minutes. What must it be like to see your mother dying, day after day, before your eyes? Suffering, hurting, struggling to be brave. No wonder Louise looked so terrible.

She came into the kitchen now, smiled at Octavia rather weakly. 'We'll go and sit in the garden, shall we?'

'Yes. Where's Dickon?'

'Daddy wanted to take him out,' said Louise, sinking on to the rather mossy wooden seat that had been set in the courtyard outside the back door for as long as anyone could remember. 'I thought it was a good idea. Do them both good.'

'And you? Are you all right?'

'Oh, you know. Yes, I think so.' Her mouth shook as she tried to smile.

'Poor Louise!'

'No, you mustn't say that. I don't deserve it. Poor Daddy, yes. Not poor me. Honestly.'

'What was the problem, then?' said Octavia, trying to lighten the mood just a little. 'That your father was going to be cross about?'

'Oh, poor Mummy. Years and years ago, when we were really tiny, her parents had an old caravan. It's in a field on a farm somewhere and we went there a couple of times. Anyway, when they died, Daddy said she had to sell it and she couldn't bear to. Now she's terrified he'll find out. She wants me to see to it.'

'Poor Anna, as if it mattered.'

'Yes, but she does get very het up about things like that at the moment.'

'Does he know about the caravan?'

'I don't think he does actually, no. Oh – hallo, Janet.'

'You want lunch, Louise? You and Octavia?'

Janet had appeared in the courtyard; to her they would alway be schoolgirls, Octavia thought. And wished fiercely, passionately that they were.

'Well, Octavia would, wouldn't you, Boot? Don't know about me.'

'Now you must eat, Louise,' Janet said. 'You can't get through this without. Even if it all comes up again. How you feeling today?'

'Oh, fine,' said Louise quickly. 'Better.'

'I'll make a salad, then. You want it out here?'

'Oh, no. It's not warm enough. We'll come in. Thank you, Janet.'

Octavia looked at Louise. 'What's the matter? Aren't you well?'

'I'm fine,' said Louise firmly. 'Absolutely fine. Just tired. And stress always makes me sick.'

'Mummy! Mummy, hallo.'

It was Dickon, tugging Charles Madison by the hand. He certainly didn't look traumatised, Octavia thought, but rosy and smiling. Janet and Derek were clearly doing a good job.

'Dickon, darling. Hug! And one for Octavia.'

Dickon hugged her.

Charles Madison came forward, kissed her too. 'It's good of you to come. Anna's been looking forward to it so much.'

'It's the least I could do.'

'Well, not everyone would. And Louise was thrilled. Weren't you, darling?'

'Yes,' said Louise. 'Of course I was.' She smiled rather anxiously at her father; she seemed ill at ease suddenly, Octavia thought. 'You're back early, Daddy. Three o'clock, you said.'

'No, it was you who said that. When you ordered me off.' He twinkled at her.

'Daddy, I didn't order you off!'

'Well, all right. Asked me to take Dickon out. I know, but Dickon wanted to get back. Said he had to work in the garden with Derek. Anyway, aren't I allowed to see your friend? She's one of my favourites, you know.'

Octavia smiled at him, rather uncertainly, puzzled by this exchange. Louise had said her father had wanted to take Dickon out: why the change of story? She supposed the stress of the situation was confusing everybody.

'She told you her news, Octavia?'

'No,' said Octavia, looking at Louise, puzzled. 'What news, Louise?'

'Can I tell her?'

'Oh, Daddy, I'd rather—'

'She's your best friend, isn't she? She'll be so pleased. Louise is pregnant, aren't you, darling? Such lovely news, don't you think, Octavia? A new life in the family. Makes things seem better. Even though she does feel so terrible.'

'Oh, Louise!' Octavia stood up, put her arms round Louise, kissed her. 'I'm so pleased. So very pleased. No wonder you look so terrible!'

'Thanks,' said Louise, slightly fretfully.

'You know what I mean. When's it due?'

'January. About.' She sounded odd; rather flat.

Octavia was puzzled. Then she remembered the innumerable times Louise had said she would never have another baby, after Juliet; never try to replace her, never risk it again. She was frightened, terrified already. It was totally understandable. She wondered what surge of courage had enabled her to go through with it: how Sandy felt about it. All things she couldn't ask.

'Well, I'm thrilled,' she said again. 'So pleased for you. What does your mother think?'

'She hasn't quite taken it in,' said Charles Madison. 'We've tried to tell her, but . . . Well, I still hope she'll understand. Before . . .'

Octavia was surprised. Anna hadn't seemed that confused.

'Lunch,' said Janet, appearing at the doorway.

*

Octavia had gone back into Anna's room to say goodbye: probably for the last time, she knew. She was finding it almost impossibly painful. She looked at the distorted, emaciated face on the pillow, and realised that not only was lovely, blithe Anna gone for ever, but so was all that she associated with her; long golden days, the first real family life she had ever known, childhood, hopefulness, and a source of great wisdom and strength. She thought of Anna welcoming her that first day, with her wide smile, her warm hug, remembered being drawn into the heart of her home, remembered realising how it must be to have a mother. She remembered how Anna had written to her often after that, not as often as to Louise, but still at least two or three times a term, remembered her pride, genuine and almost proprietory, when she had won her scholarship to Oxford, her sweetly tender little speech to Tom when she had first taken him to meet her, telling him what a lucky man he was, remembered the careful serious wisdom she had given her when she had gone to ask her advice over – well, over Minty. Anna had taken a central place in her life for so long; wrong, of course, to compare her loss with that of Louise, but it was still huge, a great fissure of pain.

Somehow she smiled down at Anna, took her hand. 'I have to go now,' she said, fighting back the tears, 'but it was lovely to see you. I'll come again soon.'

'Darling, do. But I won't be here. Of course.'

'Anna—'

'No, darling, I won't. But Louise will need you. She's so very frail. And Charles loves you.'

Clearly they had been wrong. Anna did understand about the baby. She smiled at her. 'It's lovely, isn't it? About the baby?'

'What baby, darling?'

'Louise's. Such lovely news. So brave of her.'

'I wish everyone would stop talking about Louise's baby,' said Anna fretfully. 'There is no baby. There can't be. It's impossible. I'll have to explain to Charles again. Darling, bless you for coming.'

Octavia bent and kissed her; suddenly the face looked neither ugly nor distorted, but sweetly Anna again, the blue eyes searching hers, tender and concerned.

'Look after yourself, my darling. Goodbye, Octavia. God bless.'

'Goodbye, Anna. Goodbye. Thank you for – for everything.'

She turned then, left the room, blinded with tears, and ran down to the kitchen, crying helplessly. She saw Louise looking at her, put out her hand to her, thinking to comfort her, to draw comfort for herself—

She stopped, shocked. The expression on Louise's face was not grief stricken at all, but oddly fierce, almost exultant.

'You must tell Tom about my baby,' was all she said. 'He'll be pleased. I'm sure he will.'

'Yes,' said Octavia trying to smile at Louise through her tears, too distressed to wonder at what she was saying. 'Yes, I'm sure he will too.'

CHAPTER 18

'Now this is nice,' said Ian. 'Lovely proportions, these rooms, aren't they? Right up your street, I imagine, Zoë. And how do you like them cupboards in the alcoves? These fair hands fitted them only yesterday.'

'They're really nice,' said Zoë. 'Yes, it's a – a lovely house.'

It was: a four-storey, perfectly proportioned Georgian terrace house in Cleaver Square, Kennington, but her mother's perfect taste would have been deeply affronted by the fussy wallpapers, marble flooring, fake-coal gas fires. Well, she was hardly likely to see it, Zoë thought, half horrified, half amused. Ian had lit one of the fires and now he sat back on his heels in front of it, turned and grinned up at her.

'Come and sit down, Zoë Flinders, and warm your pretty little toes. I'll fetch us some bubbly in a minute. Plenty here. Now give us a kiss. Relax, Zoë, calm down, for Christ's sake. Safe as – well, safe as houses, we are here.'

Zoë took a deep breath, forced herself to smile at him.

'Good.'

But she didn't feel it; it was more dangerous here, she knew it was . . .

'Boot? It's me.' Her voice sounded raw; raw and weak at the same time.

'Yes?' said Octavia. 'What is it?' But she knew.

'She's gone. Mummy's gone . . .'

'Oh, Louise, darling Louise, I'm so sorry.'

'I'm not,' said the voice, stronger now, fierce, angry. 'I'm glad. Glad it's over. It was so horrible for her.'

'Was she – was it . . .'

'Peaceful? Yes, in the end. Very peaceful. Only Daddy was with her. He was just there, loving her, holding her hand. He said – oh, Boot, he said he watched her go, just drift away from him, he said he could see her leave him, and all he wanted was to go with her, follow her. Poor Daddy. Poor poor Daddy, he loved her so.'

'How is he now?'

'Fine. In that odd state, you know? Quite calm, almost cheerful. Shock, I suppose. And relief of course.'

'Would you like me to come down? Come and see you?'

'No, honestly, I don't think so. I'll let you know about the funeral as soon as I can. You will come, won't you?'

'Yes, of course I'll come.' Octavia felt shocked that Louise should even doubt it, however briefly.

'Good. I'll be better if you're there. I'll ring you when I know. Thank you for being there.'

'I'm always here for you. You know that.'

'Yes, Octavia, I do.'

It was a long, sad, difficult day. Even Minty seemed subdued. After lunch, Tom took the twins cycling and Octavia tried to read the papers. They got back at five and Tom said he had to go to the office.

'The office. On a Sunday?' she said.

'Yes, the office. Aubrey and I have a crisis meeting. There could be a lot of those over the next few weeks.'

'Oh, dear,' said Octavia, icily polite.

Early in the evening, Louise phoned again. 'Wednesday, the funeral, Octavia. At twelve. In the village church.'

'Fine,' said Octavia. 'I'll be there.'

There was a silence, then Louise said, 'I know this must sound odd, but – well, could you ask Tom to come too? Mummy was very fond of him, and I do so want everyone to be there for her. And Daddy likes Tom, said he hoped he'd come with you. So – just for me. For all of us. If you could bear it.'

'I could bear it,' said Octavia, while thinking it was very odd, when Tom and Louise had so spiky a relationship. 'Of course I could. For you. Yes, I'll ask him.' The idea horrified her; she wasn't sure why.

'Thank you. Thank you very much. And, Octavia: when you come to the funeral, don't say anything about the baby to Sandy, will you? He's a bit funny about it, very unsure that it's a good idea. He'll come round, but at the moment it's best left. I've told Daddy to keep quiet, too.'

'I won't,' said Octavia.

Tom came back soon after ten, looking exhausted.

Octavia was reading. 'Tom,' she said, 'a couple of things.'

He sat down, started loosening his tie. 'Not a heavy number, Octavia, please. I'm exhausted. I've spent the evening trying to work out how to save Fleming Cotterill. You just might like to know that. What your little principled stand has done for us.'

'Really? Well, I'm sure you will. Save it, I mean.'

'I envy you your confidence. Which is, of course, based on a serious lack of knowledge. Octavia—'

'Tom, please. Not now.'

He sighed. 'All right.'

'Look, Anna Madison's funeral is on Wednesday. God knows why, but Louise is very keen that you should go.'

There was a fraction of silence, then he said, 'I can't. I've got meetings all day.'

'Well, of course you must go to them,' she said, anger swiping through her. 'The funeral of an old friend is neither here nor there, is it, compared to a meeting?'

'Octavia, Anna wasn't my friend. You know that.'

'She was very fond of you. She was saying how much she liked you when I last saw her. And how much Louise liked you. Which did surprise me, considering you're scarcely even polite to her, most of the time.'

'Yes, well. She's your friend – they all are.'

She felt angry suddenly, freshly, fiercely angry. 'Tom, I really do think you should consider coming. These are people grieving horribly. Louise has only just recovered from the death of her baby, and, Tom, she's pregnant. She asked me to tell you, God knows why, seemed to want you to know, but anyway, I think it's very brave of her. She's obviously feeling appalling. So I really do think—'

'Pregnant?' he said, and his voice sounded odd, strained. 'Louise is pregnant? Are you sure?'

'Of course I'm sure. She told me, her father told me, she's being sick every five minutes. Why shouldn't I be sure?'

'Sorry,' he said, and his voice sounded rather quiet, almost shaky. Upset, then. Good. 'Of course you must be right. I was surprised, that's all.' There was a silence, then he said, 'Maybe you're right. I will try and come. I'm – I'm going to bed now. Good night.'

'Good night, Tom,' she said.

His footsteps as he walked across the room were heavy and very slow; as he reached the door, he turned and looked at her and his face was extraordinarily drawn and seemed to have new, deep lines etched into it.

A thud of fresh fear went through her. Maybe Fleming Cotterill really were in trouble. Guilt, briefly, joined the fear; she crushed it. If losing one client could ruin them, then they could hardly have been on a very sound basis in the first place. She would not and could not be blamed for any of it. It wasn't fair.

Tom went into Aubrey's office.

'We have an angel, or a possible one. Name of Terence Foster. Funny sort of name for an angel, but there you go. Meeting on Thursday morning, eight thirty. That okay with you? I took a flyer, said yes.'

'Fine,' said Aubrey. 'Absolutely fine. Well, let's hope we like each other.'

'We'll need to,' said Tom heavily. 'He'll want a third share in the company.'

'A third! That's tough.'

'We might be able to talk him down. Anyway, not much we can do about it, but at least we'll be out of our misery by then. One way or another. Right, I must get off to the Savoy. Got a lunch with Cadogan.'

'That's working out well, isn't it?'

'Seems to be,' said Tom. 'Cheers, Aubrey.'

It amazed him how cheerful and normal he managed to appear. Given everything he was having to cope with.

'Louise, it's Octavia. How are you?'

'Oh, not too bad. A bit tired.'

'You must be. Poor you, all that sickness misery as well. You're very brave. Anyway, just to let you know that Tom will be coming on Wednesday.'

'Oh, Boot, I'm so pleased. I know it will be harder for you, but I do appreciate it. Please tell him.'

She'll be sending him her love in a minute, thought Octavia, half irritable, half amused. 'Yes, of course.'

'Any – developments on that one?' Louise's voice was cautious, careful. 'I didn't ask before. Sorry.'

'Well – a few. We've had it out. Had the conversation.'

'And?'

'I can't talk now. I'm at work. But it's over. I want out. Or rather, I want him out.'

'When – when was this conversation?'

'Louise, what does that matter? Wednesday, I think. Yes, the Wednesday before I came down to you.'

'And he's agreed?'

'He won't have any choice.'

'You've made it really plain?'

'Yes, of course I have. What is this?'

'Oh, nothing. I thought you weren't sure. About divorce.'

'Oh, I'm sure now. Very sure indeed.'

There was a silence, then, 'Good for you. I do admire you, Boot. Being so strong.'

'Well, I've hardly started yet. The worst thing will be telling Daddy. It will be horrendous. I absolutely dread it. The longer I can postpone it, the better. He'll crucify Tom.'

'Really?'

'Oh, yes. Really. Even feeling how I do about Tom, I fear for him. And I fear for the company as well. Daddy will set out to destroy him in every way he can, and that won't do me any good. I have to present it all quite carefully. Work out a way of telling him.'

'He wouldn't like to come on Wednesday, would he?' said Louise. She sounded wistful. 'I like your dad. Daddy does, too, and I remember Mummy saying how attractive he was.'

'Really? Are you sure you want him? He's hardly a close friend.'

'Yes,' said Louise slowly, 'quite sure. Will you ask him for me, Boot?'

'Of course,' said Octavia.

'And if he wants to bring Marianne, then that would be lovely too. She wrote me the sweetest note when Juliet died.'

Octavia felt rather bemused. Louise seemed to be treating her mother's funeral like a cocktail party.

'Romilly,' said Clementine Wilson, head of the music department at Queen Anne's, 'Romilly, I really cannot believe you've practised this piece at all since last Thursday.'

Romilly felt like bursting into tears. Her head ached, the period that her spot had heralded had still not arrived, she felt bloated and almost fat, and she was in a state of huge agitation about her father's arrival the following day and the effect of it upon her modelling future. Her mother had warned her he was very opposed to the whole thing.

'Well?' said Clementine Wilson.

'I haven't practised very much. No.'

'Well, Romilly, I can only say I am tempted to withdraw you from the concert and ask Primrose to play instead. Very tempted.'

Had her father not been coming over especially for the concert and his approval so crucial, Romilly would have said that was fine; under the circumstances she burst into tears.

'I'm sorry,' she said, 'very sorry, Miss Wilson. I haven't been very well.'

'Well, we'll do the full rehearsal this afternoon and then I shall make my decision in the morning, after I have heard you again.'

Romilly went down to school lunch, found Fenella.

'Hi, Rom. You look cheerful.'

'I feel cheerful.'

'I thought your life was, like, utterly wonderful.'

'It was. For five minutes. Now my mother is dead set against me doing anything that is remotely worthwhile, and Miss Wilson is threatening to replace me in the concert tomorrow. And my dad is coming over from New York especially to hear me. And he's against the modelling too. Fen, does my stomach stick out?'

Fenella studied it. 'Well, maybe compared to a board. Just a bit. Today. I didn't notice it on Saturday.'

'Oh, God,' said Romilly. 'It's my period, it's late, I'll just get fatter and fatter till it arrives. And I may have to go back to the agency on Wednesday. And then this spot. They'll cancel the contract. Fen, what'll I do?'

'Nothing,' said Fenella soothingly. 'You're often late, it'll come. Go for a run tonight. That sometimes helps.'

'Yes, I will. And I won't eat anything till it does,' said Romilly.

'Rom, don't be silly. You have to eat. They'll all start thinking you're anorexic if you're not careful and then they'll never let you do it.'

'No, you're right. Well, I won't have any lunch at least. That should help a bit. And – hey, I know what I can do. I could take some kind of laxative, couldn't I? That'd help. I remember Zoë doing that once, when she was going to a party, said it would make her stomach go flat.'

'Romilly, I really don't think this is a good idea,' said Fenella nervously. 'You'll make yourself ill, and compared to most of us your stomach is concave.'

'No, it isn't. And it's only till after Wednesday. I think it's a really good idea. I'll get something in Boots on my way home.'

Fenella looked at her friend anxiously; this was exactly what everyone said happened to models. Only it was happening to Romilly with horrible speed. She sighed. 'At least eat something. An apple, or—'

'Yes, all right,' said Romilly, reaching for the smallest apple in the bowl. 'But I don't want any more fussing, Fen. You're supposed to be my friend.'

'I know,' said Fenella with a sigh.

In New York, one of Alec Muirhead's major clients had just phoned him to say that he wanted to press ahead with a deal he had not expected to go through for at least another two months. This would clearly necessitate several days of intense activity, and probably a flight down to Texas where his head office was. He was a very major client indeed; his fee alone covered a third of Muirhead Templeman's overheads for the year. Alec Muirhead looked at the week ahead and saw that however much disappointment it might cause, there was no way he could take four days out and fly to London. After the briefest hesitation, he lifted the phone to tell Marianne to break the news to Romilly.

The packet of laxatives said to take one or two tablets on retiring; Romilly, her stomach more bloated still, after having a large bowl of spaghetti bolognese practically forced into her by Marianne, took four. She woke at five with appalling cramps and spent the next hour in the lavatory; but as she showered and dressed, having gone through her solo once more, feeling rather shaky, she noticed with great satisfaction that her stomach had become almost concave once more.

'Romilly darling, I want to talk to you about something. And do eat something, you look very pale.'

'I'm fine,' said Romilly, 'just a bit nervous.'

'Well, at least drink some nice sweet tea. Look, this is very bad news for you, I know, but—'

'They don't want me,' said Romilly. Her eyes filled with tears. All that agony for nothing.

'What? Who don't want you?'

'The Americans.'

'Darling, it has nothing to do with the Americans. It's about today. The concert. Daddy's desperately sorry, but he has some huge deal going through and can't come over today. He sends lots of love and—'

'Oh,' said Romilly. 'That's okay. It's only a crummy school concert.'

'Darling, that's not what you said when you were told you could play your solo. Anyway, it's very sweet and grown up of you to be so brave about it. Now, go and get your things and I'll drive you in. Stars shouldn't have to travel on the Tube.'

When Romilly got to school, she played her solo to Miss Wilson, who said she had certainly improved considerably and that she could play in the concert as arranged. Right in the middle of telling Fenella this, and that her father was unable to come to the concert, or indeed come to London at all, Romilly felt a familiar dull ache in her stomach and back; her recalcitrant period had finally arrived. Glancing at her face in the cloakroom mirror, she noticed that the spot had virtually disappeared. The pain in her stomach, increasing in intensity by the moment, felt almost pleasurable. She would know what to do next time; it had been really really easy.

'Sandy! What do you think?'

Sandy looked up, surprised at the tone in Louise's voice. For the first time for weeks, she sounded upbeat, cheerful, her real self.

'This one?' she said, putting a large black straw hat on her head. 'Or maybe—' removing it, replacing it with a silk turban – 'this?'

'Well,' he said carefully, 'they're both very nice. I don't know. Does it really matter?'

'Of course it matters! This is Mummy's last party. Everything's got to be right for her.'

'Louise,' said Sandy, 'you're talking about your mother's funeral. Not a party. She – well, she won't . . .'

'Won't what, Sandy? She won't what?'

'Won't be there,' he said, very quietly, afraid of saying it, afraid not to.

Louise walked forward, right up to him, stared up at his face; her own, under the black silk turban, was very white, very set. She raised her hand and struck him hard, across the face.

'Don't!' she said. 'How dare you say such a thing? Of course she'll be there. She'll *know*. She'll want it to be right.'

And then she stared up at him, horror in her eyes, and burst into tears and said, 'God, I'm sorry, Sandy. So, so sorry. I'm just so tired. Tired of trying to be brave, to be positive. Please forgive me.'

She put her arms round him; he could feel her thin body straining, pressing against his, felt almost repulsion for her. Then he hauled himself together, put his arms obediently round her.

'I forgive you,' he said, 'of course I do. I know how upset you are, how awful this all is for you. I understand.'

'I know she won't be there,' she said, leaning against him, her voice thick with tears. 'I know that, that's why it's so awful. That's why I'm trying to concentrate on other things. Like the flowers, and the food, and – and my hat. And who's coming. Anything except her not being there; or rather her being there, in her coffin. And then going into the ground. You know why she wants that, don't you, wants to be buried, not cremated?'

'No,' he said, because he knew she wanted to tell him.

'So she can go back into the earth, still be here, part of things. She said she'd really like to be buried in the orchard, where we all had such lovely times. Become part of the trees. But she said that would upset Daddy, and I think it would. So—' She seemed about to tell him something else, but stopped. 'So anyway, that's why.'

'Yes,' he said, 'I'd feel like that.'

'Would you?' She stared up at him, genuine astonishment in her face. 'Would you really? I'd have thought you'd be all for the neat and tidy way.'

'Yes,' he said just slightly coolly. 'Well, perhaps you don't know me quite as well as you think you do, Louise. I'm always telling you that.

Now, have you decided about Dickon? Whether he should be there, in the church?'

'He should be there,' said Louise. 'Not at the burial, but at the funeral, at the church. That's what I've decided. I don't think children should be shielded from death. I think they should see it as part of life. It always used to be that way. She was his granny, he adored her. He wants to come, he told me so.'

'He might have told you that. He hardly knows what it means. What he's in for.'

'He's not in for anything, Sandy. It'll be lovely, all the flowers, all the friends, the hymns. He'd think something strange and horrible was going on if he couldn't come. Surely you can see that.'

'Well . . .'

'And I know Mummy would have wanted him there. So you're outnumbered.' She managed a smile, touched his face gently, where she had struck him. 'I'm so sorry, sorry I hit you. Forgive me?'

'Of course I do.'

'Thank you. Now, I think I'll take both hats, and decide at the last minute,' said Louise, moving out of his arms, going over to the door. 'Will you be ready by teatime, Sandy? I do want to get over there for supper. Daddy's going to have trouble getting through this evening.'

'Yes, Louise,' said Sandy with a sigh, 'I'll be ready by teatime.'

God, he'd be glad when this was over. At least she was looking better. Less – well, less how she looked when she was pregnant. Which of course she wasn't. Of course she couldn't be. It had obviously been the strain of looking after her mother that had made her so ill. Obviously.

CHAPTER 19

Marianne was lying in the bath; she felt low. Romilly's concert had gone well, she had played beautifully, got a lot of applause. A vast bouquet of flowers had been delivered from her father: the four of them had all gone out to dinner, but when they had got home, she had flown to check the answering machine, come back looking faintly sulky, kissed her mother briefly, said thank you for a nice evening, and gone up to her room. A month ago, she would have been starry with pleasure and excitement, talking the evening over again and again, giggling, refusing to go to bed; Marianne would not have believed so great and so swift a change possible. It hurt: it hurt a lot. For the hundredth time she cursed her weakness in not stopping the whole wretched modelling thing before it had begun: for not listening to Zoë. She was worried about Zoë too, she seemed so secretive and moody. And now she had to drive almost a hundred miles to go to the funeral of a woman she had hardly known, in order to please Felix's daughter. It was extremely hard.

The phone rang in her bedroom; she ignored it. The answering machine would pick it up.

'Mum!' Zoë appeared in the doorway, with an irritatingly knowing expression on her face, 'Mum, it's your boyfriend.'

'Zoë, you mustn't call Felix my boyfriend, you know it annoys him,' said Marianne, struggling to sit up, covering her breasts with her arms, thinking, half amused, that it was almost impossible to express disapproval of your grown-up daughter with your nipples showing.

'It's not Felix. It's someone called Nico Cadogan. *Very* dark brown voice. You want to ring him back or not?'

'Yes. Yes, I'll ring him back,' said Marianne, trying to sound calm and unflustered. 'But he's not my boyfriend!'

'Okay, okay. The one you had the hots for the other day. I'll tell him you'll call back. Oh, and Felix is here.'

'Here! But it's only just after nine.'

'I know. He's in the drawing room, reading the papers. Hey, talking of the papers, did you know Versace had been murdered? Hideous, or what?'

'No, how dreadful,' said Marianne. 'I had no idea.'

'Well, now you do. Anyway, Felix said to tell you he didn't want to be late.'

He didn't want to be late, because it would upset Octavia, thought Marianne savagely, and then stopped herself. What an unpleasant thing to think; of course he didn't want to be late, it was a funeral, for heaven's sake.

'Tell him I'll be ten minutes. And yes, tell Mr Cadogan I'll ring him back.'

Nico was clearly amused by Zoë. 'She said you were in the bath. I'd like to see you in the bath. I will one day, quite soon, I imagine.'

'Nico, I wish you wouldn't talk like that. Of course you're not going to see me in the bath. It's ridiculous.'

'Well, we shall see. Now then, I thought you might like to have dinner with me tonight.'

'Nico, I can't possibly. Felix and I are going to a funeral.'

'I'm sorry. Whose?'

'The mother of an old friend of Octavia's.'

'Ah. Was she very close to you?'

'I only met her once,' said Marianne. That was a mistake.

'And you're going to her funeral? Why? Was Felix a great friend of hers also? Or is this a further example of your being dragged into his love affair with his daughter?'

'Felix was a great friend. So of course I must go.'

'I see. Well, I hope it's not too sad for you. I shall be thinking of you. Where is it?'

'In Gloucestershire.'

'And are you going with Octavia and Tom?'

'No. Octavia said it would be better if we were all independent. Tom has a meeting later today and—'

'Tom and his meetings. I was just talking to him, as a matter of fact.'

'What news of the takeover?' said Marianne.

'None whatsoever. Well, should you get back early, give me a ring. Otherwise tomorrow evening perhaps?'

'Nico, no, I can't.'

'Of course you can. You needn't think I'm giving up on this campaign. I'll ring you again tomorrow morning. I might even get some more intimate details about you from your daughter. Goodbye, Marianne.'

She was still smiling, slightly foolishly, as she sat down in front of the mirror to put on her make-up. She felt better. Romilly would settle down again: of course she would. And Felix . . . they had these ups and downs from time to time. They had always managed to settled peacefully down again. There was no reason to think this one was any different.

Octavia stood in the small village church, her eyes fixed on Anna's coffin, with its heap of white roses and lilies, and willed herself not to cry. If Louise could be brave – and she was being hideously brave, had come over to her and Tom in the church, and kissed them both, thanked them for coming, smiling almost radiantly at them – so could she.

Charles Madison stood beside Louise, ramrod straight, his eyes fixed directly ahead of him, and little Dickon, smiling rather tremulously across at her now, was between Louise and Sandy. A strange decision to have him here, in the church, when he had been so upset about his little sister's death. Probably Sandy thought he ought to learn to cope with such things. A bit of army discipline. He was ramrod straight too, equally stiff lipped; how alike they were, Sandy and Charles, in some ways, and how alike Anna and Louise. The two Madison brothers, Benjy and Giles, and their pretty, Sloaney wives were in the pew behind and the small church was very full.

They had already sung one hymn; the vicar had read the lesson, the inevitable 23rd Psalm, then he said, 'And now Louise will read from St Paul's Letter to the Corinthians.'

Octavia was stunned; here was Louise, wrung with grief, unable to speak on the phone the evening before for tears, standing up, perfectly composed, looking beautiful, in a black silk long-sleeved dress, her fair hair a halo under her black straw hat, smiling round the church at them all before beginning to read. Her voice was steady and musically clear, with the slight huskiness that made it so recognisable. Irrelevantly, Octavia remembered Louise saying with a laugh that she could never make an anonymous phone call to any man she knew because her voice was so recognisable.

She had mixed the texts of the King James's Version and the New English Bible to great effect, her voice ebbing and flowing with the music of the phrasing: 'Though I speak with the tongues of men and of angels – now we see through a glass, darkly . . .' Octavia felt at that moment she knew exactly where it was, her heart, or at any rate, the notional heart that was the centre of her feelings, so deeply and heavily did it hurt. And when Louise finished, when she reached the lovely end,

'And now abideth faith, hope, and love—' there was a long pause – 'but the greatest of these is love.'

For a long, long moment Louise stood there, in the sunlit silence of the church. Octavia looked at Tom, and saw that he too was deeply moved, was looking down at his hands, plaiting his fingers together, and just for a moment she forgot everything – his betrayal of her, her hatred of him – and felt only that she still loved and needed him and then the moment finally ended, and Louise stepped down from the lectern. The organ started again and a small boy's voice sang out from the shadows of the choir stalls with 'God Be in my Head', and then there were prayers, and then it was over, and they were carrying the coffin out of the church again. Octavia looked at it, and thought, all that was happiest of my childhood is there, in there, with Anna, and then thought that was disloyal to her father and looked up at him, smiling, fleetingly anxious lest he should have read her mind. His own face was sombre, heavy, but softened as he looked at her; and Marianne looked thoughtfully, sweetly sad, her green eyes smudged with tears. They could hardly be for Anna, Octavia thought, she had hardly known her; but then funerals did that, revived other sadnesses, prompted tears for other pain. As this had done for her; it had not been only for Anna she had wept, as the coffin was carried in.

Outside the church Louise was moving from group to group, being kissed, having her hand shaken, patted, held, still strangely calm, and when she reached the four of them, she kissed each in turn, and thanked them again for coming.

'Come back to the house, won't you? We shall be a little while, the – the burial is over there, in the graveyard, private this time, by Daddy's request. But we'll see you afterwards.'

'She's wonderfully composed,' said Marianne. 'I'm surprised, I'd have imagined her to be distraught.'

'Adrenalin,' said Felix Miller fiercely. 'Gets you through most things.' Thirty-three years after his wife's death, he still found funerals very painful.

'Come along,' said Marianne, slipping her arm through his. 'Let's get the car and make our way to the house. Oh, dear, look at that poor little boy, he looks so lost. I wouldn't have brought him if he was – Octavia, are you all right?'

'Yes. Yes, thank you,' said Octavia trying to smile, but she couldn't, tears suddenly engulfed her, and she started crying, quite hard. 'Sorry. So sorry.'

'Why don't you come with us?' said Felix, putting his arm round her.

'Our car is just over there and I don't see yours. Tom can collect it and join us later.'

Grateful not to have to be with Tom while she was so upset, afraid of what raw emotion would do to the gulf between them, Octavia nodded silently, and allowed Marianne to take her arm, and lead her away. As they walked to the car, her father took her other hand; she looked up at him and managed to smile, trustingly.

'This was a good idea,' she said, and pulled off her hat and rested her head briefly on his arm.

Tom was not the only person watching them to think how childlike she looked at that moment.

Over at the house, contemplating the odd quasi-cocktail party mood of the funeral reception, accentuated by the absence of the chief mourners, and sipping gratefully at a glass of champagne, Octavia suddenly saw Dickon wandering out into the garden, all alone. He had been with Janet, but she was busy, rushing round with trays of canapés, her eyes red.

'Dickon,' she said, going out through the french windows, 'Dickon, darling, are you all right?'

He looked at her and nodded, but his mouth was quivering.

Octavia bent down and put her arms round him. 'Come here. You feeling sad about Granny?'

He nodded. 'Mummy said I shouldn't. Mummy said it was wrong to be sad, that Granny was better and with Juliet. Is she?'

'Oh, most definitely,' said Octavia. 'In heaven with Juliet, playing with her, I expect. But of course you feel sad, you're going to miss Granny. I feel sad, too. No one can help that. Your mummy is very sad, I know, and—'

'If she had another baby, would that one die too?' said Dickon suddenly.

Octavia stared at him, feeling rather sick. 'No, of course not,' she said finally.

'Are you sure?' His little face was working, his dark eyes, Sandy's eyes, fixed on hers.

'Well, yes,' she said, sending a prayer up to the God she didn't believe in. 'It was just a terrible accident, what happened to Juliet, it wouldn't happen again.'

'I think it might,' he said, and she could feel him trembling. 'People keep dying in this family. And she might have another baby, you see, and that one might die. I'm frightened now . . .' And he started to cry.

Octavia couldn't see anyone who might be able to comfort him. The family were all still at the graveyard. Louise, his father, his grandfather even, all missing. She stood up suddenly, took his hand and smiled. 'Dickon, darling, let's go for a walk, shall we? Down to the little bridge. We could play pooh sticks for bit. Just till Mummy and Daddy get back.'

'Where's Octavia?' said Felix distractedly. 'She was so upset, I do hope she hasn't gone off on her own somewhere.'

'Felix, if she has, I'm sure it's because she wants to,' said Marianne briskly. 'She's not a—' She stopped herself just in time. God, how often did she say that to Felix? That Octavia was not a child. This was not the moment for it. She took a deep breath.

'She's probably gone to the loo. Shall I try and find her for you?'

'Yes. Yes, if you wouldn't mind. I'm still worried about that hysteria the other day. It's not like her. I'm sure there's something wrong.'

Octavia wasn't in any of the loos. She glanced down from the landing window on to the garden; there were several people out there now, but no sign of Octavia. Well, it was probably easier to go on looking for her than return to Felix without her. She ran downstairs and out of the front door before Felix could see her and walked quickly down the drive.

Charles Madison and his sons and one of the wives were walking down the drive, and a car, driven by Sandy, was inching its way behind them. There was no sign of Louise. In that case, she probably was with Octavia; they would be talking together, remembering the old days. That was good, then; that would comfort them both. She could go back and report to Felix that was what was happening. Or maybe she should try and warn Octavia anyway. They couldn't be far away.

Marianne suddenly decided she needed a cigarette rather badly. Felix had no idea that she smoked, albeit occasionally; no one did, certainly not her children. She'd sit in the car for a minute, with all the windows and doors open, and indulge herself. She walked down to where it was parked, about a hundred yards from the house, settled herself in the driving seat and rummaged in her bag. She kept her cigarettes in a rigid tampon container, and she smiled at herself as she pulled one out; really she was just like a naughty girl at boarding school.

She lit one with the car lighter, and then decided she really couldn't risk smoking in the car, Felix's nose was extremely sensitive. She got out and walked down to a gateway leading across a small field. It was actually a short cut, she realised, to the churchyard; she could see a few of the graves. They must have walked back that way.

And then she saw Louise. She was unmistakable, even at the hundred yards' distance, with her shining fair hair, the hat removed now, and the black silk dress. Only she wasn't with Octavia. She was with Tom. And he was holding her at arm's length. And she was hitting him, with both her fists; and across the field, in the still air, Marianne could hear their voices, although not what they were saying, and then a louder sound, Louise crying hysterically, and then she saw Tom push her almost roughly away and set out across the field.

Marianne stamped out her cigarette and walked, very quickly, back to the house.

Lucilla Sanderson settled herself into the wicker chair – her wicker chair, as she called it, although several of the other residents of Bartles House didn't regard it in quite the same way – with a sigh of pleasure. This was the best bit of the day, especially in the summer; midday, when the aches and pains of the early morning were easing, when she had had her coffee and biscuits and a good read of the paper, listened to the wireless for a bit, and then made her way from her room – slowly, on her sticks. That was part of the pleasure, really, pausing to chat to people in the corridor and the big lobby at the bottom of the stairs, popping her head in briefly to the large sitting room where the poor old things who were really well past everything were settled in front of the television, nodding off already as Richard and Judy – well, it was only Richard at the moment, Judy was in hospital having some operation or other – as Richard interviewed yet another celebrity, and that strange Savage creature talked about its frocks. Lucilla didn't approve of watching TV before six in the evening; the day was for the radio and for reading and writing letters. It was the great divide between the people like her, still completely in command of their faculties, and the poor, other ones: going into the television room, or rather being put into the television room, in the morning. One of the many wonderful things about Bartles House was that it was big enough to allow for a variation in lifestyle.

Lucilla, who had grown up in a large Queen Anne house in Wiltshire and had a very real eye for architectural virtue, had been enchanted by Bartles from the first moment she had seen it. Of course it was quite ugly outside, with its ridiculous turrets and mullioned windows, but it had charm and personality, and the interiors were really very nice; the high ceilings, the stone fireplaces, the wooden panelling, and the cornices, although plain, were rather fine. She wouldn't even have considered moving into a residential home if it had been one of those dreadful modern places, or even the thirties Tudor that seemed so popular in nursing-home culture. But somehow Bartles House had felt it could – just – be home. And the grounds were so very lovely; the gardens, neglected, of course, the small sloping meadow leading down to the wood, that charming little wood, were enchanting. Occasionally, when she was feeling very fit and strong, her daughter would walk her to the edge of the wood and they would stand looking in at its dusky, leafy heart. She had several times seen woodpeckers flying out, so rare these days; and there were jays and thrushes, and in the summer, she often lay awake at night, soothed by the sweet throbbing song of the nightingales.

She settled herself in her wicker chair, picked up the *Telegraph* to do the crossword, and allowed herself five minutes first, just to close her eyes. It was a lovely day and the sun felt warm on her face; the air was rich with birdsong, and the sunlight danced on the tips of the trees in Bartles Wood and across the little valley; she could hear the rather overgrown lambs bleating, bothering their mothers still, as adolescent children did . . .

Lucilla snapped her eyes open with an effort; she would be nodding off if she wasn't careful. She reached for her pen and glanced at her watch – nearly sherry time, only half an hour to go, good – and before she started on the crossword, drank in the view in all its lovely, graceful, mellow summer best. How lucky she was: how privileged, what a truly lovely place to end her days. They all thought so, she and her fellow travellers, as they called themselves, often said that if they had to move, leave Bartles, they would simply lie down in the drive and let the removal vans drive over them. Not that it was in the least likely to happen.

There had been this nonsense in the papers, but both Mr and Mrs Ford had assured them that they were simply silly rumours and there was absolutely no way they would ever dream of selling Bartles. 'This is our home, as it is yours. Don't worry about it.'

They didn't.

In his small neat square pen of an office at the Planning Inspectorate in Tollgate House, Bristol, John Whitlam was making out a report on his visit to Bartles House, Bartles Park, Near Felthamstone, Avon. He had found the place, he said into his dictaphone, in very bad repair; the house particularly, cold and draughty, in need of renovation, was obviously expensive to heat and generally unsuited to its purpose. Staff had to travel considerable distances, as did the relatives of the inmates to visit. The inmates would be far better in every way – as indeed Mr and Mrs Ford had stressed – housed in a modern, purpose-built establishment such as they had already earmarked on the other side of Bath. The house had no architectural merit and it would be no loss to anyone if it was pulled down.

There were no preservation orders on any of the trees in the grounds except for one, behind the house, which could remain, given a small adaptation to the plans.

It was hard to see on what grounds the local council had turned down the first planning application; the proposed development was well conceived and visually pleasing and in keeping with the best of the local architecture in Bath and Bristol. And of course there was also the added benefit of the community centre with its facilities for the disabled.

Finally, the construction of the development would bring much needed employment to the area.

His conclusion was, John Whitlam said, that planning permission should be granted to Carlton Construction without very much more delay.

Well, the funeral was over; the very worst was over. Or maybe it wasn't. Sandy took a glass of champagne from the tray, drained it and picked up another. It had been after Juliet's funeral that Louise had really fallen apart. That might happen again. Although she had seemed much better yesterday; and she had read beautifully in the church today, and had wept easy, natural tears at the graveside. Her reactions had seemed much more normal than – well, than then. And when she had said she wanted to stay on her own for a moment, after the burial, with her mother, she had sounded quite calm. Not the hysterical, taut creature he was so afraid of.

'Please, Sandy,' she had said, managing to smile at him, holding one of the white roses loosely in her hand, tears standing in her eyes, 'I want to say goodbye. By myself. Please. You go and look after Dickon. All right? Take the car, I'll walk across the field.'

'All right,' he had said, and indeed he did want to get back to Dickon, he was worried about him, and then Rosemary, Giles Madison's wife, said she wouldn't mind a lift back, so he drove her, and then went to find Dickon. Only Dickon was not to be found.

Worried, he ran upstairs and checked the little room that was his in the house, then Anna's room, even the loft room where Charles had set up a railway layout for him. He asked Janet, who said she'd last seen him in the garden, and then a few other people, and then finally Derek said he'd gone off with Octavia, down towards the stream.

That was all right, then; Dickon adored Octavia. He'd be all right with her. Sandy liked Octavia; she was a bit tense, not entirely comfortable to be with, but she was very attractive and interesting to talk to. He admired her drive, the success she had made of her life. And she had always been such a good friend to Louise. Well, they were good to each other – very loyal. Rather like an army friendship; you went through hell together and nothing could break that bond. Sandy had a brief chat with a few people, most of them complete strangers, and then saw Octavia and Dickon coming back across the lawn. Dickon was holding Octavia's hand, and waved at him happily.

'Daddy, we've been playing pooh sticks!'

'How very nice,' said Sandy, smiling at him. 'And did you thank Octavia for looking after you?'

'No. Thank you, Octavia.' His hand stole into Sandy's. 'Where were you?'

'Finding the car. Driving Auntie Rosemary back.'

'Where's Mummy?'

'She's just coming. Won't be long.'

'Is she all right?'

'Yes. Yes, she's fine.'

'Sandy,' said Octavia, in a low voice. 'Sandy, I wonder if I could have a word?'

'What? Yes, of course. Now?'

'If possible, but—' Her eyes gestured downwards towards Dickon.

'Oh – right. Dickon, old chap, like to go and find Janet? She said she'd like some help putting things on plates. Think you could do that?'

''Course I could. Come and tell me when Mummy gets back?'

'Yes, I will.' He went off.

Octavia looked up at Sandy. She was clearly embarrassed. 'Sandy – oh, dear, this is awfully difficult. I know it's nothing to do with me, and you probably don't want to talk about it, but I've been talking to Dickon. He's very – well, worried. He was saying people in the family kept dying. And that Louise had told him that his granny was better now, and she was with Juliet. I didn't want to say this to Louise today of all days, because it's *such* dangerous ground, so I thought I could tell you.'

'Yes . . .' said Sandy awkwardly.

'I know she thought it would comfort him, but it's sort of misfired. He sees everyone he loves dying, leaving him. He really is terribly upset. And terrified it's going to happen again. You know?'

'Happen again? What do you mean, happen again?'

'Well.' She hesitated. 'He said to me, if Louise had another baby, would that one die too? And go to be with Juliet. It was so awful. Seeing how frightened he was.'

'Oh, dear,' said Sandy, 'poor little chap. Octavia, thank you for telling me. I'll have a chat with him. See if I can reassure him. I think in time he should calm down about it. It's not as if there are going to be any more babies. Pity in a way, but under the circumstances, for him—' He stopped. Octavia was looking at him rather oddly. 'Anything wrong?'

'Well, Louise might change her mind. She might decide she did want another baby.'

'Er, yes,' said Sandy. God, he could have done without this conversation. 'But it just isn't going to happen. That's the thing.'

'But, Sandy—'

'Octavia, I really must be getting back to the guests. Sorry.'

'But I thought – well, I wondered . . .'

'I know why you were worried, Octavia. The sickness and so on. But honestly, it was just nerves. I do assure you, there's no possible chance Louise can have another baby.'

'Why?' said Octavia. Her voice was very low. 'Why is that, Sandy?'

'Because after Juliet she made me have a vasectomy. She said nothing else would make her feel safe.'

Octavia stood staring up at him; she was very pale, he noticed, suddenly. Very pale and she looked almost – what? Frightened.

'She hadn't told me that,' was all she said.

CHAPTER 20

'What on earth are you doing in here?'

Marianne jumped; Felix was standing in the doorway, glaring at her.

'Sorry,' she said, and then, struggling to sound light-hearted, 'So sorry, Felix. I wasn't going to touch anything. I was just passing, and I looked in. Is that a crime?'

'No, of course not. I was just – surprised.' Surprised and displeased. He hated anyone to go into this room without him: into Octavia's bedroom.

The first time she had seen it, Marianne had been touched, saddened even: a young girl's bedroom, patently waiting for its owner's return. It was all white and yellow, very pretty, with flounced curtains and a very prettily ornate brass bedstead, the bed made up with an elaborately embroidered white quilt and pillows, and a heap of lace cushions, a row of teddies arranged carefully on them in order of size.

There were fresh flowers on the windowsill, and the chest of drawers, and the walls were covered with pictures: a few Victorian watercolours, a lot of rather nice early photographs, a couple of collages; and there was a battered old school trunk in the corner of the room, with more teddies piled on it, and hanging on a bentwood hatstand, an array of hats, spelling out a life, from a baby's sunhat to a school panama, a mortar board, and the sort of confection worn to weddings.

'How sweet,' she had said, 'to keep it for her like this.'

'Well,' Felix had said, 'you never know when she might want it.'

That was before Marianne had realised that Octavia was already married.

'Come on down. I've had a drink poured you for ages,' said Felix now.

'You want me out of here, don't you?' said Marianne, turning to him, smiling, kissing him lightly. 'You're like some latterday Mrs Danvers or Miss Havisham. You don't like it touched, your little girl's room.'

He scowled at her and turned away, but she put her hand on his arm, and pulled him back.

'Felix, don't be cross. You know I'm only teasing you.' She closed the door behind her, and, almost involuntarily, sighed heavily.

'What is it?' he said. 'You've been odd, ever since we left that house today.'

'Oh, nothing. It was a strain, wasn't it? Funerals always are.'

'Yes, I suppose so. Poor woman. Octavia was very tense, I thought. Not herself at all.'

'Oh, I don't know,' said Marianne. 'She was bound to be upset, she was very fond of Anna. And she's very close to Louise.'

'Yes. I never thought she was a very good influence on her, you know. Flighty. And a bit unstable.'

'What do you think of Sandy?' said Marianne casually.

'He seems nice enough. A bit stiff necked, maybe not too bright – here's your drink.'

'Thank you. Slightly surprising husband for Louise, perhaps, wouldn't you say? He's so very conventional, so straight down the middle, and she's so – well, obviously very artistic, much more nonconformist, I would have thought.'

'God, Marianne, I hardly know either of them. I couldn't possibly comment.'

'So Octavia's never – well, implied they weren't happy?'

'Not really. She didn't think he was a very suitable husband for Louise when she first met him, but she's quite fond of him now, I think. Tom doesn't like him much apparently, but then Tom's very hard to please when it comes to people. Nobody's ever good enough for him.'

'Does he like Louise, do you think?' said Marianne casually.

'Marianne, what is all this? You've never shown any interest in these people before.'

'No, because I've never had anything much to do with them. My heart broke for Louise over that poor little baby, but otherwise—'

'I don't believe he does like her, no,' said Felix suddenly. 'I remember Octavia saying once or twice that it was difficult, having Louise to stay or anything, because Tom disapproved of her.'

'Why disapproved?'

'Oh, for heaven's sake, *I* don't know,' said Felix. 'You'll have to ask Octavia.' He stopped talking suddenly, then said in quite a different voice, 'Marianne . . .'

She looked at him; he was staring at her, sitting very still suddenly, his eyes under the white brows very fierce, very dark, and she sat equally still, smiling back at him, recognising the signal, the thud of desire, extraordinarily swift and sudden, feeling it in herself, as she always did, swooping, leaping, leading her into such a longing for release that she stood up, laughed aloud, held out her hand.

'Let's go upstairs,' was all she said.

What followed next was a distraction: a wild, extravagant, joyful distraction, from her anxiety and her fear. But afterwards, as he slept briefly and she lay stretching luxuriously, her body sweetly straightened from its tangles of pleasure, she remembered the anxiety and the fear, and wondered what, if anything, she should do. She decided, finally, nothing, nothing at all would be best. Least of all, asking Octavia how Tom might feel about Louise.

If Louise walked into the room now, Octavia thought, she would have hit her. However distraught she was about her mother. How could she have deceived her like that; allowed her to get into the awful situation, where she had almost given her secret away to Sandy, telling her all that nonsense about how he wasn't too keen on the idea of a baby and no one was to mention it? When all the time it was someone else's baby. Her lover's. A lover she hadn't told Octavia about, while listening to Octavia telling her all about Tom. Seriously, seriously awful. She felt totally betrayed.

She'd found it very difficult to be polite to her, when she'd come up to her at the house; she felt sick. She'd managed it because she'd had to, and anyway, it was hardly the place to make a scene; but she was sure Louise must have noticed that she was being rather cool. To put it mildly. On the other hand, Louise was probably too busy playing her part, acting her role, to notice anything – but maybe that was unfair, Octavia thought, struggling to be charitable. She clearly was desperately upset, had come back to the house after the burial looking pale and strained, her eyes swollen and red, but then she had rallied and moved round the room almost dutifully, mostly at her father's side. She had kissed Octavia when they left, thanked her for coming again and again. Tom had gone to fetch the car; he told Octavia he'd wait for her outside.

He had been absolutely silent in the car, said nothing to her whatsoever until the phone rang, and had then spent the rest of the journey talking first to Aubrey Cotterill, then his accountant, then to Aubrey again.

Her anger with Louise had made her feel remorseful about dragging him down there when he was so busy: in spite of everything.

'All right. All right, I give in. I won't phone you any more.'

'Thank you,' said Marianne with cool dignity.

'Today.'

'Nico. Not today, not tomorrow, not for a very long time. I wish you'd understand.' Guilt, mingled with a sense of disloyalty at betraying the man with whom her body had soared with pleasure only twelve hours earlier, made her irritable.

'A very long time? Oh, that's much too open ended. I won't phone you until – let us say Saturday. How's that? And that is a very long time – forty-eight hours.'

'Nico—'

'Mum!' Zoë's voice had never been more welcome. 'Mum, where are you?'

'Look, Nico, I have to go. I'm extremely busy.'

'Marianne, oh, all right. I'll phone you at the weekend. What a steely-hearted woman you are.'

She put the phone down; it rang again at once.

'Mrs Muirhead? This is Ritz Franklyn from Choice. We have some wonderful news for you. Donna Hanson has just called from Christie's in New York: they are all agreed she is absolutely the girl for them. I'm very excited, and I hope you both will be too.'

'Well, I—'

'I wonder if you and she could come in to the agency this afternon. After school, of course. To discuss the deal with Christie's?'

'I'm afraid this afternoon won't be possible,' said Marianne firmly. 'Early next week would be the soonest. And incidentally, I would like my lawyers to be present at any future meeting with Christie's.'

'Yes, of course.' Ritz Franklyn's voice was soothing and very calm. 'I quite understand. Well, shall we say Monday afternoon?'

'I should think so, although I must speak to my husband. He has unfortunately not been able to come over this week as I had hoped.'

'What a shame. I was looking forward to meeting him. But I really think this is the beginning of a very long and happy association between us. Goodbye, Mrs Muirhead.'

Ritz Franklyn put the phone down, picked up a very heavy, cut-glass ashtray and hurled it at the wall.

'You are being trouble,' said Ritz to the phone. 'Very big trouble. But we're going to win, Mrs Muirhead. Make no mistake about it.'

'I need to talk to you,' said Tom. They were in a taxi, going home from a drinks party at the House of Commons. For the time being, they had agreed to honour their joint obligations; it was simpler.

Octavia turned to look at him; his face was very set, his eyes fixed unseeingly out of the window, his fingers twisting endlessly at his signet ring.

'What about?' she said coldly. 'Where you're going to live? How soon we can see a solicitor? Those are the only things I want to talk to you about.'

'No,' he said, 'it's nothing to do with us personally. The company is in serious trouble, financially, that is. Losing the Carlton account was a disaster for us.'

She looked at him, and felt briefly stricken. Then she rallied. No company, if it was well run, collapsed on the loss of one client. It really wasn't her fault; she should not be blamed for it. 'I'm very sorry to hear that,' she said. 'Especially for my contribution to that.'

'Oh, it wasn't just that,' he said wearily, surprising her. 'We've been running things on a knife edge for over a year. It was certainly a last straw, but the camel's back was pretty near breaking before. The bank won't let us have any more money, the house is remortgaged, as you know, and frankly next month we won't even be able to pay the staff salaries.'

'Oh,' she said. She felt rather sick. 'So what—'

'We're trying to get further backing. From a private investor. Now it is absolutely essential that no word of this gets out. I have two prospective clients, teetering on the edge of joining us. There's no way they'd come in if they thought we were a dodgy prospect. By the same token, people like Nico Cadogan would probably question whether they wouldn't be better with someone else, as almost certainly would a couple of other clients who are not entirely satisfied at the moment. No fault of ours, things not going their way, but of course we get the blame. And having a new government has obviously made things more complex. New systems to work, new people to work with; Whitehall doesn't change, thank God, but other things – oh, it's very complicated. But none of it helps create a very easy climate for us. Anyway, please, Octavia, for God's sake, don't talk about any of this.'

'I wouldn't,' she said, genuinely indignant. 'I know at least enough to keep my mouth shut.'

'Do you?' His eyes on her were very cold.

'Yes, I do. Bartles Wood was a one-off thing, you know it was.'

'I hope so.'

'And it was just bad luck that the *Mail* put out that story about Carlton being your client as well as mine.'

'I don't see it quite like that. Actually. Not quite bad luck. It wasn't very difficult to ferret out. Tip-off or not.'

'The tip-off couldn't have helped. Have you any idea who it might have been? Some rival of yours or something?'

'Absolutely none. Anyway, there's no point talking about it. Blood on the tracks and all that. But it's also essential your father doesn't get to hear about it.'

'Why?'

'Oh, Octavia, do use your brain. He'd be delighted to spread any muck about me. You know he would. Nothing would make him happier than to see me brought down.'

'Tom, he may not see you as the ideal son-in-law—'

'Now would such a person ever exist, I wonder?'

'He was right about *you*, wasn't he?' she said, her words lashing at him. 'I should have listened when he told me I was making a mistake. That you weren't right for me. That I'd regret it.'

'I'm surprised you haven't gone running to him,' he said bitterly, 'Daddy's little girl. Asking for comfort, asking him to take you back.'

'That's a vile thing to say,' she said, tears stinging her eyes. 'You know how hard I've worked to break away from him, not to let him manipulate me, run my life. I've kept it from him most carefully, what you've done. I dread him finding out. Not really because of what he might do to you, I couldn't care less about that, but because of all the recriminations, the self justification, the "I told you so"s, the emotional blackmail to go home to him . . .'

'Well,' he said, 'I'd be grateful if you could keep my professional perfidy from him. As well as my personal. Until I've managed to sort myself out.'

'Yes, all right,' she said.

The taxi had reached the house. Tom paid it off, and they went inside. Octavia walked into the small study to check the answering machine and the pad where Caroline left messages about the children.

He followed her in. 'Any messages?'

'Only one, from Louise. Thanking us for going to the funeral.' She turned, suddenly, looked at him. 'Did you talk to her yesterday at all?'

'No,' he said. His voice was exhausted suddenly, devoid of emotion.

'Not at all?'

'No. Not at all. Should I have?'

'No, not really, I suppose, but she – well, let's just say she's not my favourite person at the moment.'

'Oh, really?' There was a silence, then he said almost reluctantly, 'Why?'

'It doesn't matter. I don't want to talk about it. Good night, Tom. And don't worry, I won't say anything about the company. To anyone. I promise.'

'Thank you. I'm sorry to have to ask you, Octavia. Sorry about all of it.'

And then he was gone.

CHAPTER 21

She recognised the voice. She was surprised to find how instantly she did recognise the public school vowels carefully slurred over: a sexy voice. 'Mrs Fleming?'

'Yes. Yes, that's me. How are you, Mr Bingham?'

'I thought we'd got past that stage. Please, call me Gabriel. Now why aren't you coming to this meeting on Friday? When it was planned carefully round my parliamentary duties, so that I can be there. I shall begin to think either that your little performance was cosmetic, put on to please your client, or that you are more under your husband's thumb than you led me to believe.'

'Of course I'm not,' she said, and then realised the indignation in her voice was out of proportion, lowered the decibel level carefully. 'I'm not in the least under his thumb. Not in the very least.'

'Good. Spoken like a truly independent woman of today. Why aren't you coming to the meeting, then? Or was my other assumption correct, that your involvement was all in aid of furthering client relations?'

'No, it wasn't. I find that rather offensive, actually.'

'Well, I'm sorry. I certainly didn't intend to give offence. But I did feel quite sure you'd be there. I was looking forward to seeing you.'

She said, surprised that he should say anything so – so what? Flattering? Charming? 'Thank you.'

'I find you a most satisfactory sparring partner.'

She felt stupid suddenly, gauche, awkward.

'Well, it might interest you to know, Mr Bingham—'

'Gabriel . . .'

'Mr Bingham, that I do have claims on my time other than my work – my children, and – and my husband.'

'Ah. So not an independent woman of today.'

'It is perfectly possible,' said Octavia, 'to be an independent woman of today, and to care about your children and your husband. In fact, it's very much an integral part of it.'

'Indeed? I've obviously got a lot to learn. Just a simple bachelor, you see.'

'I thought you had a fiancée, Mr Bingham. Or is she cosmetic too?' That was probably rude.

'What an interesting concept. No, she is not cosmetic. Nor a fiancée either, as a matter of fact. Anyway, you're in London this weekend, are you? I shall have to manage without you. Pity. If the social diary suddenly clears, give me a ring. I'll buy you another half afterwards. If that doesn't tempt you, nothing will.'

'Nothing will, I'm afraid,' she said. 'Goodbye, Mr Bingham.'

'Goodbye, Mrs Fleming.'

She could hear the amusement in his voice and felt fractious for the rest of the morning.

Especially as her diary was blank for the entire weekend.

Charles Madison was forcing himself through the painful process of clearing up Anna's most personal possessions, trying to decide which things to keep, which to store away somewhere, which he could bear to throw away. It was proving very painful indeed: her hairbrush – still with a few of her golden hairs in it – the perfume she had continued to spray herself with even that last day, the book he had been reading her – *Captain Corelli's Mandolin*, doubly poignant, since they had spent their honeymoon on a Greek island – all the letters and cards she had been sent by loving friends, her handbag, with her diary, her cheque book . . . She had been so extravagant, had always come to him with confessions just before the bank statement arrived each month – her lace handkerchiefs, a huge heap of them – she loved lace hankies, had a huge collection, and she left them everywhere, in everyone's houses, people were always having to send them back . . . Charles suddenly found himself in need of one of the lace handkerchiefs, blew his nose on it, and went to find something more substantial. And stopped dead in the hall, for he could hear Louise's voice coming from the study.

'Please!' she was saying. 'I must see you. Just this once. And try to explain. Please . . .'

She sounded tearful; she had been better lately, since the funeral, had made a clear effort to be more cheerful both for his sake and Dickon's. Sandy had wanted both of them to go back with him that night but she had refused, had said she must stay a few more days, although Charles had assured them both it wasn't necessary. She had promised Sandy that she would go back on Saturday or Sunday and he had accepted it.

He was proving to be a bit of a saint, was Sandy, endlessly patient with her; well, Charles had always liked him, always defended him against Anna's and the boys' criticism. 'He's a rock,' he had said over and over again, as they laughed at his heartiness, his old-fashioned manners, 'and Louise needs someone like that, someone reliable and strong. He loves her; he'll love her whatever she does. You mark my words.'

And he'd been right, it seemed; Sandy had been marvellous over the baby's death, supporting Louise through her breakdown without complaint, never mentioning his own misery, and he was a wonderful father to Dickon, patient, kind, loving. Charles admired him greatly. And enjoyed his company, never having been too bothered by what most of his family termed Sandy's dullness. He couldn't see it himself.

He cleared his throat loudly so that Louise would know he was there, that she could be overheard.

It obviously worked because her voice became more normal, almost cheerful, quite brisk. 'Fine,' she said, 'yes, that'll be fine. Good, thank you. Friday afternoon. I'll be there.'

She came out and smiled at him. She looked quite cheerful. 'Hallo, Daddy. You all right?'

'Yes, thank you. Bit of a bad morning, clearing up Mummy's things. What I'm going to do with—Oh, that wretched phone!'

'Shall I get it?'

'No, it's all right. Hallo? Yes. Oh, hallo, Octavia. How are you? Good. Yes, well, I hoped it was as good an occasion as possible. It was lovely to see you, and so good of Tom and your father, and Marianne, to come. What a nice woman she is. Yes, I'm fine. What? Yes, it is a difficult time. Sorting things out, you know. I don't know what we're going to do with Anna's collections of lace handkerchiefs. Some of them are so lovely it's a pity to put them away and never use them again. Perhaps you'd like a few? I know she'd like you to have them. Yes, of course. I'll sort one or two out. Now you want Louise – she was here a minute ago. I'll see if I can find her, just a minute, Octavia.' He put down the phone, went into the hall, bellowed for Louise.

A rather feeble voice came from the bathroom. 'I'm in here, Daddy. Sorry. I know it's Octavia, could I call her back?'

Charles went back to phone. 'Octavia? Sorry, my dear. She's not feeling too good. I know we're not supposed to talk about it, but you can guess the reason of course. Anyway, she'll call you back. Is that all right?'

Octavia sounded rather odd, he thought, as she said yes, it would be all right, but she really did want to speak to Louise, it was something fairly urgent.

*

Alec's voice over the phone was very cold, very clipped. 'I'm sorry, Marianne, I am just not prepared to agree to this nonsense.'

'And I think we should at least consider it.'

'It will disrupt her education, bring her into contact with unsavoury people—'

'How do you know that? I have friends in the fashion industry, perfectly responsible people.'

'Marianne, please! There is a vast difference between people your age who are fashion editors at *Vogue*, and the kind of dissolute crowd who hang around photographers' studios.'

'Look, Alec, perhaps we should accept that neither of us knows what we're talking about. In this particular instance. I do assure you I am keeping a very open mind on the subject.'

'And I do assure you mine is closed. Now I have to go. Goodbye.'

Marianne put the phone down. She was shaking and near to tears. It was twelve years now since she had left Alec, and very occasionally she had wondered quite why she had found him so intolerable as a husband. Incidents such as this reminded her with a force that was very hard to bear. Anyway, it had done one thing; it had made her want to keep an open mind on the whole thing herself. She simply would not be ordered what to do by Alec. Even on the subject of their children.

'Boot, hallo, it's me. Sorry I couldn't talk to you earlier.'

'That's all right,' said Octavia. 'How are you today?'

'I'm fine. You sound odd. What's the matter?'

'I feel rather odd, as you put it. Stupid, more like it. Louise, what are you playing at?'

'I don't know what you mean.'

'Don't you? Don't you really? Well, try this. I'm talking to your husband, about Dickon, about how he was worried about everyone dying and what if you had another baby, would that one die, and your husband says oh, don't worry about that, there won't be any more babies, and I'm about to say well, what about the one your wife is having then, and he stops me just in time, *just* in time, I might say, and tells me he's had a vasectomy. Thanks a lot, Louise, for letting me blab away to you about all my problems, and keeping it all to yourself about your own little affair. And that you're having a baby by someone else, God knows who. Funny way to run a friendship.'

There was a much longer silence, then Louise said, 'Oh, Boot. Oh, dear. I'm so so sorry. My only defence is that with Mummy dying—'

'Your mother's dying, so you forgot to mention that you just happen to be having an adulterous liaison and that you're also having your lover's baby? Sorry, Louise, but it doesn't quite wash. Whose is it, who are you pregnant by?'

'I'm not pregnant.' The voice was very sad, very shaky suddenly.

'What?'

'I'm not. It was all – all in my mind. I honestly think, Octavia, I've been a little bit mad this past few weeks.'

'But, Louise, you said – your father said—'

'I know. I thought I was, I honestly thought I was. I've had all the symptoms, missed two periods, been so sick, sore boobs, everything. But I'm not. I had a test. Negative. I feel pretty rough about it actually.' Her voice shook.

Octavia felt totally disconcerted. 'But if Sandy's had a vasectomy, how could you even have thought you were? I don't understand.'

'Those things don't always work. I've heard of a couple of people who've got pregnant afterwards. I mean, it's one in a million stuff, but – well, I obviously want a baby really, because I managed to hope myself into Sandy still being fertile. I regret making him have the vasectomy now. I really do. But at the time I thought – well, you know what I thought.'

'Yes,' said Octavia, 'yes, I do. I'm sorry, Louise. I just felt so upset. That you hadn't confided in me. And that I nearly dropped you in it.'

'I would have felt the same. Of course I would.'

'And I'm sad you're still so upset about – about Juliet as well. I didn't realise you'd changed your mind about it. About having another baby.'

''Fraid so. And short of taking a lover, there's nothing I can do about it now, is there? Silly me.'

'Can't they be reversed? Vasectomies? I read about it only the other day. Yes, it was in the *Mail*. I'll see if I can find it.'

'Could you, Boot? Goodness. What a marvellous thought!'

'Well, don't get too excited. Oh, you poor old thing. What a filthy time you've had. Poor Louise.'

'We've both been through the mill a bit, haven't we? How's things with you?'

'Bad,' said Octavia briefly. 'I've told Tom I want a divorce. I think he's hoping still I'll come round. Forgive him. All that crap.'

'No chance?'

'No chance.'

'Your dad still doesn't know?'

'No, thank God.'

'And Tom still hasn't told you who it is?'

'No. He's avoiding talking about the whole thing. I think it's partly because – oh, I shouldn't tell you. It's something quite different.'

'What sort of different? Tom's not ill or something, is he?'

'No, nothing like that. It's just that I swore I wouldn't tell anyone, and it's to do with Tom's business.'

'Boot, who am I going to tell? Living in this backwater.'

'You mustn't tell Sandy even. He might talk.'

'I won't tell Sandy, but—'

'Okay, then. I need to tell someone anyway. Fleming Cotterill are in trouble. I mean, *real* trouble. They've got to get hold of some more money fast, or they could go bust.'

'My God. Really?'

'Yes. Our house is remortgaged right up to the hilt, and so is Aubrey's. If the bank foreclosed, well . . .'

'But why so secret? I don't understand.'

'It's the pack-of-cards thing. If the clients he's got, even one of them, heard the company was dodgy, one of them might pull out too. Then he really would have had it.'

'Oh, dear. Yes, I see. So your little fun and games with the wood was really quite catastrophic?'

'It didn't help. I feel a bit bad about that.'

'You shouldn't feel bad about anything you do to Tom.'

'But it's not just him, it's the other people in the firm. Aubrey's so nice. And there are people there with young families. You can't help feeling responsible for them. And then of course, if it does go bust, what happens to our house and the children and everything? So I do feel worried, yes.'

'He can get hold of some money, it isn't difficult. They're drowning in money in the City, Daddy says. Do you want me to ask him? Maybe he could help.'

'No!' said Octavia horrified. 'Louise, you mustn't mention it to anyone. Please.'

'All right. I won't. I promise. Now then, have you forgiven me?'

'What? Yes, of course I have. I think I should be asking you the same thing, not trusting you like that. I'm sorry you're so unhappy, Louise, so sorry.'

'Oh, well,' said Louise, with a sigh, 'no doubt I'll get over it one day . . .'

Octavia felt remorseful when she put the phone down: remorseful and very sad. Poor Louise. She must find the article, maybe Sandy's vasectomy could be reversed. She buzzed for Sarah Jane, asked her to look for it and then settled down to writing a full proposal for Lauren Bartlett about the day at Brands Hatch for Next Generation.

A few lines in, she stopped, sat staring at her screen. Something was troubling her, distracting her, and she couldn't think what it was.

Something that had happened in the last hour or so, something ugly, burrowed deep now into her subconscious. What was it? What was it about? Raking through her brain, going over the experiences of the morning, revealed nothing. But there was something; she knew there was . . .

'But would you want to get into bed with him?' Aubrey's voice was thoughtful.

Tom looked at him quickly, then laughed.

'Just for a moment then, I wondered, Aubrey.'

'No, no, dear boy. Purely in the business sense. He's not just going to let us take his money and run. He's going to be there, sitting in on meetings, questioning our decisions. We won't be our own masters any more. Fair enough. Maybe we don't deserve to be. But we do need to find someone who's in sympathy with us. And I don't think Mr Foster is.'

'In a perfect world, no. Nice enough, I suppose, bloody tough, but as a partner, maybe not. Bit crass.'

'Very crass. And my father told me never to trust a man in a short-sleeved shirt.'

'I think I agree with your father. His suit was vile too. However, can we really be that picky? If he's prepared to come up with the cash. Illingworth hasn't come up with anyone else. We have two days left.'

'I know, Tom. But it would be madness to get into a relationship that wasn't tenable. I'd like to look a little further,' said Aubrey, 'hang on the cliff a bit longer. If you're game.'

Tom hesitated, then he said, 'By all means let's cast our net a bit wider, but I don't quite see where the perfect bride might be found.'

'I've got one idea,' said Aubrey. 'Old chum with a boutique-style investment bank phoned this morning, about a dinner he's giving. I hadn't thought of him before, but I mentioned it and he seemed interested. More likely to come in with us than the big boys are.'

'Sounds good,' said Tom.

'Yes, but not a lot more likely, I have to say. Anyway, I'll talk to him later today, if you're agreeable. Want to be in on it? Around four?'

'Yeah, I'd like to be there,' said Tom. 'God, if only we could get one of those two new prospects to sign, it would make such a difference.'

'One of them will,' said Aubrey easily. 'I feel it in my water.'

Romilly listened to her mother very carefully as she told her that Christie's had said they did want her for their new campaign, that they were sending over a contract for her mother to look at and talk to her solicitor about, that Ritz Franklyn also wanted them to go into the agency and discuss it with them. Romilly agreed that she couldn't possibly go into Choice before Monday, since she was going away for the weekend, and she also agreed that it was very important that Ritz understood that she was only available part time, in the school holidays and at half term, until she had done her GCSEs at the very least.

'You might hate it,' Marianne said, and Romilly said, yes, of course she might.

Marianne also said that her father was still very against the whole thing, and if they were to proceed it was very important to be able to present him with the kind of scenario which would allay his fears.

'What are the fears?' said Romilly. 'Exactly?'

'Oh, darling, your education being disrupted. You being hurt. Other dangers . . .'

'What, like drugs and all that stuff? Shooting coke in the dressing room?' She was smiling at her mother, agreeing that it was an absurd joke. 'And don't tell me. He thinks I'll go anorexic.'

'He didn't actually spell that out,' said Marianne, 'but—'

'But it's there, in his head, right?'

'Right.'

'That's obviously nonsense. You know how greedy I am. As for making myself sick – well, I'm phobic about it, aren't I?'

'You are,' said Marianne, smiling at her.

'So – think we can do it? I don't want to upset him.'

'I think so. You really are being very mature about this, darling. I'm impressed.'

'Well,' said Romilly seriously, 'it's a tough business. I'll need to be mature. Anyway, we'll go and chat to them on Monday, right?'

'Right. And maybe we should have a chat with the dentist.'

Romilly went upstairs. She could never remember feeling so happy. Happy and self-confident. It was going to be all right. They were going to come round. She just had to be mature and patient about it, that was all. Impress everyone, including her parents, show them she appreciated their point of view. Not behave like a baby. Ritz Franklyn had said as much, when she had rung her in tears at lunchtime, the day before, asking if there was any news about the contract.

'But don't quote me on this, Romilly. Show them you've thought it all through for yourself, that you're grown up enough to cope with it all. Which I know you are . . .'

Octavia was just wondering how she was going to get through yet another hostile weekend when the phone rang. It was Lauren Bartlett.

'Octavia, hi. Listen, how would next Wednesday be for the meeting? And I wondered if you and Tom were around on Sunday. Just a casual lunch, a few old friends. There's a guy coming, friend of Drew's, just bought a chain of chemist shops, looking for someone like Tom as far as I can make out, to advise him a bit. I told him I knew Tom, and he seemed interested in meeting him.'

Octavia thought fast. If Tom could get a new client, it would make everything much better; he'd be on firmer ground, she'd feel less guilty, and it would be a lot easier to begin to sort things out.

'I think that might be rather nice,' she said. 'I'll ring Tom and ask him if he's—'

'Good. About one, then. Really casual, dress comfy.'

Octavia knew what dressing comfy meant at the Bartletts'; not quite new Armani jeans, last season's JP Tods, a slightly washed-out Joseph sweater; and a really casual lunch for a few old friends meant twenty or so people, all networking furiously, over a champagne buffet of asparagus, salmon, carpaccio, wild strawberries . . . She felt tired just thinking about it, but she picked up the phone and rang Tom's office.

'Sorry, Octavia, he's not here. Gone to Birmingham. Big meeting with Bob Macintosh. All day, till late. Coming back tomorrow. You could try him there.'

She phoned Bob Macintosh's secretary, asked if Tom was with him.

'I'm not too sure, Mrs Fleming. They had an early lunch, do you want to speak to Bob?'

'Oh, yes. If that would be all right.'

Bob Macintosh was friendly, expansive, asked her how she was. 'I'm fine,' said Octavia, 'thank you. I wonder if I could possibly speak to Tom. I'm sorry to bother you but something's cropped up.'

'Tom's gone, love, an hour or so ago. It was only a fairly quick meeting we had. Said he had another appointment.'

'I see,' said Octavia slowly. Misery hit her, cold, solid in her stomach. She could imagine what the other appointment was; with *Her.* So much for it being over. There she'd been, trying to help him in his bloody business, pushing clients his way, and all the time he was rushing off to get into bed with his mistress.

She put the phone down and sat shaking slightly. Well, she supposed it was no more than that she could expect. She certainly wasn't going to go to any filthy lunch parties now, just to further the cause of Fleming Cotterill. She phoned Lauren, said she was terribly sorry, but Tom was out of London that weekend; Lauren made a rather half-hearted attempt at pretending that Octavia would be welcome without him, and was clearly relieved when she said she didn't think she could.

'The nanny's away, I'd have to bring the baby.'

'In that case, it might be better not. Well, see you on Wednesday, Octavia.'

And now the weekend stretched in front of her, empty, lonely, full of wrenching jealous misery. It wasn't fair. She couldn't even go and spend time with her father, as she often had on such occasions in the past. It would be much too difficult. And she didn't want to see any of their friends, it would be bound to lead to inquiries, speculation. So it was just her and the children. And too much time to think.

Unless . . . On the spur of the moment, she picked up the phone, dialled Pattie David's number, said she could come to the meeting, but she'd have the children with her. Was there any way Pattie could help?

Pattie was thrilled. Yes, of course she could; the twins were almost Megan's age, they could all watch a video together. 'And then my daily will be in the house, keeping an eye on Megan – she'd be delighted to look after the baby.'

'She's an awfully good baby,' said Octavia. 'Anyway, it won't take long, will it? The meeting?'

'It might,' said Pattie. 'There's never any telling with these things. And of course with Gabriel Bingham coming . . .'

'Oh, yes,' said Octavia, carefully vague, 'I'd quite forgotten he was coming . . .'

She called Caroline, told her to get the children's things packed, and then left a message for Tom saying what she was planning to do, and that she presumed he would be staying in London.

She felt much better suddenly; tough, cool decisive. A woman on her own, an independent woman, doing what she wanted, going where she liked, following the causes she was interested in. Very contemporary. The only flaw in the whole thing was that Gabriel Bingham would be there, misinterpreting all her actions, being snide about her motives. Well, maybe he wouldn't turn up. You never knew your luck . . .

Julie Springer, the young account executive in charge of press relations at Fleming Cotterill, was feeling rather pleased with herself. It had been a bit slow in her department during the last three weeks, so the call from a journalist on the *Independent*, asking her who Fleming Cotterill's major clients were, was particularly welcome. She was a very nice girl, clearly well informed on the nature of the business; she said she was doing a round-up of firms like Fleming Cotterill, for a big feature on Tony Blair's first months in power, and had already talked to the people at GJW and Fishburn Hedges. She was also more courteous than most journalists, thanked Julie for her help and warned her that she might need to ring her again.

'Just to check a couple more things. Would that be all right?'

Julie said it would be perfectly all right and put the phone down, smiling. Tom and Aubrey would be pleased.

Julie decided to follow up the information she had given her with a letter confirming it. Her last boss had always told her to do that. She addressed it to the girl, whose name was Diana Davenport, at the features department at the *Independent* and took it down to the post room herself to make sure it got the next mailing out.

'Well, that was very satisfactory, wasn't it?' said Gabriel Bingham. 'I enjoyed your little trajectory in the direction of the Newbury bypass. Very ingenious.'

'That was not ingenious,' said Octavia irritably. 'It's perfectly true. There is more development, more building planned now, just because the new road's there. It's dreadful. After all they—'

'Yes, yes. I was listening. Very intently. Anyway, I hope your colleagues are going to proceed in an ordered, professional manner now. Getting seen as a load of green do-gooders won't serve them at all well.'

'I think they – we – know that,' said Octavia. 'And you've certainly rammed the point home. Several times.'

'Inserting it firmly was more what I intended.'

'It sounded like ramming to me,' she said.

'An unattractive word, ramming.'

'Yes. Quite onomatopoeic, too.'

He looked at her and grinned suddenly. 'Shall we continue this extremely intellectual discussion over the half of bitter I promised you?'

'Most unfortunately I can't,' said Octavia coolly. 'My children are at Patricia David's house. I have to collect them and go on to the – our cottage.'

'Ah. So you've quite put yourself out to come to this thing tonight. Very exemplary. Well, I mustn't stand between a woman and her maternal duties. What about the uxorial ones?'

'What?'

'Where is your husband? On his way, is he, bombing down the M4 in a BMW, unleaded petrol obviously, green wellies and shooting stick in the boot? And a couple of bottles of vintage port for tomorrow's dinner party?'

'No,' said Octavia, and tears suddenly stung at the back of her eyes. 'No, he isn't, actually. He . . .' She heard her voice wobble, swallowed hard, turned away.

'I'm sorry.' The voice was quite different suddenly, gentle, quieter. 'Very sorry if I upset you. I didn't mean to. I was only teasing you.'

'Yes,' she said, still looking away, not trusting herself to face him. 'Well, perhaps you should choose your targets with a bit more care.'

'What's the matter?' he asked. 'It's not just what I said, is it? You're upset about something else.'

'No,' she said firmly, turning, smiling at him rather distantly. 'I'm not upset. Now I must go. Excuse me. Pattie, hi, I'm over here. I really should be getting back to the children. Do you mind if we go?'

She tried not to, but as she pulled the car door shut, she glanced up at him; he was standing quite near, staring down at her intently, his expression concerned still, pushing his hand through his wild hair.

'Sweet man, isn't he?' said Pattie, moving off with a violent jerk.

'That's not quite the adjective I'd apply,' said Octavia.

CHAPTER 22

'Mummy, there's a man at the door.'

'Just coming.'

Octavia had been engrossed in an article about the party Prince Charles had thrown for Camilla Parker-Bowles' fiftieth birthday; she struggled back to reality, hoping it was Bill Dunn, come to do the grass. It needed it very badly. But it wasn't Bill.

'Oh,' she said. 'Hallo.'

'Hallo, Mrs Fleming. Peace offering. It's not vintage, I'm afraid, but it is Bollinger.'

'I can see. Honestly, you really shouldn't have.'

'I think I should. I felt rather guilty on Friday night.'

'Oh, it didn't matter. Please come in, I was just going to make a cup of tea. Poppy, this is Mr Bingham. Darling, would you put the kettle on?'

'I remember you,' said Poppy. 'We met you in that wood.'

'Not actually in the wood,' said Gideon, who had appeared at the door. 'It was a clearing.'

'It was a clearing of the wood,' said Poppy, 'so—'

'Poppy, I said could you put the kettle on. Mr Bingham, please come in.'

'Mum, Minty's crying. I heard her from the garden.'

'Oh, I'll go and get her. That was a short sleep.'

'I hadn't realised family life was so demanding,' he said.

When she came back, he was following Gideon out of the door.

'He's going to bowl for me,' said Gideon.

'Gideon, Mr Bingham hasn't come all this way to be dragged straight into a game of cricket.'

'It's not a game, it's just so I can practise my batting. And he said to call him Gabriel.'

Gabriel Bingham's eyes met Octavia's over Gideon's head. He smiled at her, then turned and followed Gideon out into the garden.

'That was very kind of you,' she said quite a lot later, as they sat drinking tea.

'Not kind at all. I love cricket. Played for my school.'

'Did you?' said Gideon, his eyes shining.

'Yup. First Eleven, actually.'

'Golly.'

'My finest hour was when we beat – well, another school, and I made eighty-nine, not out.'

'Which other school?'

'Harrow. Not hard to beat, actually.'

'And where did you go to school?' said Gideon

'Er, Winchester,' said Gabriel Bingham, avoiding Octavia's eye.

'Winchester and Harrow. What a very egalitarian occasion it must have been,' said Octavia mildly. But she smiled at him; he smiled back.

'I'm going to Winchester, I hope,' said Gideon. 'You have to be clever to go there, though. What's your job?'

'I'm an MP.'

'Are you? Our daddy knows lots of MPs. Have you met him?'

'No.'

'Mummy, can I fill the paddling pool? It's so hot,' said Poppy. 'Minty'd like that.'

'She might not,' said Gideon.

'Of course she would.'

'How do you know?'

'Gideon, stop it,' said Octavia, wearily. 'I agree with Poppy, Minty probably would like it very much. Now go and help Poppy get the pool out and fill it, would you?'

'But, Mum—'

'Gideon. I mean it. Otherwise, no hamburger on the way back to London.'

'I can see you're a very harsh mother,' said Gabriel Bingham.

'I'm quite strict. Actually,' said Octavia.

'Well, they're very nice children. And this is a very nice place you've got here.'

He looked round; they were sitting on a small paved area outside the kitchen door, set with a wooden table and chairs, and marked out by a trellis covered in climbing roses and honeysuckle. In front of them was the daisy-covered lawn, bounded by a thick hawthorn hedge, and beyond that the rolling, tree-studded Somerset landscape.

'And nice village? Friendly? Do they approve of you?'

'I think so. I mean, we do try to join in.'

'Go to the fête, use the shop, all that sort of thing? Very commendable.' His eyes were amused, but there was an edge to his voice.

'Look,' she said, 'it's very easy for you to sneer. I might tell you that this cottage had been empty for three years when we bought it, it was derelict, so—'

'Calm down,' he said, smiling. 'My word, you're touchy. I was only teasing you. I'm sure the village are very fortunate to have you here. Anyway, where is the husband? I'm beginning to think he doesn't exist.'

'He's working. In London.'

'I see. Do you often come down here on your own?'

'Oh, yes,' she said quickly, 'quite often.'

'I see.'

There was a silence; then she said, 'How did you know where I was, anyway?'

'I asked the saintly Mrs David.'

'It was very kind of you.' She felt disproportionately touched; her life had not contained a great deal of kindness lately.

'Well, I'm quite a kindly chap. On the whole. I don't really like upsetting people.'

'Actually,' she said, after a long pause, 'it wasn't only you that upset me. I'd had a hard week.'

'And what constitutes a hard week to you? Don't look at me like that, I really want to know. Too many lunches? Too few grateful clients? Bad traffic on the M4?'

The treacherous tears stung at Octavia's eyes again; she blinked furiously, stirred some sugar into her tea.

'Mummy! Minty's nearly swimming.' Poppy stood in front of them, beaming, breathing heavily. 'On her tummy, properly, arms and legs together. Caroline said she'd been teaching her.'

'Who's Caroline?'

'Our nanny. She's very nice. You might have met her, but she's gone away this weekend. Gideon, stop that. Stop it!' Poppy ran off.

'Ah, another hardship,' said Gabriel Bingham lightly, 'no staff.'

'Oh, shut up!' said Octavia. Her voice shook. 'What have I done to you, why do you have to be so – so snide all the time?'

'Look.' He put his hand on her arm. She pulled it away.

'Don't! Don't touch me.'

'I've done it again, haven't I?' he said. 'Oh, dear. I was only teasing you. Again. How very sensitive you are, Mrs Fleming.'

'And don't call me Mrs Fleming!'

'I thought you didn't like me calling you Octavia?'

'I don't care what you call me,' she said, and burst into tears.

He was very nice, very calm. He moved into the chair next to her, gave her a handkerchief, poured her another cup of tea, added two spoons of sugar.

'Here,' he said gently, 'drink this.'

'I don't want it,' she said, blowing her nose furiously.

'It will do you good. My nanny always said sweet tea cured what ailed you. There, I've done it now. Telling you I had a nanny. Does that make you feel better, knowing what a hypocrite I am?'

'A bit,' she said, smiling reluctantly through her tears.

'I'd rather it didn't get all over the House. Don't tell your husband.'

'I don't tell him anything at all,' she said, 'at the moment.' And then froze, staring at him in alarm. 'I shouldn't have said that.'

'Don't worry,' he said, his untidy face very gentle. 'If you don't tell about my nanny, I won't tell about your husband. Promise. Bad patch? No, sorry, shouldn't have asked. Ignore the question.'

'No, it's all right. And you could say that, yes.'

'Marriage, as far as I can see, consists of one large bad patch, interspersed by a few very small good ones. Would you care to comment on that, Mrs Fleming?'

'Is that why you're not married?' she said.

'Partly. Probably more because no one would marry me.'

'So you don't have a fiancée? Putative or otherwise?'

'No, I don't. She's just given me my marching orders, wants to marry someone else, much nicer and more convenient than I am. Doesn't keep rushing off to London every five minutes.'

'I'm sorry.'

'Oh, it's all right. I think we both knew it was over months ago. Just jogging along, for the sake of convenience.'

'Specially for you,' she said briskly.

'Sorry?'

'Well, I mean, you need to have someone, don't you? In your business? Otherwise people think you're . . .'

'Gay? That wasn't why I went out with her,' he said slowly, and his face was less friendly now. 'You seem to view me as a bigtime hypocrite, which is rather a shame. I felt we were becoming friends. I'm not sure that's going to be the case after all.'

'Mr Bingham – Gabriel – I really didn't mean . . .' She felt panicky suddenly, and cold. It had been a foul and insensitive thing to say to someone who had gone out of his way to be kind and friendly to her. 'I'm sorry,' she said, rather helplessly. 'It was tactless of me.'

'Yes, it was,' he said, standing up, smiling down at her rather coolly.

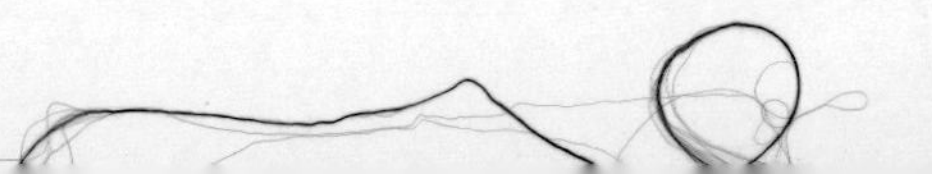

'Anyway, I must go. It's been a very pleasant afternoon. Goodbye, Mrs Fleming.'

'Are you going?' said Gideon, running over to them. 'That's a shame – I wanted to ask you about my bowling.'

'Sorry. Work to do. Nice to meet you, Gideon, I'm sure you'll make a fine batsman. For Winchester or wherever else you go. 'Bye, Poppy.'

And he was gone, striding across the lawn towards the gate and his rather battered old Golf, parked just outside it.

Octavia watched him go, feeling very sick.

'He's really nice,' said Poppy.

'Yes,' Octavia said, and heard her own voice, rather sad, 'yes, I think he is really nice.'

'Louise, are you sure you shouldn't see the doctor?'

It was early on Monday morning; Louise had gone into the lavatory to be sick three times already, had crawled back into bed and lain there shivering, resisting any attempt to be comforted.

Every time Sandy looked at Louise, he felt more afraid: a deep gnawing fear that logic tried desperately to deny. She looked like this, was ill like this, only when she was pregnant; but pregnancy, he had been assured, was a total impossibility. He had had the vasectomy over two years ago; he had had tests done, his sperm count, the doctor had cheerfully assured him, was zilch. He had been unsure about having it done, had thought in those first few months that perhaps one day Louise might feel strong enough to have another child. But he had done it for her because he loved her so much, loved her in spite of her dark moods, her impatience with him, the fear that she no longer loved him at all . . .

She looked at him now, her head turned to him on the pillows, her great blue eyes dark and shadowed with misery, and seemed genuinely puzzled at the question.

'Why should I see a doctor?'

'Darling, you keep being sick, you've lost weight, you're not sleeping, it can't be – I mean, surely it can't . . .'

'Can't be what?' she said sharply, and afraid of confronting her, confronting himself with the awful words, he said feebly, 'Can't be all grief.'

'Of course it's grief, Sandy,' she said and started to cry again, fierce angry tears. 'Of course it is. I've lost my mother. She's died. She's dead, gone. I shall never see her again. How can you be so insensitive as to think that isn't enough to make me ill, how can you?'

Sandy got up in silence, dressed and walked out of the room and out of the house. It was exactly like the time after Juliet had died, when Louise wouldn't let him near her, physically or emotionally, warded him away from her by the sheer force of her pain; there was nothing he could do but keep away from her. And try not to feel so wretchedly afraid.

'Thanks a lot!' Tom's voice was shaking with rage.

'What?'

'Telling Lauren Bartlett I wasn't around on Sunday. When you knew she had a contact for me, when you know how desperate we are. Jesus, Octavia. You, I, the children, we'll all suffer if Fleming Cotterill go down. We're on a fucking knife edge, don't you understand?'

'Tom, if I might interrupt this torrent of abuse just for a moment,' said Octavia, 'I did try to get hold of you on Friday. Actually. To tell you about the lunch at the Bartletts', to tell you Lauren had a contact for you. I was quite prepared to go. And where were you? Not with Bob Macintosh in Birmingham, as Barbara Dawson informed me, but on some mysterious assignation which nobody knew about. Presumably with your mistress. With whom, it seems, you're still involved. Well, you know, it's funny, Tom, but after that I didn't feel able to continue with arranging networking opportunities for you. So sorry.'

Octavia stood in the vast space of the Central Lobby at the House of Commons, feeling absurdly nervous. It was crowded with a huge assortment of people: parties of tourists and rather weary-looking people wearing identity badges, clearly part of the workforce, scurrying through, holding sheaves of paper and files; rather less weary-looking people, walking more slowly, often in twos or threes, heads together, the members of parliament themselves – she recognised several of them, Austin Mitchell, Harriet Harman, Virginia Bottomley, and the Earl of Longford, looking too old to be alive at all, standing courteously back to allow a group of schoolchildren through; and the elaborately dressed doorkeepers, in their white tie and tails uniform. The noise level in the great echoing space, the hum of voices, the occasional announcement (totally unintelligible) over a loudspeaker, the calls of greeting, was extremely high. The whole place wore an air of total disorder, she thought, more reminiscent of some huge marketplace or money-changers' temple than the seat of government of one of the leading countries in the world.

Julie Springer had been in a meeting all morning; when she got back to her office, her voice mail told her to ring the features department at the *Independent*. Good. It would be that nice Diana Davenport again, probably phoning to check some details.

'Hi,' she said to the person who answered the phone, 'this is Julie Springer. Could I speak to Diana Davenport?'

'No Diana Davenport here,' said the voice.

'Oh. Well, maybe she's freelance. Could I speak to someone else, then? I did have a message to call you.'

'Who is it?' said the voice, slightly impatiently.

'Julie Springer. From Fleming Cotterill.'

'Just a minute. Hold on.'

A long silence. Then, 'Yes, apparently it's about your letter. To this Davenport person. Look, I'm sorry, but we've never heard of her. Probably a freelance trying to pull one on you. They do it all the time. We have no feature planned about lobby shops, sorry. Shall I send the list back or what?'

'Oh, no, don't,' said Julie. The oldest trick in the book for freelancers getting information, and she hadn't spotted it. Now she looked a fool to the *Indie*, and if they found out at Fleming Cotterill – well, there was no reason why they should. 'No, just bin it.'

'Peace offering,' said Octavia. She held out a long narrow box. 'It's not vintage, but it is—'

'Let me guess. Bollinger. Mrs Fleming! How very kind. And to take time out of your extremely busy schedule.' The voice had an edge to it, but the eyes, moving over her face slowly, were soft, thoughtful.

'I felt I owed it to you,' she said quickly, feeling the wretched easy flush rising from her neck. 'I am so sorry about the other day. What I said.' She realised the messenger at the desk was watching her with some amusement; Gabriel Bingham realised it too.

'About my being gay, you mean?' he said loudly. The messenger glanced at him involuntarily, then returned to a intense study of his telephone directory. 'Honestly, I didn't mind. I've come to terms with it now. It's fine. If you can live with it, so can I.'

Oh—' She turned away, crossly, half hurt still.

He caught her by the shoulder, pulled her round to him, smiled down at her. 'Don't be silly. I really do appreciate your coming. Look, are you free for lunch? Or does a table full of power-dressed women await your arrival at the Ritz?'

'I never lunch at the Ritz,' she said, and then realised how absurd that sounded and smiled reluctantly.

'Well, are you awaited anywhere else?'

'No.'

'Good. Then have lunch with me? We can go up to the press dining room, I have a pass. The only thing is I must be in the chamber by three.'

'No, really, I have to get back to my office. I've a meeting at two thirty.'

'It's only a quarter to one. Where's your office?'

'South Ken,' she said, realising too late how predictable that must sound too.

He grinned at her. 'Of course. Well, what about a drink? On our famous terrace? Go on, Mrs Fleming, you can't come all this way and not let me give you at least something to wash down the humble pie. Just a small glass of mineral water. That's what you ladies who lunch drink, isn't it?'

'I'm not a lady who lunches,' she said irritably.

'I'm sorry. I thought you were. Well, anyway, you must allow the occasional drop of something to pass your lips. Clearly nothing solid, you are so admirably slim. Come on. Just a quiet one, as they say.'

She hesitated, then, 'Yes, all right. That would be very nice.'

'Marvellous. And we can discuss my sexual predilections further there.'

She smiled with pleasure as they came on to the famously lovely terrace, the river flowing surprisingly far beneath them, Westminster Bridge arching to their left.

'There's a table there, look. Grab it quickly. Busy day today.'

'Yes, I know.'

'You do?'

'Yes, of course,' she said irritably. 'Debate about taxation, isn't there? And the IMF. That's why I came today. I thought you were fairly likely to be here.'

'Good Lord,' he said, studying her, 'you must have been very keen to apprehend me.'

'Is there anything wrong with that?'

'No, of course not. Don't start getting huffy. Try this. It should be very nice. Pouilly-Fuissé. I am not entirely unaware of life's more sophisticated pleasures, you see. They keep a very good cellar here. The best in England, some say.'

'It's lovely,' she said, sipping it. She met his eyes; he smiled at her, and she felt that smile, felt it move through her, warm, intriguing.

'It was very sweet of you to come,' he said, and the word was unexpected somehow. 'I really do appreciate it.'

'I felt so bad. It was a foul thing to say.'

'Well, I've said some fairly foul ones to you. So we're quits.'

'I hope so.'

There was a silence; she looked at him. He was wearing a suit; it wasn't at all a good suit. Her eye, trained by Tom's obsessive stylishness, placed it as very mass-market indeed, Principles probably, and under it he wore a very unsuitable shirt, light woollen check, with a striped, rather battered tie, and with the navy suit he wore brown Hush Puppies. He was a sartorial nightmare; perversely she liked him for it.

'What are you thinking?' he said, looking at her.

'Oh, nothing really.'

'Yes, you were. Come on.'

'I was thinking about your clothes,' she said, 'actually. That I hadn't seen you in a suit before.'

'Do you admire my suit? I bought it in the spring, just in case I got in. And what about the shoes? Ken Clarke style, very politically correct.'

She laughed. 'But the wrong party.'

'Yes, well, you can't have everything. On such small things is political success built. I'm only joking.'

'I do realise that,' she said sharply.

'Oh, you are touchy,' he said. 'Where does it come from, this dreadful defensiveness?'

'My father,' she said, without thinking.

'Do you have any siblings?'

'No, just me and my father.'

'How very claustrophobic.'

'Not at all,' she said. 'We were very happy together.'

'Good,' he said lightly. 'And how did he react when you were stolen away from him?'

She stared at him. 'What?'

'Stolen by your husband. Surely that's how he saw it?'

'Of course he didn't,' she said. She felt alarmed, almost threatened by his swift grasp of her situation.

'Then, he must be a saint. Your father.'

'Oh, no,' she said, laughing. 'No, he's not a saint.'

'It's nice when you laugh,' he said suddenly. 'You don't do it enough. It suits you . . .'

'Dickon, I've got to go out for a couple of hours this afternoon,' said Louise. 'I've arranged for you to go and play with Timmy.'

'Can't I come with you?'

'No, darling, not today. I've got to go to the dentist.'

'You're not ill, are you?' said Dickon, his large dark eyes filling with alarm.

'Of course not. I'm fine.'

'Can we go to the swings when you get back?'

'Yes, all right. We'll take Timmy if you like.'

'That's a lot of letters.'

'Yes, business ones I'm doing for Daddy. I've got to finish them, and post them when I go to the dentist. Now we might go to McDonald's later. You deserve it, you've been such a good boy lately.'

'Yes, please!' said Dickon. 'You are a kind mummy.'

'Yes, well, I'm feeling rather kind. Just at the moment.'

'You're looking a bit flushed,' said Melanie. 'What have you been doing?'

'Oh, nothing much.'

'Good. I'm delighted.'

'What about?'

'Your lunch date.'

'I didn't have a lunch date,' said Octavia irritably.

'Okay, have it your own way. Fine by me.'

Octavia went into her office. She felt extremely lightheaded; she'd had two glasses of wine, she who never drank and certainly not at lunchtime. She felt sweetly flustered, happily disturbed; the pain, the humiliation of Tom's behaviour somehow anaesthetised by the ebb and flow of interest and amusement and sharp response that was Gabriel Bingham's speciality, by his sudden warmth, his even more sudden gentleness, by her response to those things, surprisingly eager, questing even. By the fact that her head was full of him, and that when she thought of him, his eyes on her, increasingly thoughtful, his long, rangy body moving slowly nearer her as they talked, so that by the end of the bottle of wine and the lunch hour he was pressed against her, casually perhaps, but very firmly, and if she moved, shifted even slightly, he moved too, followed her, and when she acknowledged that fact by looking at him, meeting his eyes, he smiled at her, acknowledging it too, and when that happened, something leaped in her, something half-forgotten, a sliver of sexual excitement, sensual exploration; by all those things she was most tenderly and surprisingly moved.

'We must do this again,' he had said as she left, as his lips grazed hers, 'and that is not an empty statement, not just London-speak for goodbye. I really would like it. If you would, of course.'

And she had smiled at him, said she would like it, but she didn't quite know, and he had said in that case he would know for her, and had waved her off in her taxi, and she had slithered down in the seat, and gazed out of the window on to a day that was suddenly most brilliantly coloured; and had thus arrived back at the office. Flushed. As Melanie had remarked.

Her phone rang; it was Louise.

'Boot, hallo. I just thought I'd phone. See if you were all right.'

And because it was Louise, Louise of all people, she said, 'I've just had an illicit lunch hour.'

'Boot! What have you been up to, and where and with who?'

'Well, only drinking wine. But at the House of Commons. On the terrace. With a very attractive man.'

'Really? What, an MP?'

'Yes. So funny, his name's Gabriel Bingham, he's the member for North Somerset, and I met him through the Bartles Wood thing. You know? I mean, it's only a bit of nonsense, and it certainly isn't going to lead anywhere but—'

'Why not? Why shouldn't you have an affair, if you want to?'

'Louise, I haven't even thought of having an affair,' said Octavia, truthfully, half amused, half surprised. 'Just a bit of a flirtation. That's all.'

'Is he attractive? Sexy?'

'Yes. Very. I mean, not good looking, but – yes. Very sexy. Sort of awkward and challenging. You know how I don't like easy men.'

'Well, no one could call Tom easy,' said Louise. There was an edge to her voice.

Octavia laughed. 'No, they couldn't.'

'And are you going to see this awkward person again?'

'I don't know. I shouldn't think so. It was just a lunch, Louise. That's all.'

'Well, a lot of the best affairs start with lunch,' said Louise. 'How is Tom, anyway?'

'He's all right. Why?'

'Oh, just wondered. About the business and so on.'

'Well, it is very dodgy. Like I told you. Now, can we talk about something else, please? I haven't forgotten about that article about reversing vasectomies, my secretary's going through all the papers for it.'

'How very kind of her,' said Louise. Her voice was oddly sharp. Octavia felt stung.

'Louise! Don't! You're being ridiculous. It's much more sensible for her to do things like that. It doesn't make any difference to you. It's not as if I'd forgotten about it.'

'No, of course not.'

'How are you feeling anyway?'

'Pretty bloody,' said Louise.

CHAPTER 23

If he had a gun, Tom thought, he would have shot her. Stupid, bloody, incompetent woman: how could she have? How could she? Then he pulled himself together; she was only the messenger. It really wasn't her fault. Given the same situation, at her age, and level of competence – or rather incompetence – he would probably have done the same. With the same ghastly result.

It had been Bob Macintosh who had alerted him to it. He'd phoned first thing: Tom should know, he thought, of a letter he had received that morning. He'd fax it immediately. 'Only have a stiff brandy in your hand.'

Tom had gone over to the fax machine and waited. And watched while it spewed out what he recognised to be disaster.

A memo, on plain paper, computer written: to Bob Macintosh.

> Fleming Cotterill are in serious financial trouble. One crucial client has left them and the effect of this on the cashflow has forced the company to seek further financial backing. Given the state of the company finances and its extravagant lifestyle, this could be difficult. Clients might be advised to move to other, more reliable firms.

The memo was unsigned, but copied to 'All clients, Fleming Cotterill'.

Tom was unable to move or even to speak for some time; then he picked it up and went into Aubrey's office.

'Today of all days,' he said simply, handing it over.

Aubrey knew what he meant: today they were to hear from Terence Foster.

A swift, carefully worded round of phone calls had confirmed that their other clients had received the same document. The staff had been summoned, questioned; and Julie Springer – flushed, tearful, wretched – had admitted to giving a full list of clients and their addresses over the phone to the *Independent*. 'Well, I thought it was to the *Independent*.'

'To a journalist whose name you didn't recognise?'

'Yes.'

'And whose name you did not check?'

'No.'

'Extremely stupid,' said Tom. 'Unbelievably stupid.'

'I'm so sorry. So very sorry.'

'I'm afraid that doesn't help us. In the least.'

'Julie, don't cry,' said Aubrey gently. 'Tom, all she did was send a full client list to the paper. That's not a crime in itself. There's nothing confidential in it. It's information readily available to anyone. Actually.'

Tom stared at him, then he said, 'Yes. Yes, you're right. I'm sorry, Julie. But it was inefficient not to check, and not to tell someone what happened later. Look, get back to your desk, field any calls that come through, say it's a mistake, and we're sending out a full release later today. Although Christ knows what it can say. Fucking thing's absolutely correct.'

So how had he known about their situation, the bastard who had written this, sent it out? Nobody knew how bad things were. Nobody knew in the company, except Aubrey and himself. Illingworth knew, but he was hardly likely to have talked, to have endangered one of his own clients, it would be professional suicide. What about Foster? No, those guys just didn't know.

Only one person knew, only one person outside the company. It must have been her: some insane, absurd revenge. He picked up the phone.

'How dare you?' Octavia's voice was shaking with hostility. 'How dare you even suggest such a thing? Of course I wouldn't have talked about your company and its troubles. To anyone. I have told no one, no one at all, about it. It makes me feel sick, that you could suspect such a thing. Sick and totally insulted. I'm not some little halfwit stay-at-home, I do have a brain on me, a business brain. I'm very very sorry for you, but this conversation is making me feel ill. Please make sure Aubrey isn't harbouring the same filthy suspicions, would you? I'd hate to have him think badly of me. As you so clearly do.'

She put the phone down, and sat with her head in her hands, trying to calm herself down. Bastard. Bastard! To dare even to suggest that she'd . . . God, she hated him.

Derek Illingworth, questioned more tactfully than Octavia had been, said that not a word about the Fleming Cotterill situation could have got out of his firm.

'It would be more than my own life is worth to talk about it. Bloody odd. Postmark any clue?'

''Fraid not,' said Tom. 'The only person I asked to check was Bob Macintosh, and his secretary had already binned the envelope and then chucked the dregs of her coffee in the bin. Totally illegible.'

'And you don't feel you can ask anyone else?'

'I didn't want to make a meal of it. Perhaps that was a mistake.'

'Well, it could be a clue. Anyway, I'll put some feelers out, make sure there's been no funny phone calls here, or anything.'

'You haven't heard from Foster yet?' said Tom.

'No. Hopefuly he won't get to hear of this, but . . .'

'That's a big but,' said Tom.

Half an hour later Illingworth phoned back. There had indeed been a funny phone call from someone from one of the financial papers, asking about private investors, and who they might recommend.

'The girl who took the call said we never handed out that sort of information. But it seems odd. Given the other thing. You're not that worried, are you?'

'Is the Pope Catholic?' said Tom gloomily.

At midday there was a call from the one remaining potential client, the one from whom they'd had the highest hopes: the restaurant chain. He thought he should let them know that he'd decided on another firm. 'Nothing personal, just feel I'd like the weight of one of the bigger boys behind me.'

'Yes, of course,' said Tom. 'Very understandable.' He didn't even try to put up a fight. He knew there was no point.

Octavia was finding it very hard to concentrate; she and Melanie were in the middle of their meeting with Lauren Bartlett about the day at Brands Hatch. Lauren had been in a difficult mood, questioning every point, quibbling over costs, criticising the suite they had provisionally booked – 'I really don't think it's big enough, three hundred people is nothing for us' – the programme they had drawn up – 'It's too male orientated. All the men will want to go round the circuit, but half the women will be terrified. And it's the women who are our prime target, surely.'

'But, Lauren,' said Melanie, her eyes glittering dangerously, 'you specifically said you wanted to get the men in. Said they'd spend the money.'

'Did I? Well, maybe I was wrong. I think we should make it more of a family day out. More of the go-karting, that sort of thing.'

'I thought you wanted glamour,' said Octavia wearily 'And anyway, it's not that sort of day. It's the classic touring race day, we booked into that one deliberately, agreed that would pull in what they call the tweeds and pearls. After all, you're not just going to make money from the invited guests, are you? We're targeting the other eighty-five thousand people as well.'

'Yes, yes, I know all that, but I want family fun. And glamour as well. Look, this is costing us an awful lot of money. We have to get it back. And if we're going to get the sort of publicity you promised, there's got to be more than a few races and stalls and an opportunity for the chaps to go round the rallying circuit. We need some – excitement. Something to talk about. I'm still hoping that the Princess of Wales will come. Bring the boys. She did seem interested when I told her about it. Just before she went away, you know.'

'Really?' said Melanie.

'But of course they won't come unless—'

'How about making it a vintage day?' said Melanie. 'For your guests, I mean. Since it's the classic day. Everyone come in 'twenties and 'thirties costume. The women would like that much more. We could have waiters in period costume, making cocktails, maybe a jazz band up in the hospitality suite, special posters everywhere. And then the kids could have a fancy dress prize, and—'

'Yes,' said Lauren. She smiled graciously at Melanie. 'I like that a lot. What a pity you didn't come up with something like that before. Look, would you like to rethink the whole day along those lines, get back to me in – let's see—' she consulted her small black Hermès diary – 'a week?'

'A week isn't long,' said Octavia, 'not to clear it with the Brands Hatch people, rehash the programme, the invitations, the early press release. Couldn't we—'

'We'll manage,' said Melanie quickly. 'It won't be that difficult.'

Octavia looked at her; she had an expression on her face she very well knew. Her face was alive, her eyes sparkling, her hawklike nose somehow scenting the air. It was a brilliant idea; but it annoyed her. It meant they would be in a fearful panic from now on, and Lauren Bartlett and Next Generation most certainly wouldn't pick up any more of the bill; they were doing the whole thing on a break-even basis already. It meant that the only thing that Melanie actually had in mind was the raising of the profile of Capital C. If she hadn't been so sick at heart, she might have put up a fight.

★

That evening, one of Fleming Cotterill's existing clients, the owner of a small chain of garden centres, said that he had decided most reluctantly that he was going to have dispense with their services. 'Nothing personal, just have to make sure every penny's being wisely spent in these hard times.'

Shortly after that, Derek Illingworth phoned and said that Terence Foster had declined their offer to become involved in the company.

'Someone up there doesn't like us,' said Aubrey wearily, refilling their glasses with the stiff brandy suggested by Bob Macintosh much earlier in the day.

'Or out there.'

'Sorry? Oh, yes. I see what you mean. Have you any idea at all who might have done that, Tom? Or why?'

'None whatsoever. Do you think we should have tried to check the postmarks?'

'Difficult. Under the circumstances. Mountain out of molehill stuff.'

'Yes, but he might have some other little surprise in store for us. Isn't there anyone else we could ask? Someone like Mike Dutton.'

'It could be worth a try. And look, I hestitate to say this, but there really is only one last port of call now. And you know who that is, don't you?'

'I'm afraid I do,' said Tom.

'So how are things with Tom?' said Felix. They were sitting in McDonald's with the twins, who were devouring Big Macs and strawberry milkshakes; Octavia smiled at him fondly. It had been Gideon's sports day; Tom had pleaded pressure of work, 'or should I say, the threat of enforced idleness', as an excuse, and Felix had gone with her and the children.

Felix had, rather surprisingly, covered himself with glory by coming in third in the fathers' race (having got special dispensation to compete), and Poppy even more so by winning the sisters' race. Gideon had won nothing, but had played for the First Eleven in an exhibition game and didn't care.

'Tom's fine,' said Octavia briefly. 'You were so wonderful this afternoon, Daddy. Not many grandfathers could have done that.'

'Oh, I don't know,' said Felix modestly. 'We're not all in wheelchairs.'

'I still remember you winning the fathers' race at Wycombe Abbey. I was so proud of you. And Louise said you were amazingly good looking, the most handsome father there, as well as the fastest.'

'Yes, well, she always was rather a one for the compliment. How is she, by the way?'

'Managing, just, I think. Poor Louise – and poor Charles. I spoke to him the other day. He was clearing out Anna's room. He was so upset, being so brave.' Saying that stirred something; something uneasy, something she had half forgotten. What was it?

Tom had a very large whisky and then made two phone calls. The first was to Mike Dutton, of Dutton Distilleries, to say they were looking for any kind of clue as to who might have sent the letters: would it be an awful lot to ask if the secretary could check the postmark? Dutton said she'd gone home, but he'd have a quick look in the bin himself; and came back to the phone to say the cleaners had already been and emptied the bins.

'Sorry, Tom. This is really worrying you, is it?'

'Oh, not too much,' said Tom, 'it's all such utter nonsense. But forewarned is forearmed and all that.'

'Yes, of course. Well, cheers. Sorry we couldn't help. Oh, and, Tom—'

'Yes?' said Tom, feeling his bowels turning to water.

'Please don't think we'll be taking any notice of that memo. Couldn't manage without you, and we know it.'

'Mike,' said Tom, 'you're a hero.'

The exchange had made the contemplation of the next phone call more bearable: he dialled Felix Miller's office.

Felix's secretary said that he was out that afternoon, 'At your son's sports day,' she said. Tom hoped he was imagining the edge to her voice, and said, yes of course, but could she ask Felix to call him in the morning.

'Yes, of course, Mr Fleming.'

'Mrs Fleming?'

'Yes, Mr Bingham,' said Octavia, smiling into the phone.

'I rang to see if you were coming down out of the smoke this weekend?'

'No, I don't think so. The children have got things on and I've got work to do.'

'Well, it's a pity. I was hoping to spend some more time coaching Gideon. If you change your mind, give me a ring. In Bath.'

'Yes. Yes, I will.'

'Goodbye, Mrs Fleming.'

'Goodbye, Mr Bingham. Have a nice weekend.'

'There'd be more chance of it being that if you were coming down,' he said and rang off.

Octavia sat smiling foolishly at the phone for several moments, tantalised by the thought of another weekend at the cottage. Maybe she could go. At least on Saturday night, after the twins had attended their respective parties. That would give her Sunday there. That would be fun. Only now maybe it would look a bit pushy. She didn't want him to think she was chasing him. Well, maybe she could ask someone else. Louise and Dickon, for instance. Sandy was away in France on one of his promotional wine tours. That would make it look a lot less calculating. It seemed ages anyway since she and Louise had had any time together. And Louise had said she couldn't wait to meet Gabriel. Yes, she'd ask her. She dialled Louise's number. She was out, but the cleaning lady said she'd get her to call back.

'She's gone to the dentist. I've got Dickon here. Oh, just a minute, he wants to speak to you.'

Octavia was touched. She was very fond of Dickon. 'Hallo, darling! How are you?'

'All right. Mummy's gone to the dentist again. She went the other day too.'

'Poor Mummy. Has she got toothache?'

'Yes, but she's not ill.'

'Of course she's not ill. Toothache isn't ill. I thought you might like to come and see us on Sunday. At the cottage. What do you think? The twins'll be there. And Minty.'

'Yes!'

'Well, tell Mummy to phone me when she gets back. And we'll try and arrange it.'

'All right, Octavia. 'Bye.'

''Bye, darling.'

Sweet little boy, he was, thought Octavia; obviously still desperately worried about illness. It was so sad.

Mike Dutton phoned Tom Fleming, but was informed he was on another call: would he wait?

'No, I'm in rather a hurry. Could you just give him a message from me? Tell him my secretary's just come up trumps. The postmark was Gloucester. He'll know what it means.'

Barbara Dawson said she would certainly pass the message on.

Tom arrived shortly after lunch at Nico Cadogan's penthouse office, looking appalling: drawn, pale, heavy eyed. He'd also lost weight: a good half stone, Cadogan reckoned, since their first meeting.

'You having a bad time with this memo business?' Cadogan said briefly.

'What? Oh, a bit. A couple of defectors, but most people seem to be piling in behind us.'

'It's not true about the financial problems?'

'Lord, no.'

'Good,' said Cadogan briefly. 'Coffee?'

'Yes, please.'

'The share price has steadied,' Cadogan said, 'and, rather pleasingly, some shares have been bought.'

'Really? That is good news. Obviously some speculators out there have faith in you. It always happens, of course. Now, strictly between ourselves, I have heard this morning that we are likely to go to referral.'

'Quick.'

'Yes, I know. And it's not official. But your MP got his question asked, there are a lot of signatures on the EDM – there are a great many keen new MPs wanting to look efficient. And the government is anxious to show its mettle. Supporting the individual, that sort of thing. They're no more bothered about huge conglomerates than the last lot, of course, but they like to be seen to be.'

'Can I say that in the interview?'

'Absolutely not! It would almost certainly reverse the decision. But I think you can feel more relaxed. Right, now, if we could just run through—'

'Sorry to interrupt, Mr Cadogan. There's an urgent call for Mr Fleming. A Mrs Cornish.'

Nico Cadogan was not given to clichéd thought, but looking at Tom Fleming's face at that moment, the phrase 'drained of colour' seemed totally appropriate. He set down his cup, with a slightly unsteady hand, cleared his throat.

'Nico, would you excuse me? Just for a moment?'

'Sure. Want to take it in here, in private? I'll clear out.'

'No, no, I'll call her back. On my mobile.'

'Of course. There's a meeting room empty, use that.'

'Thanks.'

He came back after a few minutes, still looking ghastly, but more in control. 'Sorry about that. Prospective client. Now then, if we could just run through this list of possible questions . . .'

Mrs Cornish was about as likely to be a prospective client, Cadogan thought, as Fleming Cotterill were to be on sound financial ground.

'Yes, all right,' said Felix, 'I can see you on Monday. Soon enough for you?'

Tom thought fast. He could probably string the bank along for the weekend. And he didn't want to rush at Felix. It would be very counterproductive. And at least it would give him a chance to talk to Octavia about it. That wasn't going to be easy. 'Yes, Felix, Monday morning would be great. Thanks. And thanks for going to the sports day yesterday. I hear you covered yourself with glory. More than I would have done.'

'Yes, well, it was nice for Gideon to have someone running in the race. Pity you couldn't go, Tom. Octavia was very upset. She sets great store by such things. I don't think I ever let her down on one official occasion, all the time she was growing up.'

'Really?' said Tom, feeling his teeth going on edge. 'See you on Monday, then.'

'Yes. Don't be late.'

'I'll try not to be,' said Tom wearily.

He put down the phone, feeling nauseated. He had never thought it would come to this. Crawling to Felix Miller. Asking for his help. Well, he probably wouldn't get it. At best he'd get his arse kicked very thoroughly. And if Felix had got word of his – behaviour . . . God, it was a miracle he hadn't. He still didn't really understand why Octavia hadn't told him. It was extraordinary. He supposed in some odd way the whole thing reflected back on her, showed her up as a failure too. Not Daddy's perfect little girl any more. Her judgment wrong, her performance as a wife seriously under question. Though Felix wouldn't see it like that. God, no!

Tom diverted his mind from the prospect of Felix seeing it any way at all, and decided he should call the bank. He buzzed for Barbara, told her to get David Jackson on the phone.

'Sure. Oh, and, Tom, a message from—'

'Barbara, I don't want any messages now. Okay? About anything. It can keep. Whatever it is. Unless it was the Bank of England waving a hundred grand at me.'

'It wasn't,' said Barbara briskly.

'Fine. Later, then.'

'I really do think,' said Felix, 'that you only have yourself to blame. You've let those children run rings round you, encouraged them to do exactly what they want, and now—'

'I'm sorry, Felix,' said Marianne, 'but I really don't think I want to listen to this.'

'Very well. Now, look, about the weekend—'

'I don't think I want to talk about the weekend, either, not just now. Goodbye, Felix.'

She put the phone down, and sat looking at it; its image blurred suddenly. She felt beleaguered. Zoë was behaving very badly, was being rude and obstructive; she was waiting to hear if she had a job at a pub near the Tower of London. So far she had had one trial evening, which had gone badly, and was waiting for another. She had found the complex orders, the 'same again' rounds, even the computerised tills, very difficult; for some reason, which Marianne was unable to understand, it was out of the question for her even to consider any other work until this was settled. She was altogether in a strange state, jumpy and irritable and more than usually protective about her comings and goings, especially at the weekends. Her financial situation was dire, and she was in a state of permanent rage with the bank, whom she saw as entirely responsible for it; Marianne had drawn a line under any further loans herself, but she knew Zoë was borrowing from Romilly. Who, as Zoë lost no opportunity to point out, had more money than anyone in the family now.

But the real problem was Romilly. At the meeting at Choice, Marianne (telling herself that, after all, she had custody of her, so was absolutely within her rights to make such a decision) had agreed to a limited amount of modelling work for Romilly during the school holidays, which (she told herself again) Alec really need not know about for the time being. What she tried to ignore was a small, dangerous, truthful voice telling her that legally she might be within her rights, but morally she was not.

Romilly herself carried with her an air of slightly distant self-confidence, and even slighter, but unmistakable, superiority; it astonished Marianne that she could have changed so much and so swiftly.

But the Christie's contract was more of a problem. The shoot was scheduled for the beginning of September, and inevitably that was going to run into the start of term. The dates would only overlap by a day or two, but it was a dangerous precedent to set so early. It would also be very high profile. A slowly growing panic was settling itself into a small area of Marianne's stomach; so far she had managed to hold off on the meeting with Serena Fox at which i's would be dotted and t's crossed and she, on Romilly's behalf, would be required to sign the contract, but she knew it was only a question of days, a week at the most. She had wanted to discuss the whole thing with Felix, get his invariably sound dispassionate judgment on the matter, but . . .

'Marianne? Nico Cadogan. Why haven't you returned my calls?'

'Nico, I—'

'Look, what are you doing on Sunday? How about dinner?'

'Nico, no. Really. I can't.'

'Why not?'

'Well, I—' She stopped. She had tickets for the last, gala performance at Covent Garden before it closed for refurbishing. She had been going to take Felix as a surprise. It suddenly occurred to her he didn't deserve it. And what was she doing, turning her back on the one person in the world who didn't appear to be openly hostile to her at the moment?

'I know you like opera,' she said, 'but how would you feel about a bit of ballet as well?'

'Passionate,' he said.

'I cannot believe you're going to do that. Seriously. Ask my father for money. After what you've done to me. Honestly, I just don't think I can continue with this conversation. It's making me feel sick.'

'Octavia, will you listen to me?' They were at home, in the drawing room. He stood up suddenly, came over to her, bent down, put his face close up to hers. 'Fleming Cotterill is on the brink of bankruptcy. The bank is about to foreclose. We've already lost two crucial clients, and we'll probably lose more, thanks to that mailing. We can't pay the rent or the rates on our building. We won't be able to pay the staff at the end of this month. Aubrey and I haven't taken any salary this time round.'

'My heart bleeds for you.'

'Oh, for God's sake, Octavia! Don't you realise what will happen to *you*, if the company goes down? I shall quite possibly be declared bankrupt. The house will go.'

'Tom, I want a divorce, I don't care what happens to the house.'

'Don't be so fucking stupid! There will be *no money*, don't you understand? No money at all. Not for the children, not for you, not for anything. Doesn't that worry you?'

She shrugged. 'I'm not going to be bankrupt. I have my own income. I'll look after the children.'

'Octavia, with the greatest respect, your salary will hardly cover the food and clothes bills. Certainly not anywhere for you to live, certainly not things like school fees.'

'We could—' She stopped herself.

'Go and stay with your father? Yes, of course you could. Without me. And what do you think that would do to the children? What sort of message would that send out?'

'Nothing like the message your behaviour will send out to them,' she said, 'when they hear about it.'

'Well, what they hear is entirely up to you.'

'I suppose you want me to lie to them? Pretend you're the perfect father still, that we're just going to live in separate houses for a bit?'

'Something like that, yes. Don't look at me like that, Octavia. I'm not looking for protection for myself, it's them I'm thinking of. Whatever I've done, do you really plan to rub their noses in it? If you're really hellbent on this divorce, we owe it to them to make it as painless as possible. They don't have to know—'

'That you're a cheat and a liar?'

'No,' he said. 'No, they don't. And they shouldn't. They'll be hurt enough by the very fact of our separating. I think we should tell them the usual things; that we're not getting along very well any more, that we're still friends, that we think we'll be happier living apart.'

'That would be very much nicer for you, wouldn't it?'

'God, you're a bitch,' he said, and he looked down at her with such distaste that she felt chilled suddenly. 'Of course I've behaved badly. Appallingly. I don't feel very happy about it, you know. I feel ashamed and wretched. I've been trying to put it right. As best I can. They shouldn't be made to feel ashamed and wretched about me. If you go down that path, it'll be an own-goal for you, Octavia.'

'Tom, I'm sorry, but you should have thought of that.'

He sighed, turned away from her. 'All right. Have it your own way. Do what you think best. But what's best for them has to be for things to go on as much as possible the same way. Staying in the same house, going to the same schools, seeing the same friends. I'll move out, if that's what you want—'

'Of course it's what I want.'

'I'll go and live in some hovel. But let's not hurt them more than we have to. It isn't fair.'

She stared at him. 'I can't believe *you're* talking of fairness.'

But he had touched something in her, some core of common sense for the children. He was right. They did deserve protection. From the truth, the ugliness. If she loved them, she should do that for them. It wasn't fair, it was hideously unfair. But it was what she should do.

She sat looking up at him, thinking how much she hated him. 'All right, Tom. Talk to my father. I won't make things any more difficult for you. But sooner or later, he's going to find out, and then God help you.'

CHAPTER 24

'I don't know how you can ask me that,' said Louise. Her large blue eyes were shocked. 'Me of all people. Your best friend. Of course I think you should divorce him. And give him the most horrible time possible. Bastard! He doesn't deserve you, Octavia, he really doesn't.'

'I know, but what he said about the children: it's true. They really are the innocent ones in all this. They shouldn't have to suffer.'

'What about you?'

'Me! Oh, Lulu, nothing is ever just one person's fault, is it? I must have done something wrong, a lot probably, to have made Tom be unfaithful.'

She pulled fretfully at a long, trailing arm of honeysuckle that was dangling down on to the table; they were sitting outside the cottage, watching Poppy patiently playing catch with Dickon. Minty was on her knee; every so often she dropped a kiss on the top of her small dark head.

'Octavia, stop it,' said Louise. 'That is just nonsense. You can't think like that, you mustn't. Tom is a cheat and a bastard. He didn't deserve you in the first place. He doesn't deserve *anyone* half decent.'

Octavia sighed. 'I must say, I have hoped that whoever she is, this woman, she's putting him through hell. Absolute hell.'

'How's his company now?'

'Very bad. One of the things I was going to tell you was that he's going to—'

'Mummy, can we take Dickon for a walk? It's getting so hot.'

'Not just yet, darling. Mr Bingham is coming over.'

'Why?'

'We have some business together, he and I.'

'What sort of business?'

'Oh – work. It's very complicated.'

'You always say that,' said Poppy, 'when you don't want to tell us something. Anyway, how long's he going to be? Me and Dickon are getting bored, aren't we, Dickon?'

Dickon, who would have jumped off a fifty-foot building if Poppy had told him it was all right, nodded vigorously.

'I'll get you some drinks,' said Octavia. 'Or what about an ice lolly?'

'Yes, *please.*'

'Louise?'

'No, thank you,' said Louise, laughing. 'They make my teeth hurt.'

'How are your teeth?'

'Sorry?'

'Weren't you at the dentist on Friday?'

'Oh, yes. Only a check-up, though.'

'You had toothache before,' said Dickon.

'No, I didn't, darling.'

'Yes, you did. When you went to the dentist the other time. When you had all those letters to post. And we went to the McDonald's when you got back and—'

'Oh, then. Yes, I'd forgotten that,' said Louise. She smiled at Octavia. 'Lost a filling. Always horrid, isn't it?'

'Yes, horrid,' said Octavia. 'I wouldn't forget it so quickly.'

'It was ages ago,' said Louise.

'No, it wasn't,' said Dickon, 'it was just the other day.'

'Dickon, it wasn't.'

'It was. I remember—'

'Mrs Fleming. Good afternoon.'

Octavia jumped up, smiling, feeling absurdly nervous. Feeling something else too, which she couldn't quite work out. Something worrying. Something odd . . .

'Boot! Aren't you going to introduce me to your friend?' Louise was smiling up at her, then stood up and held her hand out to Gabriel Bingham. 'Louise Trelawny. Old friend of Octavia's.'

'Yes, she told me. You went to school together, is that right?'

'Yes. Happiest days of our lives, weren't they, Boot?'

'In some ways, yes,' said Octavia slowly. 'Would you like some tea, Gabriel?'

'Yes, please. Now where is my cricketing partner? I hope he hasn't let me down.'

''Fraid not,' said Octavia, laughing. 'He's inside, watching the test match on television. I'm amazed he hasn't heard you. I'll tell him you're here.'

Waiting for the kettle to boil, she tried to work out what had – or what might have – been worrying her; but by the time she had made the tea, had a further argument with Poppy about the prospective walk, and set a time limit to Gideon on the cricket practice, she had completely forgotten that she had been worried at all.

'I like your friend,' said Gabriel Bingham. Louise and Dickon had gone and he looked up from the mug of coffee she had just made him, smiled at her across the kitchen. 'Very pretty. Bit neurotic, but—'

'Neurotic? Oh, I wouldn't describe Louise as neurotic,' said Octavia. 'She's very emotional, and she's had a horrid time – her mother, whom she adored, died just a few weeks ago. And she had a little daughter who died at nine months. And she isn't very happily married.'

'Dear, oh, dear. What a tragic story.'

'It is,' said Octavia defensively. 'It isn't funny.'

'Of course it isn't,' he said, looking at her rather seriously, then smiling gently. 'You really must try not to be so tetchy, Mrs Fleming.'

'I'm not tetchy,' said Octavia, 'I just don't like people's troubles being belittled. Especially my best friend's.'

'I'm not belittling poor Louise's troubles. But I stand my ground – she is neurotic. She's jumpy. Watchful. Especially with the little boy. And too careful what she says.'

'Louise? She's always getting into trouble for *not* being careful of what she says.'

'I think not. Actually. And I do assure you, I'm a very good judge of character. Had you summed up straight away. Looked at you that day in Bartles Wood, thought *there* goes a tetchy lady. Want to know what else I thought?' The hazel eyes looking at her were alight with amusement.

'Oh, for God's sake,' said Octavia. She stood up, picked up her own mug of coffee, turned to the sink.

'I'm so tired of being got at by you. All the time. When I . . .'

'Oh, dear,' he said, and she heard him get up, still didn't look round, afraid he would see the tears, the wretched easy tears; and then suddenly, there was an arm round her shoulders, a head close to hers.

'Do you want to know what else I thought? I thought there is a rather sexy lady. And beautiful. And quite nice too, unless I'm much mistaken. I wasn't, as it turned out,' he added rather complacently.

'Oh,' said Octavia. 'Oh, I see.'

She felt rather foolish, incapable of thinking of anything to say in return.

'Octavia,' he said suddenly, 'I don't know what's going on in your marriage. I'm not asking you to tell me. And I certainly don't want to add to your troubles. In any way. But if you were not married, or not married any more, or even in the process of becoming not married any more, I would like to get to know you very much better. How's that for a romantic proposal?'

'It's not bad,' she said, smiling up at him rather uncertainly through the tears.

'And could you imagine yourself accepting it?'

'I – well . . .' More than anything, she wanted to say yes. But something stopped her. Fear, she supposed; but she didn't know what of. It was ridiculous. Go on, Octavia, do it, say you'd like it, say—

'I'm sorry,' he said, drawing back. 'I've said too much. Stupid of me.'

His voice was cooler, more detached now, his eyes harder.

'No,' she said, 'you haven't. It's just that I – well, you see . . .'

She wasn't confident, that was the thing; she was desperately insecure. She hadn't realised how desperately until that moment, how hurt, how shaky Tom's rejection had made her; hadn't realised that she had studied and fretted over herself, her looks, her figure, her conversation, her performance at work, at home, at the dinner table, her performance most of all, of course, in bed. What if that was it? Why Tom had left her, discarded her? She had had so little experience, apart from him; for all she knew, she was dull, hopeless, useless in bed. And if she did go to bed with Gabriel, then that dullness, that hopelessness, would be displayed, and she would feel worse, more despairing—

'Mummy! Gideon's hurt his foot. Quick, it's bleeding.'

'Oh, God,' she said, running out of the kitchen; Gabriel followed her.

Gideon was sitting on the ground, outside their gate, looking at his bare foot in horrified fascination. Sticking out of it she could see a jagged edge of glass, and blood pumping relentlessly.

Poppy was pointing not at the foot but the glass. 'Mummy! It's horrible. Quick, pull it out.'

'No,' said Gabriel sharply, 'don't touch it. We must get him to hospital. Fast. Silly little bugger, going out there without your shoes.'

'He knows he's not allowed to,' said Poppy, sobs choking her.

'Shut up,' said Gideon. He was very white.

'I'll drive,' said Gabriel. He bent and picked up Gideon, stood cradling him in his arms. 'Can we take your car? It's faster.'

'Yes, of course. I must get Minty. Poppy, get in the back, strap yourself in. Don't worry, darling, he'll be fine.'

'Bring some towels,' shouted Gabriel as she rushed into the house.

A nightmare three hours followed. The Sunday evening traffic was beginning and it took them over an hour to reach Bath General. Casualty was full of holiday accidents: cuts, stings, minor broken bones. She looked at the foot, no longer bleeding, but ugly, swollen round the glass, experiencing wild fears about septicaemia, gangrene, amputation. Why was it taking so long, so terribly long?

Gabriel and Poppy had gone for a walk; Minty sat in her buggy, mercifully asleep.

The doctor finally looked at the foot, said it would need stitching and cleaning, but he could do it under a local. Octavia had hoped for a nice remote, surgical procedure under general anaesthetic, and Gideon then returned to her, neatly bandaged, not the horror taking place before her eyes. And Gideon's.

'Won't that be horribly painful? And traumatic, he's terribly upset already.'

'No, of course not. He won't feel a thing. This is Valium,' he said to Octavia, easing a needle into a vein in Gideon's arm. 'Works very quickly. And he won't remember much about it afterwards.'

It was just as well, thought Octavia, standing by the bed, holding Gideon's hand, stroking his hair, watching in sick horror as they cut out the glass, cleaned the wound, stitched it up.

When it was over, and they were outside, Gideon sleepily peaceful in a wheelchair, she felt suddenly faint and half fell on to a seat.

'Dear, oh, dear.' She heard Gabriel Bingham's voice from a great distance. 'How many more invalids do I have to take charge of today?'

He pushed her head down between her knees, asked a nurse to fetch her some water, sat quietly by her until she felt better.

'I'm sorry,' she said, sitting back finally, smiling rather weakly at him. 'I haven't done very well altogether today, have I?'

'You've done all right,' he said, smiling back at her, and pushed a stray bit of hair back from her face. 'Now I think we should get back to the cottage. I'd ask you to my house, but I imagine it's a bit short on things you need.'

She looked up at him; he was holding Minty in one arm, and Poppy was sucking her thumb and leaning against him. 'What's that on your shirt?' she said.

He glanced down at a large, dark stain. 'Oh, an offering from your younger daughter. I think her nappy just finally gave out or something. Doesn't matter.'

Her heart turned over.

'You've been so kind,' she said, when she joined him downstairs at the cottage, all three children finally asleep. 'No, that's ridiculous. Not kind. Just – well . . .'

'Magnificent?' he said, grinning. 'I thought so too.'

'Seriously.'

'I am being serious. I was magnificent. We all were. But I think I might like a drink. Whisky, if you have it.'

'Oh, God,' she said, stricken, 'how awful of me. Yes, of course, and you must have something to eat, you must be starving.'

'Only in parts. As the curate said.'

She made a salad, found some cheese and some fresh bread, carried it into the sitting room. 'Is this all right?'

'It's excellent. And this is very good whisky.'

'My husband drinks whisky,' she said, and then sat silent, awkward.

'Does he? Look, it's nothing to do with me, but shouldn't you phone him, tell him what's happened?'

'Yes, I suppose so.' She had been putting it off, not sure what to say.

'You do that. I think I'll go and have a wash, if that's all right.'

'Of course. Oh, and let me find you a clean shirt. That one's so awful.'

She riffled through the rack of Tom's shirts, the Ralph Laurens, the Lacostes, the Brooks Brothers; which would be the least offensive, provoke the least comment? Finally she found an old Madras cotton one from LL Bean, turned to take it down to him.

He was standing behind her, watching her from the doorway of the bedroom. 'Very pretty,' he said, looking at the label. 'Not a brand I recognise.'

'Oh, it's a really obscure American one,' she said quickly. 'Nothing smart.'

'I doubt that. Bit of a natty dresser, your husband, I would imagine. Judging from the look of that wardrobe. And this is just for the country.'

'Well. It's sort of a hobby.'

'Really? Instead of shooting, I suppose. Thanks anyway.'

She phoned the house; there was no one there. She left a message saying where they were and briefly what had happened, that Gideon was fine, and then tried his mobile. It was switched off.

'Bastard,' she said aloud, and slammed the phone down again. 'You absolute bastard.'

'Your husband?' said Gabriel Bingham.

She looked at him; the events of the day had left her more emotional, more highly strung than usual.

'Yes,' she said and burst into tears.

'I haven't told anyone else all that,' she said later, moving away from him on the sofa; he had pulled her down beside him, sat with his arm round her shoulders handing her handkerchiefs, of which he seemed to have an endless supply, while she talked. 'Well, not anyone except Louise.'

'Louise? Ah, the best friend. Yes, of course, you women always talk to your best friends.'

'And you men don't, do you?' she said, sniffing, glad of the distraction suddenly.

'No, not often. Well, I believe the really young chaps do. Sobbing into their cocoa, hugging one another, all that sort of thing. Not for me, I'm afraid.'

'How old are you?' she said

'Thirty-nine. Can't quite think how it happened, only yesterday I was nineteen. But there you are. What about you?'

'I was seventeen,' she said, 'only yesterday, I mean. Now I'm thirty-six.'

'A very good age for a woman,' he said. 'Just look at you. Beautiful. Clever. Successful. Sexy.' He grinned at her.

'You have no idea if I'm sexy or not,' she said fretfully.

'Of course I do. You're incredibly sexy. Don't look at me like that, I mean it.'

'I don't think I can be,' she said, too drained to speak anything other than directly, 'otherwise my husband wouldn't have left me.'

'Oh, now that is really ridiculous. The sexiest women in the world get left by their husbands. Look at poor Marilyn. Look at that silly Princess Diana.'

'Do you think she's silly?'

'Terribly silly. Neurotic, too. And dangerous. But gorgeous. She has charm like you wouldn't believe. And she has the most wonderful giggle. Your friend Louise reminded me of her as a matter of fact.'

'I don't think anyone could call Louise dangerous,' said Octavia.

'Good,' said Gabriel Bingham lightly.

Their table was by the window; the view from the Oxo Tower incomparable, of the river, the city, and upstream the bridges; and by the table, a bottle of Krug on ice.

'How marvellous,' Marianne said, looking out into the darkness.

'Isn't it?' he said complacently.

She smiled at him.

'Why the smile?'

'You sound smug. As if you created it. The view, I mean. It amused me.'

'I knew it would be exactly right for you. And it is. That's what I'm smug about. Does your other boyfriend never bring you here?'

'No. He goes for the more conventional places.'

'How foolish of him. When that is clearly not right for you. Never mind, I shall do much better, so let's order. I recommend the feuillettes of salmon and the veal, but you must make your up own mind. Now, did I see you crying at one point during that performance?'

'Yes, you did.'

'Do you always cry so easily?'

'No. No, I don't. I'm usually rather cool. On most occasions.'

'Something happened? To disturb your cool?'

'You don't want to hear about it.'

'Yes, I do. Very much.'

'I've got myself into a bit of a mess,' she said slowly, sipping at her champagne.

'I can't imagine it, I must say. You seem much too in control to be in a mess.'

'Well, maybe mess is too strong a word. It's tedious. Family stuff.'

'Not having a family, I find them the opposite of tedious. What are they all doing? Taking drugs, getting pregnant? Tell me about it.'

'No, really. It's very boring.'

But she did tell him about it; about Romilly and her contract, about Alec's furious opposition to it.

He listened attentively. Then he said, 'It doesn't sound too bad to me. She'll have lots of fun. And I'm sure you won't abandon her to the wicked world. You've obviously got far too strong a conscience. And are still too much in thrall to your husband. Are you still in love with him?'

'No, of course not,' she said, shocked. 'Alec wasn't a very nice man. He was bad tempered, unfaithful, he—'

'That wouldn't necessarily matter. Women don't mind anything, in my experience, unfaithfulness, physical violence even, if they're in love.'

'That is such absolute rubbish,' she said, half amused, half shocked. 'Patriarchal, establishment, male chauvinist rubbish.'

'Isn't it? Not true, of course. I don't believe it. Well, hardly. I just said it to make you cross.'

'Why do you want to make me cross?'

'Because,' he said, reaching out his hand, touching her cheek, 'because if you can make a woman cross, you can make her sexually aroused. Same set of responses.'

'That's rubbish too,' she said, confused by his touch and her response to it. 'Anyway, are you in love with your ex-wife?'

'Oh, good Lord, no,' he said, removing his hand, reaching out for his wine glass. 'She was very unpleasant to me. But the fact remains—'

'Why was she so unpleasant to you? Weren't you a very good husband?'

'I was a very good husband. I wasn't even unfaithful to her. Not strictly speaking anyway.'

'Now what do you mean by that?'

'I mean I never went to bed with anyone else. While we were together.'

'But you lunched around, I would guess?' she said.

'As in slept around? Nice concept. I like it. Yes, a bit. But she wasn't very nice to me. Even before the lunching.'

'And why do you think that was?'

'I think I outshone her,' he said, 'and she didn't like it. She was a very spoilt, difficult woman. And at the same time rather dull. In spite of her great beauty. People, especially women, preferred me. I make them laugh, and she didn't like that. She was in a permanent bait with me.'

'So why did you marry her in the first place?'

'Because she was extremely beautiful. And seemed rather nicer than she was. Oh, and she had a title. I was dazzled by such things in those days. Now she has a hugely pompous new husband, who is considerably less attractive than her, so she is very happy.'

'You are appalling,' said Marianne, laughing.

'Indeed I am. Now what about you? Have I made you feel any better?'

'Yes,' she said, surprised, 'yes, you have.'

'Good. I think the only thing you should do is warn Romilly of the dangers in her new situation, as you see it. I do think that's important. People should be always warned. If they are in danger. Not to warn them is a ducking of moral responsibility, however unpleasant it might be. Anyway, enough of this rather earnest conversation. Far too serious for dinner with a beautiful young woman.'

'Hardly young,' she said laughing, 'I'm thirty-nine!'

'That's pretty young. And certainly you are beautiful. The most beautiful woman I've had dinner with for a very long time. Now, are you going to come home with me tonight?'

'No, Nico, of course I'm not.'

'I really think you should,' he said, and he took her hand and turned it over and kissed the palm.

She tensed; she couldn't help it.

'I felt that.'

'Felt what?'

'Oh, never mind,' he said, releasing her hand, sitting back, smiling at her as their first course arrived. 'You know as well as I do. I'm a very patient man. I can wait. Well, for a bit. Now, I do have a little more serious conversation, actually. What of young Fleming? I want to discuss him. Incidentally, does the name Cornish mean anything to you? In connection with him, I mean.'

'No. I don't think so. Why?'

'A Mrs Cornish phoned him on Friday. When he was in my office. I have seldom seen a man so rattled.'

'Poor Tom. Probably just a difficult client.'

'This was a rather more – what shall we say – intense reaction than that. Rather personal. Anyway, no matter. More to the point, or rather the Fleming point, an extraordinary document arrived on my desk on Thursday. A memo. Telling me, in effect, that I should withdraw my account from his company.'

'Really?' said Marianne. 'Who was it from?'

'I have no idea.'

'You mean it was anonymous.'

'Entirely. And not a businesslike piece of writing. Although it tried to give the impression it was, at any rate.'

'How very odd,' said Marianne slowly.

'I thought so. Very odd. Well, I checked it out. And it is true, you know. His company is in trouble. Or about to be. He's been looking for funding. He's lost two accounts. One, of course, through the unfortunate little games his extremely neurotic wife has been playing.'

'Oh, God,' said Marianne. 'So you think it was a sort of poison pen letter?'

'Yes. Exactly. Someone who wishes him ill. Now can you think of anyone who wishes him ill?'

'No, of course not,' said Marianne. But something was tearing at the back of her brain, a discomforting, almost frightening memory, something she had tried to dismiss, tried to explain away.

'No sacked employees, no disappointed clients?'

'Well, I wouldn't know about them anyway, would I?'

'Maybe not. What about a scorned woman? The likes of whom hell hath no fury.'

'Now that really is ridiculous.' said Marianne.

Tom phoned Octavia at one thirty-one. She was lying in bed with Gideon, and she grabbed the phone instantly, lest it woke him, and checked on her bedside clock.

'Octavia, it's me. What the hell's going on?'

'I'll go downstairs,' she said quietly into the receiver and eased herself out of bed; Gideon stirred, restlessly, but didn't wake.

Even on her way down the stairs, concern for Gideon was replaced by a savage rage.

'Where the hell have you been? With her? You have, haven't you?'

'No, I haven't,' he said. 'I've been with Aubrey. You can phone him now and check if you don't believe me.'

'Oh, he'll tell me the truth, won't he? Your old friend and partner.

Who's bound to want to keep me sweet, since he's going to ask for money too. From my father.'

'Oh, Octavia, please. How's Gideon?'

'He has eight stitches in his foot and he's in a lot of pain, but there's no harm done.'

'And how did it happen?'

'He'd been playing cricket with Poppy in the garden.'

'In bare feet?'

'Yes. Don't ask me why. He climbed over the gate to get the ball and someone had left a broken bottle on the verge. Simple as that. He's had a tetanus shot and antibiotics and God knows what.'

'Where did you take him, which hospital?'

'Bath General. We thought—'

'We?'

'Yes. I had a – a friend here.'

'Oh, yes,' he said, 'of course, Louise.'

'How do you know she was here?'

'You told me,' he said. 'When you said you were going down. But there's a Nuffield at Bristol, why didn't you go there?'

'Tom, there's no Accident and Emergency at the Nuffield. And in a crisis the NHS is still best. Anyway, you weren't here, I coped with it, he's fine, please don't start criticising me now.'

'Sorry. When are you coming home?'

'Tomorrow maybe, or Tuesday. He certainly couldn't be moved tonight. He was wretched, in a lot of pain. And he'd lost a lot of blood.'

'Poor little bugger. Should I come down, do you think? Tomorrow?'

'There is absolutely no point. Anyway, you've got an important business meeting in the morning. As I recall. I'll call you in the morning, tell you how he is.'

'Yes, all right. Give him my love. Poppy okay?'

'Yes. She was very upset, of course, but she's all right now.'

'And you're sure he's had sufficient treatment? He doesn't need the foot X-rayed, there isn't any further damage, to ligaments or—'

'Tom, if you'd been here, you could have seen to all that. As you weren't, I had to. Gideon will be fine. Good night. I'll speak to you in the morning.'

She put the phone into the kitchen, filled the kettle. Bastard! How dare he criticise her choice of hospital, imply the treatment Gideon had had was in some way wanting? When he hadn't even had his mobile on, when she couldn't have got hold of him even if she'd wanted to . . .

'Bastard,' she said aloud. 'You absolute bastard!'

'Your husband again? He seems to attract a great deal of opprobrium from you.' Gabriel Bingham had appeared in the doorway; he was wearing the Madras shirt and what seemed to be nothing else. Octavia smiled at him uncertainly.

'It's all right,' he said, noticing her eyes travelling down him, 'I have a very stout pair of boxer shorts on. Nothing to worry about.'

'I wasn't worried,' she said. 'I'm making some tea, would you like a cup?'

'That would be very nice. I wasn't asleep anyway, I was reading. I have trouble sleeping at the best of times.'

'You do? So do I.'

'That doesn't surprise me at all,' he said, settling down at the kitchen table, sticking his long legs out in front of him, crossing them at the ankles. They were, she noticed, very nice legs.

'Why doesn't it surprise you?'

'You're not exactly relaxed, are you?' he said and grinned at her. 'I would imagine you spend quite a lot of every night fretting over the next day, the past day, the present night, and then fretting because you're not asleep. An unsettled personality, you have, Mrs Fleming.'

She was feeling extremely unsettled at that precise moment; unsettled by Gabriel, unsettled by Tom and unsettled by something else, and she couldn't think what. It kept happening, that: why, what was it?

'Still, it's very attractive,' he said. 'It's all part of what I was talking about earlier. You being sexy. Of course, serenity can be sexy. There's a certain kind that is. But it's very rare.'

She said nothing.

'Anyway, I prefer your brand. Of sexiness, I mean.'

'Good,' she said lightly. She didn't know how to react to him at all. She never did; he had her emotionally disadvantaged all the time. The last thing in the world she wanted to appear was over-eager, a sex-starved deserted wife; on the other hand, she didn't want to appear cold, frigid even. She had been slightly taken aback when he had gone up to bed, having accepted the logic of staying, after two large glasses of whisky and three of wine, with nothing more than a brief good night; it had been one of the reasons for her sleeplessness.

She smiled brightly. 'Well, I might be getting back to bed. I'm quite tired.'

'Yes,' he said, after a short silence, and his voice quite different suddenly, almost cold, 'that's probably a good idea.'

His eyes were distant, almost hard.

She felt a sudden rush of courage. 'Gabriel—'

'Yes?' But the voice was still cold, detached.

She turned away, feeling foolish: terrified that he might think she was propositioning him. 'Nothing,' she said, 'sorry.'

'I think it's I who should be saying sorry.'

'What?' She looked at him in genuine astonishment. 'What for?'

'For so clearly embarrassing you. Obviously I've been in politics too long, grown a second skin. You've made it perfectly plain, several times, that you don't find me in the least attractive, and I've just gone on and on, making ludicrous remarks—'

'Gabriel, that is nonsense.'

'I don't think so,' he said heavily. 'I really don't. You cry, I try to comfort you, you move away from me, I tell you you're sexy, you leap up, start plumping cushions, or offering me a nice cup of tea—'

'Gabriel, please.'

'Oh, go to bed,' he said wearily. 'I feel quite sober now, I think I'll chance the roads.'

'Don't be ridiculous!'

'Why ridiculous?'

'Well, think what it would do to your career. If you got caught.'

'Oh,' he said, and his expression was colder still, 'do you know, just for a moment then I thought you were going to tell me there was something else I was being ridiculous about. Idiotic of me. Good night, Octavia.'

She followed him slowly, watched him go into the spare room, shut the door, stood outside feeling utterly wretched. She hesitated, struggling with her pride; lacking the self-confidence, even then, to knock, to go in. She walked back into her own room, closed the door, close to tears of absolute despair. About herself, about Tom, about Gabriel; that she should have come to this, to such absolute failure to be, to do, what she wanted.

The moonlight falling on to the bed showed her Gideon occupying the whole of it now, sprawled across it. If she tried to move him, he might wake. She sighed; there was only the sofa left. Well, she certainly wasn't going to sleep now, she might as well lie down there and read.

She went out again, walked back towards the stairs. As she reached the spare room, Gabriel came out, fully dressed. He looked at her, clearly startled, stood quite still for a moment, his eyes moving over her; Octavia, caught in the same stillness, looked back at him, afraid almost to breathe. Then he grinned, a huge, joyful grin.

'What kept you?' he said.

What she experienced with him that night was different from anything she had known before: an amalgam of so many things, of release from tension, relief from the anxiety of the day, the restoration of her self-esteem; of emotional delight that he should want her, and of physical delight at her response to him. She lay with him, awkward at first, nervous even in the face of his desire, then relieved at her ability to respond to it, at the hunger opening up obediently in her, dark, soft, fluid. He was patient, tender with her, waiting for her, and then suddenly, before she had thought she was ready, it was there, the bright, piercing brilliance, breaking, shattering, reaching far though her, through not only her body, but her head, filling it with images, strong, strange, powerful patterns, and then finally her heart, filling it with peace.

And then she lay, looking at him, half crying, half laughing, her body damp with sweat, trembling, weakened by him, weakened and released.

'Your husband must be quite mad,' was all he said.

CHAPTER 25

'So exactly where were you last night?'

The voice was dark, heavy with anger. It annoyed her, that anger: it annoyed her a lot.

'I was out,' said Marianne, 'at the Opera House.'

'At midnight?'

'No, then I was out to dinner.'

'On your own?'

'No, with a friend. Look, Felix, I'm sorry, but I'm very busy. I really haven't got time for this kind of interrogation. I've got a houseful here.'

'I was worried about you,' he said abruptly. 'Usually you tell me what you're doing.'

It was, for him, close to an apology. Remorse filled her suddenly; remorse and guilt. She shouldn't have gone out with Nico. Not for reasons that were little more than pique. Felix, in his tough, difficult way, loved her, she knew; and she loved him. Didn't she? And they were both too old for playing games.

'I'm sorry, Felix,' she said, 'very sorry. Maybe this evening we could—'

'I don't think so,' he said, 'not this evening. I've got a very full day.'

'Well, perhaps—'

'Marianne, I really can't talk now. I'm seeing Tom in fifteen minutes. I'll try and phone you tomorrow.'

'Are you seeing Tom about his business?'

'I imagine so.'

'Well, there's something I think you should—'

'I'm sorry, Marianne, I have to go. I hope your day isn't too stressful.'

And the phone went dead. She sat looking at it, wondering if she should brave his wrath and try again. Tell him what Nico had said about Tom. She decided not to. There was no point while he was in this mood.

*

'So exactly where were you last night? I tried to phone you.'

'I was here, Louise, still at the cottage. Gideon had an accident. He cut his foot. Terribly badly. We spent the evening at Bath General.'

'Oh, no! Boot, how awful, is he all right?'

'Yes and no. Eight stitches, very painful. He's quite shocked too.'

'I'm so sorry. And you had to cope all your own as well.'

'Not really. Gabriel came with me, he was wonderful.'

'Gabriel! He's very sexy, Octavia, I could fancy him myself.'

'Well, hands off,' said Octavia without thinking. 'He's mine.'

'Boot, as if I'd steal a man of yours. Anyway, he's obviously mad about you.'

'Mum! My foot hurts.'

'Coming, Gideon. Did you really think he likes me? Gabriel, I mean.'

'Well, of course. Blatantly obvious. And just what you need.'

'Yes,' said Octavia, smiling foolishly into the phone, thinking how precisely and perfectly Gabriel was what she needed. 'Yes, he is. Just what I need. But—'

'Mum! *Mum!* Can you come? My foot's hurting so much.'

'Lulu, I have to go. I'm sorry. I'll ring you back. I do want to talk to you. About – something. Well, about everything, really.'

'Okay. Fine. I'll be here.'

Felix sat looking at Tom. He tended to forget, unless they were alone together, the full intensity of his dislike for him. 'How is Octavia?' he said abruptly, as his secretary brought in the coffee. 'Get away this weekend, did you?'

'Octavia did. I was working. Unfortunately, Gideon had an accident.'

'An accident? What sort of an accident?'

'Nothing serious. He cut his foot. Had to have it stitched. But he's fine apparently.'

'What do you mean, apparently? Haven't you seen him?'

'Well, no. It was down there, down in Somerset.'

'And Octavia had to deal with it all on her own? With the baby there as well? Or was the nanny there?'

'No, a friend of hers was with her. Anyway, she is—' He hesitated.

Felix waited. Now what was he going to say? Something self-justifying, no doubt.

'She is very good on these occasions.'

'She has to be, I suppose. Is he in hospital?'

'No, no, it was all dealt with in Casualty.'

'What a dreadful thing for them all. And today? You're not going down today?'

'Felix, it isn't necessary. I'm desperately busy, and—'

'Perhaps I should go down and help her, then,' said Felix. 'She can't cope with three children, one of them injured, all on her own.'

'I suggested the nanny went down. She said she didn't want her. She said they were fine.'

'I'll ring her anyway. Make sure there's nothing I can do. Just wait a moment, will you, while I do that. I wish you'd told me last night.'

'Felix, it was after midnight.'

'And do you think I'd have cared? In the very least?' Rage filled him; this man seemed to have no idea of the nature of love. He would most gladly have driven down to Somerset at three in the morning, if Octavia had told him she needed him. If only she had . . .

'Octavia? Darling, it's Daddy. I've got Tom here, he's just told me about Gideon. Sweetheart, I'm so sorry, how is he? Is he? Send him my love. Brave little chap. Look, Tom tells me he's too busy to come down, would you like me to? I'm more than happy to, I hate to think of you coping all on your own down there. What? Well, darling, think about it. I could be with you in a couple of hours. Just promise me to let me know if you change your mind, will you? Any time, doesn't matter if it's late. Tom said he didn't know until after midnight – I would have come immediately if I'd known. Goodbye, my darling. See you very soon.'

He put the phone down.

'She's amazing, how she copes with everything,' he said.

'She is indeed,' said Tom. 'I'm very lucky.'

'You are. Very lucky. Now then, what did you want to see me about?'

'Zoë said Octavia's friend Louise used to be a model.' Romilly stood back, studying herself in the long mirror in her mother's bedroom. 'Do you think these trousers for this casting thing, or my jeans?'

'I think you should ask Ritz,' said Marianne with a slight effort.

Romilly smiled at her. 'Good idea. I'll phone her. What was Louise's name when she was modelling? I could tell Ritz.'

'It was Louise Madison. She was quite big in the States.'

'I wonder if she misses it. Did she marry someone terribly rich and successful?'

'Not really,' said Marianne, smiling, 'but very nice. He's called Sandy. Sandy Trelawny.'

'Trelawny. That's a nice name.'

'Yes. Yes, isn't it? It's Cornish, I sup—'

She stopped suddenly, staring at Romilly. She felt hot. Hot and sick. Cornish . . . 'Do you know anyone called Cornish? . . . I never saw a man so shaken . . .'

'Oh, my God,' she said, and her voice was almost a whisper. 'Oh, dear God.'

'He's thinking about it,' said Tom, 'wants to see the all the figures and so on. I'm getting them over to him ASAP. I honestly don't know which way he'll jump, Aubrey. I think he's torn three ways, between wanting to refuse me, and making me suffer, not wanting to see his daughter dragged down into the gutter, and wanting to get his hands on this business. God, I really don't know that bankruptcy wouldn't be the better course. If he does come in with us, it'll be hideous.'

'We'll cope,' said Aubrey. 'I think if you considered bankruptcy and its implications carefully, you'd retract that statement.'

'I'm not so sure. I've had to listen to at least thirty minutes of shit already, about our extravagance, bad management, lack of foresight – it's a nightmare. I know it's only eleven thirty, but can I have a drop of that whisky? I need it pretty badly. And I'll tell you something else,' he added, raising his glass to Aubrey, 'if Mr Miller moves in here, we'll be drinking mineral water. Or, more like it, tap water. Cheers, Aubrey.'

'Cheers,' said Aubrey, 'and well done. I can hardly begin to imagine what that cost you.'

'He hasn't agreed yet.'

'I suspect he will. Unless something goes really horribly wrong . . .'

Marianne sat at her desk, staring alternately out of the window and at the phone. She couldn't ever remember feeling so terrible. She kept seeing, again and again, the image of Louise after the funeral, hitting Tom, with that savage, pent-up energy. Sexual energy, she could see that now. She heard Nico's voice: 'Can you think of anyone who wishes him ill . . . a scorned woman perhaps, the likes of whom hell hath no fury . . .'

It must be her. It must. But what was she to do? How could she possibly ring Octavia, or even Tom, what could she possibly say?

Of course she couldn't. If Tom was having an affair, that was his own business, his and Octavia's. And disregarding what was really rather slim circumstantial evidence, was it really likely that Louise, lovely affectionate Louise, would behave in such a way?

Maybe she should do nothing. That was the safest thing and certainly the easiest: but was it honourable? She heard Nico's voice again – God, was it only yesterday? – saying that people should be warned if they were in danger. 'Not to warn them is to duck moral responsibility.'

Marianne didn't like that thought. She didn't like the thought that people she was fond of were suffering and might suffer more, through her lack of moral responsibility. Suddenly, swiftly, acting on a surge of courage, Marianne dialled Tom's office number.

'They're lovely,' said the girl at *Marie Claire*, handing Romilly back her pictures. 'really nice. Great, you winning that competition.'

'Yes,' said Romilly politely.

'Have you got a composite yet?'

'No, sorry. It's not ready.' Ritz had said they'd all ask that, for the card with her pictures and measurements and details of her agency on it. 'It doesn't make any difference to whether they'll book you or not, they just like to have them for their files.' But she felt miserable about not having one; it looked inefficient.

'Well, get them to send us one, will you? Okay, Romilly, that's fine. Thanks for coming in.' She turned back to her desk, clearly dismissing her.

Romilly managed to smile, to say thank you back. They didn't like her, didn't want her. No one would, she should have known, she was too young, too inexperienced, just winning some competition didn't mean a thing, It was her third appointment that morning and everyone had looked rather perfunctorily at her pictures and then virtually told her to piss off. It had been horrible . . . and she had two more people to go and see before she could go home . . . Her eyes filled with tears.

Tom had been out when Marianne phoned; would be out for the rest of the day, Barbara Dawson said. With clients. Would Marianne like to leave a message?

'No, no,' Marianne said hastily, relief at this reprieve washing sweetly over her, 'it doesn't matter.'

'What's the matter, princess? You're not pregnant, are you?'

'God, no! No, it's just – well, I need some money. Quite badly. I got a letter from the bank this morning, and—'

'Can't you get some from Mummy and Daddy?'

'No, I can't. My dad says my allowance is more than adequate, when actually all it does is bring me back in credit, and my mum won't let me have any more either.'

'Seems a bit mean. They can't be exactly short.'

'No, they're not. They are mean, you're right. I think it's supposed to be good for me, or something. Anyway, I really need that job at the pub. Has Katrina made her mind up yet?'

'Yeah, sorry, I forgot, she said she decided on the other girl.'

'Thanks for telling me,' said Zoë. Her heart did a nasty lurch. 'Now what do I do?'

'There's plenty of other jobs, for God's sake. You can't have been relying on that one. She did warn you.'

'I know,' said Zoë, 'but I'd thought it was more certain than that.'

'Plenty of bars all down the Kings Road. Shall we go to the house?'

'No,' said Zoë. 'I really don't feel like it. Sorry.'

'Right.' Ian stood up.

'Where are you going?'

'Home.'

'Home! I thought you were taking me out.'

'I was. But you're no fun in this mood. I'm better off with me mum and a video.'

'Fine. Just fuck off, then,' said Zoë. 'That suits me really well.'

He walked out of the bar, and she looked at his tall, muscular back with a mixture of distaste and regret. He supplied just about the only pleasure she got at the moment: all her friends were away, she had only a lousy two-week holiday at Martha's Vineyard with her father to look forward to, her mother was really getting up her nose at the moment, and Romilly was fretting endlessly because magazines didn't want her. Zoë was thoroughly pissed off. And she couldn't go anywhere this evening, she had literally fifty pence in her purse until Friday when her allowance came in. And then she'd only be about ten pounds in credit. And what she hadn't told Ian, because it made her sound such a loser, was that she'd tried all the bars in the Kings Road and the Fulham Road and they all said they had enough people; she'd left it too late, most students came in in early June.

She stood up; she really couldn't face another evening of her mother being tense and Romilly being smug. She walked to the door of the pub; Ian was standing outside, talking on his mobile.

'Hi! Ian! Sorry about that. Yes, let's go to the house. Good idea.'

'Okay,' he said, grinning at her. 'I've got some grass on me as well. We can have a really good night.'

Octavia made Gideon a sandwich, settled him and Poppy in front of *Superman*, currently one of their favourites, gave Minty a drink, and took her and the phone out into the garden. The phone rang.

'Boot! I thought you were going to ring me back. How's Gideon now?'

'Much the same. I'm going back tonight. Hopefully they'll sleep.'

'What was it you were going to tell me? Talk to me about?'

'Oh . . .' She hesitated. 'Well – if you can bear it. Tom's company is in such a bad way now, he's got to ask my father for money.'

'What! After all he's done to you? Go to your father for help? Octavia, I can't believe that. You can't let him.'

'I can't stop him. And anyway, the thing is, it won't help any of us if Fleming Cotterill goes bust, will it? Not me, not the children, nobody.'

'And your father still doesn't know? About Tom?'

'No! If he did, there'd certainly be nothing forthcoming. He'd go berserk.'

'Octavia,' said Louise, 'I think you must be some kind of saint. I really do.'

Tom was at the house when Octavia and the children got back; he came out to greet them, looking as exhausted as she felt. She looked at him, hating him, filled with the new resentment that he had avoided all the traumas of Gideon's accident. Louise was right; she must be some kind of saint, to continue to shield him from her father's wrath. And to feel any kind of guilt about her behaviour.

The children greeted Tom ecstatically, the twins fighting for his attention and the opportunity to present their own version of the story. Octavia came down from handing the sleeping Minty over to Caroline, to hear Poppy saying, 'So I helped the nurse—'

'You didn't,' said Gideon.

'I did.'

'When?'

'When she was fetching you the wheelchair. And Gabriel said—'

'Gabriel?' said Tom.

'Yes. Gabriel Bingham, he was with us,' said Octavia. Easily, carelessly, as she poured herself a glass of wine. There was clearly no point trying to hide his involvement.

'What, the MP?'

'Yes.'

'What on earth was he doing there?'

'He dropped in last week, to talk about – well, about constituency matters.'

'Just a minute,' said Tom. 'Gabriel Bingham wanted to talk to you about constituency matters? What matters?'

'The wood,' said Poppy. 'You know, the one they're trying to build on. We met him there once.'

'And he came to the house to talk about that?'

'Yes,' said Octavia. He looked so angry she was quite frightened.

'I see,' said Tom. He appeared about to say something, then glanced at Poppy and Gideon and stopped again. 'We can talk about that later,' he said.

'Anyway, he was so so good,' said Poppy. 'He drove Mummy's car really fast to the hospital and made the doctor see us quickly.'

'What a paragon,' said Tom drily.

'What's a paragon? And then in case Mummy had to go back to the hospital he—'

'This hurts,' said Gideon, shifting his foot, grimacing. 'It hurts so much. I need some more of those things, Mum, the ones that stop the pain.'

'He has them up his bum,' said Poppy, giggling. 'Just—'

'Be quiet, Poppy,' said Octavia. 'It's not funny. Come on, Gideon. If Daddy can carry you up to your room, I'll see to it for you.'

She would not have wished Gideon a moment's pain, but she felt a stab of intense gratitude that he had chosen to complain about it at that precise moment. One more breathless phrase from Poppy, and Tom would have learned that Gabriel Bingham had stayed the night at the cottage. No earthly reason why not, of course – under the circumstances, she could entertain a regiment of eligible men if she wanted to – but it was still simpler if he didn't.

She was sitting at her desk an hour later; there was a pile of invitations on it that she had been setting aside day after day. Invitations to drinks parties, private views, restaurant openings, book launches, charity auctions: all addressed to Mr and Mrs Tom Fleming. Some of them would be fun, she would enjoy them, but she couldn't face going with Tom, and it wasn't her they wanted, nor was it him; it was the pair of them, the glossy, powerful pair, helping to lend some of their personal success, their own charmed lives to the gatherings. She knew that the moment the news broke of their separation, their social life would be decimated. It would be the usual problem of who was going to be loyal to whom, to the power of a hundred; which organisation could afford to offend which of them; which occasion was better suited to a single man or a single woman. Their marriage would not be broken neatly and cleanly, nobody's was of course, but theirs would be a multiple fracture, more messily painful even than most, crossing as they constantly did the lines of public and private life. They would become not only single people, but famously unsuccessful ones, would no longer effortlessly straddle two worlds, but would scarcely stand on the top of one; their association and their marriage would be no longer powerful, it would be a public as well as a private failure. At the last function they had attended together, fraudulently flaunting their marriage and its success, she had had a terrible longing at one point to tap on her glass for silence and say, 'Our marriage is over, totally over, Tom is having an affair and I want you all to know,' but of course she hadn't, she had smiled sweetly and continued to propagate the lie. The fertile, bankable, valuable lie.

As she sat leafing through the invitations, Tom came into the room, his face tight, his mouth white round the edges. She knew what that meant. Rage. Rage and recrimination.

'Can I just establish something?' he said.

'Yes, of course.'

'Thank you. Not content with alienating one of my most important clients, you're now taking your involvement with this business of the wood further. Is that correct?'

'Yes,' she said, taking a deep breath to steady herself, to keep her voice level. 'Yes, that's right.'

'To the extent of getting involved with the local MP?'

'Yes.' Getting involved with: that just about described it. Her head, her heart, her body; all very involved. Wonderfully, joyfully involved. 'Is there anything wrong with that? Now?'

'Wrong? Oh, no. Nothing wrong. Criminally stupid perhaps, epically self-interested, absurdly destructive. Not actually wrong, of course.'

'Tom, I don't know what you mean,' she said.

'You really don't, do you?' he said. 'I find it hard to believe, but you don't. You can't see that even if Carlton is a lost cause, there may be other clients out there, possibly on the brink of joining us, or even contemplating leaving us, given the rather unfortunate events of the past few days.'

'So what if there are?'

'Well, if there are, they might find the prospect of my wife continuing to act rather publicly against me and my best interests rather less than reassuring. God, Octavia, I sometimes do wonder if you've got any sense at all.'

'Oh, do you?' she said. 'Do you really? Well, that's very interesting, Tom. I mean, it's really seriously awful, isn't it, what I'm doing? Trying to preserve a bit of countryside, halt the spread of concrete just a few more miles? Much worse than having an affair, lying to me, deceiving me—'

'Oh, shut up,' he said. 'At least I have the grace to admit what I did was wrong, to express contrition for it. I don't dress it up as some piece of idealism.' His eyes were brilliant in their hostility. 'Don't you realise what you're doing, Octavia? With great success, it seems. Destroying me professionally and financially, and destroying your family and its security into the bargain. Why, in the name of God, can't you—'

'I think it's you who should shut up,' she said. 'I'm trying so hard not to destroy you. I've gone to enormous lengths to keep the details of your squalid liaison from my own father, in case he changes his mind about lending you some money. God almighty, Tom, do you think that's been easy?'

'Oh, let's not get into that,' he said. 'There's no point in this conversation, none whatsoever. If you want to ruin me, Octavia, go ahead. I'm going upstairs, I've got work to do. Just don't be surprised if you find your own extremely comfortable, feather-bedded lifestyle rather altered suddenly.'

At Reading service station on the M4, Mick Rice and his girlfriend Jackie had stopped for a cup of coffee and some chips, and for Mick to refuel his bike.

'Where's this letter got to go, then?' said Jackie.

'City. EC4. Then we can cut right up West, go to a few bars and that. I got double money for this. "It must be there first thing," she said, "absolutely first thing." Classy bird, she was. I felt sorry for her. She was really upset.'

'How do you know that?' said Jackie, her voice slightly muffled through a mouthful of chips. 'She tell you about it?'

'No,' said Mick, 'she didn't need to. She was crying. Crying quite hard, matter of fact.'

CHAPTER 26

'Oh, my God,' said Octavia. She put the phone down, sat staring at it as if might leap off the desk of its own volition. 'Oh, dear God.'

Sarah Jane, who had been with her when the phone rang, looked at her in alarm. 'You all right, Octavia? You're very pale. It's not Gideon, is it?'

'No,' she said with a great effort. 'No, he's fine. But I have to go out. To meet my father. Something's cropped up. I'll try not to be long. I'm meeting him at the Hyde Park Hotel. Could you tell Melanie?'

'Yes, of course.'

Charles Madison had finally remembered, through the foggy inefficiency of grief, to buy some large strong brown envelopes. After breakfast that morning, he went into Anna's room and picked out the prettiest half dozen of her handkerchief collection, put them into one of the envelopes and wrote a card to Octavia Fleming; he then drove down to the village himself, to post the package. He was feeling better; grieving no less, of course, but stronger at least. Pretty soon now he would want to go back to work.

Louise seemed much better too; and she looked quite rosy, was beginning to bloom. It was going to be a lovely thing, the arrival of that baby: a lovely, restorative thing . . .

'So – I ask you again, Octavia. Is it true?'

'Yes. Yes, it is, I'm afraid.'

'I would like,' said Felix Miller quite quietly, 'to flay him alive. After all you have done for him. All your loyalty.'

'Daddy, I—'

'To cheat on you in this horrible way. And then to come to me for money. It's obscene. How could you let him, Octavia, how could you allow that? God in heaven, you must be some kind of saint.'

'I most certainly am not,' said Octavia quietly. 'I can't tell you how much I hate him. But—'

'Of course you do. Well, I have to say I'm not surprised.'

'No?' She looked at him rather dully. This was the very thing she had most dreaded, feared; the appalling self-satisfaction at knowing he had been right, that she had make a mistake, that Tom was not good enough for her, was not good at all. It was one thing for her to know he was a cheat, a liar, to face that knowledge in the innermost heart of herself; quite another to be told it, to have it spoken of, recognised. And by her father of all people, who thought she was perfect; who would look at her now, and realise that this was not a universal view of her, that her own husband did not find her anything like perfect, had looked out of their marriage for distraction from her indeed, who had wanted sex with someone else, the intimate company of someone else. This was a fresh and very painful humiliation; she felt diminished, a disappointment on a most agonising scale.

'Darling,' he said, and he put out his hand to hers. 'How long have you known?'

'A few weeks.'

'Weeks! And you've gone on pretending, even to me?'

'Well, I didn't want to worry you.'

'My darling child! That's what I'm here for. What I've always been here for. To worry. To take worry off you. I can't bear to think of you enduring this on your own. You've always brought me your troubles, Octavia, always. It pleases—' he corrected himself swiftly – 'it makes me feel better. To be able to help you. Comfort you. Put things right.'

'Daddy, you can't always put things right for me.'

'I can try. Don't you remember, when those girls were being so horrible to you, at school. You said it would make things worse if I complained about it, went to the head. You were wrong. It was better, wasn't it?'

'Oh – yes,' she said, shuddering at the memory. It hadn't been better, of course; the girls in question had taken hideous revenge, forbidding everyone else to speak to her, organising events which included everyone except her, sending her what she thought were invitations through the post, had opened with shaking hands, only to read, 'There's a party next Saturday, sorry, Fatty, you're not included.'

'I've always helped you, haven't I?' her father was saying now, and she looked at him stupidly, jerked back into her present misery from the ones of the past; and 'Yes,' she said, 'yes, of course, you helped a lot.'

'And I can help now. In lots of ways. Make it up to you. And the first thing I intend to do is talk to Tom.'

'Daddy, don't! You're not to,' she said, her heart seeming quite literally to rise in her throat.

'Octavia, if you think I am going to let this pass unremarked, you are terribly wrong. Apart from anything else, I am outraged that he should have come to me for money when he was cheating on you. And therefore on me. He has no morals. No sense of honour of any kind. I presume he's still living in Phillimore Gardens? Or has he had the decency to move out?'

'He's still there, but—'

'Exactly what I would have expected of him. Dear God, when I think – oh, my darling, you must have been so unhappy.' He stopped suddenly. 'Did you know when we were all at Ascot? Is that why you were upset that day?'

'Yes,' said Octavia, flinching from the memory. 'Yes, I suppose it was.'

He sighed, looked at her. 'Anyone else know about this? Anyone at all?'

'No,' she said quickly. 'No one.' She couldn't bear the thought of him approaching people, ringing them up, leading them into a character assassination of Tom. 'And I don't want them knowing. It makes me feel worse.'

'And do you know who . . .'

'No. And he won't tell me.'

'Well – some tart, I suppose. Some vulgar little tart. You'll want a divorce of course.'

'Daddy, I don't know,' she said, and found, to her immense surprise, that it was true.

'That's absurd! You can't stay married to a man who's cheating on you. Of course you must get a divorce. As soon as possible. And get a really good lawyer, who'll see to your interests. Don't worry about the cost, I'll see to that for you. God, I'd like to see him reduced to total penury.'

'Look, I'm really not quite sure. He says it's over.'

'And you are prepared to believe a single thing he says? Octavia, you have to stand up for yourself in this, let everyone see that you—'

'That's the whole point! I don't *want* everyone to see. Can't you see how humiliating, how appalling it all is? What a failure I feel? A wretched, miserable failure . . .'

She started to cry: sitting there, in the bar of the Hyde Park Hotel, and Felix put his arm round her, found a handkerchief, wiped her eyes tenderly, hushing her grief.

'There there, darling,' he said, 'you cry if you want to. It'll help. I'm here, I'll fight your battles for you. Your old daddy'll make it up to you. Come on now, blow your nose. That's right. Good girl.'

He's actually enjoying this, thought Octavia, through her grief; enjoying having me back, being the white knight, slaying the dragons for me again, and thought, too, this was one of the things she had most dreaded when he found out. And then, with a rush of horror, of realisation that there was a crucial question she hadn't asked, her tears stopped abruptly, and she said, 'Daddy, how did you find out? Who told you?'

Zoë looked at the money. All one hundred pounds of it. Sitting in an envelope, in her bag. They had been in the kitchen in Cleaver Square, looking for a tin opener (having found a tin of peaches and Ian saying they'd go down a treat with some of the rum and raisin ice cream they had found in the freezer and indeed already sampled). Zoë had rather fancied the idea as well; they had had some extremely energetic sex and she was tired and hungry. And very lightheaded after smoking the extremely good grass Ian had brought along.

The money had been in an envelope in the drawer, with 'Mrs Kendall' written on it. It was in ten-pound notes, and it wasn't even sealed up. There was a note inside that said, 'This should be enough for the three weeks, but if you have to pay for any cleaning materials, take it out of this and we'll pay you back when we get back. Thank you so much. Lyndsay.'

'Honestly,' said Ian, looking over her shoulder at it, 'you lot. More money than sense.'

'What do you mean, us lot?' said Zoë.

'You posh lot. The ones who have cleaners and that. Fancy trusting her. Giving her all that up front. We haven't set eyes on her all the time we was working here.'

'Well, surely that's why. She wouldn't come when you lot were here.'

'No, they said someone'd be in to do the ironing and that. Water the plants. Anyway, better put it back, Zo.'

But she hadn't. She'd slipped it into her pocket without telling him. It would just be a loan: until Friday when her allowance hit the bank. Get her out of this immediate hole she was in. She could put a bit of it in the bank to shut them up, use the rest. Fine. Simple. No problem. Absolutely no problem at all.

'You mean you got an anonymous letter? Telling you Tom was having an affair with someone? How absolutely bizarre.'

Another anonymous letter: dear God. But why tell Felix, what possible point in that?

'Marianne, I'm a little puzzled by your reaction,' said Felix. 'I would have thought the information in the letter was rather more important than its form.'

'Not really. I mean, of course it's very serious that Tom's having an affair – but, Felix, who would have done such a thing? Why should you need to be told?'

'Marianne, I am Octavia's father. Don't you think it is a matter of great concern to me? All day I've been feeling so wretched. So desperately sorry for her.'

'Yes, of course you have,' said Marianne quietly. He looked dreadful, drawn and gaunt, as if it was he who had been humiliated, betrayed, as well as Octavia. Well, he would feel that.

'Do we know who it is? Who she is?' Maybe he knew now, maybe this was going to release her from her moral purgatory.

But, 'No. Tom won't tell Octavia. Shielding the woman, I suppose. And you know, he had the gall to come to me for backing. For his company? Only yesterday. Think of that, Marianne, think of him sitting there, asking me for help when he had been cheating on my daughter.'

Tom must be absolutely desperate, she thought, asking Felix for money. In spite of herself, her sympathy with Octavia, Marianne's heart went out to Tom.

'It must be true, then,' she said, without thinking.

'What must?'

'Oh, that his company's in trouble.'

'How the hell do you know that?' said Felix, staring at her. 'There's been nothing in the press. I had no idea myself until he approached me.'

'Oh, I – I heard a rumour.'

'Marianne, you'll have to do better than that. This is terribly important.'

She saw the pain, the hollow gnawing misery in his face, and decided she must tell him what she knew. 'I – that is, I had lunch with Nico Cadogan the other day.'

'You had lunch with Nico Cadogan? What on earth for?'

'He asked me.'

'Oh, I see. And you accepted. Without checking it, clearing it with me?'

'Felix, I'm sorry, but I had no idea I had to get your permission to go out to lunch.'

'Marianne, don't play games with me, please.'

She opened her mouth to say she was not playing games, but knew it to be untrue. Of course she was: and it was an insult to him to pretend otherwise. 'I'm sorry,' she said quietly, 'I should have told you.'

'Yes, you should. But I certainly don't want to talk about that now. What I don't understand is why on earth you were talking about Tom Fleming's business.'

'Nico is a client of his. As you know.'

'Yes, I must make sure he ceases to be a client pretty damn quick.'

'Felix! You can't do that.'

'Why can't I?'

'Because whatever Tom has or has not done to Octavia, his clients are his own affair. If he's looking after them well, if he's a good businessman, then it's surely up to the clients themselves to decide what they're going to do.'

Felix stared at her. 'I cannot believe you said that, Marianne. That you should consider any friend of mine would wish to have any dealings with Tom Fleming now. After what he has done to my daughter. Of course Cadogan won't wish to continue with the relationship.'

'Well, I think you're wrong,' said Marianne, 'actually. But it doesn't matter what I think.'

'Of course it does. I find it very distressing that you can't see that. Anyway,' said Felix, his face dark and brooding as he looked at her, 'how did you know the company was in trouble?'

'Nico received a sort of memo the other morning. So did all the rest of Tom's clients. Saying that the company was about to go under, and they'd all be best advised to move elsewhere. That was also anonymous.'

'And you knew this, and you didn't tell me?'

'Felix, I tried to. I tried very hard, but you said you had to go and meet Tom and you hung up on me, literally mid-sentence. I assumed he would have told you himself at your meeting. And I haven't seen you since. You haven't been overwhelming me with your attentions or with support recently.'

'Good God,' said Felix. He ran his hands through his thick white hair. 'This gets worse and worse. Not only is the man an adulterer, he's fraudulent as well. Attempting to inveigle money out of me when – oh, for Christ's sake! And why didn't Cadogan tell me about it? I can hardly credit such disloyalty.' His voice was raw with distaste and rage.

'But, Felix, Nico is Tom's client, not yours. Tom impressed him, he has served him well.'

'You seem to know a great deal about Nico Cadogan's business affairs,' said Felix, staring at her. His dark eyes had changed, had become very brilliant; she knew that change and it frightened her. 'Clearly he has talked to you about the whole thing. And at some length. Just how much did you know, Marianne? And choose not to tell me?'

'Oh, Felix, don't be absurd! Don't turn this into some sort of conspiracy.'

'I'm afraid that's rather how it seems to me,' he said, 'a conspiracy. Against me. Me and my daughter.'

'Felix, really! A conspiracy. That is truly absurd.'

'I don't think so,' he said, 'I don't think so at all.'

'For the last time: what goes on in their marriage is between Octavia and Tom. Not you.'

'Well, nothing will be going on very much longer,' he said. 'Octavia will be divorcing him.'

'Has she told you so?'

He hesitated fractionally, then said, 'No reasonable person could do otherwise. She will want a divorce. And I shall see Tom is made to pay. In every possible sense of the word. Beginning with that company of his.'

'Oh, Felix, do be careful, please. That sounds very destructive to me.'

'Destructive? Of course it's destructive. I intend to destroy Tom Fleming to the very best of my ability.'

'Including his marriage to your daughter?'

'Marianne, he's done that himself.'

'Not quite,' said Marianne, standing up, picking up her bag. 'Not necessarily quite that. And I think you complete that particular job at your peril. It's nothing to do with you, Felix, nothing at all. Octavia is married to Tom. Not to you. She's grown up, Felix. When are you ever going to realise that? She's not a child, she's not yours, she's not your property any longer. Leave her alone. Her and her marriage. For God's sake, just leave her alone!'

She could speak openly to Octavia about it, perhaps even suggest who it might be. She really had to do that: no time should be lost. It was too dangerous.

Aubrey went into Tom's office. He was carrying two tumblers and a bottle of Chivas.

'Come on, old chap. Few quiet ones. Do you good. Do us both good.'

Tom looked up at him; his eyes were red in his exhausted face. Aubrey realised with a shock that he must have been weeping.

'Aubrey, I'm so sorry. So terribly sorry.'

'Oh, now, Tom, I don't want any self-flagellation. This is no more your fault than anyone else's.'

'Of course it is,' said Tom. 'I've let everyone down; the company, you, Octavia, the children . . .'

'Tom—'

'Yes, I have. I'm an idiot, a bloody, fucking idiot. Why did I do it, Aubrey? How could I have been so stupid?'

'Had this affair, you mean?'

Tom stared at him; they had not confronted the issue before. Such conversations were not really Aubrey's style. 'Yes,' said Tom quietly, 'this affair. This awful, dreadful, hideous affair. He was so vile, Felix Miller, I mean. I did deserve it, I know, but he was unspeakable. He said he wouldn't lend us the money, said I had no right to ask. I suppose I don't. But then he started. Over and over, round and round. You name it, I've been called it. He must have had the thesaurus open at adultery. God. I feel physically sick.'

'And you just sat there? Took it?'

'No. I eventually put the phone down. When he started on my calibre as a father. Said I wasn't fit to be with my own children. That was one insult too far. Oh, Jesus, Aubrey, what am I going to do?'

'I don't know,' said Aubrey simply, handing him a huge tumbler of whisky. 'Want to talk about it?'

'I can't,' said Tom, 'it's too hideous. It wouldn't be fair.'

And then proceeded to talk about it in some detail and at some length.

By the time he had finished, Aubrey needed a second, equally large, scotch himself.

When Marianne got home, there was a message to ring Nico Cadogan.

She did so; and heard herself agreeing not only to have dinner with him the following night, but to drive out to the country with him on Saturday and look at a house he was thinking of buying near Marlborough. 'And then I thought we might have dinner down there. How would that be?'

Marianne, who knew exactly how it would be, said she wasn't sure about dinner, but seeing the house would be nice.

'Well, I shall book a table anyway. So that when you are sure, it will be ready for us.'

'Nico, I—'

'Yes?'

'Oh, nothing.'

'Are you sure?'

She had been going to warn him about Felix, to tell him how angry he had been about Tom, how dangerous his mood, but she could not formulate her thoughts and her fears into logical order. Nico was a clever man, and a hugely competent businessman; he could surely take care of himself and his affairs. Business and otherwise. 'No,' she said, 'no, really, it's nothing.'

'Well, ring me if you change your mind. Good night, Marianne.'

Octavia was in the kitchen, making herself a cup of hot milk, when Tom's taxi pulled up outside. He walked into the kitchen looking appalling. He sank down into a chair, pushed his hair back, asked her if she would give him a glass of water.

'Do you want something stronger?'

'What? Oh, no, no. I've had more than enough of that.'

He had obviously been drinking but he was strangely, heavily sober.

'I've had a phone call from your father,' he said.

'I didn't tell him,' she said. 'I want you to—'

'I know you didn't,' he said, 'he told me. He had a letter.'

'Yes. You don't know who—'

'I don't want to talk about that,' he said.

'No. No, I see. I just wondered if – well, the other letters, the memos, if they were from—'

'No,' he said sharply. 'That really is out of the question. Anyway, I really don't want to talk about it. Not now.'

'No, all right.'

'He wasn't very pleased with me,' he said, and there was the shadow of a smile on his face. It was oddly touching, that he could be humorous about it.

'No,' she said, her own half-smile echoing his, 'no, I don't suppose he was.'

'You've talked to him, then?'

'Yes, I saw him this morning.'

'Did he ask you to move out of here? To go home to him?'

'He suggested it,' she said and smiled rather weakly.

'And are you going?'

'Of course not. This is home.'

'I'm glad you see it like that,' he said, and suddenly buried his head in his arms and started weeping.

Octavia stared at him horrified: horrified that he should be so distraught; horrified at what her father must have put him through to bring him to this; horrified at her own reaction. Which was of tenderness, sorrow, pity. How could she be feeling like this, towards a man who had behaved as Tom had behaved, who had let her down, publicly and horribly? How could she want to put her arms round him, comfort him, staunch his tears? Whatever it was, she couldn't help it: she stood up, moved forward, put her hands on his shoulders, leaned down, kissed his bent head.

'I'm sorry,' he said, putting one of his hands over hers, looking up at her, his face ravaged. 'So sorry. For all of it. I am truly ashamed.'

'He refused you the money, I presume.'

'Octavia, he didn't just refuse it. He made it very plain that every fragment of energy, of power he might possess, would be put to work to destroy me totally. Professionally, that is. Personally, I think I should start to employ a bodyguard. Only I won't be able to afford it of course.'

She said nothing, just stood there, looking down at him.

'The company can't survive,' he said after a while. 'We shall have to declare insolvency. Your father was the last port of call. I don't know quite where that leaves you. You and the children. The house will have to go, I expect, but no doubt your father will see you all right.'

'Tom, I don't want him to see me all right.'

'Well, I can't, I'm afraid. Any more. I shall be absolutely without money, you see,' he said, 'no credit, nothing. That's what happens.'

'What about all these stories you hear, people starting another company the very next day, leaving their creditors behind them?'

'Mostly apocryphal. In this climate and in my line of business, and with your father at work, out of the question, I'm afraid.'

'I see.'

She stood there, appalled at the part she had played in this small, poignant tragedy. Revenge, it had been; revenge, dressed up as principles. Not pretty.

'I'm sorry,' she said finally. It was the most difficult thing she had ever had to say. 'Sorry for my part in it. About Michael Carlton.'

'Oh, it doesn't matter. We were on dodgy ground long before that. It didn't help, I can't pretend it did. But – well, blood on the tracks. As Aubrey would say.'

'How is Aubrey?'

'He's been magnificent,' said Tom. 'Not a word of reproach.'

'But, Tom, it can't just have been your fault.'

'No, it wasn't. But mine was the lion's share, I'm afraid.' He looked up at her suddenly, his eyes raw with emotion. 'I still love you, you know,' he said. 'I don't expect you to believe me, for it to make any difference, I'm not asking you for forgiveness, can't expect you to listen to me even. But – I do.'

'Please don't say that,' she said, 'don't say you love me. It hurts more than anything.'

'Why?' he said. 'I don't understand.'

'Because it simply can't be true, Tom. That's why. It just sounds – horrible to me.'

'Yes, I see,' he said.

She went up to bed after that; lay awake for a long time, examining her own feelings, trying to decide how much could be forgiven, how strong a marriage needed to be to survive such mortal blows as Tom had dealt it, whether love turned to hatred could become love ever again. And fell asleep before she even began to find any answers.

CHAPTER 27

'What did you say?'

Barbara Dawson looked at Tom in alarm; she would never have thought he was a candidate for a heart attack, but he was suddenly red in the face, a vein bulging on his forehead, white round the lips, breathing extremely fast.

'Did you say Gloucester? That postmark? Why the hell didn't you give me that message before?'

'Tom,' said Barbara, concern for him evaporating at great speed, 'I tried to give it to you. On the day it came in. You said you didn't want any messages about anything at all, unless it was from the Bank of England. I've hardly seen you since. I left a written list of messages on your desk each morning. Each night I've found it buried under a welter of paper. It's hardly my fault if this is the first time you've deigned to communicate with me properly since last Friday.'

'Yes, all right, all right,' said Tom. 'And this came from Mike Dutton, you say?'

'Yes.'

'Get him on the phone, would you?'

Mike Dutton said that yes, the postmark was definitely Gloucester. 'I've kept the envelope, Tom, if you want it.'

'Yes, please, if you wouldn't mind sending it here. Thanks.'

Barbara heard the phone slammed down; heard him making another call, his voice very low and intense: then he appeared in her doorway.

'Barbara, I'm going out. I may be some time.'

'Don't lie down in the snow,' said Barbara brightly.

'What? What the hell are you talking about?'

'Captain Oates. You know, as in Scott of the Antarctic. Got gangrene. Famous suicidal walk, never came back. At least leave your mobile on.'

Tom didn't seem to think it was very funny.

*

Octavia had usually left the house long before the postman came, but this morning Gideon was fractious, Poppy querulous and Minty, picking up on the prevailing mood, wailed relentlessly. Caroline, normally calm in the face of such traumas, clearly felt like wailing herself. Octavia looked at her: the last thing she needed was for Caroline to crack.

'Look, Caroline, I'll stay and read to Gideon for a while. You and Poppy and Minty could go down to Sainsbury's, get some treats for lunch.'

She was halfway through the first chapter of *The Hobbit* when the bell rang: 'Postman, Mrs Fleming,' called Mrs Donaldson, 'something to be signed for.'

'I'll come down. Gideon, do you want a drink while I'm about it?'

'No thanks,' said Gideon, 'I'll turn into a drink soon, the way you keep pouring them down me.'

'They're very important at the moment,' said Octavia firmly.

'Why, is my foot going to dry up or something and drop off?' He was greatly amused by his own wit; Octavia left him giggling and zapping through the TV controls.

It was a small package, sent recorded delivery, the envelope hand written and addressed to her. She didn't recognise the writing.

'Mum! Can I have a drink after all? Coke?'

'Wouldn't some nice orange juice be better? I'll put ice in it.'

'Okay,' said Gideon, his voice resonant with martyrdom.

Octavia got out a glass, filled it with juice, reached into the fridge for the ice tray. She decided she'd like a drink herself, and filled the kettle; while it was boiling, she picked up the package, started opening it with a knife. She reached into the envelope, pulled out a note from – of course, Charles Madison, she recognised his neat, rather old-fashioned writing now. A charming, slightly sad little missive, telling her he hoped the enclosed would give her pleasure and remind her of Anna – and then she pulled the handkerchiefs out of their tissue paper. The handkerchiefs. Six of them. Pretty handkerchiefs, some lacy, some embroidered, a couple obviously very old, antiques in their own way, worn quite thin. Handkerchiefs. Lying there, on the kitchen table, Anna's handkerchiefs. Anna's. Anna, who was, who had been—

'*Mum!* I'm thirsty.'

Gideon called her again and then again; but even then she didn't move, she just went on standing there, quite still, looking at Louise's mother's handkerchiefs. And thinking of the one in her filing cabinet at the office, so very like them, telling herself over and over again that they didn't, they couldn't, mean anything at all . . .

Dickon was miserable. His mother had promised to take him to

Legoland that day: 'I know it would be more fun with Daddy, but he's not back till Sunday, and it will stop us being bored and lonesome.'

He'd been really pleased and excited, she'd been talking about it for ages, and he'd begun to get ready, fetched his rucksack for sandwiches like she'd said; and then the phone had rung, and she'd been out in the garden hanging out the washing, so he'd answered it. It had been Tom, the twins' daddy, and he'd said could he speak to her, and so he'd gone to fetch her, and then she'd come upstairs looking a bit funny, with her face all red, and said she was terribly sorry, but they couldn't go that day after all. 'Uncle Tom wants me to do a few business things for him. It's important. But I promise, word of honour, we'll go tomorrow. Is that all right, darling?'

'Yes, all right,' said Dickon miserably.

'Now, I'm sorry, but I'm going to have to take you over to Mark for a bit, to play there. His mummy said she'd take you to the swings.'

'I'm bored of the swings,' said Dickon. 'And I don't like Mark.'

Octavia found getting to the office a great relief. Normal, orderly, with its own set of rules; and she was inevitably behind with her work, a great pile of papers stacked on her desk, mostly with explanatory notes from Sarah Jane. No time to think about handkerchiefs, no time to fret over her father, no time to so much as cast her mind in the direction of Gabriel Bingham . . .

Sarah Jane put her head round the door. 'It's Patricia David. She sounds upset.'

Pattie David was very upset. Michael Carlton had managed to get an interview with the local paper, and was making much of his community centre in general, and the facilities for the disabled within it in particular. The reporter in question had then gone out to visit Bartles House rest home and found the house rundown, a roomful of old people stuck in front of the television; and the grounds sadly neglected, the gardens overgrown with weeds, the lawns covered with plaintains and ragwort. There was also, she pointed out to her readers, much local unemployment in the area, and the Carlton development would create, she estimated, hundreds of jobs.

'And then she finishes by saying, "It is natural that there should be local support for saving Bartles Wood, an undeniable beauty spot, but for the rest of the estate, little can be said. The money which would be brought into the area by Mr Carlton's development would enrich it in more ways than one." Octavia, what are we going to do? This is the sort of thing that really influences people, swings public opinion.'

'I know. Well, we'll just have to have another interview with someone else.'

'Yes, but who? Do you think Gabriel Bingham would do it? You and he seem to be quite good friends now.'

'Quite good,' said Octavia cautiously, remembering with a stab of sudden white-hot pleasure Gabriel's mouth on hers, his hands exploring her body, his voice speaking of quite other delights than those of Bartles Wood. 'I could ask him.'

'Would you mind, Octavia? That's terribly good of you.'

It was a good pretext to ring him; but for some reason she was reluctant. She couldn't quite work out why. Anyway, all she could think about was handkerchiefs. She sat at her desk, staring out of the window. Of course it was absolutely ridiculous. Everyone had handkerchiefs. She was just going crazy. Deceived wives did go crazy. Looking for clues in pockets, wallets, car ashtrays. It simply didn't mean anything. She was getting obsessed.

If Louise knew she was even thinking all this, she'd never speak to her again . . .

'Octavia, Barbara Dawson is on the phone. She says do you know where Tom is?'

'No,' said Octavia wearily. 'I have no idea. If he calls me I'll make sure he gets in touch with her.'

Marianne had woken with a strong sense of foreboding. She lay in bed, raking the Octavia and Tom affair over in her mind. She really had to try and do something to help. Starting with cancelling her appointments with Nico. Apart from anything else, Felix was going to need her in the weeks ahead. Both for comfort and restraint. She shuddered at the thought of what harm he might do, unchecked. She might not be able to achieve much, but she could at least try. Starting now.

Nico was out; she left a message for him to ring her, and then decided to go and see Octavia. She rang her office; the secretary said Octavia was in back-to-back meetings all day, and right through lunch, but she'd certainly get the message to her; and yes, she would of course stress it was urgent.

Two hours later, Octavia hadn't phoned. Clearly she didn't consider Marianne as important as her back-to-back meetings. Having also been rebuffed by Felix that morning when she had phoned holding a rather puny olive branch – 'I'm sorry, Marianne, I really can't possibly talk to you now' – Marianne was feeling rather out of sorts altogether with the Miller family. And guiltily relieved that she had been unable to cancel her arrangements with Nico.

She finished what must have been her fourth cup of coffee and went down to make some more. Zoë was in the kitchen. She looked tired, Marianne thought, but a lot more cheerful than she had for some time.

'Hi, Mum.'

'Hallo, darling. Got any plans for today?'

'Not really. Might do a bit of shopping.'

'Zoë! I thought you didn't have any money.'

'Mum, we're not talking mega expense here, just a top or something. Anyway, I got some money from that bar job I did.'

'Oh, I see. Well, darling, don't go mad.'

'Mummy, hi.' It was Romilly. 'I just spoke to Serena Fox. She said had you had a chance to look at the contract yet, that it would be nice if maybe the four of us could have a meeting on Friday, get everything tied up. I would like to, Mummy, I haven't got any other work yet and—'

'Romilly, there's no earthly need for you to work, darling,' said Marianne. 'You don't exactly need the money and—' She saw Romilly's face, quickly adjusted what she was going to say. 'But I can see it's frustrating for you. Er – why were you speaking to Serena?'

'I got a card from her this morning. Look, isn't it sweet?'

Marianne looked at it: a black-and-white postcard of a famous vintage fashion shot. On the back, Serena had written, 'You'll be on one of these one day. Good luck and happy hunting. The hot chocolate session was fun. Serena.'

'Yes, I see. Very – sweet.' Marianne felt a chill of unease. 'What hot chocolate session was that, Romilly?'

'Oh, I met her in the street the other day. As I was coming out of some advertising agency. I was a bit down and she said come and have a drink. She was really, really lovely.'

'I'm sure she was.'

'Anyway, I phoned to thank her and she said can we set this meeting up? You must have had it back from your lawyers by now.'

'Well . . .'

'Mummy, what is this? I'm not going into a drugs ring or something. Please can we get it settled? I'd really really like to. If we're not careful they'll find someone else!'

Romilly looked at her, and not for the first time in the past few weeks, the expression in her eyes was not entirely pleasant to see. Suspicious, impatient, almost hard: more like Zoë. Marianne felt panicked, as if she was losing her; it was horrible.

'I'm off,' said Zoë hastily. 'See you later. If that's all right, of course, Mum.'

Her voice was also hard, sarcastic; suddenly Alec's voice, equally so, came into Marianne's head.

She looked at Romilly. 'Darling, I—'

The phone rang. It was Felix. 'Marianne? Look, we were having dinner tonight. I'll have to cancel it. I'm talking to my lawyer, getting some advice over Octavia.'

'Felix, please, please don't get too involved.'

'Marianne, I'm sorry, but I am becoming extremely tired of your attitude to all this. I have yet to hear any clear expression of sympathy with or loyalty to Octavia from you. I find that rather shocking.'

'Felix—'

But he had cut her off. Marianne felt horribly, disproportionately hurt. She looked at Romilly again; her expression was still impatient, fretful. Romilly, whom she had always been able to rely on for a ceaseless uncritical outpouring of love. She hadn't realised until now how much it had meant to her.

'Yes, darling, you're right,' she heard herself saying. 'Of course we must have that meeting. Friday, did you say? Let me just look in my diary – yes, fine. Now how would you like us to go out and buy something new to wear for it?'

Octavia felt she had lived through a week by five o'clock; she had entirely failed to come up with any further suggestions for sponsorship for Margaret Piper, the work she had done for Foothold looked pretty puny, set down on paper, and Lauren Bartlett had phoned with a long list of suggestions about the day at Brands Hatch, a very few of which were sound, and all of which would need careful attention.

Before she went home, she decided to phone Louise. Just to assuage her conscience: silly really, Louise had no idea of the heinous crime she'd been suspected of. But it would make her feel better. She'd tried to phone Marianne back, and she'd been out, in spite of leaving a message saying it was urgent she spoke to her. It clearly wasn't.

Louise sounded odd: rather over-excited.

'Boot, hallo. I'm glad you phoned. I'm going away for a few days.'

'Yes? Where?'

'Oh, just over to France with Dickon. The Loire Valley. Sandy just phoned, asked us. I thought why not?'

'It's probably just what you need,' said Octavia, 'to get away for a bit.'

'Yes, I do feel that. Away from all the pressures. And the phone. Are you all right?'

'Yes. Yes, I'm fine. Thank you.'

'How are things for Tom?'

'Terrible.'

'Good,' said Louise briefly.

It was an oddly chilling little word. Octavia frowned briefly.

'And you, darling Boot, how are you? Any more news of the Angel Gabriel?'

'Oh – not really.'

'You in love, do you think?'

'Louise, I don't know,' said Octavia. 'I'm not ready to be in love with anyone, I don't think. Last night, talking to Tom about his troubles, I felt terrible suddenly. So guilty. At what I'd done to him.'

'You haven't done anything to him.'

'Yes, I have. I've helped to scupper his company pretty effectively, haven't I?'

'What, with the Bartles Wood business, you mean?'

'Yes. And it's worse now. I mean if he knew, if anyone knew, I'd actually – well, you know . . .'

'Slept with the local MP! Who you met there! Great story, Boot.'

'Louise, I didn't actually say that I'd—'

'But you have, haven't you? Come on, you can't deceive me. Me of all people.'

'Louise, I—' Oh, for heaven's sake, what harm would it do? 'Yes, I have. But look, that's very – well, you know. Between us.' Why was she saying that? Why?

'What do you mean?' The husky voice was harsher suddenly, indignant. 'I hope you don't think I'm going to tell anyone. We're friends, I thought. Best friends. For ever and ever. Amen.'

'I'm sorry. I guess I'm just feeling vulnerable. And guilty all round. Including now about Gabriel.'

'You shouldn't be. Are you going down this weekend? To see him?'

'I don't know. It depends on Gideon's foot, Tom, all sorts of things. But I probably won't be able to resist.'

'Very sexy?'

'Yes, very sexy,' said Octavia, laughing. ''Bye Louise.'

''Bye, darling Boot. And try to remember, I love you.'

It struck Octavia as a slightly strange thing to say.

'Now, Octavia, whatever you do, get your arse in here early in the morning. Mrs Piper is getting her rather larger one up from Chichester at nine thirty for a discussion about the sponsorship and we want to be well ready for her.'

'Yes, of course, Melanie. I promise.'

'We can't afford to lose that account, Octavia.'

'I know, I've made a hash of it.'

'Well, not all of it. Just most of it.' Melanie's hawklike face softened into a wide grin. 'These things happen, but I don't want them happening again for a bit. I know things are tough for you at the moment, but . . .'

Octavia knew what the buts were. All of them. She smiled quickly at

Melanie, struggling to look cool and on top of things. 'Mells, I'll be there. Don't worry about it.'

Octavia was reading to Gideon when Tom came in. She heard the door slam, heard his footsteps on the stairs, heard him coming up the second flight to the nursery. That was nice, that he'd made the effort. 'Here's Daddy,' she said to Gideon, 'he'll probably play that horrible computer game.'

The door opened; Tom stood there, his face devoid of colour, his eyes dull, filled with something ugly and dark.

She stared at him. 'Are you all right?'

'No. No, I'm not. I want to talk to you.'

She felt angry suddenly. 'It'll have to wait, I'm afraid. Gideon's been dying for you to come home, he wants to play that computer game with you.'

'I can't play with you, Gideon. I'm sorry. Not yet. I have to talk to Mummy.'

'But, Daddy—'

'Look, Tom, I don't know what this is about, but it's hardly fair on Gideon. I really do think he should come first this evening. He's bored, he's lonely, his foot hurts. I've been reading to him for ages, but—'

'Oh, how wonderful you are,' he said. 'Such a perfect mother. Get downstairs, Octavia. If you can tear yourself away from your beloved children. If I might interrupt quality time. That's what it's called, I believe. Gideon, I'll come and play with you later, I promise.'

'I'll get Caroline to find you a video, Gideon,' said Octavia quickly. She felt very frightened suddenly.

Charles Madison was just finishing an early supper when he heard the door bell go. Cursing, he went to answer it. Louise stood there, holding Dickon's hand, looking rather pale.

'Daddy,' she said. 'Daddy, I'm sorry, but I'm feeling absolutely terrible. I just can't cope any longer. I know I should be strong for you, but . . .'

'Oh, my darling, you've done so much for me already,' said Charles. 'It's my turn now. Come along in. Dickon, you run in and see Janet. She's got some wonderful apple pie in the kitchen.'

'Is Mummy . . .' Dickon was very white, his eyes huge in his small face.

'Mummy's fine. Just tired and a bit upset. About Granny. You can stay here with me, both of you, for a few days. She'll be better in no time.'

He took Louise upstairs, to the spare room. 'Now you get into bed, darling, and I'll get the doctor.'

'No. Honestly, Daddy, there's no need for that. I just want some peace and quiet. Can I really stay here for a bit?'

'Of course you can.'

'And if anyone phones, can you tell them I'm not here? Say I'm – I know! Say I'm in France. With Sandy. That's a good idea.'

'Yes, all right, darling.'

'I do mean anyone. Even Octavia. Actually, most of all, Octavia. She's been getting me down quite badly lately. Going on and on about her work and everything, about how busy she is. It really doesn't help.'

'Yes, of course I will. Only you know I'm not a very good liar.'

'No, I know. But I thought I actually would go over and see Sandy at the weekend. He did ask us. So it will be almost true. Please, Daddy.'

'Darling, I said I would. Now do let me get Dr Hodgen. You look absolutely all in. And you have to think of the baby.'

'Yes. Yes, I know I do. I've been thinking of nothing else but the baby all day, as a matter of fact.'

'I only want to ask you one thing,' said Tom. They were in his study now, standing facing one another across the room, the door closed. 'Did you or did you not have an abortion eighteen months ago?'

For what felt like hours she stood there, absolutely still, staring at him, absorbing the question, all that it meant, absorbing the knowledge, her mind crunching on it, falling into dreadful disarray, then realigning itself, neatly, mercilessly.

'Well, did you?'

Her flesh crawled: her stomach felt as if it was about to start leaching its contents on to the floor.

'Yes, Tom. Yes, I did.'

'And – and whose was it?'

'It was yours. Of course.'

He raised his hand and struck her: hard across the face.

She didn't feel it, didn't feel anything at all. She just stood there, staring at him in silence. Then she said, 'So it was her, then, Tom. It was Louise.'

And then she turned and ran out of the room, out of the house, and into her car.

Because she now knew with absolute certainty, and somehow it was as if she had known all along, that although everyone might have handkerchiefs, the one in the hotel room had belonged to Louise. And although everyone had letters to post, the ones Louise had had in her car, the ones that Dickon had noticed, had been addressed to Tom's clients.

And it was Louise Tom had been having an affair with. For months and months. Louise. Her best friend.

CHAPTER 28

The house in Cheltenham was in darkness. Octavia stood outside, hammering on the door, shouting Louise's name: nobody came. She looked at her watch: it was only half past nine. How had that happened? She could remember nothing, nothing at all since leaving Phillimore Gardens.

What about her father? Might Louise be there? Yes, possibly. It was worth a try anyway. She went back to her own car, switched on the phone, rang the Madison house; Charles Madison answered the phone.

'No, Octavia, she's not here,' he said carefully. His voice sounded rather strained and awkward; she didn't believe him.

'Charles, are you sure?'

'Yes. She's gone to France. To join Sandy.'

Surely he wouldn't lie to her.

'All right, my dear?'

'Yes. Yes, fine. Thank you.'

She switched off the phone again, she didn't want Tom ringing her, and sat staring into the darkness.

In the kitchen at Rookston Manor, Dickon was just taking his third helping of Janet's apple pie and coating it liberally with ice cream. 'Don't you take too much of that, Dickon, you'll be sick.'

'No, I won't. I'm never sick.'

Janet smiled at him. She was very fond of Dickon. Poor little chap. What a time he'd had. And Louise too. She'd looked dreadful when she'd arrived. They both had.

She heard a car in the drive outside and looked out.

'Who's that?' said Dickon.

'It's the doctor. Come to see your mummy.'

'She's not ill, is she?' Panic filled the great dark eyes.

'Just got a bit of a tummy ache, I believe. Nothing to what you'll have if you don't stop eating that ice cream.' She called from the kitchen across the hall to the drawing room. 'Mr Madison, Doctor's here.'

'Thank you, Janet, I'll let him in.'

'Grandpa, is Mummy really ill, really really ill?'

'No, Dickon, she's just a bit – tired.'

'You don't need the doctor for being tired.'

'Sometimes you do. Evening, Dr Hodgen. Good of you to come. Dickon, you go on back to the kitchen with Janet.'

'Come on, my lovely.' Janet took his hand. 'We'll watch some TV together, shall we?'

He hesitated. 'Could I have a weeny bit more ice cream?'

'Just a weeny bit.'

Octavia was on her way to Rookston. She simply hadn't believed Charles. No doubt Louise had spun him some elaborate story or other. There was another father who was putty in his daughter's hands. She wondered if Tom would be like that with Poppy, then thought of their family by the time Poppy was old enough to manipulate him – fractured, dysfunctional beyond repair – and the road ahead blurred. She dashed the tears away furiously. This was no time for sentiment. She had to keep her mind absolutely fixed on the present.

It was dusk now, that ultra-clear half-light peculiar to late summer evenings. The whole situation seemed very surreal; she felt rather as if she was watching herself in some film, with no real idea of what was going to happen, her purpose in coming here, what it might achieve. She only knew she had to see Louise, hear her voice, watch her face, in the now certain knowledge that she had been having an affair with – no, Octavia, don't dress it up – sleeping with, having sex with, screwing her husband. Louise, who was, who had been her best friend, for ever and ever amen, always with a special place in her heart, confidante, sharer of secrets, guardian of intensely personal, intimate information, like the final dangerous piece of information. And, oh, God, what would she do with that, about Gabriel . . . yes, I have slept with him . . .

How could Louise have sat there listening, asking her things, questioning her, knowing, knowing all the time. When she was fucking Tom, kissing him, moving with him, welcoming him into her lovely, long, slender, orgasmic body . . . crying out in that pretty, husky, evil voice . . . Octavia felt bile rise suddenly in her throat, slammed on the brakes, jumped out, reached the hedge just in time, vomiting over and over again.

She got back into the car finally, wearily, sat resting on the steering wheel, wondering if even now she still had the strength to go on, whether after all she should go back to London, face Tom, face all of it.

Her car phone rang, shrilly, made her jump. Damn, she'd meant to keep it off.

'Yes?' she said wearily.

'Where are you?'

It was Tom.

'In Gloucestershire.'

'Octavia, don't go and see her. Don't. It would be madness. Believe me.'

'Tom, I've been driven to madness already. It can't get any worse. Sorry.'

She put the phone back on its hook, switched it off.

Tom was sitting in his study watching an absurd news shot of what the reporter called a Cool Britannia party at Number Ten: Eddie Izzard in a frock, Chris Evans making silly faces, Mariella Frostrup looking like the cat that swallowed the cream, the Gallagher brothers. What were they doing there, on what kind of crazy logic had they been invited? He supposed it was all part of Blair's nonsense: he'd been going on the day before on Radio Two about the people's government. Were these supposed to be the people's stars? He'd be talking about the people's Royal Family soon.

The phone rang: please, God, let that be Octavia, saying she was coming home.

It wasn't. It was Aubrey.

'Tom. Are – are things any better?'

'No, I don't think you could say that. But anyway. Let's talk about Fleming Cotterill. What news. If any?'

'Not good, I'm afraid.'

'Oh, God,' said Tom, 'it's a nightmare. And it's so frustrating. We only need a tiny bit of luck, just one more account, and a hundred grand, then we could get by.'

'I know. But tomorrow is the first of the month. We have to pay the staff, certainly by Monday. We can't do that – the bank will bounce the cheques. And then we have that huge VAT bill, due for payment today, those guys'll petition to have us wound up before you can say Customs and Excise.'

'If we could pay the staff,' said Tom slowly, 'how much time would we have?'

'Not long. The rent and rates are due September first.'

'That sounds like a long way off. After these last few days. And what about if the Customs and Excise boys do petition, how long would it take?'

'About six weeks, I think. But honestly, I think we'd just be digging ourselves an ever-deepening hole. Look, Tom, I'll see you in the morning. Think about a merger, there's a good chap. Octavia all right, is she?'

'Oh, fine, yes. Thank you. Good night, Aubrey,' said Tom. He put the phone down. 'Please, God,' he said aloud.

'Why did you do it?' said Octavia. They were sitting, she and Louise, in her car, just down the road from Rookston.

Louise had met her on the doorstep: for that at least she admired her. She was looking terrible. 'You can't come in,' she had said, 'we can't talk here. It would be dreadful for Daddy, for Dickon.'

'I don't care where we talk.'

'Let's go for a drive.'

'I couldn't help it,' Louise said simply. 'I just – fell in love with him. I'd never felt like that before. I really hadn't. It was just—'

'Don't tell me. It was bigger than both of you. You betrayed me, your best friend, and your own husband, simply because of some romantic fantasy you felt you had to live out. You always were strong on all that stuff. Jesus, Louise. How old are you?'

'I'm thirty-six. Same as you. That's the whole point. Time's passing, isn't it? We haven't got that much time left, have we?'

'Oh, the biological clock. That old thing. Next thing you'll be telling me is you felt you had to have another baby.'

'Well, I did. That as well.'

'But you're not pregnant? With Tom's baby? Tell me that at least isn't true?'

Louise looked at her. Her blue eyes were very dull and heavy. 'No, I'm not pregnant,' she said finally.

In spite of everything, all the pain, that was somehow better.

'How – how did you know it was me?' said Louise.

'He knew about the abortion. I only told one person in the whole world: your mother. And then she told me you found out. Nobody else knew, nobody at all. So it had to be you. There were other things. But I ignored them. I knew it couldn't be you. Not you. Not my best friend. Why did you tell him about that? Hadn't you betrayed me enough?'

'Because it was so awful. So unfair. I'd lost Juliet. One day I had a lovely, warm, smiling, breathing little girl, and the next day she was ice cold, dead. I had to put her in a coffin, I put her in myself, you know, and kissed her and said night night, sleep tight, and then . . . then . . .'

Octavia felt her eyes fill with tears in spite of everything, felt her heart literally ache. 'Oh, Louise.' She put out her hand, tried to take Louise's.

She snatched it away. 'No! Don't touch me. And what do you do? You just carelessly throw a baby away. Chuck it out. Oh, I don't think I want that one, you said to the doctor, it's not quite perfect, pull it out, would you, pull it out and throw it away, down the sluice, only be quick, I've got a meeting later this morning. It was safe in there, Octavia, safe and warm; it trusted you, it was alive; my baby was dead. You had a choice; I had no choice.'

'That was it, was it?' said Octavia slowly. 'You were so angry with me, so jealous, you had to hurt me the way you most could?'

'Oh, no,' said Louise, and smiled at her, her sweet, gentle smile. 'No, we'd been sleeping together long before I knew about you. About your baby. Until Mummy was ill and I found that letter you'd written her. How sweet, you coming to her for advice. Why did you do that, exactly? Why not talk to Tom about it?'

'Tom was away. In the States. He didn't even know about the baby. He'd been more or less commuting for weeks and weeks, working on some new account or other. I tried to tell him, but we had a row about something stupid; then he went back, and I had the test. And you know the rest.'

'If someone had said to me,' said Louise, '"Your baby has spina bifida," do you think I'd have cared? Do you think I'd have thrown her away, put her in an incinerator? That's what they do, you know, with those babies, those aborted babies. They burn them, they—'

'Shut up!' said Octavia. 'Just shut up. And don't try to compare the two. Juliet was a child, a person, she was nine months old; my baby was – was just a fertilised egg.'

That's what she'd kept telling herself, that it was only a fertilised egg, not a baby at all, not really, not something growing in her, being nurtured by her, not something she'd betrayed. That was what she had hung on to: what had kept her from cracking.

'Why didn't you tell Tom? It was his baby too, he might not have felt the same, he might have thought it was actually worth keeping, caring for . . .'

'I thought it was best not,' said Octavia, very quietly. 'I knew he wouldn't want it. The whole thing was a mistake, he'd said there was no way he wanted any more children, and illness, any kind of deformity, sickens him, he really can't cope with it. He can't even bear the children being sick. Everything has to be attractive for Tom, perfect, clean, wholesome. There was no way he'd want to keep a – a deformed baby.'

'But you didn't actually know that. Not for sure. You didn't give him the option even to think about it.'

'Oh, shut up,' said Octavia again. 'Shut up, shut up, shut up. Don't you start preaching morals at me. Don't you try and tell me I'm wicked. What you've been doing was disgusting. Absolutely disgusting. I can't bear to look at you, knowing you were screwing my husband. You. My best friend. And then pretending you were sorry for me, wanted to help. Asking me if I knew who it was, if we were still sleeping together, for Christ's sake. That is truly sick. What you did was a total, utter betrayal. Of years and years of affection and trust and sharing of everything – oh, God, I don't want you in the car with me, even. Get out, Louise. Get out and walk. I'm going home. I absolutely loathe you. And it hurts more than I can tell. Far more than when I first found out about Tom. The very last thing you said to me this afternoon, I can hardly bear to think about it, the very last thing, "Remember I love you." You said that. You told me you loved me. God! You don't know what love is. You have no idea. No idea at all. Get out. Go away. And don't ever come near me again. Ever.'

Louise got out of the car and walked. She walked back to the house and went in and smiled at her father and said she was fine, that the little walk with Octavia had done her good. And then she went upstairs and read a story to Dickon, who said he had a tummy ache. She went and chatted to her father for a while, about her mother, and how he was coping and what his plans were, and about Sandy's business, and about Dickon and how he would soon be at school and that he seemed to be much better and happier these days. After that she kissed him good night and went to have a bath, and lay in it for a long time, and looked at her legs and decided they needed shaving and she went to find a razor and spent quite a long time doing that, and then she massaged her favourite body lotion into herself and brushed her hair and put on a nightdress, one of her favourites, white lawn, trimmed with lace, and then she went down to the kitchen and made herself a hot drink and filled a carafe with water, and lay in bed, reading magazines until she fell asleep over them.

She woke up with a start, a few hours later, and looked at the clock. It was already half past two. She'd wasted a lot of time.

She sat up in bed and reached for the small hoard of sleeping pills she had found in her mother's medicine cabinet, and the four which Dr Hodgen had left for her, and started to swallow them, very carefully, one by one . . .

CHAPTER 29

Dickon woke up feeling horrible. His tummy hurt, he felt sick and he was rather cold; when he sat up, he felt dizzy. He stayed in bed for a bit, hoping to feel better and go back to sleep, and then realised he felt sicker than ever, slithered out of bed and made for the bathroom.

Halfway there, he realised he wasn't going to make it; he stood on the landing, alternately vomiting and crying.

Charles appeared looking anxious. 'Oh, dear, bad luck, old chap. Look, let's get you into the bathroom, that's the ticket, get those off – oh, whoops, not again, poor old soldier.'

'Janet said I shouldn't eat so much ice cream,' said Dickon, through chattering teeth.

'Well, she was right. She usually is. Come on, off with the jacket as well. Good boy. Now shall we put you in the bath, do you think?'

'Yes, please,' said Dickon, 'and get Mummy.'

'Oh, we don't want to bother poor Mummy. She was so tired. Let's just get you cleaned up, and then back to bed.'

'I want Mummy,' said Dickon and started to cry.

'Maybe. When you're all cleaned up. Come on, now, hop in here. Was it Janet's own ice cream? Yes, I thought so. Very rich. Your uncles used to make themselves sick with it too. That's better, lie right down, in the water. Now where are we going to find you some clean pyjamas, I wonder . . .'

Dickon sat in the bath, shivering; he felt much better, but he still wanted his mother. Surely she'd want to look after him if she knew he was ill, however tired she was?

His grandfather came back into the room, helped him out of the bath, and snuggled him dry in a towel. 'Feeling better?'

'Yes, much. Thank you. But I do want Mummy—'

'Look, tell you what,' said Charles, 'you get into my bed for a bit, and we'll see . . .'

'Yes, all right.'

When Charles came back to his room, Dickon was asleep, breathing steadily, his colour much better. He looked at the clock: almost half past four. It would soon be light. He'd have trouble getting back to sleep himself now. Two hours of wakeful misery, remembering, missing, longing for Anna. He decided a tiny, second nightcap would be a good idea; he went downstairs and made himself his second hot toddy of the night. As he passed Louise's room, he stopped, turned the handle and peeped in; she was sleeping soundly, quite heavily even. Good. That was exactly what she needed. Charles eased himself into bed beside his grandson and fell asleep with surprising speed.

Tom woke up at five with a start; he was still on the sofa, the screen was a whining white-out, and he was almost unbearably cold. Where was Octavia? She must have come in without him hearing her, probably realised he was there and went on up to bed, not wishing to speak to him. He'd better check.

Rubbing his eyes, he staggered out to the hall: the chain wasn't on the door, but she was always forgetting it. He went up to their room, but the bed was empty; he checked both guest rooms, even the small spare bed in the corner of the nursery. He stood there for a while looking at Minty, determinedly asleep, her bottom thrust into the air, her rosebud mouth working gently round her thumb. Thinking of the other baby, the one before Minty, the one Octavia had discarded: how could she have done that without consulting him, discussing it, how could she have not told him she was pregnant even? Whatever the reason, Minty was actually the result. Strange to think that she might never have been born, never existed. And now, oh, God, now there was another child of his, waiting to be born. A child Louise had taken from him by stealth – he had read somewhere that was the female equivalent of rape – trapping him viciously, more efficiently. What was to become of that child, who would care for it? Its half-insane mother? Its hapless, amoral father?

Tom made a sound that was half-sigh, half-groan, walked quietly out of the nursery. More important at this very moment to find Octavia. He was beginning to feel uneasy. Perhaps the cottage: yes, that wasn't so far from Rookston. He phoned it: there was no reply. He left a message, just the same. She might be on her way there. But – where was she? Where had she spent the night? Surely, surely she wouldn't have done anything – anything stupid? Or had an accident, driving in a distressed, exhausted state? Maybe he should phone the police. Or the hospitals . . .

*

Dickon wondered what the awful noise was: thunder? Something falling downstairs? No, of course, it was snoring. Loud snoring. Right next to him. His grandfather. He turned his head, looked at him. Charles was lying on his back, his mouth open. Each breath sounded louder than the last. It wasn't a very nice sound. Dickon sighed. Maybe he should try and go back to his own bed. If he went back to his room, he could at least look at the Thomas the Tank Engine book his mother had been reading to him.

Very carefully, he edged his way out of the big, rather high bed, tiptoed across the room. He let himself out, closed the door very carefully and walked down the corridor towards his own room. He looked longingly at his mother's door, but Grandpa was right, she was very tired, he shouldn't wake her up. Specially not now he was better.

He went into his own room, rather pleased with himself; and then realised that the book wasn't there. Of course; his mother had taken it away, some of the pages had been falling out and she'd said she'd mend it. So it would be in her room.

He turned the handle cautiously, looked in; she was lying on her back, she looked rather like the Sleeping Beauty. Only she wasn't going to sleep for a hundred years. He wouldn't let her. Just till breakfast. That would be quite enough.

Octavia had spent the night at one of the motels on the M4. Utterly anonymous, totally uninterested in her, caring for nothing but that her credit card should be cleared, they gave her a room number and handed her a key for it: it was exactly what she needed, a mindless, faceless, unpeopled environment. She made a cup of tea and lay down on the bed and stared at the blank television screen. The room was absolutely silent, the double glazing forming an impenetrable barrier against the roar of the motorway, and absolutely dark, the thick curtains lined with some kind of plasticised fabric, a surreal womb in which she could escape from the world.

No, no, not a womb, she thought, sipping the tea, she would never hear that word again without feeling terror and nausea. A tomb, that was more like it, it was like being sealed in a tomb, but interred by her own choice, removing her from action, demands, decisions. Here she could and would stay; no one could find her, no one trouble her, until she wished to be found and troubled. At that moment, either seemed unthinkable.

Dickon was having a bit of trouble finding the Thomas the Tank Engine book. It wasn't on the table by the window, nor was it on the chest of drawers. Dickon turned, looked at the bed. Not there, not on the bedside table. But the bedside table did have a drawer; maybe she'd put it in there. Only, opening that might wake her. Although she seemed very asleep.

Gingerly, he went over to the bed, eased himself between it and the wall; his mother slept on. He was next to the bedside table now. If he could just – Dickon reached out to the drawer handle, and the sleeve of Benjy's pyjamas, much too big for him, caught on the glass jug standing on the table. It balanced dangerously on the edge for a long moment, then in slow motion, tipped right over and fell off. On to the wooden floor. And shattered. Loudly.

He stood, holding his breath, waiting for his mother to wake up and be first frightened and then cross with him. Only she didn't.

Janet had slept badly. She wasn't sure why; she normally slept like the dead, as she herself cheerfully announced every morning if asked, but she was restless, dreaming fitfully; at five she got up and went downstairs to make herself tea and found she was down to the last teaspoon of leaves; she decided to borrow some from the house. She slipped across the yard in her dressing gown and was just tipping a handful of tea leaves into her tea caddy when she heard the crash from the floor above, where Louise slept. And after the crash a long silence.

It was the long silence that seemed strange; rather like Sherlock Holmes' dog that didn't bark, as she explained it to Derek afterwards. No exclamation, no footsteps, no creaking of the bed even, just a dead still silence.

Janet went up to investigate; and found Dickon crossing the bedroom floor, a deeply anxious expression on his small face, and beyond him, Louise, waxy pale, totally still, her body looking somehow oddly collapsed into itself.

Marianne had also, and most unusually, slept badly. Normally, she slept like the proverbial baby; although anyone who had had a baby, she always thought, would have known what an absurd comparison that was. But the night had been filled with anxiety, which filtered into what sleep she had: anxiety about her children, about Octavia and Tom, about her relationship with Nico – not of course that it was a relationship – about Felix. Finally at six, she got up, made herself a cup of camomile tea, and was just climbing back into bed when the phone rang.

It was Felix. 'Marianne, are you awake?' He sounded terrible, hoarsely agitated.

'I am now,' she said, trying not to sound petulant, the reproachful lie rising easily to her lips. God, he was inconsiderate.

'It's Octavia. She's disappeared.'

'Felix, what on earth do you mean?' An exaggeration, no doubt.

'I mean she's disappeared. Nobody knows where she is.'

'Felix, you're going to have to explain this to me a bit,' said Marianne, pushing her hair back wearily. 'How do you know she's disappeared?'

'Tom rang me. About a quarter of an hour ago.'

'Tom?' It clearly was serious; Tom must have been driven to a desperation of anxiety to have rung Felix. 'But why?'

'It seems that Charles Madison rang him. They're desperate to get hold of Octavia. Louise has taken an overdose. She's been rushed to hospital. Charles seems to think Octavia might have some idea why she did it.'

'Oh, my God,' said Marianne very slowly. 'Oh, Felix. This is very, very terrible.'

Greatly to her surprise, at some point during the long, timeless, strangely emotionless night, Octavia had actually slept; she woke to see something resembling light coming through the curtains. She was fully dressed still, lying on top of the heavy bedspread. The radio clock by her bed said it was half past six. Half past six: Minty would be waking, the twins would soon be up, looking for her, wondering where she was. They would be worried about her; it wasn't their fault, they didn't deserve that. She tried to use the phone in the room, but it wasn't connected, tried her own mobile, but it was run down. Damn. It would have to be the car. She stood up, wincing at a stiff neck, a foul mouth, caught sight of herself in the mirror, rings of smudged mascara under her eyes, her hair pushed into a bizarre shape, and almost smiled. What price stylish Octavia Fleming now?

She phoned the house; Caroline answered.

'Octavia! Where are you? We were so worried. Tom's been trying everywhere. Even the police. He wants to speak to you. And your father's terribly—'

'I can't stop,' she said quickly. 'Tell Tom I'll call again later. And my father that I'm fine. And tell the children I'll probably be back tonight.'

'Octavia, please speak to Tom. He's—'

'I can't. Sorry.' She snapped the phone back on its hook, switched it off, and went back into the motel.

She supposed she ought to go home. But she couldn't face it. She wanted to run away, disappear, never be seen again by anyone who had ever known her; start again, with a new identity, a new life.

Given the impossibility of that, she pulled out of the service station and turned down the M4 in the direction of Somerset and the cottage.

★

Tom was also on the M4: driving to Gloucestershire and the hospital where Louise lay. Mad, beautiful, radiant Louise, whom he had come at one point most dangerously near to loving, and whom now he feared and dreaded beyond everything. He would have said, indeed, that he hated her now; but since Charles' phone call, hearing his voice raw with fear and misery, he realised that was far too straightforward, too simplistic an emotion. What he felt for Louise now had no name: there was hatred in it, to be sure, but there was tenderness too, and remorse and regret, and revulsion and desire. He kept seeing her face as he had slammed the car door shut, driven away from her: distorted with misery that he had once again refused her, refused what she wanted, and at the same time, with an ugly elation that she had finally touched him, hurt him with the story of Octavia and the baby she had discarded.

'Leave me alone,' he had shouted, the last thing he had said to her. 'Stay out of my life.' And then, very slowly, 'I – don't – love – you. Understand that. For Jesus Christ's sake.'

For Jesus Christ's sake. Amen. Was that the next thing he would be saying to her? Or rather to her coffin? Was she dying, was she dead? And if she was, then was it his fault, his fault alone? Or could he at least share that guilt with the demons she lived with, who had invaded her lovely body and her tortured spirit? Should he have told someone, sought help for her when he had begun to fear for her sanity? He should; he knew that very well. Cowardice had held him back, the fear of the consequences of going to Sandy, or to Charles, telling them what he knew, revealing how he knew it. Cowardice and hope. Hope that she would come through, accept what he had told her she must accept, see what he had struggled to make her see.

But he hadn't; and the sweet, intense flirtation that had begun with a dance at a party, extended to lunch, to wild, winging afternoons in hotel rooms, and thence to magically lovely stolen nights and days, had slowly darkened into tears, dependence, demands, protestations of love, of need, and finally declarations of hatred, and of revenge: and now of the ultimate vengeance, laying her death at his door.

Barbara Dawson came through on his car phone.

'Tom, where the hell are you? You have a meeting with Bob Macintosh like now. He's come down from Birmingham, and—'

'Tell Aubrey to see him. I can't get back,' said Tom. 'Look, I'm dealing with a – a domestic emergency. Please tell everyone that. Okay? Unless my wife rings. In which case, find out where she is and get her to ring me on this. Or my mobile. I don't want to speak to anyone else. Anyone at all.'

★

Sandy had been enjoying a bowl of milky coffee and a *pain au chocolat* when his mobile rang, preparing himself for a meeting with the manager of a big chain of autoroute cafés. If he pulled this one off, he would be able to do some of the things he had been dreaming of; buy a better house, a decent car, put Dickon down for Eton, take Louise away for a holiday. Somewhere sunny, somewhere glamorous, the Caribbean or the Bahamas. A couple of weeks in the sun would see her right; and then the promise of a move, of being able to use her talents as an interior designer. She'd cheer up in no time. No time at all . . .

This might be her now; he lifted the phone, smiled.

'Hallo. Sandy Trelawny . . .'

Dickon was sitting on Janet's knee in the kitchen when his father phoned; he had hardly spoken all day. The terrifying events of the early morning, seeing his grandfather holding his mother like a limp doll, trying to force water into her mouth, the ambulance arriving, sirens screaming, the men rushing up the stairs, and then moving down swiftly, so swiftly they seemed to be flying. Seeing his mother on a stretcher, and being put into the ambulance and the ambulance driving off again, hearing the siren moving out of earshot. And then his grandfather hurling himself into his own car, driving off, his mobile telephone held to his ear. It had all been so horrible, exactly like a bad, bad dream. And now he was afraid, so afraid, that she would die too, and join Juliet and his grandmother. Janet kept saying that she wouldn't, that she'd be fine, but he was terribly afraid. Dying was what seemed to happen to everyone he loved.

'You mean you knew? Or you suspected it was Louise? And you said nothing, nothing to me, or to—'

'Felix, I didn't think I should say anything to you. For the hundredth time, it's nothing to do with you. Or me for that matter.'

'I rather beg to differ, Marianne. If you had told me I might have been able to do something about the whole thing.'

Marianne looked at him; thinking what an appalling force for danger he was. He was pacing up and down her drawing room, energised by rage and anxiety, gnawing at his knuckles. He always did that when he was distraught.

'Really?' she said, surprised at her own courage. 'And what would you have done?'

'Oh, for God's sake. Spared her some of the shock at least.'

'You're sure she knows?'

'Oh, yes, she knows. Tom told me. God, that man has a great deal to answer for.'

Marianne said nothing; but she thought of Louise lying near to death, if not dead, in hospital, and of Octavia, hurt and doubly damaged by this new deadly betrayal, and of three – no, four children, desperately hurt, Dickon most of all; of Charles Madison, who deserved no more pain at all; of Sandy who deserved none either; and she agreed with him. Tom did indeed have a great deal to answer for.

'Felix,' she said, putting her hand on his arm, trying to defuse his rage just a little, 'Felix, let's try to think calmly about this. About what we can do to help now. Rather than what we should have done.'

'What *you* should have done, you mean,' he said, shaking off the hand, and he looked at her with something so close to hatred she was almost frightened.

'Well, whatever you may feel about that, I didn't. Might she be at the cottage?'

'Do you think I haven't tried there?' he said. 'Marianne, we're wasting valuable time. I think we should go to the police.'

'We can't do that. Surely. It has to be Tom. He's her husband, he's her next-of-kin.'

'For what it's worth. In any case, Tom is on his way to Gloucestershire. He appears to be rather more worried about his mistress than his wife!'

'Felix, that is so unfair.'

'It is not unfair,' he said, his voice rising now to a roar, 'and I will not have you passing any more judgments on me, Marianne. I find your contribution, or rather your lack of contribution, to this whole affair absolutely incomprehensible. The best thing you can do from now on is stay right out of it. I'm going to my office. Octavia might phone me there. Please contact me at once if you hear anything: anything at all.'

She was standing between him and the door; he pushed her out of the way so violently she almost fell over. Marianne finally lost her temper.

'How dare you!' she said, her voice low and rich with rage. 'How dare you behave like this. When I am trying—'

'You are not trying to do anything so far as I can make out,' said Felix, 'except possibly obstruct my efforts to help my daughter.'

'Felix, I am not obstructing your efforts to help her. I am querying your methods. Which are intrusive, and, in my view, dangerous. And however you view my behaviour, it does not entitle you to manhandle me physically. Please do go. And don't come back until you feel able to apologise to me.'

'I think it is you who should be making apologies,' said Felix, 'to Octavia, as well as to me. What you have shown towards her is a near criminal irresponsibility.'

'Oh, please!' said Marianne. 'That is a truly disgusting observation.

Just get out, will you, Felix? If I hear anything of or from Octavia I'll call your secretary or your housekeeper. I have absolutely no desire to speak to you. Today, or indeed ever again.'

He stood there for a long moment, just staring at her, his face white, working with rage. Then he turned and she heard him running down the stairs and out of the front door, slamming it viciously behind him.

'What on earth is going on?' said Nico Cadogan. 'Nobody will speak to me. I leave crucial messages for Tom, asking him to ring me urgently, and I'm told he's out of town on urgent business. I ring you, and your daughter tells me you can't come to the phone, that must be the younger one, more helpful than the other. I try Felix, and he won't speak to me either. Have I been blackballed by the whole of London? Should I fall on my sword?'

'No,' said Marianne, smiling for the first time that day. 'God, Nico, I don't know where to begin. I'm sorry I didn't speak to you earlier, but I was – upset.'

'Upset? What about?'

'Just about everything. Oh, Nico, it would be so nice to see you. Is lunch still on?'

'Of course. That's why I was ringing you. I've got a table booked at the Ritz. Meet me there at twelve thirty. Do you know where Tom is, by the way?'

'I think possibly in the emergency department of Gloucester Hospital,' said Marianne soberly.

'I just wondered,' said Philip Thorburn, Nico Cadogan's accountant, or, as he preferred to style himself, financial adviser, 'if you'd noticed the share price has gone up again.'

'I hadn't actually. Not today. Rather a lot of other things on my mind. But I'm delighted to hear it. Clearly our message is getting through. The shareholders must be pleased.'

'Very. Quite a lot of movement in the shares as well, I'm told. Of course that always happens when there's a bid. Any news from your chappie about the referral?'

'No, not yet. Nothing concrete anyway. But he's pretty confident.'

'Good. Well, tell him about this, won't you?'

'I will when I can get hold of him,' said Nico, a touch of irritation in his voice.

'What on earth are you doing here?'

Charles Madison looked at Tom rather dully as he walked into the

Casualty waiting area. Tom eyed him warily back. How much did he know, how much did he have to tell him?

'I couldn't get hold of Octavia. So I thought it might help if I came instead.'

'Very good of you. Very good.'

So he didn't know. Anything. Thank Christ. He would have to, of course, but not now, not here . . .

'How – how is she?'

'Oh, they don't really know yet. Poor child. Poor, poor child. Tom, why, why should she have done such a thing? When she was pregnant, when things were going to get better for her?'

'I suppose she's – well she'd had a lot to bear,' said Tom.

'Yes, of course. But last night she seemed brighter. She came over, you know, and Octavia came down. She didn't want to see her, tried to make me say she wasn't here, don't know why, but Octavia just arrived, and after that Louise seemed happier. She was thinking of going over to France, to see Sandy. Poor chap – dreadful shock for him.'

'Have you spoken to him?'

'Oh, yes. He's on his way. Should be here by late afternoon. He's such a good man. I feel so sorry for him.'

Tom's stomach heaved. 'Yes.'

'Have you spoken to Octavia yet?'

'No. But she's on her way to the cottage apparently. I've left a message for her.'

'Her father seemed in a terrible state when I spoke to him. Have you told him you've tracked her down?'

'Yes.'

'Must have been relieved.'

'Er – yes.'

Relieved, yes. And then a bitter, vile attack.

'So – Octavia's at the cottage, is she? I did leave a message there.'

Oh, God. That was how Octavia would get the news, unless he could speak to her first; from an answering machine. The message that her best friend, the one who had been sleeping with her husband, had now taken an overdose. It would be almost unendurable.

'Excuse me,' he said, and half ran down the corridor pulling out his mobile.

'It all sounds rather like one of those splendid Greek tragedies,' said Nico, smiling at her over his glass, 'only rather less stylish. Come on, you're not drinking your champagne. You need it.'

'Nico! How can you talk about style in connection with such things?'

'Sorry. Am I not taking your family affairs seriously enough? What did she take, this girl?'
'Sleeping pills apparently.'
'Couldn't possibly kill her,' said Nico complacently. 'Just wanted to upset everyone. No intention of dying.'
'Nico, how do you know?'
'I'm frightfully well informed on such matters. As on most things. My mother was a doctor.'
'Your mother!'
'Yes. Don't look so surprised. You Americans always think you've invented female emancipation.'
'I'm only half American and I don't,' said Marianne irritably. 'Nico, I'm not really up to being—' She stopped suddenly. 'Oh, dear, I don't want to start quarrelling with you as well.'
'Did you actually quarrel with Felix?'
'Actually, yes. Yes, I did.'
'Good. That's the best news I've had all day,' said Nico, sitting back with an expression of great satisfaction.
'Nico!'
'Well, it is. It seems to me he treats you very badly. Everyone seems to treat you badly. You are obviously far too nice for your own good. In any case, I intend to treat you extremely well, to make up for the rest of them. Anyway, let's not talk about Felix any more, I think we are both on slightly unstable moral ground so far as he is concerned. What are we going to do about poor old Tom, do you think?'
'I really don't think Tom deserves any sympathy whatsoever,' said Marianne.
'I disagree. I think he deserves a great deal. His business is clearly in serious trouble, through very little fault of his own as far as I can tell, and with Felix determined to finish it off with great speed, there seems little hope for it. And then he is caught in this dreadful marital tangle—'
'He's caught in it! Nico, please! That is entirely of his own making. He's behaved appallingly. Octavia is the most wonderful wife. Loyal, clever, supportive, she's a wonderful mother—'
'And not a lot of fun, I suspect?'
'Nico, if you think not being fun is grounds for adultery – anyway, how can you possibly know?'
'I have observed her. I'm sure she is extremely virtuous. She is also very attractive. But nervy, difficult. A trifle humourless, perhaps? Anyway, let us look at this affair from Tom's position. There he is, caught up in this intense high-profile ten-year-old marriage. With a nightmare of a father-in-law for whom he can do nothing right. A hugely demanding, difficult business to run. And along comes this

extremely pretty girl, fun, flirtatious, finding him terribly attractive, looking for a diversion from her own marriage. He's flattered, he's charmed, he wants to please her in return, he suggests lunch, things go one step beyond that, just one and he's had it. Poor sod. She's clearly completely potty.'

'Do you think so?' said Marianne soberly.

'Well, of course. Look at all the dreadful things she's done. So he's trapped, helplessly so.'

'But, Nico, she's Octavia's best friend.'

'I know. That's bad. On both their parts. Don't get me wrong, I do feel very sorry for Octavia. But I still think you should have some – understanding – about what has happened to Tom. He made one fatal mistake, took one step too near the edge of the quicksands and he was done for, sucked down with no hope whatsoever of getting free again. Poor bugger. And now Felix Miller is going to have his head up on a stake on Tower Bridge. I really do feel very sorry for him.'

He sat back, looked at her.

'Anyway,' he said, 'I would like to help Tom, from a business point of view at least, and I intend to if I can. I just felt I had to make that quite clear, so that you knew where I stood. Now let us not waste any more time talking about other people. I can't tell you how much I am looking forward to our day on Saturday. I have found a few more houses I want to look at, so it's all going to take quite a long time, make us rather late for our dinner.'

Octavia stood leaning on the desk, thinking she would never again be able to look at answering machine without feeling sick.

She would have said, had anyone asked her, that nothing could have upset her further; but the news, delivered in Charles Madison's gentlemanly voice, that Louise had taken an overdose and was in hospital, had horrified her almost beyond anything. In that first moment, and for a few moments more, she remembered Louise not as treacherous enemy but loyal friend, loving, kind friend, saw her face not obscenely twisted in misery and revenge, but sweetly, generously smiling.

Then she moved on; remembered with her emotions as well as her mind, squared this new horror up with the new hatred and was surprised to find she was still upset and shocked.

She thought of Sandy, poor, innocent, well-meaning Sandy; of Charles, faced with a double loss; of Dickon, most of all: he had had to endure so much in his rather sad little short life. And of Tom: what would this do for him, how would he feel, would he be grieving, shocked – and did she care?

The phone rang sharply; she picked it up.

'Octavia Fleming.'

'Octavia? It's Tom.'

'Is there any more news yet? Of Louise?'

'No. She's still alive. Can't tell you any more than that. Sorry.'

'Yes, you must be. Sorry, I mean. Where are you?'

'At the hospital.'

'Oh, I see. Yes.'

'Octavia, are you all right?'

'I'm absolutely all right. Yes. Of course. First I find it's my best friend you're having an affair with, then I hear she's tried to kill herself.'

'What did you say to Louise last night?'

'That is nothing to do with you.'

'Of course it is.'

'It is not. Look – let me know if there's any more news. I'll be here till tonight.'

'You – wouldn't think of . . .'

'Wouldn't think of what?'

'Well, coming here? To the hospital?'

'No,' she said, and her voice was very hard and flat now. 'I absolutely wouldn't think of it.'

CHAPTER 30

Sandy finally reached the hospital at five o'clock; Louise was no longer in Casualty, she had been moved to one of the medical wards. At least that sounded like good news.

Sandy found Charles in the corridor, half asleep; he looked terrible. Sandy sat down next to him, touched his arm gently. 'Charles! I'm here. Any news?'

'Oh – Sandy! Good to see you, my boy. Yes, yes, she's going to be all right apparently – ah. Here's the doctor now. Doctor, this is my son-in-law.'

'The husband?' said the doctor. 'Is that right?'

'Yes,' said Sandy.

'She's fine. That is to say, I'm afraid—' He paused.

Sandy had often heard the phrase 'his heart stopped', and thought how absurd it was, but in that moment his own did: he actually felt it lurch and then seize entirely.

'Well, she has lost the baby. I'm sorry.'

'The – baby?'

'Yes. To be honest with you, I think it might be better. In the long run. A lot of drugs at this stage in the pregnancy could well have harmed the foetus. It's no comfort perhaps at the moment, but – well, there it is. You can go and see her if you like. We're about to send her up to the gynae ward.'

Sandy sat down; he felt as if he was isolated in some kind of sealed capsule, everything outside seemed rather hazy and muffled. So she had been pregnant; he hadn't been entirely mad. But—

Tom Fleming suddenly appeared through the swing doors; he saw Sandy, and hesitated. Only for a moment, but it was enough. Few people would have recognised that hesitation; Sandy, trained in observing the enemy, did. He looked at Tom for a long moment in silence. Then, 'What the hell are you doing here?' he said.

*

That was that, then: the end of it. The end of the baby, the end of the affair. Louise lay in her bed and stared at the nurse who was telling her she really couldn't have anything more for the pain, that her system simply could not tolerate any more drugs at the moment, and said politely no, she quite understood, and then, 'What was it?'

'What was what?'

'The baby. Was it a girl or a boy?'

The nurse was very young; she stared at Louise. 'Oh, you don't want to be worrying about that,' she said.

'What do you mean, I don't want to be worrying about it?' She could hear her own voice, loud and rather angry. 'Of course I'm worried about it. I have to know, I have a right to know.'

'Mrs Trelawny—'

Louise put out her hand, gripped the nurse's arm. 'You just go and find out what my baby was. A girl or a boy. Don't come back until you know. And don't tell me what I want or don't want either.'

The nurse shook her arm free, hurried out of the cubicle; Louise heard her talking in a low voice to someone at the end of the ward.

Another, clearly more senior nurse appeared; she looked at Louise rather sternly.

'Mrs Trelawny—'

Louise interrupted her. 'Look,' she said, 'all I want to know is whether my baby was a boy or a girl. You must know. It was quite old enough.'

'We – that is, it's impossible to—'

'Where is it?' she said. 'Where is the baby?'

'Mrs Trelawny—'

'You've thrown it away, haven't you?' she said, rage making her suddenly strong. 'Put it down the sluice. I know you have, don't lie to me. You had absolutely no right to do that, no right at all, it wasn't just a mess, you know, it was my baby. It's wicked what you've done, and what's more, illegal . . .'

And then she heard a strange, horrible, high-pitched sound, that she realised after a moment or two was her own screaming, and then a doctor appeared, and gave her an injection and she sank into a blank darkness that she hoped more fervently than ever might be death.

Sandy sat holding Dickon on his knee, smoothing his dark hair, trying to hush his sobs; he felt like crying himself. And so utterly weary, he could not imagine ever moving again. Just as well, probably; given the strength to match the violence of his rage, he would have gone out to find Tom Fleming and killed him. Or at least beaten him to pulp.

He had known at once, of course, hadn't actually needed his brutally frank confession at all, he'd known the minute he had seen him there. It had all made sense suddenly. Tom, brilliant, charming, good-looking Tom who made Louise laugh, who led the sort of life she would have loved, who spent his life in her old haunts, the smart restaurants and nightclubs of London, Tom who had money and style, Tom who could still have children . . .

'Daddy,' said Dickon, turning his small face up to him, 'Daddy, please don't cry. Mummy's better, you just said so.'

'Louise has had a complete breakdown,' said Tom. 'There's talk of a psychiatric nursing home. Some place in Bath.'

They were sitting in the drawing room in Phillimore Gardens; both more than slightly surprised to find themselves there, set back within the boundaries of normal life, so totally had the world appeared, during the past twenty-four hours, to have spun on its axis. They had even had supper together, pizzas brought in from the Pizza Express; Octavia, able suddenly to observe them all detachedly, arguing over whether a Neptune was more or less interesting than an American Hot, and passing round bits from plate to plate as they always did, wondered at the extraordinary resilience of the human spirit, and its capacity to dissemble.

'We'll come and tuck you up,' said Tom, patting the twins' bottoms gently as they started up the stairs. 'Half an hour, Okay?'

'Okay. And don't disappear again, all right?'

'They didn't both disappear,' said Gideon, 'only Mummy.'

'They did really.'

'Twins, please. Go on, see you later.'

'You must have been relieved,' said Octavia now, icily polite, 'about the baby.'

'Yes, I was. Of course.'

Charles had told her when she had finally spoken to him, asked after Louise, forced herself to, for his sake: 'You'd want to know, my dear. So that when you see her . . .' and 'Yes, of course.'

She had said, thinking of that last lie, that last act of treachery, 'I'm not pregnant,' adding politely careful, 'I'm so sorry,' and wondering how much more she was going to be asked to endure.

'That was clever of her,' she said now to Tom, 'very clever. I suppose she thought you'd have to stay with her, leave me if she was pregnant.'

'I think it was more complex than that,' he said, 'given that she knew about your baby.'

'*Our* baby,' she said, looking at him very steadily. 'Tom, it was. It was yours.'

'Was it? Was it really?'

'Yes. Yes! I so much want you to understand. The baby was – would have been – handicapped, it had spina bifida. You were away, terribly busy, I – well, I decided to – I'm so sorry.' It was strange suddenly, to find herself in the wrong, the one who had done damage, the one apologising.

He stared at her for a long time in silence, his face very drawn, quite colourless. Then 'Oh, I see,' he said. 'But whatever you felt, whatever the situation, you had no right to do what you did. It was dreadful. Not the abortion itself, I might have agreed to that, I probably would; but taking it upon yourself to make that decision. With no recourse to me whatsoever. It was very wrong.'

There was a long silence; then she said: 'I know. I can see that now. I'm sorry. Very, very sorry. I thought it would be for the best.'

'But you didn't consider what I might think?' He stopped again, looking at her as if from a long distance. 'The fact that it was my baby too?'

'No,' she said, very quietly, 'no, I didn't. I just thought you wouldn't – wouldn't want it.'

'You are very like your father,' he said, 'in some ways. I'm sorry to have to say it, but it's true.'

She was silent: hating him for saying it, knowing she deserved it.

'Did he know about it?'

'No, of course not,' she said, shocked that he should think such a thing, while recognising that he easily could. 'Only Anna knew, she – well, she gave me the advice. She was wonderful. It helped.'

'A pity you couldn't have turned to me.'

'Tom, I couldn't. Well, I thought I couldn't. You were away, terribly distracted, it would have been so difficult on the phone.'

'Do you really think I wouldn't have come home? For such a reason? Dear God, how did we come to this?' he said.

'If it's any comfort,' she said, with difficulty, 'I thought I would go mad with the misery and the guilt.'

'Now there is an interesting remark. Do you think it is? A comfort to me? Don't you think I feel the same misery, the same guilt? About what I have done to you? Ask yourself that question, Octavia, see if it helps.'

She looked at him, struggling to accept it. 'I don't know how you feel. I don't know what I feel either. About any of it, any of it at all.'

'I think,' he said carefully, 'you have to try and accept that Louise is – well, almost mad.'

'Almost mad? Or completely? Or then again not at all? Just bad. Wicked.'

'No. Not wicked. I really don't think so.'

'She's been very clever. For someone mad.'
'Mad people are clever.'
'And she's done some terrible things. Sending those letters, wrecking your business, that was almost a crime.'
'Yes, it was,' he said slowly, 'you're right. It was. Almost a crime.'
Another silence, then, 'Louise told me something else,' he said. 'I would like to know if it's true.'
She knew what that was: Gabriel. And of course Louise would have told Tom. Looking back now, she recognised the last in a long line of probing, of innocent questions, of outraged loyalty. Against all logic, she felt guilt.
'Yes?'
'I'm sure you can imagine what it was.'
'I – yes, I suppose I can.'
'Is it true? That you're involved? With this man?'
'If you mean have I slept with him,' she said, anger and a desire to hurt him suddenly striking her, 'yes, I have.'
'I see.'
He looked at her; she saw shock, hurt, anger, and – most pleasing of all – jealousy. All of them illogical, outrageous even: but most recognisably there, a source of sweet, sure revenge.
'Well, I can hardly complain. I suppose,' was all he said.
And 'No,' she had said, 'no, you can't.'
Shock and jealousy apart, he was, quite clearly, less concerned about her relationship with Gabriel Bingham than about the termination. Grudgingly, unwillingly, she liked him for that.
'Do you still want a divorce?' he said, and she said yes, most certainly she did, but she really couldn't think about it at the moment, there were enough complexities in both their lives, both professional and personal, not least the children, they must take their time, work out the best route.
'So – is it – serious? With this man?' he said, and she said she didn't want to discuss it; later lying in bed, she found herself wondering if it was, indeed, serious with Gabriel.

CHAPTER 31

'Right. That's all absolutely wonderful.' Serena Fox smiled at Marianne and Romilly, drew back the contract, replaced the cap of her Mont Blanc pen. 'Let's drink, shall we, to a very happy association. Josie, bring in the champagne!'

'Goodness!' said Romilly. 'Champagne, how exciting.'

'I won't,' said Marianne. 'I'm afraid I never drink in the middle of the day.'

She didn't look very happy, Romilly thought. That was mean of her, casting a sort of shadow over things. 'Mummy!' she said. 'Come on. Don't be a spoilsport.'

'Oh, well, all right.' Marianne accepted the glass, smiled, clearly with an effort, sipped it over-cautiously. Romilly felt irritated with her.

'Now,' said Serena. 'Donna Hanson is coming over again in ten days. With the photographer. He's going to do some preliminary shots of Romilly over here, for publicity and so on. They're arriving on Monday the eleventh, so how would the Tuesday be? Or the Wednesday. For the session?'

'Wonderful!' said Romilly. 'I'll wash my hair.' They all laughed. She looked round Serena's office at them all, smiling at her, her, Romilly, the centre of attention, laughing at her jokes, eager to fit in with her holiday dates. It was all so nice, she thought: so nice to be important, the one who mattered. Every day now she felt less shy, less unsure of herself.

It wasn't until Romilly got home to her diary that she realised that her period would be due again by the twelfth of August. Or possibly overdue. But she would know what to do this time . . .

'I'm fine, thanks,' said Tom. 'Sorry to have deserted the sinking ship.'

He smiled carefully at Aubrey; Aubrey, the least demonstrative of men, felt an urge to go over to him and put his arms round him, so white faced, so drawn, so patently and literally shaken was he. Well, it had been an appalling thirty-six hours for him; poor old Tom. He must have truly glimpsed hell.

As it was (being the least demonstrative of men), he did get up and put his hand on Tom's shoulder, refilled his coffee cup, said, 'I think you've been bloody good about it all.'

'Not a lot of choice. And I certainly don't deserve any sympathy,' said Tom. 'Now let's talk about Fleming Cotterill. Much more important.'

'Well, basically we have three choices. We can do nothing, muddle along for a bit longer, try to persuade the bank to meet the salary cheques, leave the rent and so on: that'll give us a week at the most. Or we can go down the merger route. Or petition to have ourselves declared bankrupt. That might be best. Cleanest. Get it over and done with.'

'I suppose we ought to try for the merger,' said Tom, 'but I cannot tell you how wretched it makes me feel.'

'Maybe not as wretched as the staff will feel if their salary cheques bounce,' said Aubrey.

'Aubrey, I think we have to pay them this month somehow. Out of our own assets. I could sell a painting or two, raise the money that way. Before we get everything seized. How about you?'

'I might sell my ex-wife's engagement ring,' said Aubrey thoughtfully, 'I made her give it back, you know. It was my grandmother's. I was keeping it for the next Mrs Cotterill, but she doesn't seem to be in too much of a hurry to materialise. The staff are a more deserving cause.'

'Fine. Well, let's do that. And let's wait till Monday, make our final decision then.'

'It's going to be a long weekend.'

'Ian, can we go to the house tonight?' said Zoë.

She had rung him on his mobile at midday. She had got the cash out of the bank and was longing to be rid of it. It had practically cleaned her out again, but it was worth it.

'Not tonight, darlin', no. I'm having a drink with the lads. Sorry. Tomorrow be okay?'

'Oh – yes. Yes, fine.'

'We'll go to the Ministry first. Have a really good night. See you, babe.'

She wished they could have gone that night, but it couldn't be helped. And one more day wasn't really going to make any difference . . .

Somehow, perversely that day, Octavia felt better: rather as if she had been suffering from some near fatal illness that had reached and passed its crisis, the fever broken, the pain easing. She felt exhausted, weak and yet mildly euphoric; she had, after all, survived. And the worst was surely over.

Lying weak and wretched in her hospital bed, hazy with drugs and pain, contemplating all that she had lost, and the life that she had tried to leave, Louise became slowly aware of something other than despair. It was anger: white-hot, blinding anger. She clung to it; it gave her strength and it gave her hope. That she could still get what she wanted. That she would get what she wanted. Somehow. Whatever she had to do. It wasn't finished yet.

Octavia went to see her father, to reassure him that she was all right, for his distress and anxiety over her had been intense, and told him, amongst other things, about Gabriel Bingham. She was quite surprised to find herself doing so, but decided it was because she wanted him to stop being so sorry for her, wanted to stop being the deceived, wronged wife. It wasn't exactly a glamorous role. She didn't tell him everything, merely that she was seeing a man she liked very much, an MP, and he was making her feel a great deal better.

Felix Miller had been disconcertingly benign in his reaction. 'My darling, you deserve a little happiness.'

Gabriel had sent her a dozen red roses that day, with a card that said, 'From Mr Bingham, with considerable admiration.' She had been astonished at the unexpectedness both of the gesture and the form it had taken; in her overwrought state, she had burst into tears and then felt absurdly pleased.

'Tell me about him, this young man. Would I like him?'

She told him: as little as possible.

'He sounds very interesting. Very interesting indeed. Well, I shall look forward to meeting him.'

'Daddy, it's not that sort of thing.'

'What sort of thing? You know I like to meet your friends. Well, there's no hurry. If ever you feel like bringing him, he'll be welcome. I suppose I should ask after Louise,' he added, his face very cold.

'She's going to be all right. Yes.'

He nodded. 'I hope Tom appreciates the full extent of the damage he's done, and to a great many people. I have to say I rather doubt it.'

'Daddy, of course he does. Very much so.' Why was she defending him, for God's sake?

'Well, let's talk about something else. You need a holiday. You look exhausted. How about my offer of the cottage?'

'I really can't go away just now,' she said. 'I've not been fulfilling my commitments at work. I've upset clients, let people down, I have to put some really long hours in.'

'Hard on the children.'

'Yes, but there's the weekends. We're going down to the cottage this weekend.'

'Seeing the new boyfriend?'

'No, I'm not.' Gabriel had wanted to see her, but she had told him he couldn't: that the children should have her to themselves for the weekend at least.

'What about Tom, has he moved out yet? He should. And we should have a chat about the divorce. I've alerted Bernard Moss that we want to see him, told him why.'

She felt a surge of surprisingly strong anger, heard Tom's voice saying, 'I'm afraid there is a lot of your father in you.'

'You shouldn't have,' she said sharply. 'It's absolutely no business of yours.'

'Octavia!'

'Sorry, Daddy. Sorry. But I really do want to do this in my own way. In my own time. And I don't want it all talked about publicly before I'm ready.'

'Well, of course it won't be. Bernard is very discreet. But I do beg of you, don't let the grass grow under your feet. If Tom is going to go down financially, then you need to get your—'

'If Tom is bankrupt, I have absolutely no intention of pursuing him into the ground,' said Octavia. 'Now please, Daddy, can we leave it just for now? I appreciate your concern, but I really want a bit of time to work all this out.'

'Well, I sincerely hope you know what you're doing,' said Felix Miller.

'Look,' said Marianne. 'I may be – away tomorrow night.' She felt terribly guilty about it, not only leaving the girls, but for going away in search of fun, after the drama and the horror of the past few days. But Octavia was all right, Louise was all right, Felix wasn't speaking to her, and she felt a need for normality quite badly.

They both looked at her; she felt a flush rising, cursed it, got up and went over to the kettle, switched it on. 'What are you two doing?'

They assured her, clearly amused, they were both busy: Zoë was going to the Ministry with friends, Romilly to spend the evening with Fenella.

'Anyway, Mum,' said Zoë, 'where's he taking you?'

'Who?'

'Felix. Of course.'

'Oh – no, I'm not going with Felix. I'm seeing friends. Out of town. For dinner.'

'Sounds cool.'

'She's going out with the new one,' said Zoë to Romilly later.

Romilly looked up; she was reading on her bed. 'Who is? What are you talking about?'

'Mum. Rom, do get a grip. With her new boyfriend.'

'Oh – yes. I spoke to him. He sounded rather nice.'

'Mm.'

'Well, good. I never thought Felix was nice enough to her. And who are you going out with tomorrow night, Zoë?'

'Lucy. Going back to hers.'

'Got a key?'

'What?'

'I said have you got a key?'

'Rom, what are you talking about?'

'You'll need a key to her house. She's away. Just gone. They all have. To Florida. I met her on Tuesday in the Kings Road.'

'Oh,' said Zoë, 'well, I must have got it wrong.'

'Yes, you must. Who is he, Zo? I won't tell Mum.'

'Oh, just someone I met,' said Zoë vaguely.

Sandy went upstairs. How was he going to get through this, stand the pain? He kept being sick as well. Every time he thought of Louise, in bed with Tom, the bile rose in his throat. He would lie in bed, staring into the darkness, watching them, her lovely slender body, and – and his. Moving with him, one with him, talking through it as she always did with sex, telling him how she felt, what she liked, crying out, as she always did, as she came. It was obscene, hideous. And then – and then becoming pregnant by him. Nurturing his child. Tom's child, inside her body. When she had said never, never again, I couldn't bear it, Sandy, don't ask me to risk it . . . All those lies: 'I'm going to see Mummy, don't ring me there, they hate it when they're so worried, I'd like to stay down there tonight, just in case, I'm ill because I'm so upset.' All that ugliness, that capacity for tortuous deceit, behind that beautiful, sweet face, all those lies told so gently in that beautiful husky voice . . .

Sandy felt the tears rising, buried his head in his hands.

He had fled Rookston, and Charles; he was too fond of Charles to confront him with Louise's wickedness – he and Tom had agreed on that one thing, that he shouldn't know. But he found seeing the pictures of her everywhere in the house, and of Anna who looked so like her, and Charles' adoration of her, his aching concern for her, unbearable. If it wasn't for Dickon he would have killed himself. He knew that, with great certainty.

'Very nice,' said Ian, 'very nice indeed. Like it.'

It was a new dress: she had bought it with the few pounds remaining of her allowance, black Lycra, extremely short, extremely low cut. Half the men in the pub had stopped talking as she walked in, and up to Ian, kissed him very full on the mouth; she felt really good. And really sexy.

'Let's have a few drinks here, then we'll go to the Ministry. What do you want, babe?'

'Oh, vodka and black. Thanks.'

'I've got some really good grass on me,' he said, patting his leather jacket, for when we get back to the house. And I've got the truck, so we don't need to mess with taxis. Cheers, babe, here's to a really great night.'

'Cheers,' said Zoë.

'Now come along,' said Nico. 'It really is time you admitted it.'

'Admitted what?' said Marianne, laughing.

She was quite drunk already and they were still waiting to go into the dining room. Several glasses of champagne sipped outside on the lovely terrace of the Swan in Marlborough, watching the sky slowly darken, had gone deliciously to her head.

They had spent the day together, looking at beautiful and rather large houses – far too large for just one person, Marianne felt. She had said so; Nico had laughed and said that as he intended that she should be there for much of the time, they were not for just one person at all, and that was why her approval was essential, as he didn't want her living in a house she didn't like. She had said there was no question of her living in any house with him, however much she liked it, and he had said nonsense, she didn't know what she was talking about.

'It's time you admitted,' he said again, 'that you want to go to bed with me. Very much.' He picked up her hand, traced the palm with his fingers. 'Almost as much as I want to go to bed with you.'

'I don't know how much that is,' she said, trying not to meet his eyes, knowing what he would see there.

'Immeasurable,' he said. 'I want you more than I can remember wanting anyone for a very long time.' He looked at her very intently, raised her hand to his lips. 'Thou hast ravished my heart,' he said and smiled. 'Song of Solomon. But of course you'll know that.'

'No,' said Marianne, staring at him. 'I'm afraid not.'

'Most beautiful words in the English language. In my humble opinion.'

'Nico, none of your opinions are humble,' said Marianne, laughing.

'True. And neither am I. And I am feeling extremely and unusually confident at this very moment. I suppose I shouldn't tell you that, should I?'

'Not really, no,' said Marianne. 'Women don't like it.'

'Then forget it. I was lying. I am wracked with nerves and self-doubt. Now come alone, let us go and eat our dinner. You can't make love on an empty stomach, in my experience.'

'Shit,' said Ian.

'What?'

'I left my money behind. The money for the Ministry. What a sod. You got any money, babe?'

'No. No, I haven't,' said Zoë quickly.

'Thought you got your allowance this week.'

'I did, but—'

'Well, we could go to a cash machine, then. Come on, Zo, won't hurt you just for once.'

It wouldn't give her any more; she'd already tried. The new dress had cleaned it out.

'Oh, for fuck's sake,' said Ian. 'I can't stand girls who're tight with money. Jesus, Zoë, I've paid for everything, ever since we started going out. Well, let's call it a night, then, just go home. Christ Almighty.'

He was obviously genuinely upset; Zoë hesitated. She was fond of him and she hated being thought tight; it was one of the reasons she was always in debt. And she had been looking forward to the evening so much . . .

'Wait,' she said, putting her hand on his arm. 'I'm sorry. I have got some money. I – I got it out to pay Rom back. Money she'd lent me. But I can get some more. Come on, I'll pay.'

She could get some more; do some babysitting or something. Ian looked at her. 'Okay, fine,' was all he said.

It cost a tenner each to get into the Ministry; then she bought him a couple of vodka and Red Bulls, which was what he always drank there, and the same for herself; forty quid gone already. Oh, well, she could still put half the money back.

She didn't care any more anyway; she felt wonderful. The music was fantastic; they danced for a long time. It got very hot, they consumed endless ice lollies from the buckets that were brought round. 'I'll get these,' said Ian, grinning at her. 'My treat. You're worth it.'

He had left his jacket in the car; he was wearing just black jeans and a black sleevless T-shirt. His brown arms were very muscly; he really did have a superb body. Zoë thought of the pleasures that lay just ahead of her and felt quite faint.

Marianne lay in the extremely large bed in the suite at the Swan; she was in a state of acute sexual excitement. In the end, there had been no conflict, she had simply agreed to stay there with Nico, as she had known, of course, that she would. She wanted him, he wanted her, there seemed absolutely nothing else to consider.

She moved her hands now to her own breasts, as she did when she was excited, contemplating the acute pleasure of other hands on them, moved one down to her flat stomach, smoothing it, lay looking at Nico. He was sitting on the bed, wearing a bathrobe, ordering breakfast and the papers, impressing that there should be no phone calls put through; he smiled at her, put the phone down, stood up, took off the robe. He was very slim, clearly very fit; unbidden she thought of Felix's large body, with its powerful sexuality and its capacity for giving her pleasure, recognised her own disloyalty and was shocked at it, and at the same time found it strangely and appallingly exciting.

'Dear God,' said Nico, pulling back the sheet, studying her, 'dear God, you are beautiful.' And then bent his head to kiss her breasts, moving his hand slowly down her, where her own had been, stroking, smoothing at her stomach.

'I haven't said this for a very long time,' he said finally, taking her in his arms, and she surged, felt herself move towards him, wanting him, longing for him, 'but I know that I am very much in love with you.' And then his body began to move slowly and with surprising care and tenderness on her and into her; and pleasure of such power and intensity took possession of her that she was surprised even at herself.

'Oh, my God!' Someone was shouting: a girl, it was her, Zoë thought confusedly, it must be, there was no one else there, shouting through the explosion of violence and release that was her orgasm. 'My God, my God, oh, my God.'

'Shut up,' said Ian, putting his hand over her mouth, laughing quietly, 'you'll have the neighbours in. Shush, Zoë, for God's sake.'

'Sorry. Sorry. Just – a bit much. That's all.'

'Good. Very good. Glad to hear it.'

He rolled off her, studied her thoughtfully. She looked back at him, smiling rather shakily, pushing her hair out of her eyes. It was wet with sweat. She was wet all over.

'You're quite a girl,' he said. 'You know that?'

'Yeah. 'Course.'

'Want some grass?'

'Not yet. No. Let's just – lie here.'

'Nah. I get bored. Come on, I'll go and get it.'

He eased himself up. They had been lying on the carpet, beneath them just a rug they had found; she looked at his back view, his lean muscly back, his taut buttocks, his confident, slightly swaggering walk and felt mildly irritated. He always got straight up afterwards, wanted to be doing something: let's get in the shower, have a smoke, a drink, never wanted to lie and talk and kiss and be close. She sighed; he heard her and turned.

'What's the matter?'

'Oh, nothing.'

'Yes, there is, come on. Out with it.'

'It's just that I – well, I like to be – close afterwards. You always seem to want to get up and –'

'Well, it's over, isn't it? What's the point of staying there?'

'The point,' she said more irritated still, 'is that I would like it.'

'What, the old postcoital rubbish? You've made me feel so good, all that?'

'Well – yes.'

'Zoë, what is this? You're not going all serious on me, are you? Because—'

'No, of course not,' she said, sitting up, pulling her knees to her chin, wrapping her arms round them so she was less naked, less at a disadvantage. 'But it's still nice to feel – well, close. Cared about.'

'Jesus,' he said. 'Zoë, I've been caring about you. I've given you a really good fuck. Two actually. I'm not up to all that lovey-dovey stuff. Sorry. You'll have to get one of your public school hoorays for that.'

'Don't be ridiculous,' she said. She tried to smile, to clear his mood.

'I'm not. I mean it. That's what they're good at, I believe. Not so good with their cocks, by all accounts, quick poke and they're wilting again, but—'

'Ian, how could you possibly know that?'

'Oh, I know,' he said. 'You're not the first upmarket bird I've screwed, you know. Don't flatter yourself.'

'I didn't think I was,' she said. But somehow she had; and she felt absurdly upset, almost tearful.

He disappeared, went downstairs, reappeared with some Rizlas and a bag of grass, sat on the bed rolling the joints. He passed her one; she shook her head vigorously.

'No thanks.'

'Go on. It's very good.'

'Ian, I don't want one.'

She felt cold suddenly, reached for her dress. As she met his eyes, she saw he was watching her, his expression very hard. He said nothing.

'What's wrong?' she said, trying to sound lighthearted again.

'Let's just say I don't like this,' he said.

'Don't like what?'

'This – mood.'

'Ian, I'm not in a mood.'

'Yes, you are.'

'I'm not. I just don't want to smoke, okay?'

'Yeah, okay. Fine. Well, best get going, then.'

'What? What are you talking about?'

'I'm talking about I don't want to sit here, you looking all tight arsed. Come on, get dressed.'

Zoë lost her temper. 'I am not looking tight arsed. You're being ridiculous.'

'I'll decide what I'm being. Get your clothes on, Zoë, I want to go.'

'Well, just fucking go, then,' said Zoë.

It was a stupid thing to say; she knew it at once. He stood up, pulled on his clothes and walked out of the room without even glancing at her; she heard the front door slam and the truck start.

Zoë looked at her watch; it was not quite four. She felt very frightened and very alone in the house; she pulled on her clothes, rang for a taxi on her mobile, and went outside and pulled the door shut after her, shivering. As she waited on the corner, she realised that the taxi would cost her the best part of the forty pounds she had left.

CHAPTER 32

'And how would you describe the way you're feeling now? Take your time, there's no hurry.'

Louise looked at him, and thought if she hadn't been feeling so physically exhausted, she would undoubtedly have hit him. How could you describe the effect on you of wanting to die, trying to die, thinking indeed you were safely dead, and then being sucked literally back to life by the horror of a tube pushed down your throat and into your stomach, the contents of your stomach emptying slowly and disgustingly into a bucket on the floor at your side. That was what she had awoken to; that, and then later the pain, the dreadful raw pain, starting slowly, increasing in vehemence and then through the haze of misery and nausea, feeling the bleeding begin, being told she was miscarrying, told she couldn't have anything for the pain just now, her body couldn't tolerate it, that it would soon be over. But it wasn't soon over at all, it went on right through the night, and then when it really was over, when there was no hope for this baby either, when she was weeping, mourning for it, being told briskly that she was being taken down to theatre, to have a D&C 'just to make sure you aren't hanging on to any bits'.

And then coming round, confused and sore, and lying all day in the ward, thinking that they couldn't tell her about the baby's sex because they would have just thrown it away, put it down the sluice. That was when the anger began.

And then, having endured all this, being asked how she was feeling.

She didn't answer because it was safer; just sat there, staring at him.

He waited patiently for a while, just looking at her, then, 'You're not ready for me yet, are you?' he said, smiling at her, a dreadful patronising smile. 'Never mind. We'll just let you rest for a day or two, and then we can really talk. All right?'

'No,' said Louise, 'not all right at all.'

Because it wasn't. It was horribly and hideously all wrong. And the only good thing she felt, strong and almost comforting, helping her to go forward somehow, was the anger. The anger was becoming her friend.

'I think I'd like to take the line of least resistance,' said Tom. 'If you don't mind, that is.'

'Not at all, old chap,' said Aubrey. 'I'd come to much the same conclusion myself.'

They smiled at one another; two stiff-upper-lipped Englishmen sitting on leather chairs in a book-lined room, looking more as if they were agreeing to cancel a game of golf, rather than the demise of something unique and successful, created through their own particular blend of talent and courage and commitment, something that had absorbed all their energy, ingenuity, and most of their waking hours over the past five years. No one would have thought at that moment that Tom Fleming was feeling a passion of rage so violent against the factors that had robbed him of it, including his own folly, that he was having trouble restraining himself from hurling his cup of coffee on to the pristine white wall, or that Aubrey Cotterill was looking round the room with a depth of sadness only matched on the day when the wife he had thought had married him for love had informed him she found him so unattractive she was moving out of his bedroom permanently.

'I did talk to DTN,' he said now. 'We'd be lackeys, office boys, forced to sit in meetings with our own clients while the decisions we knew were right for them were reversed.'

'Aubrey,' said Tom, 'I did hate that idea. And I tried the bank: no joy. Not a penny piece. But I did pop into a few galleries over the weekend. I can cover the salaries if I empty my walls into Cork Street.'

'I can't match that, I'm afraid. But I can probably keep the wolves from our personal doors for a week or two, if I visit an old friend in Hatton Garden with Bernadette's ring.'

'Well, what do we do first? Talk to the staff, inform the clients?'

'Go down to the courts, I should think, get the form. I shall find it easier telling everyone if it's actually a *fait accompli*. Three hundred and fifty quid, you said?'

'Yup. I wonder if the bank will lend it to us,' said Tom, and actually managed to smile.

'Oh, my God,' said Octavia. 'Oh, my God.'

'No,' said Gabriel Bingham modestly, 'no. Just me. Mr Bingham. I'm surprised you've forgotten me already.'

He smiled at her; she smiled back.

'It's so nice to see you,' she said and meant it.

'Well, I thought I'd come and see your modest little workplace. Don't worry, I'm not staying.'

'Absolutely you are not,' said Melanie Faulks walking in. 'She's very busy.' She settled herself on the edge of Octavia's desk, held out her hand. 'Hi. You must be the Angel Gabriel. I'm Melanie. Loved the roses you sent on Friday. Nice touch. She cried, you know.'

'She cried?' He was clearly astonished. 'Why did she cry, for God's sake?'

'Oh, she's like that,' said Melanie. 'Very emotionally labile. I have a lot of trouble with her.'

Octavia felt a stab of irritation. She could see it was all good fun, that they were enjoying it, but in her fragile – or indeed labile – emotional state, it was hard to keep smiling. The faint euphoria of Friday had been brief lived. She had had a difficult and lonely weekend with the children and had actually longed by Saturday evening for adult company, someone to talk to; Gabriel had phoned several times, but she simply didn't feel ready for the emotional pressure of seeing him. She had begun to recognise slowly, and with a sense of dreadful irony, the true implications and complexity of the loss of Louise from her life, Louise who had always listened, always understood: who had counselled, sympathised, teased, been on her side. Who would, who could replace her? It was not just a betrayal, she could see that now; it was a death in her life, and one she would never recover from.

'I just wondered,' said Gabriel now, still talking to Melanie, 'I just wondered if you had any idea if she was avoiding me. I rang her three times over the weekend and she just said she wanted to be alone.'

'Look,' said Octavia, forcing a smile, trying to sound bright and in charge of things, 'I am here, you know. I can talk. You could try asking me yourself.'

'I did,' said Gabriel, 'all weekend.'

'He did,' said Melanie.

Octavia burst into tears.

Later, when Melanie had gone – 'You can have ten minutes, Gabriel, then I'll be in with a large bowl of cold water to throw over you both, we really do have work to do,' – and she was sipping some strong coffee, she said, 'I'm sorry. I just felt so wretched all weekend. I feel as if I've had – no, I've still got – some terrible illness. There's a lot I haven't told you. It's so – oh, I don't know. I'm sorry. But it is lovely to see you.'

'Well, it's not bad seeing you,' he said, 'and it's all right, I understand. I think. But when can I see you? Or are you still not ready?'

'I would like it,' she said quickly. 'I really would. It's difficult though, and the children are very upset, specially Poppy.'

'Of course they are. But they could surely spare you for an hour or two? This evening maybe.'

'That would be lovely,' said Octavia. 'Yes, we could have an early supper. But I mustn't be long.'

She and Tom had agreed to meet that evening at home, to talk, to try and decide what to do with their lives. Or what was left of them.

'You're on. How about high tea? Very appropriate. I'll pick you up here – when?'

'Six?'

'Fine.'

She reached up to kiss him; the door opened.

'I said ten minutes,' said Melanie. 'Sarah Jane, bucket of cold water please.'

'I'm going,' said Gabriel. 'Right now.'

He disappeared, his shambling body in its unpressed trousers and checked country shirt incongruous in the chic office. Octavia looked after him smiling. He was so . . .

'Nice,' said Melanie, looking after him. 'Really nice. Very sexy. As sexy as his voice. Just what you need, Fleming. Now come on, we have work to do, remember?'

Nico Cadogan had been heard to describe himself a mischief connoisseur. 'I would never make the stuff myself, but I do know a good sample when I see it. Like wine. I can smell it.'

He did of course make it himself from time to time; but he found the true pleasure in adding to a brew, stirring in whatever ingredients came to hand. And just at the moment, he found himself confronted by an excellent sample. The fun to be extracted by helping, just slightly unorthodoxically, a man whom he not only liked and admired, both personally and professionally, but who was also loathed and under attack by the rival for his lady love's hand. 'This, Cadogan,' he said, smiling into the mirror that Monday morning, 'is truly vintage stuff.'

It had been true, what he had told Marianne on Saturday; he was in love with her. She seemed to him what he had been seeking for many years: beautiful, intelligent, charming and – most surprising of all perhaps – nice. Extremely nice. Her struggles over her disloyalty to Felix – however justified – had been tiresome but at the same time infinitely touching and rather pleasing. There was, in spite of her sense of humour, and sense of fun, an underlying seriousness to her. She thought carefully about everything, both large and small; none of her judgments was reckless or even haphazard, whether they concerned a choice of pudding, of politics – or something much more personal. He loved her too for her intense concern for her children. Nico had no children, no experience of true parental love, having been raised in nanny-run nurseries and dispatched to school at eight, but he could sense nevertheless that the way Marianne directed her family was the right one.

And then she was easy to please: in a sophisticated woman it was a rare quality. She enjoyed things: food, wine, clothes, conversation, her wretched golf, and, it seemed, sex. He was quite shaken by how wonderfully sexy she was. He had expected responsiveness, a capacity for pleasure, a desire to please; he had not expected quite the level of energy, the exuberance and – as she slowly grew more familiar to him – the creativity.

'Intelligent, that's what it is, that body of yours,' he had said, stroking it, smiling at her, as they drank buck's fizz in bed, and she had said intelligent maybe, but it had seen thirty-nine summers and it wasn't quite what it had been.

'Nonsense. So you were married at—' and she had said eighteen, she was a child bride, and that her parents had been very worried about it. 'Quite right, too,' he had said, so they should have been. What kind of man would have taken advantage of someone so young, so inexperienced, and landed her with a child just a year later?

'Ten months later, actually,' she had said, 'and I wanted it, I wanted that desperately. And I was right, you see. Here I am with three nearly grown-up friends.' Adding more soberly that she felt she was hardly grown up herself.

'I find you quite grown up enough,' he had said, and removing her champagne glass, had set about proving it.

That was the occasion he had discovered the inventiveness.

He was thinking about it now, when the phone rang: it was Felix.

Nico Cadogan was not a natural villain. He felt a stab of guilt. 'Good morning, Felix.'

'Look, just a quick call. I want you to do me a favour.'

'Yes?'

'Reconsider resigning your account from Fleming Cotterill.'

The guilt eased. 'I'm sorry, Felix. I have no intention of doing that.'

'I don't think you understand. The man is not to be trusted. I wouldn't let him have a farthing of my own money. Not now.'

'But why not? What's he done?'

'He has set out to destroy Octavia, destroy their marriage.'

'That doesn't affect his business judgment.'

'I disagree. He's a liar, a cheat. Not the sort of person you'd want to do business with.'

'Felix, the City is full of liars and cheats. All conducting their financial affairs with great acumen. Look, if you want to do down your own son-in-law, for what are clearly purely personal reasons, you must do so. I'm not interested in helping you.'

'But it's a lot worse than you think. Far worse things have been going on. He—'

'Felix, no offence, but I really don't want grisly extramarital details just now. Too early, in the day and in the week and indeed any time. I'm sorry. Good morning to you.'

Absolutely no guilt left. Felix was a monster. And in danger of making a total fool of himself. When it came to Octavia, the brilliant mind was dull and blunted. It was almost frightening.

Marianne phoned; briefly, he told her what Felix had said. 'Oh God,' she said, 'poor Felix. I'll have to talk to him. Nico, what have I done?'

'What any sensible person would have done,' he said. 'The man's mad. Now don't start feeling guilty. He still has Octavia.'

He still had Octavia, Felix thought, putting the phone down with a hand that shook horribly. He felt very dizzy suddenly; dizzy and faint.

He found it very hard to believe what Marianne had just said to him, what she had done. That she could not continue to see him while he was working so savagely against Tom. And when he had asked her how she knew, she told him. That Nico Cadogan had told her.

'And why is he talking to you? Are you seeing him? A lot of him?'

And she had taken a deep breath and said that yes, she was seeing him. 'I do realise you will probably never forgive me. But I simply cannot continue any longer in our relationship while this – insanity over Octavia continues.'

'What insanity?' he had said. 'I'm only trying to protect her, help her, get that – that creature out of her life, where he can't hurt her any more.'

'You can't protect her,' she had said, her voice very low, very intense. 'I've been telling you for so long, she's an adult, Felix, she's thirty-six years old, she's not yours to protect any more, leave her alone for just once in her life, let her be. Let her work things out for herself in her own way.'

'I am shocked at you,' he had said simply, 'shocked and very hurt. She would be too. As you must know.'

The shock and hurt he felt himself were far greater on Octavia's behalf than on his own.

'I'm going out,' Tom said to Barbara briefly, 'be about an hour. Then

Aubrey and I have a lunchtime meeting. I don't want to be disturbed by anybody.'

'Tom, Nico Cadogan phoned. Twice. He wants to speak to you very urgently.'

Tom really couldn't face telling Cadogan of all people that Fleming Cotterill was about to go belly up. Not until it was beyond argument.

'Tell him I'm out of town,' he said, 'tell him I'll phone him later this afternoon.'

It would be done by then: the bankruptcy petition would have been filed. There would be no going back.

Without anything being known quite for sure, the talk had begun about the Fleming marriage; had anything been heard about it, people were saying; and then did anyone think that whatever it was might be true; and then had anyone heard what had actually happened; fed, perversely, by the marriage's apparent earlier perfection, by jealousy, by resentment, by *schadenfreude* the rumour grew, until it was 'of course you knew', and 'of course I always said' and 'of course it was inevitable'; and thus in days, hours almost, the story became fact, discussed and debated in restaurants, across bars, over lunch, through dinner. The details were hazy, the possibility of a break-up were vague, nobody knew quite what had brought it about (although a lot of people knew people who did), only that something assuredly must have done. As both the Flemings were constantly and separately with all manner of people, stories ran swiftly wild: Tom was having an affair with a researcher, Octavia with an editor; Tom had been seen with an actress, Octavia with an entrepreneur. Most people were sorry, a few were pleased; hardly anyone was indifferent. The marriage had been too well known, too much of an entity for that; it was something impossible not to have a view on.

One of the people who had a view – and who was if not pleased, then certainly not sorry – was Lauren Bartlett. She had always found Octavia sanctimonious, too good to be true, undeserving of Tom's easy, charming devotion. And the marriage had always seemed just a bit too perfect: they just didn't come like that. Not in real life.

Tom had been certainly looking a bit rough recently, she reflected. He was obviously under a lot of strain. And he was actually so loyal to Octavia, supporting her in her career while his own was so demanding.

Well, it was gloves-off time. She'd been waiting a while for the opportunity to get to work on Tom Fleming. Absolutely one of the most attractive men she knew. It wasn't just the looks and the charm, not even the style; it was that slight touch of awkwardness under the smooth that was so tantalising. A bit of grit in the mix. Very sexy. A quick lunch maybe, that would be best, under the guise of a possible new contract. At least she could find out if there was someone else. Someone serious, that was. She could use the device of the friend with the account, the one with the chemist's chain. Probably too late, but she could string things along. And Tom had obviously been desperate for the business.

Yes, that would be the way to go. She'd ring Tom's mobile straight away.

He answered it at once; there was an odd hum in the background.

'Tom?'

'Yes. Who is this?'

'Tom, it's Lauren. Lauren Bartlett. Hi. Tom, I just wondered if—'

'Lauren, I'm sorry, I'm a bit tied up right now.'

'Of course. It's just that I spoke to my friend again, the one who might have wanted to appoint you, you know?'

'Oh, yes?' He didn't sound very enthusiastic.

'There still might be a chance. If you're interested. I can fix a meeting, I think.'

'Really? Look, I can't talk about it now. Can I get back to you?'

'Yes, of course. Of course. We could have a drink maybe. Talk about it. I'll ring him, see what I can fix. Then get back to you. How's that?'

'Maybe. I'm sorry not to be more responsive. Bit difficult just at the moment.' He was clearly making an effort to be nice.

'Of course. I'll phone you at your office.'

'Thanks, Lauren.'

'My pleasure. I'll see you soon. Look forward to it.'

'Me too.'

He was gone. She smiled into the phone, dialled the offices of Oliver Nichols Pharmaceuticals, plc, in the City.

'I'd like to speak to Mr Nichols,' she said, 'immediately, please. It's Mrs Bartlett speaking. It's quite urgent.'

Tom got back to Fleming Cotterill at one thirty. Barbara Dawson looked at him through rather bleary eyes. 'I wish you wouldn't do this to me,' she said. 'I've got a dozen calls, all urgent. Please let me at least give you the really important messages.'

'Barbara, I can't take any calls until mid-afternoon. I told you.'

'Not even from Nico Cadogan? He's rung again. Twice.'

'No, sorry. Not yet.' He looked at her. 'You all right?'

'No, I think I'm getting flu. I feel ghastly.'

'Look, why not go home? Now. Get someone to sit in here, just say no calls. I'll take one from Cadogan in – let's see – an hour, and I'd also like a Mrs Bartlett put through then, she's trying to do me a favour. Otherwise, everyone can wait.'

'All right, Tom. Thanks.'

It was neither Barbara's fault nor Tom's that this message became just slightly garbled and the temporary from the accounts department who was the only person free to take the calls conveyed a message to Mrs Octavia Fleming that she was very sorry but she had strict instructions only to put through calls from a Mr Cadogan and a Mrs Bartlett and no one else at all until after four o'clock.

'Bastard!' said Octavia. She sat staring at her telephone. 'Absolute bastard.'

'Is it your husband of whom you speak?'

'What? Oh – yes, Mells. Who else? He won't even speak to me. Only taking calls from Nico Cadogan and – and wait for this, Melanie – Lauren Bartlett. God, I hate that woman. He's off already. Louise hardly out of his bed. I just don't understand it, Melanie, I really don't.'

'Look, I don't ever like to give a man the benefit of the doubt,' said Melanie, 'but is there even a possibility here that the message was wrongly conveyed? It sounds very unlikely to me. Anyway, funnily enough I just came in to say I've got the costings on the day at Brands Hatch. Could you bear to look at them or not?'

'All right, then,' said Octavia fretfully. 'What do I care what she's up to with my husband? She's welcome to him. She really is. Give them to me, Mells. I'm a professional, aren't I, for God's sake?' She managed a rather feeble smile.

'That's my girl. And you've got the Angel Gabriel. Don't forget that.'

'No,' said Octavia, thoughtfully, 'no, I won't forget that. Not again.'

'Right, that seems to be about it,' said Tom, pushing back his chair, handing the bankruptcy petition to Aubrey for signature. 'I'll take it back right now. Get it over. Stop hanging about. Now the great thing is, can we afford three hundred and fifty pounds to make the application?' He grinned slightly shakily. 'Quite a lot of money, just to go bankrupt, isn't it? Let's have a cheque, Aubrey, there's a good fellow.'

'Right. Shall we have a last drink? On Fleming Cotterill?'

'I think I'd rather do that when I get back. Give me courage for the next stage. Breaking the news.'

'Fine. I'll have it ready for you. Cheers, Tom.'

'Cheers, Aubrey.'

'Look,' said Nico Cadogan, 'I don't care if he's with God. I want to speak to him. It's terribly important. Now will you please put me through?'

'I can't, Mr Cadogan. He's just gone out.'

'Oh, Jesus. Is Mr Cotterill there?'

'Well – yes.'

'Look,' said Nico, 'you sound a bright girl. If they fire you for putting me through, I'll take you on in my company. It's a deal. How's that? Go on,' he said, 'live dangerously.'

She put him through.

Rather less than two minutes later, she was startled to see Mr Cotterill running extremely fast through reception and down the stairs.

'Look, I know it's only a piss in a pot,' said Nico Cadogan modestly, 'but you can have it. Five months' fee, in advance. That's a hundred grand. Any good to you?'

For one terrible moment, Aubrey Cotterill thought he might break down. Then he rallied, reached for the bottle of Chivas Regal and poured three very large glasses.

'A great deal of good,' he said, 'and I have no idea why you should be doing it.'

'Easy,' said Cadogan. 'I'm impressed by excellence. I've found it here. Cheers!'

'Come on, Mrs Fleming. Come over here and have a good old-fashioned cuddle.'

She looked at him; he was sitting on a rather lumpy sofa in the sitting room of his flat in Pimlico.

'It's all right. I'm not going to try and seduce you. I'm perfectly resigned to our first and rather splendid sexual encounter being our last.'

'Gabriel—'

'All right. Not perfectly resigned. But temporarily at any rate. Right now I don't feel very inspired anyway. And I want to tell you something. I think it might take that shrivelled look off your face.'

She went over to the sofa and he put his arms round her. It was soothing, cosy, brought back her childhood . . .

'It was this,' said Gabriel. 'Now, I'm not very used to having this sort of conversation, so you'll have to be patient with me. But I – well, I do find myself extremely . . . engaged by you. I can't stop thinking about you, and I haven't been in love with anyone for a long time.'

'Gabriel! What about the fiancée?'

'That was a long time ago. When it began. But I think I could be now. In love, I mean. Only I know this is a dreadful time for you, and you probably don't know what you think about anything.'

'I don't,' said Octavia, 'that's exactly it. I don't know what I'm doing half the time, I can't remember my own phone number, and I got in the car this morning and I literally couldn't remember where to put the key.'

'Not the dynamic Mrs Fleming at all.'

'Not at all. And I hate it. Hate feeling out of control. All the things that were important to me, that I was sure about – my marriage, my career, my best friend – none of them is there any more. And the other really important person in my life—'

'Me?' said Gabriel hopefully.

'Well . . .'

'It's all right. I know I'm a new ingredient. Your father? Your omnipotent father?'

'Yes. At any time at all I could go to him for help and advice. I'd learned not always to take it, but at least it was there. Now I just daren't. He'd kill Tom if I so much as indicated I'd like it. He's out to destroy him professionally as it is.'

'Can he do that?'

'Well, he can make things much more difficult for him.'

'And does that matter to you?'

'There's nothing I'd like more in some ways than to see Tom destroyed. But in another – it wouldn't help the children. It won't help me. And – oh, God, I don't know.' She found she was crying again. 'Sorry, Gabriel, I'm so sorry.'

'I think,' he said carefully, handing her one of the large unironed handkerchiefs he always seemed to have in good supply, 'I think actually you still care about Tom. Rather a lot.'

'Oh, no, I don't, Gabriel. I actually think I hate him. I find it hard to be in the same room as him. At this very moment he's with some woman.'

Tom had phoned her, apologetic, had said could they defer their conversation, he had urgent business to see to, and a meeting with—

'Lauren Bartlet,' she had said. 'Don't tell me you haven't been talking to her because I know you have.' And clearly too taken by surprise to deny it, he had said yes, actually, he had, and she had arranged a meeting with a friend of hers who just might be able to help him.

'Good for him,' she had said and put the phone down.

'Now listen,' Gabriel said, 'all I'm trying to say is that for the foreseeable future, I'm here if you want me. And I'll bugger off if you don't. How's that?'

'It's pretty good,' she said, smiling. 'Thank you.'

She bent to kiss him; he was nice to kiss, gentle, responsive, careful.

Just for a moment, she wanted to do more; but only for a moment. It was too soon; too soon and too confusing.

CHAPTER 33

'For various complex reasons,' said Tom, 'I think we can still survive. Just about.'

'I presume you mean Fleming Cotterill,' said Octavia, 'rather than us? Much more important, of course.'

Tom looked at her and sighed. 'Yes. Yes, I do mean that. We've had some pretty tangible expressions of loyalty. Which is nice.'

'Very nice. Good.'

'Octavia, the Macintoshes are in town tomorrow. They've asked us to dinner.'

'Tom, I can't believe we're having this conversation. Of course I'm not going out to dinner with you and the Macintoshes. It's *over*. You've seen to that. I no longer wish to function as your wife. You'll have to take someone else to dinner. What about Lauren Bartlett?'

'Don't be so bloody silly,' said Tom. 'Octavia, I've told you so many times. I cannot stand Lauren Bartlett.'

'Then why instruct your secretary to put her calls through and block mine?'

'Oh, Jesus. That was a stupid mistake. Look – can we just keep to the matter in hand? It's terribly important. If you'd only come out to dinner tomorrow. With the Macintoshes. He's so fond of you and—'

'Well, in that case, he'll understand why I'm not there.'

'Octavia!' He stood up suddenly, moved across the room, smashed his fist down on the small table next to her.

She jumped, stared up at him. 'Will you please listen to me?' he said, and the expression in his eyes was frantic, almost violent. 'I can imagine how you feel. About me, about everything. But can't you get it into your head I am fighting to survive? Yesterday I went down to the courts, to file a petition for my own bankruptcy. It seemed the only thing to do. There was nowhere else to go, nothing else to do. If that had happened, we would have lost everything. The house, our personal assets, everything we've worked for. God knows what you think that would have done to the children. Oh, I suppose you could have gone to your father, but – anyway. We were saved by Nico Cadogan.'

'Nico!'

'Yes. He came forward with a hundred grand.'

'Why on earth did he do that?' said Octavia. She was genuinely amazed.

'I imagine because he felt we were worth it. That's what he said anyway.'

'My God. I wonder if my father knows about that.'

'I have no idea. Neither do I care. Anyway, as a result, we're in a position to battle on a bit longer. But we're still on a knife edge. The bank won't let us have another penny, we need a couple more accounts, and above all I need to keep the ones we've got. Even that hasn't been easy. As you know. Anyway, Bob has been an absolute brick. And this is not a business occasion tomorrow; he phoned and said he reckoned things must have been very tough and he'd like to give us a nice evening. I don't want to throw that in his face.'

'Take Aubrey. What's wrong with that?'

'I am taking Aubrey. But he specially asked for you as well. He's terribly fond of you, so is Maureen.'

'Tom, I really don't believe he'll withdraw his account if I don't come.'

'He won't. Of course he won't. But it will be easier, happier if you do, it will mean one less thing for me to sweat through, have to smooth over. I don't want to hurt him, I don't want to throw his kindness and support back in his face – Jesus, Octavia, I run that company for all of us, you know, for the children, for—'

'No, you don't. You run it largely for your own gratification. To feed your own ego.'

Even in her own hurt and misery, she could feel that one going home. She stared up at him, actually saw him wince physically.

'All right,' he said after a pause, 'have it your own way.'

And walked out of the room.

She sat there for a long time after that; she felt shaky. Shaky and something else. Uncomfortable. Uneasy with herself. She had no idea why. She had every justification for saying anything at all to him, she knew. He had absolutely no claims on her loyalty, no right to call on her kindness. He had forfeited those things long ago, when he had first become involved with Louise.

She stood up, heaped up the untidy pile of newspapers and picked up the mugs and glasses. She looked round the room: she loved it, the small sitting room, where guests were not invited. It was the family's own, not a playroom, but somewhere they all shared, with its heap of games on the shelves, the big television, the family library of books, from *Thomas the Tank Engine* through Roald Dahl, to the bound volumes of classics she had brought from her father's house. It was warm and comfortable, that room, all shades of red and pinks, with hundreds of photographs; in the winter, a real fire was kept burning in the pretty grate, and whenever it was warm enough, the small french windows were open, bringing the garden into the house. The children would come and find them there, if they felt in need of company, help or comfort in the evenings; it was where family business was conducted, holidays planned, arrangements discussed, reports read, Christmas presents wrapped. A happy room: or so it had been.

Well, time to move on. No use looking back. Tom had stolen the past as well as the future; and it could never be the same again.

She walked slowly up the stairs; the house was very quiet. Tom's study light was on, but there was no sound from the room. Maybe he'd gone to bed, left the light on. She pushed the door open gently; he hadn't gone to bed, but he was asleep, sprawled across the desk, his head on his arms, his face hidden. He looked, in that moment, like a large version of Gideon, the tumble of dark curls, the thin neck, the long, slender hands. He did not stir as she went across to the desk; his exhaustion was absolute. There was a note on the desk: to Bob Macintosh. He had scribbled it and intended to fax it.

'Bob: about tomorrow. Dinner would be great. Just what we need. Octavia can't make it, something on at . . .' and then he had written 'school', crossed that out, 'work', crossed that out too, finally 'her father's not well', and had started to write a new version. 'Bob. About tomorrow . . .'

Something stirred in Octavia, something painful and unwelcome, which she was still quite powerless to resist. She couldn't even put a name to it, give it a character of any kind. Whatever it was, it prompted her to reach for a piece of paper, and a pen, and to write on it, in her neat script, 'Tom, I'll come tomorrow night.' She had no idea even why she did it.

She went out of the study, closing the door quietly behind her. She had no wish to be there when he read it, no desire to see his gratitude. That really would be more than she could bear.

A rumour that John Whitlam had found that there was no reason, in his opinion, why the development at Bartles Wood should not go ahead, arrived at the offices of the *Felthamstone Advertiser* on the Wednesday evening, just as the features editor was looking for a good story to lead his weekend edition.

He phoned several people and received a firm denial, was told that it was far too early for anyone to have begun to have made a decision, and then tried Bartles House itself. Mrs Ford, the matron, said she would be the first person to know if it was true, so clearly it wasn't, and put the phone down on him rather briskly. The features editor, whose nickname was not Bulldog for nothing, then phoned the one person from whom he knew he would at least get a reaction one way or the other, Mrs Patricia David, and asked her for her comment. Mrs David gave him a very long one.

Octavia was just putting on her black dress – a low-cut one that Tom disliked – to go out to dinner with the Macintoshes when Pattie phoned with the news. She listened slightly impatiently, trying to do up her zip with one hand while tucking the phone under her chin with the other. Tom, who had come into the spare room in search of a book he had lost, automatically reached out and completed the job for her. He noticed as he did so that she was extremely warm, and that she was wearing a scent that he disliked as much as the dress, both clearly and deliberately chosen to displease him; nevertheless, despite his dislike, he found both the warmth and the strong, rich fragrance disturbing.

She scowled at him, turned away; he left the room.

'Pattie, I'm sorry, I really can't talk about it now. Look, I'll be down this weekend, we can meet then. Come to the cottage, bring Megan if you like. Yes, of course. That's okay. 'Bye.'

'So,' said Betty Carlton, looking at her husband shrewdly across the supper table, 'you've done it, then?'

'I'm sorry?'

'Got your planning permission. For Bartles Park.'

'No, I haven't. Nothing definite, nothing at all.'

'Oh, really? So what was the long conversation with Mr Ford about, then? I could have sworn I heard the words "on account" mentioned.'

'You're imagining things, love. More's the pity. This is very good. How would you like a weekend in Venice in a couple of weeks? For your birthday?'

'How would you like a weekend in Venice?' said Nico Cadogan. 'No, forget I said that, it's an appalling idea. Hot, crowded, smelly. We'll go in the spring. Tell you what, let's go to Glasgow. There's a delicious hotel there I'd like to take you to, and I adore Glasgow. All that wonderful architecture. Do you know it?'

'No, Nico, I don't. And I really can't go away this weekend.'
'Why not?'
'Well . . .'
'Right, I'll book it.'
'No!'
'Next weekend, then?'
'No, really, I can't.'
'Of course you can. I'll book that one. And I'll see you tomorrow. For dinner. All right?'
'Well – yes, Nico. Yes, all right.'

'How would you like a weekend away?' said Donald Ford. 'When this is all over? Somewhere nice, somewhere like Venice. We'll be able to afford it.'
'Oh, Donald, I can't think about anything at the moment, except getting through all this, all the upheaval and upsets. I don't know how we're going to break it to them, I really don't if it ever happens . . .'
'You're not getting cold feet, are you?'
'No, of course not. I just wish it was over.'
'It won't be over for a long time yet, love. Better make your mind up to that one.'

'Thank you, Octavia,' said Tom. 'Thank you so much for that.'
He was rather drunk; they had just arrived home after the dinner with the Macintoshes. Bob Macintosh had pushed the boat out, as he had promised he would, taken them to the Connaught. It hadn't been easy, but they'd got through it. Aubrey had been marvellous, making a fuss of Octavia, devoting himself to her comfort, had engineered that he was sitting next to her, with Bob on her other side. She had been very good too; having decided to go, had applied herself to the evening with her usual thoroughness, had listened politely to Bob while he told her about their proposed holiday in the Scilly Isles, admired the pictures of the children, asked Bob if he would take a page in a charity ball brochure. No one except him, Tom thought, watching them, would have thought anything was amiss; no one else would have noticed the fiercely hostile eyes as she occasionally had to look at him, the way she refused all his suggestions of what she should eat, the way, when he raised his glass of champagne round the table, she alone did not raise hers in return. Just for that one evening, through some huge effort of will, the marriage had become apparently whole again, no longer terminally damaged, but a positive, constructive thing. Even in his gratitude, Tom had found it disorienting, disturbing even: to know that so totally and competently could hatred, mistrust, despair be disguised.

'Thank you,' he said again now.

'That's all right. I hope it helped.'

He stood in the hall watching her; as she passed him, on her way to the kitchen, he caught the rich scent again. She was slightly tanned, and her breasts, spilling out of the vulgar dress, looked richer and fuller, not their usual neat small selves. She saw him looking at them and frowned, hurried on.

Tom sighed, started up the stairs himself; he was in his study when he heard her pass the door.

'Good night,' he said. She was silent.

Later, he passed the spare room, on his own way to bed. The light was still on, the door ajar. She was sitting up in bed, reading; she was naked, but the sheet was pulled up, covering her breasts.

He looked in. 'All right?'

'Yes, thank you,' she said.

Upstairs, there was a sudden cry, then another: it was Minty. She looked at him, swung her legs out of bed, pulled on a cotton robe.

'Excuse me.'

He watched her go up, heard her soothing the baby, heard her talking quietly to Caroline, then silence; he was half undressed himself when he realised he had still not found the book he had wanted earlier. He knocked on the spare room door; she wasn't there. He went in, was looking through the books when she came in. The robe was unfastened, swinging free; she was exposed to him, her breasts, her stomach, her thighs . . .

Tom could not move or look away. He knew he should, he knew he should say he was sorry, that he should hurry from the room, that at the very least, he should stop staring at her. But he couldn't. He couldn't because he wanted her more than at any time he could remember: a violent, sad hunger for her filled him. He stood there like a drowning man observing his own life and saw all the other naked Octavias he had loved; the one he had first seduced, first loved, plumper, younger than now, uncertain, laughing, nervous; the more confident creature she had become by their honeymoon, drunk with pleasure and sunshine and love; the swollen ripe-bodied woman bearing his children, infinitely desirable and lovely; the thin, tautly sensuous one she had become. And now, this new one: hurt by him, damaged by him, still beautiful, still desirable, lost to him irrevocably, and in love, it seemed, with someone else.

He managed it finally, said, 'I'm sorry,' hurried from the room. When he turned to close the door, he saw that she had not moved at all herself, but was standing carved into time, utterly still, staring at him in return.

And there was an expression in her eyes that he could not begin to read or understand.

Ian had still not rung, and it was Friday. Zoë could feel herself getting very edgy. For two reasons. She couldn't quite remember when the people were coming back to Cleaver Square, but it had to be soon; and if they found the money missing, Ian would work out pretty fast that it was her. Not that she had any money: she'd spent the lot and done one bit of babysitting which earned precisely fifteen pounds. Ten of which she'd already spent. But maybe she could talk the bank into letting her have just a bit more. Or borrow it from her mother. Or even Romilly. Anyway, she would worry about actually getting the money when she knew she was in a position to put it back. That was the main thing. She could hardly do it without Ian. And anyway, she was missing him. It wasn't just the sex, he was fun and funny. And it annoyed her that he'd been able to dump her. She was the one who did the dumping: or always had in the past. And she had nothing whatever to do all weekend . . . She dialled, let the number ring.

'Ian?'

'Yeah?' God, even his voice made her feel horny.

'Look – I lost an earring. You haven't got it, have you? Silver, big hoop thing.'

There was a silence, then, 'You know I haven't got it, Zoë. Don't you?'

'No,' she said determinedly.

''Course you do.' She could hear him smile. 'How are you?'

'Fine,' she said, trying to sound dignified.

'Good.'

'I just wondered – well . . .'

'I got to go away this weekend,' he said. 'One of my mates is having a stag do. So I can't see you. Sorry. But next weekend could be good. Last one in that house, matter of fact. They get back middle of the next week. I'll give you a bell.'

Now all she had to do was get hold of a hundred pounds.

'Please can we go and see the twins?' said Dickon. 'You said we could, this weekend. Please.'

Sandy hesitated; the thought of facing Octavia was, for some reason he couldn't quite understand, very difficult. It was absurd; here they were, the two innocent parties in this awful affair. Maybe that was why: the guilt was there, by implication, almost infecting them. Or was it that they were the two fools, the two duped fools? Either way it was almost unbearable. On the other hand, it had to be got over some time. Somehow.

'Well, if she can have us,' he said rather weakly.

'Ring her. Ask her. Please.'

Octavia sounded quite pleased. She said she had a friend coming. 'And someone else, to do with this wood business. You know? No? It's a wood down here, really beautiful, under threat from a developer. Well, anyway, I'll explain. Yes, come to tea, Sandy. The twins will be pleased.'

The twins certainly seemed pleased; Poppy rushed importantly to the car, helped to unbuckle Dickon from his seat.

'Come on,' she said to Sandy, 'Gabriel's here, he's playing cricket. Gideon's having to hop. It's so funny.'

'Who's Gabriel?'

'A friend. Of Mummy's.' Her face was slightly wary as she said it.

'Your father's not here?'

'No. He had to work this weekend. He just might come down tomorrow.'

It was plainly not true; Sandy wondered how much she had managed to interpret for herself from the situation, from the carefully presented version she would have been given.

'Sandy, hallo. Come in.' Octavia kissed him; slightly awkward, determinedly bright. 'How – how are you?'

'Not too bad considering. You know.'

'Yes,' she said. 'Yes, I do know.' She smiled at him, then suddenly drew him to her and kissed him again, more warmly, more easily. 'I'm so glad you came. We both need it. Now come on in. This is a friend of mine, Pattie David. And this is her daughter Megan. And that—' she pointed at a rather odd-looking figure wearing baggy khaki shorts and old-fashioned plimsolls, bowling at Gideon – 'that is Gabriel Bingham. The local MP. And cricket coach. Come and sit down, we're all talking about the wood . . .'

Sandy neither knew nor cared about the wood, only that he was grateful for it. He sat down next to Pattie David.

'Hallo,' she said, smiling at him. She had a nice smile; it made her look ten years younger. She was rather pretty in a worn, faded sort of way. 'Will you be able to help us with this, do you think?'

'What, the wood? Oh, not really my thing, protests and all that.'

'What is your thing?'

'I'm in the wine trade. Before that I was in the army. Pretty good at crawling through undergrowth, that's about all I could manage.'

'That could be jolly helpful,' she said, 'we're thinking of adopting

Swampy-type tactics. You could help us with the tunnels. Only joking! My father was in the army,' she added.

'Really? Which regiment?'

'DCLI.'

'No! My father was in the Somersets.'

'Heavens,' said Pattie, 'they probably knew one another. When did you leave?'

'About three years ago. After twelve years.'

'Do you miss it?'

'More than I can possibly tell you,' said Sandy. He didn't often admit it; most people didn't understand. He wasn't quite sure why he had now.

Pattie David smiled at him again. 'I bet you do,' she said.

Pattie had had a phone call: from a Mrs Lucilla Sanderson.

'She lives at Bartles House. Poor old soul, she sounded so upset. She'd read the article in the paper yesterday, and wanted to know if I thought it was true. She said the matron kept saying it wasn't, but she didn't believe her.'

'Quite right,' said Gabriel, sitting down, chewing on a long stalk of grass. 'I wouldn't believe a word that woman said, not even if it was that my name was Gabriel Bingham.'

'"This is our home," she kept saying, "we love it, we don't want to move."'

'Poor old things. Do you really think it's true? Or just a rumour?'

'We pray it's a rumour, of course,' said Pattie, 'but the man from the *Advertiser* kept saying that he'd heard every objection had been overruled. And most important of all, he said, the developer has offered six more small houses. I don't know why that's so important.'

'Planning gain,' said Octavia. 'It's a sort of trade-off. You have to include ten per cent of what's called socially affordable housing, along with your executive homes.'

'You know a lot about this sort of thing, don't you?' said Sandy. 'I'm impressed.'

'Oh, it's the sort of thing I've picked up, being married to . . .'

'Married to a sort of politician,' said Poppy. 'That's what Daddy is. Isn't he, Mummy?'

'Well, not exactly.'

'Daddy is terribly clever,' said Poppy. 'He knows so much about everything. I wish he was here. Don't you, Mummy? He could help such a lot.'

'Yes,' said Octavia, 'yes, I expect he could.'

Sandy looked at her thoughtfully; she was flushed. He saw her glance at Gabriel Bingham, saw him raise his eyebrows at her imperceptibly. So that was it. Lucky Octavia; she had someone else to ease her through this awful thing, she wasn't quite alone – as he was. He sighed. He felt very bleak suddenly.

'We have to stop them,' said Megan. 'We really do.'

She was a dear little thing, Sandy thought, so pretty and frail and quiet, fair like her mother, sitting there in her wheelchair, watching the other boisterous children, smiling at them rather like an elderly maiden aunt.

'How would you suggest we do that?' he said to her gently.

'There are trees for a start. We might be able to get them preserved.'

'Now that's worth a try,' said Octavia. 'Good thinking, Megan.'

'And the house. The land's no good unless they knock that down, is it, Mummy? It's awfully interesting looking. Maybe it could be listed.'

'Darling, I don't think so. It's not that old or anything.'

'Doesn't have to be old,' said Gabriel, 'just special. Unique. Well unique-ish.'

'It's certainly that,' said Octavia laughing, ''twenties Gothic.'

'Have you tried that one? Getting it listed?'

'Only as much as to know it's almost impossible. In theory. But we can try.'

'I think you should,' he said.

Pattie looked at him. 'Does this mean you're definitely on our side, Mr Bingham?'

'Oh, no. Not definitely.'

'Your backside must be getting quite sore,' said Octavia briskly, 'sitting on the fence so long.'

He grinned at her lazily. 'I have my reputation to consider. My political future. Bartles Wood could come between me and the premiership.'

'That's no contest,' said Octavia.

They agreed that Pattie should go up to the house, try and talk to the Fords, and that someone should investigate the possibility of getting the house listed.

'I'll do that,' said Sandy. 'I know a bit about it. My parents got their house listed. That stopped a bit of progress, in the form of a supermarket car park.'

They all stared at him.

'Sandy! Do you really not mind? It's not exactly on your doorstep,' said Octavia.

'I know. But I've – well, I've got a bit of spare time at the moment. Dickon and I can put our minds to it. Can't we, old chap?'

'That's so very good of you,' said Pattie David.

★

'Thank you for coming,' said Octavia as Sandy and Dickon left after family tea.

'No, Octavia, thank you for having us. It was such a help. Dickon hasn't had much fun lately.'

'No, I don't suppose he has. Actually, I've been meaning to ask you. We're having a big charity do in September, at Brands Hatch. It's a vintage car day, everyone's dressing up. And bringing their children. I'm taking all mine. If you'd like to come, please do. Dickon would love it.'

'Yes, he probably would. I'll let you know, if I may.' He was strapping Dickon into his car seat; she couldn't see his face. It was an easy time to ask.

'Have you seen her yet?'

'No,' he said, not turning, and she could see he found it as hard to confront the awful ugly thing that lay between them as she did. 'No, not yet. Tomorrow.'

'I hope it goes well.'

'So do I,' he said, 'for Dickon's sake.'

Octavia felt suddenly awkward when they had all gone; when they were reduced to a family-size group. A false family.

She went upstairs and bathed Minty, gave her a cup of milk, told the twins to kiss her good night; they scarcely looked up from the game of jacks Gabriel had brought with him for Gideon.

She went and tucked Minty up, sat with her for a bit, watching her drift off to sleep, her small face sweetly composed. She looked down on the garden; the sun was still quite strong, but the shadows on the lawn were lengthening. Gabriel was reading the paper, occasionally going off to adjudicate in the game; he looked utterly relaxed, the picture of – what? What was he, for God's sake, in her new, strange, unfamiliar life, its new unworked-out structure? Something permanent? Or something simply holding it – and her – together while the new, tenuous forms began to grow strong?

Later they all ate some pasta, and watched *Noel's House Party*; at nine o'clock the twins went reluctantly up to their room.

She tidied up, poured herself a glass of wine, settled down with a magazine. Gabriel was amazing with the children, so patient and such fun, the children seemed to like him so much.

'Mummy.'

It was Poppy; her small face oddly taut and wary.

'Yes, darling?'

'I can't sleep.'

Poppy stayed downstairs, sitting sucking her thumb beside Octavia, reverted suddenly to babyhood, while she and Gabriel watched the news. She was half asleep.

'Come on, darling. I'll take you up.'

'I'm watching this.'

'No, you're not. Come on. You're so tired.'

'When is Gabriel going?' said Poppy, carefully not addressing him.

'Oh, pretty soon,' he said. 'When this is over.'

She nodded, went rather forlornly upstairs. Octavia went up after her, tucked her in.

'He's not staying tonight, is he?' said Poppy. 'He doesn't need to, does he?'

'No, of course he doesn't.'

'I'm sorry,' she said carefully to Gabriel when finally they were alone. 'I can't let you stay.'

'That's all right,' he said.

She knew he was disappointed.

'Could I stay for a bit?' he said.

'Well . . .' Octavia hesitated. Torn between a desire to please him, to thank him, a longing to have the comfort of him, and anxiety about the children, what they might discern if they awoke. It would hardly be an easy, joyful piece of lovemaking.

'Okay,' he said, interpreting her silence. 'I understand. Tell me one thing, though. It will make it easier. Do you – I mean . . .'

Octavia leaned over, kissed him very hard, very deliberately on the mouth. 'Oh, Gabriel,' she said. 'I do. I really do.'

Just the same, when he left an hour later, she sensed a growing impatience, a tension in him. She tried to feel cool, lighthearted even, about it: but it troubled her quite a lot. And it was another pressure; just when she didn't need it.

'She's still quite confused,' said the matron to Sandy, 'so don't expect too much. But she's looking forward to seeing you.'

He hadn't known what to expect in himself: coldness, distaste, anger. The sense of total unreality he experienced when he saw her sitting in a chair by the window, smiling at them, very pale and thin, but dressed, in trousers and a pale pink shirt, her hair washed and brushed, Louise again, not some wretched shell, lying on a hospital bed in a paper gown, that took him totally by surprise.

She held out her arms; Dickon flew into them.

'Mummy, you look so better! When are you coming home?'

Only her voice was changed: somehow slower, rather quiet and weak. 'Not just yet, darling. I'm feeling a bit wobbly. You look wonderful. Daddy's obviously looking after you very well.' She covered his face with kisses. 'What have you been doing?'

'Lots of things. Yesterday we went to see the twins.'

'The twins! Did you? How were they? How was their mummy?'

She was showing no sign of tension, of wariness. Just the rather frail voice.

'She was all right. Megan was there, a girl in a wheelchair, she was nice. And Gabriel, the man who plays cricket.'

'Oh, really? Was he?' She hugged Dickon closer, was silent.

Finally her eyes met Sandy. 'How are you, Sandy?' she said.

'Oh – fine.'

'Good. Well, sit down.' She waved her hand towards another chair. 'They're bringing tea. I asked for chocolate biscuits, Dickon, for you.'

'Yeah!' he said.

It was extraordinary. She had done her nails, was even wearing lipstick. She smiled and made an effort to chat, asked Dickon questions about going swimming, asked Sandy about his business; it was as if she was some close friend, who knew them well, and who was enjoying an afternoon tea party, rather than – rather than what?

She put her hand out, put it on his arm; Sandy looked at it. She had beautiful hands, they were one of the things he had first noticed about her; now it looked ugly to him, that hand, ugly and out of place. He had to struggle not to shake it off.

'How are you, Sandy?' she said again.

'I'm – fine,' he said. 'Yes. You know.'

'It must be very difficult. Managing with Dickon and everything.'

'Well, I've taken a bit of a holiday and your father's having him next week – I've got to get some work done then.'

'Of course. Daddy's coming tomorrow. Have you seen him?'

'No. Not yet.'

'I'll be home soon,' she said quite firmly. 'I told the doctor I needed to get back. To look after you both. But he said – well, not for a week or two.'

Sandy looked at her; he didn't know what to do or say. What could he say? That he didn't want her at home, ever again, didn't want her near him, ever again? Simply to get her hand off his arm, he stood up, went over to the window.

'I think I might go outside for a bit,' he said, 'leave you and Dickon to have a chat.'

Outside was reality; the nightmare receded. He walked about the grounds rather briskly, avoiding people's eyes. Then he made for the gate, walked down the road a few yards. The nursing home was on the outskirts of Bath, in a wide tree-lined road. That was even better: there were ordinary people walking about, leading proper ordered, ordinary lives, not mad, lying fantasies. He found a newsagent, bought some peppermints, ate his way through the whole packet. They were oddly refreshing. He turned back to the gates, walked purposefully towards them; but when he got there, he stopped, had to make a huge effort of will to go through them. Back into the madness.

'Mrs Trelawny is very tired.' The nurse's face was reproachful. 'You shouldn't have left her with the little boy. Not really. You weren't to know, of course. But another time . . .'

'No,' Sandy said, 'I'm sorry, I thought she and he – well . . .'

Louise was lying on the bed again, smiling drowsily. 'Sorry, darling. So sorry. Come again very soon.'

'We will.'

Dickon gave her a kiss, walked over to Sandy, took his hand. 'You're all right, aren't you, Mummy?'

'Of course I'm all right. Just tired. Sandy, come and kiss me goodbye.'

He managed it; but it was the hardest thing he had ever done.

CHAPTER 34

'Oh, God! Oh, no. What am I going to do?'

Loud sobs came out of the girls' bathroom; racked, anguished, deeply distressed.

Zoë banged on the door. 'Romilly, what is it? What's the matter?'

Very slowly the door opened; a tear-stained, white face looked round it. 'Look . . .' She pointed to her chin; there beneath the fine translucent skin, silky smooth, was an undeniable ripple.

Zoë gazed at it very seriously. 'Spot?'

'Yes. Coming. Isn't it? In two days it'll be huge.'

It wouldn't be huge; but it would be there. Zoë understood. And sympathised. 'And you've got your session? Oh, Rom, what a shame. Is it your period?'

'Yes. It's just about due. Can't you tell? Look at my stomach, it's huge.'

'Yeah, right,' said Zoë, glancing at the concave flatness that was Romilly's stomach. 'Really huge. Rom, you're getting obsessed.'

'I'm not! I'm not obsessed.'

'It would hardly be surprising if you were,' said Zoë. 'Well, you have to say something, I think. Would you like me to call Ritz?'

Romilly stared at her. 'But what would you say?'

'I'd tell them the truth. I'd say you were getting a spot, and did it matter?'

'And then what?'

'Well, then it's up to them. It's hardly your fault.'

'No, but I'm still letting them down.'

''Course you're not. In all probability they can retouch the picture, so the spot won't show anyway. But you should tell them.'

Ritz was very good; she said of course she understood, that it was nice of Zoë to let them know, and also helpful. 'Is it her period?'

'Yes. Yes, it is.'

'It's often a problem with very young girls. We should have asked her, really.'

'God, she'd have died.'

'I'm afraid she'll have to get used to that,' said Ritz, and her voice was harsher suddenly.

'I see,' said Zoë.

Her own voice must have sounded different, because Ritz said hastily, 'Sorry. That came out wrong. What I mean is, she'll have to get used to anticipating it, letting us know – she can say she's going to be away or something if that makes her feel better. Anyway, it's only Monday, maybe by Friday . . .'

'Yup. Thanks, Ritz.'

'That's okay.'

Romilly received the news that she was to go in for some test shots on the Wednesday, 'so they can decide for themselves', in a state approaching total anguish. She sat down with her diary and spent the next half hour counting not only days, but hours. Finally, she decided that it must be all right, she was always a bit early, and tomorrow was the full four weeks. And her back did ache a bit: and she did have the swollen stomach. That had to go as well, though. Maybe she should play it safe.

She reached into the back of the large dolls' house that still sat in the corner of her bedroom and pulled out the hidden stack of laxatives. She swallowed four; and then she could take four more at bedtime. That should work. God, it *had* to work. She had read in a magazine somewhere that the girls who swallowed laxatives to lose weight took a lot of exercise to increase their efficiency; she put on her cycling shorts and running shoes and set out along the street in the direction of the park.

Felix Miller was unaccustomed to feeling unsure of himself. He had always known precisely not only what he was doing, but also that he was absolutely right in doing it. From the earliest days at the bank, as one small piece of shrewd judgment followed another and earned him the gravitas to make larger ones: as his client list, carefully harvested and still more carefully pruned, grew in stature and status: as he married the right girl – rich, well connected, dutiful: as he watched Octavia grow up into beauty and brilliance and success: as his relationship with Marianne proved emotionally fulfilling and sexually pleasurable: as his own fortune grew beyond his wildest dreams and his collection of fine paintings and sculpture soared in value: as his own health and vigour continued unabated into his late fifties: all these things he put down entirely to his own ability to take hold of and run his life with skill and intelligence.

The dark things contained within it – the death of the perfect wife, the loss of a child, Octavia's marriage to Tom Fleming – he could set at the door of a malevolent chance, unforeseeable, unpreventable.

Until now. He was being forced to recognise that the loss of Marianne was actually very painful; and he was also, with greater difficulty, beginning to accept that it was, if not exactly within his control, then certainly not entirely outside it. He had treated her badly, he knew. He had neglected her over the previous few weeks, he had been distracted from her needs, thoughtless of her concerns, hostile to her unhappiness. He told himself that he had been driven to it: that some of it at least was justified, that she had seemed less than sympathetic to his anguish over Octavia, that she been less than forceful in her own response to the situation. But he also knew that those things could be put down to her own gentleness of spirit and her own rather non-directional style of parenting.

And now, at least for a while, he had lost her.

That she should have left him for Cadogan, a man who had betrayed a friendship in so many ways, he found doubly painful. Cadogan had made his move on Marianne quite ruthlessly at a time when she was vulnerable and unhappy, and no possible excuse could be made for him. None the less, it was he, Felix, who had made her unhappy in the first place; and the sense that he could blame himself added to his misery, his sense of panic. And casting about for a scapegoat, as he had done all his life, one was very easily to be found. A person who had caused him certainly indirectly to be neglectful, blind to Marianne's needs, and who had made her receptive to the approaches of Cadogan. Tom Fleming. The dislike he had always felt for Tom now became a loathing that he felt physically, a putrid, suppurating presence somewhere deep within him. He could not bear it; it could not go on.

'I'm having lunch with Tom Fleming tomorrow,' said Lauren Bartlett.

Drew Bartlett glanced up at her. He knew that hyper-casual tone very well. 'Oh, yes? What on earth for?'

'I think I might have persuaded Oliver Nichols to consider appointing him after all. He's joining us. And he's really up against it, poor old Tom. Company's right back on the ropes.'

'Good Lord. Poor old Tom. And didn't you say the marriage wasn't too hot either?'

'Yes, I did. Poor old Tom,' said Lauren.

She was meeting Tom and Oliver Nichols at the Pont de la Tour. She had planned with great care: Tom at twelve thirty, Nichols at one fifteen. In theory so that she could brief Tom, actually to try and find out how things really were between him and Octavia. She had always wondered why he didn't have affairs: she had heard the occasional rumour, but generally he seemed to lead a blameless life. Too busy making money, she supposed. Like Drew. Lauren was totally confident of her husband's sexual loyalty to her. He talked big, he flirted loudly, but that was all. Out of the social arena, he worked seven days a week, ten hours a day. His company consumed his energy, on all levels. On their increasingly rare couplings, he displayed less and less confidence and skill; time and again recently, he had rolled off her, saying he was sorry, and gone straight to sleep. It suited Lauren well; in spite of her overt sexiness, the pleasure she took in pursuit, she didn't actually like sex very much. It bored her. Few men had made her come; and when she did she only enjoyed that for a short moment. It was a release, no more, quite removed from actual pleasure. She preferred to fake it, and then lie there, clenching and unclenching her taut, well-exercised pelvic floor, observing dispassionately what seemed to her the rather pathetic and unseemly spectacle of the male orgasm. She would enjoy observing that in Tom Fleming.

He looked terrible, she thought, when he arrived. He had lost weight, he looked drawn and pale; there were more grey hairs amongst the dark brown. But he was beautifully dressed as always, in a cream linen suit and black silk shirt; he smiled at her, bent to kiss her.

'You look lovely,' he said.

'Oh, please! I've put on about five pounds since I saw you last week. Drew and I were staying with friends in the country, nothing to do all weekend but eat and drink. Anyway, I've been at the gym ever since. Diana was there this morning. She looked fabulous.'

'Diana who?'

'Tom! The Princess.'

'Oh.'

'Yes. I really do think this man is making her happy. Dodi Fayed, I mean. And she deserves it. She's had a lousy time. Now then, what do you want to drink? Champagne?'

'I'll stick to water, thanks. For now.'

'How very disappointing. I was planning on getting you deliciously drunk.'

'Not at lunchtime, Lauren. Sorry.'

He smiled at her. She took it as encouragement. 'Well, I shall have to take you to dinner instead, then. How's Octavia?'

'She's fine. Thanks.'

Not prepared to admit anything, then.

'She and her partner are doing marvellous things for our charity day. I expect you've heard about it.'

'No. I haven't had much time even to talk to Octavia recently.'

That was encouraging. 'Well, it's at Brands Hatch. In early September. I'm hoping Diana will be there. With the boys. They're such fun, those two, especially little Harry. What a charmer. Anyway, I hope you'll be there.'

'I don't think so.' He smiled at her, sipped at his water. 'Tell me about your friend, Lauren.'

'Oh, yes.' The intimate chat was clearly not going to materialise. 'Well, he has just bought this chain of chemist's shops. He owns among other things a pharmaceutical company. And I don't need to tell you, that's a minefield.'

'Yes,' said Tom slowly, 'I can see that.'

'He just needs a lot of advice. About presentation, legislation, all that sort of thing.'

'But I thought he'd appointed someone else.'

'Well, nothing's actually signed. Apparently. And he is having second thoughts. So – over to you. But he can't get here till one fifteen. I did tell you that, didn't I?'

'No,' said Tom, 'no, I don't think you did.'

'Oh, I'm sorry. Well, we'll have to fill in the time somehow. Are you going away this summer . . . ?'

'Mrs Trelawny doesn't really take part in the group therapy at all,' said the nurse.

'Oh, really?' Dr Brandon frowned. 'I thought she was attending now. She's become slightly more communicative now the Prozac is beginning to take effect.'

'With you, I expect. And she does come to the sessions. But she hardly says a word.'

'Not formed any relationships?'

'No. None.'

'What impression did you get of the husband when he came?'

'He seemed very nice. And the little boy was sweet. She obviously adores him.'

'Yes. Well, she insists the marriage isn't a problem, says they're very happy.'

'I think that's probably true. He's obviously very upset, poor man. I think it's a simple case of everything being too much for her. The cot death, her mother's death, then this miscarriage. Poor woman.'

'Yes. Yes, I daresay. I still haven't managed to get her to talk about the baby. She shies away from it. I'll try again soon. I'll talk to the husband, too. It may be he's not as supportive as she claims. Bit bluff, isn't he? Army type. Probably none too sensitive.'

'Probably,' said the nurse.

It went very well, she thought. Oliver Nichols had seemed to like Tom; they virtually ignored her for the final hour. She didn't mind that, just sat watching them, smiling indulgently at them from time to time. They emerged into the sunshine together after three. The river had a holiday look to it, studded with small craft, and to their left Tower Bridge's Meccano-like structure rose from the blue water.

Lauren put her arm through both theirs, smiled up at them. 'It's lovely here, isn't it? Sad to leave. Now, I have a cab waiting. Either of you want a lift to the West End?'

'Not me,' said Oliver, 'back to the City.'

'I'm going to Westminster, I'm afraid,' said Tom. Rather hastily, she thought.

'I call that West End. I can drop you off. I have some heavy shopping to do after that. We're off to Tuscany in a week.'

'How marvellous,' said Tom.

'I wish I was coming with you,' said Oliver.

'I wish you were coming with us, too, Oliver. And you, Tom. What are your plans for the summer?'

'We don't really have any,' said Tom quickly.

'That's a shame. Camilla would adore to be with Poppy. No one of her age going. Now if you brought her . . .'

'Well . . .'

'Look, you two, I'll leave you discussing your holiday arrangements. I've got work to do. Tom, I'll be in touch. You've given me lots to think about.'

In one of those quirks of fate that reveal her determination to interfere with the affairs of men, Oliver Nichols went to a dinner that night at the Mansion House and found himself seated at the same table as Felix Miller, whom he had met several times at other such functions. He told him he had had lunch only that day 'with your son-in-law, Tom Fleming. Nice chap, very impressive.'

'He's very good on presentation,' Felix said, his tone unenthusiastic.

'Well, that's precisely what I'm looking for. Presentation skills. We had a very pleasant lunch at the Pont de la Tour.'

'Oh, yes? I'm surprised he could afford it, the company's in serious trouble, you know.'

'Really?' Nichols looked at him sharply. 'He didn't give me that impression. Anyway, he wasn't paying, I was. It was organised by a mutual friend, gorgeous girl, Lauren Bartlett. Dead ringer for the Princess of Wales. When I left, she and Tom were climbing into a very cosy-looking taxi, seemed to be fixing up some holiday together.'

'A holiday?' said Felix. 'Surely not!'

'Oh, not just the two of them. Some jaunt to a villa. Their daughters are friends, I believe. Pass that bottle, would you, good sir. I need some more of its contents rather badly. Bit of a tough day . . .'

When Felix got home he was physically sick. He lay awake most of the night, torn between the desire to inform Octavia of Tom's apparently fast-blossoming relationship with Lauren Bartlett and his plans to go on holiday with her, and the desire to spare her further pain. In the end, in the interests of her ultimate good, he decided he should tell her.

Marianne had also spent a sleepless night: but not unhappily. She was filled all the time now with a throbbing, pervading energy; and she lay through the night, alternately reading and then dozing, tossing on her pillow, smiling foolishly into the darkness, overwhelmed, invaded by – what? Love? Too early to call it that. Infatuation? That was more like it. Nico called her half a dozen times a day now, to tell her she was beautiful, that he adored her, that he loved her, that he wanted to marry her; that he was buying the house for her, that he wanted her to look at it again, make sure it was what she wanted. She tried to dismiss it as nonsense, told him that of course she wasn't going to marry him, he wasn't to buy anything for her, anything at all, and certainly not a house, that she was a respectable middle-aged woman, that—

'Hardly, my darling. Just. Respectable, no. Not with the things you are capable of. Behind closed doors. What your children would say I dare not even think.'

'Don't,' said Marianne with a shudder.

She went into her bathroom, took a shower then looked at her watch. Still only eight. Romilly had her session today; she was terribly jumpy about it. They had to be at the studio at ten: Marianne had insisted on going too. Romilly had complained vociferously; called her neurotic, over-protective, mad, tears welling in her great green eyes. This whole thing had brought on a very acute attack of adolescence; she had been so level and easy before. Finally, Marianne had said she would stay for a while until things were under way and then go shopping.

She would wake her soon; she would want to spend hours getting ready. Marianne made a cup of tea and took it up to Romilly's room. She wasn't there. The bedclothes were thrown back, the door wide open; it looked as if she had rushed out of bed.

She looked down the landing; the door of their bathroom was shut. Clearly she was already at work on herself. Marianne put the tea down on the bedside table, went along to the bathroom.

'Tea in your room, darling. I'm very impressed you're up.'

Silence.

She tried again. 'Rom? You in there?'

'Yes.' Her voice sounded odd, rather weak.

'Darling? You all right?'

'Yes, I'm fine. Thanks.'

'Well, see you in a bit. I'll be downstairs.'

Another silence.

Romilly finally emerged from the bathroom rather shakily ten minutes later. She'd obviously overdone it with the pills. It had been agony; she'd been on the loo what felt like half the night. Horrible cramps, going on and on. But – no period. It wasn't fair. God, it wasn't fair. She got dressed slowly, had to sit down from time to time. Once she thought she was going to faint. She felt terribly thirsty; surely it would be all right to have something to drink. She just wouldn't eat anything; not until after the session. It would get her stomach going again, sticking out. Oh, God, why wouldn't it come, why?

'You're looking much better anyway,' said Dr Brandon.

Louise said nothing, just smiled.

'How are you feeling?'

'Better,' she said dutifully. She was beginning to enjoy this game a lot; it was indeed making her feel better. Telling them what she wanted to; painting her own view. Much better than the stupid Prozac, which didn't seem to make any difference at all.

'I'd like to talk to you some more about your husband . . .' he said.

'Yes?' This was the bit of the game she enjoyed most.

'Now, you've been married – what?'

'Seven years.'

'Yes. And always been happy?'

'Very happy.'

'Louise, there's one thing that puzzles me a bit.'

'Yes?'

'I understand your husband had a vasectomy? Why did he do that?'

She shrugged. 'We didn't want any more children.'

'Even though the baby had died? You didn't want to try again?'

'It was before that,' said Louise quickly.

'Before she died?'

'Yes.'

'I see. They must have got the dates confused.'

She fixed her large blue eyes on him. 'Please, Dr Brandon.'

'Sorry. We'll leave that for now. Anyway, he was happy to have the vasectomy?'

'Oh, yes. Very happy.'

'I see. But you became pregnant?'

'Yes.'

'How did that happen, do you think?'

She smiled at him. She knew he liked her, was interested not only by her, but in her. Looking at the other patients, it was pretty obvious he would. 'The usual way. Obviously. Vasectomies do fail, don't they? I can't be the first person it's happened to.'

'No,' he said, 'no, of course you're not.'

'Romilly, hallo. Come in. And Mrs Muirhead. It's so nice you came too.' Serena smiled at them across the studio reception area. 'Now, I think you know everyone. Except the photographer. Here he is: the great great man himself. Straight from the pages of *Vanity Fair* and American *Harper's*. Alix Stefanidis.'

Romilly had seen pictures of him with some of his subjects in *Vanity Fair*. He'd photographed them all, Nicole Kidman, Cindy Crawford, Naomi, the Princess of Wales ... He was tall, blond, impossibly handsome, with brown eyes and a hundred-volt smile.

He bowed slightly over Marianne's hand as he shook it, then turned to Romilly, took hers. 'So you are the famous new face-to-be,' he said, smiling. 'How very very lucky for me, to be the first to work with you.' His accent was middle-European-American; his voice was throaty, fairly light.

Romilly smiled uncertainly up at him.

'Well,' he said, turning to Serena and Donna, who were sitting side by side on a reception sofa, 'she's *so* much prettier than you said. Wonderful eyes. And that skin!'

'I've got a spot,' said Romilly abruptly. Everyone laughed; she felt like crying.

After they had had coffee, Alix Stefanidis said, 'Well, little baby, I'd like to get going. Just work around a little, get you used to the camera, to me, let me get used to you. These are just for us. Our own special pictures.'

Romilly smiled at him rather uncertainly; she wasn't sure she liked being called 'little baby', but she supposed it was partly him being foreign.

'Fine,' she said.

'Let's go, then. Follow me.'

'Ritz, when shall I come back for Romilly?' said Marianne.

'Oh, I don't know. Can we put her in a cab when it's time to go home? Alix may take all day or he may take an hour.'

'Well – look, Romilly, I have my mobile. Call me if you want me.'

'Mum! I think I can sit in a cab on my own. I'll see you at home.'

Afterwards, Marianne realised it was the first time Romilly had not called her the babyish, dutiful 'Mummy'.

Being photographed by Alix was rather different from being photographed by Jonty.

It started all right; he set her down on a stool on the background paper, told her to relax, to smile, to think, to look around, and then did some polaroids which he studied for a long time in silence by the window. She looked at him anxiously, waiting for a reaction; finally he threw them all on the floor and turned back to her, smiling rather remotely. His assistant, Tang, a Japanese boy dressed entirely in black, picked the pictures up and carried them reverently over to a low table where he set them very precisely in neat rows.

Romilly began to feel rather edgy. She also felt the opposite of someone who was about to be the latest famous face; she had no make-up on, she had expected someone to do that for her, and at least to brush her hair out, all she had done was wash it. She knew she was pale, and she was miserable about the spot. And she still felt a bit odd.

Alix worked much more silently than Jonty, played music she couldn't recognise, and apart from issuing increasingly abrupt instructions, hardly spoke to her, occasionally having intense little exchanges with Tang in which Romilly presumed to be Japanese while they both stared at her.

After half an hour, he turned to Ritz and Serena and told them to leave. 'None of us can concentrate with you all here. Donna, you stay for a little while, I want to go through those layouts again.'

Ritz stood up reluctantly. 'You okay, Romilly?'

'Yes. Yes, I'm fine. Really I am. Could I just go to the loo?'

'Of course. You should have asked before.'

She sat there for a few minutes, taking deep breaths. Her tummy still ached, and she felt very nervous.

When she came out, Serena was waiting. She smiled at her, gave her a brief hug. 'Are you really all right?'

'Yes. Yes, I think so. He's a bit scary. So – grand.'

'Romilly, darling, let me tell you a little secret about Mr Stefanidis. He was born in a slum in Athens, he only went to school for about three years, and he still has table manners like a pig.'

Romilly giggled.

'It's true. All that talk about Diana and Jemima and which of them he enjoyed working with more, it's to impress you, make you feel small. Which is stupid of him. He has a rather rocky ego, even if it looks like the size of the Empire State. You have twice as much class as he does. In every way. Now Ritz and I will be right here if you need us.'

Romilly smiled at her; she was so nice. Impulsively she leaned forward and gave her a kiss. 'Thank you. Thank you so much. That does help.'

It did: for a bit. Then he moved closer, his lens probing her face.

'You have the most wonderful eyes,' he said to her, 'widen them for me. Now drop them. Yes. Good. Beautiful. Lovely. Now look at me as if it was the very first time.'

She supposed he must mean she should look surprised, interested. She tried.

'No, no, little baby. You know what I mean. The first time. The very first.'

Romilly flushed; she did know what he meant. She dropped her eyes again, naturally, automatically, then looked at him: awkwardly shy.

'That's a little bit better. Let's do it again. Try to show it more. Yes. And more, and again more, look at me now, now, yes, and now, think, Romilly, think . . .'

She heard a cough; saw Donna shake her head imperceptibly at Alix. He took no notice.

'Alix, can I have a word?'

'Not now, darling, not while I'm working.'

'Alix, please.'

'Donna, I can't work like this, I really can't. I think it would be better if you left too.'

Tension had risen in the room; Romilly's stomach was twisting again.

'Romilly, is that all right?' said Donna.

'Of course. Of course it is.'

'Good girl. More coffee?'

'Yeah, more coffee, great,' said Alix. 'And could someone send for some cigarettes for me, I really really need one. Romilly, do you smoke?'

She shook her head.

'Of course no,' he said, the famous, the beautiful smile breaking suddenly across his face. 'No vices at all. Yet. Now relax, darling, just try to relax. Let's try the floor, sitting on the floor – no, baby, not like that. Stretch out, now ease yourself to the camera, to me . . .'

She became increasingly nervous. The more he told her to relax, the more she tensed. She could feel his tension, his impatience.

'Fine,' he said finally. 'This will be the last roll for today. Now I want you to – let me see. I'd like that hair to start working. Drop your head, baby, shake it all about. No, no, more, as if you were shampooing.'

She dropped her head obediently, pushed her hands through her hair, pretending she was washing it.

'No no,' he said, and there was real anger in his voice. 'Not like that. Silly little one. No. Go and brush it out, start again.'

She brushed her hair smooth, flushed, near to tears.

'Right. Now then, lean over, so it hangs straight, right over your face. Now quickly, fling back, so it flies. Yes! Yes, that's better. But this time, the eyes wide, wide. And again. Wider. And again.'

Suddenly she felt hopelessly dizzy. She said, 'I must sit down,' and sank rather helplessly on to the floor. 'Dizzy. I'm so sorry.'

She heard him calling impatiently for Donna; then heard him say, 'It's very difficult. I hadn't expected it, she's so tense. I can't get her to relax. And now she is not well. Dizzy, she said. I suppose she has her period or something. These very young girls, all the same problem, the hormones, so unreliable. I think we should stop for today. Anyway, the skin is not good enough. I can't work with her any more today.'

When Serena and Donna came in, Romilly had her face in her hands, crying quietly.

'I'm so so sorry,' said Serena. Donna had gone in pursuit of Alix to upbraid him. 'He's a pig! I never wanted him in the first place, but they insisted.'

'No, no,' said Romilly sniffing, 'it's my fault. I'm no good, and it's true, I have got a spot. I told you.'

'Yes, but it will be gone by Friday, when we start shooting for real. Or we could make it Saturday. How would that be?'

Romilly thought fast; Saturday. Another whole day. Surely by then everything would have sorted itself out.

She smiled at Serena. 'It could help. Yes. I seem to have got some sort of – bug.'

'Yes, I know. Zoë told us. We understand.'

God, she was nice. So nice.

'Look, how would you like another of our hot chocolate sessions?'

'That would be *lovely*.'

'Jesus,' said Ritz to Donna as she watched Serena and Romilly leave the building, 'I hope she's not up to what I think she might be up to.'

CHAPTER 35

Megan David was alone in the house that afternoon; her mother had begun to leave her occasionally now, and Megan liked that, to feel she could manage, that she did not always need someone with her. It made her feel more normal, less of a freak. She loved having the kitchen to herself, to pour herself an extra Coca-cola, to find a packet of biscuits, to steal a lolly from the fridge; innocent, forbidden pleasures taken for granted by most children. As she rummaged through the low cupboard by the sink, in search of the miniature cookies her mother had bought only that morning, the phone rang. She swivelled her chair, drove it forward importantly towards the low table by the kitchen sofa where the phone sat; she picked it up in triumph. 'Hallo. Felthamstone 6721. Megan David speaking.'

'Oh,' said a slightly shaky, but very posh voice (as Megan described it later to her mother), 'I wonder, is that Mrs David?'

'No, she's my mum. I can take a message.'

'It's very important.'

'I can take an important message,' said Megan, 'or unimportant, it's all the same, you know.'

There was a silence; then a deep laugh came down the phone, throaty, infectious. 'Of course it is. How silly of me. I'm sorry.'

'Not at all. Who am I speaking to? I have a pen and paper here.'

'You're speaking, my dear, to Mrs Lucilla Sanderson. Have you got that?'

'Yes,' said Megan writing fast. 'Yes, I have.'

'From Bartles House.'

'Oh,' said Megan, 'is it about the protest?'

'It's about *my* protest, yes. I want to stop this development more than anything.'

'My protest too,' said Megan. 'I want to save the wood so much. Well, all of it of course, the house and everything, but specially the wood. We had a meeting the other day. I had some quite good ideas, I think,' she added modestly.

'Well, that's splendid. I'm glad somebody has. Now could you ask your mother to ring me, please? Is your father involved in this as well?'

'Er – no,' said Megan. 'He doesn't live with us any more.'

'Oh, my dear, I'm sorry. How very tactless of me.'

'It's all right. You couldn't have known. Anyway, it was ages ago he left.' When the strains of living with a handicapped child and a distracted wife had become too uncomfortable for him. 'My mum divorced him years and years back.'

'I see.'

'I'll get my mum to ring you,' said Megan.

She sounded lovely, Megan thought, putting down the phone, starting immediately to rewrite the message in careful, coherent prose. Maybe they could go up there and meet her. She'd like that, get a better look at the house.

Octavia Fleming was by coincidence focusing on Bartles Wood at the very same time. She had just received a call from Gabriel Bingham telling her that he really felt the most pressing need in the whole business was to raise some money, since Michael Carlton – so he had heard on the local grapevine – was determined to fight for the project right up to the highest courts in the land. 'Just gave the quote to the *Advertiser*, apparently. He'll have loads of dosh. And you will need some. I've seen these cases before. They can drag on for years, and every day of every year seems to cost thousands.'

'Yes, well, thanks,' said Octavia with a sigh.

'That's all right. Just felt you ought to be aware of it. When am I going to see you?'

'Oh, Gabriel, I don't really quite know.'

'Okay.' His voice sounded more distant suddenly. 'Just let me know. 'Bye.' He put the phone down.

Two hours later, her father phoned.

'All right, darling?'

'I'm fine. Thanks. Very busy, though.'

'Yes, of course. I won't keep you. Just wondered if you'd thought any more about holidays. About the cottage.'

'Dad, I really can't leave the children just now.'

'Oh, really? I heard – oh, it must have been a mistake.'

'Heard what?'

'That Tom had plans for a holiday with them. I met someone who'd been talking to him about it.'

'Met someone? Someone who?'

'Man called Oliver Nichols. Nice chap. He's considering becoming a client of Tom's apparently. I was very surprised. Judgment's usually very good. Anyway, he's a friend of your client, what was her name, some woman, looks like the Princess of Wales, I think you said.'

'Lauren Bartlett?'

'Yes. He said they'd all been at a lunch together, and she and Tom were discussing a holiday in Tuscany. With their respective children.'

'What?' That hurt so much, she felt it physically. 'Daddy, when was this?'

'Oh, last night, I think. Yes.'

Last night; when she and Tom, by mutual agreement, had had supper with the children, had made a huge effort to be courteous to one another for their sake, when he had gone up to his study when everyone was asleep, saying, 'I am trying, Octavia. To get some things at least right. I really am.'

Trying. To get another woman into bed. Already.

Reckless with rage, she picked up the phone, dialled his direct line.

'Tom?'

'Oh, hallo. I'm in a meeting just at the moment, so if you—'

'I'm so sorry to have interrupted it. Is Mrs Bartlett one of the participants?'

'I'm sorry?'

'I said was Mrs Bartlett one of the participants? Is planning a holiday with her the purpose of the meeting? Tom, just answer me one thing. Have you or have you not discussed a holiday with Lauren Bartlett? With the children?'

'I'm sorry,' he said, 'I really cannot have this conversation with you now.'

And the phone went dead.

The Cadogan share price was continuing to rise. Nothing dramatic, nothing remarkable even, but still unarguable, a steady day-by-day, point-by-point climb. Philip Thorburn, Nico Cadogan's financial adviser, was watching it and worrying over it; it was – odd. The company was under threat of a takeover bid certainly; but the takeover was under threat of referral to the MMC. And if it went to referral, the shares would almost certainly fall again. So what was going on? Someone, somewhere, was moving in on the company; but why? It didn't make an awful lot of sense.

It was mad, she knew, mad, undignified, stupid, terrible; but Octavia phoned Lauren. She hated herself as she did it, watched herself, listened to herself in horror, but she still went on.

'Lauren? Octavia.'

'Oh, hi, Octavia. How are you?' The throaty voice sounded particularly self-confident.

'Oh, fine. You know. Look, ridiculous, I know, but I can't get hold of Tom and Poppy just said something – well, about a holiday? With you?'

'Oh, yes. Did Tom mention it to her? Or you? Good. Yes, we talked about it the other day. You know I'm trying to help him with this client? We had lunch together, the three of us, and he said you had nothing planned. I'd be so utterly thrilled if it could be arranged. We all would.'

'Yes,' said Octavia, 'yes, I expect you would. How very – thoughtful of you, Lauren. Well, I'll have to get back to you.'

She put the phone down and thought for a minute, then she picked it up again, and dialled Gabriel Bingham's number.

'Gabriel,' she said, 'Gabriel, how would you like to spend a few days in Barbados with me?'

Zoë pushed her card into the cash machine. She had had an idea. If she asked for ten pounds at a time, all over the place, it would probably give them to her. Stupid to have thought a hundred would get shunted out. But if her account was only, say, seventy over the limit, it might easily let her have ten. It didn't.

'Refer to Lloyds Bank,' it said firmly.

She went into a branch of Lloyds with her cheque book: wrote out a cheque for fifty pounds. The girl smiled at her, passed her card through a machine, looked at it, tried again, then said, still smiling very nicely, 'I'm sorry, Miss Muirhead, your account seems to be over the limit.'

She was very nice; Zoë hated her.

Shit, what was she going to do? She asked Romilly, who was in a foul mood and said she had hardly money at all; she got a quarter of Zoë's allowance, and she needed what was left for a top for Saturday.

Maybe she could sell something. She looked through her jewellery; there was a necklace, left her by her grandmother, an elaborate thing on a gold chain, an opal spider crawling after a ruby fly. She hated it; maybe she could sell that. No one would ever know.

She went into a shop whose sign read, 'Antique and modern jewellery. Turn your unwanted trinkets into cash.'

She went in, offered them her necklace. The man said he'd take it off her hands for fifteen pounds.

'Fifteen pounds?' said Zoë. 'That's outrageous. It's real gold. Those are real rubies.'

'Yes, but totally unfashionable. I'd be doing you a real favour at that price. I mean – frankly, it is interesting, but it's not pretty. Spiders and that. Tell you what, I'll make it twenty.'

'No, you won't,' said Zoë. Even in her panic and misery, she wasn't prepared to sell for that. She took it home again, and threw it into her jewellery box. It really was the end of the line. Unless of course she asked her mother. And maybe, just maybe, if her A-level results – due at the end of this week – were good, she'd agree . . .

It was not like Nico Cadogan to be nervous; his supreme self-confidence, so much part of his charm, was virtually unshakable. But a few people could at least cause it to tremble a little. His dentist was one; his ex-housemaster at his prep school, who had bullied him mercilessly, another. His ex-wife was certainly of their number.

'Good Lord,' he said now, and nearly dropped the telephone. 'Portia, my dear. How are you?'

'Perfectly well, Nico, thank you. And you?'

'Yes, I'm fine. Thank you.'

'I wondered if we could meet,' she said. 'To discuss something.'

'Yes, of course. Is it something important?'

'Quite important. Certainly for you.'

'Well, no time like the present. Tea?'

'No, I'm afraid I can't possibly manage anything until Monday. Monday morning, about eleven, would suit me.'

'Well, I'm not sure. I'll have to check—'

'I know what that means, Nico. I'll come to your office. Good afternoon to you.' She rang off.

Nico sat staring at the telephone. 'What on earth could that be about?' he said.

'Aubrey, there is a God,' said Tom. He had just walked into Aubrey's office and sat down heavily. 'The Drapers have come back. Just like that.'

'Good God!'

'Yes. They've bought some poor sod out, some other provincial newspaper chain or other, and they need help.'

'How extraordinary. Are you sure? They're not just talking?'

'No. I have to go and see them next week, it's all fixed, with a contract. Incredible.' He paused and grinned. 'All we need now is Oliver Nichols, and we're home and dry. God! Should I ring Nichols, do you think, while the fates seem to be on our side? I think I will. I feel bullish for the first time in weeks.'

'Up to you, old chap.'

'I think I will,' said Tom and dialled Oliver Nichols' number.

He wasn't in his office: 'He's gone out to meet someone, Mr Fleming. But I can get him on his mobile, if it's important.'

'Oh, don't do that,' said Tom. 'It can wait.'

'He did say if anyone phoned, I could call him. He doesn't usually leave the office at this time.'

'Well, if it's really okay . . .'

Five minutes later, she called back. Oliver Nichols was at the Connaught, in the American Bar. He said why didn't Tom go down and join him. He had a few more points he'd like to run past him.

'He said I could give you his mobile number, Mr Fleming, you can call him yourself.'

That was good: that was very good. Someone who wasn't even yet a client, giving you their mobile number. Tom felt the great surging wave of ease that had been lifting him all afternoon gather speed, hurl him further forward still.

He dialled Nichols' number; he could hear the hum of the bar in the background.

'Oh, Tom, hi. Yes, do come on round if you like. I've got – oh, sorry, got to go. Been ticked off by the *oberführer* here. Switching right off now, sir. See you in a bit, Tom.'

As Tom walked into the American Bar, amused as always that even on so brilliant a summer day, the management should see fit to set their clients down in a book-lined, winter-dark library, complete with paintings of rather odd-looking dogs, he saw Oliver Nichols sitting in the furthest corner, on the sofa next to the bar. He was with Lauren Bartlett.

'Gin and tonic, Mum! At this time of day. What is this new man doing to you?' Zoë grinned at her, pulled a can of Coke out of the fridge.

'What new man?' said Marianne. 'And it isn't gin and tonic. It's mineral water.' She tried hard not to sound defensive.

'Mum! We're not *that* stupid. Of course there's a new man. You look great, it's nice. Much better for you than Felix. Nice watch! Present?'

'Well – yes. As a matter of fact.'

'Tiffany,' said Zoë to Romilly, tapping the side of her nose. 'Rich, that's good.'

'Not specially,' said Marianne. 'Just generous.'

'Uh-huh. Nice, isn't it, Rom?'

'Very nice,' said Romilly politely.

She looked pale, Marianne thought; a flash of alarm went through her. Maybe she was ill, maybe she shouldn't go . . .

'Romilly, darling, are you all right?'

'I am absolutely fine,' said Romilly. 'I wish everyone would stop treating me like an invalid. I feel extremely well.'

'Nervous still? About the session on Saturday?'

'I'm not nervous,' she said, 'not in the least. Alix Stefanidis said he was very pleased with the early shots. Ritz phoned to tell me.'

'Good. Well, now I want to talk to you about the weekend.'

'Oh, yeah? Off with him? Where you going this time? Paris? Venice?'

'No, we're going to Glasgow.'

'Glasgow? Oh, please! The man clearly has no soul,' said Zoë.

'Glasgow is a very beautiful city,' said Marianne. 'You'd love it – it's full of Charles Rennie Mackintosh.'

'Yeah? Maybe I should come too. I'd like that. Okay, Mum, only joking.'

'You'd be very welcome,' said Marianne briskly.

'Yeah, right. No thanks. Never did like being a gooseberry. But yes, if that's your thing.'

'Only if I know you are all all right.'

'Oh, God,' said Zoë, 'this again. Rom, when are you leaving kindergarten, moving up to Form One? I'm taking my exam to my prep next week.'

'Zoë, darling, please. I just want to know you're going to be all right.'

'I'll be partying, I hope. Results tomorrow, you know. God, you're a bad mother. You'd forgotten all about them, hadn't you?'

'Oh, Zoë. How awful, I'm so sorry, darling, when will you—'

'We're going to meet about midday. With Lucy and so on. Then we'll hit the town. You won't see me for a long time. Whatever they're like.'

'But you will let me know?'

'Mum, of course I'll let you know. Don't be ridiculous.'

'Romilly, darling, what about you?'

'Oh, I'll be with Fenella. She's specially asked me this weekend, her granny's coming to stay. Really wild.'

'At least I won't have to worry about you. So you're both quite happy about it?'

'Yes, of course we are,' said Zoë. 'Want to tell us about the new boyfriend now?'

'Only that he's very nice and I think you'll like him,' said Marianne, smiling at them, feeling herself relax.

*

'Tom, come and sit down.' Oliver Nichols beamed. 'Drink? We're on dry martinis, they make the best in London here. I'm not usually out at this time, but Lauren and I had a little tryst, only don't ever tell my rather strict secretary. It's Jodie's birthday next week and I needed some help with her present. It's the big four-o, so it had to be good. Lauren took me to Tiffany's.' He indicated the bag on the seat next to him. 'Gold heart on a chain, you might have seen them. Very pretty indeed.'

Tom looked at it, at that bag, in that unmistakable turquoise colour, caught a glimpse of the box inside, the same colour, tied up with white ribbon, and was transported with hideous, heart-churning accuracy and speed back to the night at the hotel, when he had told Louise finally that the affair was over. He had given her that gold heart on that chain, in that self-same box, tied in that self-same ribbon, and set into that self-same bag; he looked at it, and he could see her lovely face, hear her small cries of joy, as she pulled it out of the box, watched her putting it on her long, slender neck, felt her kisses as she thanked him, smelt her perfume again, and then, God, the next vision, Louise, naked except for the heart, lying, holding out her arms to him on the bed, her beautiful, responsive body wonderfully, sweetly ready for him; and then finally, Christ, her face swollen with tears, ugly now, her voice wailing, dreadful with grief, telling him she couldn't bear it, she wouldn't bear it, that he must—

'Tom? You all right, my dear chap?'

'Oh – yes. Sorry.' Tom managed to smile. He felt very dizzy, almost faint. 'Had a bit of a day, no lunch.'

'Maybe you'd better not have a martini, then,' said Lauren briskly. 'Michael, could we have some mineral water, please?'

'I'll be fine,' said Tom, managing to smile at her. 'I want my martini. And some of those crisps will help.'

'Just the same, you must drink the water first. Here. Now are you sure you're all right?'

'I'm absolutely sure. Yes. Thanks. So sorry. Very pretty, those hearts. Your wife will be thrilled.'

'Bloody well better be. Yes, you do look better. Doesn't he, Lauren?'

'He looks wonderful,' said Lauren, smiling, her eyes moving over his face, down his body, 'as always. Lovely suit, Tom.'

'Thanks. Little Paul Smith number,' said Tom lightly.

'God, I wish Drew would get himself some decent clothes. He'd wear suits from Marks and Spencer if he had his way.'

'He always looks perfectly smart to me,' said Tom, 'and banking maybe isn't quite the place for Paul Smith.'

'Of course it is. When you're the chairman, surely you can wear what you like.'

'Maybe,' said Oliver Nichols. 'Look, Lauren, I don't want to keep you, I'm sure you're busy. I have a few details to go over with Tom, so . . .'

'I'm not busy at all,' said Lauren, crossing one long brown leg over the other and smiling at them. 'My children are out with the nanny, my husband is in Munich, I would be sitting twiddling my thumbs at home if it wasn't for you two. So may I stay? I'll be very good and I won't interrupt. I love business talk. It's so sexy.'

Oliver Nichols looked at her and grinned; then he turned to Tom. 'She might be disappointed, but let's try. Now look, I like your proposals very much. Your fees are high, but they're comparable with other firms, the top ones, that is, I checked them out. I liked your partner. Just two straight questions. One is that I feel we might have a clash of interests with Axfords and—'

'No clash of interest,' said Tom bluntly. 'They've resigned their account.'

Nichols' eyes on him were probing, very direct. 'Why was that?'

'We had just reached the end of the line.'

'I see. That leads me to the second question. I had heard, and from your father-in-law in particular, that your company had been in trouble. Was in trouble. Can you give me your absolute assurance that that is not so?'

Tom sipped his martini; he suddenly felt quite different, very steady, very confident.

'My absolute assurance, yes,' he said. 'We've signed a new account today, a big one, we have a new injection of capital and I'm very happy to give you bankers' references. And I would never, ever, allow anyone to sign up with us, if I wasn't totally confident that we had the substructure to support them.'

Slightly less steady then; a few more crisps might help. He was aware Lauren was watching him, had anticipated his need, had passed him not only the crisps but a bowl of cheese biscuits as well. She said nothing, just smiled a quick, almost distant smile. He felt a slug of gratitude to her. She was being great.

There was a silence. Then Nichols said, 'Fine. Well, that's all. I really would like to work with you. I go further. I look forward to working with you. Maybe we could get together early next week, dot the i's, cross the t's and so on.'

'Yes,' said Tom, 'yes, that'd be great. Excellent.' He held out his hand, and Nichols took it. 'Thanks, Oliver. Thanks very much.'

'Thank you,' said Oliver Nichols, 'and now I really must go. Lauren, darling, thank you again. I'll let you know what Jodie says. I wanted to give her a party, but she says she has to hide away, now she's so old, so

I'm taking her to Paris for a couple of days instead. Not the best time, of course, but still.'

He stood up, bent and kissed Lauren, shook Tom's hand again. 'You finish your drink. Order a club sandwich or something, I would. I don't want my new management consultant dying on me. Very untidy.'

'I won't,' said Tom.

'I won't let him,' said Lauren.

They watched Oliver Nichols leave the bar; Tom felt, childlike, as if he could have literally stood up and floated after him. He had done it; he was not a failure, not a bankrupt, he was successful again, he had money again, he was his glossy, flying, sleek self. He would enjoy this, savour it, drink it in. Just for a while, he would allow himself to shed his guilt over Louise, his anguish over Octavia, the grisly misery of a divorce. He smiled at Lauren. She was smiling at him too, leaning against the back of the sofa. She was wearing a black linen suit with a very short skirt. Her eyes were very blue, and how had he never noticed the mole perfectly placed on the crest of her bosom? His dislike and suspicion of her seemed suddenly very unjust. She had worked this for him, hustled tirelessly away, and he could only feel grateful, deeply pleased with her.

'You are a wonderful girl,' he said. 'I have you and you alone to thank for that.' She shifted, imperceptibly, in her seat; Tom found her body suddenly pressed, albeit lightly, against his. She smelt wonderful: of something rich and raw. It was the same scent he hated on Octavia; funny, that it should suit Lauren so well.

'I think I owe you a bottle of champagne,' he said, 'at the very least.'

'That'll do for a start,' she said.

CHAPTER 36

Ridiculous, really. That just three letters should be so extremely dangerous. Should spell longterm the end of any truly high hopes, short term the triggering of intense wrath and disappointment.

'Zo! That them? What'd you get?'

'DDE,' said Zoë, very quickly.

'Ah,' said Romilly.

At least she wasn't pretending to be bright about it, to say, 'Well, that's not too bad.'

'Yeah. Exactly.'

'What was the E?'

'Geography.'

'So D for English.'

'Yup. Shit, Rom, why was I so stupid about it? I could have got a B for that, if I'd worked. Why didn't I, what the fuck was I doing, why did I think it didn't matter?' She was crying now, tears of panic rather than misery.

'Zoë, don't cry. It's not that bad.' Her pale face was earnest, the huge green eyes wide and anxious.

'What am I going to do? How am I going to tell Mum? She'll be so upset. And as for Dad . . .'

'Just tell them,' said Romilly. 'She's all over the place today anyway, with her weekend and everything. Tell her you're sorry, tell her you'll retake, tell her you know you've been stupid.'

'Yes. Yes, I suppose you're right . . .'

'I really don't think I can come,' said Marianne. Her voice was shaky.

Nico, accustomed to her cool, was alarmed. 'Why not? What's happened?'

'Mayhem's broken out here. Zoë's A-levels are appalling, and I do mean appalling, and she's very upset. I feel absolutely wretched.'

'All the more reason for a break for you.'

'Nico, I have to be here. Alec is going to go mad when he hears.'

'With you?'

'Oh, yes,' said Marianne, 'with me. It will be my fault. My fault for not overseeing Zoë, making her work – probably quite right.'

'What an appalling load of rubbish,' said Nico. 'I may not be a parent, but I do have godchildren. I do know that you can lead those little fillies to the fountains of knowledge but you can't make them drink at it. Zoë is a wilful, lazy, silly girl who hasn't done any work. Locking her in her bedroom wouldn't have changed that. In any way. You have the decency and the wisdom to treat her like an adult; she's behaved like the adult she can see now she doesn't want to be. She might be just young enough to learn lessons from it. Any other problems?'

'Yes. Romilly's photographic session has been postponed to the Saturday. So I really should—'

'Marianne, as I understand it, Romilly has legs and a tongue in her head, she can hire a taxi and get herself to her photo session. Her sister could go with her, if you're really worried about it, as a small token of her contrition. That's my view of all this, as a non-father. Now will you please go and put some clothes, as few as possible, into a bag, and I'll send the car at five as arranged.'

Marianne said yes quite meekly, and put the phone down without saying another word. It was a long time since anyone had told her so clearly what she should do and made her feel she should do it.

It was a great pity Nico Cadogan had never been a father. He would clearly have been a very good one; and moreover one after her very own heart . . .

'I'm going to Barbados for a few days,' said Octavia. 'To stay at the cottage. While you're in Tuscany, you understand, with the twins. And Mrs Bartlett.'

Tom turned to her; he had been up and working at his desk since six. He was very pale. There was a heavy bruise and a swelling on the side of his forehead.

'Octavia, I do wish we could talk about this.'

'I really don't think there's anything to talk about. I'm clearly not mistaken. That's where you're going and who you're going with.'

There was a long silence; then he said, very quietly, 'So you seem to have decided.'

'Good. Well, then, we shall both have a break. We both need it. When we're back, there will obviously be a great deal of discussion, about the future. When are you leaving?'

'We're going tonight!' It was Poppy, her eyes shining, rucksack in tow. 'Lauren – Camilla says we're to call her Lauren – she said we had to be at Camilla's house at six. It's so exciting, going at night!'

'Yes, I suppose it is,' said Octavia, and walked out of the room.

Tom looked after her helplessly. He could have tried to explain, but he had reached a level of emotional exhaustion that made even uttering the simplest sentence daunting.

He had been very stupid the previous night. Very stupid indeed. But somehow, it had been so good, just for once, to be having fun, not sitting out of control on an endless hellish rollercoaster of misery and guilt and anxiety and fear.

They had drunk the bottle of champagne at the Connaght, he and Lauren, and she had been very sweet, very flattering (but not over so), had made him feel better about himself, albeit briefly. She had been quite tactful too, not tried to pump him about Octavia, about what, if anything, had gone wrong; it was only when she said that she supposed he needed to be getting back to Octavia that he had suddenly found himself telling her at least something of what had happened. Not the grisly detail, of course, not the really bad things: just that he had had an affair, that Octavia had found out.

'Well, we all have to deal with these things,' Lauren had said lightly, and 'Do we?' he had said, his voice infinitely heavier.

'Yes, of course. God, it's hardly realistic, is it, one partner for life? I mean, of course one should stay put, with the family and everything, I do feel that terribly strongly and I'm sure you will, but—' She had looked at him, the blue eyes with the heavy black lashes very serious, very concerned for once. She seemed a different person suddenly. 'You are, I presume? Staying put?'

'I want to,' he said. 'I want it very much.'

'That's what counts. The other is – well, I always think of it as shopping.'

'Shopping!' said Tom, and it was so ridiculous he laughed.

'That's nice,' she said, 'nice that you can laugh.'

'I'm sorry. Have I been such a dreary companion?'

'No, but not Tom Fleming. Not quite. Anyway, yes, shopping. I mean, life is fine for me, I live in a nice house, and I have a good husband and great kids, and we have a good time, but it's all rather predictable. I get – I don't know. A bit flat. So I go shopping. I go and buy myself things. Spend probably more than I ought to, on myself. And then I feel quite different. No more resentment at having to do what Drew and the kids want, no more boredom at entertaining endless dreary clients. I take those bags home, and look at what I've given myself, and I feel special again. Ready for anything. For a bit. Does that sound crazy?'

'Not really,' Tom had said. It was a philosophy so totally at odds with Octavia's ascetic, almost puritanical approach to life, he had found it hard to comprehend. It had a certain charm.

'Well, anyway, that's what I do. And having lunch or whatever, with lovely men, makes me feel the same. Sort of – soothed.'

'I see.'

'Trouble is,' she had said carefully, not really looking at him, 'it can get a bit out of control. The shopping. I mean, I do more than I mean to.'

'And the lunches?'

'Yes, sometimes. One minute it's flirting, the next it's – well, danger. Serious. Huge.'

'Yes,' said Tom. 'Yes, that's exactly right.'

'But still fun. Still making you feel better.'

He was silent.

'Would I be right in thinking that's what happened to you?' she said. 'Thin ice, and all that?'

'Yes, very thin ice. I should never have got on the pond, though, I'm not trying to make excuses.'

'Tom,' said Lauren, 'from where I'm sitting you're a great husband. You back Octavia in that career of hers – how many men are big enough to do that? – you've been incredibly loyal to her and—'

'Don't,' he said, and to his horror there were tears in his eyes, 'don't talk about loyalty, Lauren. I'm afraid I don't know the meaning of the word.'

'Oh, of course you do,' she said, 'you just slipped a bit. On that ice. You wouldn't be feeling so bad, if you weren't so loyal. God, you know what I'd like to do now, I feel so terribly drunk and hot?'

'No,' he said, smiling at her, happy to be having fun again.

'I'd like to go and swim. At the Harbour Club. Lovely! Come with me. And then maybe another drink and then we should probably go off to our respective families. How does that sound?'

Tom heard himself saying it sounded wonderful.

They had gone to the Harbour Club; it was fairly quiet. Half London was away. He had hired a swimsuit, walked through to the pool, arrived just in time to see Lauren diving in, her slender body and long legs one perfect arch. She resurfaced, swam over to him with an efficient crawl.

'It's heaven. Come on, just what we need.'

He swam for a while; she was right. He felt sober suddenly, sober and exhilarated at the same time. 'This is such a good idea,' he said.

'I have a lot of good ideas.'

'Yes, it seems you do.'

She pulled herself up on to the side. Her body was intriguing: slim, but very strong, her breasts, with the tantalising mole, full and high, her stomach board-flat, the swelling of her pubic mound sweetly full, the skin smoothly and perfectly tanned. A pampered body, with time and money clearly lavished on it; a body to be looked at and admired. It was there for that purpose, and the purpose made it sexier. Much sexier.

Afterwards they sat drinking spritzers: 'Almost harmless,' said Lauren, smiling at him again. 'Like our evening.'

'Yes,' he had said, determinedly firm, 'yes, that's exactly right.'

She had kicked her shoes off, tucked one leg underneath her. Her extremely short skirt just failed to reveal her knickers. It was hard, Tom found, not to check that it hadn't succeeded. She caught him doing that once or twice and smiled at him: a slow, confident smile. She was extraordinarily sexy.

'Well,' she had said, finally, setting her glass down, 'enough shopping for one day. I must get back.'

He had been surprised; surprised and relieved. This was enough: he wanted no more. He had the stomach for no more, and certainly not the sexual energy. But it had been a wonderfully soothing, revitalising encounter.

'Now look,' she had said, 'I suppose there's no possible chance you could come to Tuscany for a few days, get the kids settled in? I know we could find you a corner.'

'No chance,' he said. 'Very sadly.'

They had parted at the entrance with the lightest of kisses; her mouth was very warm, very inviting. It had been quite hard not to prolong it. Suddenly, as she turned away, he had pulled her back towards him, gave her a hug. No more than a hug.

'Thank you, Lauren,' he said, 'for everything. You've saved my sanity tonight. And not just tonight, with fixing Nichols for me as well. You're a great girl.'

'I'm just pleased you feel better,' she said, and jumped into her car, drove it off rather fast. It was a bright red BMW. Very sexy, very much of a statement, very Princess of Wales.

He had got home at about nine. Octavia had looked at him with an icy dislike. Tom's warmth, his sense of wellbeing, had shrivelled.

'Where have you been?' she said. 'With Mrs Bartlett, perhaps? Planning your holiday?'

'No,' he said. 'No, of course not.'

'Well, who have you been with?'

'I . . .'

'Tom, I don't actually care, obviously, but it would have been helpful to know. I've been trying to find you. I do have things to do for the children, you know. Aubrey said the last time he saw you you were off to the Connaught.'

'Yes. Yes, that's true.'

'With?'

'Oh, for Christ's sake,' he said, 'it was a business meeting. With Oliver Nichols.'

'Ah. Mrs Bartlett's friend.'

'Yes.'

'And was she there? Please, don't lie to me.'

'Yes,' he said, very quietly, 'yes, she was there. As a matter of fact.'

'And then?'

'Oh, Octavia, for Christ's sake! This is ridiculous.'

'In a way, yes, I agree. Ridiculous and even amusing. I can't quite believe it, that you're starting again so soon, but—'

'Octavia, I am not starting again, as you put it. I'm trying to sort our life out.'

'Tom, I have no intention of sharing a life with you, let alone Lauren Bartlett. Anyway, let's not talk about her any more, shall we? I find the subject intensely wearying.'

'You started it,' he said. His headache was growing worse. 'All she has done is helped me. Largely thanks to her I've got Fleming Cotterill back on a safer footing. And this evening we—'

'Yes? We? You were together?'

'Oh, fuck off,' he said. He suddenly had a vision of Lauren, smiling, warm, sexy, making excuses for him; looked at Octavia, so thin, miserable, shrewish, sending him back to his own small piece of purgatory, and wanted to hurt her.

'Yes, we were together. She at least seemed to think I wasn't the devil incarnate. It was nice – just for a moment.'

'Well, I'm so pleased for you,' she had said, and her voice was rich and thick with disgust. 'So very pleased. It must be so awful to feel bad about yourself. Whatever filthy things you've done. No, that's really marvellous, Tom. I must ring her and say thank you. Well, clearly you'll be very happy on this jaunt to Tuscany. The children are beside themselves with excitement. Camilla's been on the phone to Poppy. I'm so sorry I can't come too.'

'Octavia. I am not—' he said and caught her arm, but she swung her hand up and hit him, very very hard on the side of the head. It really hurt; rage gave her strength. He sat down abruptly, the stinging pain confusing him, adding to the throbbing headache. She looked at him, picked up a book from the table and hit him in the same place again with it.

'I hate you,' she said. 'For everything you've done, but this most of all. It's disgusting. Disgusting. I wish you well of her, Tom. I'm going to bed. As soon as I get back from Barbados, I'm going to take the children and move into my father's house. There's at least a code of honour of some sort there.'

That did it; that made him so angry he couldn't talk to her any more. Didn't want to try to explain, hadn't the strength.

'Oh, just go,' he said wearily. 'Why don't you go tonight, at once? I'll help you pack.'

But she said nothing, just walked out of the room.

Tom sat down at the table, and buried his head in his arms.

'Oh, bloody hell,' said Lyndsay Forbes to her husband, as she pulled aside the blind of their room at the Loew's Harbour Cove Hotel on Paradise Island, Bahama. 'It's raining again. Tim, why don't we try and get a flight back today? Three weeks is enough for anyone, and it's been great, but I'd like to go home now. I'm missing my lovely new house, and anyway, I want to see what they've done. Please? Sweetie?'

Tim Forbes, who was also extremely tired of watching the Bahamian rain fall, as it had in interminable stormy bursts for the past four days, said that he would see what he could do.

Gabriel Bingham wasn't sure if he really wanted to go to Barbados or not. He wanted to be with Octavia, and the thought of being with her, away from everything else – her children, her work, her household, her clients, and the husband who seemed to be consuming her now in a fire of hatred and rage – was extremely attractive. He had somehow managed to fall in love with her, to be in love with her, while hardly knowing her at all. The thought of being able to talk to her, learn about her, trace her tortuous past, and help her disentangle her troubled present was engaging. He also found her intensely sexually desirable.

The problem was Barbados.

Gabriel didn't like the sun and he didn't like lying on white, palm-fringed beaches, which was what he imagined he would be doing; he became bored swiftly. He liked doing things, and he liked them to be English things: walking in the wind and the rain, sitting in the pub, working in the garden, reading by the fire.

And there was another alarming element to the venture; it meant a modicum, at least, of shopping. The only garments in Gabriel's wardrobe that could have been regarded as remotely suitable for a hot holiday of any kind were his rather baggy swimming trunks which he had had at school, and his even baggier khaki shorts. And then he possessed a few T-shirts, and his old plimsolls. It was clearly not enough.

Shopping was to Gabriel what the dentist was to most people: something to be dreaded. Gabriel sighed and got out his bicycle, which was by far the best mode of transport in Bath, and made for Marks & Spencers.

On that hot August day there was very little available; no shorts in his size at all, only some rather lurid purple and yellow swimming trunks, which he bought two pairs of, a pair of brown leather sandals which he didn't like, but bought because they fitted him – and a small range of short-sleeved shirts in colours as lurid as the swimming trunks. He bought a couple of them as well. There were no white T-shirts, which were the only ones he really liked, but he found a beige one and a bright turquoise; and then, warming to his task, decided to buy a panama hat as a protection against the sun. The only ones left were slightly too big, but he felt that was all right. Nothing worse than a too-small hat.

The flight was out of Heathrow at midday on the Saturday, Sarah Jane told him, when he rang to check. 'British Airways. You can go through the express check-in, so you don't need to get there quite so early.'

'How come?' said Gabriel.

'Oh, club class perk,' she said. 'And you get your visa when you get out there.'

Gabriel felt his stomach lurch rather uncomfortably. He had no idea how much club class would cost, but he knew he couldn't afford it.

'I – that is – when will Octavia be back?'

'In about an hour. Shall I get her to call you?'

'Yes, please.'

She phoned at three thirty. 'Hi,' she said.

'Octavia, I'm sorry, but I can't afford club class,' said Gabriel. 'I'll go tourist.'

'You can't. There aren't any seats.'

'Well, I can't go, then. I'm sorry. I really don't have two and a half thousand pounds. Not to spend on five days, anyway.'

'Gabriel, this is on me.'

'Oh, no!' he said. 'No, I'm sorry. Bollinger Socialist or not, I don't like being paid for. I won't be paid for.'

She sighed. 'Oh, dear. This is all coming out wrong. Listen. My father has this cottage there, okay? He likes it used. He specially likes it used by me. His company just buys the tickets for me when I want them. It doesn't cost him anything, it's – well, think of it as a sort of tax dodge.'

'I don't approve of tax dodges,' he said, 'as you should know.'

She was silent.

'If it was for your husband or your kids, I can see that would be all right. But it's not for me. I think maybe I'd better not come.'

'Oh, shit, Gabriel.' Her voice wobbled; she sounded almost frightened. 'You've got to come! I can't bear it. Please. Please don't be silly about it. My dad has so much money, he doesn't know what to do with it. Those tickets are – well, they're like buying a packet of Kleenex to him. Think of it like that, using his Kleenex.'

'I never use Kleenex,' he said, 'sorry,' and put the phone down.

Ten minutes later it rang again; it was Melanie. 'Look,' she said, 'don't be an arsehole.'

'I'm sorry?'

'Making her miserable over some fucking stupid principles. Just swallow them, Gabriel. Her old man's an evil manipulative bugger. He's also as rich as Croesus. He's doing something good for her for once. Let him, for Christ's sake. Don't be so bloody – male.'

This was clearly to her the ultimate insult; Gabriel found himself smiling, reluctantly. 'Okay,' he said, after a moment. 'Okay, put her on.'

Not for the first time, after he had said, just a little shortly, that he was sorry, and he'd see her at the airport next day, he felt a pang of sympathy for Tom Fleming.

The phone call had come from Alec. Cold, reproachful, lined in venom. How had it happened that Zoë had been allowed to do no work, had she been out partying all summer, why hadn't Marianne been in touch with her teachers, why had Zoë fallen so short of her predicted BBC? Marianne said she had no idea; she knew there was no point defending herself or Zoë.

'Well, I'll have a very serious talk with her next week. She can't be allowed to get away with this. No Sydney, obviously, she'll have to go to a crammer, do retakes. And she must understand, absolutely no going out, no seeing her friends even, until she's got herself in order. I think, too, I should stop her allowance with immediate effect.'

'Alec! You can't punish her like that. She's eighteen years old.'

'It's not a punishment. It's an attempt at discipline. Which you should have made yourself, I might say. I can't believe you've been quite so stupid about her. And so – neglectful.'

'Alec! That is outrageous.'

'I'm sorry. I don't think so. I've always trusted you, Marianne. To deal with the children, to oversee their lives. It seems I was wrong.'

She said nothing.

'Well,' he said finally, 'I'll meet the girls at Kennedy as arranged on Monday. How is Romilly? Over that nonsense, I hope?'

'Romilly's fine,' said Marianne very firmly. 'Goodbye, Alec.' And she put the phone down.

Octavia looked at her watch. It was already after five. Even if she left at once, she'd be lucky to get to Phillimore Gardens by six, which was the time Caroline was taking the children up to the Bartletts' house. Shit! She wasn't going to make it. Wasn't going to be able to say goodbye to them. Maybe if—

'So would that be a possibility, Mrs Fleming?' Margaret Piper's voice pushed into her consciousness. 'Is there any future in that one?'

'Oh – yes. Yes, I'm sure there is, Mrs Piper.'

'Good. Because I really don't want to be let down again. I was bitterly disappointed in you over Mr Carlton. Now look, I have here the budgets for next year, if we could just run over them now, and then—'

'I wonder if I could take them with me, Mrs Piper? I think they need a really careful examination.'

'Well, I'm afraid I see no reason why they shouldn't have that now, Mrs Fleming. I am in no hurry. In fact rather the reverse. I'm having dinner with my brother in town. So . . .'

'Yes, of course. Er – could you excuse me just one moment?'

She half ran out of the office, put her head round Melanie's door. 'Mells! Is there any chance at all you could take over my meeting with Mrs Piper? She wants to go over the budgets for next year now and—'

'Reasonable, I'd have thought,' said Melanie, 'given how we've had to mess her around recently.' Her expression was hard; Octavia winced.

'Yes, of course. And I would do it. But – well, the children are about to go away. I promised to go home to see them off.'

'Look, Octavia. I appreciate that you have your familial duties to attend to. I also appreciate that you're very tired and you've had an extremely difficult time recently. That's why I've agreed to manage without you next week. But I would point out that we are hanging on to the Cultivate account with our rather chewed fingernails. It's *your* account, it's *your* fault we've nearly lost it, so just get the fuck back in there, would you, and do your job. Thanks.'

Octavia stared at Melanie in a frozen silence; then she said, 'Yes, of course,' and phoned Caroline to say she'd try to make it to the Bartletts' to say goodbye, but meanwhile to go on there without her. Caroline said she would, sounding as cold and as hostile as Melanie. And as Gabriel. She didn't seem to be doing very well altogether, Octavia thought, walking back into her office and sitting down to Mrs Piper's budgets. If she didn't pull herself together soon, she wouldn't have anything at all.

*

'Bye, Mum,' said Zoë, as Marianne appeared at the bottom of the stairs, holding her leather Gladstone bag, her slightly embarrassed expression clearly indicating she was about to leave for her weekend. 'Have a great time.'

'Thank you, darling,' said Marianne. 'Thank you very much. Now you will keep an eye on Romilly tomorrow, won't you, take her to the session and so on?'

'I promise, Mum.'

'Thank you.' The doorbell rang. 'That'll be the car now. I must go. 'Bye, Zoë, I'll see you on Sunday night. You've got my number in Glasgow, haven't you?'

'Yes, Mum. Er – Mum, could you – could you possibly lend me a hundred pounds. *Please?*'

Zoë very seldom saw her mother angry; it wasn't her style. She was angry now.

'I really can't quite believe you said that, Zoë. Of course I won't lend you a hundred pounds. I actually wouldn't lend you ten at the moment. You have simply got to learn some self-discipline – you failed your exams because you never exert any. You have a perfectly adequate allowance, and if it doesn't cover your extravagant requirements, then you must change them. In any case, I imagine you want the money to go out celebrating, and I think even you must realise you have absolutely nothing to celebrate. So – sorry, but no. Goodbye.'

And she was gone, without even a kiss.

Zoë sat down and burst into tears.

'Okay, hon,' said Tim Forbes, coming into the bar where Lyndsay was reading a rather elderly *Vogue*. 'We leave early in the morning. Home to sunny old England. It's eighty over there apparently. We'll get to Heathrow about nine, local time. Home by midnight. How does that sound?'

Octavia dialled the Bartlett house; a foreign voice answered. Lauren would have a Filipino, exploitative bitch.

'This is Mrs Fleming. Mrs Tom Fleming. Could I speak to Mrs Bartlett, please?'

'Oh – I am sorry, Mrs Bartlett has gone. And the children.'

'To the airport?'

'Yes, to the airport. They were delayed, the taxi did not come. But Mr Fleming, your children's father, yes?'

'Yes,' said Octavia, 'yes, that is correct.'

'Mrs Fleming, he arrived and so they have all gone together. So there was no more problem.'

'No. No, I see. No, absolutely no more problem. Well, thank you.'

As Zoë had done, half an hour earlier, Octavia too sat down and burst into tears.

'Tom, hi!'

It was Bob Macintosh; Tom had rarely been so pleased to see anyone in his entire life. Waving the children off through Departures, seeing them hardly glance backwards, had left him feeling totally alone and very bleak. He had planned to have dinner with Aubrey, but Aubrey's father wasn't well and wanted to see him. So he had seemed destined to an evening at Phillimore Gardens alone with an icy Caroline, and an even icier Octavia: the only mitigating circumstance being that Octavia would be forced finally to concede he wasn't actually in Tuscany with Lauren Bartlett.

He turned and took Bob's outstretched hand like a drowning man reaching for a log. 'Bob! Good to see you.'

'What are you doing here?'

'Oh, just seen the kids off on holiday. Going home on my own.'

'No Octavia?'

'No, she's – working late.'

'Great. Come and have dinner with me. I'm on my own tonight as well. Maureen's at some absurd hen night, one of her friends is getting married. We're staying at the Berkeley, we could eat there. Bloody good restaurant. How does that sound?'

'It sounds magnificent,' said Tom.

'Darling, why don't you come and have dinner with me tonight? There are a few things I'd like to go over with you, things I want you to tell Elvira and—'

'Daddy, I can't. Honestly. It's my last night with Minty for a week, and I really really want to be with her. I've missed saying goodbye to the twins as it is.'

'Oh – very well.' He sounded disappointed. 'I'd have thought she'd be asleep by now anyway. And you can see her in the morning.'

Octavia hesitated; it was a serious temptation, she was so tired, so dispirited. And she needed to talk to him about the sponsorship of Cultivate. But she was going to miss Minty terribly; it was her last chance to be with her.

'No, really. I'm sorry. I'll call you about the cottage.'

'Very well.' He was clearly disappointed.

She phoned the house; a rather brisk Caroline informed her that Minty was already asleep. 'Absolutely exhausted, Octavia. And rather upset at the twins being away. I certainly don't think you should wake her.'

Octavia assured her she would do no such thing, and phoned her father back. The thought of an evening alone with a hostile Caroline was hideous.

'Is the invitation still open? Apparently Minty's already asleep. Had my hand slapped by Caroline very hard. Metaphorically.'

'My darling, of course you can. Nothing would give me more pleasure. Do you want to go out, or shall I get Mrs Harrington to cook something special?'

'It's a bit late for that, surely.'

'Well, she could do you some fish, or some steak. What would you fancy?'

Octavia didn't fancy anything; the thought of food made her feel sick, but it seemed churlish to say so. She had an inspiration. 'Tell you what I'd like. Fish pie – that wouldn't be very difficult, would it?'

'Fish pie, eh? Our favourite. Of course not. Plenty of fish in the freezer. Might not be ready till nine.'

'That's fine. I might not be there till nine.'

It really was too bad, Caroline thought. Octavia had promised to see the children off and failed; Poppy in particular had clearly been upset by it. Octavia had also promised to get back that night, spend the evening with her and Minty; the poor child had hardly set eyes on her mother for days. She had been very cranky as Caroline put her to bed.

She had no idea when Tom would be back; he'd not even spoken to her at the Bartletts', except to nod at her briefly and tell her to check the children's luggage, before driving off. She didn't like the way any of it was going; her last employers had divorced, and she could see that the Flemings were hardly on steady ground at the moment. She had planned to talk to Octavia that night, try and make her understand how unsettling it all was, for her as well as the children. But now she was out with her father. Monstrous man! In Caroline's view, he was largely to blame for whatever had gone wrong with the Fleming marriage.

The phone rang: Caroline sighed, went to answer it. It was her mother.

'Darling? How are you?'

'Oh – fine. Thanks. All alone here, with Minty.'

'That's what I thought. Darling, why not bring her here for the weekend? If Mrs Fleming is willing? I'd love to have you and her, and your father's gone off sailing. What about it?'

'What a wonderful idea. And of course Octavia wouldn't mind.' She had done it several times before; taken Minty to her parents' house in the New Forest. 'I'll have to check with her, obviously, and then I'll come down first thing in the morning.'

'Splendid. I'll expect you mid-morning unless I hear to the contrary. It'll be lovely to see Minty again.'

Octavia's mobile was on message, and Felix Miller's phone picked up by an answering machine. Caroline left a slightly terse message on both to the effect that she would like to take Minty to stay with her mother and, unless she heard to the contrary, by nine in the morning, that was where she would be.

This was lovely, Felix thought, smiling at Octavia across the dining table, heaping her plate with the fish pie that had been their favourite celebration dish right through her childhood, that had been served on both their birthdays every year, on the awarding of her scholarship to Wycombe Abbey, her brilliant O- and A-level results, her 2:1 in Law – should have been a First, he knew, but he had smiled away his disappointment of course, assured her it was marvellous.

They did not, however have fish pie the night Octavia had arrived home, flushed with excitement and joy, bearing a bottle of champagne, to tell her father she had fallen in love with Tom Fleming; indeed, after that, they had never eaten it together again, until now.

It was a very special recipe, worked on and fussed over down the years by Mrs Harrington, haddock and scallops cooked in a white wine sauce with prawns under a wonderful flaky pastry lid; served always with new potatoes and Octavia's favourite vegetables, runner beans.

When she had been little, she had gobbled it up greedily, always asking for more; then as caution and concern over her figure took over, she had rationed herself carefully. That change had saddened Felix; he had loved to watch her, plump and glowing, tucking in unselfconsciously, her little round face watching him closely as he cut into the pastry, ladled the wonderful contents on to her plate. The tense teenager who had pushed her prawns on and off her fork, piled her plate high with the beans, rejected the potatoes, had been a worrying stranger.

Tonight, she was actually eating more than he had expected. 'Do you know, I'm starving,' she said as they sat down, 'I haven't eaten since breakfast.'

'Octavia, that is madness. When you work so hard, why not?'

'Oh – too busy. Frantic, you know, finishing up to go away. Dad, don't look at me like that, I'm hardly fading away.'

'I think you are actually,' he said, studying the sharp cheekbones, the thin arms.

'You can't be too rich or too thin, you should know that. It's all right, I'm only joking. No, it has been difficult lately, what with one thing and another. And I've been so upset about this Tuscany business. For some reason it seems – well, the very last straw.'

He was encouraged by that; that she should, finally, be talking in such terms. He had been so afraid she was going to accept what Tom had done, stay with him, take him back even.

'I know it doesn't alter what he's done, but it's so brutal, so – oh, I don't know. I honestly think if he'd stayed, if we could have had some time together, time to talk – well . . .' She smiled at him rather weakly.

'I'm sorry, Bob,' said Tom Fleming. He leaned forward slightly hazily across the table, put his hand over Bob's. 'Terribly, terribly sorry. To have embarrassed you. So terribly sorry.'

'Tom,' said Bob, signalling to the waiter for the bill, 'you haven't embarrassed me. Not in the least. I wish I could help more.'

'Helped a lot. Just having you to talk to. Really, really helped. Not good at talking, us men, are we, Bob? Oh, God. What a fool I am! Bloody, bloody fool. Wonderful girl like Octavia and I have to go and do that to her. I love her so much still, Bob, you know. So much.'

Half an hour later, Bob Macintosh gave a ten-pound tip to the young porter who had helped him get Tom Fleming up in the lift, and settle him on to the bed which Maureen would be occupying the following night. Then he removed Tom's shoes and tie, got into the other bed himself and lay in the darkness, listening to Tom's snores and worrying slightly that Maureen might not actually be at a hen party.

Octavia lay in bed in her room: it felt very strange. She looked round, smiling at its absurd familiarity, at the way it was so unchanged; as she had got ready for bed, she had felt almost frightened, so easily did she slip back into its rituals, putting her used underwear into the linen bag hanging on the door, showering away the strains of the day in the adjacent bathroom, pulling a cotton lawn nightdress out of the chest of drawers, opening both the windows, settling into the bed – God it was soft, so wonderfully soft, she had forgotten, opened the book she had pulled out of the bookcase. Even the bookcase was kept fresh and up to date, like the flowers; there were all her old favourites of course, but on the top shelf, her father kept a steady supply of the new novels, the bestsellers that she called junkfood reading. There was a new Maeve Binchy there: wonderful. Just what she needed. She had only just opened it when there was a knock at the door: it was her father. He was carrying a tray, with a blue and white mug on it.

'I've brought you a milky cure. I thought you needed one.'

'Dad! I'm fine.'

'Octavia, you are not fine. You practically fainted down there, when you said you were going to drive home. You're exhausted, you need taking care of. I hope this Mr Bingham of yours is going to realise that.'

'I think he will.'

'Good. Well, anyway, you drink this. It's got a dash of whisky in it, and loads of honey. And real, full cream milk.'

'Daddy, honestly. I'll put on—' She realised she was saying absolutely the wrong thing, amended it hastily. 'I'll never wake up in the morning. And I have to get packed. And anyway, I have to see Minty, we're going to be apart for a week.'

'That's all right. I'll wake you up, drive you down to the house. And then you can get a cab to the airport if that's what you prefer.'

'We'll have to be away from Phillimore Gardens by eight.'

'That's all right. Not a problem. Oh, by the way, there's a message from Caroline, the nanny.'

'Caroline? What is it, is there something wrong?'

'No, nothing. She says she would like to take Minty to stay with her mother for the weekend, and if she doesn't hear from you, she'll do that. She's left a number.'

'That's a very good idea,' said Octavia, who had been worrying about Caroline and Minty being alone in the house. 'Oh, dear, it's a bit late to ring now. Caroline does like her sleep. But I'll see her first thing of course, when we go down, won't I?'

'Yes, of course you will. I presume Caroline is to be trusted, and that her mother is a decent sort of woman?'

'Daddy, you are such an old snob. Caroline's mother is an extremely decent sort of woman, as you put it. She went to Roedean, as did Caroline.'

'Really? How extraordinary. That's all right, then. Drink that up, darling, before it gets cold. Now look, there's one thing I'd like you to do for me, out in Barbados. There's some new legislation coming in apparently, relating to property held by offshore trusts, as of course Mossaenda is. They have to be reregistered in Barbados, and subject to a transfer tax. Bloody nuisance, and probably expensive, but there it is. So you might go and see Nicholas Greenidge, find out a bit more about it, tell him I'd like to have a look at all the bumf. I could do it on the phone and so on, but it's a bit complex, and I know he'd like to see you. Would you mind?'

'Of course not. It's the least I can do. And thank you for being so positive about the sponsorship thing. You're so good to me. 'Night, Daddy.'

'Good night, my darling. It's so lovely to have you home.'

CHAPTER 37

Romilly woke up feeling sick. She looked at her clock: only half past five. Her period had finally started the night before and her stomach still hurt. But she pushed the sheet down, examined her stomach carefully – it was very satisfyingly flat. So it had all been worth it. But she did feel very odd still. She reached out for the small magnifying mirror she kept by her bed, examined her spot. Gone. Quite gone. Just a slight, dry, rough bit of skin where it had been. That couldn't be a problem. And she'd know what he meant when he told her to do things today, wouldn't be so nervous. She just wished he wouldn't call her 'little baby' all the time. It really didn't help.

Caroline was also awake. Minty had been restless and miserable all night; it had been very hot, and she was cutting a huge molar. Anyway, it was nice and cool now. And London was quiet. No traffic, anywhere. Pity they couldn't leave now for Hampshire. It would only take about an hour and a half.

She heard Minty start to whimper and went in to the nursery. Minty was standing in her cot, her small face crumpled with sleep, the tooth-cutting side livid and red.

She looked at Caroline, held out her arms. 'Up up up,' she said, imperiously.

Caroline picked her out of the cot; she smelt awful, the tooth was taking its toll on her nappies. She went into the bathroom, ran her a bath. Minty sat in it, filling and refilling the plastic beaker that was her favourite toy, her small head bent over it, intent on her task, happy and calm again.

Outside the pigeons were cooing; a small breeze had got up. It was very peaceful, it really would be an ideal time to go.

And then she thought that of course they could. Octavia hadn't rung back, so Caroline felt no obligation to wait for her. Tom had clearly done a runner, probably off with his ladyfriend, whoever she was. Why wait for the heat and the traffic to get up and subject herself to a ghastly drive with a fretful child?

Caroline picked Minty out of the bath, gave her a banana and a drink, packed a small bag for them both, wrote a polite, if cool note to Octavia, explaining what she had done, and was halfway down the M3 before Octavia had even left Hampstead.

Serena Fox had hardly slept at all. She was very upset. The affair she had been conducting with a young girl from the Paris office was beginning to go badly wrong; the girl had made it very plain that she found Serena unbearably possessive.

Serena knew she was possessive, it was her worst sin, but the girl was so very lovely and so very young; Serena knew perfectly well that at thirty-five, she was regarded by her more as a meal ticket than a lover. In a few weeks, it would be quite over, Marie France would have found someone else, and she would be alone again. It was always happening to her. And she didn't like being alone. Solitude frightened Serena, left her feeling confused and threatened.

Well, today should be fun, a distraction; she and Ritz were both going to the session with Romilly, and Ritz had even suggested dinner together. Ritz, who had an extremely aggressive heterosexual sex life, rather surprisingly enjoyed such evenings; quiet, introspective, gossipy. And she had one thing in common with Serena: she had a very low opinion of men in general, and Alix Stefanidis in particular.

Marianne lay, smiling, in Nico's arms, in the vast bed at Number One Devonshire Gardens, one of Glasgow's most beautiful hotels. She was flushed with love, with sex, with triumph, with release; happiness soared though her, winged, birdlike.

'My darling, I love you. God, I do.' He sat up on his elbow, studied her, his eyes probing her face. 'And you are so very very beautiful. And so very, very – young.'

She reached up, pulled him down again, kissed him, laughing. 'Nico, you're allowed to say I'm sexy, and I really don't mind you saying I'm beautiful, but I really can't lie here and let you call me young. It devalues the rest.'

'My darling, you are young. You're not yet forty. To me that's a child.'

'Oh, don't be silly,' said Marianne. 'And don't present yourself as an old man either, you're only forty – what?'

'Forty-six. I'm hurt that you don't remember.'

'Sorry. Anyway, of course I'm not a child, I have three grown-up children of my own.'

'That's precisely why you don't see yourself as young. Just because you went into this absurd slavery of a marriage straight from the nursery. Plenty of women of your age are having their first children these days.'

'I know. And very silly it is too, in my opinion. You find yourself dealing with teenagers when you're sixty. When you should be having grandchildren.'

'Nonsense. Absolute bloody nonsense. Imagine you with grandchildren, sitting in a rocker . . .'

'I hope I will be. Well, not sitting in a rocker, I plan to be a very fun grandmother.'

'Marianne, you have the body of a twenty-year-old, and a face your daughters no doubt envy. Do stop talking about becoming a grandmother. Look, why don't we go and climb into that enormous and rather vulgar marble bath and I'll order some coffee and we can plan our day. Or we could just lie in the bath – or possibly not even just lie there . . .'

An hour later, as she lay limp with exhaustion on the bed, he sat beside her, playing with a lock of her hair, sipping thoughtfully at a glass of orange juice.

'I love you,' he said, 'I love you very much. Tell me you love me, Marianne. Please tell me. Or tell me you think you might be beginning to at least. That's not very much to ask, surely.'

And finally, setting the past, her difficult past with Felix, more firmly in its proper place, she said, 'I think, Nico, that I might be beginning to, yes.'

'You're up early, Daddy. Are we going to see Mummy today?'

'Yes, we are. Just for a bit. Then we're going on to see that nice little girl Megan, the one in the wheelchair. I've said I'll go up to Bartles House with her, to take some photographs. You know, the one they want to pull down. And then her mummy has very kindly invited us to lunch.'

'That'll be nice. I like her mummy. She has a very good face.'

'She does, doesn't she?'

Tom woke at seven thirty feeling appalling. Bloody hell, where was he? Not at home, surely? Maybe in some hotel room – yes, in some hotel room. Jesus, he needed a pee; he swung his throbbing legs over the edge of the bed, closed his eyes again against the whirling room.

The room whirled further; better get the eyes open, then it would steady again. He opened them determinedly, and found himself staring into the kindly face of Bob Macintosh.

'God, Bob,' he said, 'what on earth have we been up to?'

And then made it to the bathroom just in time.

'I have to get home,' he said twenty minutes later, sipping alternately iced water and weak tea. 'I have to sort out this bloody mess with Octavia before she goes to Barbados. She probably still thinks I've gone to Tuscany with that wretched woman . . .'

'Oh, no!' said Octavia. 'They've gone. I wondered why she didn't answer the phone. Daddy, this is awful. I haven't even seen Minty, haven't kissed her goodbye. Oh, I feel so terrible—'

Her eyes filled with tears, staring at Caroline's terse note; she felt terribly remorseful. How could she have done that, stayed away from Minty just because she didn't want to see Caroline?

'I'm such a lousy mother,' she said. 'I don't deserve those children.'

'My darling, you're a wonderful mother. You do as much as you possibly can. More, if anything. That's why you're so exhausted. Look, Minty will have a wonderful time with Caroline and her mother, and it is only a week.'

'I know,' she said, blowing her nose, 'I know. But – well, it's too late now. I'll try and phone Caroline from the airport, she'll be at her mother's by then. I'd better go and sort out my stuff.'

It was almost eight when Tom finally phoned Phillimore Gardens, Bob Macintosh having persuaded him that attempting to get there under present circumstances was not only unwise but virtually impossible. Felix Miller answered the phone.

'Felix? Felix, it's Tom.'

'Tom? Oh, really. Where are you calling from?'

'The Mayfair Hotel.'

'The Mayfair? I thought you were in Tuscany.'

'Of course I'm not in bloody Tuscany! There never was any question of my going to Tuscany, and I need to talk to Octavia to tell her so. Is she there, Felix, can I speak to her?'

'No, Tom, I'm sorry, she's not. She's on her way to the airport. She's going to Barbados, you know. With this man Gabriel Bingham. Who, I might say, seems to have a little more respect for her than you do. I really cannot begin to tell you—'

'Yes, Felix, I know what you cannot begin to tell me. Well, I'll just have to ring her on her mobile.'

He slammed the phone down.

*

'Daddy! Was that the cab? I'm just about ready. Oh, damn, I've forgotten my sunglasses. Hang on – shit, they're in the study, I remember. I'll have to go and get them. Now what was I saying – oh, yes, was that the cab?'

'Yes,' said Felix Miller, 'yes, that was the cab. Just coming down the street now apparently. Now goodbye, my darling. Have a wonderful time. Don't worry about anything, just enjoy yourself. And eat something, every day. Promise me.'

'I promise you. I'll just get my glasses. Hold my bag, would you, just a second . . . Right. Here I am. You don't think I ought to try and get hold of Caroline, do you? Before I go?'

'No, I don't. Go on, darling, quickly, you don't want to keep the cab waiting. Here's your bag. 'Bye, sweetheart. Send your old daddy a postcard.'

'I will. Big hug.'

As the car pulled away, Octavia realised, just slightly anxiously, that she didn't after all have her mobile phone with her. Odd, she'd been so sure she'd put it in her bag. Well, too bad. It wouldn't be much use to her in Barbados. She could ring Caroline from the airport. That would be all right.

Felix Miller, left alone in the house, carefully rinsed out the coffee cups he and Octavia had been using, checked that the burglar alarm was on and all the gas taps off, and went out of the front door. Octavia's mobile phone, placed by him in the kitchen drawer under some tea towels ten minutes earlier, was still ringing intermittently as he drove down the street . . .

CHAPTER 38

Zoë looked at her watch: time she and Romilly left. She went to the bottom of the stairs and called her.

'I'm just coming.'

Romilly appeared in the hall; she was wearing a white very low-cut top, new black satin skintight trousers and high-wedge trainers, and she had tied her hair up on top of her head. She had made up her eyes with very heavy shadow and her lips with a rather dull, flat colour, outlined in heavy pencil. She looked older, less fresh; Zoë felt she was making a mistake, but didn't say so. Romilly was nervous enough already.

'How do I look?'

'Fine. Great. Really great.'

'You don't sound exactly sure.'

'Well, I suppose I'm used to how you usually look. That's all.'

'You sound like Mummy! I am just sick and tired of being seen as a silly little baby. Even the photographer calls me little baby! I'm not, I'm nearly sixteen and I just happen to have signed a very big contract with a cosmetic company. So clearly I'm not just a silly little baby. And it's time I stopped looking like one, okay?'

'Yes, Rom, okay.'

Ritz and Serena were waiting in the studio reception. Zoë liked Ritz; she was a bit less sure about Serena. She didn't actually trust either of them, but Ritz she felt was an honest rogue.

'Hallo, Zoë. Nice to see you,' said Ritz. 'Goodness, Romilly, you look very grown up.'

Zoë could tell from her voice she didn't like what she saw.

Romilly looked at her warily. 'It's only because I'm not in my school clothes.'

'Yes. Yes, of course. Well, we have a make-up artist and everything here, so we may change what you've done a bit.'

'I realise that.' Romilly's voice was just slightly irritable. 'Is Alix here?'

'No, not yet. He's going to be late, apparently. Out on the tiles last night. Anyway, we can start getting you ready. Come in here. This is Frances, she runs the studio.'

Frances was tiny, skinny, with spiked black hair; she was wearing ripped cut-offs and a top that revealed almost all her breasts. 'Hi. This way, Romilly. Jan, who's going to do your hair and make-up, has just popped out. She'll be back in a minute. Want a coffee or a Coke or anything?'

'Look,' said Zoë, 'I've just got to go and do a few things. I'll be back later. Romilly doesn't want me hanging around anyway, do you, Rom? Or shall I wait?'

'No,' said Romilly. 'I'll ring you on your mobile when we're through. I mean, we might be hours.'

Sandy looked at Louise warily. She did appear to be better. She had put on a bit of weight, there was some colour in her face and she was rather full of having had her hair done, had told him now the hairdresser came every Friday, it was so nice, and on Monday a beautician came as well, she was going to have a massage and a facial.

'Daddy said he'd treat me. He's been so wonderful, came in three times this week. I missed you, Sandy.' Her voice was reproachful.

'I'm sorry,' he said, trying not to sound short, 'I do still have a business to run and a small boy to look after. And it's quite a trek over here from Cheltenham.'

'Sandy! I know that. But I get very lonely, you know.'

'Yes,' he said. 'Yes, I'm sorry.'

How could she talk to him like this, after what she'd done, how could she behave as if everything was all right, as if she'd just had an operation or something? He was about to try and make her at least understand how difficult life was for him, when he caught himself back; he must try to remember what the doctor said; that however difficult, he had to realise she had been, indeed was, extremely ill, that he must be patient, must try to understand what had been happening in her poor, confused brain.

It was all right for the doctor; he hadn't loved Louise, hadn't thought she loved him, hadn't properly had to realise what she had done, hadn't had to confront the thought not only of her infidelity, but of her carrying another man's child. They all seemed to think that when Louise was better she would come home again; how could he even contemplate living with her again? And what could he do instead? And who could he talk to about that, who would not be shocked that he felt he hated her, never wanted to see her again, felt incapable ever of even beginning to forgive her?

'Well, I'm sorry,' he said again, his voice very quiet.

'I'm sure Dickon would like to see me more, wouldn't you, darling?'

'Yes, I would. I keep asking Daddy.'

'Well,' said Louise with her sweet, quick smile, 'you'll have to ask some more.'

'We're going to do something so exciting,' said Dickon.

'Really?' Her voice was sharp. 'What's that?'

'Go to a car race. With Octavia.'

'A car race! Sandy, what is he talking about?'

'Oh, it's some charity do of Octavia's. At Brands Hatch. Everyone's dressing up and there will be vintage car racing.'

'And Octavia has asked you?'

'Yes,' he said, 'yes, she has. Very kindly.'

'How extraordinary,' she said. She was flushed. 'When is it?'

'September the seventh,' said Dickon. 'I had a postcard from Poppy this morning. Daddy read it to me. It said see you on the seventh. She's going. Maybe you'll be better by then, Mummy, maybe you could come.'

'Maybe I could,' said Louise, 'if anyone was kind enough to take me.' Her voice was very sharp, then it changed again, swiftly. She smiled at Sandy. The soft, flirtatious smile. 'Sandy, I would love to go out. Lots of the people here do. I would love it. The doctor said maybe next week I could. Just for a drive, and maybe tea. But only with you. Or Daddy of course. I'm sure Daddy would take me. Only I'd much rather go with you. You and Dickon.'

'Yes, all right, Louise. I'll – well, I'll see what I can do,' said Sandy.

He felt sick suddenly; he didn't want Louise sitting in the car beside him. He didn't want to see her again. Ever. He had actually found himself wishing sometimes that she had died from her overdose. Having to entertain that thought in his head kept him from sleeping, was driving him mad . . .

'I really will try,' he said firmly, trying to make amends for the thought.

'Octavia? I thought it was you!'

Gabriel looked up. There was a man smiling down at Octavia, whom he didn't like the look of at all. He was rather as he had imagined Octavia's husband must be: tall, slim, tanned, very smooth, very well dressed. Only he was American.

'Fergie! How very nice to see you. Where have you sprung from?'

'First class, darling. You know I never slum it in club. I've been asleep, but I thought I heard your name earlier and I came to look for you. Nice surprise.' He smiled rather uncertainly at Gabriel.

'It is a nice surprise,' said Octavia. 'For me, anyway.'

'Tom on board?'

'Er – no. No, he's not. This is – this is a friend, Gabriel Bingham. Gabriel, this is Fergus Payne. Our fathers were at Harvard Business School together.'

'Hi, Gabriel,' said Fergus Payne, with a brief flash of perfect teeth.

'How do you do,' said Gabriel. He knew it was absurd to feel hostile to this person, but he couldn't help it.

'Gabriel's coming out to stay for a few days, at Mossaenda. Where are you staying?'

'At Cobblers Cove. You must come and have a drink one night. Both of you.'

'That'd be lovely. I'll phone you there. You on your own?'

'Yes and no. I'm with a friend. Divorce just came through. Third time lucky, I hope.' He hesitated, clearly hoping, Gabriel could see, Octavia was going to volunteer some information about her own marital state; she smiled at him.

'I'd heard. I'm sorry. Very sorry.'

'Anyway, darling, better get back to the safety of first class. See you at the airport maybe.'

Octavia looked at Gabriel rather intently as Fergus Payne disappeared up the stairs. 'Not your type?'

'Not exactly.'

'He's okay. I've known him since he was about ten. He's a wonderful tennis player.'

'How very nice for him.'

'Gabriel! Don't look like that. Honestly, he's very nice when you get to know him. Which you will, I hope. I'd like you to see Cobblers Cove, it's a gorgeous hotel, the nicest on the whole island.'

'I thought we were going to be on our own?'

'Well, we will mostly. But you might get tired of me.'

She smiled at him. She seemed much happier now; she had been in tears at the airport, unable to get hold of Caroline, the nanny, hadn't said goodbye to Minty.

'You don't understand,' she had said, 'I didn't even kiss her goodbye, or the twins, I feel so terrible about it all—'

Gabriel said he thought he did understand, just, but that it was only a week, and he was sure Minty would be all right, then when she continued to be distressed, even suggested cancelling the whole trip, 'But the twins are away anyway, so—'

Octavia had said of course they couldn't cancel the trip, and that of course Minty would be all right, she knew that. 'It's me that won't be. Oh, dear. I am a complete disaster.'

Gabriel tried to tell her she was nothing of the sort, but she continued to berate herself until long after the plane was in the air, when she surprised him by suddenly falling asleep. He looked at her tenderly; she was clearly completely exhausted . . .

'More of the Californian chardonnay, Mr Bingham? Or would you like to try something else? And would you like a cigar?'

Gabriel said he'd have some more of the chardonnay, and that he'd like a cigar very much. If you couldn't beat the buggers, and he clearly couldn't, you might as well join them. It was only for a week. And it did have its brighter side . . .

'Now come on, little baby, you're not thinking. This business is all about thinking, you know, what goes on in your head. Concentrate, really concentrate on me now. Nothing else. Give it to me now, now, come on, come on – that's it. Yes! Good! And again and again, now a little little smile – no, no, too much, too much, back, back – no, darling, I don't mean move, I mean – oh, God. Frances, get me some more cigarettes, would you? And, Tang, bring me those polaroids again. And send this film off for clipping, please, now now now.'

Tang, moving on his silent, slippered feet, his blank pale face turned permanently away from her, gave Romilly the creeps. They were all alone in there, in the studio, just the three of them; she felt desperately uncomfortable. Alix had had a screaming row with Ritz before the session began and Ritz had stormed out of the building, returned ten minutes later and apologised horribly publicly – it had clearly been demanded of her – and even then Serena and she had been banned from the actual studio, were confined to the reception area.

Frances was sent in and out with the polaroids, asking them for comments, which Alix was quite clearly ignoring. Once she came in and said, her cool little face quite amused, that they had said he was not to go below shoulder level; that they wanted the pictures cropped really tightly. He had looked at her and raised his eyebrows and grinned, that awful grin, and said, 'They have the wrong photographer, I think, darling, don't you? Tell them I crop where I fucking crop, darling,' and turned back to peering at Romilly through the camera.

He had made Romilly take off the white T-shirt she had worn last time, and wrap a length of muslin round her body, just above her breasts, so that her shoulders were bare. She had tied it quite high up, but he had come and eased it down, not actually very low, but she had hated the feel of his hands on her. She had begun to get cross with him then; it had helped with the nervousness.

And for a bit it had all gone better.

'It's the place where she had the pimple. It's going to show, look, here, see? Dry, rough little patch. Darling, can you do anything about it? Anything at all?' He was in the dressing room now, lounging on the stool, talking to Jan. Romilly sat down on the stool in front of the mirror.

Jan stood back looked at her. 'Yes, I see what you mean. Thing is, Alix, if I put more on now, it's going to get a build-up. Really I should start again.'

'Well, darling, start again. We have to try and get it right.' He made it sound an extremely unlikely outcome.

They were both looking at her, talking about her, as if she was a jar of cream or a piece of furniture, not a person, not there at all. It was horrible. Calm down, Romilly, don't get upset, it won't help.

'Well, do what you can. I'm going to go out for an hour or so, get a drink.'

An hour: another hour of waiting, of feeling nervous, feeling sick. They'd waited nearly three hours for him this morning.

'Fine. It'll take an hour, give the skin a chance to rest. Hair okay?'

'The hair is wonderful. Thank God.'

Romilly knew what he meant: nothing else was.

'We had such fun,' said Megan, beaming at her mother. 'Sandy was wonderful. We took about ten pictures and then Mrs Ford appeared and said what were we doing, and did we know we were trespassing. Sandy said he was terribly sorry, he'd thought the house was open to the public, he was interested in architecture and could we possibly do some from the back of the house. And she said no, we couldn't, and then her husband appeared and got really stroppy, and then one of the old ladies came out and she turned out to be Mrs Sanderson, and she was really, really great and said she'd take some pictures for us. So it was all very successful.' She smiled up at Sandy. 'And then we went and had a drink, didn't we, Dickon, at the Coach and Horses, and—'

'Sorry we were so long,' said Sandy, smiling at Pattie, interrupting this monologue, 'but they were so great, both the kids.'

'It couldn't matter less,' she said. 'I was enjoying the peace and quiet. Oh, I'm sorry, I didn't mean to sound rude!'

'You didn't.'

'Beer? And then I've just made a big salad, so it's hardly spoilt.'

'Great idea. Both of them. Megan, let me lift you out of the car . . .' She was very light; horribly light. She was a sweet child, he thought: uncomplaining, cheerful even, highly intelligent, full of funny, blithe comments about everything. Dickon adored her.

'Pattie, I've had a very nice morning with your charming daughter, and it's taken my mind off my troubles.'

Now why had he said that? Sandy wasn't given to talking about his troubles; that wasn't what you did. Troubles were your own business, nobody else's.

'I'm sorry you have troubles.'

That was all she said: but accompanied with her sweet, rather tired smile, it was absolutely right. Not pressing, not over-sympathetic, not do tell me about them, not can I help, just that she was sorry.

'Yes, well; we all do, don't we? You certainly do.'

He looked over at the children; they were drinking lemonade and giggling over some card trick Megan was showing Dickon.

'Yes, I do. But I'm pretty used to them.'

'I'm afraid I'm not used to mine yet,' he said suddenly and was shocked at himself again.

'Look – if you feel up to talking about them, do. I mean, don't feel embarrassed or anything. Just because you don't know me very well. Sometimes that's better. And it can help.'

'Thank you. I'll bear it in mind.'

She was right: someone who didn't know him, didn't know all about him, didn't know his friends, or his history. It would be better. He probably wouldn't talk to her, certainly wouldn't tell her much. But the thought that he could, if he got desperate, was oddly soothing.

'When my husband left me,' she said suddenly, abruptly almost, 'I was so ashamed, I didn't tell anyone for months. Pretended he was away. When finally I did manage to talk about it, I felt a million times better. I was surprised. Having been brought up to the stiff upper lip and all that.'

'Oh, that ruddy upper lip,' said Sandy and laughed. 'My father's was so stiff, he could hardly talk through it. Poor old Dad.'

'What's he do now? Retired, I suppose?'

'I'm afraid he's in God's regiment now,' said Sandy.

'Oh, Lord. Oh, Sandy, I'm sorry.' It was the first time she'd said his name, not called him Mr Trelawny. It was warming, nice.

Sandy smiled at her. 'Don't be silly. It was a couple of years ago now. I'm quite recovered.' He decided to return the warmth. 'Pattie, could I have another beer? And then maybe we could get the kids over, start our lunch? I'm famished.'

'Yes. Yes, do let's. Oh, dear, now I haven't brought out any more beer.'

'I'll go. Relax. In the fridge?'

'Yes. Yes, well, I hope so.'

It wasn't in the fridge, it was on the work surface warming up nicely. He picked it up and went out and told her he'd found it in the fridge.

*

'Okay, little baby.' Stop it, stop calling me that, thought Romilly, gritting her teeth. 'Now let's try it another way. Sit with your back to me. No. No, that doesn't work. Lean back on the stool. Yes, that's better. That's definitely better. Only now the neck is strained. Maybe a chair would be better. Tang, get a chair. Now now now!'

Tang ran silently out of the room, ran in again, holding one of the Lloyd Loom chairs from reception.

'Put it down there. Romilly, sit on it. Not like that, darling, not like a chicken on a perch. Push your bottom into the back of the chair. That's better. Okay, let your arms hang free over the sides. Relax, darling, relax. You mustn't be so tense. I'm not frightening you, am I?'

He bent over her, smiled into her eyes; he had been drinking wine and was slightly drunk. His breath smelt horrible; she had to fight not to turn her head away. 'No, of course not.'

'Good. Because I think we are beginning to get somewhere.'

Beginning! Only beginning. She was so tired. Her head ached unbearably and she hadn't dared ask for an aspirin. Her back ached too, and she wanted to go the loo, but didn't dare say that either.

'Right, lean back. Right back. That's it. Good. Only – here, let me pull that down a bit more,' he said, gesturing at the muslin.

'I'll do it,' said Romilly quickly. She couldn't see how it could go any lower, without showing her nipples. She pulled it cautiously; it moved a couple of millimetres. He nodded, started shooting again.

He had taken the camera off the tripod now, was moving round her, shooting from the top, the side, then the back of her. 'Now, darling, turn, now, yes, that's better. No, no, no, too much. Much too much. Romilly, don't be silly, darling. Not your head, just your eyes. Tang, I'm still getting the muslin.'

Tang came over, eased the muslin down further.

'Not enough. That's it. Now Romilly, again. Yes, yes, that's better. Beginning to get better. Think, darling, think about what you're doing. No! No, too stiff. Start again, relax. Deep breath, darling, move your bottom again, back into the chair. Right! Now then, stretch your neck right up, think of a bird, darling, think of a swan, yes, yes, that's good, good, yes – shit, fucking muslin. Darling, take it off, would you? Just take it off.'

'Off? But—'

'Oh, darling, don't go all virginal on me. I've seen breasts before. They're not going to show, I just keep getting the shadow of the fucking muslin, and I can't manage.'

Romilly thought of sitting there, with her breasts bare, knowing both he and Tang were looking at them, knowing they'd be in the pictures, and she tried and tried to cope with it. It didn't matter. It really didn't matter. Of course he'd seen breasts before. It was like – well, it was like being at the doctor's. It would mean no more than that. And they wouldn't show in the pictures. Not when they were printed. Only on the actual prints. All the models had pictures taken with bare breasts. She'd seen some of Kate Moss and Naomi Campbell. It wasn't as if he wanted her to show her pubes. Of course it was all right. Of course she had to do it.

'Darling, just do it, would you? Take the muslin off. Come on.'

Very slowly, very miserably, she pulled it down. Right down. Tang came over to her, stretched out his hand for it. She sat there, her arms crossed over her breasts; she felt very hot suddenly, hot and scared.

'Right. Now then. Arms over the sides again, just like before.'

So easy. All she had to do was move her arms, let them hang over the arms of the chair. But she couldn't do it. She really couldn't. It was as if they were glued to her breasts. She swallowed, stared at Alix.

'Darling, please. I'm getting a little bit tired here. Come on. Like this, look.'

He walked over to her, tried to move one of her arms.

Panic shot through Romilly; she pulled away from him. 'No! No, don't. I'll – I'll do it.'

She managed it. Her arms felt rigid.

'Right. Let them fall. Now, look at me. Come on, come on. Jesus, Romilly, relax. Just relax.'

'I can't,' she said and burst into tears.

'Dear sweet Jesus,' he said and stalked out of the studio. She could hear him shouting, hear the door bang.

When Ritz and Serena came in, she was sitting, her head buried in her hands, crying quietly.

Tang was being very sweet and standing by her, draping her shoulders with the muslin and offering her his handkerchief.

Gabriel felt quite panicky already. And he was only on the airport tarmac. The heat was stifling, blanket thick. How as he going to stand it?

The airport building was slightly cooler, and Octavia was waving excitedly to someone in a gallery over their heads.

'Who's that?' said Gabriel gloomily. 'Another friend of your father's?'

She smiled at him; she seemed oddly cheerful and relaxed, in spite of the heat and the long flight. 'You are in a grump. No, it's Bob. Elvira's husband. I told you about Elvira, didn't I?'

'No, I don't think you did.' He tried not to sound sulky.

'Elvira's our cook – well, housekeeper, I suppose.'

'Your housekeeper! I thought we were going to be on our own in this house.'

'Gabriel, we are. She lives with her husband and some of her children in Holetown. She comes in every day. For heaven's sake, calm down. Bobby, hallo.'

'Hallo, Octavia. Good to see you. This way now.'

Bob was tall, thin, grizzled, very relaxed. Gabriel liked the way he called Octavia Octavia, not Mrs Fleming. He followed him over to a rather battered car.

'This is Gabriel, Bob. Gabriel Bingham. He's a politician from England. Gabriel, you sit in the front, then you can see more.'

Outside again, the blanket of heat had descended. He had thought the car might be air conditioned. It wasn't.

'How's your dad, Octavia?'

'He's very well, Bob. Working too hard.'

'And Mrs Muirhead?'

'She's fine too,' said Octavia quickly. 'How's Elvira?'

'Elvira's fine. She's very happy about the new baby. And he's beautiful.'

'I'm sure. Gabriel, look, you see that great palace over there?'

It did appear to be a palace: Moorish in style, vast, painted purple and aqua green, with glittering minarets. 'Who lives there, for God's sake?'

'It's the supermarket. Isn't it wonderful? Waitrose, eat your heart out. Now look, over there, Gabriel, that's sugar cane. See? And over there . . .'

He tried to smile, to appear pleased and interested. The drive seemed to go on for ever: hot, blindingly sunny, the old car lurching over the road. It wasn't very pretty, not as he had imagined it, just an endless, rather narrow, two-lane highway, lined with small wooden houses set on stilts. He felt a bit sick: and very depressed. What was he doing here, why had he come?

'Zoë? Zoë, hallo, it's Ritz. Look, is your mum there? Oh, she's not. Oh, I see. No, nothing's wrong. Well, Romilly's a bit upset. No, nothing serious. Yes, if you could. How long do you think you might be? Oh, fine. Yes, we're both here.'

'I'm fine,' said Romilly. 'Honestly. I'm just so sorry I was – well, silly.'

'Romilly, you weren't silly,' said Ritz. Her voice sounded rather shaky.

'Yes, I was. Next time—'

'There won't be a next time,' said Serena smoothly, 'not with Alix Stefanidis. I do wish these bloody people would remember who's paying the bill.'

'Serena—' said Ritz. Her voice had an edge to it. 'Not now. Now look, Romilly, what do you want to do? Go out for a drink, go home, call your mum?'

'I certainly don't want to call my mum,' said Romilly. She managed a rather shaky smile. 'It's exactly the sort of thing she was worrying about, I expect. She'd be on the next plane down. Hideous! Honestly, I'm fine, please don't worry about me. I—' Her mobile rang suddenly, from the depths of her bag; she pulled it out. 'Sorry, I thought it was switched off. Hallo, this is Romilly. Oh – hi, Fen. Yes. What? Oh, okay. I'm a bit tired. What? Oh, oh, I see. No, that's fine. Honestly. I can spend it with my sister.'

Zoë's stomach lurched. Now what?

''Bye, Fen.' She switched off the phone, smiled the same shaky smile. 'That was Fenella. Her grandmother's taking them all out to the ballet, apparently. Surprise treat. So they can't have me tonight after all. Fancy a video, Zoë?'

'Well – I . . .' Shit! That was all she needed. To miss the one good night she was going to get for a long time; she'd be off to the States on Monday, probably wouldn't see Ian again.

'What's the problem?' said Ritz.

'Well, Rom can't stay home on her own. I did have plans. But – doesn't matter.'

'What sort of plans did you have? Share your exciting young lifestyle with us,' said Ritz, grinning. She was clearly glad of a distraction from the horrors of the day.

'Oh, just going to the Ministry of Sound. With some – some friends.'

'Sounds good. I hate going there these days, I feel so old. I do, occasionally, talent spotting, but not any more often than I have to. Shame, Zoë. Was it for anything special?'

'Celebrating her A-levels,' said Romilly, 'well, hers and her friends'.'

'Oh, Zoë, you can't miss that. Romilly, how would you like to come out to supper with us? We were going to have a quiet evening together. Honestly, it would be a pleasure. We could go somewhere fun, like the Hard Rock. Or the Fashion Café.'

'No,' said Zoë, quickly. 'No, honestly. I'll stay home with her. I haven't got much to celebrate anyway!'

'I don't want you to stay home and look after me, Zoë. Look, I really would like to go out with Ritz and Serena tonight. The Fashion Café'd be great, really cool.'

'Rom, if I go out, I won't be home till four or five in the morning. You can't stay at the house alone. Mum would never forgive me.'

'Why not? God, I really am not a child! But look, tell you what. Mrs Blake would come over. Just to sleep at the house. She offered yesterday when she was doing the ironing, before I fixed to stay with Fenella. How's that?'

Zoë hesitated. It was very tempting.

'I'll ring Mrs Blake,' she said finally, 'just to make sure she can come.'

Mrs Blake said she'd be glad to come over. *Steel Magnolias* was on Sky and she had been going on to Mr Blake about how she wished they could get it.

'I'll order a cab for you, Mrs Blake. On Mum's account. About half past eight, that all right?'

That way she could see her safely into the house before she went off herself. Romilly was right, she told herself, they really should stop treating her like a baby. When Zoë had been sixteen, she'd flown out to Sydney to stay with her aunt Bella, all by herself, and then travelled on the train down to Melbourne, also by herself, to meet her cousins there. There was no way her parents would think Romilly was old enough to do that. It was the curse of the youngest child, that Romilly was always going on about. And she did seem to have recovered from her ordeal now. Nothing had happened to her after all; she'd just been a bit embarrassed. It would do her good to have a grown-up evening with Ritz and Serena. Put it in perspective. And she probably did need to do a bit of PR on them, if she was going to make this modelling thing work. She really did seem fine. Absolutely fine. Nothing to worry about at all.

It just wasn't fair of Sandy, Louise thought: not to come and see her more. She needed people to talk to, ordinary people, not the wretched other patients and the ghastly nurses, and the doctor with his endless questions. Why couldn't Sandy see that? She was trying so hard to cope with it all, and he just wasn't doing anything. Obviously, she hadn't behaved exactly well: but for heaven's sake, Sandy of all people should understand why. Nobody seemed to understand how much she hurt. What it had been like, all of it. First losing Juliet, then her mother. And discovering what Octavia had done. She still couldn't believe that of her. Having an abortion, getting rid of a baby. After all the things she had said when Juliet had died, about how she admired Louise so much for her courage, about how she wouldn't be able to bear it, about how she could hardly begin to imagine how much it hurt, about how she had cried for nights out of sympathy with Louise. She'd been able to bear it, all right: she had just trotted along to the clinic one morning, let them scrape the baby out of her and throw it away, and then go off to her busy life, her important meetings, without another thought for her dead baby. Killed, incinerated, that's what they did to them, she had read about it. Just because it wasn't quite perfect enough for her perfect family, and perfect marriage.

Octavia deserved to lose her husband, she really did. She deserved to lose her baby. She needed to be shown how much it could hurt, how much Louise had hurt. But how did you do that, to a woman who was so hard, so tough, she could just throw her baby away, in between breakfast and lunch? How could she have ever loved Octavia, thought she was her friend? Louise wouldn't have had an abortion if they'd said her baby had had two heads. You looked after babies, you didn't murder them. And then Octavia had had another. Just like that. Less than a year later. A healthy, beautiful baby. Who was still alive: Octavia's baby hadn't been found dead in her cot one morning, white and cold and still. Octavia's baby could sit up and laugh and say dad-dad.

Juliet had just started to talk; she hadn't said dad-dad though. She'd said Mum-my. Not mum, not mum-mum, but Mum-my, very beautifully, only the day before she had died. She had been sitting on Louise's lap, and she had looked up at her and smiled that beautiful, perfect smile and reached out her fat little hand and touched her hair and then said, 'Mum-my.' It was the first and the last thing she had ever said. Mummy. And now she was lying under the earth, in her little coffin, with her toys in it, wrapped in her blanket, and she would never say or do anything, ever again. And the other baby, the baby she had managed to make with Tom, that was dead too, washed so painfully out of her that terrible day. Two cold, dead babies: when she needed them so much. And Octavia, who didn't need any babies, who had everything else she could possibly wish for, including Tom, had a baby as well. Octavia deserved to lose that baby. Lose her for ever. Then she would know how it felt, what the pain was like.

Louise sat there, in the settling dusk, savouring her anger, the helpful, strong anger, looking over the garden, and thinking very hard indeed about Octavia losing Minty. It made her own pain feel much better. It really did.

'We'd better be on our way,' said Sandy, 'it's after six.' How had that happened, how had the whole afternoon just disappeared, how had he managed not to notice it, when for the past two and a half weeks, every hour had crawled painfully, sickeningly past?

'Could we go and see Mummy again on the way back?'

'No. Visiting hours are over. And she'll be tired.'

'She won't. She said she missed us, she said she wanted to see us more.'

'Dickon, no, old chap.'

Pattie was watching him closely; she said suddenly, 'If you want to go on your own, we could keep Dickon here . . .'

'No,' said Sandy, 'thank you all the same.' His voice sounded sharp, even to him; it shocked him, that sharpness. It was a giveaway.

Pattie looked at him, her pale blue eyes very calm suddenly. 'Just a thought.'

'It was very kind. But – one visit is enough, in one day. For Louise, I mean. Come on, Dickon, off we go. Say thank you to Mrs David.'

'Pattie,' said Pattie, 'please.'

'Thank you, Pattie,' said Dickon solemnly. 'Thank you for having me. Thank you, Megan.'

'We loved it,' said Megan, 'come again soon.'

'Yes, do,' said Pattie, 'any time. Whenever you visit your wife, we'd like it.'

'Thanks. I'd like that. Good luck with your application, Megan. Don't forget to send the pictures.'

'Of course not. I've got one frame left on the film, might as well finish it. Mum, stand up, next to Sandy. Smile, that's right. Great. Mum can get them developed. Sandy, thank you very much for your help. I wish you'd stay for supper.'

'Maybe next time,' said Sandy, 'if your mother could face it.'

'She could face it,' said Megan, 'she'd like it, she gets ever so lonely.'

'Megan!' said Pattie. 'Please! You make me sound very pathetic.'

She was flushed; Sandy realised she was upset. 'I get ever so lonely too,' he said, and realised it was the second time that day he had spoken seriously out of character.

Romilly sat back in her seat at the Fashion Café and smiled at Serena and Ritz. She felt rather lightheaded. Not only had they ordered her a glass of champagne – but only one, had then insisted she moved on to Pepsi Max – but Serena had produced a present for her, as they settled down at the table. It was a Donna Karan sweater, black, very sexy. 'It's to make up for today. With love from us both.'

She had insisted on going to change in the ladies'; it was quite perfect. It made her look more sophisticated without looking older.

'I love it,' she said happily, sitting down again next to Serena, kissing her impulsively, blowing a kiss across the table at Ritz. 'It's absolutely gorgeous. But you really didn't have to.'

'Well, we thought we did,' said Serena. 'You had a horrid day, and we felt responsible. Anyway, Alix Stefanidis won't be working for Christie's again. That's for sure. Will he, Ritz?'

'Absolutely not,' said Ritz. 'And there's some more news, Romilly. Very exciting. I think Mario Testino might do the campaign instead.

You'll like him, he's so gentle and sweet. He did these marvellous pictures of Diana, look, in *Vanity Fair*, I brought them to show you.'

'They are lovely,' said Romilly, looking at the pictures of a new, utterly different Diana, her hair unstyled, slicked back, what could only be described as a grin on her lovely face, 'but . . .'

'But what?'

'Oh – doesn't matter.' How could she tell them she found the very thought of being photographed by another world-class photographer totally scary?

'Yes, it does. Come on, tell your old aunties.'

'Don't!' said Romilly, sharply. 'Don't talk to me like I'm a baby. Like everyone else.'

'Oh, Romilly.' Serena looked at Ritz swiftly, then at her. 'Romilly, we don't think you're a baby. We think you're very special. A real discovery. We're very proud of you. It isn't easy, being catapulted into all this. No one can cope with it at first. No one. Whoever they are, however old they are.'

'Of course they can,' said Romilly. She was shocked to find tears rising in her eyes. 'I was so feeble. As if it mattered. That – that bit of material coming off. Off my boobs,' she said loudly and clearly. The people at the next table stared at her; she stared back at them boldly. She didn't care. It seemed important: to stop behaving as if she couldn't bear to talk about it. When it had actually been quite – well, quite funny.

'Romilly,' said Ritz, putting down her glass, looking at her very seriously, 'of course it mattered. Let me tell you something. When Kate Moss was just starting, she arrived at a session and some dirty old man tried to make her take her bra off. And you know what? She just refused and left. Listen, you don't have to do *anything* you don't want to. You hold all the cards. You're the face of the millennium. Everyone's going to be talking about you soon. And if you don't want to take your bra off, you certainly don't have to.'

'Really?' said Romilly.

'*Really*. More chips?'

'Yes, *please*!'

Marie France Auguste sat in the first-class compartment of the Paris to London Eurostar, sipping at a glass of champagne, and thinking complacently how pleased Serena would be to see her. It would be good to give her a surprise. She knew she hadn't been terribly nice to Serena lately, and she felt remorseful about it. She might not be exactly madly in love with her, but she was fond of her, and she owed her a lot and certainly didn't want to upset her. Well, actually, she couldn't afford to upset her: her career would go right on the skids if she did. Marketing directors could do a lot for junior product development executives if they felt so inclined. And so far, Serena had felt very much inclined. She looked at her watch; nine. The train got into Waterloo at ten thirty; she could be with Serena by eleven. And then they could have a really good night together.

It never occurred to her for a moment that she might not be entirely welcome.

Steel Magnolias was just drawing to its tear-stained conclusion when the phone rang: Mrs Blake swore and went to answer it. It was her husband. 'Sorry to disturb you,' he said, 'but I think you'd better get over to St Thomas's. It's your mum, love. I'm sorry, but she's had a stroke.'

'A stroke! Oh, God, Phil, a bad one?'

'I'm not sure. I don't think anyone knows yet.'

'Poor Mum. You'll come, too, won't you?'

''Course I will. What about that little lot there?'

'Oh, I'll ring Zoë. She said she could get back if there was a problem.'

'All right, love. Best get a cab.'

Mrs Blake phoned Zoë on the number she had given her; it told her that Zoë would get right back to her. That didn't sound too good. Now what did she do? Distractedly she flipped open the telephone book, looked down the list of numbers under Emergency. Not a lot of help: doctor, dentist, gasman, plumber. Oh, and here were all the children's mobile phone numbers. Spoilt brats, thought Mrs Blake. Still – useful. And yes, here was Romilly's. At least she would know that she'd be coming home to an empty house; she could probably make other arrangements. She dialled the number.

'Then you'll have to stay with me,' said Serena. 'That's absolutely no problem. There's no way you can go back to an empty house. I've got a very nice spare room and—'

'Serena,' said Ritz, 'Serena, perhaps it would be better if Romilly stayed with me.'

Romilly saw Serena look at Ritz, saw a very strange expression in her face: if she hadn't known better, she would have said it was anger.

'I really don't see that,' she said. 'You haven't even got a spare bed, let alone a spare room.'

'Yes, I know, but—'

'But what, Ritz?' The blue eyes were icy cold, the mouth tight and hard.

Romilly suddenly felt very uncomfortable. 'Look,' she said, 'look, it really doesn't matter. I'll be fine for a bit. Zoë'll be in later . . .'

'No,' said Ritz, 'no, we have to look after you. Of course you can't go home alone. Sorry, Serena, I – I just didn't want you to be – well, put out in any way.'

'I won't be,' said Serena briefly. 'I'm surprised you thought I would be. Very surprised.'

Romilly suddenly felt she had to prove to them that she was actually more grown up than they thought. And improve the mood of things at the same time. 'Let's have another glass of champagne, shall we?' she said. 'My treat. Mummy always says it's the best thing at the end of an evening. Ends it on a high.'

'Your mother,' said Ritz, smiling at her, 'is a woman after my own heart. But I've got my car, so I daren't have another glass of anything. Let's go back to your flat, shall we, Serena, have it there? How would that be?'

'Fine,' said Serena. She was still icy cool. But at least she managed a smile. At Romilly at least.

The house was nearly finished; the kitchen looked wonderful, the units in the obligatory distressed greeny-blue wood, a blue Aga in place, Fired Earth tiles on the floor.

'Looks good, doesn't it? And wait till you see the bathroom. Bath came yesterday. Black.'

It wasn't quite black, more dark grey and white marble, with gold taps and jacuzzi jets. He led her into the bedroom; that was finished as well, done in what her mother would have described as wedding-cake style; ruched blinds, fringed lampshades, silk wallpaper, the bed an absurd confection, made up in white and cream lace-trimmed linen, with curtains hanging from a brass coronet hung over it, and a heap of teddies piled on to a mountain of lace cushions.

'Teddies!' said Ian, his voice thick with distaste.

'I think they're rather sweet,' said Zoë, 'and I love the drapes. Um – Ian . . .'

She had decided, while they were dancing, to come clean about the money. He might be cross, but he'd be bound to lend it to her – it'd be worth more than his job if he didn't, actually; and he had a great stash of fifty-pound notes in his wallet, she'd seen them.

'Yeah? Get your clothes off, princess, there's a good girl – we haven't got all night.'

Serena's flat was lovely, Romilly thought: on the first floor of a modern building just behind Lowndes Square. It was very cool, very minimal. She asked if she could use the loo and sat there staring at endlessly repeated images of herself, disappearing into infinity, from all four mirrored walls. It was quite a nice idea, she supposed, but the loo didn't seem the right place for it; you were hardly at your best. Next to the loo was a study, white carpeted, with a big black desk, dauntingly neat, and on the walls a set of framed Christie's advertisements, dating back to the 'sixties. She went, rather reluctantly, to find Ritz and Serena, but they seemed to have called a truce and were chatting fairly easily in the kitchen, which was all white-and-chrome with an endless battery of chrome and stainless steel cookery appliances, toasters, processors, juicers, and a kettle that looked like no kettle Romilly had ever seen. The fridge was silver too; Serena was removing a bottle of champagne from it.

'I feel bad now,' said Romilly. 'I meant the champagne to be on me.'

'Another time,' said Serena easily. 'Let's go into the sitting room.'

She put some music on, strange, high pitched, other worldly. Romilly settled herself on the sofa, next to Serena, smiled across at Ritz.

'To Romilly,' said Ritz, raising her glass. 'Romilly and – and . . .'

'Us,' said Serena.

'Yes, us.'

'Feeling better?' said Serena.

'Much,' said Romilly.'

'Good.'

Romilly felt a sudden lurch of affection for her; for both of them. They had been so kind to her, so thoughtful and patient. She moved slightly nearer Serena, smiled at her. 'You've both been so . . .'

'Cool?' said Ritz and grinned.

'Yes. Really cool,' said Romilly. She took a large gulp of the champagne and then another.

'Romilly! I'm sorry, but there is a limit, even to our indulgence. That is no way to drink champagne. You're meant to sip it. It's not Coca-cola!'

'Sorry. Mummy always says exactly the same thing.' She giggled; and having started, couldn't stop. It was partly the champagne itself, partly relief that the day was over, not too disastrously after all, and partly that she could never stop giggling once she'd begun. Tears began to stream down her face.

'Here,' said Serena, laughing too, handing her a hanky; she wiped her eyes, handed it back, then collapsed against Serena's side, still giggling, in between exaggeratedly genteel sips of champagne. The others began to do the same thing.

The doorbell went.

'I'll go,' said Ritz.

Romilly, no longer giggling, was wiping her eyes, still leaning against Serena, when a girl walked in. A very pretty girl, blonde, blue eyed, very slim, wearing trousers and a sweater exactly like the one they had given her that evening.

She stood there, looking at them, a rather cool smile on her face; Romilly felt Serena stiffen suddenly, then sit up very straight.

'Well,' said the girl, in a thick French accent, 'I see you are having a little party, Serena. Am I too late to join in?'

Marianne lay, half-asleep in Nico's arms. She felt easy, sweetly at peace. She could not remember feeling like this before; love for her had meant always darkness, complexity, tension. Nico, she realised, was that rare thing, a man at peace with himself. She had no illusions about him; he was vain, arrogant, pragmatic to the point of amorality. But those very things made him easy; sure of who he was, what he wanted. Self-doubt, and its more difficult companion, self-mistrust, were unknown to him; the result was a personality that was blithely straightforward. And then he was fun: Marianne's life-companions, her children apart, had been short on fun. And he said he loved her. And seemed to mean it.

She lay there, contemplating him, listening to his heavy breathing, reliving the evening, reliving his last words to her: 'Go on, Marianne. Promise to marry me,' before he fell asleep and she felt quite tempted to wake him up and tell him she would. For why not? Because she had not known him long? Because she hardly knew him at all? She had known Felix for years and still not been sure. She had known Alec extremely well, and still read him wrong. Marriage, love itself indeed, was a gamble; there was no way to be sure of a winning hand. You could see there was a hand to play, and that was the best you could hope for. So – why not take it, Marianne? she thought, shifting just slightly, smiling at Nico's sleeping face. It would be a very different marriage, this one, if she made it: very grown up. She and Nico could lead a life of total selfishness. There would be no one to worry about, no one to be concerned for but one another. She rather liked that concept. She had always been rather critical of childless marriages, seeing them as incomplete, inconclusive: but second time around, that was surely different. It would simply be fun: self-indulgent, self-centred fun . . .

Marianne lay there, beside Nico, half smiling, thinking about fun. But her sleep when it came was uneasy and her dreams troubled.

Afterwards, Romilly thought, almost the worst thing was knowing (again) how stupid, how naive she had been, not realising at once what was going on. Thinking the girl introduced to her and Ritz by Serena as a colleague from Paris, was just that: a colleague or a friend. Misunderstanding Ritz's embarrassment, thinking she was being silly in suggesting she and Ritz leave at once, feeling sorry for Serena, who was also embarrassed, thinking it was because she had offered the spare room to her, when the girl from Paris clearly needed it more. She said that of course she would go with Ritz, that she wouldn't dream of staying, but the girl, whose name was Marie France, said not to rush off on her account, that she could go to a hotel if necessary. But 'Don't be silly,' Serena had said. 'Have some champagne, Marie France, there's plenty of room for everybody. We've just been out celebrating Romilly's success, she is our new face for the—'

'Yes, I can see she is your new face. And a very pretty one too.' Marie France walked over to Romilly, tipped her chin up, studied her closely. 'How old are you, Romilly?'

'Sixteen,' said Romilly firmly.

'Sixteen! Serena, really!'

'Serena, I think Romilly and I should go,' said Ritz.

'No, don't go,' said Marie France. 'We can have a little party here. All of us. That's a very nice sweater you have on, Romilly.'

'Yes. Isn't it? It was a present, from—'

'From Serena. Mine too. She obviously gives it to all her *jeunes filles* just at the moment.'

Romilly was silent; she couldn't think of anything remotely sensible to say.

'Marie France, come into the kitchen. Let me fix you a coffee,' said Serena.

'I don't want any coffee, thank you. I will stay with the champagne. I think we should all sit and have some more to drink and a little chat. Don't you, Ritz?'

'Not really, no,' said Ritz firmly. 'Serena, call a cab for us, would you? I'll pick up my car in the morning.'

'Could I just call Zoë on your phone?' said Romilly. 'My mobile's battery's run down. I think she might be home, you see . . .'

'Yes, of course,' said Serena, 'in there.' She nodded in the direction of the study; Romilly went in and shut the door, grateful to be away from the tension.

She dialled the number at Eaton Square; as she did so, she must have touched the playback button on the answering machine. Alix Stefanidis' voice came out of it.

'I'm not going to apologise for today,' it said. 'It is you should apologise to me. That girl is crap. She may be pretty, but she has no real idea. And her skin is lousy. I think you made a big mistake, Serena, picking her. I think you know it, too. She's a silly, awkward little girl. You should find someone else. I just spoke to Donna, and she's in agreement with me.'

Romilly felt tears filling her eyes; it hurt, hearing what he had said, because it was true. She was quite sure it was true. She was silly, and she had been awkward and tense. She didn't have an instinct for the camera. She hadn't actually realised her skin was lousy, but clearly it was. Serena had indeed made a big mistake. She stood there, taking deep breaths, trying to cope with the misery and the humiliation, wondering if they had been thinking this all evening, had just been humouring her, taking her out, giving her presents. God, she was a fool, such a fool!

The door opened abruptly; Marie France came in. She smiled at Romilly, closed the door behind her, stood leaning against it. She was holding a large wineglass of champagne, obviously very drunk indeed. She studied Romilly with her head slightly on one side.

'Wonderful legs, you have, Romilly. I suppose that's what caught Serena's eye. She loves good legs. Good long legs. Mine are a little bit short, maybe that's where I went wrong.' She walked towards Romilly. 'You have a wonderful figure altogether. You're a very lucky girl. So slim and yet so – voluptuous. I wonder, would you mind if I—'

She reached out suddenly, caressed one of Romilly's breasts with her hand; Romilly stood there, just for one moment, frozen with horror. Then she dashed the hand away and pushed past her, out of the room, and down the hall towards the front door.

'Oh, my God,' said Zoë. 'Oh, my God!' The second time the words came out like a wail, punctuating the thick, rich pleasure that was being pulled from her, slowly, agonisingly by Ian. This was like nothing, nothing she had ever known before, deeper, longer, stronger, it was unbearable, it was agonising . . . She tensed, held herself, wanting to keep it there, there, now. 'Now,' she shouted, and again, 'Now now now!'

'Shut up,' he said suddenly, 'shut up, Zoë.' She stopped, frozen, the pleasure suspended, frightened by the urgency in his voice.

And as she lay there, fear slowly crawling into her, she heard the front door open, and then shut, the thud of luggage put down and a girl's voice saying, 'Darling, those builders are the absolute end, there's a light on up there, up in our bedroom, and why isn't the alarm on, the door's not even double locked?' and then, unable to move, unable to do anything, heard footsteps on the stairs and then the door opening very slowly, and a man's voice saying into the fear and the horror, 'Lyndsay, call the police. Now. Quickly.'

CHAPTER 39

God knew what the time was in England, Gabriel thought confusedly. He had hardly slept; an extraordinary noise, shrill, insistent, which Octavia had said was the tree frogs 'calling for sex', had filled the hot night, replaced now by the sweet throbbing of birdsong. It was still half dark; he looked at his watch. Seven o'clock. Octavia was fast asleep, relaxed as he had never seen her; he eased himself out of the bed, out of the mosquito net that hung around it and walked over to the window. Yet another mosquito guard filled that; the window itself was wide open, letting in the sweet morning air and the sound of the sea, fifty yards away, just beyond the garden. The steep, sloping beach was overhung with trees, not the palm trees he had expected, but great tall things with sweeping, drooping branches that could have stood in an English wood, and then the wonderfully coloured warm water which could not. It was very beautiful. Nobody could deny that.

He had begun to feel better as soon as they had arrived; the cottage – actually quite a large, four-bedroomed house, white painted, grey roofed, with a long verandah at garden level – was built backing on to the beach, Gibbes Beach, a perfectly curving small bay with water that was not the characterless blue he had feared but a most distinctive greeny-blue. 'We'll swim straight away,' said Octavia after they had greeted Elvira, 'cool ourselves down. You'll feel better then, Gabriel.'

He had: immediately. The water was perfect, silkily warm, the beach tipping swiftly into deep water, with gentle waves lurching on to the bleached-gold sand, and breaking as well on to a small edge of rocks a hundred yards out.

'Those rocks are lovely, lots of pretty fish, we can snorkel on them tomorrow. But don't put your feet on them – they're a mass of sea urchins.'

Octavia swam swiftly out to sea, then returned to him smiling, her hair slicked back, her lashes starry with water. She looked absurdly young, almost childlike. He told her so.

'Already! Goodness. I always thought this place had magical properties. Doesn't the house look lovely from here? You see those trees in the garden, with what looks like bunches of pink Kleenex hanging from them? They're mossaenda trees, and that's why the house is called Mossaenda. And those trees all along the beach, they're manchineal trees – don't even *touch* the fruit, it's poisonous. So poisonous that if you stand under them in the rain, you can get blistered.'

'Rain?' said Gabriel hopefully.

'Yes. It never stops in the rainy season. But that isn't likely now, don't worry.'

They swam for a long time; then went in and sat on the verandah, and drank the most delicious rum punches made for them by Elvira. He liked Elvira; she was large and cheerful, and clearly very fond of Octavia. The relationship between her and the servants intrigued him; it was friendly, easy, as close to equal as could be imagined. If anything, Octavia was almost deferential to them.

Later, as they ate a wonderful dinner of fish and rice, she talked about the island: in affectionate, rather proprietory terms, a bit like a parent talking about a child.

'It's the size of the Isle of Wight, but there are half a million people living here and the white population is only about two per cent. They wouldn't inter-marry, but they have great respect for one another. The posh white Bajans go to private schools, and are very snobbish. The high-up black Bajans are equally snobbish, with titles bestowed upon them by the British government, and really important jobs. Honestly, Gabriel, this place provides the most fascinating social study in the world, I think. You could have a ball here.'

He said he found Elvira's accent hard to understand. 'It is till you get used to it,' she said. 'It's a sort of cross between Southern States American and West Country English. There's a settlement here called Chalky Mount, where Cromwell sent a whole load of unrepentant English aristos who have kept absolutely to themselves. Now they're very poor, and look terrible, very pale, almost albino-looking, because of all the inter-marrying. But you could just find the true heir to the Duke of Marlborough there.'

'My God,' said Gabriel, 'I must hurry over.'

'Yes, I thought that would intrigue you. Truly, it is the most fascinating place. More wine?'

'Yes, please.'

She poured him some, and a glass for herself.

He looked at her. 'You're drinking! You had a rum punch, too.'

'Yes, I always do here. I feel so – oh, I don't know . . .'

'Safe?'

She hesitated. 'Yes. Yes, maybe that's it. Well, I risk it anyway. Let's go for a walk on the beach.'

She took his hand and they walked towards a small haze of light to their left.

'That's Glitter Bay over there. Very expensive hotel. Very glitzy. You'd love it.' She looked up at him and smiled.

He put his arm round her, kissed the top of her head. 'I could try it. You seem to be undergoing a personality change. Perhaps I will, too.'

'Perhaps you will.'

Huge crabs scuttled away from them, and a picture-book moon had risen and was gleaming on to the water. The soft sound of the waves was very soothing, very musical. Gabriel felt hugely happy suddenly: happy and absurdly grateful and tender towards her for bringing him.

'Let's go back to the house,' he said, 'I feel an urge to get into bed with you . . .'

He had expected too much of himself and of her, he realised; the heat and the length of the day, the strong cocktails, the wine, the dinner, combined with a certain anxiety, all conspired to make them both tense, and 'Uninspired, I'm afraid,' said Octavia, as she kissed him, reassured him that she had not even wanted to make love that night, had been surprised that he had been able to arouse her at all. It was sweet of her, he thought; but he had still fallen asleep distressed at himself. It had been all right; but only just. Tomorrow, he had thought, as he drifted into an awkward, hot sleep, tomorrow would be different. Surely. Yes, it would.

He was sitting out on the verandah, eating a chunk of extraordinarily sweet pineapple and gazing slightly gloomily at the sea, when Octavia suddenly appeared, smiling, still slightly hazy with sleep; she bent and kissed him, then sat down, holding out her hand for the pineapple. He had never seen her like this; he told her so.

'I know,' she said. 'Everyone says that. Even Daddy says I'm different here.'

She was: happy, easy, less watchful of herself.

She stretched, yawned, looked at the sea. 'We should swim now. Then we could drive along to Glitter Bay. They do a mean breakfast at the hotel.'

'Wouldn't I have to look – glitzy?' he said.

He was joking, but she took the question seriously, looked at him, her eyes thoughtful. 'Not for breakfast. Just bring a T-shirt and some shorts. Which reminds me, tonight we're going over to Cobblers Cove to meet Fergus for a drink. It's beautiful, there. Stunning. You sit right on a terrace on the edge of the beach looking over the sea and drink the best cocktails on the island.'

'Why should my clothes remind you of that?'

'Well, because it's very upmarket and you'll need to look just a bit smart. Nothing too much obviously, but a shirt and a pair of decent trousers. Shall we swim now, do you like that idea?'

Gabriel said he did very much and followed her inside to find his swimming trunks and a towel, trying to ignore the drift of unease that this talk of clothes and drinks at upmarket places had drawn out of the blue, perfect morning.

Marianne rose with difficulty from a thick, heavy sleep, to hear Nico shouting down the telephone, saying it was four in the morning for Christ's sake, what the hell was the hotel doing, putting calls through at such an hour, and then he was saying, 'Oh, oh, I see,' and handing her the phone. 'It's for you. It's the police.'

She took the phone, looked at her watch: four a.m. This was no ordinary call; this was the one, the one every mother dreaded, the one that would impart the information that a beloved child had been attacked, raped, mutilated. She closed her eyes, swallowed hard. 'Yes?' The blood was pounding so hard in her ears that she could hardly hear.

'Mrs Muirhead? This is Kennington East police station.'

'Yes,' she said again, her voice so faint she could hardly hear it herself.

'We have your daughter here, Mrs Muirhead. Zoë Muirhead.'

'Is – is she – all right?'

'Yes, she's perfectly all right. But she's been arrested for burglary.'

'Burglary? Zoë? Oh, no, there must be some mistake!'

'I'm afraid not. Perhaps you'd like to speak to her. She can tell you about it.' She heard a hum in the background, then his voice saying, 'Take it over there, other side of the room. Putting you on to her now, Mrs Muirhead.'

Marianne shut her eyes; that might do it, turn it into a dream.

Of all the things she had feared for Zoë, being arrested for burglary was not even on the agenda. She licked her lips; they were very dry.

'Mum?' It was Zoë's voice: subdued, shaky even, but unmistakable.

'Zoë, darling, what's happened? It must be some mistake, I don't understand.'

'Oh, Mum. Please, please come!'

'Zoë? Darling, you must tell me what's happened, please.'

There was a long silence; she could hear the heavy breathing that always indicated Zoë was struggling not to cry, heard her blow her nose, heard her say, 'Could I have another tissue, please?'

'Zoë? Come on, darling, please . . .'

'I – oh, God. God, Mum, I'm so sorry. I'm so so sorry.'

'Zoë, have you really been arrested? You must tell me, it's obviously a mistake, we must—'

'No, no, it's not a mistake. I have.'

The room swam. Marianne grasped Nico's hand. It was warm, strong, reassuring. 'But whatever for, for heaven's sake?'

'For – for burglary. Like they said.'

'But, Zoë, that's absurd. You don't need to steal anything.'

She saw shock begin to register in Nico's eyes.

'I know, I know, but . . .' The voice rose in a wail, then turned to sobs. 'Just get here, will you? Please?'

'Zoë, are you all right? Do you want a solicitor or anything? Let me speak to them.'

A silence; then, 'Mrs Muirhead?'

'Yes.'

'I'm sorry, Mrs Muirhead. Your daughter was found in a house in Kennington. With a young man. We have him here, also. Your daughter has admitted taking one hundred pounds in cash from the owners of the house. And it seems other things had been taken, by the young man.'

'But what were they doing there? In this house? I don't understand, it's absurd.'

'I think perhaps your daughter should tell you that herself, Mrs Muirhead. She was also in possession of drugs.'

'Oh, my God,' said Marianne. She looked at Nico, and her fear must have shown in her eyes, for he put his hand out and took hers. It was warm, strong, oddly comforting.

'I imagine you'll want to get down here as soon as possible. I realise it may take a few hours.'

'Yes. Yes, of course. I will get there as soon as I can.' How did you do that, in the middle of the night? Panic rose in her, the blood pounded harder in her ears. 'Can I – can I speak to her again, please?'

'You may.' She heard the voice turn from the phone, say, 'It's your mother. She wants to speak to you again.'

And then, through the nightmare, the confusion, Zoë's voice, childlike, frightened, very shaky, saying again and again, 'Mum, I'm so sorry. Please, please come . . .'

Zoë lay on her bed in the cell, trembling. Her teeth were chattering. Not only with cold, but shock and fright. It had been so terrible. She could see, with strange foresight, this night would set a yardstick for the whole of the rest of her life. Everything bad that ever happened to her from now on would be set against it, compared with it: the frozen terror as the man had come into the room, the humiliation of being caught there, with Ian, both of them stark naked, him rolling off her, seeing his penis shrivelled suddenly, him pulling the sheet over it, trying to cover it. It seemed to sum up the whole ghastly scene, that penis and its transformation, no longer bold and pleasure giving, but small and wretched, something to be ashamed of: and then the horror as a girl came into the room, said, 'There is something missing, Tim, the money I left for Mrs Kendall, a hundred pounds. She's left a note, said the envelope was empty, had I forgotten to put it in.' Sensing, rather than seeing, Ian's eyes on her, shocked and accusing.

And then the ghastly nightmare of the police arriving. Being questioned, asked if they could explain what they were doing there. It was like a bad dream; no, a bad film. Hearing the words 'You are under arrest for burglary.' Being cautioned, being told anything they said might be given in evidence. Definitely a bad dream. She'd wake up, any minute now. Being taken to another room by the woman officer, being searched, the Ecstasy being found in her pocket. 'They're nothing,' she said, 'they're codeine.' And then, fearing it might make things worse for her if she lied, saying no, they were Ecstasy. Being charged again, cautioned again, this time for being in possession of an illegal drug.

Being taken out to one of the cars, Ian being put in the other, being driven to the police station; taken into it at the back, led through a kind of caged area, with a locked door at each side into the custody area. She didn't seem to be waking up; and she couldn't have dreamt this, she didn't know about it. It was very, very frightening.

Then being questioned, where did she live, what was her date of birth, all that sort of thing. And then things got really bad; she asked if she could go to the lavatory, and they said no, not until she'd been searched.

'I have been searched,' she said.

'No,' they said, 'you have to be strip searched.'

She was taken to a cell; told to take all her clothes off. It was vile, but she refused to cry.

'Now you can use the toilet,' said the WPC, pulling off her rubber gloves. She nodded at it; it was in the corner of the cell. That was when Zoë did cry. And asked them to phone her mother.

Later they were interviewed separately. The interview was taped. On and on it went: what had they been doing there, had she taken anything else, what had she used the money for, was she going to buy drugs with it, who had supplied the tablets, was Ian involved in procuring them?

Zoë stuck stolidly to the truth. Speaking to her mother had both helped and made her feel worse: hearing Marianne's shock and disbelief, and at the same time her calm assurance that she would be there as soon as she possibly could be. 'But it won't be much before mid-morning, darling, it can't be. Try to keep calm. We'll do everything we can.' She was concentrating now with every fibre of her being on keeping calm, not screaming, not bursting into hysterical sobs. It was extremely difficult. And even in her wretchedness, she thanked God that she had arranged for Mrs Blake to be with Romilly. If she was not going to get home till midday, Romilly was going to need looking after.

Romilly lay in her bed, her face buried in the pillow. She felt herself on some kind of ghastly fairground ride of humiliation and misery and distaste and confusion; a ride she had got herself on to through a mixture of arrogance and stupidity and from which there seemed no prospect of escape.

She had run out of the building, and mercifully a taxi had been passing; she had hailed it and directed it to Eaton Square, ignoring the cries and gestures of Ritz and Serena. She had half expected them to follow her, had shot into the house and double locked it, put the chain on the door. The phone started to ring at once; because it seemed simplest, she picked it up. It was Ritz, telling her not to be silly, not to stay alone in the house, to let her at least come and join her there.

'I'd rather not,' Romilly had said, the polite child in her adding, 'thank you. My sister is here now,' she said firmly, 'please leave me alone,' and then put the phone down, checked that the answering machine was on, and then went and stood in the shower for a long time. She felt dirty, wretched, and she ached all over; the hot water was soothing, almost cathartic. Afterwards she had made herself a cup of cocoa and tried to watch an old film on television, but it was useless, the scene at Serena's house intruding, ugly, shocking, more vivid than the one on the screen.

After a while, she went upstairs to her room, too exhausted and wretched to be frightened of any creaks and noises, and hoped that she would sleep; but three came and then four and then five, and she heard the grandfather clock in the hall striking every time, and the half and quarter hour in between as well.

Finally, at six, she got up and made herself a cup of tea, and sat in the kitchen, listening to Capital Radio, oddly reassuring in its banal familiarity, her mind fixed now only on Zoë's return and a huge thankfulness that she was not going to have to face her mother until she had worked out some kind of sanitised and face-saving explanation for her determination never to enter a photographic studio again as long as she lived.

'What on earth am I going to tell Donna?' said Serena to Ritz. They too had been awake all night; the rift between them closed sharply and completely by what had happened. Marie France lay in a drunken sleep in the guest room; Serena had no idea what to do about her in the morning either. But it seemed a minor problem by comparison.

'I have no idea,' said Ritz. 'No idea at all.'

'You don't think . . .'

'I don't think what?'

'Well, that Romilly might – get over it. Decide it was all a lot of silly nonsense and – come back.'

'Frankly, Serena, no, I don't. That is a very innocent, very sensitive girl. You could see how appalled she was. And then she'd heard that message from fucking Alix.'

'I could kill that man,' said Serena, 'slowly and painfully. Cut off his balls and then—'

'Serena,' said Ritz, 'don't start talking about cutting off men's balls. It doesn't help. He did behave very badly. Of course. But—'

'I know. I know,' said Serena. 'Jesus, what a mess. Oh, Ritz, I'm so sorry.'

'It wasn't your fault,' said Ritz, with a sigh, 'not really. Well, I suppose you could choose your girlfriends with more care . . .'

'Stupid bitch,' said Serena. Her eyes were very hard suddenly. Clearly any relationship with Marie France had become history. 'But – God, Ritz, it isn't just Donna, is it? I've blown it. Just blown it. Oh, God . . .' She started to cry, very quietly. Ritz looked at her uncertainly for a while, then put her arm round her.

'Don't be so hard on yourself, Serena. It wasn't actually your fault. Just a hideous series of accidents. And you certainly can't be blamed for Alix Stefanidis. It was Donna who insisted on him. Personally I'm much more concerned about Mrs Muirhead. What she might do when she finds out. As for Mr Muirhead . . .'

'Maybe we should both flee the country,' said Serena with a rather shaky smile.

'Right. Come with me, please.'

Zoë had been back in the cell, sitting with her head in her hands. She was so frightened by now she would not have been surprised to find herself facing a firing squad. The custody sergeant, almost fatherly, telling her she was simply to receive a caution was such a shock she burst into tears again.

'But you do now have a police record. And if you commit any further offences, it will be taken into consideration. Now we want your fingerprints and to photograph you and then you can go.'

'Go?' she said stupidly. 'But my mother's coming here to collect me.'

'We'll tell her you've gone. You can't stay here.'

'But how will I get home?'

He gave her a look of grim patience. 'There are Tubes. Buses.'

'But I haven't got any money.' She felt helpless, incapable of any kind of coherent thought.

'Then you'll have to walk.' He shook his head. 'Now sign this here, please, and then go along with PC Manning and he'll take your fingerprints.'

Given that an extremely carefully planned – and expensive – weekend had been most efficiently wrecked by a combination of an avenging fate and a great deal of bad behaviour on the part of children who were nothing whatsoever to do with him, Nico was behaving extraordinarily well, Marianne thought. Felix would have conducted himself quite differently. Nico had rung some private plane service he had used on various occasions and organised a flight that got them to Heathrow by seven: and had his driver meet them there and drive them direct to the police station. He didn't even lose his temper when they were told Zoë had gone home, expressed satisfaction and relief that she had been let off with a caution, and then dropped Marianne off at Eaton Square, refusing to come in for so much as a cup of coffee.

'You have a lot to talk about,' he said, 'and you don't want anyone in the way. I'll phone you later today.'

Zoë greeted her mother on the doorstep. She was very pale. 'Hallo,' she said.

'Hallo, Zoë. Are you all right?'

'Yes, I think so. Thanks for coming. I am so terribly sorry.'

'We can talk about it later,' said Marianne. 'Right now, I want a strong coffee.'

'I'll make one.'

'Is Romilly here?'

'Yes,' said Zoë, 'she's here. And – Mum, you're going to need that coffee.'

'Why?'

'Well, I think you'd better let her tell you herself.' She met her mother's eyes, tried to smile. 'This is not a good day,' she said. 'Not a good day at all.'

'Gabriel,' said Octavia, shaking him gently, 'Gabriel, wake up.'

He surfaced slowly and smiled at her. He felt good: even if he was hotter than he would have liked, and there was a certain tautness to the skin on his shoulders that he knew would become first soreness then agonising irritation. It had been a very pleasing day: so far. She had taken him out to the little reef and shown him how to snorkel; he had swum about for ages – dangerously careless of the sun on his back – gazing in wonderment at the slow and peaceful world beneath him and the water, at the fish, with their sweetly smiling faces and dazzlingly brilliant colours, moving about in shoals with almost military precision, swerving first this way then that. Finally she had said they should go in, and they had changed – she into something chic and beige and he into his spare pair of brilliantly coloured trunks and a blue T-shirt that went with them rather well, he thought, and then they drove to the Glitter Bay Hotel and had a wonderful breakfast of fruit and yoghurt and honey and wheat toast and glass after glass of orange juice. And then they had walked through the grounds and she had shown him the blue water lilies that grew on the ornamental pool and the house that formed the main part of the hotel.

'It used to belong to Emerald Cunard,' she said. 'Isn't it lovely?'

'Who's Emerald Cunard? You know how ignorant I am.'

'You are,' she said laughing. 'Famous beauty in the 'thirties who was actually called Maud. I suppose she thought Emerald was smarter.'

'Sounds like my sort of person,' he said.

Back at Gibbes Beach, they had sat under the trees for a while; and then she had remarked that it was midday and really the time for resting, for siesta; and then they had been in bed together and not doing a great deal of resting, but making love, and it had been immensely better than the night before. He had felt confident and in command of her, of her thin pliable body, had felt his own body moving in her, through her, had felt her responding to him, softening, tautening, easing again, had been as surprised as he had the first time by the swiftness and greed of her, had heard her cry out with pleasure, loudly, sharply, and then after that he followed her and after that they had slept. Holding her, watching her sleep, her face soft and unwatchful, already flushed with the sun, her body utterly at rest, perfectly relaxed, one arm flung across him, her legs entwined in his, a hand occasionally lifting to brush her hair off her face, she seemed quite a different creature from the well-ordered, carefully controlled one he had thought he knew. And he had thought how ironic it was that coming to this place, about which he had had such misgivings, was changing her into a person about whom he had no misgivings at all.

Until . . .

'Gabriel, do wake up. Please.' She was smiling at him, but was anxiously serious as well. 'It's almost four, we have to eat something and then get ready and be across at Cobblers Cove by six.'

'What's so great about Cobblers Cove?'

'Gabriel! I told you. We're meeting Fergus there. For drinks.'

'Can't we go tomorrow instead? Don't they have a phone?'

'No, we can't go tomorrow. They're expecting us today. Anyway, I want to go, I want to show it to you.'

'I'd rather be shown it without Fergus.'

'Oh, Gabriel! He's perfectly nice really. Come on, get up. Elvira's left a perfectly gorgeous Caesar's salad. We must eat it.'

'Can't we have it for dinner?'

'No, we're going out for dinner.'

'Out!'

'Yes. My treat. To a place just along the beach. Don't look like that – only the two of us. It's so heavenly, the food is just fantastic and—'

'I'd rather eat here,' he said.

'Why?'

'I just would.'

She hesitated. Then, as if it settled things, 'Well, we can't. There isn't anything.'

'Whyever not?'

'Because I told Elvira we'd be out for dinner.'

'Without asking me? What I'd like?'

'Yes. *Mea culpa.*' She smiled, then saw he wasn't smiling back. 'Gabriel, please don't be difficult, I just know you'll like it. The place is so lovely. And the food is wonderful. Come on, get up. Or shall I bring you a plate of salad in bed?'

'No,' he said with a sigh. 'No, I'm terribly hot.'

'It's cooler in the dining room. The fan's been going full speed.'

It was cooler. And the salad was excellent. He drank a very cold beer, felt his irritability easing.

'Now, what are you going to wear?' she said, as they sipped iced coffee on the verandah.

'Wear? God, I don't know.'

'Well, what trousers have you brought?'

'Octavia, I haven't brought any trousers. Only the flannels I had on on the plane.'

'No others at all?'

'No. Sorry. No others.'

She was clearly struggling to say the right thing, not to sound dismayed. She failed. 'Gabriel, that's – that's a pity.'

'Why? You said we'd be alone, at the cottage, as you call it. Why should I have thought I had to bring lots of trousers?'

'You must have thought we'd go out a bit. To restaurants and so on. Come prepared for it. Most people would.'

'I'm not most people.'

'No, I know,' she said, kissing him, clearly struggling to make a joke of it. 'Well – you'll have to wear your flannels, then. What about a shirt?'

'Again, I've only got the one I wore on the plane.'

'What – the white one? Is that really all you've got with you?'

'Yes. And it's sitting in the linen bag in the bedroom.'

'Elvira's probably washed it,' she said, jumping up. 'I'll go and see.'

Elvira had; but it was still very wet.

'Damn. Well, you will have to borrow one of Daddy's. It may be a bit wide, but it'll do.'

'Can't I wear a T-shirt?'

'No, Gabriel, you can't. Not to Cobblers Cove.'

He suddenly felt violently irritated. 'Look, Octavia, why don't you go without me? I don't want to go, I'm perfectly happy here, I had no idea I had to bring a half my wardrobe with me, I'll just stay and read. My back's sore anyway.'

'I told you you should wear a T-shirt snorkelling,' she said, her tone crisply bossy.

'Yes, well, I thought that cream stuff would do. Must be something wrong with it.'

'There's nothing wrong with it, Gabriel, it's just not a high enough factor. You should have asked me.'

'Octavia, I've hardly had a chance to ask you anything at all over the past few days. If I had, I wouldn't have wasted it on bloody silly rubbish like suncream. For God's sake, just stop bugging me, will you? And go off to meet your friends on your own. I don't want to come.'

'Gabriel—' She put out her hand, covered his. Her face was very concerned, her dark eyes brilliant with tears. 'Gabriel, this is awful. We mustn't quarrel. This is supposed to be our time together. To get to know each other.'

'Exactly,' he said.

'What do you mean?'

'I mean why waste it going to meet bloody silly people for drinks, which means I have to wear clothes which I patently don't possess?'

She was silent for a moment; then she said, 'I'm going for a swim. I think you're being very unfair.'

He opened another beer and sat glaring out at the beach.

She was gone for about ten minutes; when she came back, she smiled at him awkwardly. 'I'm – sorry, Gabriel,' she said, 'very sorry. I didn't think.'

He looked at her. She found it hard to apologise for anything, he knew, so great was her need to get everything right, to know she had done so. She was wearing a one-piece navy swimsuit; with her hair slicked back, her anxious expression, she looked like a little girl. He stood up, went over to her, kissed her.

'I'm sorry too,' he said. 'Of course I should have brought some more clothes. It's just that – well, I didn't think I'd need them. I haven't got them anyway,' he added and grinned at her.

'No. I know.'

Suddenly he wanted her very badly. Her nipples stood out very clearly under the swimsuit, drops of water hung on her mouth. He bent and kissed it; she tasted salty, earthy.

'Let's go back to bed now,' he said, 'and I swear we'll go and meet your friends tomorrow instead. I'll even ring them, if you like, say you're not well. So you don't feel you're letting them down.'

She hesitated, then smiled and said slowly, 'No, I'll ring them. I – think that's a nice idea, Gabriel. Very nice indeed.'

Later, much later, as they lay finally apart, shaken, sated with pleasure, he said, 'I tell you what. Tomorrow morning, we could go into Bridgetown and buy me a couple of shirts. How would that be?'

She leaned over and kissed him, very gently. 'The sex must have been very good,' was all she said.

Tom couldn't ever remember feeling so lonely. Like all over-busy people, he fantasised about having time, space, life to himself; thought wistfully of a day filled with only a neat and orderly structure of appointments, rather than a mountain of them, heaped furiously one upon the next; of having an evening to himself to read, watch TV, rather than sharing every one with clients or even friends, over dinners, drinks, theatres, exhibitions; dreamed of spending a quietly self-indulgent weekend, a day even, alone in the house, doing what he wanted, pleasing himself. Now, at the end of just such a weekend, he felt strange, disoriented, longed as he would never have believed for noise to fill the silence – even the twins arguing, Minty crying, Octavia playing the chamber music she so loved and he so hated on the stereo; longed for people to fill the space – even interrupting him as he read the papers, taking the pen he was doing the crossword with, taking the water he had just boiled for coffee to make tea or hot lemonade with – longed for demands to disturb his thoughts, stress to wreck his peace. It did not come; and his sense of loss, planted in solitude, nurtured by silence, burgeoned and grew into a vast, oppressive misery.

He thought of the twins, playing with their friends by some swimming pool in the Tuscan countryside, of Minty, smiling and giggling, over-indulged by Caroline's parents, of Octavia, lying in the sunshine on the golden Barbadian beach, and not only on the beach, but in the large, white-veiled bed where he and she had spent most of their honeymoon; and not alone either, but with her lover, and although he knew that he deserved some of the loneliness, much of the pain, he also knew that other factors, avenging furies even, had played their part, and not entirely fairly, in creating it. And as he drank himself into sleep, staring at an appalling film on the movie channel, he found himself filled with anger and outrage at those furies. And at the one that had played the largest part, the human, inhuman man who had set out most wilfully to wreck whatever it was he had made for and with Octavia; and was forced to recognise that, barring some rather unlikely miracle, he had probably, finally, succeeded. And Tom did not believe in miracles.

Marianne sat on the floor of Romilly's bedroom; Romilly lay on the bed, looking at her, her large green eyes cloudy with tears and some kind of strange sullen defiance.

Marianne felt very sick. Finally, haltingly, prompted gently by Zoë, who was now asleep herself, released briefly from her own troubles, the story had come out; the terrible session with Stefanidis, his criticism of her, the humiliation, physical and emotional, of the whole, terrible, drawn-out day, culminating in the naked breasts, bared to two men, total strangers, not so dreadful perhaps in absolute terms, but an outrage against someone as innocent, as eager to please as Romilly: and then, as if that was not enough for her to bear, the appalling episode with Serena Fox and her lesbian lover. And then coming home to an empty house, with no one to hold her, comfort her, say there there, it doesn't matter, you're quite safe, nothing matters, I'm here.

What kind of mother was she, that she could have allowed even the possibility of such a situation developing: so engrossed in her own affairs – or affair – her own pleasures, her own concerns. While one daughter was running wild in London, committing God knew what crimes, or near-crimes, and another was being confronted by the reality of a world she had no business even to be near, never mind forced into. Briefly, wildly, she contemplated what Alec would have to say to her on the matter of her motherhood now, and shuddered and tried to turn away from it; and then thought that whatever he might say, she deserved it and more.

'Darling,' she said rather helplessly, 'darling, would you like to come down, maybe watch TV with me for a bit?'

'No,' Romilly said, still with the strange closed expression. 'I really don't feel too good, I'd rather stay up here.'

'But, Romilly, sweetheart—'

'Mum, don't make so much of it. It was no big deal. I'm fine. Stop fussing.'

She sounded like Zoë: older, hostile, difficult; Marianne sighed and turned away from her, looked rather wildly round the room, still a child's room, with its Roald Dahl books on the shelf, and her noticeboard, covered with tickets to theatres and pop concerts and the teenage balls she had gone to, and postcards and pictures taken in photo booths of herself and her friends, and posters of Leonardo di Caprio and Robbie Williams, and her rollerblades and her riding hat slung untidily into a corner, and the endless collages of family holidays, and the dolls' house, standing next to the desk. Romilly had always loved that dolls' house; Alec had bought it for her in America, a lucky find, a house very like the one they stayed in at Martha's Vineyard every year.

She reached forward now, to close the front door, which was hanging open. Something stopped it.

'Don't,' said Romilly sharply. 'Leave it alone.'

Marianne didn't leave it alone. She pushed again, and then when it didn't yield, she opened it, and against the background of Romilly saying, 'Mummy, please!' and feeling sicker than ever, pulled out an almost-empty packet of laxative tablets.

'Romilly, darling, why on earth were you taking those? Horrible things, for heaven's sake, couldn't you have asked me? Why take them? For God's sake, Romilly, you've got to tell me. Got to let me help you.'

And then finally, the spell broke, and Romilly flung herself off the bed and into her arms, and was saying, 'I had to, I had to.'

'But, darling, why?'

'I had this spot. My skin was horrible and my stomach was all bloated, and it was the session. I thought – I thought they'd help. They did.'

'But, darling, help what?'

'Help bring it on. My period,' said Romilly, her voice louder, thick with tears. 'It was late. Days and days late. I had to do something about it, I had to, it was so terrible, you don't understand.'

And Marianne sat there, holding Romilly, feeling the sobs shaking her body, feeling more ashamed of herself than she could ever remember, and realising exactly how badly out of order her own life had become.

CHAPTER 40

Playing God is a dangerous game for mortals. It requires breathtaking arrogance, an iron nerve and an absolute determination to see it through, whatever the cost and whatever the consequences. Felix Miller, who possessed all those things, had been playing God with some success; he was lacking, however, in that other crucial quality, granted only to the Almighty; the ability to see what further moves, if any, might need to be made . . .

He simply considered his job done, and well done: Octavia dispatched, alone with her lover, into the loveliness and peace of Barbados; and in the knowledge moreover that her husband was disporting himself in the pleasure-domes of Tuscany with his mistress. He had done that, Felix thought, studying the financial pages that sunny Monday morning; he had created a set of circumstances whereby Octavia could go away, guilt free, knowing that her marriage must be finally and absolutely over. And whereby Tom Fleming had been typecast, correctly of course, but in a manner in which there could be no doubt, as the unarguable villain of the piece. All that was needed now was the divorce to be set in motion, and Octavia would be safe again. There could surely be no possible reason for her to postpone it any longer now: no reason either for him not to ring his solicitor and establish exactly what Octavia should and should not do in order to bring about a legal end to her marriage, as final and unarguable as its emotional counterpart. He picked up the phone and dialled Bernard Moss's number.

'We'll go to Cave Shepherd tomorrow morning,' said Octavia, 'to get your shirts. It's a marvellous shop, a bit like – well, like Harrods.'

'Sounds my kind of place.'

He grinned at her. They had spent the day at Crane, on the northern side of the island, a glorious white-sanded beach with rolling white-edged turquoise surf. They had taken belly boards and Octavia had tried to teach Gabriel to catch the waves; he had been hopeless at it, missed the moment every time, but he hadn't minded, had watched her from the beach, laughing, as she rode in through the surf, and felt a stab of something very close to love for her. Afterwards, she lay stretched out on her board, half asleep, her body already turned golden brown, a clutch of rather surprising freckles on her small perfect nose. Octavia would not have been expected to have freckles, Gabriel thought, they were somehow too childlike, too random, for her neat orderly beauty. But they suited her. The sun suited her altogether, Gabriel thought, more than half envious; he had woken pink shouldered and sore, had kept his T-shirt on all morning, even in the sea, feeling slightly foolish and somehow adolescent. He wondered if Tom Fleming burned in the sun and decided it was unlikely.

At lunchtime they went up to the terrace restaurant at the Crane Hotel, set on the cliffs high above the beach, and ordered swordfish salads and fries; while they waited Gabriel had a milk punch.

'I warn you,' said Octavia, 'that might sound innocent, but it's lethal.'

It was; his head was spinning long before the food arrived.

Later, they swam again, and then she went fast asleep on her board, in the shade of some trees; Gabriel, feeling the heat badly now, walked along the water's edge, and tried to ignore a determinedly developing headache. He needed some time out of the sun; but she had organised a boat-trip the next day, and was so excited about the wonders it was going to offer that he didn't have the heart to say he couldn't go.

The dreaded cocktails had been postponed until the next day: Fergus and the blonde were going to a dinner party that night. For that, at least, Gabriel was grateful.

He had walked as far as he could, stopped by some cliffs jutting far out into the sea, and turned; he swam for a few minutes, trying to get cool. The water was warm as well as wild; his headache eased as he dived under the waves. A quiet evening and he'd be fine tomorrow . . .

'We're going to dinner at a restaurant called Pisces tonight,' said Octavia, sitting up, refreshed from her sleep, waking to his kiss. 'It goes right out into the sea. You'll really enjoy it.'

He tried to look enthusiastic but his headache had stabbed back into life. 'Good. Shall we go back now?'

'Yes, I think we'd better. You look as if you've had quite enough sun. Your face is terribly pink, Gabriel. I wish you'd—'

'You wish I'd what?' he said, irritably conscious of his burned face.

'Wear a hat.'

'I will tomorrow,' he said. 'I did bring one. A panama.'

'Really? How nice, I love men in panamas. So old-worldish. Come on, let's get you back. We can have a – well, a rest before we go out.'

She smiled at him, jumped up and kissed him. He knew what she meant, and tried to look enthusiastic, but his headache was so bad when they did get back that all he could do was fall gratefully asleep.

Pisces was a very nice restaurant; cooler now (in spite of wearing his grey flannels), and with several painkillers inside him, Gabriel managed at least to appear to appreciate it. He decided he should stick to water, but Octavia said the wine list was incredible, and he should have at least a glass. Sipping a Californian chardonnay at one of the tables at beach level, looking appreciatively at the menu, he felt almost human again.

Octavia, dressed in a white linen dress, unbuttoned dangerously low to show her brown breasts, smiled at him, picked up his hand and kissed it. 'I'm enjoying this so much,' she said. 'So very much. I hope you are too.'

Gabriel said he was. 'Much more than I expected,' he said.

'Really? I find that mildly insulting.'

'Only because of the heat,' he said hastily.

'I hoped that was what you meant. Now this menu is wonderful, a perfect blend of Caribbean and smart London. My advice is ignore the smart London bit, stick to the Caribbean.'

'I'm not actually very familiar with smart London menus,' he said. He had meant to sound lighthearted but it didn't quite come off.

'Oh, Gabriel,' said Octavia, 'you do run on about your humble lifestyle. It could get boring.' He hoped that, too, was meant to be a joke, but there was something approaching an edge to her voice. He knew her well enough now to recognise that edge; he hadn't heard it much out here, it belonged to the other Octavia. He had wondered when she might come back.

He smiled at her, picked up the menu. It really was very near perfect. The moon was just rising, reflecting in the water; the stars were brilliant. The waves – gentle, foamy, quite unlike the pounding surf of Crane – were drifting on to the shore. Just the sound was cooling. It was all a cliché. A luxurious cliché. But really very very nice. He was very lucky: only a fool would knock it. He'd have the crab, he thought, and after that—

'Octavia! Hallo, my dear, how are you?'

'Bertie! What a lovely surprise. I'm very well.'

Bertie was sixtyish, tall, handsome, white haired, very tanned. Gabriel hated him on sight. 'And your father? How is the old rogue? He's not here, I suppose?'

'No, he's not. He's fine. Coming over later in the year.'

'Hope he'll bring the lovely Marianne. I could use a decent golf partner. Got the children with you? Look, why don't you join us? We'd love some company. Clem, darling, look, it's Octavia.'

And then Clem joined them: also tall, also good looking, blonde, very slim, beautifully dressed. She bent and kissed Octavia. 'Darling girl. How lovely.' She looked rather uncertainly at Gabriel.

Octavia kissed her, then said, 'This is Gabriel Bingham. A friend of mine from England. Gabriel, this is Bertie and Clem Richardson. Old friends of my father's. They live here, in the most wonderful house.'

Gabriel stood up, shook their hands dutifully. He felt unreasonably outraged by their arrival.

'Now, do join us, won't you?' said Clem and Gabriel was almost prepared for Octavia to say that would be lovely, saw her glance at him, was overwhelmingly relieved to hear her say, 'Well – just for a drink. But I think we might stay on our own, if that wouldn't seem terribly rude. We're a bit – tired. Long day.'

'Oh, nonsense. Tired! Young things like you,' said Bertie, but Clem cut in and said, 'Bertie, do use your head. They want to be alone. Not spending the evening with a pair of old geriatrics.' Gabriel could have kissed her. 'Tell you what, though,' she said, smiling a dazzling smile at them, 'why don't you both come to lunch on Thursday? At the house. We're having a small party.'

'That would be heavenly,' said Octavia. 'Wouldn't it, Gabriel? Their house is glorious, one of the old plantation houses, I'd love you to see it.'

'Yes,' he said, 'that sounds very nice.' His desire to kiss Clem had died.

He felt instinctively that even a new shirt would hardly cover a lunch party with the Richardsons. His headache had come back; beating right through him, down his neck and his back. As he got up to follow the Richardsons to their table, he saw Bertie turn, take in his baggy flannel trousers and distinctly crumpled white shirt, saw his expression of slight disdain.

Bertie saw that he had seen, adjusted his expression hastily, clapped him heavily on the back to make amends, said, 'After you, dear boy.'

The last thing in the world Gabriel wanted was to be Bertie's dear boy. And the clap had hurt his sore shoulders terribly.

'I simply cannot understand it,' said Alec. They hadn't gone to Martha's. Alec was sitting in the drawing room in Eaton Square. Marianne had decided he should know everything, that she owed it to her children that there should not be the slightest necessity for deceit or connivance.

It had taken great courage, but she had done it. Had asked him to come to London, saying there were problems with the girls, had met him off the first available flight and told him what the problems were on the drive from the airport. At least she was able to tell him Zoë had been let off with a caution.

He had listened in silence, his jaw taut and set, his mouth downturned and supercilious, physical manifestations of the mental superiority he had always assumed over her. The intense dread that seeing them induced in her had been one of the major reasons for finally deciding to leave him.

When they got back to the flat, he saw the girls separately; Zoë first. She never told her mother what he had said to her, but she emerged from the drawing room white faced and shaking, and ran up the stairs to her room. When Marianne went up, asked if she was all right, she told her to go away.

'Zoë! Please! Let me come in.'

'Mum, I'm all right. I just can't take any more, okay?'

Romilly emerged from her interview brilliant eyed and defiant, less subdued than Zoë. She smiled at her mother, kissed her briefly, said, 'I told him none of it was your fault. None of it. But he does seem to think it was. I can't understand it.'

Marianne, who could, but who was none the less outraged that Alec should express such a view to Romilly, went into the drawing room. Alec gestured to her to sit down.

'I'll stand, thank you, Alec.'

That was when he told her he couldn't understand it.

'Leaving the two of them, Romilly still a child, and at the mercy of those dreadful people. You knew I was opposed to it, Marianne, I'm appalled you should have allowed it to go ahead at all, let alone without your being there with her. I really can't remember when I felt so – shocked.'

She was silent.

'As for Zoë, I am completely defeated. It seems she has no moral code of her own, she clearly needs constant guidance.'

'Alec, she was led astray. That's all.'

'And how was that, Marianne? How did that happen, that you allowed such a thing?'

'I can't watch her every minute of the day, know where she is, what she's doing . . .'

'Well, I'm afraid it seems that is what she needs. If she's not properly and constantly supervised, she'll end up in prison.'

'Oh, Alec, really.'

'Marianne, she's been arrested, caught in possession of drugs—'

'Two Ecstasy tablets!'

He stood up then, stalked over to her; his face literally livid with rage.

'How dare you talk like that! You, her mother, supposed to be responsible for her, granted custody of her. Dear God, I wonder why. Only two Ecstasy tablets, was it, Marianne? I can hardly believe I'm hearing you correctly. It's that sort of attitude that has allowed her to fall into this situation. Next you'll be saying only a hundred pounds.'

'No,' said Marianne quietly, 'no, I won't be saying that.'

God, she felt terrible about that hundred pounds. If only she'd had the time, time and attention to spare for Zoë, she might have noticed how distressed she was, might have got the whole story out of her.

'How long has she known this boy?'

'I don't know. I didn't know he was – well, he was in her life at all.'

'You didn't know! How is that possible, Marianne, how can you not know what sort of boys your daughter is spending her time with? What have you been busying yourself with for the past few weeks, for God's sake? Your golf?'

The withering contempt with which he said that hurt Marianne so much that tears stung her eyes. She blinked them away. She couldn't start crying. Not now. She'd never stop.

'Does Felix Miller know about any of this?'

'No, of course not. Anyway, I haven't seen much of Felix lately.'

'Oh, really? So who were you in Glasgow with, then?'

'A – friend.'

'A man friend?'

'Alec, I really don't think that is anything to do with you.'

'I disagree. I think everything in your life is to do with me. Insofar as it affects the way you are looking after, or rather failing to look after, our children.'

'Yes, all right, Alec. I get the idea. Yes, it was a man.'

'I see. So you were in Glasgow, with a man, while one of our children, underage, was left alone to fend for herself in a situation which any fool could see was potentially dangerous. Who was looking after her, in God's name?'

Useless to go into the explanation: to travel down the sad series of coincidences that had left Romilly alone. As useless to try to explain how it was that Zoë could have been allowed to have had a boyfriend who was so dangerously influential. She was silent.

Alec stood up. 'Well, I think I should still take them to Martha's anyway. It will do Romilly good to get away, and although Zoë doesn't deserve a holiday, I can keep a very close eye on her, and sailing and so on will be a lot better for her than dragging round the nightclubs of London. I'll just phone my secretary, see if she can organise their flights.'

'I can do that,' said Marianne.

'I'd rather you didn't,' he said. 'I'd rather you didn't have anything to do with the girls for a few weeks at least. You're clearly very busy with your own life. You'd better confine your energies to that, I think. It would benefit everyone.'

At which point she really did have to hurry out of the room and shut herself in the downstairs cloakroom where she sat on the lavatory and cried, like a naughty child ticked off by her headmaster.

They left at four that afternoon, Zoë sullen and miserable, Romilly quietly excited. Alec had been right about that at least: getting away was exactly what she had needed. He had made a curt phone call to Serena Fox, telling her that she should consider any contract with Romilly terminated, and that it would be followed by a letter. She could see that Romilly was actually relieved to have matters taken so totally out of her hands.

I should have seen that myself, Marianne thought, I should have known how frightened and threatened she felt. Her only comfort was that Zoë had flung herself into her arms at the last minute, and said how sorry she was, and how she mustn't blame herself for a moment.

But Marianne blamed herself totally. She, who prided herself above all in being a good mother, had sacrificed her children and their welfare on the altar of her own vanity and emotional requirements. She wasn't fit to have the care of those children. She couldn't ever remember feeling so wretched.

Few things were able to shake Nico Cadogan's self-confidence; the interview with his ex-wife that morning did so. For at least five minutes after she had left, he sat staring at the space she had occupied opposite his desk; then he picked up the phone and rang Tom Fleming.

'I think we have a problem,' he said.

'I feel so much better,' said Louise. She smiled at the doctor. 'Really so much better.'

'Good. I'm delighted. And the nurse in charge tells me you're sleeping better too, with less medication.'

'Yes.' She wasn't; but she wanted to go home, and she knew the insomnia worried them. It was the Prozac apparently; a little-known side effect. They were afraid they'd have to take her off it. And that would mean, possibly, staying at the Cloisters longer. So she lied. It was quite easy. Well, the lying was easy. Not sleeping was very difficult. It meant less escape, less oblivion. But if she could get home it would be worth it.

'At this rate,' he was saying, 'you'll be home in a few weeks.'

A few weeks. That wasn't soon enough. She needed to be out by Sunday, 7 September. It was essential.

She smiled at him. 'I do miss them so much, you know, my husband and my little boy. They don't – that is, they can't come to see me very often. And then it upsets Dickon, terribly, seeing me here. And of course that upsets me . . .'

'Well, let's see how you are in a few days. Are you getting more physical exercise now?'

'Oh, yes. I went for a long walk yesterday, with Alice, you know?'

Alice was one of the nurses; Louise hated her. 'She's so kind and she seemed happy to come with me. We must have walked miles. I love the outdoors so much. I always feel better there.'

'Yes, well, it's important you do the things you enjoy. You certainly look better.'

She felt better: in spite of being so tired. It was having the plan: that was what was getting her through.

Pattie David was lost in Ambridge when the phone rang: she jumped. 'Hallo?'

'Pattie? It's Sandy Trelawny. You all right? You sound a bit – odd.'

'Oh – yes, I'm fine. Sorry. Listening to the radio.'

'Look, we're coming over to see Louise on Saturday again. I wondered if Megan needed any help with her application. To get the house listed? I have to tell you, I'm not very hopeful. But don't let her know that.'

'Of course not. It's been so good for her, all this. Actually, she's sent the application off. Did it on Monday. But I'm sure she'd like to see you. And, Sandy, stay to lunch, won't you? Megan would love it.'

'Well—' he hesitated – 'we don't want to intrude . . .'

'You wouldn't be. I'd like it too,' she added, surprising herself.

Octavia looked at Gabriel and had to try very hard not to laugh. He was wearing his baggy Boy Scout shorts, a T-shirt that was just slightly too small, and a panama hat that was more than slightly too big. It slithered down over his forehead, almost meeting his eyebrows: the combination of that and his pink, peeling nose and slightly pained expression was very funny indeed.

'I think the hat's a bit big,' she said finally.

'So what, if it's comfortable?'

'Fine. Of course. But we might try and get you one the right size. In Cave Shepherd.'

'Octavia,' said Gabriel, and there was a distinctly raw note to his voice, 'I have no intention of buying another panama hat. This one is brand new, it cost me twenty-five pounds, I like it, all right?'

'Yes,' she said hastily, 'yes, all right.' His temper was not as equable as she had imagined; she was learning to respect it. 'Well, let's go. Got your swimming things? We pick the boat up in Bridgetown.'

'Yes, thank you.'

'It's a gorgeous day. Last time I did this trip was with Dad and it rained all day. We were warmer in the water than out of it.'

'It sounds rather nice to me,' he said.

She felt a stab of irritation. He didn't make much effort to hide his antipathy to the sun. Or to people, come to that. He'd been less than charming to Clem and Bertie Richardson the night before; on the other hand, he had apologised on the way back, pleaded a bad headache. She'd made some joke about his avoiding sex, but he hadn't laughed. He hadn't made love to her either . . .

'While we're here, I have to go and see my father's lawyers,' she said. 'There's some change in regulation about property ownership here. He wants the records and so on.'

He shrugged. 'Fine.'

'Right. Let's go.'

She liked Bridgetown, it was so alive, swarming with people; liked the central square by the big bridge, with its statue of Nelson; liked particularly the toytown dense suburbs edging it, street after street of little wooden houses, all painted different colours, perfectly kept. She drove Gabriel through it now.

'Isn't it amazing? Families of ten or more live here. When they were first built, the houses had no water or anything, just one big room. The children slept under the bed, the parents slept in it, with possibly a couple more children. Often, even now, the sink's outside at the back and there might be a gas ring on a shelf. Yet they're very happy, close families. There's very little violent crime here.'

'You'll be telling me next they're happy with their lot,' he said.

'They are,' she said. 'Really happy.'

'Octavia, please don't insult me with that nonsense.'

'It's not nonsense, and you don't know anything about it,' she said, and was silent. He didn't speak either, sat glaring out of the window. A little later, anxious to improve matters, she said, 'We might go and see Elvira's daughter tonight, on our way back. She lives here.'

'No more socialising, Octavia, please.'

'Gabriel, it's hardly socialising,' she said without thinking.

'Oh, really? And why would that be? Because she's black? Because she's the daughter of a servant?'

'Oh, don't be so bloody ridiculous,' she said, suddenly sharply angry with him.

They went into Cave Shepherd and she felt him making an effort, aware of her mood; picking out hideous shirts, asking her opinion. His taste really was terrible.

She struggled to be tactful, allowed him one of the hideous ones – brilliantly patterned, short sleeved – and then steered him towards a striped Ralph Lauren, in pink and white. 'This is nice too. And there's the same in blue. And while we're here, shall we look at trousers?'

'Octavia, I really don't want to—' He stopped.

'Don't want to what?'

'To spend a fortune. On bloody silly clothes I'll never wear again.'

'Of course you'll wear them again. Why on earth shouldn't you?'

'Well – I won't. And they're terribly expensive. It's ridiculous.'

'Everything is here. It's the import tax. Anyway, the rest of the holiday hasn't cost you anything,' she said lightly and then stared at him appalled, realising what she had said.

He stared back, his pink face bright red suddenly.

'I'm sorry,' she said, 'very, very sorry. I didn't mean – that is, that came out wrong.'

'It certainly did,' he said.

'I'm really sorry. Please forgive me, Gabriel.'

'Oh, forget it,' he said. 'Let's just go, shall we?'

'Are you – getting these?'

'What? Oh, yes, I'll get the shirts. If that's what you want.'

She left him in a café, drinking orange juice, while she went to see the lawyers. 'I'll be about half an hour. Is that all right?'

'Yes, of course. Be as long as you like.'

He was clearly angry: with good reason, she supposed. That was a terrible thing she'd said; she felt quite sick, just thinking about it. It was so unlike her, to be tactless; she was usually so careful about everything she said. On the other hand he was being – difficult. Ungracious. That was what had prompted it. When she looked back he was sitting staring at his glass like a sulky child; she sighed.

The lawyers were in one of the small side streets behind the main square; next door to one of the innumerable diamond shops. She glanced into the window of the shop; there was a very pretty emerald and diamond pendant, simple, almost deco in design. She liked it. She wondered if she might buy it, treat herself. Jewellery was one of the few things that was cheaper here. Then she remembered that she was an about-to-be-divorced woman, and no longer allowed such extravagance. She went up the small stairs into the office of Myers and Greenidge, her father's lawyers.

Nicholas Greenidge, a large, charming white Bajan, greeted her with a kiss. He had known her since she was a baby. 'It's really lovely to see you, Octavia. How you doing?'

'I'm doing just fine, Nicholas. Thank you.' She hoped she was, anyway. 'How about yourself?'

'Oh, you know. Pretty good, I would say. We're very busy, that's for sure.' His accent was thick, the rolling vowels hard to understand at first.

'Good. I'm pleased for you. Dad sends his regards. Now, you know why I'm here. To pick up the stuff from the trustees in BVI. Have you got it?'

'Yes, it's all here. The deeds of the house, all the trust fund details. If I was your dad, I'd want to be pretty damn careful before I registered the house in Barbados. I wouldn't want the officials here having a claim on the money. The transfer tax when he sells will be bad enough. He'll have to pay that. But tell him I said to strip all the money out of that trust fund.'

'You think he should?'

'I do. There's a lot there at the moment, you know.'

'Really? I suppose with the stock market doing so well . . .'

'Nothing to do with the stock market, Octavia. It's the extra funds which have been put in that he wants to watch.'

'Extra funds?'

'Yup. Quite a bit. Paid in over the past two months or so.'

'Really?' she said. She was touched. It was so like her father, that: to pay money quietly into the trust fund, of which she was a beneficiary. He obviously knew she wouldn't take money from him directly, and this was his way of keeping her safe.

'Yup. About twenty thousand dollars paid in.'

'Twenty thousand! Goodness.'

It was the divorce of course, his fears for her over that. He clearly saw her living on the street without his help.

'So you don't want to lose it. Anyway, Octavia, you take all this back with you, talk to him about it. I don't think this legislation is going to happen yet awhile. But best to be ahead of the game. That is my advice to you.'

'Yes, of course. And we should follow it. It's always good, your advice, Nicholas.'

'Glad you think so.' He grinned at her. 'He keeping well, your dad?'

'Very well. Thank you.'

'And how's Mr Fleming? And the children? You got them with you?'

'No. No, I haven't. Unfortunately,' said Octavia. 'They're in Italy and I miss them.' She realised, with a sudden pang, just how much.

'I bet you do. He's a very good man, Mr Fleming. I always did like him a lot.'

'I didn't mean—' said Octavia, and stopped. It was far too complicated to explain.

'You send him my best regards, too.'

'Yes, I will. And Mary, is she all right?'

'She's very all right. We've got another little varmint on the way.'

'How lovely! Congratulations. Well – lovely to see you, Nicholas.'

'And you too, Octavia.'

She went to find Gabriel, hoping he was in a better temper.

If Felix Miller had been present at that interview, he would have been more than a little troubled by it. God, on the other hand, of course, would not . . .

Hugh Shepherd leaned back in the rather luxurious leather chair that was one of the perks of his job with the Planning Inspectorate and called Michael Carlton on his direct line. He smiled out of the window as he waited for a reply; it was very good to be able to impart welcome news. And this was welcome news: with a lot of noughts attached to it.

'It was so wise of you not to take this to a full public inquiry, Mike,' he said. 'Always a temptation, but it wastes so much time. Anyway, a little bird told me this morning that the news is very positive. Very positive indeed. Can't say more than that, of course, but – well, of course it should never have been turned down by the LPA in the first place.'

'Really? I'm delighted.'

'Yes. I mean, John Whitlam's report was pretty watertight. And genuine, nothing remotely dodgy about it. Straight as a die, our John. Can be tiresome in his own way, but a useful name to have at the bottom of a report.'

'Marvellous.'

'Sure. Now there's just one thing. I had a call from the DOE this morning. Some fool of a woman is trying to get the house listed. Now if she succeeds – which I'm pretty sure she won't—'

'Jesus, Hugh. That would really put the kybosh on it. I can't build this place with the house standing there.'

'No, of course not. But it won't happen. That house was built in the 'twenties. God, Mike, you can hardly get Georgian houses listed these days.'

'I know that. But that house is rather extraordinary. The DOE might think it worth saving.'

'They won't. Anyway, the man from the DOE is going to have a look at it next week. Quickly, as a personal favour to me. But I am confident they won't list it. And that is their last card. There's nothing else they can do. They don't have a leg to stand on. So I reckon by – well, let's say, by next March, you can lay your foundation stone. And Bartles Wood will be history.'

'Good God,' said Tom. He stared at Nico. 'That is appalling.'

'Isn't it? He's clearly going to make a bid. Portia's won't be the only shares he's after. They've been creeping up in value for days now. I didn't think too much about it.'

'And are you absolutely confident this consortium had Miller behind it?'

'Oh, yes. He's not making any real effort to hide the fact. The London Wall Bank is one of the biggest components of the consortium's backers. Portia's advisers did a bit of homework, being intrigued by the rather high offer.'

'Which was?'

'Two pounds eighty-five.'

'God. He really wants them.'

'Yup. It seems he's ferreting around, seeing just how many he can find.'

'And how many has she got?'

'Oh, five per cent. Helped with the tax at the time, of course, and I was younger and less wise. Accountants always advise giving shares to wives. My solicitor said I'd regret it if things went wrong, but I didn't listen to him. He was right. Shrewd as well as shrewish, my ex-wife. As is now proven. She's very excited about it. Going to make a packet.'

'Well, he'll have to declare his intentions soon. On the takeover, I mean. If he's got any substantial holding together. Stock Exchange regulations. But—' He stopped.

'Yes?'

'Oh – I was going to ask a really crass question. Of course we know why he wants the company.'

'Marianne?'

'Well – yes. But rather more, I'd say because you've helped me.'

'What? Oh, now, Tom, that can't be right. Is he really that – tortured?'

'I'm afraid,' said Tom, 'Felix Miller can be a lot more tortured than that.'

'You look very nice,' said Octavia.

'Well, that's all right, then. Nothing else matters, does it?'

'Gabriel, please! Please try to enjoy this.'

They were driving to the lunch party with the Richardsons; to their plantation house in the heart of the island.

Gabriel felt wretched. He had got burned on the boat the day before, despite thick haze, wearing a T-shirt in the water and Octavia's factor 10 suncream. He had also drunk too much beer, in an attempt to improve his mood – very black after the shopping trip – and had spent the afternoon asleep on deck, waking to another filthy headache.

The trip itself had been fun; the catamaran she had chartered had seemed to fly through the intensely blue water and he and Octavia had lain on the nets between the two prows and managed to become friends again. The snorkelling had been spectacular. She had produced an underwater camera and he had taken endless pictures of the electric-blue and yellow striped and spotted fish; and he had enjoyed swimming with the turtles, sweet, gentle creatures who took little fish from his hand. But it was hot: very hot, and there was a new heavy humidity in the air that added to his misery.

He had arrived home feeling terrible, had hoped she might say there was no need to go and meet Fergus and the blonde; but all she did was hurtle into a shower as soon as they got back and call to him from it to hurry and use one of the others.

He had pulled on the grey flannels – more scratchy by the day over his sore legs – and then the Ralph Lauren shirt.

'You look really nice in that,' she said.

'Don't sound so surprised.'

'I'm not. I just thought you'd like to know.'

'Not specially,' he said, tying up the laces of his old plimsolls.

'Gabriel, are you going to wear those?'

'Yes,' he said, 'yes, I am.'

He had half hoped she'd say he couldn't, just so that he could refuse to go; but she hesitated, and then said, 'Come on, then, let's go.'

It had been a long, lurchy drive in the car; Cobbler's Cove, pink and excessive, offered him no comfort. Fergus and the blonde were waiting on the terrace by the sea; a lot of kissing went on.

'Having a good time?' Fergus had said to him.

'Yes, great, thanks,' he had said, 'but could we sit under one of those umbrella things, do you think?'

'Oh, no need this time of day. What sun there is is going down fast. I think it's going to rain. Octavia, what do you want to drink?'

He had asked for water, sitting sulkily squinting into the sea; they had told him he couldn't possibly drink water at Cobbler's Cove, and ordered a Bellini for him.

'Only place here you can get one,' said Fergus. 'Superb. Do you good. Octavia, are you by any chance going to the Richardsons' tomorrow?'

Gabriel had not thought his heart could sink any lower. He was wrong.

Nico Cadogan's temper, hard to ignite, was nevertheless very slow burning. Felix Miller's clear intention to move in on his company for reasons of nothing but personal revenge infuriated him; after a day of intense anxiety over it, discussing tactics with Tom Fleming, he arrived home to a note from Marianne that added to his sense of outrage. He had behaved magnificently, he thought, over the weekend, had not complained about having it cut short, had hired planes and cars, been supportive and patient with Marianne, courteous to the difficult daughter – pretty, though, she was going to be a dead ringer for her mother – and then slipped tactfully away, left them all in peace. And what did he get for it? A thankyou note that might have been from someone he'd invited to a cocktail party, and a plea to be left alone 'for a few days'.

He telephoned her immediately, and asked her, slightly tersely, to join him for dinner.

'I'm really sorry, Nico. I can't. I just feel so dreadful about everything.'

'Then you need something to make you feel less dreadful,' he said, trying to sound lighthearted.

'No. No, Nico, I don't. I really need to be on my own.'

Irritation stabbed him. 'Marianne, I need to be with you. I want to talk to you. And things aren't that bad. Surely.'

'To me they are.'

'But why?'

'You wouldn't understand. You couldn't understand. Please, Nico, leave me alone.'

The rage flared. Illogically, he knew: she had no idea what Felix Miller had done, and it was he who had pursued her and provoked Felix into revenge, not the other way round. Just the same, he felt she owed him at the very least some time. If he requested it.

'Very well,' he said and put the phone down.

'Isn't this lovely?' said Octavia. 'Mahogany trees.' They were driving through a long tunnel of them, arching tall and graceful over the road. 'Amazing, aren't they?'

'Yes. Amazing.'

'And those feathery things are called casuarina trees, they were introduced to Barbados by Prince Albert. It's said to be the best firewood in the world.'

'Not much use here, then,' said Gabriel.

She didn't answer. They left the mahogany trees behind, drove on a straight road between surprisingly lush fields, where cows grazed alongside brown creatures with floppy ears he assumed to be goats.

'Those are tropical sheep,' she said. 'Aren't they sweet? Very biblical looking. They're all tethered because—'

'Octavia, I really think I've had enough of the guidebook stuff for now. If you don't mind.'

She looked at him, her eyes suddenly dark with anger, and said nothing more.

The Richardsons' house was remarkable; built in 1700, it would have been more at home in Wiltshire or Suffolk, he thought, three graceful storeys high, with fine tall windows complete with shutters, exquisite mouldings on the ceilings, wooden floors and, astonishingly, fireplaces in all the main rooms.

'They thought houses needed fireplaces,' said Clem, laughing, seeing Gabriel's face – Octavia had ceased speaking to him altogether. 'The man who built it came over here from England to start a sugar plantation. He only knew about Queen Anne houses.'

'Do you grow sugar still?' Gabriel said, making a great effort to be polite.

'Goodness no, the sugar market here is dead, I'm afraid. No, we sold off the land in the early 'sixties. My husband is a businessman. A banker actually. Champagne, Gabriel?'

'Er – yes. Thank you.'

'Follow me,' she said and led him into what seemed to be an English drawing room; a black girl, in a black dress and white frilled apron, stood holding a tray of champagne glasses by the door. She gave him a minimal and polite smile. Clem took two glasses, motioned to her to move further into the room.

'Thank you,' said Gabriel loudly to the girl. 'Thank you very much indeed. Gabriel Bingham. I'm from England. Can't shake your hand, unfortunately, but very nice to meet you.'

The girl looked embarrassed; Clem Richardson amused.

'Come through and meet some more people. Now, Fergus I know you've met, and Harriet, of course, but let me see, oh, yes, this is Lady Browning. Lady Browning, Gabriel Bingham. He's here with Octavia Fleming.'

Lady Browning was plump, middle aged, beautifully dressed – and black. She smiled graciously at Gabriel. 'And what do you do in England, Mr Bingham?'

'I'm in politics,' he said.

'Oh, really? Like my husband. He's in the Civil Service. And my son, Alistair, over there—' she pointed out a slim, flashily dressed man – 'he's in property. That's the thing here, you know. All these great mansions going up, have you seen any of them?'

Gabriel said he hadn't.

'Huge places, costing four or five million dollars. They're going to cause trouble here.'

'Why?' said Gabriel.

'Well, because they will have to have security gates, guards, dogs, all that sort of thing. And it's against the culture here. It's always been a very open society and that sort of thing will lead to crime. I hear London has a terrible crime problem these days.'

'Not good, no,' said Gabriel. 'I think it's because—'

'Maria, come and meet Douglas Bird.' It was Bertie Richardson, beaming at them both. 'And you, Bingham. Interesting chap, into the charter airline business. Good name for it, Bird, don't you think?'

Gabriel followed them dutifully across the room. He didn't want to meet anyone in the charter airline business. He didn't want to meet any of them: although Lady Browning seemed like fun. The whole thing was like the worst sort of middle-class English dinner party. And with his luck he'd be sat down next to Harriet, the blonde . . .

'Octavia, I said I'm sorry.'

'Yes, I heard you. But I'm afraid that can't put right what seemed like downright rudeness. Doesn't matter to me, but the Richardsons are old friends of my father's. I could see they were feeling terribly uncomfortable. And Fergus is an old friend of mine.'

'I wasn't anywhere near Fergus.'

'You were next to Harriet. You ignored her through the whole meal. I just don't understand—' She stopped. She felt horribly near to tears. She had been genuinely embarrassed and upset. She had taken Gabriel along as her guest, and he had abused the hospitality. It just wasn't fair. Unbidden, social occasions with Tom came into her mind: however dreadful the people, however tired he was, he was always charming, interested, made an effort. She tried to crush the thought again, found it difficult: the effort made her feel more upset still.

'I'm going to try phoning Tuscany again,' she said, 'before it's too late.'

Gabriel shrugged, went out to the verandah.

She had tried to get through the night before and failed; then had tried the house, in order to speak to Caroline, to achieve some kind of contact with at least one of her children. Caroline wasn't there either: presumably still with her parents. Their number was on the answering machine, anyway, but she couldn't get through. The whole thing had unsettled her, upset her; she felt cast adrift. And the ghastly evening at

Cobbler's Cove with Gabriel being difficult, obtuse, not responding to what was a genuine effort on Fergus's part to be friendly, his wanting to get home early, had left her very much in need of hearing small, friendly voices.

He had obviously wanted to make love to her when they went to bed; upset, she couldn't face it, had made an excuse, said she was hot, had gone into the spare room. Later, lying awake, she felt wretched; another relationship going wrong already. Maybe it was her, as much as Tom; maybe she just wasn't good at relationships, and that was all there was to it; maybe she was a control freak, as Tom had said; maybe she was frigid even. No wonder Tom had turned to someone like Louise, warm, easy, funny; no wonder he had gone off with Lauren.

Panic had hit her; she was suddenly hot, stifling. She had got up, made herself a cold drink, and gone out to sit on the verandah, staring at the moonlit sea, trying to calm herself, failing. It was ironic, she had thought, that this holiday which she had thought would start to rebuild her self-esteem, was threatening to wreck it further . . .

'Hallo? Hallo? Is that the Villa Vittorio?'

'*Scusi?*'

'I said – oh, dear, could I speak to – to Signora Bartlett?'

'Signora is not 'ere.'

Thank God for that, she thought.

'Signor Bartlett, he speak. I fetch.'

'Thank you.'

Drew Bartlett's deep, over-smooth, tones came down the line. 'Octavia! Wonderful to hear from you. How are you, how's Barbados?'

'Oh – marvellous. Thank you. Last day tomorrow, though.'

'Really? Short trip.'

'Yes, well, I've got to get back. Are – are the children being good?'

'Marvellous. Really marvellous. That Gideon is a little trouper. He's swimming today for the first time, marvellous dive he's got. Hasn't complained once about not swimming either.'

'Is his foot all right?'

'Absolutely fine. We had the local doctor check it over, just to make sure. Right as rain.'

'That was kind of you. Thank you so much. And Poppy?'

'She's a peach. Really. Now the girls are all out, I'm afraid, gone to Florence for the day. Lauren's pretending they were going for the culture, but actually, between you and me, they're just shopping. But Gideon's here. Want a word?'

'Yes. Yes, please.'

She stood there, feeling slightly weak at the knees. She had been so afraid Tom would answer the phone, her heart was still thudding.

Gideon's cheerful voice came over the miles. 'Hi, Mum!'

'Hallo, darling. Is your foot all right? Having a good time?'

'Brilliant. It was a bit hot till now, but I could swim today. There's another boy here, he's good fun. He let me play with his Nintendo while I couldn't swim. And Drew – Mr Bartlett – was really kind, taught me chess.'

And what was Tom doing, she wondered tartly, swimming with Lauren, no doubt . . .

'How's Poppy?'

'She's a pain. She and Camilla spend all the time giggling. Really gross. She's out. They're going to be really late back. They went to Florence on the train. I could have gone, but it's so hot. Drew said it'd be more fun here.'

'I see. And – and Dad?' She brought the word out with a struggle. 'How's he?'

There was a silence; then Gideon said, 'Dad? He's okay, I expect.'

'Has he gone to Florence, too?'

'What? Dad's not here, Mum.' Gideon sounded puzzled.

'He's in Florence?'

'No, he's not here at all. He never was. I mean, he didn't come. I don't know why you thought he did . . .'

'He didn't – come?' she said stupidly. The floor seemed to shift under her feet; she felt dizzy.

'No. He's at home. In London.'

'But I thought—'

'Mum? Of course he couldn't come. There's no room for him. Poppy shares with Camilla and I sleep on a camp bed in the dining room.'

'Oh,' she said, 'oh, I see. I thought – well, that was silly of me.'

'It was a bit. Anyway, how's it there? Even hotter, I expect.'

'Yes, pretty hot. Anyway, darling, I'll be home in London on Sunday morning. Give Poppy a big hug from me. Drew says you're both being very good. I've got to go now. Sorry. I'll ring again when I get home.'

She felt an urgent, a pressing need to get off the phone, to be by herself, with her whirling thoughts. Everything seemed to have shifted again: black had become white. And two and two clearly didn't quite add up to four. How had she reached that conclusion? How was it possible? How could Tom have let her reach it? Had he been hoping to go, perhaps, thinking he was going even? Or – had she just been stupid? Angrily, dangerously stupid?

Quickly, swiftly, before she could lose her courage, she dialled the house; it rang for a while, then the answering machine picked it up.

She took a deep breath, started to leave a message, and then Tom's voice cut in. 'Hallo, Tom Fleming speaking.'

'Oh – Tom,' she said. 'Tom, hallo. It's me. Octavia.' She felt like a schoolgirl: silly, nervous.

'Hallo, Octavia. How is Barbados?'

'Oh – very nice thank you. Yes.'

'Good time?'

'Yes. Yes, very good. Thank you.'

'Good. Everything's fine here. I spoke to Caroline last night, she's bringing Minty back tomorrow.'

'Tom—'

'Yes?'

'Tom, I thought you were – that is, I thought you were in Italy.'

'Did you?' he said and his voice was cold, hostile suddenly.

'Yes. Yes, I did. I – don't know how – why . . .'

'I don't know either,' he said.

There was a long silence; clearly he wasn't going to help her out of this one.

'I suppose I just got the wrong end of the stick.'

'Yes. Very much the wrong end.'

'Why didn't you explain?'

'Have you ever tried to explain to a fly there's glass in the window, Octavia?'

She said nothing.

'Well, I did try. Once or twice, actually. But you went on buzzing furiously and I just couldn't get through to you. Gave up in the end. Bit of a shame.'

'Yes,' she said. 'A bit of a shame. But – but I thought – when they said you'd all gone to the airport . . .'

'We did all go to the airport. I drove them, waved them off and then went out to dinner.'

'Oh,' she said again, trying to digest this, to make sense of it. 'Yes, I see. Well – anyway, I'll be home on Sunday.'

'Fine. Goodbye, Octavia.'

'Goodbye, Tom.'

She put the phone down; she felt very sick. It was more than a bit of a shame. It was an appalling shame. It was the only reason, really, she had asked Gabriel to come with her. Because she was feeling so hurt, so angry. How stupid of her. How extremely stupid. Not that it mattered really of course. It didn't make any real difference. The marriage was over anyway. She and Tom were over. One more misunderstanding, one bit less communication, didn't really matter. It didn't matter at all. It was just a further example of how far apart they had grown. It just didn't matter.

She just didn't care . . .

'Why are you crying?' said Gabriel. For the first time for days he looked at her kindly, with concern. 'Is something wrong?'

'No,' she said, 'not really. Everything's fine.'

But she went on crying uncontrollably, just the same.

CHAPTER 41

Time was running out on him, Felix Miller reflected. No, that put a rather negative spin on the situation. In the dreadful modern phraseology. He was doing so well, acquiring the Cadogan shares, he'd have to declare very soon. And that would be pure pleasure. He'd have to put in a pretty high bid to the shareholders: probably three pounds a share. He's worked the price up himself. Well, the company was probably worth it. All his research indicated that Cadogan had made a good job of overhauling the company. Done his work for him. That afforded Felix some pleasure as well. Of course hotels ran on borrowed money; but the properties alone were worth a small fortune. And he could undoubtedly make the thing pay. Not that it mattered; no price was too high. The first thing, the very first thing he would do, after robbing Cadogan of the company that was as much a part of him as his own name, he had once told Felix, was get him voted off the board. There was the little matter of the merger referral of course; but since he had no hotels of his own, then there should probably be no problem. He wasn't creating a monopoly. Just an unemployed hotel owner. That would teach Nico Cadogan how it felt to lose something very dear to him. It would teach him very swiftly indeed. It had been really a very clever idea. Very clever indeed . . .

Marianne felt worse about Felix every day. She had treated him appallingly; and he didn't deserve it. He often treated her at best thoughtlessly and at worst harshly. She did not come first in his heart: Octavia did. She was used to that. She had not come first in Alec's either: his career did. Nevertheless, she owed Felix a great deal; they had had a marriage of a sort. He had not been some casual boyfriend, to be discarded on a whim, and her feelings for him remained very intense. Although he had treated her particularly thoughtlessly over their final few weeks together, she had too easily betrayed his trust and their past, had turned her back on him when probably he needed her most. And he was, at heart, a good man. Of course it had been outrageous, trying to destroy Tom's business, desperately urging the marriage towards a final conclusion. But he had been driven by the best motive, however misguided: had been driven by love. And she, without doubt the person he loved next best in the world, the person to whom he had turned in his awkward, truculent way, had not been there for him, had left him to do his worst. And she was afraid that worst might be very dreadful.

She felt guilty about Nico of course, but she wasn't in love with him; she felt she knew that very certainly now. He had just been there, when she needed someone. Love, in all its complex difficulty, was what, in spite of everything, she still felt for Felix. It was time to make amends; time to stop betraying Felix.

'So when will Octavia be home?' said Caroline. She was spooning cereal rather briskly into Minty.

'Oh – early on Sunday morning,' said Tom. Then, noticing that Minty was rubbing her cereal into her neck, added, 'Minty, that's not what Weetabix is for.'

'Oh, dear, I'd better get you another bib,' said Caroline. 'She needs some new ones, these are all too small. I think I've got some bigger ones in this drawer – good heavens!'

'What's that?' said Tom.

'Mrs Fleming's mobile phone. What an extraordinary place for it to be. Underneath all the tea towels.'

'Well, maybe Mrs Donaldson put it there.'

'She's away this week. Visiting her daughter and new grandson. Well – it doesn't matter.'

'No,' said Tom. 'No, it doesn't matter at all.' It was true, he realised: Mrs Donaldson had been away. The house had lacked its usual sparkling order. Trained to neatness by Octavia, he always cleared up his dirty coffee cups, put his clothes in the dirty linen basket, made his bed, but this week the bed had not been changed, nor the towels, and nor had the waste paper baskets been emptied; in his depressed distraction he had failed to notice it until now. Anyway, clearly Mrs Donaldson had not put the phone in the tea-towel drawer. So who . . .

'Well – I must get Minty out,' said Caroline. 'It's a lovely day.'

'She looks awfully well, Caroline. Obviously the country air, down at your parents'. Thank you for taking her. Anyway, I must get off to the office. 'Bye for now.'

'Goodbye, Tom. Should I get you any supper for this evening?'

'No, that's all right. I'll be out. Thank you all the same.'

He drove off, flicking his mind on to the day ahead: he had a meeting with Nico Cadogan at ten. Nico was frantic with worry about Felix Miller's intentions and needed to be steadied. And something more than an upbeat letter to the shareholders would be necessary this time. But a tiny portion of Tom's mind refused to be flicked, stayed fixed on the mobile phone hidden underneath the tea towels. For some reason, it troubled him. He couldn't quite think why.

'It hasn't really worked, has it?' said Gabriel.

He put out a hand, stroked Octavia's flat brown stomach gently. She tensed, then relaxed and half smiled at him. They were lying on the beach, in the shade of the great heavy trees; they had become oddly, quietly close, in the aftermath of a long and raging row, a sleepless night, an acknowledgement from him finally that he had been less than courteous at lunch, less than easy altogether over the previous few days, and from her that she had made demands of him throughout the holiday that he could not reasonably have expected.

'No,' she said finally and with huge difficulty, 'no, it hasn't worked, I'm afraid.'

'I blame the sun,' he said, with an embarrassed grin. 'The sun and Marks and Spencer.'

'Marks and Spencer? How can you blame Marks and Spencer?'

'They didn't have any decent summer clothes when I went in that day. Just sale stuff. And winter woollies. So I couldn't get properly kitted out.'

'Oh,' she said, 'yes, I see. Well – certainly partly their fault, then.' She smiled at him. Nearly a week of his company had taught her not even to suggest that there were other shops he might have gone to.

'It's very sad,' he said. 'I'm sorry.'

'Well, just one of those things. And maybe, in a way, just as well.'

'Now how do you work that one out?' he said.

'Well, at least it's settled things. Otherwise it might have dragged on for months, mightn't it? We could have gone on and on, trying to make it work, not getting anywhere, disrupting our lives . . .'

'Yes, and that would have been a serious waste of time,' he said. 'I can see that. Your pragmatism is breathtaking, Octavia. I really must try and pick up a few tips. Before we part.' He stood up. 'I'm going for a walk.'

'Gabriel, you're being silly,' she said.

'I'm not being silly. I find your attitude very hurtful. Incomprehensible, even. Regarding a love affair as a – as a sort of marketing exercise. A bit of research. It's horrible.'

'Look,' she said, and there was an underlying panic in her voice, 'all I meant was we'd have made one another unhappy for longer. Longer than we have.'

'Oh, so we're happy now, are we? Start an affair, find it doesn't work, finish it, all inside a week, phew, that's all right, then, no time or energy lost.'

She reached up and took his hand, pulling him down on to the beach again. 'Think of what might have happened. We'd have gone on and on for weeks, months, the occasional night here and there, all more and more unsatisfactory. And in the end, the same, miserable finale. Better to – well, to find out now. That's all I meant. You must see that.'

'I do see it,' he said. 'Of course. But I'm afraid I can't parcel up my emotions quite so neatly, Octavia, set time limits on them. One of the reasons, I daresay, we could never have – well, made things work.'

'Oh, God,' she said, and buried her face in her hands.

'Octavia – I'm sorry.'

'No, no, don't say you're sorry. I deserved that. You're right. I am – well, I am all the things you said last night. Controlling. Ruthless. Manipulative. Arrogant.'

'Did I say you were all those things?'

'You did. And—' she gave him a watery smile – 'and that I was a concrete-skinned, self-aggrandising bitch. Gabriel, you were right. Maybe not concrete skinned. But all the rest. I have to be – in charge. Don't I? That's my problem.'

'Well, to a degree. You do seem to need to be in control at any rate. Have everything on time, in order—'

'I know I do,' she said, very quietly.

'But is that really your problem, as you put it? It's made you a very successful person.'

'Oh, very successful,' she said bitterly, 'so successful my marriage is over.'

'Is it?'

'Of course it is! My children are neglected – apart from a little quality time, at the fag end of the day. My job is at this moment in jeopardy—'

'I really do doubt that,' he said.

'I'm afraid you don't know anything about it. Melanie is absolutely sick of me and my carryings on. Always away, always upset, letting people down, ducking out of meetings – that is no way to run a company. I do know that.'

'Well, that really is all temporary, surely,' he said. 'When you get back to real life – and at least in real life you won't have me hanging about any more – and it's true, it would have gone on and on, never any time together, you rushing back to your children, me to my constituents.'

'Perhaps even your putative fiancée?'

'Oh, no,' he said, 'no, not her. Definitely not her. Not after you.'

'Well,' she said, 'thank you for that at least.'

Her voice was very quiet suddenly, quiet and shaky; he looked at her sharply.

'Octavia?'

'Yes?'

'This thing not working out. It's no reflection on how I feel – felt – about you.'

'Of course it is!' she said. She was crying, rummaged furiously in her beach bag for a tissue.

'Oh, God,' he said, 'you're seeing this as another rejection, aren't you? Another failure?'

'So – isn't it?'

'No!'

'Well, tell me what it is, then.'

'It's got nothing to do with you. You as a woman. I still think you're one of the sexiest women I've ever known.'

'Gabriel, please don't. Don't try and humour me. Flatter me . . .' Her eyes were full of tears again. 'The fact is, however you dress it up, I've made a hash of our relationship, our time together and – oh, God . . .'

Gabriel put his arm round her. 'You may have made a hash of it,' he said gently, 'but so have I, for God's sake. I've been brought here, to this glorious place, by a beautiful and sexy woman and done nothing but whinge about it. Most men would think I was off my trolley. I can hardly believe it myself. I regret it terribly. But it has nothing at all to do with you, how I feel about you.'

'Oh, Gabriel, of course it reflects on how you feel about me. You've hardly made love to me since we got here.'

'Yes, well, you can blame the sun for that. I've been feeling lousy most of the time. Chronic headache. Agonising skin. Sick. Sore throat.'

'Yes, all right,' she said. 'I get the idea.'

'Sorry. Nor does it mean I don't like you.'

'How could you like me? When you see me so clearly?'

'I haven't told you some other things I see in you.'

'Do I really want to know?'

'Yes, you do. You're hugely intelligent. You have a great and engaging capacity for enjoying things. You're curious, interested, generous. Thoughtful, kind—'

'Oh, stop it,' she said, laughing.

'In a minute. And beautiful, as I said, and very, very sexy, as I said. Nobody's perfect, Octavia. Stop trying to be.'

'I don't suppose you can remember what I said about you,' she said. She was smiling now, through her tears.

'I can. Self-centred, self-satisfied, paranoid, immature – those were a few of them.'

'Ah. Well . . .'

'Anyway, for whatever reason, we clearly have to kiss and part and know we're not meant for each other. Not really. Not for more than – well, more than a few days.'

'If that,' she said and smiled again.

'Well, in a cold climate, maybe. But the real thing is – well . . .'

'Yes?' she said. 'What is the real thing? As you put it. Apart from a basic incompatibility?'

'The real thing is,' he said simply, after a long pause, 'you're still in love with your husband.'

'Marianne, this is Nico.'

'Oh,' she said, 'hallo.'

It was very good to hear his voice; she had missed him more than she would have admitted. Missed the nonsense, the attention, the affection. Missed him. But . . .

'I – wonder if you'd like to have dinner with me.'

He sounded different; rather low, less sure of himself.

'Well, I – Nico, the thing is . . .'

'Yes?'

'I really can't.'

He sighed. 'Hot date with your delinquent children?'

'No, it's not that.'

'Tomorrow, then?'

'No. Not tomorrow, either.'

A silence. Then, 'Am I to deduce from this you're trying to avoid me? On a longterm basis?'

'I—' She hesitated, then gathering her courage said, 'Yes. Yes, I'm afraid so.'

'I see.' The voice became icy suddenly; changed in a way she would not have thought possible. Terrifyingly, it reminded her of Alec's. 'And would you like to tell me what has brought about this change of heart? Was it something I did? Was I not quick enough, getting you down to London on Sunday morning? Did I not express sufficient sympathy with you over your domestic tribulations?'

'Nico, no, of course not, it's nothing like that. You were wonderful. It's just that I've been doing a lot of thinking.'

'About?'

'About—' She hesitated. 'Felix.'

'Felix!'

'Yes. You see, I feel, whatever I may have said, I . . .'

'Yes. Do go on. Whatever you may have said?'

'I feel that I still owe him my loyalty,' she said.

'Loyalty! Well, that's very amusing. Very amusing indeed. Let me tell you, Marianne, Felix Miller doesn't have the faintest idea of the meaning of the word. Or honour. Or decency. Any of those things.'

'Nico—'

'The man is a bastard. A conniving, unscrupulous bastard. Who just happens to be in love with his own daughter.'

'Nico, stop it! Don't talk about Felix like that.'

'I shall talk about him how I bloody well please. And I find it deeply distressing that you should place him before me in your priorities, Marianne. Deeply. Well, you are most welcome to one another. You will receive no more opposition from me. Good morning to you.'

The phone went dead. Marianne burst into tears.

Octavia stared at Gabriel. 'Don't be so ridiculous,' she said. She felt very hot suddenly, and her mouth was dry. 'Of course I'm not still in love with Tom. I *loathe* him.'

'No, you don't.'

'Gabriel, I do. Every time I think about him I feel sick. What he did – not just having an affair, but having an affair with my best friend—'

'Who is clearly a complete nutcase.'

'What's that got to do with it?'

'Quite a lot. He got trapped. Very nastily trapped.'

'And that makes it all right, does it? Gabriel, please. I don't think I like the turn this conversation is taking. One man defending another, poor chap didn't really mean any harm . . .'

'I'm not saying that. Not really. Look,' he said, taking her hand, 'I think I can understand how you felt. It was a double betrayal. Very ugly, very hard to bear. It turned your life into a sort of minefield. What, where, who next.'

'Yes,' she said slowly, 'it was exactly that.'

'The fact remains,' he said, 'you're still in love with him. I know you are. He's what you really want, he's right for you, right for your life. You hate what he did. You don't hate him.'

'Gabriel, I do.'

He shrugged. 'All right. I won't argue any more. But I shall wait for news of you with more than usual interest. Now what are we going to do with our last day? It would be nice to enjoy it.'

'You can't enjoy it, can you?' she said, her voice irritable. 'You hate it here, you hate the sun, you feel rotten—'

'I don't feel rotten today,' he said, 'actually. I slept much better last night. Once we'd finished our little – exchange. Maybe I'm getting used to it. Maybe if we stayed for another week—'

'We can't possibly do that,' she said quickly.

'Why not? Is someone coming over to take the cottage?'

'No. But I have to get back to work.'

'I was only teasing you. Of course we have to get back.'

He looked at her thoughtfully; she was sitting hunched up now, sifting sand through her fingers, not looking at him. The body language was interesting: defensive, watchful, self-aware.

'You'll be going ahead with the divorce, then, when you get back?' he said lightly.

'Oh – absolutely, yes. Look, let's not talk about that. Is there anything at all you've enjoyed that you'd like to do again?'

'Just stay here,' he said, 'swim, snorkel, snooze, talk. Maybe have dinner at that nice place just along the beach. That would be lovely. A lovely day.'

'Oh, dear,' she said, 'maybe if I'd let you do that every day, we'd still be happy together. Don't look at me like that, I'm only joking. We'd better get on with it, then. Our happy last day. Shall I go and get the snorkelling things?'

'Yes,' he said, 'only give me a kiss first. And if you don't hate me too much, the idea of a siesta seems a pretty nice ingredient. For our happy last day. Or would that offend you?'

'I'm really sorry,' she said simply, her face very serious as she looked at him, 'but I think it would. Well, not offend me. But I – well, I don't feel I could be very wholehearted about it now. It's hard to explain.'

'It's all right,' he said, 'I understand. And I'm not offended. Yes, go and get the snorkels. And that dreadful thick white stuff that seems to stop me getting burned.'

He watched her as she walked up the beach. He knew he was right. She was still in love with Tom Fleming. It was going to be agony for her to have to recognise it even, but the simple fact remained: she was.

CHAPTER 42

'You must be thrilled,' said Pattie David. Her plain face was flushed as she looked at Sandy, her sweet smile slightly strained. 'I mean that she's getting better so – so quickly.'

'Yes, indeed,' said Sandy. 'Of course I am.'

He longed to say he wasn't thrilled, that he was horrified at the prospect of Louise being home in less than a fortnight. But he couldn't explain. It really wasn't on.

'Well – if you want to pop in next week again, after your visit, we'd love to see you.'

'Thanks. Yes. That'd be very nice. If we have time.' He really mustn't get too much in the habit of coming here, enjoying her – her and Megan's – company. It would have to stop all too soon.

'No, if you don't have time, I shall understand.'

She looked hurt; he couldn't bear it, hurried to reassure her.

'No, no, we'd love it. Let's make that a definite. Tea, if that's all right. We'll probably take Louise out to lunch again. She enjoyed that today.'

She had: sitting there, smiling in the sunshine in the garden of a pub, cuddling Dickon endlessly, flirting – that was the only word for it – with him. She obviously had decided he was what she wanted – for now. And she was working on it. Working on making him want her. He thought of her being at home again, thought of her being in the house, in every room, not being able to get away from her, thought of the horror if she wanted to share his bed, have sex with him, and felt physically sick. How was he going to stand it, what was he going to do?

'Oh – hi,' said Octavia. Her voice she knew sounded odd: strained and shaky, not the cool, controlled one she would have hoped for. She felt shaky altogether; her hand had had difficulty turning the key in the lock and the twenty-pound note had shaken rather humiliatingly as she handed it to the cab driver. Absurd really to be so nervous: but it wasn't nervousness at all, of course, it was simply stress. She had done her best with her appearance, had cleaned her teeth, changed her T-shirt, done her make-up, sprayed on some perfume at the airport: but she still felt frowsty, somehow grubby. And sick. And very tired. She had not slept at all.

She didn't care in the least what she looked like, of course: not for Tom anyway. She had no desire to impress or to please him. She wanted only to proceed with the divorce. She had given it a great deal of thought, particularly on the journey home, and there really was no option. She could not continue to live with someone she didn't trust; it was unthinkable.

No, the only reason she wanted to look – well, reasonable – was that her mood was always affected by her appearance. She wanted to feel confident and in control, from the moment she walked in the door, and she couldn't do that if she was looking scruffy. She never had been able to.

And somehow, Tom being in the hall, looking far from scruffy, dressed in a collarless white shirt and jeans, and his deck shoes, rattled her, dislodged her. She had expected – hoped actually – that he wouldn't be there at all. If he had been there, then she had thought he would have stayed in his study, doing whatever it was. Not come down the stairs to greet her. It was disconcerting. She wished he hadn't.

'Hi,' he said, taking her bag. 'Good trip?'

'Very. Thank you.'

She smiled at him. That was all right. Ideally, she would like them to be friends. Not close friends, that was impossible. But – well, friends was essential for the children.

'You look very good.'

'Tom, I don't! I've been awake all night.'

'Well, all right, you don't.' He smiled back at her. 'I know better than to argue. Do you want anything to eat?'

'Oh – no. No, thank you. I feel sick.'

'Coffee, then?'

'Yes. That would be nice. Where's Caroline?'

'She's taken Minty for a short walk. We didn't expect you quite so soon. Your plane must have been very prompt.'

'It was. And there's no traffic, of course.'

'No, of course not.'

'I'm going to have a shower. Then I'll come down and have a coffee. Are you going to be here for a bit?'

'Yes. Of course. Why shouldn't I be? It's Sunday.'

'I know but—'

Somehow she'd thought he'd at least be going out. Not sitting there, in the house, as if – well as if things were normal. All right, even.

'But what?'

'Oh – nothing. Look, I'll go on up.'

She walked rather wearily upstairs. She didn't feel as if she'd had a holiday at all, felt worn out. That in itself was disappointing. Maybe tomorrow . . .

She felt better when she'd had her shower. She put on a white polo shirt and some shorts, and then pulled out the bag of dirty washing from her luggage, so that she could put it in the linen basket. As she tipped it in, a shower of sand fell out with it: Bajan sand. It had travelled back with her: along with her disappointment, her despair at herself, a sorry souvenir. She remembered lying on that sand the day before with Gabriel, agreeing that their relationship was not to be the joyful thing she had hoped for, that she had set her heart on, that would restore her self-confidence and her faith in herself, something that meant she could face Tom, bid farewell to him and her marriage feeling desirable and fearless again, but a sad shadow of a love affair. Suddenly, foolishly, she missed Gabriel, in spite of everything: wanted him back with her. They had parted, tenderly, quite cheerfully, even, at the airport; he had promised to ring her in a few weeks.

'Not too soon, it might be painful. But after that: well, I hope we can be friends. And there's Bartles Wood to settle, of course.'

'Yes. Of course.'

'And one day I'd like to meet your dad. Your legendary dad.'

'I won't say you'd like him, because you probably wouldn't.'

'I thought you adored him?'

'I do. But he is very – difficult.'

'And – good luck with everything. With Tom . . .'

'You mean the divorce.'

'Yes, all right. With the divorce.'

So foolish: his insistence that she still loved Tom. Absurd. A measure of their incompatibility really.

'Well – thank you, Octavia. For a lovely week.'

'You don't mean that,' she had said, laughing.

'I do. There were lovely bits, every day. And whatever I said, Barbados is a much more interesting and beautiful place than I imagined. Like you,' he had added.

His words came back to her now and she felt very near to tears. Don't, Octavia, just don't. Don't be silly.

She pushed the rest of her washing into the basket and went downstairs. Tom was waiting for her with a large pot of coffee and some orange juice.

'Here you are. The coffee's really strong.'

'Thank you. I wish Minty would come back. I missed her so much. And I miss the twins. Any news from them?'

'No, they haven't rung. They'll be home on Friday.'

'Yes.'

'So – it was a success, was it?'

'Yes, of course it was,' she said, irritable at the implication. 'The weather was perfect and I saw lots of friends.'

'Sounds good. Did you go to Crane?'

'Of course.' He always liked Crane best; they had once made love there early in their marriage, in the small beach beyond the bay, in the shelter of a cave. She could remember it still, so vividly; they had been surfing, riding the waves, laughing as they were swept in on them, and afterwards he had looked at her as they lay exhausted on the hot white sand and leaned over and kissed her and said, 'Come on, let's go for a walk.' She had known what he meant, had felt a stab of pleasure, of anticipation and had taken his hand and they had run along the beach, scrambling over the rocks and the rough steps at the end, and into the next cove, grateful for its desertedness, frantic now for each other. They had gone into a small cave, tearing off their clothes, lain down on the damp sand, and she had taken him into her at once, into her wet, greedy self, the taste and sound of the sea mingling with the taste of Tom and the sound of her own pleasure, looking out from the cave afterwards at the dazzling, blazing sky, watching the waves rising, gathering, breaking, just like her own orgasm, thinking she had never been so happy.

She looked up at Tom now, met his eyes; he was reliving it too, she could see, and she felt awkward, discomfited by the shared, vivid memory, of the pleasure, the happiness, the desire for one another, sex by proxy, remembering too his words after that, knowing he would be remembering them too. 'I shall never forget this,' he had said, kissing her bare breasts, 'never, as long as I live, and no matter what happens to us.' And it was if she was naked there in front of him now, pleasured by him, not neatly dressed for Sunday breakfast, not hating him, not betrayed by him at all.

'I'm glad you enjoyed yourself. And how was Elvira?'

'Fine. She sent her love.' She was back in the kitchen now, hating him; even passing someone else's love on was difficult, she didn't want to do it.

'Thank you.'

'So what have you been doing? Given that you weren't in Tuscany. So silly, me thinking that.'

'Extremely silly,' he said.

'Not that it really mattered.'

'Didn't it?'

There was something in his voice that startled her: something raw, something angry.

'It mattered to me, Octavia. It mattered a lot. That you should think I would have – well, I was very upset about it.'

'I'm very sorry you were upset,' she said and her voice was harsh. That he should complain that a suspicion of hers should be unfounded, that he should be upset. When—

'I still don't know quite how it happened,' he said.

'No, nor do I.'

'I tried to ring you,' he said, 'that morning. The morning you left.'

'Where were you?'

'In a hotel,' he said and his eyes were almost amused. 'With Bob Macintosh and the worst hangover I can ever remember.'

'Oh, Tom, really.'

'I got drunk because it was so bloody awful, seeing them go off without me.'

'Who, Lauren, you mean?' It was petty, she knew, but she couldn't help it.

'No, not Lauren, Octavia. I keep telling you, I don't even like Lauren.'

'You were with her the night before you – she – went away,' she said and her voice was rather loud.

'Yes, I know, I know I was. But I was only swimming with her, for God's sake.'

'Swimming! Tom, as stories go, that's not very clever. I'd have thought you could do better than that.'

'Oh, for Christ's sake,' he said wearily, 'this is ridiculous.'

'Yes, I quite agree with you. Totally ridiculous. Anyway, I don't care what you were doing with Lauren, not really. Whatever it was, it hardly compares with what you did with Louise, does it? With my best friend?'

'No, Octavia, it doesn't. God, do we have to have it all over again, so soon? When you've just got back. I was hoping we could be at least civilised about it all.'

'Nothing could please me more,' she said, 'than a little civilisation in our relationship. Unfortunately—'

He sighed. 'Octavia,' he said, 'I would like to get one thing at least cleared up. I did try to ring you before you went away. Over and over again. Here. In the morning.'

'Yes, well, I was at my father's house. We were only here for about ten minutes. The taxi came at eight fifteen.'

'Yes,' he said, 'yes, I've worked that out now.'

'How?'

'Because I spoke to him.'

'You spoke to him?'

'Yes. And he said you'd gone.'

'Well, obviously I had by then.'

'Yes,' he said, 'yes, of course you had. But then I tried to get you on your mobile. So that I could speak to you on your way to the airport. Let you know – well, I suppose it doesn't matter.'

'My mobile! But I didn't have it with me.'

'No, I know you didn't. So the bloody thing kept telling me. Or rather that it was switched off. Octavia, you never go anywhere without your mobile. What on earth made you leave it behind?'

'I couldn't find it, the taxi was waiting.'

'You couldn't find it,' he said, his voice quieter suddenly. 'Oh, I see. Well, that's – different. I suppose.'

'Yes. I must find it today, actually. I hope I didn't leave it up in Hampstead that morning.'

'You didn't,' he said.

'I didn't?'

'No. It's here. Caroline found it. In the drawer where we keep the tea towels.'

'Well, that's really ridiculous. I'd never have put it there!'

'No,' he said, 'no, I don't think you would. Anyway, it being there stopped me getting in touch with you that morning.'

'Yes. But it doesn't matter, does it? I was going anyway.'

'Yes, of course,' he said. 'Of course you were.'

There was an extraordinary expression in his eyes as he looked at her; sadness, despair, and something else. Anger. But it didn't seem to be directed at her. A strange silence formed between them; she wanted to break it and couldn't, just sat there, looking at him, trying to make sense of his mood, of what he was saying. She had just taken a deep breath, found the courage to ask him, when the door opened and Caroline came in with Minty in her arms, and there was a joyful shout of 'Ma-ma.'

Octavia scooped her into her arms, and thought of nothing else for several hours.

'Daddy! How lovely to see you.'

'It's lovely to see you, too, darling. And you look so much better.'

Louise smiled at him, hugged him. He was an important part of her plan; she needed him to trust her totally. 'I feel so much better. They say I can go home in a week or so.'

'A week! I didn't think it would be that soon.'

'Maybe a bit more than a week. But anyway. Very soon. I went out to lunch with Sandy and Dickon yesterday, to a pub, a real pub. It was wonderful.'

'Good. And what does your doctor say?'

'That I'm really much better. The pills are working beautifully. I'm sleeping well. Going for walks every day, with one of the nurses. All I want now is to be home again. With Dickon and Sandy. Start leading a normal life.'

'Darling, you mustn't try and run before you can walk.'

'No, I know that. But I do so want to get back to normal. I worry about Dickon as well, he's had such a horrible time.'

'Yes, he has. He's such a fine little chap. Been so plucky all the time you've been away. Sandy's been marvellous too. He's a good man, Louise, you're very lucky.'

'I know I am. I'll tell you what I'd really like. If they'd let me.'

'What's that, darling?'

'To come and have lunch with you at Rookston. One day next week. Do you think I could?'

'Well, I'd love it of course. But I'd have to make sure the doctor was happy about it.'

'I'm sure he would be. Could you – could you ask him?'

'Yes, darling, of course I will. It would be so nice. Janet would be thrilled.'

'Thank you. Thank you so much. Anyway, how are you?'

'I'm coping. Back at work at my little part-time job.'

Louise smiled. His little part-time job was board director of one of the biggest stockbroking firms in the country; it absorbed three long days a week.

'I suppose you've cleared out all Mummy's things now,' she said after a pause, her voice wistful.

'Not really. Still a lot of work to do there.'

'Her clothes . . . ?'

'All still there, I'm afraid. I can't face going through them.'

'And – her jewellery?' said Louise. She struggled to keep her voice level; she was terrified it would shake, give her away.

'Oh, darling, I don't know what to do with it, all the less valuable stuff, it's all in her—'

'In her box?' Still the slight tremble in her voice; still he didn't notice.

'Yes. All there still.'

Thank God! She'd been half afraid that he'd have got rid of it, emptied the wooden Victorian jewellery box that held all Anna's earrings, dozens of pairs, she'd been such a magpie, mostly pearl or gold studs, her charm bracelet that Charles had given her as a simple chain on their wedding day and which had grown into a collection in itself forty years later, some very expensive costume stuff, a Chanel crucifix, a Saint Laurent brooch – and a few other things. Things she'd treasured, wanted a safe place for: first teeth, first bangles, rings from Woolworth's the children had given her for Christmas presents. And something else was in that box. Something Louise needed. The most valuable thing of all.

'Well,' she said now, 'I'd love to go through it for you. And her clothes, of course. With you, if you like, maybe when I come over for lunch.'

'Darling, would you? I'd be so grateful. It wouldn't upset you?'

'Not too much, I don't think,' said Louise. 'And I'd like to do it, I'd like to help you. You've done so much for me. Now go and ask the doctor, see what he says. And also, ask him if we can go out to lunch today. Tell him how well you think I am.'

Marianne stood in the hall, waiting for Felix to appear. It had taken all her courage to do this, to come to the house; to make the phone call even, inviting herself over. He had been pleasant, but no more; had suggested a drink before Sunday lunch. No mention of lunch itself. It was not exactly encouraging.

'Marianne, good morning.'

'Hallo, Felix.' He looked perfectly normal. She had half expected him to have changed, that he would be drawn, thinner, pale, but he looked as near to cheerful as his brooding face would allow, and perfectly well. She felt rather foolish suddenly; clearly, she had been flattering herself.

'It's very nice to see you,' he said stiffly.

'It's nice to see you, Felix.'

'Do come in. Drink?'

'Nothing alcoholic. I'm driving. But I'd like a coffee.'

'Yes, of course. I'll go and organise one. Go into the drawing room.'

'Yes. Thank you.'

The papers were all over the coffee table; *The Sunday Times* and the *Observer* were both open at the financial section. Of course. Those were always the first he read. There was a picture of Felix over some article: that wasn't particularly unusual. 'FIVE STAR TAKEOVER?' was the headline. She wondered what it was about, but didn't like to start reading in case he came in and thought she was prying. She felt uneasy, unwelcome; she sat down on the window seat and stared out at the garden.

Felix came in with a tray. 'Here you are. You're looking well, Marianne.'

'Yes, I feel well. Thank you.'

'Octavia's coming over shortly. She's been in Barbados, you know.'

'Yes. Yes, I did know.'

'Really? Have you been talking to Tom?' The eyes were very brilliant, very fierce under the heavy brows.

'No, Felix, I've been talking to you. You told me she was going.'

'Oh, did I? I don't remember. Anyway, she's had a marvellous time. Took the new man in her life.'

'I didn't know there was one.'

'Oh, good Lord, yes. Of course, I don't know if it's going to come to anything, but she seems pretty fond of him. That's what she needs, you know, a happy, uncomplicated relationship. With a decent man who cares about her, won't upset her. Nothing too serious.'

'Well – I'm glad she enjoyed her holiday,' said Marianne carefully.

'Yes. She needed it desperately of course. I'm hoping she's going to move in here for a while, with the children. That husband of hers seems to be hanging on in the house indefinitely, and so she can't possibly stay there. And it's practically a second home to the children. They love it here. Much better for them than being in the house with a horrible atmosphere.'

'Yes. Yes, I suppose so.'

'So what can I do for you?' he said. 'Sorry about last night, didn't mean to sound bad tempered, I'd just got off to sleep.'

She had rung quite late, having spent most of the solitary evening plucking up her courage. 'Yes, I'm sorry, Felix. I thought you'd still be up. You usually are at eleven. I just – wanted to make sure you were all right.'

'Of course I'm all right. Why shouldn't I be? I'm not ill.'

'No, I know. But—'

'You thought I might be pining for you, did you?' he said suddenly. 'No, I'm fine, Marianne. Not fading away, not going into a decline. Sorry if I disappointed you.'

'I didn't think you'd be pining for me,' she said, 'but I was – worried about you.'

'How kind.' His voice was very hard. 'But no, I do assure you, there's nothing to worry about. I'm quite good at looking after myself. As you may recall. I did it for many years.'

'Yes, Felix, I know that. Of course I do. But I felt very – guilty. About the way we – well, we parted.'

'*We* didn't part, Marianne. You did the parting. However, that's perfectly all right. I won't say I don't feel a little regretful. We had quite a long history. But it's not as if we were married. Still plenty of time ahead of us. To do other things. As I keep telling Octavia. All the time in the world. To continue with her career, enjoy herself . . .'

'Yes, of course. But—'

'I hope he didn't send you,' he said.

'Who?' she said, stupidly.

'Cadogan. My onetime friend. My Judas.'

'No, of course he didn't send me,' she said, 'he has no idea I'm here. Why should he have? Anyway, we—'

He interrupted her. 'Are you sure about that? He didn't ask you to wheedle your way in, ask if I really intend to buy his company. Try to persuade me not to, even?'

'Buy his company? What are you talking about?'

'Marianne, I'm not that naive. Nor can you be, surely. There are rumours, it's even in the papers today. I'd like to believe you didn't know about it, but it's – well, it's a little difficult. Especially your timing. I haven't noticed any of this concern for my welfare before.'

She was genuinely and fiercely hurt. 'I do assure you,' she said, and she could hear her voice shaking slightly, 'I have come here only out of concern for your welfare. I had no idea you were bidding for Nico's company.'

'I didn't say I was. Merely that there were rumours.'

'All right. I had no idea there were rumours. Are they true?'

'I hardly think you can expect me to tell you of all people.'

'Why not? Because you think I'll go running back to Nico? You seem to have a very low opinion of me, Felix. I have no interest whatsoever in whether you want to buy his company or not. As I said, I was only concerned for you. I can see now it was rather foolish.'

'Yes,' he said glaring at her, 'I think I would agree. Foolish and arrogant, if I might be allowed to say so.'

'You are allowed to say whatever you like, Felix. You always did.'

'Then allow me to say something else,' he said. 'I would really rather prefer you left. There is absolutely no point your being here. Our relationship is over. Quite over. The major concerns in my life, Marianne, continue to be my daughter and my business. Octavia has always needed me, and never more than now. In fact, I really must ask you to excuse me. She is coming up here with little Araminta for tea, and I have to make sure everything is ready for her.'

Marianne managed to get to the car and to drive away before bursting into tears of humiliation, of rage – and of very deep, raw hurt. She was not to know that inside the house, Felix Miller was sitting at his desk, his study door locked, his great head buried in his arms, and Elgar's cello concerto playing very loud on the stereo to drown the sound of his weeping.

CHAPTER 43

'My father's in terrific form, thank you,' said Octavia briefly. Tom had greeted her – for the second time that day – when she arrived back from Hampstead with Minty.

'Good. Did you talk about – business at all?'

'If you mean, did he tell me if he was buying Nico Cadogan's company or not,' she said briskly, 'no. He didn't. He just said it was an interesting idea. He's enjoying all the fuss though. He loves talking to the papers.'

'Is he going to do it, do you think?'

'I really don't know. If he does, it would be revenge, I suppose.'

'For what?' said Tom lightly.

'Well, for Nico stealing Marianne from under his nose. Wouldn't you say?'

'I wouldn't know what to say, I'm afraid. When it comes to your father.'

'I'm going to bath Minty,' she said, ignoring this, 'you must excuse me.'

'Sure.'

She spent a long time in the nursery bathroom: partly because she was enjoying having Minty back, partly because she didn't want to go back downstairs. She thought she might have an early night.

Tired as she was, she couldn't sleep. Her body was restless, full of energy. She considered a sleeping pill and rejected it: it was too early. She'd simply wake at four with a thick head. She sighed, sat up, staring out at the still-light garden. What she needed was some kind of physical exercise; but wakeful as she was, she was also tired; running, or even walking, was unthinkable.

The gym: that seemed better. She could do something like the treadmill and work herself into a well-tuned torpor. And then maybe a quick swim: yes. That was the answer.

She pulled on some leggings and a T-shirt, ran downstairs, decided reluctantly she should tell Tom. Minty might wake, Caroline was out . . .

The gym was August-empty, no need to chat. She worked herself hard, rowed, cycled, walked, felt herself begin to relax. A quick swim and then she'd be fine.

She went down to the pool: dived in, swam fiercely up and down for ten lengths, then climbed out, suddenly shaky. She felt very thirsty, as she often did when she was tired, and went to the bar to order a fruit juice.

'You look very well, Mrs Fleming,' said the boy behind the bar. 'Been somewhere nice?'

'Pretty nice. Barbados. Only a week, though.'

'Did Mr Fleming enjoy it?'

'He – yes, he did.' That was easier.

'He looked very tired last time I saw him,' he slipped some lemon and ice into her fruit cocktail.

'Really? When was that?'

'Not too sure, Mrs Fleming. Time flies when you're having fun.' He looked uneasy suddenly, aware he had broken one of the club's cardinal rules, talking about members, to anyone else, even their husbands or wives. Especially to their husbands or wives.

'Look, it's okay,' she said. She tried to laugh, to sound easily relaxed. 'I know he was here with Mrs Bartlett about ten days ago. You're not setting a divorce in motion or anything. They were on their way back to our house for dinner.' She laughed again, saw relief on his face, saw him relax.

'Yes,' he said, 'yes, must have been then. They'd been swimming.'

'And you thought he looked really tired? Poor old Tom. He works too hard.'

She sat absorbing this new piece of information. So they had been here together. Swimming. As Tom had said. God. The news was almost unwelcome, so foolish did she feel. Of course they could have gone somewhere afterwards. But – he'd been home by nine. Before? No, Aubrey had told her he was at the Connaught. With a client. Aubrey wouldn't lie. He just wouldn't. God, oh, God. Another bit of paranoia. She remembered hitting Tom that night and winced. Not very clever. Not very clever at all.

Lucilla Sanderson was also unable to sleep. It was a very hot night, and although she had the window open, there was no air anywhere. Everything was still: even the birds were exhaustedly silent. The only movement in the still, dark blue air was made by her small friends. Swooping about, silently, gracefully swift. She believed they made a noise, but so high-pitched that human ears couldn't hear them. She loved to sit and watch them until the darkness swallowed them up, Nora Greenly hated them, said they frightened her, gave her the creeps. She wouldn't have her window open if they were about, some nonsense about them getting in her hair. Well, she was a pretty feeble creature altogether, thought Lucilla. Most of them were. She sometimes felt she was the only inhabitant of Bartles House with any real gumption at all. Especially at the moment. Everyone was so worried, and nobody else would so much as broach the subject with the Fords. She continued to broach it; and the Fords continued to deny there was anything to worry about at all. Mrs Ford, she could tell, was getting rattled by her persistence; Mr Ford was smoothly, patronisingly calm.

'I don't know where you've got these ideas from, Lucilla,' he had said only yesterday. 'I really don't.'

She'd said from the newspapers, that was where, and he'd said only very foolish people took any notice of what they read in the papers. 'If we were planning to move from here, Lucilla, you'd be the first to know. Of course you would. I keep telling you, this is your home. And ours. Home sweet home and all that. Now, then, I have to get on with my work, so if you'll excuse me . . .'

She knew he was lying: she knew that they were all in great danger. And soon there would be no more nights like this, no sweet summer nights, with the moon rising over Bartles Wood and the sky thick with stars and the raw sound of the foxes calling out across the valley. And no bats, wings outstretched, making their joyous evening journey through the growing darkness . . . Just the hideous permanent neon-twilight of the city, and a centrally heated, air-conditioned cell to observe it from. It was not to be borne, thought Lucilla, it really was not to be borne; she had to think of something. But she was beginning to fear that she never would.

Octavia stood outside the study door for a long time, feeling absurdly nervous, wondering why she was putting herself through this when there was no need, when she could just leave it. But it was all part of her sense of rightness, of moral order, of her painful conscience. Finally, she knocked.

'Yes?' Tom sounded irritable.

'Can I speak to you? It won't take long.'

'Right.'

He swung round in his chair, looked at her. He was clearly exhausted; his face was drawn, his voice sounded heavy and almost hoarse.

'Tom, I just wanted to say I'm very sorry. I – that is, the thing is – I – misjudged you,' she said quickly.

'Misjudged me? What on earth is this about, Octavia?'

'I – I didn't believe that you were swimming with Lauren. That night. I – was wrong.'

'And how did you make this discovery?' he said.

'I've just been to the Harbour Club. Someone said you'd been there. With her. Swimming. I – was wrong,' she said again. 'I shouldn't have hit you.'

'Not then, perhaps,' he said quietly.

'No. Anyway, I just wanted to say – that.' She turned away from him, to leave the room. Then 'Octavia,' he said.

'Yes?'

'Look at me.'

She did so, reluctantly; was amazed to see him smiling. A real smile: amused, friendly, affectionate.

'You really are extraordinary,' he said. 'Quite extraordinary.'

'Of course I'm not,' she said, irritable again. 'What do you mean?'

'I mean I've done some fairly terrible things to you. Correction. Some *very* terrible things to you.'

'Well, that's certainly true.'

'And yet you feel you have to apologise for some minor dismeanour towards me.'

She didn't say anything. He stood up, walked over towards her. She backed into the corridor; she didn't want him near her.

'One of the reasons,' he said, his eyes moving over her face, 'one of the reasons I have always loved you—'

'Don't say that! Please!'

'One of the reasons I have always loved you,' he said, 'was your scrupulousness. Your sense of justice. It's very – special. *You* are very special.'

She said nothing. She felt confused, disoriented. He reached out suddenly, and touched her cheek, very gently. She shied away, pushed his hand down.

'Don't!'

'Sorry.'

Suddenly, startlingly, she wanted his hand there again, wanted him to touch her. It was frightening, how much she wanted it.

'Octavia,' he said, very slowly, and she realised he had seen it, and was horried at herself, at her foolishness. And still she didn't move.

'You look very tired,' he said gently, and then bent and kissed her on the mouth. Just briefly, lightly. 'Go to bed, get some sleep.'

'Good night, Tom,' she said. And then he bent and kissed her again, still lightly, but very carefully; and she could not help it then, it was as if she had become herself again, the self she had forgotten, the self who had loved and wanted Tom, and her lips parted under his. She felt him pause, hesitate, then felt his mouth moving gently, with infinite care, the rest of him not moving, utterly still. She knew that stillness, she could remember it, her body remembered it, preceding in him, as it always did, an intense, urgent sexual excitement. And then she felt the echoes of it herself, felt a warmth creeping into her somewhere, felt a stirring and a softness: and then almost frightened, she pulled her mouth away.

'Good night,' she said quickly, and half ran to her room and slammed the door and lay on the bed, breathing very fast, appalled at the power of her body to betray her, to want him, and still more at the fact, the terrifying fact, that however hard she denied it, she was able to consider beginning at least to forgive him.

CHAPTER 44

'I want a divorce,' she said. 'As quickly as possible. So – can you help?'
Melanie grinned at her. 'As co-respondent? Not too sure about that.'
'No. With a lawyer.'
'Oh, yes. I certainly can help you there.'
She'd known Melanie was the person to ask. Lying awake, afraid that she might weaken, find herself feebly accepting the whole thing, she had suddenly thought of Melanie, of her famously successful departure from married life. If ever anyone had been given absolutely superb advice about their divorce, it was her.
Melanie smiled at Octavia now. 'Does this mean you and the Angel Gabriel are an ongoing item?'
'Um – no,' said Octavia quickly.
'Oh, dear. Don't tell me his powers were a little less than heavenly?'
'Well, I – actually, no. I mean, he's lovely and funny and we got on really well, had a great time but – not quite right, I'm afraid.'
'Shame,' said Melanie. 'I'm really sorry about that.'
Her large, brilliant eyes were gentler suddenly as she looked at Octavia.
'Oh – it's not important. Honestly. I mean I never thought it was going to be the love affair of the century.'
'Didn't you? I thought you were pretty smitten with him. What went wrong?'
'I messed it up, basically,' said Octavia quietly. 'I was ghastly. Bossy, controlling, all my worst things, expected him to fit in with everything there, the people we know, the things we do. As if he had been – been . . .'
'Tom?' said Melanie helpfully.
'Well – no, not Tom. Obviously. But used to it all, liking the things we do there, getting on with the people . . .'
'Like Tom?'

'No, Melanie, not like Tom. What is this?'

'Just testing!'

'Well, don't. I can't cope with it.'

'Is he still in the house?'

'Well – yes.'

'You've got to throw him out.'

'I know.'

'Octavia, you have. Fiona – my lawyer – will have a great deal to say about that, I can tell you.'

'Don't! You sound like my father. He's practically got the divorce papers ready for me.'

'Good on him. Now I'm going to give you Fiona's number and you're to ring her, and then, if you could possibly get your nicely sunburnt little nose down to the grindstone, we have a few nightmares on our hands. Mostly to do with the dreaded day at Brands Hatch. I tell you, we, personally, are going to make a huge loss out of that thing.'

'Mells, I'm sorry.'

'Not your fault – you didn't want to do it. And the publicity and the association with the charity will more than make up for it. I've already had two inquiries from other children's charities, as a direct result. Largely because of Diana, of course.'

'I don't suppose we know if she's coming or not?'

We don't. She likes to keep people hopping. At the moment she's still disporting herself all over Europe with Dodi Fayed. Have you seen the picture today? Obviously posed with the supplements in mind.'

The picture showed the Princess sitting alone on the prow of Dodi Fayed's yacht, wearing a pale blue swimsuit, lovely legs swinging. She looked very alone, a tragic, beautiful figure.

'What on earth is to become of her?' said Octavia. And went back to her office, thinking that the same question might have been asked of her.

'He's called a press conference. For Thursday morning,' sid Tom. 'I fear that confirms it.'

'Have you talked to him?'

'Would he talk to me? Of course not. But I've had my spies out. He's still in denial, of course, about a takeover. Although he's declared his holding to the Stock Exchange, he'll have to notify you of course before the press conference. But I can't think whatever else it could possibly be.'

'Shit!' said Nico Cadogan. 'God, I don't like this.'

'Nor do I. More coffee?'

'Thanks. Well, I suppose I have only myself to blame.'

'No,' said Tom, 'you don't. Much of it has to be set at my door.'

'It still seems to me that I'm the major culprit. I walked off with his woman. Although . . .'

'Although what?'

'Oh, nothing.' He sighed, then said, 'I suppose I should tell you. Marianne has – well, she's back with him.'

Tom stared at him, fighting to keep his face blank. 'Really? But—'

'I know what you're thinking. If he's got her back, why does he still want the hotels?'

'I was right, you see,' said Tom. 'This is all about me. Me and Octavia, your helping me. The man's crazy. He—' He stopped, looked at Nico suddenly. 'Jesus!' he said.

'Tom, are you all right? You've gone the most ghastly colour.'

'Have I? Sorry.'

'What is it?'

'Oh – just remembered something. Doesn't matter. Let's go over those figures again, shall we? There's still a chance your shareholders might back you, isn't there?'

'A chance, yes, I suppose,' said Nico Cadogan, 'but I wouldn't put money on it.' He looked at Tom. He seemed rather different: older, worn down, his air of sleek confidence quite gone. 'I feel pretty grim about this, I have to tell you. I really can't imagine life without Cadogan Hotels.'

'Maybe you won't have to,' said Tom.

Commuters were informed by their *Evening Standards* that night that Nico Cadogan was really rather likely to have to imagine life without Cadogan Hotels.

The press conference, called for Thursday morning by financier Felix Miller, of the London Wall Bank, was likely to announce his bid for the company. A consortium, headed jointly by London Wall and stockbrokers George Martindale, were said to have substantial funds in place; the shares now stood at over three pounds. The earlier bid from Western Provincial would be trumped by this one. Mr Miller had stated earlier that day that although he had no intention of pre-empting what he had to say at his press conference, he was prepared to admit he had no objection in principle to the idea of owning a hotel chain: 'I travel a lot and it would be useful always to be sure of somewhere decent to stay.'

'Bastard!' said Nico Cadogan, hurling the paper across the room. 'Bastard!'

Nice thought of the first Cadogan Royal: the one that had set the pattern and standard for all the rest, in the beautiful house in Bath. He hadn't lost a single feature of that house: every cornice, every shutter, every lovely window and stairway and piece of ironwork was still there. It had cost him a fortune, had taken years to see back, but he had done it. He had sacked two interior designers before he had found one sufficiently in sympathy with the house and its mood; had thrown back drawings that showed fancy furnishings, overdressed windows, elaborate wallpapers. The hotel when it was finished remained a beautiful and elegant house that could be lived in by up to forty guests; but it could also be imagined as the home of one civilised and privileged family. It was still cited as an example of how to style an exclusive hotel, photographed and written about in all the design magazines, and it was still his favourite, as dear to him as his own home. And the company as dear to him as anything could be: in the absence of a family, it seemed a part of him, had done so for many years. It held his heart, absorbed his attention, satisfied his pride. Without it he would feel absolutely bereft.

And the irony was that Marianne, who had inadvertently brought about its loss, had left his life as well . . .

Marianne was one of the many readers of the *Standard* who read about the bid for Cadogan; it finally gave her the courage to ring Tom, who seemed delighted to hear from her.

'I was thinking of calling you. I've got a client who's a great golfer, he's coming to London for a few days, for a conference, so where might he be able to get a game?'

Marianne suggested a couple of clubs, and then said, 'Tom – is it true? That Felix is putting in a bid for Nico's company?'

''Fraid so,' said Tom. 'That is, it hasn't been confirmed, but the writing's pretty clearly on the wall. You hadn't heard before?'

'No. No, I haven't seen Nico for – for a few days. I saw something in the paper today.'

'I see. Yes, the poor old boy's in a terrible state about it. Very upset.'

'I expect he is,' said Marianne. 'Oh, dear. How dreadful. I feel . . .'

'Feel what?' said Tom?

'A bit responsible. Somehow.'

'Don't be silly,' said Tom. His voice was very soothing, very kind. 'You ought to know Felix well enough to realise he's much too good a businessman to do something like this on some kind of a personal whim. The company's worth having. He wants it. Simple as that.'

'Yes, of course,' said Marianne. But she knew he wasn't being entirely truthful.

Tom called Nico.

'For what it's worth, Marianne doesn't seem to be – what shall I say?

– in very close contact with Felix. She phoned me to ask me if it was true about the takeover.'

'It's worth nothing to me at all,' said Nico shortly.

'Fine. Sorry to have troubled you. I'll fax those circulation figures over to you later today.'

'Thanks,' said Nico.

Felix had several times tried to teach Marianne chess. It had been a disaster; she lacked the intellect, or so she told him, to play. He had told her that her intellect was more than adequate, it was her powers of concentration that were lacking.

'Octavia is a very good chess player. But it's mostly because she has the capacity to put everything else out of her mind. You just need to develop that.'

Marianne said briskly that she had no desire to try to develop it, and that was the end of the chess lessons; but she did remember being much intrigued by the concept of checkmate, of being in a position from which there could be absolutely no escape, where absolutely no move was possible. She felt herself checkmated now. She was the king on the board, trapped helplessly by the all-powerful queen: only the queen was not another person, it was her own emotions, her own folly. That was what had trapped her. She had left Nico Cadogan – who she did miss quite painfully – to return to Felix, because that was where she belonged, where her duty lay; and because it was him – in spite of everything – she believed she loved; and Felix had told her he didn't want her. She could hardly go back to Nico and explain that, say she would now like to return to him. The only purpose served by Felix's rejection had been to show her how wrong she had been about him. He didn't want her: he was no longer in love with her, if indeed he ever had been; he was managing perfectly well without her – and he was more ruthless even than she had thought. But that didn't really help her, in fact it made her feel more wretched still. She had made a hideous mistake, and the game was over. There was absolutely nothing left for her to play with.

All the way to Rookston, Louise thought of nothing but the jewellery box. It was all she could do not to rush up there the minute they arrived. But Dickon was waiting for her, scarlet with excitement, Janet had coffee and homemade biscuits waiting in the morning room, and even when she went up to the loo Dickon came with her, sat outside singing loudly.

It was only when Charles said, 'Well, I must go and make a couple of phone calls, if you'll excuse me,' that she managed to make her own excuse, say could she just take a look at her mother's things, get a measure of what needed to be done.

Dickon went with her, of course, hanging on to her hand limpet-like; she tried not to feel irritated, not to shake him off. It didn't matter; she could look for it with him there, he wouldn't know.

Her mother's room was painfully tidy, everything set in its place still. Things like her alarm clock, her silver dressing-table set, the endless photographs of them all as children. Her letter rack and stationery on the small desk, her precious collection of Staffordshire dogs on the fireplace. All there, all looking at her. The only thing missing was the jewellery box.

Panic hit Louise; she started pulling drawers open, then tried the wardrobe, the drawers in that. No box. Under the bed, in the shoe cupboard. No box. She felt absurdly upset, tears filling her eyes; she realised Dickon was looking at her, blinked them back, tried to smile.

'What are you looking for, Mummy?'

'Oh – something of Granny's. Something that I thought would be here.'

'But what?'

She realised he might know. 'The wooden box that she kept all her jewellery and things in. Remember? I showed you once, a funny bracelet I made her when I was little, about your age. Oh, and my first tooth when the fairy brought it back. Do you know?'

He nodded solemnly.

'You do! Oh good, Dickon. Where is it?'

'I don't know where it is. I just remember it.'

'Oh. Oh, I see. Now—'

Janet came in. 'Everything all right, Louise?'

'Oh – yes, thank you, Janet. Fine. Um – you haven't moved anything out of here, have you?'

'Certainly not,' said Janet. 'Mr Madison said he wanted it left exactly as it was. What were you looking for?'

'Oh – nothing much,' said Louise quickly. 'It's just that I promised him – my father – that I'd do some sorting out today and I wanted to make sure it was all here.'

'She wants—' said Dickon.

Louise interrupted him quickly. She didn't want Janet to think the jewellery box mattered particularly. Not that she could possibly put two and two together: but you never knew. Safer not to risk even the slightest thing. 'Anyway, doesn't matter. Come on, Dickon, let's go in the garden for a bit. It's such a lovely day.'

Sitting outside in the garden, panic hit her again, the blind panic that threatened to engulf her from time to time, the racing heart, the shaking, the hot sweaty sickness. Was she ever going to be better, ever going to—

'Mummy, are you all right?'

'Yes, darling. I'm fine.' She smiled at him, gave him a kiss. Having to pretend was helpful, she found; she had learned that at the Cloisters. But she had to find it, the jewellery box; she really had to.

Octavia dialled Fiona Michael's number. She noticed her hand was rather shaky and felt irritated with herself. It was so clearly the right thing to do. She had completely got over the frightening madness that had threatened her on Sunday evening. It had simply been exhaustion that had done it to her. Made her think, however briefly, that she had wanted Tom. Not hated him. A marriage could not be built – or rather rebuilt – on mistrust, fear, lies, betrayal. It just couldn't. She had to end it, start again. There was no choice. She would talk to him that night: tell him what she had decided, that she wanted him out of the house, that she was instigating divorce proceedings . . .

Fiona Michael's voice was low, soothing, not the strident bark Octavia had somehow imagined. She was very nice, very helpful; said the first thing was to meet, that she would like to get the background details. Her office was in the Strand: when could Octavia go in? Octavia said she was too busy to take time off work; were the evenings any good?

They settled on the Friday, at seven.

She'd never liked Bernard Moss, her father's lawyer. Maybe she should ring her father, tell him what she's done. Then he could stop threatening to involve Bernard Moss. If he hadn't already . . .

Her father was pleased. Delighted even. The last time he'd sounded like that was when she'd got her degree. Warm, almost congratulatory.

'Darling, well done. I'm so pleased, so proud of you. I know it's the right thing to do. Even if it is hard.'

'Well – I hope so.'

'Octavia, of course it is.'

'Yes. Yes, of course. So – no need to bother Bernard about it.'

'No. I presume this woman is competent.'

'Oh, very. She did Melanie's divorce. That's how I got on to her. Anyway, I've done it now – so there's no need to nag me any more.'

'I promise I won't. By the way, Greenidge is nagging me about the documents you brought back, and I haven't even looked at the stuff yet.'

'Oh, that reminds me of something. I forgot to mention it on Sunday, forgot to thank you. Daddy, you are naughty.'

'In what way?' he said.

'Putting all that money into the BVI trust fund. Very naughty. But very sweet. Thank you.'

'Darling. I haven't put any money into it. Not recently. It must be an accumulation of interest.'

'No, I don't think so. Well – I suppose just possibly. But . . .'

'But what?'

'But it's a lot. I thought – oh, well. Doesn't matter. Doesn't matter at all.'

Felix put the phone down; he felt extremely happy suddenly. All his rage and misery over Marianne seemed unimportant; he would have Octavia back. Soon she would be free, safe, his again. Her and her children. She'd probably be much happier completely on her own in the future: only she wouldn't be alone, she'd have him.

And the children of course: he hoped this lawyer woman would see that Tom Fleming got as little access to them as possible. He didn't deserve any at all. He must make that point to Octavia, next time they spoke. She must be very firm about it.

He was puzzled, though, about the reference to funds in the BVI account. He couldn't think what that was about. Anyway, he'd have a look at the statements that evening. There was obviously a perfectly good explanation . . .

God could have provided it of course; and could have provided a warning of other, equally dangerous situations that were developing. But Felix was still too busy playing Him to listen . . .

It was there: safely at the bottom of the box, where Anna had left it, tucked under the silk lining. Where Charles was most unlikely to see it. Lucky it had been there; he'd had the box, had locked it in his safe, might well have seen it.

'I thought some of the things were slightly valuable,' he'd said when finally she asked him about it, feeling so sick she couldn't swallow, 'so I put it away. I'll get it for you, after lunch. Or now, if you like.'

'No, no,' she said (miraculously hungry suddenly), 'there's absolutely no rush. We'll do the clothes first. As long as I can check it through for you before I go, that'll be fine.'

She picked it out of the box, slipped it into her bag, into the little zip section where it would be safe. Nobody saw her, not even Dickon. He was out in the garden, playing Fench cricket with Janet, laughing. Charles had gone to fetch some tea for them, to help them in their task. Nobody knew she had it, nobody knew it existed even. She was safe now. She could do it. She had somewhere to go . . .

★

'Octavia! Octavia, it's Lauren. Lauren Bartlett. Can you hear me?'

The low, throaty voice was very clear.

'Yes,' she said, 'yes, I can hear you fine, Lauren. Thank you.'

She felt guilty immediately; had Lauren been talking to Tom? Was she ringing to accuse her of being neurotic, paranoid? Was she going to laugh at her, say—

'Your children are fantastic. Just fantastic. They've both been so good, and Gideon has been marvellous. About his foot. So brave. It's fine now, no need to worry, completely healed, we've had the doctor here have a look at it, just in case.'

God, thought Octavia, she isn't a bitch at all. She'd misjudged her so horribly . . .

'Octavia, are you there?'

'Yes. Yes, I'm here. Sorry. I'm so glad the children have been good.'

'They have. And Gideon is so good looking, and such a little charmer. Tom all over again. Camilla is madly smitten with him.'

Yes. Well, she was allowed to say that. If she wanted to.

'Anyway, they'll be back on Friday night.'

'Yes, so – so Tom said. Lauren, thank you so much for taking them. I'm really grateful.'

'Oh, honestly, it's been a help. You know how dreadful children are on holiday, always at one to play with them. I've had plenty of time to work on my tan. How was Barbados? Lucky you, I adore it there. We always stay at the Sandy Lane, do you know it? Yes, of course, you would. Poor old Tom, no holiday for him. Still, someone has to do some work. Now then, talking of work, I want to have a quick word about the seventh. I believe it's all going forward well. But the food – I don't like those menus Melanie faxed over at all. *Very* coronation chicken. I thought something much more imaginative. And lighter. And I don't want sparkling wine, Octavia. I want champagne. I said that at the beginning, so if your quote doesn't allow for it, then I'm afraid that's your mistake. You'll have to find the money from somewhere else. Poppy says she's very excited about it, she and Camilla are planning their dresses. And Tom, I can't wait to see him in a Prince of Wales suit. I've got a marvellous outfit, from Bermans, and the most divine hat. What? Well, of course Tom must come. Apart from anything else, Oliver Nichols is coming. Tom's new client, you know? The one I was able to help with? He's got the most marvellous Mr Toad outfit. He's driving down in his own car. It's a most lovely thing, 1935 BMW. Anyway, come back to me on the food, would you, Octavia? And the champagne. I'll be in the office Monday for our meeting.'

Octavia heard herself saying that she was sure Tom would come to Brands Hatch and that she'd get some more menus faxed out to Lauren next day . . .

She'd meant to tell Tom that night that she'd spoken to Fiona Michael, that she wanted to press ahead with the divorce; but first she had to ask him to come to the day at Brands Hatch. 'And in 'thirties dress,' she added.

He looked at her as if she'd asked him to come dressed as a chicken.

'Octavia, I have no intention of coming at all. Let alone dressed up in some damnfool costume.'

'Tom, please! It's so important to me, this day, and anyway, you always like fancy dress things usually, and—'

'And what? I really cannot imagine why you want me there. It's your day, your show. When did we last make a joint appearance anywhere?'

'A couple of weeks ago actually,' she said, thankful that she had done it for him. It had after all been a much bigger concession. 'When we had dinner with Bob Macintosh. I did that for you.'

'And for Fleming Cotterill.'

'Yes. And this is for me and for Capital C. And I know Lauren is expecting you to be there. Wants you to be there.'

'I'm very surprised you should be so concerned with what Mrs Bartlett wants,' he said lightly.

She looked at him; his eyes were gleaming.

She felt very foolish suddenly. 'I'm not. Exactly. But she – well, she is—'

'The client,' he said. 'Ah. Suddenly, we have to please the client. Together. A trip down memory lane, eh?'

'Tom—'

'Yes, Octavia?'

'Just this once. It would be – helpful. And anyway,' she added, 'apparently Oliver Nichols is going to be there.'

'Yes. Yes, all right, Octavia, I'll come. In the cause of our joint commercial futures. How does that sound?'

'Fine,' she said. 'Thank you very much.' Somehow it didn't seem quite the moment to tell him she was seeing a solicitor about divorcing him.

'Darling, don't cry. Please, don't cry.'

'I can't help it,' said Louise, and she couldn't. 'I just hate it there so much, I want to go home so badly. I don't see why they won't let me.'

'I'm sure they have their reasons.'

'Yes. Getting more money out of you,' she said, blowing her nose, trying to smile at him.

'Nonsense! I have far too much respect for them to think that. Dr Brandon is a very highly qualified, highly respected psychiatrist. There is no way he would keep you there unless he thought it was really necessary. You have been quite – ill, you know, darling.'

'Yes. Yes, I know. It's just that I get so homesick. Perhaps if you spoke to Dr Brandon, or to Sandy, even. I don't think Sandy wants me home, either.'

'What nonsense. He misses you terribly, of course he does. Look, I will ring Dr Brandon in the morning, see what he says. How would that be?'

'That would be lovely,' said Louise, 'really lovely.'

Time was running out on her; she had to get home very soon . . .

'I want to ask you something,' said Tom. He had appeared at her study door; it was quite late.

'Yes?'

He looked rather nervous; Octavia wondered wildly if he was going to make it easy for her, tell her he wanted a divorce, had seen his own solicitor. She sat back in her chair. That would be marvellous: really marvellous.

'It's about – well, about the morning you went away. I know it sounds silly, but – are you sure you had your mobile phone up at your father's house?'

'Yes. Quite sure. I went there straight from the office. Why on earth do you want to know that?'

'Oh, I'm just querying the bill. It came in while you were away.'

'Well, that's your answer. But where it went after that, I have no idea. I didn't use it on holiday, or even that morning. Okay? Now can I get on, please?'

'Yes,' said Tom, 'you can get on.'

'I've had a letter,' said Nico Cadogan, 'it just arrived. By hand.'

'From?'

'Miller.'

'And?'

'Oh, nothing too important in it. Just that he's declaring a bid tomorrow for the company. He's called a press conference. At the bank, at noon. That's all. I wouldn't mind quite so much if he actually wanted it. But he doesn't. He just wants *me*. Or rather my head. On a plate. God, Tom, I could kill the bugger.'

'Please don't before tomorrow,' said Tom.

Felix Miller was just about to go to bed when the front doorbell went.

Damn. Mrs Harrington had forgotten her key again. She was always doing it, in spite of having at least three of the things. Stupid woman.

He hauled himself out of the deep leather chair in his study and walked through the hall. 'Just coming, Mrs Harrington,' he called, fumbling slightly with the two locks. 'We shall have to find somewhere we can keep a key for you. There we are, now . . .'

But it wasn't Mrs Harrington. It was Tom Fleming.

'Evening, Felix. Can I come in?' He looked rather cheerful; and very spruce, beautifully dressed as always, with a bottle of what looked like claret in his hand. He held it out. 'For you.'

Felix glared at him. 'I have no intention of asking you into this house, and certainly not of accepting anything from you.'

'Pity. Because I intend to come in. Whether you ask me or not. I have a – proposition for you. And I think we might share this bottle while I outline it.'

'I have no interest in any proposition of yours,' said Felix, 'and that information is all I wish to share with you. Good night.'

'Felix, this concerns Octavia. I would advise you very strongly to listen to me. Very strongly indeed. It's about you. You and her. You and her, and a certain misunderstanding, just before she went away. Felix, do let me in, there's a good chap. You don't want to hear me out on the doorstep, I do assure you.'

A streak of panic went through Felix; he felt slightly dizzy. He put out his hand to steady himself on the doorframe. He could see Tom had noticed it as a sign of weakness, and cursed it.

'Well,' he said finally, 'well, you'd better come in.'

'It's very simple,' said Tom, setting two of Felix's rather fine claret glasses down on the dining-room table, 'very simple indeed. Really. Where do you keep your corkscrews? Oh, yes. Right. Now let me just pour this out and then – no? Well, it's awfully good, you know. You're missing a treat. Margaux, 'ninety-six. Now where was I? Oh, yes. This takeover Of Cadogan Hotels.'

'I thought you'd come to talk about Octavia,' said Felix. He felt very panicky now. There was a nasty lump in his throat. Against his will, he took a small sip of the Margaux. It was extremely good; even in his sick anxiety he could appreciate that.

'I have. And about the takeover.'

'I'm afraid I fail to see my connection whatsoever between the two.'

'Well, you will. Now, you're making the announcement at this press conference tomorrow, I understand?'

'I'm afraid I have no intention of discussing any of it with you. So—'

'Pity, Felix, you're obviously not going to make this easy for me. Or yourself. Now please listen to me, very carefully . . .' He leaned forward, and his dark blue eyes were very brilliant suddenly, full of menace. Felix swallowed hard; he could feel his heart thumping, his hands sweating.

'Right,' said Tom. 'I don't want you to announce your takeover bid for Cadogan Hotels in the morning. I want you either to cancel the press conference or find some other pretext for calling it.'

'Oh, really?' said Felix. 'And how do you imagine you are going to persuade me to do that?'

'Quite easily. Actually,' said Tom. 'You can't have Cadogan Hotels. You really can't, Felix. I'm very sorry.'

'And why not? How exactly are you and Cadogan going to stop me?'

'Oh, Cadogan has nothing to do with it. He has no idea I'm here. Nobody has. Fortunately for you.'

'Are you threatening me?'

'Yes. I suppose so. Now then, Felix, this is it. Unless you pull out of that bid in the morning and find a feasible reason for doing so, I shall tell Octavia what you did just before she left the house that morning. When she was going to Barbados.'

'What do you mean?' said Felix. He felt dizzy again.

'I think you know what I mean. That you first lied to me and told me she'd left when she hadn't. And then you hid her mobile phone, so that I had no way of contacting her once she'd left the house. Or of telling her that I wasn't in Tuscany with a new mistress, as you had so carefully encouraged her to think, but in London, desperately trying to get hold of her. Now, how do you think that would make her feel about you, Felix? Do you think she would still see you as her knight in shining armour, her perfect and beloved daddy, the source of all goodness, who can do no wrong, and who shields her from any evil that might come her way? Eh? What about it, Felix? Do you think she'd love you quite as much after that?'

CHAPTER 45

'Darling, don't be so upset. Please. I'm sure something can be done.'

'I'm sure it can't.' Megan looked at her mother, tears streaming down her cheeks. 'That was our last chance. Stopping them knocking the house down.'

The letter stated quite unequivocally that, in the opinion of their inspector, the Department of the Environment had to inform Megan that Bartles House, while being an interesting example of its kind, was of no real architectural value and could not therefore be considered for listing.

'So it'll go. And the land will go and the wood will go and they'll build their horrible houses and shops and it's not right. It's just not just right.'

'Look, why don't we tell Octavia?' said Pattie. She didn't actually feel very hopeful about that either, but it was a way of diverting Megan from her misery. 'She'll know what to do next.'

'I don't think there's anything we can do next,' said Megan. 'It's down to chaining ourselves to trees and things now. We must tell Sandy. He'll be very sorry.'

'Sandy's coming to tea tomorrow,' said Pattie. 'You can tell him then.' She smiled at Megan.

'Mum! You're blushing. You really like him, don't you?'

'I do, yes.'

'He's very good looking. I'm not surprised.'

'Now, Megan, don't be ridiculous,' said Pattie primly. 'I don't like him in that way. Anyway he's married.'

'Of course I want her home,' said Sandy. He felt himself flush; he forced himself to meet Charles' slightly reproachful eyes. 'But not unless she's really better.'

'But it seems she is. I've had a word with Dr Brandon, and really, he feels she could leave early next week. But I think a call from you would help. To confirm that you could cope, take a week off, settle her in properly. Apparently, you rather gave Louise the impression that might be difficult. Which – upset her, I'm afraid.'

'Well, I'm sorry about that,' said Sandy. He was finding it very hard to speak.

'She's so very vulnerable at the moment,' said Charles. 'And she misses you and Dickon so much. She needs all the love and support we can give her. So – I wonder if you'd have a word with Dr Brandon. Tell him how much you'd like to have Louise home. There's a good chap. I know it would be best for her.'

'Have you heard anything from Felix Miller?' said Tom casually.

'No,' said Nico. 'Why on earth should I? Today of all days.'

'Oh.' He was mildly disappointed – that would have been the best, the most dramatic outcome – but not really surprised. 'Oh, I just thought you might. As today's the day.'

'Indeed. Today is the day.'

He looked ghastly, Tom thought, white and exhausted, drained of his vitality. He felt a surge of vast sympathy for him.

'Nico, would you excuse me a minute, I just want to make a couple of calls.'

He went into his office, spoke to a couple of financial journalists, one at *The Times*, one at the *Mail*. Was the press conference called by Felix Miller still on?

It was. A sliver of unease went through Tom. Maybe this wasn't going to work after all. It had been a huge gamble but he really had thought it would pay off. Had thought that the spectre of being revealed to his daughter as an out-and-out baddie would have frightened Felix into silence. Suddenly he saw that it could easily not frighten him at all. He could lie his way out of it. He could lie his way out of anything. Just the same – surely, surely he would be afraid that Octavia would at least half believe it. He had his own mobile phone print-out, showing the time he had called her that morning; she wasn't stupid, wasn't that blind. Even to Felix's faults. There was also the fact that it was Felix who had first put the idea of the Tuscan holiday with Lauren into her head. It would be a huge risk for him to run. Surely, surely he wouldn't do it.

Tom felt himself beginning to sweat. This was going to be a long morning.

Pat Ford was very tired. Tired and upset. This whole thing was beginning to get her down. The tension, the waiting, keeping it from the patients – especially sharp-eared and -eyed old Lucilla Sanderson.

She was beginning to think it just wasn't going to happen, that she would be trapped at Bartles House for the rest of her life, with the endless stairs, the eccentric plumbing, the impossibility of attracting staff. And the last straw that had laid itself on her increasingly narrow back this morning had been when Mrs Tims, one of the two cleaners, had given notice. 'I'm going to have to leave, Mrs Ford. The work is just too hard. Those floors are murder. And it's the hours as well, what with the journey and everything. I'm sorry, but I really can't stay any longer. I can get better-paid, easier work in Felthamstone.'

When Mrs Tims had left the office, Pat Ford sat down at her desk and burst into tears. She was so tired, it hurt. Suddenly she decided she had to know. Or try and find out. One way or another. Even if the news was bad, knowing would help.

She got up and shut the office door; and then did what Mr Ford had always forbidden her to do – she phoned Michael Carlton. He was such a nice man, so helpful and reasonable. Surely she could at least ask him if he knew anything yet, when they might at least be able to look towards moving. If ever.

Mr Carlton was out, his secretary said; she was very sorry, could she help?

'No, I don't think so,' said Pat. A fresh wave of weariness and despair hit her and she felt a sob rising in her throat again. 'No, I need to speak to him myself.'

'Well, can you at least tell me what it's about? So that I can tell him, make sure he has all the necessary information when he does call you back?'

'It's about – about Bartles House,' she said, 'whether – whether the scheme is going ahead or not. I – well, I really do have to know. Soon.'

'Of course,' said the secretary soothingly. 'Of course you do.'

'So – could he ring me, do you think? I'll give you the number.'

'I'm sure he will, Mrs Ford. Yes.'

Sheila Edwards, Michael Carlton's secretary, put the phone down. Poor woman had sounded desperate. She was the matron, of course, looked after all those old people. What a dreadful life. Well, from what Sheila had heard that morning, she was going to get some good news. Some very good news indeed.

She scribbled a note to Michael Carlton which said, 'Mrs Ford from Bartles House phoned. She sounded really very upset. Is there any chance we could let her know it's all going through all right, cheer the poor woman up? Sheila.'

Then she looked at her watch. God. Almost eleven. She and Michael Carlton had a site meeting at eleven thirty, with the borough surveyor.

She needed to get her skates on. She picked up her coat and bag and hurried out of her office, calling to Sharon Parker, the junior secretary, to take messages carefully, and to get on with photocopying the plans for the Warminster development and that she'd be back by one. Oh, and could Sharon have some sandwiches ready for her and Mr Carlton?

Sharon said yes, she would, but she had a dental appointment at one. Sheila said she would be back in plenty of time. 'I promise. But I'd rather you didn't go until then, Sharon.'

Tom phoned one of his favourite journalists, a girl called Jenny Angus on the *Daily Sketch*. Would she do him a great favour, call him from the London Wall Bank the minute the press conference was over, tell him what had happened?

'Yes, of course I will,' she said. 'What's up?'

'Let's just say it really rather matters to me,' he said.

Nico and he were in his office; Nico was pacing up and down.

'You look like an expectant father,' said Tom, in an attempt to cheer him up.

'Expectant fathers are in at the off these days, I thought,' said Nico gloomily, 'not waiting until the obstetrician's good enough to let him know what's emerged. God, this is bloody agony.'

Pat Ford looked at the clock. Twenty to one. Any minute now Donald would be back, and he might get the phone call from Carlton's office. And he'd be so angry with her; so terribly angry, tell her what a fool she was, how dangerously stupid she'd been. She really couldn't risk it.

She picked up the phone again, dialled the number.

Sharon was getting very annoyed. Sheila Edwards had phoned to say the meeting was dragging on, and she might be slightly delayed.

'The dentist's only just down the street, isn't he, and he's bound to be running late. Sorry, Sharon, but there's a very important client phoning. I really don't want the phone unattended. Do please wait for me.'

The phone was ringing now: obviously the important client. Sharon put on her personal secretary voice. 'Mr Carlton's office. Sharon Parker speaking, how may I help you?'

'Oh – hallo. Yes. This is Mrs Ford again. Is Sheila Edwards not there?'

'No, she's out, Mrs Ford. Perhaps I can help you.'

'Oh – it's just that I phoned earlier. I'm from Bartles House. To see if there was any news.'

'Bartles House. Yes?'

'We're – well, we're waiting for news. About what was going happen to it. I just wondered if . . .'

She sounded nice: and as wound up and edgy as Sharon herself. 'There's a note here about Bartles House, actually, Mrs Ford,' she said, noticing it suddenly. 'I wonder if that's what you want?'

'It might be. What – what does it say?'

'It says – oh, yes. It does look like good news for you. It says it's going through all right, and that that should cheer you up. Does that make any sense to you, Mrs Ford?'

'Oh, yes,' said Pat Ford. 'Yes, it certainly does.'

Donald Ford walked in through the door.

She turned to face him, shining eyed. 'Wonderful, wonderful news. Guess what?'

'What?'

'That was Michael Carlton's office. It's all going through. It's all right. Do you realise what that means? It means we can leave this awful place, and go to the new one. Oh, Donald, I can't believe it. No more Bartles House, no more struggling with the stairs and the plumbing and the awful draughty doorways.'

She went over to him and kissed him; over her shoulder she suddenly saw Lucilla Sanderson, standing very still, looking stricken. She had obviously heard every word.

'Jesus,' said Tom, 'what the fuck are they doing over there? Having a party?'

'Probably, yes. Look, shall we give up and just go out to lunch ourselves? I need to get seriously drunk.'

'No, I think we should wait,' said Tom. He felt very sick. He had failed Nico, as Nico had not failed him; it was not a good feeling.

'I just want to make quite—'

The phone on his desk shrilled. He snatched it up.

'Tom Fleming.'

'Hi. This is Jenny. With a full news report.'

'Yes?' said Tom. 'Yes?'

'Okay. Well, he went through a whole rigmarole about the London Wall Bank, what a great place it was, how careful management and investment and really good client services had placed it in the top fifty investment banks in the country. And then he made his announcement.'

'About . . . ?'

He was so sure she was going to say about Cadogan Hotels, he actually heard it, heard the words. And then realised rather slowly that she hadn't. That those words hadn't come. That she was saying something quite different. He tried to concentrate, to make sense of it.

'So they're opening a telephone banking arm. Called London Wall Direct. I mean, boring or what? And then he served some rather nice champagne and then we all left again. And I called you.'

'Jenny,' said Tom, 'Jenny, I love you. Thanks. Come round here and I'll give you some more. Nice champagne, I mean.'

He looked at Nico, who was standing staring out of the window, every line in his tall, thin body an agony of tension.

'Nico,' he said. 'Nico, we have work to do. We have to improve that cashflow situation further.'

Nico turned to him; his face was very drawn.

'He's made the bid?'

Tom waited for a just a moment, then, sensing the cruelty, smiled at him. 'No. No, he hasn't. Old bugger didn't even mention the hotels. Clearly doesn't think they're worth bothering about. They're safe – from him, at any rate.'

'Jesus!' said Cadogan. 'Jesus. I don't bloody believe it.'

'You'd better.'

'You had something to do with this, didn't you, Fleming? What was it, what the fuck did you do?'

'Oh – nothing much,' said Tom. 'Certainly nothing worth talking about anyway.'

CHAPTER 46

'Now one thing I must ask you, of course. Have you given careful consideration to the idea of reconciliation?'

'No.' said Octavia. 'I mean yes. I have considered it.'

'And?'

'And—' she paused. She had been warned about this by Melanie: that Fiona Michael was bound – by professional regulation – to ask her. It was surprisingly hard to say. 'And I – I, well, it isn't an option.'

'You're sure?'

Another pause. She realised Fiona Michael's expression was very piercing. It was obviously important to get the answer right.

'Yes. Yes, of course. I mean—'

'Because it is important that you are absolutely sure. That it can be ruled out. Have you discussed it with your husband?'

'I don't discuss anything with my husband,' said Octavia briskly.

'It's important that you do. Divorce is a complex procedure. This is only one thing that requires you cooperate with one another.'

'Oh. Oh, I see. I thought – thought that you'd do it all. See to it.'

'Most of it,' said Fiona. 'Not all.'

She smiled at Octavia coolly, crossed one long leg over the other. She was tall and very slim, with dark red hair and very white skin; immensely attractive. Her office resembled a sitting room; they were sitting on sofas, on either side of a low table. A large box of Kleenex was placed beside the vase of flowers on the table. Octavia wondered what they were for.

'Now then,' she said, 'just let me have as much background as possible. When the marriage first began to break down, why you're so sure there's no hope of reconciliation. Does he know you're seeing me?'

'No. No, not yet.'

'Well, that's absolutely the first step. You must tell him. Unless you want things to become very unpleasant indeed.'

'Oh – no, I don't. Of course not.'

'Well – let's go through it, shall we?'

At the end of forty minutes, Octavia discovered what the Kleenex were for.

'Don't worry,' said Fiona, passing her the box, 'everyone cries. Men and women. Everyone. However much they come in feeling and talking tough, they cry. It's natural. This is your marriage you're planning to say goodbye to. Coffee?'

'Yes, please,' said Octavia. She felt horribly upset.

The coffee was very strong; it made her feel better. She managed to smile at Fiona. 'Sorry.'

'It's all right. Where is your husband living now?'

'At home,' said Octavia.

'At home? You mean, with you?'

'Well – yes.'

'That is rather – unwise.'

'Why? We're not sleeping together any more.' She felt absurdly defensive suddenly. Of Tom, for God's sake. What was the matter with her?

'You're suing him for adultery. If you and he are cohabiting, that weakens your case. You really should press him to leave. Although you can't force him unless he's being violent. I presume that isn't the case.'

'No,' said Octavia, thinking of the night she had hit Tom, starting to cry again. 'No, he isn't.'

Her father had been very insistent that Tom moved out; maybe that was why.

'He's been having problems with his business,' she said after a while. 'Financial problems. It would have been – difficult for him.'

'That's really rather accommodating of you, Mrs Fleming. Not many wives would see things quite that way. Are the problems over now?'

'Oh – yes. Things are much better.'

'That's good. We shall be able to press for a more substantial settlement. Bankrupt husbands are never good news.'

'No. No, of course not.'

Fiona Michael hesitated. Then she said, 'Mrs Fleming this won't be pleasant. I do urge you to talk about it to your husband one more time.'

Octavia looked at her; she waited for a moment, trying to find order in her whirling thoughts. Then she said, 'No. No, I don't want to do that. I want to go ahead.'

'Very well. Now I'd like you to take this form and fill it in for me.

Before we talk any more. All rather tedious, I'm afraid, but it will save a lot of time in the long run. More coffee?'

Fiona Michael saw Octavia out of her office after an hour, and went over to the window, watched her walking slowly down the street. She liked her; but she felt it was unlikely she'd be handling her divorce. If ever a woman was still in love with her husband, it was Octavia Fleming.

It was all arranged: Louise was to come home on Sunday. Every time he thought about it, Sandy felt ill. He spent a long time on Friday evening cleaning the house, making up the bed in the spare room – there was no way he could even contemplate having Louise sleeping with him – putting flowers in their own room for her.

He could cope with it; of course he could. And it wasn't for ever after all.

'Tom, I want to talk to you.'

Tom looked at her over the financial section of *The Times*. He was sitting at the kitchen table, a half-drunk bottle of chardonnay in front of him; he looked tired, but extremely cheerful. 'Sure. Want some of this?'

'No. No, thank you. I wouldn't mind some fruit juice though.'

'Fine. Sit down, you look tired.'

'I don't feel tired,' said Octavia coolly.

'Good.'

'I expect you're pleased about the takeover. Or rather that there wasn't one.'

'Yes. Yes, I am. Did your father call you about it?'

'No. I haven't heard from him. I just read it in the papers. Is there any post?'

'Over there.'

He had his back to her, was standing at the fridge. She flicked through the letters; there was one from Barbados. Nicholas Greenidge. He said he'd write about the mysterious money in the trust fund.

Dear Octavia

I have looked into the matter of the monies in your BVI trust fund, and it would appear that two payments of ten thousand dollars each were made over the course of the past six weeks. There is no record of where they came from. A nice surprise for you, perhaps! I have spoken to your father about the house and everything is in order, but no doubt he will have told you that.

So glad you enjoyed your week with us.

Come back soon.
Nicholas.

'How extraordinary,' said Octavia.

'What's that?'

'Well – someone has paid twenty thousand American dollars, that's – God, that's about fifteen thousand pounds, into the BVI trust fund. The one my father set up for me. Ages ago. It's rather odd. I mean, Daddy didn't put the money in. I asked him. So who . . .'

'Very odd,' said Tom. 'I shouldn't worry about it, if I were you.'

There was something in his voice, in his attitude, that made her suddenly suspicious.

'Tom?'

'Yes, Octavia?'

'Tom – you don't know anything about this, do you? About the money? You do? Who put it there? What's it got to do with you?'

'I put it there,' he said quietly.

'You? But why, how?'

'I wanted you to have a bit of money that would be safely yours,' he said finally. 'If I'd gone bankrupt, you'd have lost an awful lot as well.'

'But you didn't have any money! You told me you were absolutely desperate.'

'I know. But I cashed in a couple of insurance policies, paid the money into the trust fund. It wasn't much, but it was the best I could do for you. I thought it was much better you had it than the bailiffs or whoever.'

'Oh,' she said. She felt absurdly distressed; she wasn't sure why. Certainly disturbed. 'But why didn't you tell me?'

'You weren't awfully keen on talking to me at the time,' he said briefly. 'Anyway, there was arguably some virtue in your not knowing. If the crunch had actually come.'

'Oh, I see,' she said again. 'Well, I'm very – very grateful. Thank you.'

'That's all right. In the event, touch wood, you didn't need it. I might even take it back.' He smiled at her, went back to the paper.

'Yes. Yes, of course you must.'

And then she'd take it back again; when the divorce settlement went through. She felt very confused suddenly; confused and upset.

'I think I'll go and see Minty,' she said.

'Yes, do. She was wailing just now.'

Halfway up the stairs, she remembered she'd been going to tell him about the divorce. Well, it could wait. A bit longer wouldn't hurt.

*

'Hi, Mum!'

Marianne looked up. In front of her, framed in the doorway of her sitting room, stood a tall, immensely thin figure, dressed in ragged jeans and a tie-dyed shirt. Its rather long straight hair was streaked ash blond and it was extremely tanned and rather dirty looking. But through the tan and the dirt shone a wide, joyful grin showing a set of unmistakably American-nurtured teeth.

'Marc! Oh, my darling!'

She flew at him, hugging him and kissing him; found she was crying, stood back, wiping her eyes, laughing at the same time.

'Hey,' he said, 'easy, Mum. Take your tie off.' It was one of his favourite expressions.

'But what are you doing here? I thought you were in the Himalayas.'

'I was. But I wanted a bath and some English grub. Wanted to see you as well, of course, and I thought I'd give you a surprise.'

'Well, you certainly did that. Oh, I'm so pleased to see you, you can't imagine, it's too good to be true . . .'

Later, sitting watching him as he devoured a huge plateful of chicken and chips and an even huger one of strawberries and ice cream, she said, 'If someone had said to me this evening I could have anything in the world, I'd have said I wanted you to come home.'

'Well, that's good,' he said, grinning at her again. 'I didn't think you'd be exactly upset. But I was afraid you might be with old Felix.'

'Er – no,' said Marianne. 'Not tonight. Or any other night, for that matter.'

'Yeah? All washed up? I can't pretend I'm too upset,' he said, 'but I'm sorry if you are.'

'Thank you,' said Marianne. 'I am. Very.'

Octavia went down to the kitchen to make herself a sandwich. Tom was there, reading the papers. She looked at him slightly warily.

'What are your plans for the evening?' he said politely.

'I was going to work, but—' She hesitated. It was actually a very good time: the twins still away, it would be easy to talk, get the initial and inevitable unpleasantness over, make plans.

'But what?'

'Well, I do want to – to talk to you about something.'

'Yes.'

'Yes. I . . .'

'I wondered if it would be all right if I went out this evening.' Caroline had come into the kitchen, wearing her smarter clothes and a slightly aggressive expression.

'Caroline, of course you must go.' Octavia smiled at her. 'And why don't you take tomorrow off as well?'

'I did actually agree with you that I should take the whole weekend anyway,' said Caroline. 'Perhaps you'd forgotten.'

'Oh, dear. Yes, obviously I had.'

'As you've been away, and—'

'Yes, yes, Caroline, of course. Do you want to leave now for the weekend?'

'It's too late for that,' said Caroline. 'I had hoped to, as a matter of fact, but—'

'Caroline, I was here,' said Tom. 'I've been here since five. You could easily have gone, you should have asked.'

'I know you were here,' said Caroline graciously, 'but Minty was very upset. Perhaps you didn't notice.'

'Caroline, of course I noticed. But I didn't want to interfere.'

'Well, I assumed that must be the reason. That you didn't come up. Anyway, it was her mother she really wanted – needed. As I said to you, Octavia, she's still very unsettled from your being away. It was a pity you had to go straight back to work, a whole day at home with her—'

'Yes, I realise that, Caroline. But I had a great deal of work to do in the office. And of course we did have Sunday together.'

'I suppose so. And the twins will be back tomorrow and they always cheer her up. Hopefully a family weekend will settle her. And them. I expect they will have missed you, too. I presume there won't be a proper family holiday this summer?'

'Not now, I'm afraid,' said Tom briskly, 'as it's September the first on Sunday. Summer's over, as well as the opportunity.'

'Well, at least the twins have had a proper break. We all need one, don't we?'

'We do, Caroline,' said Octavia. 'And that reminds me, we must arrange your holiday. Late September, you usually like, don't you?' (Best to get that over before the inevitable turmoil of the divorce, she thought.)

'I do, yes. Well, I must go, I was hoping to catch the cinema, but it's a bit late now.'

'Oh, not really,' said Tom. 'Only just after eight. Do you want me to run you down, save you parking?'

'No, no, it's quite all right. I think, actually, I might just go for a walk down to Kensington Gardens, it's such a beautiful evening.'

'Fine. 'Bye, Caroline.'

As the front door closed finally behind her, Octavia looked at Tom. He was a rather odd colour; he looked back at her, exhaled loudly and started laughing.

'God,' he said, 'that was a tough one. Six of the best, wouldn't you say?'

'A dozen, more like it,' said Octavia. She started to laugh as well. 'Look at the pair of us, sitting here, feet together, hands folded, in ticked-off mode. I just didn't dare even look in your direction when she started about the twins missing us. I wish!'

'Actually,' said Tom, 'the most priceless moment was when she said I didn't care about Minty crying.'

'Did she say that?'

'Not in so many words. But it was printed out on the wall. In twenty-four-point letters.'

'Well, we'd better write a hundred lines,' said Octavia, still laughing. '"We must not neglect our children."'

'Go on, then. I dare you. And leave it out on the table.'

'I'm not going to. You do it.'

He got up, fetched some paper and a pen, sat down again next to her and started writing.

'Tom, she'll leave! You're not to. Tom, don't . . .'

She was leaning just slightly against him, looking at what he was writing, still laughing; relaxed, not watchful of herself, of what she was doing. 'Here, you need two pens. Then you can write two lines at a time.'

'Really?'

'Yes, that's what I used to do.'

'Octavia, I've known you all these years, and I had no idea you ever did anything naughty to write lines about.'

'Of course I did.'

'What was the worst?'

'Oh, God. It was terrible. It was at my day school. Well, me and my friend—'

'I didn't think you had any friends. I thought everyone hated you.'

'I had one. Horrid girl, fat like me. We used to climb up on each other's shoulders in the lavatory, and look over the wall down on the girl in the next one. It was so funny, such fun.'

'How disgraceful. I'm appalled.'

'Anyway, one day, it was a prefect. She'd just pulled down her pants and was settling her great white bum on the seat when I giggled. She looked up, and – well, that was it. We had to write a hundred lines. "I must not look at people sitting on the lavatory." Even though I was a bit scared, I still giggled every single line.'

'Well, this is a new facet of you, I must say. Dear, oh dear. I'm married to a voyeur. I had no idea.'

'Sorry, I should have told you before.'

And then he looked down at her, suddenly serious and said, 'It's nice to see you laughing. So nice . . .'

And she realised how closely she was sitting to him, and pulled just very slightly away, realised also that it was actually quite difficult to do so, that she didn't want to lose the warmth and the comfort. And then he leaned towards her and kissed her and, eased by laughter, she did not immediately pull away. And when she did, she realised that there was the stillness in him again, the intense, hungry stillness; and, somehow, some strange treacherous piece of desire stirred in her in return, and it was as if her mouth, and indeed her body, did not in any way belong to her, and she watched it, felt it even, observed her mouth returning the kiss, gently at first, then more urgently, and his mouth became harder, more probing on hers: and she felt the probe echoed deep within her body, warm, pushing, urging through her; and even as she knew she mustn't do it, that it was lethal, a betrayal of her very self, she put her arms round his neck and pulled his face down to hers and kissed him harder; and when he pulled back just a very little, and said, 'Upstairs, then?' she saw his eyes on her very brilliant, and perhaps, yes, yes, there were tears in them, and 'Yes,' she said, feeling her own eyes filling in sympathy, 'yes.' And then, dizzy with confusion, shocked at what she was doing, recognising the danger of it, even as she wanted him more than she could remember doing for a very long time, she took his hand and followed him upstairs.

As she pulled her clothes off – half amused at the haste, the urgency with which she was doing it – she knew that she must, she had, to stop – and knew that of course she couldn't, that she was as helpless to resist the demands and commands of her body as she was a while later to stop the great surging rollercoaster of her orgasm. She lay there, quite out of control, moving, pushing, working with and round and on him, kissing him greedily, frantically, feeling his hands on her, taking them, guiding them to where she needed them to be, moving her own on him, remembering with her body as much as with her head how perfect, how driven, how controlled, sex with him could be. And as the lightness and the brightness began, as she fought towards it, pulled back again to prolong it, as she mounted finally the piercing jagged heights of pleasure, fell noisily grateful into the fluid ease beyond it, she heard him say, just before he came himself, 'I love you,' and realised properly then, a rush of panic interspersing the peace, what a horribly dangerous thing she had done . . .

CHAPTER 47

It had been a very beautiful day. Well, it was August, everyone said, albeit the very end of August: all the more unusual actually, everyone then said. August usually went out, along with the summer, in a great driving sheet of rain. It was a wonderful bonus, anyway; everyone agreed they should enjoy it.

In London, the Fleming family were in their garden, the twins rather over-confident and full of themselves at accomplishing their first holiday away from their parents, more full of energy even than usual, at one and the same time happy to be reunited with them and querulous at the loss of freedom, the pool, and several other children to play with. Minty, having recovered from her first intense joy at seeing them, was fractious and restless with the heat. Tom, cautiously relaxed, was cooking a barbecue; Octavia jumpy, wary, watched him and wondered and worried at how she could have allowed herself to do what she had done, how much it might affect the final outcome of her divorce petition, whether anyone actually needed to know about it, and when and how she was going to break the news of that divorce petition to Tom. For, of course, that was still what she wanted.

Louise Trelawny was packing, reflecting upon her escape from the Cloisters, now little more than twelve hours ahead, remembering with something approaching savage rage her final interview with Dr Brandon when he told her he thought she seemed so very much better – how could he think that, a doctor, how could he not see still how much she hurt, how angry she was – but grateful at the same time that he should think it. At least she would be away from this horrible place; at least she could begin to take her revenge. Indeed, in little more than a week, in eight days' time, she would have taken it; or rather be in the very midst of the pleasure of taking it. Then she really would feel better.

Every so often she opened her bag, checked the zipped pocket, just to make sure it hadn't fallen out. It was still there; she could go ahead.

Sandy Trelawny was sitting in the garden with Dickon and Megan and Pattie David, eating a very nice lasagne Pattie had cooked, and thinking this was the last time for many weeks, or even months, that he would be able to see her – or rather them – and that he would be feeling calm and at peace. Tomorrow he would be at home with Louise, trying to suppress his anger, his distaste, trying at the same time to care for her, because, until she was quite, quite better, there was nothing he could do to get away from her. Pattie had already said how much she would miss seeing him and Dickon, and that he must let her know if there was anything she could do to help over the next few weeks, but he knew there was no prospect even of seeing her, let alone her being able to help him.

But as they left, finally and reluctantly, he did allow himself to kiss her lightly – only on the cheek – and to say that he was more grateful than she would ever know for all her help, and that he hoped very much that he would see her and Megan again before too long.

He had thought he could say no more than that; but somehow, when she said, 'You must be so much looking forward to having Louise back home,' he heard his voice, harsh and raw, saying that actually, no, he wasn't, not at all. Pattie then said (her pale face slightly pink) that it would obviously be a great strain for him, and he had actually been about to try and tell her that was not quite the reason, when Dickon ran up and said to come and see – Megan's rabbit had just had babies.

And after that, there was no more opportunity and it was time to set out on the long drive home.

Lucilla Sanderson sat watching her friends the bats swooping through the twilight, and wondering what she should do next; she had phoned the Davids and they were coming to see her the next day, and she had also spoken to her MP, Gabriel Bingham, who seemed a very nice young man, and didn't sound at all like a Socialist, but you never knew these days, look at Tony Blair. He had said there was very little that could be done, if planning permission had definitely been given, but that he had no idea if that was the case. If it was, he said, then the democratic process must take its course, and he very much hoped Mrs Sanderson was not going to take to living in the trees or in a burrow underground. This was intended as a joke, but Lucilla told him that that was precisely what she would do if and when the bulldozers arrived at Bartles Park.

'I'm very old, you know,' she said, 'and I would see that as quite a good way to go. Actually.'

Gabriel Bingham had laughed and said he would be in touch with her as soon as he had some definite news.

Suddenly, across the valley, a rush of wind heralded the beginning of a storm. The bats disappeared.

In London, Marianne Muirhead sat alone in her house, working her way through a bottle of Sancerre and thinking about Nico Cadogan and Felix Miller and the incredible mess she had made of her relationships with both of them. And about being checkmate and how there really was nothing at all she could do about it. Upstairs, Marc was playing some appalling music rather loudly; it was amazing how the young managed to sleep, talk and even work against the background of that noise.

Suddenly he appeared in the doorway; he looked different today, cleaner and a bit paler, but still very thin and extraordinarily beautiful. Marianne would have died rather than admit it, but she did know that, deep down, at the bottom of her heart, Marc was her favourite. She had once heard a friend say, 'I love my daughters more than anything in the world, but I love my son more than more than anything in the world.' That described her own feelings about Marc.

'I can't sleep,' he said. 'I've come for a chat, if that's all right. We did a lot of chatting at night in Nepal. Under the stars. The stars were amazing. Huge.'

Marc was a great chatterer: more than either of the girls. It was one of the things that she most loved about him, made him so easy to talk to.

'Did you do anything else?' she said.

'Yeah, played cards a lot. And chess.'

'Ah,' she said, 'chess. It's been much on my mind at the moment, chess has.'

'I didn't think you played.'

'I don't. But I find myself in a situation that I can only describe as checkmate.'

'Oh, really? Want to tell me about it?'

She hesitated, then said, 'No. No, it's a bit – personal.'

He shrugged. 'Okay. That's cool. But I won't tell anyone. If you want to talk.'

Over a third glass of Sancerre, Marianne started to talk. When she had finished, Marc was silent for a while; then he said, 'That's not quite checkmate, Mum. Checkmate's when you can't do anything at all. I'd call it check.'

'And how do you get out of check?'

'You do something of a defensive nature.'

'Marc, I did that. When I went to see Felix. It didn't work.'

He stared at her. 'And this Cadogan guy. How do you feel about him?'

'I just can't tell you,' said Marianne fretfully. 'If it wasn't for Felix, I suppose I'd be—' she hesitated – 'in love with him. As there is Felix, I – well, I just can't be.'

Marc looked at her thoughtfully. 'Yeah,' he said slowly. 'Yeah, maybe it is checkmate.'

In Bath, Gabriel Bingham sat in his tiny courtyard of a garden and thought rather sadly of Octavia, and also how thankful he was that the day which had been so extremely hot – although not nearly as bad as Barbados – was cooling down now with the help of a wind that was rather strong for August. The sky was growing stormy, too; it looked as if it might even rain. That really would be extremely nice. The whole week had been rather too hot.

He was missing Octavia; but he had come round quite swiftly to her pragmatic point of view, that it was as well they had discovered their incompatibility so soon. For that alone, the week in Barbados had been worth while. He hoped he wouldn't lose her from his life entirely; he enjoyed her company, her clear, incisive mind, her rather engaging seriousness. He wondered if her inevitable reunion with her husband had yet been accomplished; he genuinely hoped so (and admired himself at the same time for hoping it). He might phone her during the week, on the pretext of checking whether she had heard from the poor old soul at Bartles House. He had very little hope that Bartles Park could be saved – from the beginning it had seemed a foregone conclusion to him. And from his viewpoint, there was much to be said for it; much-needed housing, local employment, and whatever they all said, the community centre and its facilities for the disabled would be extremely valuable. These Nimbys were all the same. They would never admit it, but it was true. If Michael Carlton had wanted to put up his development on the other side of Bath, none of them would have made a murmur . . .

Sailing off Martha's Vineyard, Zoë Muirhead lay on the deck of a dinghy, watching the clouds scudding above her, and occasionally smiling at the immensely good-looking boy at the helm. The holiday hadn't been nearly as bad as she had feared. One big abasement session with her father and he'd been sweet as a pie, let her out every night so long as he knew her escorts' parents – God, adults were naive – and Romilly had had a ball, getting off with half the sixteen-year-olds on the island, cured of the worst of her shyness by her foray into modelling. Zoë had even told her father she might like to go to an American university when the time came: that had been a very smart move, and

Ian and Cleaver Square and the police station all seemed like nothing more than an extremely bad dream . . .

In Edinburgh, Felix Miller sat morosely alone in his hotel room, having left the friends with whom he had been having dinner, after attending the wedding of another friend's son, drinking whisky and mourning the death of his relationship with Marianne. For it was undoubtedly dead. He knew that. And it was his fault. He had forfeited for ever any chance of getting her back. Even as a friend. She had come to him, swallowing her pride, concerned, anxious even for him, and he had rejected her, harshly, horribly. He was a fool: a complete fool. He missed her more and more painfully every day; physically, emotionally, intellectually. He felt very alone. And he was also somehow frightened. That he had come so close to being caught out, shown up, to Octavia, to the person he loved most, by far the most in the world, had shaken him badly. He had thought himself inviolate and now knew that he was very much the reverse; it had been an extremely salutary experience.

But there was something else, something equally disturbing. The encounter in the house over Nico Cadogan that night had another result: one that Tom could certainly never have envisaged, that Felix would not have believed possible. It had changed his opinion, just very slightly, of Tom Fleming, nudged him just a very little near respect. Of course, Tom had been very clever, very devious. But he had also wished to spare Octavia pain. It would have been very easy for him to tell her, to say look what your father did to me, to you, to disillusion her about him. But he had not; he had kept his counsel. Even before he discovered the need for a bargaining point. For that Felix had to admit Tom was not all bad.

In Paris, Diana, Princess of Wales had arrived at the Ritz Hotel in the company of Dodi Fayed; the gang of paparazzi who had pursued them there from Le Bourget airport were now pitched up outside the entrance to the hotel in the Place Vendôme waiting to see where their quarry might lead them next.

Whether she'd enjoyed it or not, she'd given them a wonderful summer . . .

CHAPTER 48

Louise went into the dining room for breakfast singing under her breath. Her last meal there: her last day. It was too good to be true.

It seemed very quiet; everyone was hushed, bent over their papers. She poured herself some orange juice and some coffee and went over to one of the empty tables. She didn't need to pretend to be friendly any more.

The woman at the next table, whom she'd always particularly disliked, looked up. 'Isn't it dreadful?' she said.

'What?' said Louise carelessly.

'About Diana.'

'Diana who?'

'Princess Diana, of course. Didn't you know? She's been killed. In a car crash.'

Louise felt as if she had been struck by a very heavy weight in her solar plexus; she was shocked at how shocked she was. She felt as if she had lost not a friend, but an essential part of her life. She had grown up with the Princess; she was almost the same age. She had watched her change from pudgy, pretty teenager into first princess, then goddess and finally neurotic divorcee; she had been influenced by her appearance, fascinated by her power over the media, sympathetic with her patent loneliness. She had always been there, it seemed; an endless focus for gossip, interest and admiration. And now she was gone; it simply didn't seem possible.

'Can – can I see?' she said.

The woman passed her the paper. 'Those poor boys,' she said. 'Those poor, poor boys.'

The story was bald, there was little detail: only that Diana had died in the early hours of the morning at La Pitie Hospital in Paris. Dodi had died too, and so had the driver of the car. The paparazzi were being held to blame, for chasing them, forcing the driver to speed, blinding him with their flashbulbs.

Louise sat reading it, thinking of her, of that lovely tragic life quenched finally and so much too soon, and began to weep herself.

When Sandy arrived she was calmer but still pale and swollen eyed. 'Isn't it awful? I feel so sad.'

And 'Yes,' he said, knowing at once what she meant. 'Yes, it is, very sad. Come along, let me get your things. I've seen Dr Brandon, maybe you should go and say goodbye to him while I put your things in the car.'

Even Dr Brandon seemed upset, said what a beautiful young woman Diana had been, what a dreadful waste it was; all the way home, they sat and listened to the radio, bringing them the endlessly repeated story, the details slowly filling in. There was no music, not even on the pop stations; Capital played the National Anthem dutifully with every bulletin.

Louise was surprised that Sandy was willing to listen to it all; normally he was impatient with any interest in the Royal Family. It was only later that she realised he was grateful for something, anything, to fill in the ugly silence that existed whenever they were together.

Dickon was rather quiet; he went to sleep on the way back.

'I expect he's bored,' said Sandy briefly, 'and then he was rather late last night.'

'Why?'

'Oh – we had supper with – with friends.'

'Which friends? You didn't mention it.'

'Pattie David and her little daughter, Megan, you remember, the one in a wheelchair?'

'Why on earth did you have supper with them?'

'They've been very kind to us. We've been there quite often, after visiting you.'

'Oh, yes, I remember now. Dickon mentioned it once or twice. She seemed very dull to me.'

'She's not dull at all actually,' said Sandy briefly.

'And Megan is lovely,' said Dickon sleepily.

'Well,' said Louise. A stab of jealousy had shot through her. 'I can see I'm going to have some catching up to do; you've obviously been having a high old time without me. What other new friends have you got?'

'None,' said Sandy, 'don't be silly.'

He gave her the brief half smile that she was beginning to know rather well.

*

'Darling,' she said, when they finally reached the house, 'it all looks so lovely. You must have worked so hard. And gorgeous flowers in our room, you are sweet.'

She reached up to kiss him; he half shied away. Gave her the smile again.

'Your room,' he said quickly.

'My room? What do you mean?'

'I thought you'd want to be on your own. Sleep better and so on. I've moved into the spare room.'

'Sandy! I don't want to sleep on my own. One of the things I've been most looking forward to is being with you again.'

'Well—' he hesitated – 'maybe for a few days at least, I think it would be best. You know how much I snore. Perhaps you've forgotten.' He smiled at her, the same smile. 'Dr Brandon said you needed a lot of rest.'

She felt a shoot of panic suddenly; this wasn't going quite right. But – best not to argue now. She could get him into her bed if she wanted to. And she did want to. She needed some sex. Rather badly.

She sat and watched the television for a while; it was hideously sad, endless shots of the Royal Wedding, of Diana with the boys, the heartbreaking sequence of her arriving on the royal yacht, holding out her arms to the tiny Harry. People pontificating about the reasons for the crash, people talking about the paparazzi, the car, the driver, the road itself, a dangerous underpass it seemed. A heap of flowers was growing slowly, outside both Kensington and Buckingham palaces. Ordinary people, weeping into the camera, said they felt they had lost a friend. The Prime Minister made an emotional statement about Diana being the People's Princess. More shots of Diana with the boys. More pontificating; more flowers. In the end she couldn't bear it any longer. Her own happiness, fragile at best, was threatened, damaged by it; she began to feel frightened, to feel a panic attack lurking somewhere in her head. She switched off the television and left Sandy cooking the lunch while she took Dickon for a walk.

'Tell me a bit more about your new friends, the Davids,' she said to him.

'The People's Princess indeed,' said Tom. 'I wonder who wrote that line for him.'

'Don't be so cynical,' said Octavia. She felt very upset. 'Anyway, even if they did, whoever it was did better than William Hague's speech writer.'

'Yes, that's true. Oh, God, this is going on for ever. I think I might go for a walk. Want to come, anyone?'

'Can we bring our rollerblades?'

'Yes, if you like.'

'Mummy, will you come?'

'I don't think so,' said Octavia quickly. She needed some time on her own; Fiona had given her a long form to fill in, and she needed to think; about what she was going to do, how and when she was going to tell Tom about the divorce. She still hadn't done it. Almost the last thing he had said before they fell asleep together on Friday night had been, 'What did you want to talk to me about?'

And 'Nothing,' she had said. Of course. How could she have told him then? Really, she needed some advice: but how could she ask for it? 'Er – Fiona, I slept with my husband on Friday night. Does that matter?'

Oh, God. Why had she done it, why? One fit of madness and she'd endangered her whole case. And made her relationship with Tom far more complex. And since then he'd been sort of quietly confident. As well he might be. God, what a mess. It wasn't as if she'd been unwilling either, that she could claim any kind of pressure from him. She'd been hideously, horribly enthusiastic. Rushing upstairs with him, tearing her clothes off. Making such a noise he'd put his hand over her mouth, telling her she'd wake Minty. Fallen asleep against him, heavily, happily sated by him. And then woken to remorse, anxiety, confusion.

It had been the money, she decided, that had done it. Well, not the money itself, of course, but the way he had given it to her. What was the biblical expression? Oh, yes. Do good by stealth. But then, did that cancel out doing bad by stealth? It had been very bad, what he had done, and very stealthy. She was still damaged, deeply damaged and humiliated. She could still not think about him with anything other than mistrust. The foundations of her life had been shaken: by something which, measured on a Richter scale of emotion, had not just rocked but come very near to ruining it. And ruining her. And how was she to know it would not happen again? When remorse had faded, memories become shadowy, pain eased? She wasn't to know it; she couldn't. For the rest of her life she would mistrust him; and she didn't think she could cope with that. Better, far better to make a break, as clean and as final as it could be. That was what she had decided: nothing had really changed. Except a piece of truly appalling folly . . .

'It's dreadful, isn't it?' said Lucilla. 'So terribly sad. Such a beautiful young woman, such a waste. And those poor, poor boys. I cannot imagine how they will be able to bear it.'

'Neither can I,' said Pattie. 'And poor Prince Charles as well, he must feel so guilty.'

'With good reason, in my opinion,' said Lucilla briskly. 'They all should. I'm sure she was very difficult, but she should never have been robbed of her royal status. And her bodyguard. If she'd had a decent English bodyguard, I feel quite sure she would have been safe. Animals, they are, those photographers.'

'Did you see the pictures of the flowers?' said Megan.

'Haven't seen anything, my dear. The TV's on the blink. All I've heard all day is people moaning about that, not poor Diana at all. Of course, a couple of the old people—' she always referred to her fellow residents at Bartles House as old people, as if she herself was young – 'have their own televisions. But I don't care for any of them, so I've seen nothing. Just the radio. Oh, Nora, dear, do you want to join us? This is a friend, Mrs David, and her daughter Megan. They've been trying to help save the house, and the wood, of course. But I'm afraid, as I was saying, we rather seem to have been beaten. Progress and greed once again are triumphing. And a little more of England is going under concrete.'

'It isn't over yet,' said Pattie, 'and we haven't lost. We're planning protests, a legal challenge, all sorts of things.'

'Waste of time, I'm very much afraid,' said Lucilla. 'They'll tell you it's all gone through the democratic process, as they're so fond of saying. About as democratic a process as Stalin's purges!'

'Lucilla, dear, that's a slight exaggeration.'

'Not at all. It's appalling what these councils get up to. Everyone with their hands in everyone else's pockets, bribery and corruption wherever you look – Nora, dear, would you like a drink? The sun's getting over the yard arm now. Not that you can see much of the sun. So different from yesterday.'

'I won't, thank you,' said Nora. 'I'm terribly tired. And I can't sleep at the moment. I know you like those bats, Lucilla, but they frighten me. And they make a dreadful noise up there in the roof. Right above me, you know. I hate them.'

'Bats are sweet things,' said Megan. 'Like dear little flying mice.'

'Quite right,' said Lucilla, 'a girl after my own heart. They are very sweet little things. I adore them. I think of them as my friends, my companions here, sharing my home.'

'Well, I wish they didn't share mine,' said Nora. 'I wish they lived outside. I really do.'

This was like Sunday used to be in the 'fifties, Nico Cadogan thought to himself, as he drove through a series of seemingly deserted Wiltshire villages. It was very strange; the entire country was still and grieving, indoors with their television sets and the images of their beloved

Princess. Even the weather had changed, as if in sympathy, with the tragedy; it had become cloudy and windy, the warm golden sunshine of the day before quite gone. He felt very odd himself; the exhilaration of Felix Miller's withdrawal, of having his company safely restored to him, had slightly faded now, to be replaced by a certain melancholy at having no one to share it with. Well, Tom Fleming had done his best, of course; but it wasn't quite the same. He missed Marianne dreadfully; he would not have believed how much. They had, after all, only been together a very short time. But it had been a very intense, a very joyful time; it had changed him, irrevocably.

But not her, it seemed; she had remained in thrall to Felix. Had preferred Felix to him. And whether that was working or not was fairly irrelevant. Nico had no intention of playing understudy to anyone. His pride would not allow it.

'I just cannot believe it.' Lauren's voice was heavy, not with the grief that might have been expected, from one who had professed friendship with Diana, but exasperation. 'What are we going to do? How can we have our day now? Or do you think it'll be all right?'

'I don't know,' said Octavia slowly. 'If the funeral's going to be on Saturday it'll definitely cast a bit of a shadow. But on the other hand, if we cancel we'll lose so much money.'

'It's a bloody disaster,' said Lauren. She put her coffee cup down on Octavia's desk rather sharply: then, seeing Octavia looking at her, hastily adjusted her expression. 'Of course it's heartbreaking. I feel devastated myself. And those boys, those poor little boys. Forced to go to church like that yesterday, it's appalling.'

'Yes,' said Octavia, 'it is all very sad. But as you say, we have a practical problem. Let's see what Melanie says. She'll be here in about ten minutes.'

'Fine. Twins all right?'

'Yes. Yes, they're fine. They had a wonderful time – thank you so much again for taking them.'

'My pleasure. Thank you for the flowers, sweet of you, quite unnecessary. And you enjoyed Barbados? I presume Tom couldn't go?'

'No,' said Octavia quickly, 'no, he couldn't.'

'Well, it's marvellous his company is doing so well. I always think it's so clever, the way you two work away together. What does he think about Sunday, by the way?'

'I don't know,' said Octavia. She hadn't thought to ask him; other years, another life, she would have done so before anyone else. It had always been one of the good things about their relationship, the other's valuable, informed opinion, always available, criss-crossing their personal and professional lives. She would miss that. Well, it hadn't gone yet . . .

'I'll ask him,' she said.

Tom, clearly pleased to be asked, said he thought they should go ahead. 'Clearly not if it was the Saturday, of course. I mean, they're cancelling football matches, for God's sake, and the supermarkets are shutting in the morning. But – Sunday. Not ideal in some ways, but people will be pleased, I reckon, to have something to do by then. They'll be sated with the stuff. I think you'll get a good turnout.'

'Thanks,' said Octavia.

'You in tonight?'

'No. No, I'm not. I'll be quite late.'

She had a meeting with Melanie; and then she thought she would sit in the office and fill in Fiona's form. Because it was easier there. Less interruptions. And when she'd done it, when it was more – formal, she would find it easier to tell Tom.

'Pity. I wanted to have a chat. And you wanted to talk to me about something, didn't you?'

'Oh – yes. But not tonight, I don't think. Sorry.'

She put the phone down.

'Darling, you look tired. I hope you're not doing too much.'

'No, of course not. I'm fine. It's just a bit of a strain, getting back to real life. And I can't sleep very well.'

'Why's that?'

'Oh – don't know. The pills, maybe.'

How could she tell her father, of all people, she had lain awake for hours angry, raging even; that she had gone to Sandy on two nights now, had got into bed beside him, had tried to arouse him, had used all the means she knew, pressing her naked body against his, using her hands, her mouth, even her voice, all quite uselessly: he had rejected her totally, had tried at first to make a joke of it, to say no, no, she mustn't waste her energies on him; then, when she persisted, had finally turned from her, saying in that tired, distant voice she was coming to know so well, 'Louise, please. Please leave me alone.'

She had left swiftly, hurrying along the corridor, arms crossed over her breasts, feeling horribly, vulnerably undesirable, ugly even, feeling that no one must see, must know – absurd, for who could? – back to her own room and lain there, weeping first sad, then angry tears, had lain masturbating wretchedly, trying to rid herself of the aching, hungry desire, and then finally slept fitfully, only to wake and remember, freshly humiliated . . .

'Well, you'll settle down, I'm sure,' her father said. 'I thought we might go out for lunch, you and Dickon and I, give Sandy a chance to do some work.'

'Oh – yes, all right. Good idea.'

It was Wednesday; the mood was growing ugly now, the tabloids taking it upon themselves to speak for the nation, whipping up a mood of anger that the Royal Family were staying in Balmoral, not coming to grieve publicly in London, as (again) the tabloids felt they should. Pictures of the mountains of flowers filled the papers; the flowers and the sobbing public. It was all very sombre; it did not help Louise's mood.

She sat studying the *Daily Mail* in the pub garden, as her father ordered the food, thinking about Diana, about her rejection by her husband and her lover. Well, Diana had taken her revenge; it was different from the one Louise was planning, but revenge it had been just the same, blackening Charles' name and his image, talking on television about how James Hewitt had let her down. It had helped her: most clearly it had helped her.

'I wondered,' she said, lightly, to her father when he came back, 'if I could possibly come over on Saturday some time, stay the night?'

'Darling, of course you can. That would be lovely. Will you all come?'

'No, no, just me. Sandy and Dickon are going off early on Sunday morning, to this charity car race day. I don't want to be left alone.'

'Why don't you go too?'

'Bit too much, I think. Long drive. No, I'd rather stay with you.'

'I wish you would come,' said Dickon. '*Everyone*'s going. The twins, and some new friends of the twins, that they went on holiday with.'

'And what about Minty?'

'Oh, yes, she's going. They've got her a special pram thing, an old one. Poppy told me last night.'

'And the twins' mummy and – and daddy?'

Yes. All of them.'

So Tom had had his cake and eaten it; he and Octavia were still together, still there in their perfect marriage with their perfect family. Octavia was still no doubt being made love to; not rejected, not creeping away, humiliated in the middle of the night. Octavia had still got a baby, too . . .

'It'll be so fun. I wish you'd come.'

'No, darling, not this time. I'll get too tired. Next time, maybe.'

'All right,' said Dickon with a sigh.

*

'How extremely – liberal you are,' said Louise to Sandy that night.

'Sorry?'

'Going to this thing on Sunday. Octavia's charity day. Won't you feel a little – what shall we say? Uncomfortable?'

'I hope not,' said Sandy. 'And Octavia has been very kind to me.'

'Yes, so I keep hearing. And Mrs David, is she going?'

'No. It's too far for Megan.'

'And how will you feel when you have to make polite conversation about the weather with Tom?'

'Tom's not going.'

'Yes, he is. You can ask Dickon if you don't believe me.'

'Oh. Oh, I see,' said Sandy. He was silent for a while; then he said, 'I think I'll just go upstairs, do a bit of work before I go to bed. If you'll excuse me. Leave this, I'll clear it up.'

After he had gone, Louise went into the sitting room, to see what was on television. Predictably, there was a great deal of stuff about Diana. With two days to go before the funeral, the Royal Family had come down from Balmoral and the Queen was to broadcast to the nation. The attitude of the tabloid press was softening; Charles had appeared with the boys at the gates of Balmoral, and they had received nothing but sympathy; Prince Andrew and Prince Edward had run the gauntlet and done a walkabout in the Strand, and not been lynched; the final details of a funeral on a scale as impressive as Churchill's were being put in place.

Louise watched it for a while and then decided she wanted some chocolate. Since she had been – ill, she had had a craving for chocolate; it soothed and comforted her in a way she would never have believed. She went to the cupboard, but there was none there. Damn. She'd eaten it all. She'd have to go and get some more. The corner shop would still be open.

She picked up her purse, but it was empty. Never mind, Sandy always had cash. His wallet was lying on the kitchen table; she rummaged through it, found a five-pound note. That would do: that would buy several bars of fruit and nut, which she liked best.

As she pulled the note out, a photograph came with it; Louise stared at it. It was of Sandy, Sandy smiling, looking very happy – happier than she had seen him for a long time – and some woman. Some plain, dreary woman. Pattie David, no doubt. Beaming into the camera, and holding Sandy's arm. For God's sake! How pathetic. How absolutely pathetic.

'Louise! Louise, I—'

She turned round; he saw her, saw her holding the picture.

'Well,' she said, 'my goodness, Sandy. How sweet. The minute my back was turned. A new girlfriend. Bit plain. But then she probably won't give you the run around. You might be able to hang on to this one. I don't suppose she's very experienced in the bed department.'

Sandy flushed, a very deep dark red. 'Please give me that,' he said quietly.

'Of course. You can put it under your pillow. Well, no wonder you can't cope with me, Sandy. Not a lot of it left, I don't suppose. You never were exactly over-burdened with testosterone.'

'Shut up,' said Sandy. 'Just shut up, will you?'

She said nothing, just leaned on the kitchen table, looking at the picture, then at him, smiling. 'I really do hand it to you, Sandy. You didn't waste much time. Of course she must be pretty lonely, pretty frustrated. Easy pickings, I suppose.'

'Louise—' He walked over to her, and raised his hand; for one minute she thought he was going to hit her. Then he simply grabbed her wrist and took the picture, and stalked out of the room, without another word. Louise stared after him, feeling very sick.

Two men had appeared on the other side of the valley; Lucilla could see them through her binoculars. If her late husband Douglas, who had used them for his birdwatching, only knew how useful those binoculars of his were proving now! The men had what looked like a camera, set up on a tripod. No, that wasn't a tripod, Lucilla thought wretchedly, she knew exactly what it was; it was a surveyor's instrument, and they weren't taking photographs, they were studying the pitch of the valley, how best to plan their assault on it, where to park their vehicles, their chainsaws, their diggers, which trees to hack down first, which foundations to sink into which slaughtered piece of woodland. The picture blurred through her binoculars; she set them down and wiped her eyes. Those harmless-looking men, with their quiet innocent-looking instrument, foreran chaos and noise and destruction. Those men were not harmless at all.

'Sandy? Sandy, hallo, it's Megan. I wondered if you'd heard about – well, about anything?'

'No, Megan, I'm afraid not.'

He sounded slightly impatient. She felt hurt.

'Oh. Well, all right. Lucilla's getting the reporter up to the house tomorrow. I thought you might – might like to come.'

'Megan, I'm sorry, I would come if I could. You know I would. Is Lucilla very upset?'

'Terribly. She says she's going to chain herself to the trees. In the wood.'

'Good for her. You going to join her?'

''Course. Her friend Nora might, but she's a bit feeble. We were talking to her on Sunday as well. She can't sleep because of the bats, which doesn't help.'

There was a long silence: then 'Bats?' said Sandy, and his voice was quite different suddenly, excited, not irritable at all. 'Did you say bats, Megan?'

Megan said yes, she had said bats. 'They're in the roof of Bartles House. So sweet, I saw one of them on Sunday.'

'God,' said Sandy. 'Bats. Good God.'

'Now who is acting for your husband?' said Fiona Michael. 'In the divorce petition?'

'Oh. Yes. Well, I'm not sure. Actually.'

'Mrs Fleming—'

'Please, call me Octavia.'

'Thank you. Octavia, you have told him now, I hope.'

'Oh. Oh, he does know. Yes.'

'And what was his reaction?'

'Oh, I think – that is, of course he's not stupid.'

'I'm pleased to hear that,' said Fiona Michael.

'Sandy? Thank you for ringing. Now is this really really true? Pattie phoned me earlier, told me. It sounded like a fairy story to me.'

'Not a fairy story at all, Octavia. No. No, I think we've – *you've* got them. Stopped them pulling the house down anyway. And from what Pattie said, that means they can't proceed with the development.'

'She says she's been talking to the local paper. They're on their way to see Lucilla now. To interview her about her little friends, as she calls them. Friends indeed. Who'd have thought it? Pattie sounded over the moon, you should have heard her.'

'I'd like to,' said Sandy.

'Well – call her. She'd love to hear from you. She's so grateful.'

'It's a bit – difficult,' said Sandy, 'just at the moment.'

'Oh, of course. How stupid. How – how is Louise?'

'Oh, she's coming along. You know. Tired. But – yes, definitely better.'

'Good.' Octavia's voice was brisk; he heard her carefully change tack. 'Sandy, you are an absolute hero. We're all just thrilled. Hopefully you'll get loads of publicity in the local papers, do your business no end of good. Now look, you are still coming on Sunday, aren't you?'

'No. No, I don't think I will after all,' said Sandy.

'Why not?'

'Because I heard that – that Tom was going. I really don't think—'

'Oh, Sandy! Oh, God, I hadn't thought. I'm so sorry. How stupid of me. But of course I see. Oh, dear, Dickon will be so disappointed.'

'I know. I wondered – well, if you could take him with you.'

'We'd love to. Can you get him up here? He'll have to come with Tom and the children. I have to be down at Brands Hatch by nine at the latest, I've got stalls to set up, banners to hang, all sorts of glamorous things . . .'

'Yes, of course. Thanks, Octavia.'

'No, thank you. You're the hero of the hour. The story will be out on Saturday. I can't wait.'

This time it was a heart attack: it had to be. He was the most terrible colour, sweat breaking out on his forehead.

'Sit down, Michael,' she said, 'sit down here, for heaven's sake. Take deep breaths. I'll fetch you some water. Would you like me to phone the doctor?'

'No, of course I don't want you to phone the bloody doctor! I don't need a bloody doctor. You're not going to believe this, Betty, you really are not. I can't believe it myself. Bloody meddling old woman! And why didn't the chap from the DOE think of it? God, I feel such a fool. Such a total fool.'

'Michael, what on earth are you talking about?'

'Bartles House, Betty, that's what. I'm afraid they've got us. And there really isn't anything we can do about it, it seems. And if that's the bloody reporter again, tell her I don't want to talk to her, all right?'

'All right, dear,' said Betty. 'But at least could you talk to me about it? I'm really completely baffled.'

Zoë and Romilly arrived home: tanned, glowing, full of stories about their holiday, about people they had met, parties they had been to, overjoyed to see Marc.

Zoë seemed particularly pleased to be home. 'It was good,' she said in response to Marianne's rather anxious questioning. 'Fine. Rom had a ball.'

'And – Daddy?'

'He was okay. Really quite human. Oz seems back on.'

'You pleased about that?' said Marianne, sounding upbeat, dreading a year of her absence.

'Yeah, really pleased. Oh, yes, and some woman came down for the middle weekend. It's obviously quite serious. I mean they're obviously very much an item.'

'What – what was she like?'

A slug of alarm hit Marianne suddenly; why, why should that be, as if she cared?

'Oh – you know. Very New York. Very thin, very well dressed, obsessed with charity and culture.'

'Pretty?'

'Probably once, yes.'

She smiled. She always forgot how extremely old they all must seem to the children, how absurd the concept that anyone over forty could possibly be described as pretty.

'What was her name?'

'Marcia. Mum, you seem very interested. You jealous or something?'

And no, she said, of course not, she was just interested; and of course she wasn't jealous. But she was left with an odd sense of unease: of lonely, getting-older unease.

'Mum seems a bit down,' said Zoë to Marc later.

'Yeah, she is.'

'Met the new boyfriend? He's really cool.'

Marc said he hadn't. 'Not likely to, either. He's history. Like Felix.'

'Oh, no. What happened? He was really good for her, Marc. Not a bit like Felix.'

Marc told her. 'Only we haven't had this conversation, Zoë.'

''Course not.'

'She says she's got herself checkmated.'

'What?'

'As in chess.'

'Maybe a knight could leap on to the board.'

'I don't know what he'd do. It's a bit of a no-hope situation. She really loves that old bugger, Zoë, God knows why. Or she thinks she does, anyway.'

'Love defies logic,' said Zoë. 'I found that out for myself this summer.'

'Sounds intriguing. Want to tell me about it?'

'How long have you got?' said Zoë.

The night before Diana's funeral, Octavia went for a walk. She hadn't exactly planned it, but she was watching the news at nine o'clock, watching the crowds, the extraordinary scenes, and someone said something about a page of history being turned and she suddenly felt she had to go. Tom was out, the children were all asleep, there was no reason for her not to.

It was an extraordinary experience. The flowers by Kensington Palace, the crowds there, the queue to sign the book of condolence, she had seen, it was just down the road; but this was different. She took the Tube to the Embankment, and crossed the road into Parliament Square; it was already packed, every available bit of grass and pavement taken up by people: some under makeshift tents or tarpaulins, others with rather impressive structures, some just wrapped up in sleeping bags and silver foil for warmth. There were a great many people in wheelchairs, also clearly there until some time late the following day. All because they wanted to say goodbye to their princess. The People's Princess. The awful phrase had stuck; it was actually, she thought, strangely apt.

Everyone was quiet, friendly, good humoured. Traffic waited patiently all round the square for people to cross; policemen walked about in pairs, relaxed and good tempered.

She moved along towards the Abbey; the bank of arc lights there was brilliant, already in place for the next day. The huge press box was built very high, opposite the main door, and already it seemed fully staffed. People walked past her endlessly, carrying flowers; a lot of them young men holding lilies. She followed them. She had brought a bunch of her own.

All down the Mall, the camps were set up; two or three thick, people sitting and lying on the hard pavements, quietly patient. On almost every lamp-post shrines had been set up, pictures of Diana surrounded by flowers and flickering nightlights. All across St James's Park, she could see more lights, Diana's candles, shining in the darkness. For the hundredth time since it had all begun, Octavia thought how much Diana would have loved it, would have felt vindicated in everything she had done; and thought, absurdly, what a shame it was she couldn't be there . . .

She walked on, down to the Palace; the Victoria monument was covered in shrines. The queue of people waiting to lay their flowers in what they felt was the proper place, at the Palace Gates, was still, she was told, two hours long: orderly, quiet, sober. Police took the flowers from them, laid them most carefully down, each bunch of the half million clearly important. She looked up at the Palace, with the flag now hanging at half mast, looked at the lighted windows, thought of the two young princes, their adored mother lost to them, gathering their courage for their ordeal tomorrow. She felt her eyes fill with tears.

The smell of the flowers was immensely sweet and strong; Octavia began to feel rather strange. She laid her own flowers down on the steps of the Victoria monument, not wishing to queue for two hours, and began to walk very slowly back. The composition of the crowd fascinated her: many young people, black people, a lot of families three or four strong, arms linked, walking soberly alone, many many young, clearly gay men. A vast, disparate group, all with just one thought in their heads: Diana. She had their hearts: everyone's hearts. In that week, her own dreadfully sentimental phrase had become reality.

When she got home, Tom was there, in the kitchen. He looked at her. 'Where have you been?'

She told him, too tired, too emotional to care what he thought.

He had been very cynical about the whole thing, absolutely on Charles' side, defending him, deploring the tabloids' behaviour.

'Me too,' he said, astonishing her.

'What?'

'Yes. I couldn't resist it in the end. Extraordinary, wasn't it? Very moving. History in the making.'

'That's exactly what I thought. In fact I wished I'd taken the children.'

'Yes, so did I. We should have done. All gone together. Well, good night, Octavia.'

He had returned, without discussion, to sleeping alone in their bedroom; he was clearly waiting for her next move.

She had to make it; she had to tell him.

But she didn't; she simply went upstairs and fell asleep, thinking of what he had said, and wishing that they had indeed all gone to see Diana's crowds together . . .

It was the boys' flowers that did it: the white posy on the coffin, with the card saying simply 'Mummy'.

Until then she had felt quite brave, quite in control.

She had put white flowers on Juliet's coffin: with a card saying, 'Juliet. From Mummy.'

It was more than she could bear. She switched off the television, went up to her room and pulled the curtains and lay there for a long time, weeping, remembering, trying to forget.

Sandy heard her; knocked on the door. 'Louise? Can I help?'

She didn't answer; he tried the door. She had locked it.

'Louise. Please let me in.'

'No. I'm all right. Just go away. Leave me alone.'

Later he brought her some tea and she let him in and drank it, but refused to talk to him, just sat there, the tears stopped now, her emotions bled white, exhausted by grief.

Dickon was with a friend for the day, had gone off excitedly soon after breakfast. She knew he was disappointed by her return, by her weariness, her short temper. She didn't know what to do about that. If only she could sleep, it would help.

At teatime her father appeared, looking anxious.

'Darling, you all right? Sandy said Diana's funeral had upset you.'

'It did – a bit. But – yes, I'm all right.'

She had her plan to cling to: she mustn't let that go. That was going to make her feel better.

Felix Miller had resolved not to watch the funeral; he knew it would add to his mood of misery and loneliness. But, glancing at the order of service in *The Times*, he could see that the music would be glorious; he might just listen to it on the radio while he had some coffee and leafed through his mail.

When Mrs Harrington brought in the coffee, she found him watching the television intently. She wasn't sure it was a good idea, he had been very down that week, and she didn't think he'd been looking at all well, a bit puffy somehow, and very pale; but maybe it would serve to distract him from what she supposed must be his business worries, the takeover bid not happening. And then there was Octavia, of course, Octavia and her divorce. And however brave a face he was putting on, he must be missing Mrs Muirhead terribly.

There wasn't much Mrs Harrington didn't know about Felix Miller.

When the funeral was over, Felix went out for a walk on the Heath. It was deserted, served to reinforce his sense of isolation. Octavia had phoned him, of course, to chat, to make sure he was all right, but he wouldn't be able to see her until the following week, she was so preoccupied with her big charity function tomorrow. She was so clever; so successful. He smiled with pride, thinking about her, then frowned as a pain in his left arm suddenly stabbed at him. It wasn't the first time; he'd been aware of it several times over the past few days. He knew what it was; he'd been doing a lot of lifting, clearing out some boxes in the room which he'd thought would make a room for the nanny, if Octavia came to stay. Rooms for the children already existed, of course, had done ever since the twins had been born. They weren't used very often, but they were there. Ready. Waiting. Although Bernard Moss had told him there should be no question of them all moving in, that the wife should never leave the matrimonial home. 'Unless there is violence. I don't know if—'

'No,' said Felix, sharply, 'no violence.'

Although, of course, what Tom had done amounted to violence. Of its own kind.

The pain stabbed again; more sharply. He might go back, take some paracetamol. And then get down to some work. He had nothing else to do this weekend. Nothing else at all.

*

'Isn't it wonderful?' said Megan. Her large blue eyes were shining. 'Just wonderful.'

'It is. And look, they've even got the bit about you in. Ringing to check with the Department of the Environment.'

'"BATS TO SAVE THE BELFRY,"' said Megan and giggled. 'What a good headline. Not that there is a belfry at Bartles House. It's just so scary, isn't it, to think that if Nora hadn't said about the bats, and then if I hadn't told Sandy, no one would ever have known. Listen, it mentions Sandy, 'Successful Gloucestershire businessman', it calls him. He'll like that.'

The phone rang: it was Octavia. 'I hear the story's in the paper. Gabriel just phoned me.'

'I'll get Megan to read it to you,' said Pattie. 'Here she is.'

'Octavia? Isn't it wonderful? Listen, this is what it says. "Local beauty spot Bartles Wood has almost certainly been saved from the developers. A chance discovery this week by little Megan David that bats nested in the roof of Bartles House, adjacent to the wood, could prove bad news for builder Michael Carlton. Bats are, of course, an endangered species and as such any building which shelters them is automatically protected. Mr Carlton was unavailable for comment when the *Post* called him. Mrs Ford, the matron of Bartles House Nursing Home, said that she had no idea that bats were in need of protection, although, of course, she knew they lived in the roof. Lucilla Sanderson, a resident at Bartles House, said the discovery and subsequent decision struck a blow for sanity, and for the preservation of the fast-disappearing beauty of England."'

'That's a good phase,' said Octavia.

'Yes. Then it says that it was successful Gloucestershire businessman, Sandy Trelawny, who first alerted the protesters to the importance of the discovery about the bats and – well, that's about it.'

'That's all that's necessary,' said Octavia. 'Well done, Megan. I think you should open a bottle of champagne.'

The good news had lifted her mood from the inevitable low induced by the funeral. She was making lunch in the kitchen, feeling quite cheerful, when Caroline came in.

'Octavia, I'm a bit worried about Minty. She's running a slight temperature. I think it's only a tooth, but she's very unhappy.'

'I'll come and see her. Is she in her cot?'

'Yes. She's just had her sleep, but it hasn't done much good.'

Minty was feverish and fretful; her right cheek burning.

'It's her tooth, by the look of her. Poor little thing. Well, if she's no better tomorrow, she can't come. Oh, God.' Her mind zoomed over the complex repercussions of that. 'Caroline could you – could you possibly stay with her? I know we said take the day off, but—'

'Octavia, I have arranged a day out with friends.'

'I know, but it is such an important day for me.'

'It's an important day for me, too, Octavia. My oldest friend's birthday. I really do have to go.'

'Oh, dear. Yes, I see.' She managed to smile at Caroline. 'Well, maybe it won't happen. Maybe she'll be all right.'

'Couldn't Tom stay with her?'

'No, I don't think he can. It's an important day for him, too. Let's see how she is later. I don't think we can leave it till the morning to decide. Too late.'

'Yes, indeed.'

'Louise, darling, you're all right, are you? You look quite flushed.'

'Daddy, I'm fine, thank you. Feeling much better already. Um – I might go for a little drive. If that's all right. Could I take Mummy's car?'

'Of course you can. I was actually going to ask you if you'd like to have it. Such a waste, sitting there, unused.'

'Oh, Daddy, that would be marvellous! I'd love it. I've never said anything to Sandy, but having only one car and him always needing it is awfully – well, it doesn't make my life any easier.'

'Of course it doesn't. No, I'd love you to have it.'

The car was a sprightly little Renault Five. As she drove off down the lane she felt quite different suddenly, free, excited. And – yes, a little feverish. She was nearly there now; the start at least was in sight.

The car was very low in petrol: she stopped at the garage, filled it up. It was one of the reasons she'd wanted to take it now: she didn't want anything to delay her in the morning. She was going to have to leave early enough as it was. She'd told her father she was going to see some friends. She did hope she'd be able to sleep tonight; she had a lot of driving ahead of her next day. Right across to Kent, then all the way down to Cornwall. She'd be terribly tired. And when she got there, it would be difficult, too. Sorting everything out in the dark. The other thing she had to do, why she needed the car, was to stow all the things away in it. She'd been squirrelling them away for days. Food, drinks, nappies, baby food. She'd dug out some cot sheets and blankets and it had all gone into her suitcase when Sandy had brought her over. She was afraid he might ask her why she was taking such a big case, but he hadn't. He was speaking to her as little as possible anyway, and especially since the fight over the David woman. There was a carrycot at Rookston, she could fit that in the boot – just. And the baby seat that her mother had got for Dickon, that had still been in the garage. She must fix that in the car, once it was dark. She'd been such a good granny, her mother had; so loving and involved and enthusiastic. She felt the tears rising in her eyes again, wiped them impatiently away. She couldn't afford any more crying, any more grieving. From now on, she had to have her wits about her.

She had studied the map, the route she would take to Brands Hatch: very simple really, just up the M4 then down on to the M25. She knew where it was, she'd been there once before. Once there, of course, it wasn't going to be easy. She might fail altogether, she was prepared for that. But she didn't think she would. She had checked out her disguise, the dark glasses, the short wig she'd worn for modelling in the 'sixties, the tacky Crimplete trousers and tunic she'd got from a catalogue. The last things anyone would expect her to wear. She had gone into the corner shop wearing it all: none of them had recognised her and they knew her very well. She'd been worried about Sandy and Dickon spotting her, but Sandy wasn't going now, and Dickon would be so excited, haring about with the twins. He had no idea she was going, he wouldn't be expecting her, and in her disguise . . . And in a crowd, it was so easy to hide. She'd once followed a boyfriend about all day, one she'd been suspicious of, thought he was seeing someone else; he'd never known she was there. Of course it would be terribly difficult; she would just have to follow them everywhere, waiting for a moment when she could grab Minty. It was bound to happen, there would be a moment when everyone would be distracted, and it wouldn't take a second. No one would be on their guard, none would be being specially watchful of her. She could do it; she knew she could. It was just a question of persistence and keeping her nerve. It might take hours, might take nearly all day, but she knew she could do it. And then she'd have a baby again. A baby almost exactly the age Juliet was when she died. A baby to love and take care of and hold and tuck into a cot at night. And Tom and Octavia would know what it was like to lose one.

CHAPTER 49

'I really don't think Minty can go tomorrow,' said Octavia. 'She's not well, I mean, I know it's only teeth, but she's still got a bit of a temperature . . .'

'Well, let's leave her here,' said Tom easily. 'She was going to be a bit of a worry anyway.'

'It's not that easy. Caroline can't stay with her.'

'Oh, Lord.'

'And I've tried the agency, to see if Mrs Thorpe could come, but she can't. They didn't have anyone else I was happy with. I don't suppose – well, that you could . . .'

'Not now, Octavia, no. I've promised Oliver Nicholas I'll be there, and Nico Cadogan's coming. I really can't.'

'No, all right, all right.'

'Mrs Donaldson?'

'She can't come. I've already tried. Obviously.'

'What about Marianne's girls? They're pretty reliable. Minty knows them.'

'Oh, I don't know. Suppose she got worse?'

'If she got worse, they could phone us and one of us could go back. It's only a tooth, for God's sake.'

'Well, I'll see what they're doing. I suppose if she's better, just cranky . . .'

Zoë wasn't doing anything next day; she said she'd be happy to look after Minty.

'I'm only going to ask you if she's pretty well all right,' said Octavia.

'All right. But I coped when your friend's little boy had chickenpox. You can check with her.'

'Yes, of course. I'd forgotten that. All right, Zoë, you're probably on. I'll ring you first thing in the morning, just confirm it. Could you be here by eight?'

There was a groan the other end of phone. 'Yes, I suppose so.'
'Thanks.'

'Octavia, could you spare me a minute? For a quick chat?'
'Not now, Tom, I have a million last-minute things to do. And I've got to go over to Melanie, to pick up some collecting tins. She just might not be there before the ladies. They're going to be at the gates by ten.'
'All right. Well, maybe later?'
'Maybe. I'm pretty frantic.'
He smiled at her. 'I hope tomorrow goes well for you, I really do. You certainly deserve it, you've worked like a demon.'
'Thank you,' she said, quickly. 'And – and thank you for coming.'
'Well, as you know, I have to now. Quite like old times, isn't it?'
'A bit, I suppose. Yes.'
She smiled at him, carefully distant. It was true; they had been working together that day, discussing the guest list, who would need looking after at the reception, finetuning the table plan: 'Not her next to him, you've forgotten, her husband's agency lost his account last year, she took it very personally . . . why not put Drew Bartlett next to Veronica Stepford, she's setting up a sharedealing shop . . . then Nico Cadogan can be on her other side, tell her stories about takeovers . . .' He had cut her vote of thanks – 'much too long' – asked her to decide which of two ties he should wear with his wide-legged, Prince of Wales check suit, she had promised to see that Oliver Nichols' wife met the New Zealand racing driver . . .

They had a pizza with the children then put the twins to bed. Minty was sleeping peacefully, but only with a generous dose of Calpol.
'Don't fuss,' Tom had said, finding her leaning over the cot, 'she's fine. And she'll be fine with Zoë.'
'Well – yes, I suppose so. But if she's really better in the morning, I still want to take her.'
'Of course.'
'But then – she'll still be a worry.'
'Yes, she will. And you'll have enough on your plate. Look, why don't we make a decision now, to leave her. It'll be one less thing to worry about in the morning.'
Octavia hesitated, then she said, 'Yes. Yes, all right. I think it would be better. I don't want to but – yes, I'll go and call Zoë now.'

Felix Miller went to bed early. He felt terribly tired, and his arm was still painful. He had listened to a concert on Radio Three, eaten (surprisingly hungry) the lasagne Mrs Harrington had made for him, and then two helpings of chocolate mousse, had drunk a couple of large brandies, and then feeling sleep might still elude him, as it had for most of the week, he took a sleeping pill. He had a lot of work to do next day, and there was a meeting of the Music for Children in Hospital committee in the evening. Marianne would have been there, she was Secretary to his Chair: perhaps she still would be, perhaps – Felix felt his painful arm stab once more before the Nitrazepam carried him effectively away . . .

Louise could hardly eat her supper, she was so excited. She felt as she had as a child, when a long-awaited treat was about to happen. Tomorrow! Only one more night. She was as ready as she could be, the car was full of petrol, the boot loaded up. She had drawn lots of cash out – she didn't want to leave a trail of credit card receipts – transferred all her things, make-up, wallet, hairbrush and, of course, the precious key – how many times had she checked that was there – into an old bag of her mother's. A large, anonymous-looking, black leather bag. Not her own distinctive Mulberry one. She really did believe she'd thought of everything. She thought of Tom and Octavia, eating their supper, with no idea of what was going to happen to them next day; just planning their stupid event. And then she thought of Minty, sleeping peacefully in her cot, with no idea either. Just for a moment, guilt stabbed Louise; guilt at alarming Minty, disturbing her, taking her away from everyone she knew.

Then she righted herself. She would soon settle down. She was very young. She'd always seemed to like her, and she was a sweet, placid little thing. And it might not even be for that long. She'd be all right. Of course she would.

Tom went into his study while Octavia was fetching the collection tins from Melanie, to make notes for a speech he was giving on Tuesday night. He felt rather cheerful. It had been a good week. What with the new account – Oliver Nichols seemed to be an ideal client, enthusiastic, responsive, accessible – the taming of Felix Miller and the gratitude of Nico Cadogan, he seemed to be able to walk on water. Again. And – he didn't want to be over-optimistic, but he was at least hopeful that things would work out between him and Octavia. She was, quite apart from her extraordinary performance in bed on Friday night, distinctly less hostile. She was wary of him, which was inevitable; he was not so naive as to think she was going to forgive, let alone forget, for a very long time. But she seemed to be prepared to draw closer to him again. She had said nothing more about wanting a divorce, or even about him moving out of the house. And the holiday with Bingham had clearly not been a success – she hadn't admitted it, but he knew her so well, knew what a vague, slightly defensive attitude meant. He was pretty sure she hadn't seen Bingham since; and it had been the very evening of her return that she had first responded to him, sexually, had – almost – returned his kiss, and then rushed upstairs away from him. That had not the behaviour of a woman in the throes of a satisfactory love affair.

God, he hoped he was right. He missed her, in every possible way, more dreadfully than he would have believed.

It had been a very odd day: pooling their knowledge, their instincts, their skills again. Watching her mind work, seeing the odd blend of confidence and nerviness that made her so successful. She was very clever, and not just clever, skilful. He found that skilfulness, that deployment of her own talent and of those who worked for her, intriguing, charming, attractive. It was one of the things that had always attracted him to her: that made her desirable. It was odd the way their relationship had always been so acutely work-based. He could not imagine finding her as sexy if she was simply a housewife, however fervently he wished it at times. He had never thought – until Louise – that he would find any woman without a career properly attractive, that it would be possible for her to engage his mind and his professional admiration as well as his emotions. Louise had broken all the rules: in every way. Please God they were safe from her now.

He decided he needed a quotation for his speech, and looked for his dictionary of quotations; it was missing. Octavia would have taken it; she was always doing that, borrowing his books, not putting them back. He went downstairs and into her study; yes, there it was, sitting on her desk. Six months earlier, he would have berated her for it; now he knew he could not.

He smiled, looking round the small room; everything pin-neat, none of the messy piles of bills and unanswered letters that lay on his own desk. Even on the memory board, everything was perfectly squared up. It spoke so clearly of the real Octavia, that room: not just her efficiency and her neatness, but her fierce pride in her work and her success – the odd award, her degree, a personal letter of congratulation from Lord Denning over some legal charity she had worked for – all carefully framed, alongside endless pictures of the children, the children's works of art – and pictures of her father. Several of them: Tom stood looking at them. Old bugger; God, he'd worked hard to break up their marriage. If it didn't survive, it would be as much down to Felix's machinations as his own.

Well, it was going to survive: he was determined. Determined and beginning to be confident.

The top drawer of Octavia's desk was slightly open, a piece of paper protruding from it. He smiled, went to close it; it was an outrage in this shrine of neatness. The drawer was slightly stuck: he had to tug it out before closing it again. The piece of paper fell out.

It was only a piece of paper: a photocopy of another piece of paper. Or rather several, neatly – of course – stapled together.

'Confidential Client Questionnaire', it said, under the logo 'Fisher Lewin Frances. Family Law Department'. He knew about Fisher Lewin Frances, they were a very high-profile firm, specialising in matrimonial and family law. The form then required to know a great many things about Octavia and her husband and family; it had been neatly filled in and was dated 1 September, 1997. Very recent. Since the holiday with Gabriel Bingham.

Tom stood staring at it, studying what it said. After a while he found it was blurred and he couldn't see well enough to read it any more; he put it carefully back and closed the drawer.

CHAPTER 50

Everything had gone so well: so very well. Louise smiled to herself; her careful planning, not something she was normally very good at, had been worthwhile. She had slipped out of the house at five thirty, had left a loving message for her father, saying she'd see him very soon, that she hadn't been able to sleep and had decided to go home and do some chores before going out for the day; the little car was flying up the M4 by six. She was going to change into her disguise at Reading services, before hitting the M25. There was the faint danger that others on their way to Brands Hatch, stopping at the service station there, might recognise her. Of course there was a danger of that anywhere, but it was less likely at Reading. She would have to fill up with petrol at the last minute, but that would be less dangerous. She had calculated that, with a full tank, she could make Cornwall. She certainly didn't want to have to stop to buy petrol, with Minty in the car.

She pulled into the car park, went in and had a coffee before going into the ladies'. She was going to need a lot of caffeine to get her through today.

She slipped out of her leggings and T-shirt and into the tunic and trousers. And the wig. The wig wasn't too bad, short and dark, and cut in the Sassoon pudding basin style Joanna Lumley had made famous in the Avengers; but even in her excitement, she found it hard to look at herself in the mirror in those clothes. So horrible; so absolutely horrible. Well, it wasn't for long. Just till she'd made her getaway. Then she could change again. In any case, Minty would need to recognise her, to know who she was.

She didn't feel at all nervous any more: just excited. Excited and confident and rather happy . . . If only they knew, Tom and Octavia. If only . . .

Octavia was already on her way down the M25 by seven o'clock. She knew she would be much too early, but it was better than worrying about being late, getting stuck in a traffic jam. Tom was coming later with the twins and Dickon. She still felt worried about leaving Minty: about whether Zoë would be able to cope. Maybe – she suddenly had an idea, dialled the house on the car phone, listened to it ringing endlessly. Tom must have gone back to sleep.

He had been very odd last night, when she'd got in. Cold. Very detached. He'd been in his study working, and when she put her head in to say she was going to bed, that everything was in place for the morning, the children's costumes, Zoë's instructions for the day, he'd looked at her as if he hardly knew who she was. Well, he was sometimes like that when he was working. It wasn't as if it mattered, as if she cared. In fact, it was quite good, really. She didn't want him to be friendly. It would be easier to tell him she was filing for divorce if he wasn't. She would do it tonight. When today was safely over.

His voice now answered the phone: 'Yes? Tom Fleming here.'

'Tom, I've had an idea . . .'

'Zoë? This is Tom Fleming.'

'Oh, hi, Tom. It's all right, I'm up, dressed, sober. Don't worry. How is Minty?'

'She's much better.'

'You decided to take her?'

'Yes, I think so. But I'd like you to come too. Look after her, be nanny for the day. That all right with you?'

'Yes, fine.'

'Good. Want me to come and fetch you?'

'No, it's all right, Tom. Mum's booked a cab – she was worried I'd be late. You know what she's like.'

'Great. Well, see you in a bit, then.'

Felix Miller woke up feeling much better, apart from a touch of indigestion – his own fault, no doubt, having a second helping of Mrs Harrington's mousse. But his arm was less painful, clearly the muscle was recovering and he felt refreshed from his long sleep. Just as well: there were a lot of things he wanted to do that day.

Felix decided to do a couple of hours' work, and then go down to the health club at Swiss Cottage and have a swim before lunch. He often did that on Sunday. Nothing too strenuous: but he always felt better afterwards, and it would probably benefit his arm. He might skip breakfast, though: make up for the lasagne. Anyway, the indigestion wasn't doing a lot for his appetite.

*

Octavia stood at the window of the top floor suite of the John Foulston building gazing out at the breathtaking view across the Brands Hatch course. The whole place was empty and orderly; still just a few people walking about, the occasional car zooming round the track. Just for a moment she stopped feeling nervous and jittery about the day, and her responsibility for it, and thought what fun it was going to be. Eighty-five thousand people they got here on a good day; probably they'd get nothing like that because of Diana. But there would still be a large crowd: 'And because it's a classic race day,' the marketing manager had told her, 'you'll get what we call the tweed and pearls set. Lot of money: your charity should do very well.'

Certainly virtually all their three hundred guests were still coming: a nervous ring round by Lauren had confirmed that. A champagne reception at twelve thirty, followed by a lunch; races beginning at two. Loads of OTG – opportunities to give – as Melanie had observed – from the raffle at the lunch to buying hot rides – ten per cent to the charity, that was very good of the Brands Hatch people. Ladies with collecting tins were everywhere, and Next Generation had a large stall on the road between the building and the paddock.

The suite looked impressive: the flowers had been done at a knock-down rate by a friend of Melanie's, in return for a generous plug in the programme, and dear Bob Macintosh had managed somehow to twist the arm of one of his suppliers over the champagne – also for a plug in the programme – and they hadn't lost nearly as much as they had feared. When she'd phoned to thank him, he'd said, 'My dear Octavia, it's a very little thankyou for your input earlier in the year. Invaluable. I don't know what we'd do without you and Tom.'

She knew what he meant: over the photocall. But he was going to have to settle just for Tom in the future . . .

After Marianne had seen Zoë off, she settled down to the papers; Marc and Romilly were still fast asleep. Probably would be for hours yet. She had been almost envious of Zoë going to Brands Hatch with Minty; had been tempted to go herself. Then she had thought Nico might be there and decided against it. Felix certainly wouldn't go, he wouldn't want to see Tom.

Thinking of Felix reminded her of the committee meeting tonight. She had decided to go to that. She mustn't start neglecting responsibilities, just because of her personal difficulties. It was wrong, she had always tried to instil that into the children. Without much success.

She decided to ring Felix, let him know. He might even decide not to go himself, of course . . . She sighed, and dialled the number.

Felix wasn't there: Mrs Harrington answered the phone. 'Oh, hallo, Mrs Muirhead. How nice to hear from you.'

'Nice to hear you, as well, Mrs Harrington. Is Mr Miller there?'

'I'm afraid he isn't, no. He's at the health club.'

'Oh, right. Well, look, could you give him a message?'

'Yes, of course.'

'Tell him I will be there tonight. At Sadlers Wells. All right?'

'Yes. Yes, of course, Mrs Muirhead. I'm sure he'll be very pleased.'

He probably won't, thought Marianne, putting the phone down. He probably won't be pleased at all . . .

'Mummy! Isn't it fun! Gosh, what a good view. Is Camilla here?' It was Poppy, flushed and excited, wearing a smocked flowery dress, a Christopher Robin hat jammed down over her dark curls.

'Not yet. You look terrific, Poppy! Where's Daddy?'

'Talking to Lauren. Over there, look.'

Octavia looked; Tom wasn't just talking to Lauren. He was standing very close to her, smiling down at her, and she was on tiptoes, pulling his head down, whispering something in his ear. She looked stunning, in wide navy palazzo trousers, a very low-cut cream silk blouse revealing her deep brown cleavage, long pearls and a small tipped hat on her streaky blonde hair. Bitch, thought Octavia, silly bitch, and then wondered why on earth she cared.

'Octavia, morning.' It was Drew. Drew not dressed up at all, looking refreshingly ordinary in a linen suit. 'You look marvellous. Jolly good show you've put on here. Now where is the lovely Anthea, I can't wait to sell her a raffle ticket or two . . .'

Octavia managed to smile at him, went over to Lauren and Tom.

Lauren's smiling, flirtatious face hardened when she saw her. 'Octavia! Lovely hat. But I did think the collecting ladies should be in costume – what happened?'

'It saved us a thousand pounds, that's what happened,' said Octavia coolly. 'I honestly don't think it matters, Lauren, they've got their sashes.'

'I know, but they look as if they ought to be outside Tesco's or something. Oh, well. Never mind, can't be helped. Now then, when are we going to start serving the champagne?'

'Twelve thirty. As we agreed.'

'I think that's too late. I mean, several chums are here already. I can't just let them stand around with nothing to drink.'

'Well, there's only thirty bottles,' said Octavia, 'so it's up to you. It did say quite clearly on the programme twelve thirty. Any more and it will cost you, I'm afraid.'

'I know that,' said Lauren coolly, 'but quite honestly, if one's friends feel – well, not properly looked after – I mean, they're simply not going to come again. Or dip their little hands into their pockets while they're here. I think we have to start sooner than that.'

'All right,' said Octavia with a sigh. 'Let's start sooner. We'll have to find some waiters, though, they're—'

'Could you do that, Octavia? I've got enough to worry about, so many friends arriving, the Nichols will need looking after . . .'

'Yes, I'll see what I can do.'

She looked at Tom, smiled slightly nervously. 'Where are Minty and Zoë?'

'She's taken her off in her buggy,' he said. He didn't smile back. 'Come on, Gideon, want to go over to the paddock?'

'Yes, please!'

'Good. Poppy?'

'No, Camilla and I want to stay here and look at everyone's clothes.'

'Boring!' said Gideon.

'Not as boring as the cars.'

'Yes, it is.'

'No, it's not!'

'Oh, shut up,' said Tom. 'You coming with us, Dickon?'

'Yes, please!'

He looked rather nervous, Octavia thought. Poor little boy. He'd had such a horrible time lately.

'Don't be long, Tom,' she said. 'You heard what Lauren said, your friend Oliver Nichols will be here soon.'

'I think I know how to look after my own clients,' he said and walked away holding the boys' hands. She looked after him, feeling rather bereft.

Zoë pushed Minty along the path towards the paddock area. It was lined with shops selling things she wasn't in the least interested in; expensive-looking anoraks, picnic baskets, rugs. There was a large sort of shop affair with the name of Octavia's charity all over it, and a lot of earnest-looking ladies inside, smiling brightly. Nobody much seemed to be going in.

Zoë hoped they were going to pay her well for today; she wouldn't say she was exactly enjoying herself. Minty was very miserable, grizzling all the time, and she'd just had to change her nappy which had been disgusting. She hadn't slept at all in the car, just thrashed around in her seat throwing her cup endlessly on the floor and then wailing for it again. Zoë had sat in the front seat next to Tom, trying not to listen to her, and telling herself she was never going to have any kids.

The place was filling up now; mostly with families, but there were a lot of young men, some of them clearly officials with large mobile phones hurrying about, and a few drivers in racing overalls. A couple of them were in thirties-style kit, with leather helmets and goggles. She supposed they must be guests at the luncheon. She hoped she'd get to meet Kit Curtis, the racing driver. She'd seen a picture of him and he was seriously cool.

Minty wailed harder; Zoë sighed, tried to interest her in her drink. Minty threw it on the ground. This was going to be a long day . . .

Louise drove past the entrance to the course soon after eleven. It was much too early; there was hardly anyone there. She drove on for a couple of miles, stopped the car in a layby and tried to read the paper for half an hour. It was all about Diana and the funeral; she couldn't concentrate. At twelve she turned the car round and went back; there was a tailback in both directions, waiting to get in. That was much better. Her heart was thudding so hard she could hardly breathe; she turned on the radio to Classic FM to try and calm herself down, but it was some dreadful programme about other people's romances and simply got on her nerves. The car beside her in the queue held a large family, with a baby of about Minty's age: they all looked at her and smiled. How dreadful if she had mistimed it; no hiding place here. But, once in the car park, she felt safer: wonderful, hundreds and hundreds of cars. That meant thousands of people.

She parked carefully and sat there for a bit, fiddling with her wig, painting on a bright fuschia lipstick, a colour she'd never wear. It was those sort of details that helped.

She took a deep breath and pulled the key out of the ignition. Now that the moment had actually arrived, she felt very sick, tempted just to leave again, go home. So strong was the temptation, indeed, that she actually reinserted the key; then caught sight of herself in the mirror, so unfamiliar she wouldn't have known herself, and pulled it out again. She hadn't come all this way for nothing.

She got out, locked the car. She must make very careful note of where it was parked; she couldn't afford to waste time on that later. At the end of the row was a large Bentley; that would serve very nicely as a marker. She had also – an old trick of her father's at Badminton – tied a red ribbon on the top of her aerial. You could see that from quite a long way away.

Then, picking up her bag, she started to walk quite slowly – but not too slowly – towards the gate. In no time at all, she was part of the crowd.

*

Felix swam rhythmically up and down the rather small pool at the health club. He liked swimming; most people said it was boring, but he had always found it a rather good way of problem solving. The way it left the brain almost but not quite free meant that it could survey and explore situations in a slightly detached way: often more effective than an intense brainstorm. And the setting up of a direct banking service, initially a face-saving operation which had become a rather intriguing reality, was presenting him with several problems to solve. He swam for about twenty minutes, then got out; his arm was certainly easier, and he'd cracked at least two of the problems, but the indigestion was still with him. Worse, if anything. A light lunch, then, and maybe a rest before going to the meeting . . .

Louise went up to one of the officials at the edge of the car park. 'I'm looking for some friends,' she said. 'They're at some function, a charity lunch.'

'Oh, yes,' he said, 'in there, in the John Foulston building. Top floor. Just go on up.'

'Thank you.'

She looked at the building thoughtfully. It looked rather formal; she'd imagined a marquee, something like that, possibly just a roped-off area, on the edge of the course, that they'd spend much of the day just wandering about. She hadn't anticipated having to get in and out of a building. Stupid of her, really. Still, surely, surely they'd come out at some point: to go and look at the cars, watch the racing. And then – well, then she could follow them. And play it by ear.

Suddenly she felt a rush of panic. Two people she knew, two friends from Gloucestershire, she'd actually been to a drinks party in their house for heaven's sake, were coming towards her. Now what did she do? Useless to run, that really would attract attention to herself. She took a deep breath, stood still, studying her programme. They drew nearer, were talking.

'Hallo,' the man called suddenly. 'How are you?'

She lifted her head, forced a smile. So much for her wonderful disguise. Then she realised they had walked past her, were waving at someone behind her. She began to feel very much more confident.

'Octavia, you look great.' It was Melanie.

'So do you,' said Octavia, laughing. Perverse to the last, Melanie was dressed as a man, in tweed suit, with a deerstalker cap on her head. 'Absolutely wonderful.'

'Thanks. Everything going all right?'

'I think so. But Lauren has insisted on starting on the champagne half an hour early.'

'Fine. If it runs out, that's her problem.'

'I told her that. She didn't seem to care.'

'There's big business going on down at the unit. Lots of people milling round in there. Several people signing up to become Friends. We must tell Lauren to mention that in her speech.'

'You can do that,' said Octavia. 'I don't want to speak to her any more than I have to.'

'Christ,' said Tom. 'Christ, where is the bloody child?'

'I don't know,' said Gideon.

'Well, surely you must have – oh, God. This is all I need. Jesus. Stay there, Gideon, just stay there. Don't move or I'll kill you.'

'Okay, Dad,' said Gideon equably.

He'd been there just a minute ago, holding his hand so tightly. He seemed very nervous altogether, poor little sod. Which was hardly surprising.

Now he'd disappeared.

Tom stood at the top of the slope just above the entrance to the paddock, where all the shops were, trying to spot Dickon in the crowd. Trouble was he was so small. He couldn't see him anywhere.

He walked back down to Gideon, said, 'No sign.' He tried to keep calm. It was difficult.

'We could try the Sega place. He wanted to go in there.'

'Really? You stay here, Gideon, in case he reappears.'

He went into the Sega World shop; it was a mass of small boys. None as small as Dickon though. Tom pushed through them, went outside again.

An official stood at the entrance.

'Lost a kiddie?'

'Yes. Yes, I have.'

'What you do is go to the BBC tower, tell them his name and so on, ask them to put out an announcement. Don't worry, sir, happens all the time. He'll turn up, don't you worry.'

Tom felt sick. He'd lost a child already, rather publicly if it had to be announced, and it wasn't even lunchtime. And suppose they couldn't find him, suppose he'd been abducted? You heard about things like that happening in these places. All the time.

'Dad! Dad, he's here!'

'What?' He rushed over to him, grabbed him, shook him not very gently. 'Dickon, where the hell have you been?'

'Sorry,' said Dickon. 'I'm very sorry.' His large brown eyes, full of tears, met Tom's.

'Oh – it's all right. I was worried, though. Where were you?'

'He was in the model shop. Just coming out. I stopped him,' said Gideon self-righteously.

'Good. Well, we'd better get back to the suite for lunch,' said Tom. His breathing and his heart had steadied. Terrible how quickly you panicked in these situations. Abduction! Absurd!

'Isn't it fun?' said Lauren happily. She was very excited, her blue eyes brilliant in her tanned face. She looked stunning. He should have gone to Tuscany with them all, thought Tom gloomily. In the event, there had been no point staying loyally at home.

'Yes,' he said, 'yes, great fun.'

'We've done awfully well. Sold absolutely masses of raffle tickets.'

'Good.'

'Bit of a shame, Anthea Turner can't come apparently. She's ill. So Kit Curtis is going to draw the raffle.'

'I'm sure he's nearly as pretty as Anthea,' he said and smiled at her.

'Maybe you should do it. You're prettier than both of them. Oh – Oliver. Nice to see you. Great costume. Sorry, got waylaid into the Sega shop by my children.'

'I'll join you all there after lunch,' said Oliver Nichols, grinning. 'You going to have one of those hot rides, Tom?'

'Don't know. They look pretty tempting. Are you?'

'Of course you must,' said Lauren. 'I'm going to.'

'Octavia! Hallo, my dear. I'm sorry I'm late.' It was Nico Cadogan; he bent to give her a kiss, then raised his glass of champagne to her. 'God, you look marvellous.'

Octavia smiled at him. He was exactly what she needed just at that moment. He was rather like a glass of champagne himself; spirit lifting, morale boosting.

'You're not late,' she said, 'and it's lovely to see you. I'm – I'm sorry about Marianne.'

'Oh,' he sighed. 'Yes. Well, all part of life's rich pattern, I suppose.'

'You must be pleased about – well, about how the takeover turned out. Or rather didn't turn out.'

'I was. Something of a volte-face on your father's part, most unexpected, but – yes, very welcome. I don't suppose Tom talked to you about it at all?' His voice was carefully casual.

'No, he didn't. Why?'

'Oh, I just thought he might have done. No matter.' He smiled at her, helped himself to a couple of canapés. 'Where is the dear boy?'

'Over there, talking to Lauren Bartlett.'

'Ah, yes. I seem to remember her from somewhere. Oh, yes, Ascot. Very pretty but lays it on with a trowel rather, as I recall.'

Octavia smiled at him again. He really was better than champagne. Marianne must be a little mad to have dumped him. Adore her father as she did, she would have thought Nico was actually a much more suitable companion for Marianne.

They sat down to lunch. Tom had had two glasses of champagne rather fast and realised he was already feeling quite lightheaded. He also realised he was sitting next to Lauren.

'You've changed the table plan,' he said.

'Yes. I thought I'd like to sit next to you. Tell you about the wonderful holiday you missed. And get you to look over my speech. You are an expert on speeches, aren't you?'

'Oh, absolutely,' he said. She had that rich, raw-smelling perfume on again; her cleavage was as deep and as dangerous as usual. Tom allowed a waiter to pour him a large glass of claret and decided to enjoy Lauren's sexiness at least for the duration of the lunch.

Louise had bought a hot dog and, encouraged by the success of her disguise, was standing eating it outside the John Foulston building. She had actually seen Tom hurrying inside, holding Dickon's hand. Dickon looked rather anxious and upset; it worried her, she wanted to rush over and hug him. But of course she couldn't. He had even glanced over in her direction; she had held her breath, studied her programme again. But it was all right; he hadn't recognised her.

She wondered if Minty was inside. She supposed she must be. She'd be having lunch with them. How on earth was she going to get in there? Or out again. She couldn't. It was impossible. But – if Tom had brought Dickon and Gideon out, then surely someone would do the same with Minty. Don't panic, Louise, stay calm. You'll manage something.

Then she saw Minty. Sitting in her buggy, crying loudly. Being pushed. Not by the dreadful Caroline – how Octavia could employ that woman Louise had never understood, so bossy and harsh, typical really – but by Zoë Muirhead. What was Zoë doing here, looking after Minty, for heaven's sake?

An official had come down the steps, was helping Zoë to pull the buggy up them backwards. Louise could almost, but not quite, hear what she was saying. She inched forwards, munching on her hot dog, rummaging in her bag so her face was down.

'. . . not mine,' came Zoe's drawling, rather loud voice. 'God, no. I'm just nanny for the day.'

Nanny for the day. Zoë Muirhead, whom Louise had always got on rather well with. Well, that really was interesting. Very interesting indeed.

She didn't care. She did not care. Tom could climb into Lauren Bartlett's blouse and her trousers, he could run away with her, he could marry her if he liked. Why not? She was going to divorce him after all. Lauren was welcome to him. Stupid bitch. Octavia saw her look over in her direction suddenly, and then whisper something else in Tom's ear; he glanced over at her himself, and then they both laughed. It wasn't exactly the way to behave, she thought, on such an occasion; why on earth had she wanted Tom to come? She glared at them: Tom noticed, looked away, turned hastily to Mrs Nichols on his other side. She should have left him at home with Minty.

Minty was behaving fairly well at the moment. They had produced a highchair for her and Zoë was making quite a success of spooning fruit salad into her. Zoë looked wonderful; dressed in her jeans and a white T-shirt, brown as a nut, her short spiky hair very blonde. She was sex on legs; Octavia had lost count of how many of the male guests had asked her where she got her nanny from.

Now, was she more or less sexy than Lauren? That was a good one. She – she was interrupted in her miserable musings by the toastmaster asking for quiet: for a few words from the Chair of the luncheon today, 'Mrs Lauren Bartlett.' Huge applause. 'After which Mr Kit Curtis will draw the raffle.' Even huger.

Lauren stood up. She was suddenly coolly, wonderfully sober. She made a sweetly sad reference to Diana, about what a shadow her death had cast over her day, thanked everyone for coming in spite of it, 'as I know she would have wanted,' paid careful tribute to her committee, to the organisers, and to 'wonderful Octavia Fleming and Melanie Faulks of Capital C who have done so much to ensure the day's success.' She was orderly, efficient, absolutely in control. How does she do that? thought Octavia, and then realised the giggling tipsiness was simply a cover, behind which she could flirt foolishly as much as she wished. With *her* husband. Bitch. Silly bitch.

Kit Curtis the New Zealand racing driver was very pretty indeed. Tall, dark, gangly, with wonderful hazel eyes and freckles. Perhaps Lauren would switch her attentions to him.

He said a few rather dull words in his rolling New Zealand accent and then started to pull tickets out of the bowl. God, this was going on for ever. And she'd got to make her speech next. With Lauren and Tom looking at her and laughing at her. It wasn't fair! It just wasn't fair.

Just before she got up to speak, Minty began to cry: on and on. Zoë pushed the buggy backwards and forwards, kept saying shush rather ineffectively. It had no effect whatsoever. God, why had she brought her, why hadn't she left her at home?

Octavia got up, went over to her quickly. 'Take her for another walk, Zoë, if you don't mind. She'll probably go to sleep.'

'Okay. Cool.'

She got up, walked out of the room with Minty. Every man in the place stopped looking at his raffle tickets.

Louise had waited outside, because there was nothing else to do. Minty was in the building and she had to wait for her to come out. Simple as that. She seemed to have been standing there for a very long time. It was very tedious, and inactivity was making her feel nervous again. This wasn't going to work. It just wasn't. She might as well go home. She'd just drive home and have a nice evening with her father, maybe get Sandy to bring Dickon over when he got back. Poor little boy, he obviously wasn't having a very nice day. And this was hopeless.

And then Minty did come out of the building. Strapped into her buggy, half asleep, her thumb in her mouth. Zoë, looking at once stressed and bored, was pushing her. Away into the direction of the crowds.

Louise followed her.

Mrs Harrington had just finished stacking the dishwasher, thinking that Mr Miller hadn't eaten much of his lunch, when the kitchen door burst violently open. So violently indeed that she feared an intruder; she swung round, startled, wondering wildly where the carving knife was.

It wasn't an intruder; it was Felix Miller, standing in the doorway, a ghastly colour, his face clammy with sweat, clutching his chest and struggling to breathe.

His voice when he spoke was hoarse and rasping. 'Please call an ambulance, Mrs Harrington,' he said, 'I fear I am having a heart attack.'

And then he fell down where he had been standing; his great body suddenly frail and less substantial.

After dialling 999, Mrs Harrington, who had done a first aid course, propped his head up on a pillow and made him as comfortable as she could; as he lay there, clearly in considerable pain, he lifted his hand, fumbled for hers.

'Octavia . . .' he said with immense effort.

'I'll ring her, Mr Miller. Don't worry.'

'No, no, don't. Please not. She's not at home – important day for her . . .'

And then he lost consciousness altogether.

The speech had gone all right; it had all gone all right. Flowers had been presented to Lauren by the committee; it was announced the raffle had made over four thousand pounds, everyone had cheered. Octavia was beginning to feel much better.

She saw Drew go over to Tom, saw Tom stand up, pump his hand, clearly congratulating him – on what? His choice of wife? She'd better warn him about the dangers of Tom getting friendly with wives. Then she saw Tom look at her.

He walked over to her.

'I'm off to have one of these hot rides. They're doing them now, before the racing starts. Drew and Oliver Nichols are very keen. Okay with you if I leave you with the kids?'

'Absolutely,' she said coldly. 'You do what you like. Is Mrs Bartlett going to have a hot ride with you? Or have you already given her one?'

'Oh, for Christ's sake,' he said. 'Don't be so pathetic.'

'What do you mean by that?'

'I mean your jealousy is pathetic.'

'I don't think so. Actually. I've felt pretty bloody silly, sitting here, watching you two practically snogging all through lunch.'

Suddenly he took hold of her arm; very hard. It hurt. She winced.

'Don't do that.'

'You come over here,' he said. His voice was savagely quiet. He led her towards the service doors, pushed her through them. They were in a lobby, full of tables and trolleys and trays covered now in coffee things. The waiters looked at them curiously. Beyond them was another set of swing doors; he pushed her through those too, on to a small outside landing.

'How dare you criticise the way I behave,' he said, his voice low but shaky with rage. 'How dare you! What right have you to any say in my behaviour when you've got a divorce lawyer all lined up?'

She stared at him.

'Well, haven't you?'

She swallowed. 'Yes. Yes, I have. I want a divorce and I want it very soon. I take it you're not surprised. And don't talk to me about rights. After the way you've behaved.'

'You really are a cow,' he said. 'A self-righteous cow.'

'Tom, this is ridiculous,' she said. 'We have guests to see to, this is not the place—'

'No, I don't suppose it is,' he said. 'There have been other far more suitable places, but this will have to do. God, I can't believe you did that, saw a solicitor without telling me. Whatever I did or didn't do, you owed me that. Well, didn't you? Answer me.'

'Yes. Yes, I did,' she said, remorse of a sort hitting her, 'and I was going to, but—'

'But you didn't. Why not? Why the fuck not?'

'Because – well, because . . .'

'God, you're pathetic,' he said. 'Cowardly as well as a cow. A cowardly cow. Have you told her what happened last week? Your solicitor?'

'What do you mean?'

'You know what I mean. Your magnificent performance in bed. Our bed.'

She looked back into the building. There was no one there in the lobby. Beyond it, people were finishing their lunch, not sure quite what was happening next, probably wondering where they were, where they had gone. She was failing, failing in the most important day of her career. God, this was a nightmare; there were cars roaring round the track now, she could hear them, hear the rhythmic roar coming up to her.

'No. No, of course I haven't told her. It was – well, it was . . .'

'I'll tell you what it was for a start, Octavia. It was the end of any hopes you have for a quick divorce.'

'Oh, don't be absurd!'

'It's true. If I choose. Legally, as you may or may not know; that indicates that you don't really want a divorce at all. If I told a court . . .'

'You wouldn't,' she said. 'You couldn't!'

'I might,' he said. 'It might be – amusing. You obviously want to be rid of me very fast.'

'Yes,' she said, 'yes, I do. And I presume you feel the same?'

'I don't know what I feel,' he said, sounding suddenly weary, 'I really don't. I wish I did. I – oh, God, there's Oliver Nichols. I must go. Do this bloody ride. I'll – I'll see you later, Octavia.'

'Unfortunately yes,' she said. 'I suppose you will.'

It had to be now, Louise told herself: she might not get the chance again. While everyone else was still in the building, while no one else could observe her. No one who would know. The plan formed swiftly, with astonishing clarity; she pulled off the wig, tucked it into her bag, pushed a comb through her hair, wiped off the fuschia lipstick. Quickened her step, walked after Zoë, caught her up, tapped her on the shoulder, smiled, said, 'Zoë! I thought it was you! What a lovely surprise.'

The ambulance had come for Felix, had lifted him up from where he lay, placed him on a stretcher and carried him carefully out of the house. He had regained consciousness briefly; they asked him if he was in a lot of pain and he had said yes, he was; they had given him some oxygen and an injection of some kind of painkiller. Mrs Harrington watched, feeling helpless; he had been in dreadful pain as they waited for the ambulance, had tried to be brave, but every so often he groaned loudly. He had clung, rather pathetically, to her hand (crushing it painfully, but she would not have removed it for the world), and twice, deeply distressed and humiliated, he had vomited.

Mrs Harrington felt terribly upset, watching him being loaded into the ambulance like a large piece of furniture. Poor man; it had been a dreadful time for him lately. Hardly surprising, she thought, that he'd had the heart attack; first the trouble with his daughter, the upset with Mrs Muirhead, all the business worries. She felt dreadfully guilty about his supper last night: it couldn't have helped, full of cholesterol. She usually tried to watch his diet, but had cooked it specially for him, comfort food, she had thought. Comfort food indeed!

Back in the house she made herself a strong cup of sweet tea and sat down. She felt dreadful. She looked at the clock; nearly three. It seemed terrible not to let Octavia know. She'd want to know, surely, whatever her father said. On the other hand, she didn't want to upset him. That was the last thing to do with coronary patients, she knew that. And it was true, of course, Octavia was somewhere in the wilds of the countryside, with this car racing day. Mr Miller had told her about it, had been so proud of Octavia.

'She's doing so well with that company of hers,' he had said, 'really extremely well.'

She had no idea where she was anyway: she couldn't contact her even if she'd wanted to. She supposed she had a mobile phone, but she had no idea of the number. Perhaps she could find it, perhaps Mr Miller had a note of it. Mrs Harrington went into the study, found Felix's address book. He had all Octavia's other numbers – the cottage, the house, the office – but not that one. Maybe that was a sign.

But then she thought of Octavia's grief if anything should happen to her beloved father, if she wasn't there; and thought of him all alone in the hospital, nobody to be with him, nobody he cared about. If only Mrs Muirhead – and then she remembered. Mrs Muirhead had phoned that day; had said she would see Mr Miller that night. At the committee meeting. They had obviously cleared things up between them, to a degree at least. She would ring Mrs Muirhead, tell her. She would know what to do about Octavia. She would probably want to go to the hospital herself . . .

Tom sat in the car and gripped the bar just above his head. It was a very tight fit; he was jammed against Kit. The helmet he was wearing was also a very tight fit; it felt as if it was crushing into his skull. In the mood he was in, that was quite welcome.

'Okay,' said Kit, 'here we go. I'm going to go round the track once or twice, see how we get on; then I'll accelerate. We'll be doing about a hundred and twenty, ninety on the corners. It'll feel more though because we're so low on the ground.'

They moved off: slowly through the paddock, gathering speed on the hill. Up the hill again, round the first curve, a comparably gentle one, then back into the straight and down the hill, and then a bend of incredible ferocity. The sensation was extraordinary, of speed, of pressure, of excitement, of – absurdly, for what could happen? – fear. The car vibrated violently all the time, he was shaken it seemed into his bones; he gripped the bar, swallowed. Down round, up the straight, then the fierce angular bend: and then again and then again. It was not like driving at all, it was like in some way flying through the earth, he had become part of it, part of the speed and the surface and the tension. Five times they went round; he looked at the speedometer: almost a hundred now on the vicious curve, a hundred and thirty on the straight. He was beginning to feel very sick, very dizzy; he clung visually to the track, tried not to look to left or right. And then at last, at last they were slowing, slowing to a feeble eighty, seventy, fifty, thirty – grinning, pulling off the tight helmet, climbing out, standing on legs that were weak, trembling, looking for Oliver Nichols, his partner in the adventure: but Nichols wasn't there, Octavia was there, ashen, her eyes huge, somehow sunk into her face, and she rushed over to him and pulled at his arm and said, her voice hysterical, raw with terror, 'Tom, Tom . . .' and 'What is it?' he said. 'Whatever is it?' and 'It's Minty,' she said, 'it's Minty, she's gone. Louise has taken her.'

It took a while for him to understand what had actually happened, that Louise had actually stolen Minty, kidnapped her. Or so Octavia was saying, gasping out in between sobs; it just didn't seem to be possible. He felt he was in the car again, back on the track, dizzy, sick, confused; Zoë must have just wandered off with her, he said to her, his mind refusing to engage in this new horror, this new latest episode in his love affair turned horror story; that's no problem, we just go to the BBC tower, ask them to make an announcement, someone will have her, don't be silly, calm down.

But no, no, she had said, no, you don't understand. Louise is here, she has Minty, she stole her from Zoë; now how could she have done that, he said, how could she possibly be here, she's ill, she's in a nursing home in Bath.

But gradually the foolish, hysterical lie had become sober, horrible truth. Louise had been, was there; she had gone up to Zoë, talked to her, been friendly, so friendly, asked what she was doing, said where was Dickson, she must go and find him, she'd suddenly decided to come, maybe they could have a cup of tea first, she and Zoë, and Zoë had said yes, why not, as you would; and they'd gone to a café and Louise had said I'll wait here with Minty, you go and get the tea, and Zoë had gone up to the counter and bought two cups of tea, and when she came back, Minty and Louise were gone.

'I thought at first she must be somewhere else,' said Zoë, who had been waiting a few yards behind Octavia, white and shaking; they were standing, the three of them, frozen with fear. 'I thought she'd gone to sit on the grass or something, so I looked, you know, for a bit, wasted time, I suppose. Oh, God, I'm so sorry, so dreadfully sorry, I feel so terrible.'

'No, you mustn't,' Tom said soberly. 'Anyone would have done the same. I would. You didn't know she'd been – ill?'

'No, not really. I knew there was some – problem.' She looked awkwardly at Octavia. 'I'd kind of gathered it from Mum, but not that she was ill. She seemed so normal today, she was so nice, asked me if I was still going to Oz, said she had friends in Sydney. I did think she was wearing some rather odd clothes, but – oh, God. God, I wish Mum was here . . .'

She started to cry and Octavia put her arm round her. 'It's all right, Zoë. It's not your fault.'

'It is, it is. I – God, I feel so stupid, so . . .'

'We must get an announcement put out,' said Tom, 'and have the gates closed. At once.'

'We've told the police,' said Octavia dully. 'They're putting out an announcement. In fact – yes, listen.'

'Ladies and gentlemen. If I could have your attention, please. A baby is missing. Name Araminta Fleming, known as Minty, aged ten months, dark hair, blue eyes, wearing a pink dress. Probably in a baby buggy. If you have seen her, or if you've found her, if you are looking after her . . .' Looking after her, thought Tom, what an absurd phrase, but he supposed the police knew what they were doing, that they must be careful, tactful. And maybe Louise was just looking after her, maybe it had been a genuine error, that she had wandered off, lost Zoë, was looking for her. 'If you are looking after her,' went on the voice, 'please bring her immediately to the control tower, so that we can reunite her with her parents . . .'

They were standing just underneath the control tower; they all looked rather helplessly round, as if expecting Minty immediately to reappear.

A large policeman came over to them, walking rather ponderously. That didn't bode well, the slow walk. It meant they hadn't found her. 'That should do it, Mrs Fleming. If she is indeed here.'

'Yes. Yes, thank you.'

'Try not to worry. People are very good. I daresay she toddled off, someone found her, is bringing her over here even now.'

'She couldn't walk,' said Octavia dully. 'She's too little.'

'Can you close the gates?' said Tom. 'To stop her going out?'

'We've got someone watching the gates now, sir, with a description of the little girl and the lady she was last seen with. Can't actually close them, no.'

'Why the hell not?'

'It's virtually impossible, sir, this not being quite an emergency.'

'Of course it's an emergency!'

The policeman ignored him. 'And other people are still arriving, all the time.'

'And my daughter meanwhile gets kidnapped? I'm not very impressed. I do warn you, I shall hold you responsible if—'

'Let's all just look for her,' said Octavia. She was very pale still, but oddly calm. 'It's true, we don't yet know how much of an emergency it is. Tom, you stay here, just in case. Zoë, you go back towards the building. I'll go the other way.'

'And we have people looking for her as well, of course,' said the policeman. 'All our people and the Brands Hatch security guards as well, all on the alert.'

'Yes. Yes, all right,' said Tom. 'Where are the other children?'

'Lauren and Drew have them.'

'Dickon as well?'

'Yes,' said Octavia very quietly.

Octavia set off down in the direction of the restaurant; walking first forwards, then backwards, so that she could keep looking all around her. The crowds were thick; she kept bumping into people. At first she apologised, then became angry with them, simply for being there, for being in her way, for keeping her from looking, from finding Minty. The day itself had become nightmarish; the screaming of the cars on the track, the endless announcements, inaudibly loud, the crowds, the smell of oil and petrol and hot dogs and chips. She felt sick, utterly alone; she began to hallucinate, to see Minty, to see Louise, walking towards her. Twice she saw Minty's dark curls over the top of a buggy, rushed forward, crying, 'Minty Minty,' only to see a puzzled face, a strange baby. And she saw Louise, saw golden flowing hair, a slender graceful body, long slim legs, ran after her too, wanting to shake her, hit her, grab Minty back: only each time it wasn't Louise, simply another blonde, without her lovely face, without her crazy, evil mind.

She had made it; she had done it. She was out of the car park, back on the road, driving towards the M25. Minty had protested, cried a lot while she pulled her out of the buggy, strapped her into the car seat. Now she was sitting hiccuping, her thumb in her mouth, her eyes big with anxiety. Well, it couldn't be helped. She would comfort her, take care of her later.

She had expected to be stopped all the way to the car, to feel a hand on her shoulder, a voice calling her; she hadn't dared run, it would have looked suspicious, but she'd walked very fast, steering the buggy in and out of the crowds. She found the car all right, but someone had parked just a bit too close on the side the baby seat was and it had been hard to get Minty in, she'd had to hold her sideways, squeeze her in. Minty had screamed in protest. And then she'd had to climb in the other side, sit on the back seat beside her to strap her in. And while she was about it, she pulled off the horrible nylon top; she'd kept her T-shirt on underneath. That way she was less likely to match any description. It was all taking so long, though. Surely someone would come? Zoë would have raised the alarm by now. But they didn't; and looking at her watch, incredibly only three and a half minutes had passed since she had walked away from the table in the café.

She climbed out of the car, leaped into the driving seat, started the engine: the most terrifying moment had been driving out of the gates, she was sure there would be a security alert by now, that the man would have been told to stop her. But there was a great flood of cars coming in, he was very busy; she drove out, carefully, not too fast, to avoid attracting attention, but once on the A20, then she could put her foot down, really get moving. Not too fast of course, she didn't want to be stopped for speeding, that really would be counterproductive; but at the top of the speed limit. And there was a lot of traffic, of course, going in the other direction, making for Brands Hatch. She seemed to have the road practically to herself.

She kept looking at Minty in the driving mirror, still wide eyed, still obviously frightened. 'I'm sorry, Minty darling,' she kept saying, her voice soothing, soft. 'Sorry. Won't be long.'

She wondered if Minty would like a drink; she had prepared a couple of non-spill cups with juice in them, but she didn't dare stop to give her one. Maybe at the service station . . . No, that would be dangerous, they might be looking for her there. She'd slip off at one of the turn-offs, do it there.

Marianne went for a short walk after lunch, it was such a lovely day. Romilly had gone out with friends to Richmond, Marc to meet some girl. The answering machine was bleeping when she got back. Probably Romilly to say she was going back to someone's house. But it wasn't Romilly. It was Mrs Harrington.

Sandy was half asleep in front of a football match that he'd recorded, when the phone went. He sighed. Hopefully this wasn't going to be Louise, wanting to be fetched already.

He even debated leaving it, letting the answering machine pick it up, then thought that no, he really shouldn't do that, it would be very irresponsible. And anyway it might be nothing to do with Louise; it might be Dickon. Or Megan or Pattie. He picked up the phone.

'Sandy Trelawny.'

But it was to do with Louise.

'I spoke to Charles,' said Octavia. 'He couldn't believe it, said we must have made a mistake.'

How could anyone be upset about anything, Tom thought, except their child being in danger? Possibly deadly danger. How could he have been upset about anything himself – his wife having an abortion, wanting to divorce him, his father-in-law hating him, his company going bust, his mistress taking an overdose – how could he have thought any of it important, any of it mattered in the least?

'And she's in Anna's old car. I have the number, I've given it to the police. I wish they'd take it more seriously, they don't seem to—'

'I know, I know. But they've heard this all before, remember. It happens here all the time. Kids getting lost. As far as they're concerned, ninety-nine times out of a hundred, they turn up. And all the stuff about Louise, it just sounds like so much fantasy to them. And to be fair, I thought I'd lost Dickon earlier.'

'Yes, but, Tom, Dickon's five. He can walk about on his own, wander off. They must realise Minty can't do that.'

'Yes. I know.'

'And meanwhile, Louise has probably been gone for ages. Miles away by now.' Her voice was rising, shaking with panic.

'Maybe not. It's only—' He looked at his watch. What had happened to time, how could this endless nightmare have been going on for only twenty minutes?

'Where on earth do you think she might go? Take Minty. It doesn't make sense. I mean, she can't take her home, can't take her to Rookston . . .'

'She might. Who knows what she might do? Octavia, she's mad.'

'Mad and very clever. Talking to Zoë about Australia while they walked to the café, getting her confidence. Coming here at all. She's obviously been planning it for ages, she knew we were coming, that Dickon was coming.'

'Yes, of course she did. Poor Zoë's completely hysterical. Nico's been terrific. He's managed to calm her down.'

'It seems so dreadful, so – so ironic,' said Octavia, her voice very low suddenly, 'that this happened while we were – were quarrelling. If we hadn't, if I'd been out there, finding Zoë, seeing if Minty was all right, if you'd been going over to the paddock – oh, God.'

'Oh, Octavia,' he said heavily, 'if we'd left her at home, if Caroline had been here . . . that way lies madness. In ifs and if onlys. I should know.'

'Yes,' she said, looking at him soberly. 'Yes, I suppose so.'

'So – what do we do? Go on looking? Go home? One of us go home? In case she – well, tries to contact us.'

'Why should she do that? That's the last thing she'd do.'

'You don't know what she'd do,' said Tom. 'She's mad. Completely mad.'

'Don't keep saying that! It's so frightening.'

'Sorry.'

'And anyway, I want us to stay together. I couldn't bear it on my own.'

He looked at her for a moment, his face very sombre. They went over to the window together and stared down, out of the control tower, helplessly, feebly, frantic, at the milling crowds below them.

Marianne arrived at St Matthew's Hospital in Hampstead and ran into Reception.

'I've come to see – to see how Mr Felix Miller is.'

'Which ward is he on?'

'I don't know. He's just been admitted.'

'For?'

'Heart attack.'

'Probably still in Casualty.'

'Oh, he can't be. It was two hours ago, almost.'

'Doesn't mean much,' said the woman, 'not these days.'

'It was a major heart attack.'

'He'll be in Coronary Care, in that case. What did you say his name was?'

'Miller. Felix Miller.'

'Just wait.'

She turned to her computer: the inevitable endless clicking went on. What did they do, these machines? Marianne wondered, watching her, trying not to scream while she tapped, stared at the screen, tapped some more, stared again, tutted, said aloud, 'Let's see if it's this one,' tapped yet again.

Finally she turned to her. 'Yes, he's in Coronary Care.'

'Can I see him?'

'Are you a relation?'

'Not exactly.'

'They usually only let in next-of-kin. But you could try. Third floor, main building, turn right out of the lift, down the end, then ask at the unit.'

She arrived at what they called the nursing station at the Coronary Care Unit; a nurse who looked not a lot older than Romilly asked if she could help.

'I've come to see Mr Miller,' said Marianne firmly.

'Mr Miller. Let me see –' More tapping. 'Oh, yes. Well, I'll have to ask Sister. Are you a relative?'

'I . . .' Marianne paused. She could see it was important to give the right answer. 'I'm his wife,' she said firmly. It was probably the first major lie she had told in twenty years.

Felix lay on a seemingly rather small bed in a small room, an enormous number of machines bleeping all around him. He was wired up to a drip. 'That's just for fluids,' said the nurse, 'to help him cope with the shock.' There was a small oxygen mask over his face. 'We're taking that off from time to time, to see how he's doing. He does seem to need it.'

'How – how is he doing?' said Marianne.

'Oh – difficult to say. Yet. He's holding his own. Excuse me.' She went over to one of the monitors, studied it intently, adjusted it slightly. 'This records his heart rhythms.'

'And . . .'

'Not terribly steady, I'm afraid. But we're giving him anti-arrhythmic drugs, to control it, and betablockers to reduce the loss of further muscle damage. The doctor will be coming up shortly to assess him further, we'll know a bit more then.'

'May I stay?'

'Yes, of course. You can talk to him quietly, if you like. Probably a good thing – he's pretty well conscious – but I'm sure you know not to do anything which might distress or disturb him.'

'I won't have hysterics,' said Marianne.

She stood by Felix's bed, looking at him. His eyes were closed, his colour very bad. She took his hand, stroked it gently. 'Felix,' she said very quietly.

After quite a long time, he turned his head, and very slowly opened his eyes and looked at her. It seemed to take a moment or two for him to focus and then to register who she was; then there was a squeeze on her hand and he tried to smile at her.

'I'm here,' she said rather unnecessarily. He nodded feebly and closed his eyes again.

She sat and talked to him, quietly and gently, as she had heard you should. She told him he was doing very well, and that the medical staff were pleased with him; that everything was fine, that Octavia had no idea there was anything wrong – Mrs Harrington had impressed this upon her – that Zoë had gone to Brands Hatch looking after Minty, that it was all going splendidly. 'When you're better, she can tell you all about it.' She began to run out of things to say, and began at the beginning again. She was very worried about not telling Octavia; but he had seemed so pleased when she had said that, had even managed to smile very weakly. Once the day at Brands Hatch was over, then she could ring. She mighty even ring Tom, talk to him . . .

A doctor appeared. He nodded to her, didn't introduce himself, checked all the monitors, stood looking at Felix.

'How is he?' she said.

'Holding his own,' he said briefly. 'Too early to say.'

'Will you be operating on him, or anything like that?'

'Hopefully not,' he said. 'Certainly not yet.'

'What – what has actually happened?'

'He's had what we call a myocardial infarction. In plain language, a heart attack. It means there's been the death of part of the heart muscle. So the heart simply isn't functioning properly. But the treatment we are giving him will hopefully compensate for that. I really can't tell you any more now. Except that the next few hours are crucial.'

'Is it all right if I stay?'

'Yes. Of course. Don't tire him, though.'

Marianne wondered how on earth she would tire Felix. Force him into a political debate, or try and make him sing?

'I won't,' she said humbly.

Minty was asleep now; she had taken the drink greedily, and then eaten a biscuit Louise had given her. She had started to cry again after that.

Louise had longed to cuddle her, to comfort her, but didn't dare, and pulled back on to the motorway; the rhythm of the car had soothed her back into sleep.

Her nappy needed changing; Louise could smell it. She'd have to leave it for now; she wanted to get off the M25, she was too visible, take to the side roads. Then she could change the nappy at a garage toilet, give Minty some milk, try to reassure her. Not for too long though, they had a very long way to go. Her plan was to turn off on to the Reigate road, make her way towards Dorking, then Guildford and across to the M3 and then to the M4 via Newbury. It was a long way round, but it was much safer.

The temptation to go faster was intense; but she didn't dare. She must just trundle along at seventy, and pray. The thought of praying amused her: asking God for help with her kidnapping. She almost giggled. Her mood of elation had held; she still felt absolutely clear headed, calm, not in the least tired. And very very pleased with herself; they might now realise what she had done, indeed they must do. But they had no idea, they couldn't possibly have any idea, where she was going.

That was her trump card. Nobody could possibly know that.

CHAPTER 51

Felix seemed a little better. There was more colour in his face, and he was breathing slightly more easily. The nurse had taken his oxygen mask off.

He had been sleeping; he opened his eyes and looked at Marianne. 'Hallo, Marianne . . .' His voice was very faint and slurry.

'Hallo, Felix. How are you?' She hoped that didn't come under the heading of tiring him.

'All right. Yes. Thank you. Thank you for coming.'

'Felix, it's all right. I'm so glad I – so glad to be here.'

There was a long silence; then, 'I'm sorry,' he said.

Marianne felt as if she might have a heart attack herself. In all their years together she had never heard Felix say he was sorry about anything.

'Sorry about – when you came. So sorry.'

'Felix, it's all right. I – I understood.'

'Mmm . . .' He nodded, closed his eyes again for a while. 'Missed you,' he said. 'Very much.'

'Oh, Felix.' She felt a sob rising in her throat. 'Felix, I missed you too.'

Another silence, and then he said, 'Tonight. You must go.'

'I will. Of course I will.' To what, for God's sake? Then she remembered. Music for Children in Hospital. 'Yes, Felix, I'll be there.'

'Good. I'm – rather tired.'

'Yes, you must rest. Don't talk any more.'

He didn't, for over an hour. Marianne decided she couldn't put off phoning Tom any longer.

It was still very hot: in the car at least. The late afternoon sun, beating in at the windows, slanting in through the windscreen as they drove westward, was unpleasant. Minty was awake, miserable, crying again. Her nappy smelt awful. She'd have to stop.

She pulled into a garage, lifted Minty out of the car. She felt very hot, damp with sweat. Her dark curls were stuck to her head. She looked at Louise and started to cry.

'Shush, darling, shush. Don't cry. Here, have your nice drink.'

Minty shook her head violently, lashed out with her little fist, knocked the cup on the floor.

'All right. I'll get you something else. Ice cream? Ice lolly, how about that?' Juliet had loved ice lollies, especially when she was teething. That was a good idea.

She carried Minty into the ladies', armed with her nappy, nappy sack, baby wipes, all in a neat plastic bag. How lovely it was, to be doing all this again. Even in her anxiety, her fear, she felt happy, soothed.

'Come on, poppet.' She gave her a kiss.

'Isn't she lovely?' said a woman in front of her in the queue. 'Here, you go first, love, get her sorted. I know what it's like. How old is she?'

'Ten months,' said Louise. She smiled at the woman; this was wonderful. This was what she had dreamed of. This made it all worth while.

'Minty's what? Been kidnapped? How, why – Oh, my God, Tom. Was Zoë – oh, no. Let me speak to her, will you?'

Zoë was subdued, but calm. 'It was my fault. I know it was. But Octavia and Tom have been so good about it. Both of them. And Nico's been great. He's going to bring me home, quite soon, I think. He's so nice, Mum. So really nice.'

'Can I – speak to him?'

'Yes, sure.'

This really was a nightmare; now what did she do? How could Octavia stand more bad news, more tragedy?

Nico listened to her carefully; he was absolutely calm, behaved as if the situation between them was quite normal, that of two friends discussing a problem, not as if the life of the man who had come between them hung in the balance.

'I'll talk to Tom,' he said finally, 'see what he thinks. And then ring you back. You say he's all right at the moment?'

'Well, not all right. But he's not in imminent danger. As far as they know. He's stabilising, with all the drugs.'

'All right, I'll ring you back.'

'You can't. I'll ring you in five minutes.'

When she rang back, Tom was on Nico's mobile. He sounded dreadful, his voice heavy, lifeless.

'Nico's put me in the picture. I don't know what to think, I really don't. I don't know how Octavia would take it, how she'd cope. What does the doctor say?'

'Oh – you know. They won't ever say much. They can't. Just that he's holding his own. No more than that.'

'I think,' said Tom finally, 'I'll have to tell her. I can't not. Maybe she could talk to the medical staff herself. Do you think that's possible?'

'Yes, I'm sure it is.'

'Right. Well, give me the name of the ward. I mean, I'd like to come back to London, but she wants to stay here. They're setting up some sort of an incident centre here. Interviewing people who might have seen anything, that sort of thing. And they're searching the woods now.'

'Oh, Tom, I'm sorry. So dreadfully sorry. You must be beside yourselves. But . . .'

'Yes?'

'Well, I really don't think Louise could possibly mean Minty any harm. I don't want to sound like an amateur psychologist, but I'm sure she just wants a substitute baby. That's why she's taken her.'

'Well,' he said, 'I hope you're right. I do hope you're right.'

The police had set up what they called their incident centre in one of the hospitality suites. Octavia and Tom had been interviewed: so had Zoë. A large number of people had responded to their plea for information: people who said they had seen Louise with the baby, without the baby, driving away. Most of it was probably useless, one of the policemen had said, 'But we have to treat every piece of information very seriously.'

'Yes, of course,' Octavia had said. She was sitting in the room where they had had lunch, twisting a handkerchief backwards and forwards in her hands; she looked dreadful.

Tom felt rather sick. 'Octavia?' he said gently. 'I have to talk to you, I have something to tell you.'

'What is it? is there any news? Have they – is she—'

'No. This is nothing to do with Minty. This is to do with your father.'

'Daddy?' She sounded stupefied. 'What about him?'

'He's – well, he's had a heart attack.'

She stared at him; seemed not to have understood. 'A heart attack?'

'Yes. But he's alive. In fact, he's doing well. Well enough to say he doesn't want you to know, doesn't want you to be worried.' God, he hoped it was true.

'He can't have,' she said. 'He can't be ill. Not today. It's impossible!'

'Octavia, I'm afraid he is.'

She stared at him, a flush rising in her face. The expression in her eyes was suddenly angry. 'Well, it's just not fair,' she said, her voice raw with rage. 'It's awful, terrible. What am I supposed to do? Leave here, go rushing back to London, forget about Minty? I can't, it's absolutely impossible, you'll just have to tell them, Tom, say of course I can't come, they can't expect it.'

'Octavia, no one's expecting anything. That's the whole point, they—'

'Yes, they are. Of course they are. They all will – expect me to be there, just like that. It's too bad of them. I just don't understand – don't – oh, God, Tom. 'And then she started crying, quite quietly at first, then increasingly loudly, until she was screaming, raging at him, at her father, the doctors. He tried at first to comfort her, to hold her, but she pushed him away, stood there, crying, arms hanging at her sides, fists clenched. And then she suddenly stopped. 'I'm sorry,' she said, hauling herself back under control. 'So sorry.'

'It's all right. I understand.'

'Is he in hospital?'

'Yes. Would you like to speak to the doctor yourself? Or the Sister in charge?'

'Yes,' she said, 'yes, I would. Please.' She wiped her eyes, blew her nose. 'I can't go up there,' she said, 'I really can't.'

'Of course you can't. I told you. He doesn't want you to, doesn't want you worried. On your big day.' He was struck rather forcibly by the irony of this, but she didn't appear to notice.

'It's so like him,' she said rather vaguely, 'thinking of me, not wanting the day spoilt. Oh, God.' She almost smiled suddenly. 'Imagine if it wasn't, Tom. Imagine if we were all going home, now, all of us, Minty and the twins, all together, singing in the car, saying what fun it had been, saying what a success . . .' She started to cry again. 'Oh, Tom, I can't bear it, any of it, I just can't. And now Daddy . . .'

He put his arms round her then, held her, stroked her hair, made the sort of noises he made to the children when they were crying.

She stayed there for a long time; then pulled away from him. 'I'd better phone the hospital,' she said, quite calm suddenly, 'speak to them. Find out how bad it is.'

'Yes. Here's the number, here's my phone.'

'I really think,' she said slowly, when she had finished, handing it back to him, 'I really think it sounds as if he's all right. As all right as he could be. That was the Sister, she was very helpful. I – I sort of explained. Said we had a crisis with one of the children, couldn't get back yet. She said he was stable, that he was responding to the treatment, that he was very strong. She wasn't giving any guarantees, but – I mean, normally of course I'd want to rush back and be with him, but I just can't, Tom. I can't leave here, not yet. I feel we'd be abandoning Minty. I know it's mad, but – this was the last place she was, and she might – well, you never know. Louise might just be keeping her here for a while, then planning to give her back to us. I want to stay. The police are here, and until we know she's somewhere else for certain, I think we should stay.'

'Suppose Louise tries to contact us, at home?' he said. 'Isn't that possible?'

'Well, if she does, Caroline can tell us. She'll be back very soon.' She looked at her watch. 'God, it's half past six.'

'Yes, but the other children, they're so upset. Don't you think . . . ?'

'Look, you go,' she said finally. 'Yes, that's a good idea. They'll be fine with you. I'll stay here. For now. For a while.'

'I thought you said you – you wanted to be with me,' he said quietly.

'I did. I do. But you're right, the children are horribly upset. They need one of us. You go, then – no, perhaps not.' She managed a half smile. 'I was going to say you could go and see my father.'

'I don't think that would do him any good at all,' he said and managed to smile back at her.

'But you will go home?'

'Yes, I'll go. I wish you'd come too.'

'No. No, I want to stay a bit longer at least. Just – just in case.'

He was too exhausted, too confused to argue with her; he didn't actually feel himself it made any difference where they were. Or what they did. Or for that matter what anybody did.

Everyone had gone: she was alone there now with the police. The twins had gone with Tom, hardly protesting, so distressed were they by what had happened. Dickon, large eyed, silent, sucking his thumb, understanding that Minty was gone, but not why and with whom, had gone with them; Sandy was meeting them at one of the service stations, to take Dickon home. Nico had taken Zoë; she too was silent with shock, beyond tears, beyond anything. Only Melanie had stayed, to keep her company.

Octavia wasn't allowed to stay in the incident room; she sat outside, with Melanie, alternately talking compulsively and silent. A line search was going on in the woods around the race track; police and dogs, pushing through the trees. That was somehow sinister, she found, she didn't like it, even while she was grateful.

'She'll be so frightened,' she said to Melanie, 'frightened and tired. And she'll need feeding and changing and her tooth will be hurting, she'll need Calpol, how will she get all those things, who will see to her?

Do you think Louise will look after her properly, know what she wants?'

'Of course she will,' said Melanie, 'of course. She's a mother herself, isn't she? She'll know.'

'She's got an upset tummy too, she needs changing a lot, she's got awful nappy rash. Oh, God, Melanie, how did I let this happen?'

'You didn't let it happen!'

'I did, I did. I was quarrelling with Tom, jealous because he was all over Lauren. I should have been outside, helping Zoë look after Minty. Oh, Melanie, God, oh, God, where can she be, where can Louise have taken her?'

'I don't know, Octavia. I really don't know.'

'I mean, she won't go to a hotel. The police said they'd put out alerts, there'll be announcements on the radio, television, all those things. I think we were right to agree to that, don't you?'

'Of course you were.'

'So – where? Where can she go? No friend would take her in. She can't explain Minty to anyone. Where can she hide? Melanie, where would you go? If you had a baby with you, and you wanted no one to know?'

'I don't know. I can't imagine. Somewhere I knew about, that nobody else did, I suppose.'

'Yes. Yes, I know that, but – but where, what?'

'Has the family got some holiday house anywhere?'

'Well, a house in Spain. I suppose she might try to go there. But then she'd know we'd all think of it. No, I don't think she'd do that. And how would she get there? On a train, I suppose. What about a train? A train is a good hiding place, you can keep moving about, hide in the lavatory and so on. Or she could drive, go through the Channel tunnel, that would be so easy, then we'd never find her.'

'She couldn't get Minty through passport control, surely.'

'No, maybe not. The police said they would put out what they call a port stop. That's all stations, ports, airports.'

'Well, there you are. They have the number of the car, a description of Louise and Minty.'

'She could be in disguise.'

'Yes. But Minty can't be. Or the car.'

'She could get another car. Easily. She could hide Minty in the boot. I bet that's what she'd do. Oh, God, think of that, she might suffocate. And suppose there was an accident? Oh, Mells, I can't stand this, I really can't!'

Melanie said nothing.

'I'm going to ring Charles. Louise's father. You're right, she might have gone somewhere, some family house or cottage I don't know about. Charles? Charles, it's Octavia. No, nothing. Have you? No. Charles, is there anywhere you can think of Louise might go? Some friend who might help her, lend her somewhere, a flat or a cottage or something? No. No, I don't know, but— Yes. Yes, let me know if you do think of anywhere. Could you ring the boys, see if they've heard anything? If they can think of anywhere. Oh, I see. Yes. Yes, please do, Charles. If you do come up with anything, anything at all, ring me on this number, it's my mobile. Yes, of course. Yes, maybe. 'Bye, Charles.

'Poor old chap,' she said gently, putting the phone down. 'He's so terribly, terribly upset. He still keeps saying he's sure it's a mistake, that Louise would never do such a thing.'

'But no ideas?'

'No ideas. Only the house in Spain. Oh, God. It's getting late, look, nearly half past seven. Minty'll be so tired, and she'll be crying. Suppose Louise is driving too fast, suppose she has a crash? Melanie, I can't bear it for her, I just can't bear it.' She started to cry again.

Melanie put her arm round her. 'I know it's hard,' she said, 'but you must try to stay calm. You must. For Minty's sake. You have to keep thinking straight. There has to be an answer to this, something you haven't thought of.'

'Yes,' she said, wiping her eyes, blowing her nose. 'Yes, you're right. I must keep calm. I must think. And she won't hurt her, she won't let her come to any harm, you're right about that too. She's taken her because she wants her. I must keep telling myself that. She's taken her because she wants a baby. She's lost two.'

'Two?'

'Yes, Juliet and – well . . . the one she was having earlier this year And she was so angry with me about – about the . . .'

'About what?'

'I – had an abortion a year before Minty. She found out. She accused me of throwing it away.'

'Ah . . .'

'So – yes, I suppose, in her mad logic, she has a right to Minty. But she's mad, Melanie. Mad people don't look after babies properly. They don't, they don't. Maybe she's planning to – to . . .'

'No,' said Melanie, 'no, Octavia. Don't even think about that.'

Poor little baby. Asleep at last. Exhausted. Louise had put some readymade formula into a bottle, asked them behind the counter in a Little Chef to warm it up for her. It was a risk, but she didn't want to give it to her cold. Then she sat in the car, trying to feed her; Minty had thrashed about screaming for quite a long time, but finally hunger was too much for her, and she'd drunk it all. And then eaten a couple of chocolate biscuits. It wasn't exactly a good diet, but she'd make it up to her tomorrow. When they were there, when they were safe. She had quite a few fresh vegetables in the chill box. And some fruit. Minty loved fruit; the last time she'd seen her, that day at Octavia's cottage, when her rather odd, badly dressed boyfriend had been there, and she'd met him for the first time, Minty had eaten about three bananas, and some strawberries. Louise remembered that day so well; she'd been caught out – nearly – in her lie about going to the dentist. She'd seen Octavia's face, just on the edge of being puzzled, realised she had to be more careful.

She was doing well anyway, with her journey. On the M4 now, almost at Bristol, which meant – she did a swift calculation – God, still three hours to go. At least. And the last bit of the journey would be difficult. She hadn't done it for so long. And then she had to get the place ready, it would be difficult in the dark. And it would probably be filthy. She'd brought lots of torches and nightlights and things, but it would still be difficult. Well, never mind. It got light very early. She could do everything in the morning. She could give Minty another bottle, maybe it would have to be cold, and then they could just lie down together, on one of the beds, tucked together into a sleeping bag. Minty was so tired; she would surely settle.

'I'll stay here with you,' Nico said, 'until your mother gets back.'

'No, honestly, there's no need.'

'I know that, but I'd like to. And I could meet your sister and – ah, hallo. You must be Marc.' He held out his hand. 'Nico Cadogan. Nice to meet you.'

'How do you do, sir,' said Marc. 'Is there any news?'

'No. Not at all. Still, I'm sure it will all be all right in the end. Zoë, why don't you make us all a pot of coffee? That's what we need.'

'Yes, all right,' said Zoë. She looked very white, and almost dazed. 'Any news from Mum, Marc?'

'Only that she's staying there for a bit longer. Said she'd be home about nine.'

'I wish she was here now,' said Zoë and burst into tears again.

'Now look,' said Nico sternly, 'I take that as a personal insult. Your crying because your mother's not here. I'm here, and that should be a perfectly good alternative. Just for now. Come on, Zoë, come over here and let me give you a hug. I hope that doesn't seem presumptuous when I haven't known you very long, but I do know what to do with girls when they cry. Here, take my hanky. Marc, you fix the coffee, there's a good chap. And oh, hallo, you must be Romilly. I'm Nico, how do you do? Got any spare Kleenex, Romilly? I think we're going to need them.'

Nobody walking into the Muirhead kitchen at that moment would have dreamed that Nico Cadogan was not a family man of considerable experience.

'Coffee?' said Melanie.

'Yes. Thanks.'

Octavia had stopped talking, was sitting silent, staring out of the window at the beginnings of the dusk. 'I might just ring the hospital again,' she said, putting the cup down. 'It's at least something to do.'

She did: the news was the same.

'Poor Daddy. How horrible for him, to be there, all alone. At least Marianne's there. It's very good of her. I wonder if . . .'

'Tell me about Marianne,' said Melanie.

'Do you really want to know?'

'Well – sort of. Yes.'

Octavia smiled at he. 'You're a good friend,' she said.

'I'm doing my best. And I am quite interested in Marianne. And your father. Good Lord! Look at that old caravan in the field. We had one just like that when I was a child. My father used to take us all over England in it. I love caravans, they're so— Octavia, are you all right?'

'What did you say?' said Octavia. Something in there had been important. Had stirred something important. What was it? She couldn't think. 'Marianne is wonderful,' she said, 'I'm sorry she couldn't have been here today. She's a real life enhancer and—' She stopped. There had been something. 'Melanie, what did you say then? Apart from asking me to tell you about Marianne.'

'I said I was interested in your father.'

'No, it wasn't that. Something else.'

'I don't think so. Except that I said my parents had once had a caravan. That's seriously interesting, isn't it? Now tell me some more about Marianne. She's rather beautiful, I do remember her from your party.'

One of the policemen came in. 'Nothing very positive yet, I'm afraid,' he said, 'and we're calling off the search now. It's getting dark.'

'I know,' said Octavia. The growing darkness had been frightening her: it was the childhood thing, of there being more to be afraid of, more things you couldn't see. And Minty hated the dark . . .

'But we'll start again in the morning,' said the policeman, seeing her face. 'First thing. And do a door-to-door in the area. The husband's been interviewed, of course.'

'Sandy! Why, he's hundreds of miles away, he doesn't – he couldn't . . .'

'Still her husband. He might know something that we don't.'

'You don't understand,' said Octavia, 'he's the nicest man in the world. He'd have told me—'

'Mrs Fleming, no one's saying he knows where your baby is. But it's possible he might have heard his wife say something, talk to someone. You'd be surprised how the smallest thing is important.'

'Yes. Yes, I suppose so,' said Octavia. She sighed. 'And – nothing else?'

'No, nothing concrete. I would advise you to try and get some rest, Mrs Fleming. I know it's hard, but why don't you book into the Thistle Hotel here? It's very comfortable and you'll still be – well, available.'

'All right,' said Octavia, 'yes, I suppose I could.' He was nice; he seemed to understand how she felt about staying there. Where Minty had been.

'I'll stay with you,' said Melanie.

'No, don't.' Suddenly she wanted to be alone. Quite alone. To think, to think about Minty. She didn't want to talk any more.

'I won't be a bother,' said Melanie, reading her thoughts.

'Of course, you won't. But – no, Mells, you must get back. It's Monday tomorrow, there's all the follow-up on today.'

'Fleming! Do you really think I'm concerned about that?'

'Well . . .'

'No, I'll stay,' said Melanie. 'I can't bear the thought of you being here all on your own. I won't even have dinner with you if you don't want to, just stay quietly in my room.'

'Melanie! I'll be all right. I swear. If I feel really bad, I'll get Tom to come down. It'll only take him just over an hour, with the roads clear.'

'Well, if you're sure . . .'

'I'm sure. I really appreciate the offer, but I think I want to be by myself.'

'I'll try not to take it personally. I shall probably weep tears of rejection all the way back to London.'

Octavia smiled at her. 'Like I said, you're a really good friend.'

After Melanie had gone, she did feel very alone. Alone and scared. Visions kept rising in front of her of Minty: Minty crying and frightened, Minty hidden away from her somewhere, Minty threatened, Minty – so far at that point she managed to drag her mind away.

She booked into the Thistle Hotel, went up to her room, stared out of the window for a bit, wondered what on earth she was going to do. It was only eight thirty; she couldn't sleep, she didn't want to eat, she had nothing to read, anyway, she wouldn't be able to concentrate. She had a rush of panic. Why had she sent Melanie away: why?

Melanie. She was the best sort of friend: understanding, supportive, loyal, funny. And quite tough when it was necessary.

Melanie. What was it now? She'd been talking and something had stirred. Muted, almost imperceptible and then gone again, rather like the first tug of pain that heralded labour. She'd been talking about Marianne. And her father. And – what? No, she couldn't remember.

She was rummaging through her bag looking for her mobile when the tug came again: slightly stronger, troubling, determined.

She sat down on the bed. Think, Octavia, think. What was it, what did she say, why did it matter?

Her phone rang. It was Tom. They were home, the children were watching *Star Wars*, they didn't seem so upset any more. 'I think they're too exhausted.' He'd handed Dickon over to Sandy. Sandy had been very low. 'I felt so sorry for him,' he said.

The irony that it was Tom who had been the immediate cause of most of Sandy's troubles did not escape Octavia. But she didn't say so.

'And your father? I haven't rung. Any more news?'

'No. He's the same. Marianne is still there. I think she feels it's something she can do. It's very good of her.'

'I'm here,' he said, 'if you need me. I can get down there, in no time.'

'Yes, I know. Thank you.'

'Well – goodbye for now, I'll ring again.'

'I think I'll just go for a walk for a bit,' said Zoë, 'I can't stand sitting here waiting for the phone to ring any longer.'

Nico was leafing through the Sunday supplements, a large gin and tonic by his side. He looked at ease, very much at home. 'Of course. Good idea.'

He was trying to find something to read that wasn't about Diana and the funeral when Marc came in.

'Hi,' said Nico, smiling at him. Nice boy; very nice. Her children were a great credit to Marianne.

'Hallo. Where's Zoë?' said Marc.

'Gone for a walk, feeling claustrophobic. Can I get you a drink? If that wouldn't sound to presumptuous in your own house?'

'No, it's okay. I've had a few beers.' He clearly had; and he looked dishevelled, upset. 'It's very – kind of you to stay here, with us.'

'Not at all. I didn't think you should be alone. Specially Zoë. And your mother could be in something of a bad way when she gets home.'

'Yeah. Doesn't sound as if Felix is going to make it.'

'Oh, I don't know. He's very strong.' He looked at Marc. 'I expect you're very – fond of him.'

'He's – okay.'

Nico was silent, turned his attention back to the paper. 'He's an old friend of yours, I believe?' said Marc after a moment.

'Well, more of a business associate really.'

'Zoë said – she said you'd been really cool about her little adventure.'

'Oh, I don't know. I like Zoë, she's great fun. And she looks very like your mother, which is an advantage as far as I'm concerned. Unfortunately, I haven't seen your mother much since then.'

'No. No, she told me. We – do talk a bit. We get on very well.'

'Yes, I see. She's very nice to talk to, I discovered that. She's very nice altogether. I've missed her. Quite a lot.'

There was a silence; Nico stood up, poured himself another drink, sat down again, staring into it. He probably shouldn't have said that; he'd embarrassed the boy now.

'She's missed you too,' said Marc. He had spoken suddenly, as if taking some dangerous leap, impelled by a sudden surge of courage.

'Oh, really? I'm afraid not. I had the impression she was very happily back with Felix Miller.' He certainly shouldn't have said that.

'No. No, she isn't. It didn't work out. She's really miserable about it.'

'I see,' said Nico Cadogan politely. He wondered where this was leading.

'Yeah. She told me—'

The phone shrilled; Marc leaped up to answer it. He stood there, pushing his hands through his hair, saying 'yes' and 'no' and 'I see', and then finally, 'No, we're fine. Mr Cadogan's here, with us. Yeah, that's right. He's being very kind. Yes, I will. Cheers, Mum.' He put the phone down, looked at Nico, opened another can of beer. 'She said to thank you.'

'How's Felix?'

'About the same.'

He nodded; went back to the papers. He felt confused, almost irritable; without knowing quite why. It was all very well, Marc telling him Marianne was no longer with Felix; she was keeping a deathbed vigil by him, which by any standards would seem to indicate a fair degree of commitment. He sighed.

Marc looked at him, drained the can, pulled open yet another.

'Sir,' he said. 'There's something – that is—' and then stopped again.

'Look,' said Nico Cadogan, 'nothing to do with me, but you've had an awful lot of those. And I've had several of these. Why don't I make us both some coffee?

'Yeah, cool,' said Marc.

*

Marc felt awful: awkward, miserable. But somehow the drama of the occasion, liking Nico, his anxiety about both his mother and Zoë – and, he supposed, being rather drunk – all these things combined to make him feel he not only could, but should, talk to him. He had to try to explain. For his mother's sake.

Cadogan came back into the room, with a large jug of coffee. 'Now look,' he said, 'forgive me if I'm wrong, but I get the impression you want to tell me something.'

'Yes,' said Marc, half afraid to speak at all, 'yes, I do.'

'About?'

'About—' He hesitated. 'About Mum. But I – well, I promised her I wouldn't tell anyone.'

'You'd better not, then,' said Nico Cadogan firmly. 'Definitely not gentlemanly behaviour.'

Marc felt a flood of relief. It was true. It was better not. He'd done his best, he'd tried, and if Cadogan didn't think he should go on, then he certainly shouldn't.

'Especially,' Nico went on, 'especially as my relationship with your mother is over.'

He sighed, picked up his coffee. He looked genuinely wretched. That did it really for Marc. The pair of them being wretched. When he could probably help.

'But it shouldn't be,' Marc said quickly, before he could stop again, 'that's the whole point. That's why she's so miserable. She's really upset about it. She said – she said . . .'

'Yes?' said Nico.

'She said you made her really happy, were really good for her. She said she—' He stopped. God, this was difficult. Embarrassing.

'Liked me?' said Nico, carefully helpful.

'Um – well – yes. Yes. A lot,' said Marc. He looked into his coffee cup. 'But Felix kind of stopped her feeling it. I mean, God, I don't really understand. It seems very complicated. But that's what she said. And she said,' he grinned, feeling with relief his way back into safer territory, 'she said in a game of chess it would be checkmate. I thought it sounded a bit like that. But Zoë said she just needed a knight to move on to the board.'

There was a long silence. Then, 'I always rather fancied a knighthood,' said Nico Cadogan.

Octavia switched on the TV, in lieu of anything else to do. A terrible film was just ending, and then there was the news. More endless footage about the funeral, the procession to Althorp: Mother Teresa had died.

Apart from film of her own life, there were endless shots of her with Diana when she had visited her clinic in Calcutta. More reactions about that round the world, very little else. Then the local news.

'A small girl is missing tonight, after disappearing from Brands Hatch racecourse. Minty Fleming, aged ten months . . .' The picture of Minty she had given them, sitting and laughing in her highchair, the only recent one she had had with her, appeared on the screen: Octavia stared at it, frozen with horror and shock, even though she had known it would happen. 'Minty was at Brands Hatch with her parents when she disappeared, apparently with a friend of the family . . . Police have been searching the course and the surrounding area, so far without success.'

Nothing could have prepared Octavia for the horror of that moment: when the deadly, dreadful item about a missing child, so often at that point during the news, the one over which normally she tutted, sympathised, said, how dreadful, poor things, I don't know how people stand it, and went on very often then to say she didn't know why people let their children walk down roads on their own, or play unattended: when that item had been about her, her child, her missing child, her unattended child. She didn't know how they stood it, those parents; and she didn't know how she would stand it. She didn't even know yet what she had to stand.

She felt violently sick, rushed into the bathroom, threw up; and then feeling slightly better, washed her face, and walked back slowly in the bedroom. She sat down on a chair by the window, staring out. It was almost dark, a horribly lovely night, warm and starry, with an almost new moon. Louise didn't deserve that night, she deserved something stormy and ugly, threatening her. And then she thought that Minty did deserve, did need a lovely night, as warm, and as tender as it could be.

'Oh, Minty,' she said aloud, as she said to her every night tucked safely into her cot, 'darling Minty, God Bless. Keep safe. I do hope you're safe.'

Her own foolish words made her start to cry again: don't, Octavia, don't. Try to remember what it was Melanie said, keep calm, think clearly.

The tug came again; the important thing struggling to surface, forcing its way up into her brain. What was it, what? Something Melanie had been saying: something so important.

Marianne. Her father. And something about going round the country when she was small. In a caravan. Yes. The tug was harder that time. That was definitely it.

'God,' said Octavia aloud. 'God, what is it, what?'

She stood up, started pacing up and down the room. A caravan. What about a caravan? A harder tug, the flash of a picture then in her head. Just for a moment, then gone again. This was like that psychometric testing they did, when they were interviewing people for top jobs, the modern equivalent of the ink blot test. Flash a picture in front of their eyes, and if they said it made them think of their mother or something equally uncompetitive, you didn't hire them. Or maybe you did. She couldn't remember. Lot of nonsense anyway.

Concentrate, Octavia, concentrate.

Travelling round the country. In a caravan. Another hazy picture.

And then it came: beaming into her head, brightly brilliant, a proper vision. Anna, the last time she'd seen her: before she died. Anna worried, saying to Louise, 'Daddy mustn't know about this, he'd be so cross.'

Asking Louise what Charles would be cross about and Louise saying, carelessly, 'Her parents had an old caravan.' And then – yes: 'In a field on a farm somewhere. Daddy said she had to sell it but she couldn't bear to.'

'Oh, God,' said Octavia in a whisper. She stood up, staring into the darkness as if it could tell her more still. 'Oh, my God.'

That was where Louise would have gone: to the caravan. Who would know she was there, dumped in a field on a farm? She would be there, in it, with Minty, thinking she was safe. Octavia felt faint, her head swirling, had to sit down on the bed again. She realised her fists were clenched, her hands sweating. But – yes. She felt quite quite sure. It was where she would go, what she would do. So anonymous, so secret, so safe. When everyone was watching hotels, airports, buildings. An old caravan in a field. What could be more perfect? She must go there, quickly. But – where? Where was it, where was the caravan, where was the farm?

Charles would know. It would be terrible having to ask him, she shrank from the thought of it, but he would know. She picked up the phone, took a deep breath, dialled the number. It rang for a long time; Janet answered it.

'Oh, hallo, Octavia,' she said, her voice with its lovely rolling accent heavy. 'I'm so sorry about all this. Very very sorry.'

'Yes. Yes, Janet, thank you. Um – is Mr Madison there?'

'He is, yes. Shall I get him for you?'

'Yes. Well . . .' She hesitated. Janet might know; she'd been with the family since Louise had been born.

'Janet, can I ask you something? In confidence. I mean I'd rather not worry Mr Madison with it, if I don't have to.'

''Course you can, Octavia. I'd save him all the worry I could, poor man, at the moment.'

'There was an old caravan. It – it belonged to Mrs Madison's parents.'

'Yes, that's right. It did. Sold, though, long time ago.'

'Well – yes. But, Janet, do you know where it was? Where it was kept?'

'Yes, of course. I went there once or twice, with Mrs Madison and Louise. When she was really tiny, before the boys were born. Lovely place, in Cornwall.'

'Cornwall!'

So far away. Impossibly far. No, not impossibly far. Nothing was impossible.

'Yes, near a place called Constantine Bay, little bay just further along called Tresilith. There was a farm there, down one of the lanes at Tresilith, one that led to the sea. Now what was it called? Plenty Farm, yes, that's right. And the lane was called Plenty Lane. Anyway, it was two or three fields across from the farmhouse, out of sight, all on its own. Lovely spot, you could see the sea from it. Probably a car park now.'

'Yes, probably.'

There was a silence; then Janet said, 'Octavia, you don't think that – that Louise is – that she's gone there?'

'I don't know, Janet. I think perhaps she has. But I'm trusting you not to say anything. It's important.'

'I won't, Octavia. You'll – you'll let me know, won't you?'

'Yes, Janet, of course I will. Thank you. Good night.'

She went down to Reception, asked them if they had a road atlas. Found Cornwall, found Constantine Bay. And – yes, there was Tresilith. God, it was a long way. Poor, poor little Minty. Dragged right across England, in a hot, strange car.

But at least now she knew where she was. She was sure of it. And at this time of night, she could be there in four or five hours. Nothing.

Octavia took the map and left the hotel; she got into the Range Rover, filled it up with petrol, and turned on to the M20.

Nearly there. Well, at least in the right county. In Cornwall, at last. Driving across Bodmin Moor, Louise felt desperately tired. She had had to stop twice, stand outside the car, take deep breaths of air, to keep awake. She had vast supplies of sweets, had munched them steadily; that always helped. She would have liked to play the radio loudly, another trick, but she didn't dare. Minty was asleep again, after a long spell of screaming, another dirty nappy; she'd changed her in the car this time, it had been terribly difficult, on the back seat, Minty's legs flailing, she'd got mess on her jeans and her T-shirt, and Minty's little pink dress was filthy and smelly. She couldn't wait to get her there, change her into something clean, wash her – she wasn't quite sure what with, maybe just the baby wipes until tomorrow, when she could get the caravan's water tank filled up – soothe her, cuddle her to sleep. Well, not long now.

She reached Bodmin, turned in the direction of Padstow. The lovely names that had meant nearly journey's end as a child, nearly nearly there, Land-end, Washaway: then through Wadebridge, asleep, silent, much bigger than she remembered, and then St Issey Little Petherick. And finally, actually a signpost to Constantine Bay and Tresilith. She had done it. She was alone, all alone in the night, no one had followed her, nobody knew where she was . . .

She paused, looked up at the stars; behind her, Minty woke, looked as if she might start to cry again, but then saw her and for the first time smiled a sleepy smile.

That had to be a good omen.

Felix woke up; suddenly, and clearly painfully. It hurt to watch him. Marianne had been half asleep herself; she looked anxiously at the monitors. They meant nothing to her.

They meant something to the medical staff; they had set off an alarm somewhere. Sister half ran in, looked at Felix, examined the machines, checked the drip.

The doctor followed her. 'I'm sorry,' he said to Marianne, 'his condition's worsening. I must ask you to leave for a while. I'm sorry.'

She went out and sat in the corridor. She felt oddly calm. At least she was here, at least he knew she was here. For the moment, that seemed all that mattered.

'Mrs Miller?'

Marianne started. She had been nearly asleep, on her chair, out in the corridor.

'Yes?'

'Mrs Miller, I'm afraid – I'm afraid he's had another heart attack. Not so severe this time, but on top of the other one . . . You might like to go and see him.'

She went back in. Felix's eyes were closed. She took his hand again; he opened his eyes. It was all like a grisly, well-rehearsed play.

He began to pull at the oxygen mask with both his hands; she watched him anxiously. The nurse had come in.

'He seems to want it off,' said Marianne.

'Maybe he wants to speak. Say something.'

'Yes. Could I – just for a moment?'

'I will.' The nurse removed the mask.

Felix licked his dry lips very slowly. Marianne watched him. He opened his mouth, clearly wanted to speak.

'Felix, do you want to – to say something?'

'Yes. Yes – please.' He reached for her hand again, kissed it. She looked down at him, at the great head bent over her hand, and thought she couldn't bear it. She stroked his hair, his thick white hair, so symbolic, she had always thought, of his own vigour and strength.

'Octavia—' he said with huge difficulty.

A slug of disappointment went through Marianne. 'Yes? What about Octavia? Do you want her to come?'

'No. Not today. But tell – tell her . . .' A long pause; he was clearly exhausted. He closed his eyes again, waited.

'Yes, Felix, tell her what?'

'Tell her Tom – Tom loves her.'

'Tom?' She was so astonished to hear this, she felt breathless indeed herself: that Felix, who hated Tom, who had wished only for Octavia to hate him too, to see him gone from her life, should say such a thing.

'Loves her – very – very . . .'

And then there was a great shudder through him, and then a gentler sigh: and then the cardiac monitor stopped its regular bleep and orderly zigzag on the screen and sent out instead a gentle high-pitched buzz and the line became dreadfully and hopelessly level. And before Marianne had told him how much she loved him, as she had intended and wanted to do, stolen from her by Octavia in death as he had been in life, Felix had died.

CHAPTER 52

Octavia looked at the dashboard clock: eleven thirty. She was doing well. Almost at the M5 turn-off. She would stop at the next place, fill the car up again, have a coffee. She felt very calm, very confident.

She had switched her mobile off; she didn't want anyone, anyone at all, not even Tom, to know where she was going. Whatever she said, whatever he promised, he might tell the police. He should tell the police, she should tell the police. But she couldn't. This was between her and Louise: nobody else. If she was to get Minty back safely, she had to talk to Louise quietly, and listen to her too. That would not be achieved by a mass of police swarming round the caravan. She was not persuaded by all the people who had told her Louise wouldn't hurt Minty. Louise was mad; she was capable of anything.

She had also, once, been her best friend. That had to count for something.

'We have to tell her,' said Tom. 'She has to know. I think – maybe I should go down there. Tell her that way. Not over the phone. What do you think?'

'Yes. Possibly.' Marianne sounded very upset.

'Look, Marianne, you should get home. There's nothing more you can do.' God, what an absurd thing to say. How death produced clichés.

'Yes. Yes, of course.'

'Is your car there? At the hospital?'

'No. I came in a cab. I'll call one. Or maybe Marc or Zoë could come and get me. I feel a bit shaky. I'll call home.'

'I'll do it for you. I know how hard it is in those places. You need endless change. 'Bye, Marianne. You've been so wonderful today. Thank you for everything.'

Fifteen minutes later, as Marianne sat, shaking slightly now with shock and grief, Nico Cadogan walked into Reception. She was somehow not remotely surprised to see him; his presence there seemed entirely natural, what she would against all logic have expected. She needed him and he was there; it was as simple as that.

'Don't say anything,' he said, sitting down beside her, putting his arm round her, 'anything at all. I've come to get you safely home. No more than that.'

'Oh, Nico,' said Marianne, burying her face against him, trying and failing to blank out the picture of the shell that had been Felix lying on the high bed, the machines about him silent and still, his strength finally spent, his vitality lost for ever. 'Nico, you'll never know how pleased I am to see you.'

'Maybe some day you'll be able to tell me,' he said, kissing the top of her head. 'Come along now. Let's take you home.'

Tom dialled Octavia's mobile. It was switched off. Damn! Why had she done that? Surely she couldn't have gone to sleep, surely. Must have been a mistake. Well, he could call the hotel, get them to ring up to her room . . .

'No reply from her room, Mr Fleming.'

'Are you sure? Try again.'

Another long wait. 'Sorry, no. She's not answering.' The voice was beginning to sound bored.

'Well – could someone go up? Maybe she's asleep, maybe she's ill. She's a very light sleeper, it's unlike her . . .'

She wouldn't, couldn't – Christ – have taken an overdose, would she? She'd been so distraught, she always had sleeping pills with her, anything was possible. No. No, she wouldn't. That really would be out of character.

'The room's empty, sir. No one is there.'

'Oh, God. But she has the key still?'

'She hasn't handed it in, sir.'

'What about the dining room, or something. Could you have her paged?'

'The dining room is closed now, sir.'

'I see. Well – is her car there?'

'I can't tell you that, I'm afraid.'

'Why not? You must have a car park, go and bloody well check. This is an emergency, for God's sake. It's a Ranger Rover, N reg, N459 AGR.'

'Very well, sir. If you'll just wait while I find someone.'

Another interminable wait. Then, 'No, the car has gone. I'm sorry.'

Jesus! What had happened to her? Where had she gone?

'Thank you,' he said, 'please let me know if she comes back.'

'Certainly, sir.'

There it was; in spite of her mother having told her it was still weatherproof, still there, that she had phoned Mr Briggs a few months earlier to warn him she was thinking of selling it, she had worried increasingly as she got nearer. Mr Briggs might have been being economical with the truth, afraid of losing his annual rent cheque. Quite a large cheque, actually, she'd discovered, in return for what was after all a very small piece of land indeed that nobody ever visited any more. He must be quite an old man now, and these were not exactly easy times for farmers. Anyway, it seemed to be all right. Thank God. Parked in the corner at the bottom of the field; looking as if it had put roots down into the ground. Sunk on its haunches a bit, very rusty no doubt, but still there, still with its roof. Hopefully it would be dry. If only there was a bit more moonlight. Still, her torch was very powerful. She could pick it out. Under the apple tree, in the corner. Yes, it was fine. No cows in the field, just a few sheep. Well, that was all right, they wouldn't make much noise.

It was amazing how she'd remembered it all so vividly: the other way to reach it, so she didn't have to drive through the farm, down the farm track even, so the dogs didn't bark. She remembered that even now; Mrs Briggs asking her mother to go that way round. It was along a very rutted track, and quite often when it had rained a lot, the car got stuck in the mud. There wasn't any mud now: it was very dry.

She had parked the car in the gateway of the first field; Minty was asleep. She wondered if she dared leave her there while she did a quick recce; she'd have to. She locked all the doors and climbed over the gate.

The field was blessedly dry; she made her way down towards the corner where the caravan was. Below the field were some woods, beyond them the sea. It was a beautiful place; they'd only had a few holidays here, but she still remembered them as being very special. It had all been so exciting, like an Enid Blyton story, getting milk and eggs from the farm, water from a tap in the corner of the field that fed the sheep trough – that was very lucky, she presumed it was still there – endless picnics, exploring beaches and caves, scrambling up and down cliff paths.

The caravan wasn't even that rusty: it looked remarkably sturdy. She pulled the key out, put it in the lock. Please, please let it work, don't let it be rusted. There was a bit of resistance, but it opened. She beamed her torch inside: filthy, cobwebs everywhere, but it was dry. A neat pile of sleeping bags, no doubt spider infested, on one of the bunks, saucepans still on the stove, a few old postcards jammed jauntily into the window frames, a vase set on the table, a Cornish pixie toastrack on the side.

Even the old curtains hung still at the windows, and a battered travel cot stood in the corner. That was wonderful: Minty was much too big for a carrycot; she'd been worrying about it. And a picture of the four of them, her mother, herself, Benjy and Dominic, all quite small, smiling over the farm gate, set in a frame on one of the shelves.

'Oh, Mummy,' she said aloud, a catch in her voice, 'oh, Mummy, I wish you'd come back.'

Well, she wouldn't She was gone. For ever. She had to manage without her now. And she had to look after Minty.

She looked back at the car; probably best to take the stuff in first, then Minty. She could make up the travel cot with the bedclothes, put her in that while she sorted out another bottle and a nappy and so on.

A wave of happiness swept over Louise. This was just as she had imagined it. Possibly even better.

The best way was across the A30 from Exeter. It was a good fast road and at this time of night there was no traffic on it. Octavia turned on to it; she felt almost happy. She had always loved night driving. God knows how she was going to find the caravan. Or even Plenty Farm. But she would. She could do anything now. Anything at all. She was going to get Minty back.

'Perhaps you should try Mr Trelawny,' said Caroline to Tom. 'He might have heard from Octavia.' She was very subdued, very shaken.

'Yes, maybe I should.'

'I feel so bad,' she said suddenly.

'Caroline, for heaven's sake why, why should you feel bad?'

'If I'd stayed behind, looked after Minty, this wouldn't have happened. I'm so sorry.'

'Look,' said Tom, 'that really is absurd. I never heard such nonsense. If it's anyone's fault, it was ours, not looking after her properly. But yes, you're right, I'll ring Sandy Trelawny. And Charles Madison, that wouldn't be a bad idea either.'

Sandy was clearly sitting by the phone; he snatched it up. He said he'd heard nothing. 'But I'll ring you immediately, if I do.'

'Thanks,' said Tom.

He phoned Rookston Manor. No answer for a long time, then Charles Madison's courteous voice, heavy with anxiety.

'Charles, it's Tom. Tom Fleming.'

'Tom! Is there any news?'

So – that was no good.

'No. I just wondered if by any chance you'd heard from Octavia.'

'Octavia? No, I'm afraid not. Why?'

'She's disappeared,' said Tom, 'we have no idea where she is. And – you see, I have to contact her. Her father's died.'

'Her father? Oh, how dreadful. What was it?'

'Heart attack,' said Tom briefly.

'I always liked him so much. He was so kind, coming to Anna's funeral.'

'Yes. But you see, I do have to find Octavia. Apart from anything else.'

'Yes, of course. And I'll tell Janet too in the morning. She's gone to bed.'

'You couldn't check now?' said Tom hopefully.

'Tom, it is quite late. She lives in a separate flat. Over the stables. She would have told me if Octavia – or Louise for that matter – had phoned. She really would.'

'Yes, of course. Well – thank you, Charles, anyway.'

'Not at all, not at all. I feel so dreadful myself. I feel – oh, I don't know.' He sounded very tired, absolutely defeated.

'Charles don't feel that. No one could have helped all this.' Except me, he thought, me, by not starting the affair, not damaging that fragile psyche further.

'Have you told the police? About Octavia disappearing?'

'No,' said Tom, 'no, not yet.'

He knew he should; but he kept putting it off. It made it too official.

Minty was all right at first. She let Louise change her nappy – God, where was she going to put these things? There were a lot of things, after all, she hadn't thought of. She'd have to find somewhere tomorrow. Minty took a bottle from her, a cold bottle, but then it was a hot night, even let her wipe her face and hands with some baby wipes. She couldn't start stumbling about looking for the sheep trough in the dark. It was when Louise tried to take her dress off that she started. It was as if the dress was her connection with familiarity, safety, places and people she knew. She screamed and screamed, on and on. Loudly, relentlessly.

Louise was terrified; it was a very still night, someone might hear her, would come down to see what was happening. She had hidden the car as best she could, halfway down the track; in the morning she'd have to move it, park it somewhere in the village maybe, where it wouldn't attract any attention.

She rocked Minty, trying to soothe her, holding her close: or trying to. Minty struggled and pushed at her; every so often the crying stopped, turning to panicky hiccups, then started again. Poor little girl: what a dreadful day she'd had. Well, tomorrow would be quite different. She could lie under the apple tree, while Louise cleared up, set up house in the caravan; they could go for a walk, down to the beach – she could remember it so well, a lovely scrambly path, bordered by fields, leading to the brilliant sea, they could play on the beach, she could even dangle Minty's toes in the water. She'd love that. Juliet had loved that, when they'd taken her to the seaside. Screaming with delight, kicking her little fat legs, her brown pudgy feet. Minty would love it too.

But Juliet had stopped crying when she held her close and talked to her. Minty wouldn't let her hold her close and was crying too loudly to hear anything she said. Louise began to feel desperate. She was so tired; so very tired. She only wanted to sleep.

She put Minty down in the travel cot; she promptly stood up in it, shaking the sides, screaming on. Louise turned all the torches out. Maybe in the darkness she'd settle down. She would give her ten minutes, that was the magic time. They always went to sleep after ten minutes. Minty screamed on, lying down now, jammed into a corner of the cot.

Maybe she was frightened of the dark; she'd brought some nightlights. Maybe she should light a couple of them, see if that helped.

Louise rummaged in her bag for the nightlights, set them in saucers, lit them. The light was very gentle, casting soft shadows in the caravan; the effect was magical. Minty lay staring at the shadows fascinated, her screams slowly quietening.

Thank God, thought Louise, thank God. At last she could go to sleep . . .

Janet couldn't sleep; she had a dreadful headache and she felt terribly worried – and something else. Not quite guilt, but a sense of dreadful responsibility. The more she thought about Octavia driving off in the middle of the night to find Louise, the more she felt it was dangerous. Louise's behaviour had become dangerous; therefore she might be capable of dangerous things.

She got up: Derek, as usual, was snoring. She looked at the clock: half past two. A very long time till morning. A very long time too since Octavia had phoned.

She looked across the yard at the house; it was dark and still. Hopefully Mr Madison was managing to get some sleep. Poor poor man. He was being asked to bear a great deal.

Then she saw the kitchen light go on, saw Charles, fully dressed, walk in, go over to the sink, fill the kettle.

Janet made her decision; she pulled on her old dressing gown and went over to the house.

★

Three o'clock. It had been a long night. She'd been awake for nearly twenty-four hours, Octavia realised. She'd got up at five the day before. But she felt fine: alert, energised, ready for anything.

She was nearly there; she'd seen a sign to Constantine Bay. Somehow she'd expected a pretty little village; it was more of a settlement of bungalows. A sign there directed her on to Tresilith: only five more miles. Tresilith was a proper village: tiny, a pub, some houses, a shop, not much more. Now what did she do? How did she find Plenty Farm, for God's sake? In the pitch darkness. Thank heavens the Range Rover lights were so good.

It must be on the sea side of the village. Janet had said it was by the sea. She would just have to explore all the roads leading in a seawards direction. In the event there were only three. The first and the second were dead ends – or rather they joined up. The third meandered about in a hopeful sort of way, but led finally inland again. But then she saw it as she turned back: little more than a track, leading off it, with a sign wedged into the bank: Plenty Lane.

Octavia turned down it, her heart thudding very hard.

A third of a mile or so along it, she could see some farm buildings just ahead and down to her left. A dog barked furiously; she backed up to the lane again, parked there, waited, waited for a long time, until the dog was a quiet once more, dreading lights going on, an angry farmer asking her what the hell she was doing. No lights came on, no angry farmer.

She got out, took the torch from the dashboard pocket and walked carefully down the lane. There were so many fields; how was she to know which one it was?

She would just have to explore them all, she supposed, until she found one with a caravan in it. In the dark. The thick darkness.

The fields up to her right had cows in them: she hoped it wouldn't be in one of them. Cows put up a huge racket, and anyway, she didn't terribly like them. They were so big. Big and powerful. Louise had always teased her about it, called her a townie and a scaredy cat, used to go up the cows and hug them, try and make her do it, too. She never had. Anyway, these fields had no caravans in them. Thank God.

She walked on. She suddenly felt herself slipping and nearly fell over; she staggered, clutched at the hedge, caught a branch just in time. Mud, she supposed: or – no, not mud, a cowpat, all over her shoes, her new pale pink suede JP Tod loafers. They'd cost her a fortune; it would never come off . . .

For heaven's sake, Octavia, your baby's been kidnapped, is possibly in danger, what on earth are you doing, worrying about your shoes? And then she slid again and then again, and the track seemed to be disintegrating, increasingly rough and stony. It was hopeless; she would simply have to go back to the car and wait until it was at least half light.

There was something outside the caravan, it had woken her up: what was it? Louise sat up in her sleeping bag, breathing heavily, her heart thudding. Then she relaxed; only the sheep. How stupid. The nightlights had burned out though; better light some more – if Minty woke up to the dark, she'd be frightened again. Thank God she'd brought them. She'd brought some candles, too, but she didn't want to light them, they were much more dangerous. Those curtain would go up in flames in a second.

Carefully, afraid of Minty waking, she lit three more nightlights, and got back into her sleeping bag. She looked at her watch. Half past five. Soon it would be light. And the first lovely proper day would begin.

Octavia could see the caravan now: just as Janet had said, in a corner of a far field, through the grey early mist, drifting across the countryside. See the sea beyond it, grey too; seagulls whirled overhead, crying, the noise somehow sinister and disturbing.

There was no sign of a car anywhere. That was worrying. Could she have been wrong, could Louise, after all, not be there?

The caravan was beyond the first field, in a second; bounded by yet another. So maybe there was another way into it, on the far side, maybe the car was there. Well, the caravan was what mattered: Octavia took a deep breath and started to scramble over the gate.

Louise woke up again, feeling cold. If she was cold, Minty must be. She got up, checked her; she was sweetly asleep, lying on her back, one arm flung above her head. It was incredible how serene she looked: after her long frightening day. Maybe she would settle down quickly. She had always seemed a placid little thing. Juliet had been placid too: always smiling, sweet natured. Like Dickon. Poor little Dickon; she hoped he wouldn't be too upset by everything that had happened. Perhaps, when everything had settled down, he would be able to join her and Minty. She hadn't quite worked it out yet, how she would manage that: but she'd worked everything else out, she was sure it would be all right. It was funny how she'd never felt the same about Dickon, after Juliet had died, had never loved him so much: in a funny way, she blamed him. For being alive, still, while Juliet was dead. She'd denied that when Dr Brandon had suggested it, because she didn't like him getting anything right; but it was true.

She looked at Minty; when she woke up she'd be hungry. And a bottle wouldn't do this time. Juliet had been eating cereal, toast, yoghurt, all sorts of things. Louise had bought cereal and yoghurt; but she wasn't sure if she'd brought it from the car or not. She'd been so tired by then, so confused, so longing for sleep. She got up cautiously, started rummaging through the boxes; she could hear the sheep outside, rustling through the grass. They obviously like the caravan, regarded it as their home. One of them was even coming up the steps, and – no. Not a sheep. God. Maybe the farmer, or some other local, having noticed the car. Knocking quite gently at the door; then after a few moments, carefully, very slowly, opening it. Maybe not even someone as benign as the farmer or a local, maybe someone dangerous, a psychopath, a—

'Hallo, Louise,' said Octavia, putting her head round the door, smiling at her. 'Hallo. I've come to collect Minty.'

Louise looked perfectly normal, really. Tired, but not in the least mad. Octavia studied her. She was sitting on the bed, wearing a rather grubby T-shirt and leggings, and her hair was very dishevelled, but her face was quite relaxed and the lovely blue eyes were very calm as she looked at her. She didn't even seem particularly surprised to see her.

'Hallo,' Louise said. 'You must have been driving all night.'

'Most of it, yes.'

'How did you know I was here?'

'Oh – put two and two together. I was always quite good at that, you know.'

'Obviously.'

'I'm sorry if I frightened you then. Just walking in like that.' What a stupid thing to say: when Louise had frightened her more than she had ever been frightened in her whole life. 'How's Minty?'

'She's fine. Absolutely fine. Fast asleep, look.'

'Yes, she looks – fine. That dress is a bit dirty.'

'Yes, she wouldn't let me take it off.'

'She hates being undressed,' said Octavia conversationally. She sounded very normal, very calm, even to herself, rather as if she was at a coffee morning or the baby clinic. 'What time did you get here?'

'Oh – about twelve.'

'And she's been asleep since then?'

'Well, you know. She took a bit of settling. But she was very tired.'

'Yes, she must have been. You must be quite tired too.'

'I'm fine. Thank you.'

'I don't suppose I could have a cup of tea?' Octavia said.

'No. Sorry. There's no gas for the stove yet. Water, orange juice?'

'Water'd do. Yes, thanks. Well – cheers, Louise. It's nice to see you.'

*

Stupid bitch. Standing there in her perfectly cut trousers and jacket – at least her shoes were ruined – thinking she could do anything, that everything was all right, thinking she could humour her, like they had at the Cloisters, that she was mad, that she could trick her into giving her Minty. Well, she couldn't. She hadn't gone through all this to lose her now.

'Was she good on the journey?'

'Yes, very good. She hardly cried at all.'

'You were lucky. She gets car sick sometimes now.'

'No, she was fine.'

'And she'd had an upset tummy, did she have endless dirty nappies?'

'A few.'

'I thought so. Louise . . .'

'Yes?'

She had that expression on her face, the one that Louise had always hated, ever since school, a slightly smug I'm-cleverer-than-you-even-if-you-have-got-other-advantages.

Only then, the other advantages had been a pretty face and friends and being thin; this time it was Minty.

'Louise, I really would rather like to take Minty now. I think it would be a good idea if you let me have her.'

'Why?'

'Well – because she is mine. She is my baby. Not yours.'

'You've got the twins.'

'Yes, of course I have—' patient, humouring her again – 'but Minty is mine too. I would like you to give her to me.'

She was doing that assertiveness stuff, that she'd learned on some course or other; she'd told Louise about it, said it worked brilliantly, no aggressiveness, no fuss, you just stated calmly what you wanted over and over again, and in the end you got it.

'Well, I'm really sorry, but I can't. I want her now. You've had her for quite a long time. As long as I had Juliet. Actually.'

'Louise, I know that. But you must realise you can't keep her.'

'Why not?'

'Because I told you. She's mine. She's my baby.'

'No, Octavia. Not any more.'

It was getting more difficult; Louise was getting more difficult. Looking less normal: very tense, rather flushed. She supposed she'd expected that. 'Lulu—'

'Don't call me that.' Louise's face was very hard suddenly. Hard and less calm. 'Don't pretend we're friends. You can't have her because you don't deserve her. You got rid of one of your babies. You got over that one. You'll get over this one too.'

'Louise, that just doesn't make sense.'

'None of it makes sense, Octavia. Me having an affair with Tom didn't make sense. My getting pregnant by him didn't make sense. Nor did me taking an overdose. I'm not too bothered about what makes sense, actually. *I'm* going to have Minty now. That's all. Whether it's sensible or not, I'm going to have her.'

'Yes. Yes, I see.'

Octavia waited, trying to think. She looked at Minty, sleeping miraculously through all this; she had given a little sigh, and turned over, her thumb in her mouth, her bottom stuck up in the air. She looked absolutely normal, perfectly well. That, at least, was all right.

She could grab her, make a run for it; but that would be very difficult in the bumpy field; and Louise, unencumbered, not carrying quite a heavy baby, would run faster. She could go on arguing, reasoning with her; but it was becoming clear that wasn't going to work. She could pretend to go away, phone for help; or she could go to the farm. But she was afraid to leave Minty again, now that she had found her. On the other hand, it was probably her only hope.

'Well,' she said, 'well, Louise, all right. I'll leave you. You can keep her. For now.'

'Oh, no,' said Louise, 'you're not leaving, Octavia. I'm not that stupid. You'll just go and tell everyone I'm here and they'll come and take her away. No, you stay here, and I'll go.'

'Don't be silly. Where can you possibly go? This is the best place – for a few days, anyway. It's very clever. Nobody except me knows you're here. Nobody at all. Even your father doesn't know about it. He thinks your mother sold the caravan.'

'I bet you told someone,' said Louise.

'No. I didn't. I really didn't. Do you think Tom would have let me come alone if I had? Don't you think the police would be here, looking for you? I swear to you, Louise, I didn't tell anybody.'

Louise hesitated. Then she said, 'No, I don't believe you.'

'That's fine. You'll just have to trust me. Tell you what – here's my mobile. Ring Sandy. Ask him if he knows where you are.'

Louise looked at her, looked the phone; hesitated just for a minute, staring at the numbers. Just long enough. Octavia reached forward, grabbed Minty, who woke with a start, began to scream.

She'd thought she could get out; but Louise was quicker. She moved between her and the door and then reached, not for Minty, but one of the candles that lay on the table, next to a still-burning nightlight, and lit it from the small flame. And with the other hand, she reached behind her, locked the door.

'Give her to me,' she said. 'Now, Octavia.'

'Louise, no. Look, try to think properly. How can you possibly keep her? The police know you've got her, you can't stay here for long, the locals will know you're here; if you run away with her, you'll get caught. I'm so so sorry for you, I understand why you want her, but—'

'I don't want you to be sorry for me, Octavia, and you don't understand. You don't understand how much it hurts, all the time, losing Juliet. You don't understand how happy I was with Tom, being pregnant with his baby, how much it hurt to lose it. You don't understand what it was like, watching Mummy die. You don't understand how much *I* wanted to die. Don't patronise me, telling me you understand, because you don't. You don't understand any of it.'

'No, perhaps I don't,' said Octavia quietly. 'You're right. But I am sorry for you, so sorry. And whatever you've done to me, I still care about you. Very much.' She wasn't trying to be clever, to out-manoeuvre Louise any more; she meant every word. She saw Louise's expression soften just a little, grow less wary. 'You can't just forget fifteen years of friendship like we had. I can't, and I don't think you can either.'

Louise's eyes filled suddenly with tears. 'Well,' she said, her voice quite different, 'well, I suppose . . .' and Octavia thought in that moment, she was going to do it, talk her round, felt a surge of confidence.

And then Minty wailed again, and instinctively she drew her more closely to her. Louise saw that, saw it as a threat and her face changed again, become harder, cunning. 'Give her to me,' she said. 'If you don't, I'll just set fire to the caravan. With all of us in it. I could, you know. I could. I'd rather do that than lose her now.' She held the candle flame near one of the old curtains.

Octavia felt very calm suddenly; time was moving very slowly. She was able to think, to recognise that Louise was indeed quite capable in that moment of doing what she said, that she was extremely dangerous. The curtains were tinder dry: they would go up in a trice. And then the sleeping bags, heaped on the bunk under one of the windows; they would catch. There was a lot of wood in the rest of the caravan – the table, two wooden stools; it might take a while to catch, but it was potentially lethal.

But if Louise had Minty . . .

'All right,' she said, her voice amazingly steady, 'all right, Louise. You take her.'

Minty didn't want to be taken; she screamed, tried to cling to her.

'Go on, darling,' said Octavia quietly, soothingly, amazed at herself that she could do it, stay so calm. 'It's all right, go to Louise. Here, Louise, take her.'

Louise took Minty, held her tight. She blew the candle out. 'Right. Now get out.'

'I'm going.'

'And don't come back. And don't bring anyone back. If you do, I'll burn the place down with me and Minty in it. I mean it.'

'I won't,' said Octavia. 'I won't bring anyone back.'

'Leave the phone.'

'I'm leaving it.'

'And don't go to the farm.'

'I won't go to the farm.'

'Go on. Get out.'

Octavia got out.

Minty was screaming; she had been screaming ever since Louise had taken her from her mother, and quite a long time seemed to have passed. The metal walls of the caravan made her screams louder, it echoed with them; Louise tried again and again to comfort her, soothe her, but she screamed on. It was a dreadful noise, so insistent it hurt. It was like the night before, only much worse, the noise boring into her head. For twenty minutes, half an hour now the noise had been going on; Louise began to feel desperate. What was she going to do? Perhaps she should take her outside for a bit, for a walk. Just round the field. But she didn't dare. Not yet. Octavia had gone, had climbed over the gate, she had watched her, had disappeared up the track; but if she did come back, if anyone came, and she and Minty weren't in the caravan, she wouldn't be able to use her threat.

'Shush, Minty, please,' she said, and then louder, 'Please! Minty, please, please stop it.'

Minty's face was scarlet, her curls stuck to her head. She felt very hot. It was beginning to be frightening. Louise tried to give her a drink from a beaker, tipping it into the screaming mouth; Minty spat it out. She was growing rigid in her fear and her misery; less human, just a stiff, boardlike little body and two thrashing flailing arms, two kicking legs. Louise couldn't hold her, couldn't even try to cuddle her any more. In the end she put her down in the cot; Minty lay there, still rigid, screaming, red faced, sweaty. Louise looked at her, almost afraid.

She tried the drink again, tried giving it to her as she lay in her cot; Minty turned her head away from it, pushing it away, screaming more loudly still. This was awful. If she wouldn't drink, she'd get dehydrated, she'd be ill.

She hadn't thought of that, of Minty being ill. How could she take her to a doctor, get her made better?

She tried to pick her up again, and Minty went rigid again, throwing her head back now, her body arched against Louise. Louise paced up and down the caravan, fighting down the panic, telling herself it couldn't last for ever, Minty would tire in the end. She looked out of the window, at the still-grey morning, the swirling mist; some crows had settled on the cattle trough, seemed to be staring at her. It was nightmarish. She looked down at Minty and saw her face was almost blue, veins bulging on the sides of her small forehead. It was a horrible sight. Louise felt a rush of pure, liquid panic, ran over to the cot, half dropped her into it; the shock made Minty silent, suddenly. Horribly silent.

Louise stared at her; she lay there very still. Very very still.

'No,' she shouted, 'no, Minty, no.' Minty stared up at her, not moving at all, her blue eyes absolutely blank. Louise burst into tears herself.

Octavia could never remember afterwards walking across the field, climbing over the gate; she would have sworn under oath she hadn't moved. But she must have done, because she was on the other side of the gate, sitting with her head buried in her arms, hoping Louise couldn't see her, trying desperately to think what to do, horrified at herself for her own arrogance, at thinking she could handle something so dangerous, so lethal, all by herself, without help or advice of any kind, when she heard Louise's voice, loud, violent, raw with terror, getting nearer to her, calling to someone, anyone, for help; and as she stood up, she saw Louise stumbling alone across the field, without Minty, her face white, working, her eyes huge and dark with terror, and when she saw Octavia, she ran over to her, grabbed her arm, and said, 'Please, please come, Octavia, I think I've done something terrible to Minty. I think she's dead.'

CHAPTER 53

'It's down here,' said Charles. 'I only came here once, always hated it, hated camping of any sort, so uncomfortable, but – ah. Here it is. Plenty Lane. There's the farm. Now, as I recall – yes, turn left here. Down this track. The caravan's beyond that field there. In the corner.'

Tom could just make it out; the mist was quite thick, and much of it anyway was hidden by the hill. 'But where's Octavia's car? God, I hope this hasn't been a wild goose chase.'

'Probably on the other lane,' said Charles, 'it runs past the farm. But that's Anna's car. There, look. Just a minute . . .' He got out, walked down the track, peered inside. He came back, couldn't quite look Tom in the face. 'Yes. There's a baby seat in it. Oh, God, I'm so sorry.'

He looked much older suddenly. Older and frail. He had clearly been hoping desperately that this had all been a mistake, that Octavia had been wrong, that Louise was somewhere else, far away, that Minty, if she had been abducted, had been abducted by someone else.

'Yes,' he said finally, 'yes, it seems she's here. With Minty.'

Tom was too exhausted, too afraid, to be tactful or reassuring. He pulled the car into the gateway, climbed over it, started running across the field. His legs felt rather odd, a bit numb; he was surprised any part of him was functioning at all.

He could see it now, the caravan; it was more of an orchard than a field that it was in, full of apple trees and sheep. Very old, very battered looking, collapsed slightly on to one wheel, but perfectly functional.

A few sheep nosed round the caravan; there was a water trough just behind it, and a very rusty hayrack tucked to one side, the land side, where it was sheltered from the sea. Clearly, it had become part of their livestyle.

It was the most beautiful place; he was astonished to find himself able to notice it, the field halfway down a small valley, with a wood below it, tipping on downwards, edging the sloping cliffs, and through the tops of the trees, he could see the sea, glittering now in the early sun, breaking through the mist.

As the mist cleared, so did the silence; he could hear dogs barking at the farm, the sheep bleating foolishly as he approached them, some cows mooing in the distance, the crying of the gulls, waves breaking on the shore far below him. He could even hear Charles, panting behind him. But from the caravan there came no sound at all.

It was eerie, sinister. Weren't they there? After all this? They had to be, surely. Even if Octavia wasn't, Louise must be. Louise and Minty.

Tom went up the caravan steps and knocked on the door. Very quietly, very gently. There was no answer. He waited, knocked again; then opened the door very carefully.

Louise was sitting on a bunk bed, very pale and still, staring at the floor, and Octavia had one arm round her. The other encased a filthy but remarkably cheerful-looking Minty, who was sitting on her mother's lap, munching her way through what appeared to be an entire packet of chocolate biscuits.

Minty was the first to smile.

'Dada,' she said, holding out a chocolatey fist.

'That was Tom,' said Marianne, putting down the phone. Tears streamed down her face. 'They're safe, all of them.'

'And Minty?'

'Minty's absolutely fine.'

'Thank God,' said Zoë and burst into tears.

'Now poor Octavia has to hear about her father,' said Romilly and started to cry too.

Nico looked at them all. 'I think,' he said, 'this might be my cue to exit. Just for now.'

Octavia had occasionally contemplated the death of her father. Far, far into the future, of course, but none the less inevitable. How she would feel, what she would do, how she would be able to bear it?

In the event, and at first at any rate, she felt almost nothing. She was too exhausted, too drained, too overwhelmingly thankful to have Minty back. She listened to Tom as he told her what had happened, nodding as he reassured her that Felix had still been insisting she was not bothered, that her not being there was exactly what he wanted. She said, politely, how wonderful that Marianne at least had been there, agreed dutifully that it was the best possible way for him to go, that it would have been far more dreadful if he had been ill, asked where he was now, and whether she would be able to see him. And then – having endured the rigours of a brief press conference and witnessing the arrest of a totally silent, oddly still Louise – slept all the way back to London, curled up on the back seat beside Minty, holding her small hand.

When they got back to the house the tumultous demands of the twins held back any emotions she might have experienced. There was also the gauntlet to be run of a handful of journalists on the doorstep; Tom told them to go away, that they'd said all they were going to that morning in Cornwall, but they were reluctant to accept that, had to be pushed aside while they carried Minty in and the flashbulbs went. That was quite distressing. Octavia sat with all three children in the kitchen, while Minty ate an enormous lunch of fishfingers and peas and sweetcorn in between submitting to the interminable embraces of her brother and sister. They seemed unable to stop touching her, hugging her, kissing her, holding her hands, arguing about who would have her on their lap first when she had finished, where they might go with her that afternoon, what she would like to do. In between arguing and hugging Octavia, they questioned her about how she had found her, how she had known where to go, what Louise had done and said.

Octavia started to tell them that Louise had been very upset, that she shouldn't really be blamed too much for taking Minty, and the twins virtually attacked her, saying that of course she should be blamed, they were always being told that being upset was no excuse for behaving badly, that she should be sent to prison in case she tried to do it again.

'But, Poppy,' said Octavia carefully, 'she's – not well. You know her own baby died, poor little Juliet, she's never really got over that, it's all very complicated.'

'Just because she lost her baby doesn't make it all right for her to take ours,' said Poppy. 'You're too nice, Mummy, that's your trouble.'

'Not really,' said Octavia. 'She was my best friend for an awfully long time, you know. I can't forget that.'

'Mum, she kidnapped Minty,' said Gideon, his face very reproachful. 'That's an awful thing to do to your best friend. That's a crime.'

'But she didn't exactly kidnap her,' said Octavia, 'and it wasn't quite a crime. Just – well, almost one.'

'Well, I think it was a proper one,' said Gideon.

'So do I,' said Poppy.

It was so remarkable to find them agreeing on anything, Octavia wearily decided to leave it at that.

'There's something else you have to know, I'm afraid,' she said, and sat with an arm round each of them as she told them about their grandfather.

Tom drove her to the house in Hampstead; she had asked that her father should be taken there.

'Do you want me to come with you?' he said, as she stood at the bottom of the stairs looking up to the first floor, and the room where Felix lay.

'No. No, thank you. I'd rather be on my own.'

'Of course.'

She stood there, looking at him, this man whom she had loved more than anyone in the world for much more than half her life, this man who had made her what she was, for better and for worse, and the pain began. It was so fierce that she thought she simply couldn't bear it, had to bite her fist to stop herself crying out. All the clichés she had heard and read, that it wasn't really the person any more, that what you saw was simply a shell, seemed to her to be so much nonsense; it was her father who lay there, her brilliant, loving, inspiring, demanding, wonderfully imperfect father. Only he was powerless, helpless, unable to be brilliant or loving or demanding any more, because he was dead. He was gone, lost to her, and she could never have him back. Never go to him for advice again, never argue with him, listen to music with him, enjoy meals with him, walk with him, tease him. Never hear his voice lift with pleasure when she invited him to the house, never enjoy his admiration, laugh at his fussing; it was over, he was over, lost to her for ever, and she had never even said goodbye.

The last conversation they had had was the night before the charity day; he had phoned to wish her good luck, to say he wished he could be there with her, but it really wasn't his sort of thing. She knew that wasn't actually the reason: or not the whole reason. There were to be too many uncomfortable elements for him in that day, preventing him from going: Tom, Nico Cadogan, Marianne. She hated them all, fiercely, for doing that, for keeping Felix from her when he needed her most, hated especially Marianne for being the person who had been allowed to be with him, who had held his hand, soothed him, talked to him.

She could remember her last words: ''Bye Daddy,' she had said, 'see you very soon,' had been deliberately vague, avoided designating a day in the week ahead, as she knew he had wanted to do. 'Goodbye darling,' he had said, 'and I do hope it all goes wonderfully well. Now do get to bed early, it'll be a long exhausting day for you,' and 'Don't fuss, Daddy,' she had said, laughing, and put the phone down. 'Don't fuss.' Those were the last words, the very last words he had had from her to carry with him to eternity: not 'Thank you for everything,' or 'Now you take care of yourself,' or even 'I love you.'

Just 'Don't fuss.'

'I'm sorry,' she said aloud, her voice thick with tears, 'and I do love you so very much.' And then she bent and kissed his cold forehead and said, 'Goodbye,' and half ran out of the room, so full of anger and wretchedness she quite literally did not know where she was.

She spent the evening on the phone, notifying people, forming plans for the funeral; she felt feverish now, full of energy, sleep seemed a remote possibility. She refused the meal Tom offered her, managed to read to the twins, to put Minty to bed, but she felt all the time so far removed from reality, it was as if she was watching herself in a film or a play. After a while people began to ring her, people who had heard the news, who wanted to offer their sympathy; she took the calls mechanically, listened to the platitudes, mouthed her own in return.

Some time after midnight, Tom came in: 'Come to bed,' he said.

'I can't,' she said. 'I can't possibly come to bed. What would be the point? I couldn't sleep.'

'I thought perhaps we could talk about – well, about your father,' he said rather helplessly and then stopped.

'Tom,' she said, 'you're the last person I'd want to talk to about my father. Now please go away and leave me alone.'

She felt most angry with him: him and Marianne of course. The rush of emotion she had experienced when she saw him in the caravan – the relief, the warmth, the astonishment that he could work such a miracle, be there, appear from nowhere when she needed him so much – had faded already; he had become again the person she could not trust, did not need – and the person who had come between her father and her. Until she had met Tom, she thought that night, increasingly wretched, increasingly remorseful, Felix and she had been together, perfectly happy, all the world to one another; Tom it was who had come between them, Tom who had driven them apart.

Had the marriage worked, had Tom still loved her, it might have been justified; but Tom had proved faithless and worthless and the whole thing in vain. Her father had been right; she should have listened to him, stayed with him, stayed safe, stayed properly loved.

She went to work next day; she felt she had to. She had meetings later with the priest, with the undertakers, solicitors, all the dreadful compulsory ritual that follows a death. But for the morning at least she could pretend life was normal; could smile and talk and pretend things were the same.

Melanie, recognising this, recognising the therapy she was providing, piled her desk with memos, reports, accounts, to be read, studied, made out; nothing difficult, nothing dangerous, nothing that exposed her to a press that only wanted to know about her baby being kidnapped by her best friend.

Sarah Jane, magnificently, fought them off, lying, denying, confusing them. 'It's all right,' she said when Octavia wearily thanked her at the end of the morning, 'they'll get bored with it soon.'

Sandy phoned, awkwardly inarticulate, saying how sorry he was; she thanked him, asked about Dickon.

'He's pretty upset. But Charles is here, that's helping a bit.'

'And Louise?'

'She's all right,' said Sandy briefly. 'They – well, she was sent to Holloway, to the hospital wing. But probably she can go back to the Cloisters on bail.'

'Poor Louise,' said Octavia, and meant it.

Gabriel phoned too; to say he was sorry about her father, to ask after Minty. She thanked him, rather formally, could find nothing else to say to him. He had assumed an oddly unreal quality; it seemed impossible now to believe she had known him at all, let alone slept with him, laughed with him, quarrelled with him, imagined herself, albeit briefly, to be in love with him, all so recently ago.

Marianne phoned, several times; Octavia refused to speak to her. She couldn't bear the thought even of being in the same room as her: Marianne who had been where she should have been, said the things she should have said, stolen her father's last hours from her. She knew it was absurd, illogical, hysterical, but she shouldn't help it; she could no more have smiled at Marianne, listened politely to anything she had to say, than danced on her father's grave.

Tom, too, she could not speak to; as with Marianne, his patience, his refusal to take any kind of offence made her more angry, more outraged, not less. Finally, just as she was leaving the office to go up to Hampstead, he got through on her direct line.

'Tom,' she said, 'Tom, will you please, please just leave me alone.'

'What about this evening, what do you want me to do?'

'I don't want you to do anything. I just want you to go away,' she said. 'It's all over, Tom, nothing's changed.'

'Octavia—'

'Tom, I know you were wonderful over Minty. I know you mean well now. But I don't want to be with you any more. Don't you understand? Is it really so difficult?'

'No, not really, I suppose,' he said and rang off without another word.

She arrived home at half past five, early enough to bath Minty, play with her, put her to bed. Minty seemed totally unaffected by her ordeal, indeed was exceptionally cheerful. Her tooth had come through, her appetite was enormous and she was embarking on what was clearly destined to be crawling, creeping on her stomach, with some rather intensive help from the twins, who were each holding one hand and one plump ankle and half pushing, half pulling her along. Usually she would have been screaming indignantly; tonight she was giggling and trying to co-operate.

'It's as if she knows how fortunate she is to be safely home,' said Caroline, smiling down at them indulgently. Relief and remorse had transformed her rather brusque, touchy personality into something rather softer and almost sentimental; Octavia felt it unlikely it would last.

'Yes, well, maybe she does. Has she been all right today?'

'Perfectly all right. Really. You wouldn't think anything had ever happened to her. Oh, now before I forget, Mr Fleming phoned. He's going to be very late, he said to tell you, probably not back until well after midnight. Dinner with a client, at the Savoy, I think. Yes, the Savoy.'

'Fine,' said Octavia briskly, and wondered why, when Tom was doing exactly what she had asked him to do, she should feel so bleak and bereft at the prospect of spending the evening all alone.

'And Mr Cadogan phoned, wants to speak to you.'

'Well, I don't want to speak to him,' said Octavia.

Nico rang again: at about seven thirty, while the twins were having their supper. Poppy answered the phone before Octavia could stop her. 'Yes, she's here, just hold on, will you?'

Cursing, Octavia took the phone.

'Octavia? Nico Cadogan. I'm so sorry about your father.'

'Thank you,' said Octavia.

'You must be very – upset.'

'I am, yes, Nico, as a matter of fact.'

Surely he must hear the hostility in her voice. He didn't appear to.

'Look, I know Marianne wants to talk to you. I also know you're avoiding her for some reason.'

Octavia suddenly felt very angry. And oddly brave. It was as if the anger in its white heat had burned out her careful self-control, set her free to say and do what she wanted.

'I wouldn't say I was avoiding her, Nico. I simply don't want to talk to her.'

'That's all right,' said Nico Cadogan calmly, 'you don't have to say a word. Just listen. She has something very important to tell you, apparently. I have no idea what it is, because she won't tell me. But it's to do with your father.'

'I don't want to talk to Marianne about my father,' said Octavia, 'and

I would be grateful, Nico, if you would stay out of this anyway. It's nothing to do with you. Absolutely nothing at all.'

'I'm afraid you're wrong there,' said Nico. 'It is something to do with me, because it's distressing Marianne considerably that you won't speak to her. And that, in turn, distresses me.'

'I'm afraid I don't care very much if either of you is distressed,' said Octavia. 'I don't see you have anything much to be distressed about. Actually. I mean, I've just lost my father. For ever. And I didn't even get to say goodbye to him. Marianne, on the other hand, spent a great deal of the day saying goodbye to him. And all the other things that one wants to say on such an occasion. Clearing up misunderstandings, righting wrongs. Lucky her. No distress due for her, as far as I can see.'

'Octavia—'

'And if you hadn't had an affair with Marianne, Nico, if you hadn't persuaded her away from my father, then he would probably have been with us yesterday. Have you thought of that?'

'Yes, actually, I have,' said Nico Cadogan quietly. 'And that is one reason why I do feel distressed.'

'Well, how very unfortunate. Were you coerced into your relationship with Marianne? Was it somehow rather less voluntary than I had imagined?'

There was no reply. Octavia suddenly realised the twins were standing at the door to the study, listening to her conversation, goggled eyed.

'Look,' she said, 'I have to go now. Please tell Marianne I really don't want to have any kind of communication with her. About my father or indeed anything else. Goodbye, Mr Cadogan.'

She was rather pleased with that 'Mr Cadogan'. Childishly pleased. She put the phone down feeling much better altogether. For about five minutes. Then she found herself crying helplessly again and little Poppy sitting with her arm round her, saying, 'Poor Mummy, I was thinking about you today, you're an orphan now, aren't you?'

'Well, you must be feeling pretty good,' said Bob Macintosh, raising his glass to Tom. They were sitting in the River Room at the Savoy, by the window; outside, hundreds, thousands of lights reflected in the water broke up the darkness. Normally Tom loved that view, the graceful timeless shape of the river studded with all the uncompromising, contradictory styles of the buildings; the curving dome of the Festival Hall, the stark hump of the National Theatre, the tall, fairgroundy Oxo Tower. Tonight the whole thing seemed pointless, not worth looking at; he might have been underground for all he cared. He would rather be underground. Several feet.

He looked at Bob. 'Sorry?'

'I said you must be feeling pretty good. About things.'

'Well – yes. Yes, in a way,' he said carefully. He had given up even trying to work out what or how he felt, so swiftly had relief and euphoria been replaced by hurt and confusion.

'How is Octavia?'

'Oh, pretty upset about her father, you know,' said Tom.

'Of course. Of course. She was very fond of him, wasn't she?'

'Very fond, yes. Very close.'

'Dreadful, both things happening on the same day. Anyway – at least the baby was safe. What a nightmare that must have been.'

'It was. Yes.'

'So – I should think you both need a good holiday, don't you? For all sorts of reasons. Got anything planned?'

'No,' said Tom. 'No, not really.'

Bob looked at him. 'Er – forgive me, but things are better between you two now, aren't they? I kind of got that impression. None of my business of course, but—'

'Of course it's your business, Bob,' said Tom. 'I seem to remember bending your ear with the sordid details for hours and hours only a very few weeks ago. Lying beside you right through the night, wasn't I?'

'Well, what are friends for? Anyway, it is all right now, is it, between the two of you?'

'No,' said Tom, 'no, as a matter of fact, Bob, it isn't. As a matter of fact, Octavia and I are – well, we've agreed to get a divorce. I'm afraid there really doesn't seem to be an alternative.'

'I've got to talk to her,' said Marianne, 'I've got to. It's so important. Nico, what am I going to do?'

'Maybe you could write to her,' said Nico.

Marianne stared at him. 'That's a very good idea. Why didn't I think of that? Only thing is, she might just tear it up.'

'She might not. It's worth a try. It's as good as you're going to get at the moment anyway.'

'Yes,' said Marianne, 'yes, you're right. I'll give it a try. Nico, what would I do without you?'

'For the time being at least, my darling, you're not going to find out.'

She smiled at him rather weakly. She couldn't think how she would have got through the past twenty-four hours without him. It was extraordinary.

Octavia had just come downstairs after watching the first half-hour of *Aladdin* with the twins, when there was a ring at the doorbell. Damn.

Couldn't be the press, the last journalist had left that morning, having finally been persuaded by Tom that there was no more story, no point in staying. Maybe it was one of those wretched young people trying to persuade her to buy a bunch of dusters for some monstrous amount of money. She always found it very hard to refuse, tried to imagine how she would feel in ten years' time, if Gideon had run away from home and was living on the streets, and some rich bitch refused so much as to listen to his sales pitch. She had a vast collection of the dusters, which were all thin and useless, and the tea towels, which shrank hopelessly when you washed them.

She peered through the stained glass of the door, trying to make out who it was. She couldn't see anyone; moved on, thank God.

The bell went again. Go on. You got Minty back, Octavia, surely you can spare a fiver. She opened the door.

'Look, I really don't—'

It wasn't a homeless teenager: it was one with several homes. It was Zoë.

'Don't turn me away, Octavia,' she said, 'please don't. Just because you're upset with Mum.'

'Zoë, if she's—'

'She hasn't sent me. I swear. She doesn't know I'm here. Nobody does.'

'So . . .'

'So I've come to ask you to see her. I can see how bad you must feel about her.'

'Can you?'

'Yes, of course,' said Zoë, sounding surprised that she should say such a thing. 'She was there with your dad when you should have been. God, I'd be upset.'

'I think you'd better come in,' said Octavia. She had felt as if she had been travelling through some foreign country where nobody understood a word she said ever since her father had died, and now here was Zoë, who seemed to be able to act as interpreter.

'Thanks,' said Zoë and followed her into the house.

Marianne was just beginning the third draft of her letter to Octavia when Zoë appeared in the doorway.

'Mum—'

'Oh, hallo, darling. I thought you'd gone out.'

'I did. But I'm back now. Anyway, I thought you might like to know—'

'Zoë, darling, not now. I'm terribly busy, I'm trying to do something very difficult.'

'But, Mum—'

'Zoë, please.'

'It's not Zoë who's here to bother you, Marianne. It's me,' said Octavia.

'I was just writing you a letter. Or rather, trying to,' said Marianne.

They were in the morning room, looking at each other warily over a jug of rather strong coffee that Zoë had brought in.

'Really?'

'Yes.'

'About my father?'

'Yes. Well, you wouldn't talk to me and . . .'

'I'm – sorry if I was rude,' said Octavia, with great difficulty. 'I've been feeling rather upset.'

'Octavia, it's all right. Of course you're upset. I think I understood. Not all of it, but – well, look. We don't want to get too embroiled in guilt and remorse. Either of us. The important thing is something your father said to me. When he – just before he died.'

'Oh, yes?' said Octavia politely. 'Do please tell me about it.' A casual visitor might have assumed she was inviting information about a holiday venue or a good place to buy a new hat.

'He said to tell you . . .'

'Yes?' She felt terrified. As terrified as when she had opened the caravan door, fearing for what she might find inside. As terrified as when she had watched the orange juice seeping into Anna's handkerchiefs. She cleared her throat, swallowed, took a sip of coffee, then wondered if it might have been mistake, if she was going to throw up. 'What did he want you to tell me, Marianne?'

That she had been a disappointment to him? That he was dying broken hearted because she hadn't been there? That he would never forgive her for marrying Tom?

'He said – well, he said to tell you that Tom loved you. Very very much.'

'I'm sorry?' said Octavia. She felt very hot and sick, and rather as if she might faint. 'What did you – did he say?'

'He said that Tom loved you. Very very much. Those were his exact words.'

'Oh. Oh, I see.'

She sat there, staring at Marianne, and the sickness and the faintness slowly passed. She waited, waited to discover that hearing those words was an aberration, a fantasy, a dream even; but that didn't happen. Everything seemed to be quite normal, quite real. Marianne continued to sit there, the coffee continued to be too strong, above their heads continued the subliminal thump of teenage music.

'Um – did he say anything else?' she said finally. 'About Tom, I mean?'

'No. Or you. He – well, he hadn't talked much at all. But – that was what mattered to him. In the end. That you should know that. You were his only thought, his only concern.'

'Yes, I see,' said Octavia again. So Marianne had not stolen him from her, he had remained hers. The knowledge was sweet, healing. 'Well – thank you, Marianne. Thank you for telling me. I – I don't quite know what to make of it.'

'No,' said Marianne. 'I can see that. Nor could I.'

'You *couldn't.* Does that mean you can now?'

'No. Not really. Of course. But it seemed to me that – something must have changed his mind. About Tom. Changed his view of him, that is. Something very radical indeed.'

'Yes. Yes, I suppose so. And you – you couldn't have any idea? I certainly don't.'

'No. But you see how important it was. That you knew.'

'Yes.' Yes, of course. It changes a few things. I mean, until – until very recently, he regarded Tom as the devil incarnate. Always did. He was so jealous of him, you see.'

'Yes, said Marianne with a shadow of a smile, 'I think I realised that.'

'And with the business about – you know – Louise – he could scarcely even bear to think about him. He did actually hate him. He thought he was the most disastrous thing that could ever have happened to me. He was hell bent on ruining him. In every possible way. Especially my view of him.'

'I do know. I knew your father fairly well.'

'Yes, of course you did.' She looked at her awkwardly. 'Marianne, I do realise he took a lot of his – distress over Tom and me out on you.'

'Now who on earth told you that? If it was Zoë—'

'It wasn't Zoë,' said Octavia smoothly. 'Or Nico, if that's what you thought. It's fairly obvious to me. Nobody knew Daddy better than I did. He could be – difficult.'

'Just a little,' said Marianne. Her eyes, suddenly brilliant, met Octavia's; her mouth curved upwards in a half smile.

Octavia smiled back at her. 'I'm so sorry,' she said, 'sorry I was so hostile. I'm sure you had a lot to put up with. For a long time.'

'I did,' said Marianne with a sigh, 'but I loved him. For a long time. Well, until he died.'

'So – Nico?'

'Nico comforted me. Distracted me. To an extent, I think I was in love with him.' She smiled. 'Still am. But I did still feel I belonged with your father. I couldn't quite break away from him. Even though in the end didn't make me at all happy. Wasn't what I needed, any more. Or even wanted.'

'I felt much the same at times,' said Octavia and managed to smile. 'But he did inspire – great love.'

'He did indeed. Great love.'

They were both silent; remembering the love, the difficult, demanding love. And both freed from it now, recognising it was time to move on, move away.

'Marianne,' said Octavia after a while, 'what do you think Tom could possibly have done, what could have changed Daddy's mind about him to that extent?'

'I don't know,' said Marianne, 'but whatever it was, it must have been pretty astounding.'

'Well, I'd better try and find out,' said Octavia. 'If you'll excuse me, Marianne, I have a hot date at the Savoy Hotel.'

'Tom! Hallo! It's the hero of the hour. I saw you on telly. How do you manage to look so handsome, even after twenty-four hours or something on a cross-country chase?'

It was Lauren; she was holding Drew's arm, smiling down at them. She was wearing a scarlet crêpe trouser suit. It beamed, briefly, through the fog of depression that was enveloping Tom.

'Hallo, Lauren, Drew,' he said, 'just a natural facility, I suppose. I'm being signed up by *GQ* any minute now. I don't know if you've met Bob Macintosh, client of mine. Bob, Lauren and Drew Bartlett. Old friends.'

Lauren smiled briefly at Bob, clearly not perceiving him as worth any more attention. 'Where's Octavia?' she said.

'Oh – at home. She's feeling pretty done in. And wants to be with Minty.'

'Yes. Yes, of course. How is Minty? Quite recovered?'

'If she could talk,' said Tom, 'she's say recovered from what? I honestly think she enjoyed the whole thing.'

'Good for her. Obviously a chip off the old block. Look, what are you two doing now? We're off to Annabel's with some chums. Why don't you join us?'

'Oh, no, I don't—' Tom stopped. What was the point of going home, re-enveloped in his fog, to be greeted by Octavia's hostility? If indeed she greeted him at all. He might as well go to Annabel's with the Bartletts. It might just cheer him up.

'I think that would be rather nice,' he said.

'Good. And you, Bob?'

'Oh – not me,' said Bob Macintosh. 'Got an early start. Thanks all the same.'

'Bob!' said Tom. He felt he needed a partner in this piece of unsuitable behaviour. 'Go on. You'll enjoy it. You know how much you liked it there last time we took you and Maureen.'

He hesitated. 'Oh, all right. Why not? Just for an hour or so.'

'Great,' said Lauren. 'We're meeting our friends in the foyer, they're staying here. See you there in five minutes? I just have to powder my nose.'

She gave Tom a dazzling smile and left the restaurant; the men slowly followed her.

Octavia sat in the taxi en route to the Savoy; she still felt very odd. Her father's concession – the equivalent, surely, of a deathbed confession – had shifted the whole world on its axis and her own position in it. She could now see things that before she had been unable to see, consider things that before she would not have considered. Whatever it was that Tom had done or said must have been of a quite extraordinary magnitude. Not only to have changed her father's opinion of him – that was perhaps just imaginable – but to have persuaded him to admit it, and more unimaginably still, to insist that she knew it. It was a humbling, a recognition and admission of his bad judgment that probably nothing but death could have forced from him. Contemplating that humbling, Octavia felt not just astonished, but awed. It was as if – she tried to think of an analogy, but couldn't. The nearest was that Darwin had said sorry, got it all wrong, as you were, everything began in the Garden of Eden after all. That extraordinary, that prodigious, that far beyond not just belief but reason.

The thought made her smile in its absurdity: but the fact remained, it had happened. Her father had recanted, repented, confessed; and it was she who could obtain absolution. Absolution from humiliation, wretchedness, hostility: so that at worst she could stop hating Tom, at best admit that she might still love him . . .

'Traffic's terrible, love,' said the cab driver, as they turned into Birdcage Walk, 'don't know why. They've been clearing up the flowers, round the Palace, you know, maybe that's got something to do with it. I'll have to go round the other way, along up Piccadilly. That all right?'

'Oh – yes,' said Octavia, coming back to reality from Charles Darwin and her marriage with difficulty, 'yes, of course. Whatever you think.'

'Right,' said Lauren. 'Here we are. I look a bit more human now, I think. Tom, why don't you and Bob come in one cab with me, and Drew, you take Marcia and David in another. How's that?'

'Look,' said Bob. He was clearly becoming increasingly unhappy about the prospective outing. 'Look, I think I won't come after all. If you don't mind.'

'Oh, what a shame,' said Lauren. She didn't look too deeply disappointed. 'Can we give you a lift anywhere?'

'No, no, I'll walk, thanks. Clear my head. Tom, I'll see you soon. Give my love to Octavia.'

'Well – if you're sure,' said Tom. 'I wish you would come. Look, I'll call you in the morning. About that press release.'

'Fine. Do that. Cheers, old man. 'Bye, Lauren, Drew. Nice to have met you.'

He set off through the Savoy courtyard; Tom watched him, wishing more than half-heartedly that he was going too. But it was too late now; Lauren had her arm firmly through his, was briefing the doorman to find two cabs.

'Not many about, madam. Some hold-up somewhere.'

'Oh, damn. Drew, I told you we should have brought the car.'

'So you did,' said Drew, smiling at her. I must remember that one, thought Tom, much better than arguing with a wife; and then remembered also that he would very shortly not have a wife at all, whether to argue with or not.

Lauren pressed herself up closer to him. 'I think autumn's beginning,' she said, 'there's quite a nip in the air. Drew, why don't you try and find a cab yourself, out in the Strand.'

'I'm sure the doorman knows what he's doing,' said Drew.

'That's better,' said the cab driver. 'We can just nip down here, down Chandos Place, and Bob's your uncle.'

'Good,' said Octavia absently. 'I'm glad about that.'

She was suddenly aware that she had no make-up on, that she had been crying earlier and her mascara was probably smudged, that her trousers had had egg deposited on them by Minty at teatime, and her silk shirt was extremely crumpled. She didn't even have a comb, she realised, rummaging in her bag; damn. Well, never mind. Within the space of forty-eight hours she had recovered her baby from kidnapping, her father metaphorically at least from the dead, and she was possibly about to reclaim her husband from the divorce lawyers. On a scale of one to ten, and within that framework, a slightly ruffled hairdo and a pair of dirty trousers probably rated about a nought point one.

'Here's one cab,' said Lauren. 'Drew, you three take that one, get us a decent table, we never seem to have one worth sitting at. Go on, off you go.'

'Right,' said Drew.

The taxi pulled out of the courtyard; Lauren pulled Tom's arm round her shoulders. 'I'm really cold,' she said.

Tom stood there, half wishing to remove his arm, half enjoying the warmth of her, the raw rich smell, and thinking absently also that anyone coming into the courtyard now would find the sight of them fairly compromising. Not that it mattered. Not that it mattered in the very least.

And then, 'Oh, shit,' said Lauren. 'Shit, I've just realised I've left my scent behind in the ladies'. I'll have to get it, Tom, sorry. Won't be a second, hold the cab would you, if it comes?'

'Sure,' said Tom.

And thus it was, that as Octavia's cab pulled into the courtyard of the Savoy, she saw her husband standing there, all alone. She got out, threw a fiver at the driver, and walked over to Tom rather slowly.

'Hallo,' she said, 'I wondered if we could have a – a talk.'

'A talk?'

'Yes. If you – if you don't mind.'

'No. I don't mind.' His eyes were very brilliant as he looked down at her; he smiled. She smiled back: carefully, rather cautiously.

'I'm very glad I caught you,' she said, 'I've obviously made it just in time.'

'Only just,' said Tom.

EPILOGUE

Pattie David was giving a party. It was to celebrate the final withdrawal of Bartles House, and consequently the wood, from the shadow of the developers, and she had called it, rather wittily she thought, a Batty Party.

It was to be at lunchtime in her garden – a slightly brave idea, as the Indian summer just might not hold, although if it started to rain or became really cold, they could of course move inside. She and Megan, and Meg Browning and Mrs Johnston, had not only worked very hard, making sandwiches and vol-au-vents and quiches and marinating chicken pieces and baking cheese straws, they had also all, unbeknown to one another, prayed quite earnestly for a fine day. Their prayers so far had been answered.

'I'm so looking forward to seeing Dickon,' said Megan, looking up from her tub of margarine and pile of cut-off crusts, wiping her fair hair out of her face, 'and I bet you're looking forward to seeing Sandy. Aren't you, Mum?'

'Well – yes, of course I am,' said Pattie primly. 'He's become a very good friend.'

She hoped she wasn't blushing too much. She had felt very nervous about ringing Sandy, after his wife had gone home to him, and then all the dreadful business with Octavia's baby; she had even consulted Octavia about it. Octavia had said briskly that she knew Sandy would love to come, and that the last time she'd seen Dickon he'd talked almost nonstop about Megan and what he called the Bat House. 'They both need a bit of fun. And in any case, the house would probably be bulldozed down by now, if Sandy hadn't known about the bats. He should be guest of honour. Of course you must ask them.'

And Sandy had indeed sounded not just pleased, but delighted, had offered to come early to help get things ready, set out garden chairs, light the barbecue if that was what she had in mind. Pattie had said it would be lovely if he came early, even if he didn't help, and then fearing that might sound forward, said hastily that Megan was pining for Dickon.

Sandy said he'd be there by eleven at the very latest.

Lucilla Sanderson was up early; it took her a long time to get ready these days and she wanted to look at her very best for the party. She was going to wear – it being such a lovely day – the blue and white silk afternoon dress that had last had an outing when she and her husband had gone to a garden party at Buckingham Palace. That and the hat she had also worn that day, a wide-brimmed navy straw – and her new Jaeger jacket in case it got colder – and she'd be ready for anything. Nora Greenly, who was also coming, along with a couple of the other old people, had appeared in the room wearing a dreadful shapeless old cardigan and skirt and said would that do. Lucilla had told her she supposed it would; she decided afterwards it was quite a relief, as Nora dressed up looked rather – well, rather common. There was no other word for it. She also tended to wear a too-bright lipstick, which was never put on quite straight, her eyesight being so very poor, and then got smudged all over the place when she ate. So on the whole the shapeless clothes would be best.

The Fords were leaving Bartles House in a couple of weeks, but the new matron and her husband, Mr and Mrs Duncan, a lovely couple who had run a nursing home in Scotland, had come to spend the day at the nursing home the previous Sunday and had said they might pop in after lunch for an hour or so, if they would be welcome. Lucilla said she knew they would be most welcome and told them they would be able to meet the local MP, who would be there.

'He's very charming and clearly went to a decent school, you'd never dream he was a Socialist.'

Gabriel had phoned Capital C to check how Octavia felt about his being there: she said she'd love to see him and that of course he must come. 'And anyway, Gideon is dying to see you again.'

'And – Mr Fleming?'

'Mr Fleming won't be there. That's because – well, Sandy, Louise's husband, he'll be there. Not an entirely easy situation, so Tom's staying at home. And besides, the wood is still a slightly fraught subject. In our lives. Professionally, I mean.' She hesitated, then said, 'He's going to the cottage and we're joining him there. At the end of the day.'

Gabriel said he was delighted to hear things had improved so radically between them that they were going anywhere together, even to something so socially undesirable as a second home.

Later that day, he decided to phone her and tease her about what he should wear: she was out. Melanie spoke to him.

'Angel Gabriel, how nice. How are you? Can I help?'

'Oh – not really. I was just going to ask Octavia what I should wear to this party.'

'Wear! Does it matter?'

'No, of course not. It's a kind of an in-joke.'

'I should think just your robe and wings,' said Melanie.

'Fine. Will you be there?'

'I was thinking of going, yes. No right to an invitation really, except the whole thing's caused me a lot of grief, but . . .'

'Oh, please come,' said Gabriel. The thought of Melanie, with her rather wild beauty, her raw sense of humour, at what might he feared might be a rather prissy occasion, appealed to him.

'Well – okay. I'll come 'Bye for now.'

'Goodbye,' said Gabriel. The idea of the party had suddenly become more attractive.

Charles had been asked to the party, but had refused.

'I've no right to be there, didn't do anything to help and I won't know anyone.'

'You'll know us,' said Dickon, 'and you can meet Megan. And Pattie. She's very nice.'

'Please, do come, Charles,' said Sandy.

Charles looked at them both, Dickon more cheerful and talkative than he'd been for weeks, Sandy clearly anxious for his moral support, contemplated yet another lonely Saturday, alone with his remorse over Louise and memories of Anna, and agreed rather reluctantly that he would. 'But I'll come under my own steam. Then I won't cramp your style if I want to leave early.'

'You won't,' said Dickon. 'We never want to leave there, do we, Daddy?'

'Octavia going?' said Charles casually.

'Oh – yes. With the children. But not Tom,' said Sandy.

'I see.'

They looked at each other and smiled briefly: two self-contained men, unable to say much of what they would like, and especially about the sad, dreadful ghost so uncompromisingly part of both their lives, for whom they each felt so responsible. It said much for both of them that they were still able to feel such affection for one another.

Neither of them noticed that Dickon had left the room rather suddenly.

*

Marianne would not have gone to the party, having no connection whatever with Bartles House, but it so happened that she and Nico were going to look at a house near Bath that very day – not really the coincidence it appeared, as she said to Octavia, they spent their entire weekends in the West Country at the moment looking at houses – and when Octavia heard about it, she said why didn't they drop in at the party for a cup of tea or something.

'Melanie was saying only the other day how much she'd like to see you again, and Gabriel, you know, my – well, my friend, the Socialist MP, will be there, and I'd just love to set Nico on him.'

Marianne said they just might come, if the day went well and the house was nice, if it wasn't, Nico would be in such a bad temper she wouldn't want him set on anyone. Octavia said she couldn't imagine Nico in a bad temper and left it at that.

Marianne was sweetly, serenely surprised by the ease with which she had resumed her relationship with Nico. Or rather embarked on a new one: easier, unshadowed by guilt or remorse. What she felt for Nico bore no relation to what she had felt for Felix; but it was no less valuable, it lacked nothing in quality. It seemed sad to her at times, even shocking, that only Felix's death could have enabled her properly to love Nico; but that was what had happened and she was intensely and happily grateful for it. Grateful, too, that in his pragmatic way, he seemed to have no problem with it either; did not appear to feel second best, second choice. She had tried to explain that was anyway not how she saw him, that his place in her life was simply different from what it had been before, that she herself was different now.

'It's all right,' he said, 'I understand. I'm extraordinarily well adjusted. As you must agree.'

Marianne said she did agree.

Zoë put her head round the door. 'Have a good day, Mum. Give my love to Nico.'

'I will.'

'He's so cool. You ought to marry him, you know.'

'Zoë,' said Marianne, 'I don't think I want to marry anyone. Ever. Not even Nico.' It was true, in spite of her happiness she shied away from the thought of real commitment. It was much too soon; it felt disloyal.

''Course you do. You'll be all alone here, soon. I'll be in Oz, Marc back at Harvard, Rom'll be going away to do her A-levels, then you'll be sorry.'

'That's no reason to marry someone. Just to avoid a bit of loneliness,' said Marianne briskly.

'It's a very good reason, I think,' said Zoë, 'specially if the person's handsome and nice. And rich. I think you're mad, Mum, I really do. Well, see you tonight.'

'See you tonight,' said Marianne.

Nico arrived, in high spirits. 'I've bought a picnic from Fortnum's – I thought it would make a change. We can eat in the garden of the house. Look: isn't it lovely?'

It was indeed stunning; Queen Anne, a small, perfect jewel, set in what she could see, even if the agent's blurb had not informed her of the fact, were the most glorious grounds, the gardens landscaped by a pupil of Capability Brown, and even a small lake.

'Imagine yourself mistress of that, my darling. How can you refuse?'

Marianne said nothing, just smiled nervously.

Octavia was late; driving too fast, as usual, down the M4. Minty was asleep, the twins arguing about who had seen the wood first the first day they had gone there. It was naughty of her to be late; Pattie was relying on her to make a little speech. She knew why she was late; she hadn't got up early enough. Or rather, she had got up early enough, of course, had the whole day planned with clockwork precision: a careful countdown planned backwards from ten thirty when they had to leave. This being Saturday morning, and the traffic undoubtedly bad. But then as she'd stood sleepily by the bathroom mirror, looking at herself, thinking her hair needed cutting, Tom had appeared behind her, smiling at her in it, the slightly lopsided, rueful smile that meant – well, that meant she was probably going to have to go back to bed. That she was definitely going to have to go back to bed. A few months earlier, she wouldn't have done, would have clung stubbornly to her schedule; now, falling just slightly painfully back into love, easing into her just slightly less controlled and controlling self, she could see what she must do. What she wanted to do, indeed; and had proceeded to do it. Very enthusiastically. And rather slowly and sweetly. And now she was an hour late. It was terrible. So unlike her. But then: all other things being equal, did it really matter? She caught sight of herself in the rearview mirror as she checked for the police; she was still tanned, she looked relaxed and well. No, it didn't. It just didn't matter.

Megan was worried about Dickon. He didn't seem quite himself. She knew he'd had a horrid time, but he was very quiet, rather jumpy, seemed less pleased to see her than she'd expected, and clinging to his father's side, instead of rushing over to her, clambering on to her lap in her wheelchair. She'd twice tried to find out if there was anything the matter, and both times he'd hurried off as if he was frightened of something. Oh, well. Maybe he was feeling shy with all the extra people here. He'd probably come out of himself later, as Mrs Johnston would say. She decided to stop worrying about him, and just enjoy herself. She hadn't been to many parties.

The party seemed to be going well. Pattie looked across her garden – Sandy had actually come early enough to strim the grass round the flowerbeds, something she never got around to usually – thinking how lovely it looked, how nice to see it full of people, resolving to entertain more in future. There was no excuse not to, really, now that Megan was older; it was just always so difficult to do it on your own, to see to things like pouring the wine and working out the table plan when you also had to make the last-minute preparations to the food and serve it up. That was why it was so marvellous having Sandy here; he was moving round constantly topping up people's glasses – topping them up rather too often, perhaps, the wine was going to run out at this rate, she wasn't used to calculating these things and people seemed to drink more than she remembered.

'Hallo,' he said, smiling at her, waving the bottle he was holding. 'Can I give you a little more?'

'Oh – no, thank you. Sandy – is Dickon all right? He seems very quiet.'

'He's fine, aren't you, old chap?' said Sandy, looking down at Dickon, who had reappeared and was clinging on to his hand. 'Just a bit tired, I expect. He said he felt sick in the car coming over.'

'Well, hopefully he'll feel better later. Sandy, I think we might be in danger of running out of wine. I wonder if we ought to get a bit more in, if you'd mind popping down to the off-licence.'

'I'll pop to the shed,' he said, 'how's that? I hope you don't mind, but I brought a case of white and a case of red with me, put them in there. Forgot to mention it in the excitement of doing the strimming. The white's in a chill-bin, shouldn't be too bad.'

'You shouldn't have done that,' she said, blushing. 'I feel embarrassed now, you must let me—'

'I wouldn't let you do anything, if you mean pay for it. It's my business, remember? The mark-up's outrageous. Whole twenty-four bottles cost me less than a couple of beers.'

Pattie felt sure that wasn't quite true, but decided it would be bad form to pursue the matter. 'Thank you very much. You're so kind,' she said. And then something came over her, probably too much of the wine, and she reached up and kissed Sandy gently on the cheek. He blushed, stood back quickly, tried to smile at her. Oh, God, she thought, horrified, now I've embarrassed him. He's obviously still in love with his wife, and he'll think I'm after him, like all those single women.

'Excuse me,' she said quickly and turned away, saw Meg Browning and hurried in her direction. She felt near to tears; the day for her quite ruined.

'It's the Angel Gabriel. Hi!' It was Melanie; looking marvellous, he thought, in a kind of long floating dress, and what looked like half a ton of silver jewellery round her neck and on her wrists, her wild hair held back from her face with a scarlet bandana.

'Hallo,' he said, 'how are you?'

'All the better for seeing you,' she said, with her wide grin. And then added under her breath, 'Have you ever see so many dreadful people?'

Gabriel said he had; many times, and told her she must lead a very sheltered life.

'But if we go over there, to the garden shed, there's a vast store of wine I've just discovered, and we can sit quietly and work our way through it. I'll grab a few of those sausages. Food's very good.'

'You could have fooled me,' said Melanie.

'Yes, well, we don't all spend our days at the Ritz. You should try a few nights on the rubber chicken circuit. I'll take you to a couple if you like.'

'No, thanks,' said Melanie with a shudder.

'Well?' said Nico. 'What do you think?'

'It's heavenly,' said Marianne. 'Quite heavenly.'

'Good. I'm glad you like it. Not too big, you don't feel?'

'Well . . .'

'Six bedrooms. Lot for one chap, I suppose.'

'Well – yes.'

'Still. That brings me to a certain matter. Marianne . . .'

Marianne felt a rush of pure panic. 'Nico—'

Octavia had made a very good speech, celebrating what she called 'the deliverance of a little bit of England', paying charming tribute to Megan, Pattie, and Sandy, 'who clearly knows more about bats than most of us would ever think to ask.'

Everyone clapped. Gabriel went over to congratulate her. 'If you ever think of going into politics, Mrs Fleming, I'll be delighted to sponsor you.'

'Thank you.'

'And I wore my hat specially for you, look.'

Octavia smiled at him. 'It looks much better here,' she said. '*You* look much better here altogether. You didn't suit Barbados. One of my many mistakes.'

'Not at all. I was an ungrateful swine. Anyway, you look great. Really very, very well.'

'Oh, God,' said Octavia, 'I know what that means, what it always means, people saying that.'

'What does it mean?'

'It means I've put on weight. Oh, God.'

'Well, it suits you,' said Gabriel, 'if you have. You look terrific. Doesn't she, Melanie?'

'All right, I suppose,' said Melanie, grinning. 'Yes, of course she does. Why don't you come and join us, Octavia? We're having our own little party, over there by the potting shed. Away from all the do-gooders. We've got our own hoard of food and everything.'

'No thanks,' said Octavia, 'I must stop eating immediately. I thought my trousers felt a bit tight this morning.'

'Oh, for God's sake shut up,' said Melanie. 'There are other sizes in the world beside ten, you know. Here, have a sausage roll. They're magic. Go on, Fleming. Let yourself go just for once.'

Octavia reached for a sausage roll and bit into it. 'I'm learning to,' she said very seriously. 'I think.'

'Hallo, Dickon,' said Poppy.

'Hallo,' said Dickon. He looked at her rather uncertainly, not returning her smile.

'It's nice to see you.'

He didn't answer.

'Are you all right?' she said.

'Yes,' he said, still not smiling. 'Yes, I'm all right.'

'Want to play cricket?'

'No. Not now.'

He turned his back on her and walked away. Poppy hesitated, then ran after him, grabbed his hand. 'Dickon, what's the matter?'

'Nothing,' he said, and shook her hand off, looked wildly round him, saw his grandfather, rushed over to him, clung to his legs.

Poppy looked after him thoughtfully, then went over to Megan. 'Do you know what's wrong with Dickon?'

'No. He's been funny with me, though. I tried to ask him and he wouldn't talk to me.'

'Nor me. I like that top,' she added, 'it's the same as Mel B wears. I wanted one but Mummy said I was too young.'

'They're like that, mothers,' said Megan with a sigh.

'How's Louise?' said Octavia to Charles.

'Oh – you know. She's had what they now call a complete breakdown. But I think she's in a much better place this time. That fellow at the Cloisters is a complete idiot, I've decided. I feel dreadful about it, insisting she went there, thinking I knew best. Quite dreadful.'

'Charles,' said Octavia gently, 'you must stop blaming yourself. We all must, actually. Louise was always—' she hesitated – 'very highly strung. My father always said so, and looking back, I can see we all missed the signs. And she had so much to bear. Impossibly much.'

'Do you really think so?'

'Yes, I do. And if I can see that, then it must be true,' she added with a quick, rather awkward smile.

'You're very generous,' said Charles, bending down impulsively to give her a kiss. 'Too generous, some would say. But you've made me feel better. Thank you, my dear. And may I say you're looking very much better yourself. Extremely well.'

'I'm really sorry, Charles,' said Octavia, 'but I don't want anyone else to tell me I look extremely well.'

Charles had actually been rather enjoying himself. He had had a very nice and interesting conversation with a rather beautiful old lady called Lucilla, who had spent most of her youth in India, and she had introduced him to Iris Duncan, the new matron of Bartles House. After another glass or two of the excellent wine, and a discussion on the charitable trust that the Duncans told him they had discovered in connection with Bartles House, Charles heard himself offering his services as professional fundraiser.

'That would be marvellous,' said Iris Duncan carefully, 'but I expect you'd want paying rather a lot of money, wouldn't you? I've had some rather unhappy dealings with professional fundraisers, not that I'm sure you're in the least like that.'

'No,' said Charles, 'I'm not. I'd do it for nothing. Really.'

'For nothing? Why should you do that?'

'Well,' he said carefully, looking across at Octavia who was chatting to Pattie David, 'let's say for – for love. Gratitude. That sort of thing.'

'That sounds wonderful,' said Iris Duncan, who was sensitive enough not to ask him what he meant, or to pursue the matter any further.

Dickon was standing behind a bush, eating a sausage roll and wondering why he had ever wanted to come today, when he heard someone calling him. Two people. Poppy and Megan. Two people he didn't want to talk to.

He ducked down, so they couldn't see him, turned towards the house – and found his way blocked by Megan's wheelchair. He turned to run; but Poppy's strong little arm shot out, stopped him.

'Leave me alone,' he said crossly.

'No,' said Poppy, 'not till you tell us what the matter is.'

'Nothing's the matter.'

'Well, come and play with us, then.'

'No, I don't want to.'

'Dickon,' said Megan gently, 'Dickon, come here.'

'No.'

'Dickon, please,' said Poppy.

Dickon looked from one to the other of them and burst into tears.

'Dickon, what is it?' said Poppy, alarmed.

He gulped, wiped his hand across his eyes. 'Aren't you cross with me?' he said to her.

'Why should I be cross with you?'

'Because – because Mummy stole Minty. That's – that's wrong.' His large dark eyes filled with tears.

Poppy hesitated, then she put her arms round him, gave him a hug. 'My mum said it wasn't wrong. And she didn't steal her. Not exactly.'

'Daddy said that, too. But she did, I know she did.'

'Well, she took her, yes. But it was because she was so upset. Sort of ill.'

'Don't say that,' said Dickon sharply, 'don't say she's ill.'

'But Dickon, she is. That's why—'

'She's not ill, she's not! She's all right, she's just gone away for a bit!' He pulled himself free, ran away again.

Megan looked at Poppy, made a face and propelled her wheelchair across the garden. 'Mum . . .'

'Yes, dear?'

'Where's Sandy?'

'I'm afraid I have no idea,' said Pattie slightly stiffly.

Megan sighed. The lovely day seemed to be going rather wrong.

'Right,' said Nico, 'you've had your lunch, which I hope you'll agree was excellent. Fortnum's did us proud.'

'They did,' said Marianne. She actually felt rather sick.

'Now, let's talk about the future. I have a proposition for you.'

'Nico—'

'Let me finish.'

'Nico, I can't . . .'

'Can't what?'

'I can't marry you.'

'I wasn't going to ask you to marry me,' he said.

'What?'

'Of course I wasn't. I'm not that insensitive. It's much too soon. I understand that.'

'Oh,' she said. 'Oh, yes, I see.' She felt odd, somehow disquieted. She didn't want it; she wasn't ready for it. But she felt just the same that something had been taken from her.

'Look at me,' he said.

She looked at him, smiled brightly, brilliantly.

'You're not – disappointed, are you?'

'No. No, of course not.' She felt foolish now, added to the rest. Tears, always near these days, rose to the back of her eyes.

'I've upset you,' he said. 'I'm sorry.'

She was silent. Felt to her horror a tear roll down her cheek. She brushed it irritably away.

'You're not crying, are you?' he said.

'Of course I'm not.' What was the matter with her? When she knew quite certainly that she didn't want to marry him. Wasn't prepared even to consider it.

'Look at me,' he said.

She didn't move.

'Look at me, Marianne.'

She raised her head. Reluctantly. Met his eyes. His brilliant, amused eyes. She felt more foolish still. He picked up her hand and kissed it, reached out and smudged the tear across her cheek with his hand.

'Let me try again,' he said. 'I love you, Marianne. Very much. As I've been telling you for months now. And I've been very patient, wouldn't you agree?'

'Yes,' she said, 'very patient. You've been wonderful, Nico, it's just that—'

'I know. I understand.'

'No, you don't.'

'Yes, I do. You don't want to get married – yet. Although it seems you do feel some kind of interest in the subject. Which encourages me. So could I express my quite extraordinary pragmatism and generosity, and ask you to become betrothed to me? Such a nice, old-fashioned word, don't you think? And rather more interesting and substantial than engaged. Of course if in five or ten years' time you feel ready to take things any further, we can discuss it then. How would that be? I've got a ring in the car, I think you'll like it.'

Marianne looked at him very seriously; then rather reluctantly smiled; and then finally she started to laugh. Her loud, rather hoydenish laugh.

'That would be absolutely wonderful,' she said. 'I accept. As long as it is only a betrothal.'

'Right!' Gabriel Bingham stood in the middle of the lawn, clapped his hands.. 'Who's for cricket?'

There was a roar of pleasure from the children, a slightly more muffled one from the adults, mixed with groans.

'Sorry. Compulsory,' said Gabriel. 'Two teams. I'll captain one. Gideon here will captain the other. Now, we may not have quite the full complement but . . .'

'Dickon,' said Poppy, 'Dickon, come on, we want you in our team.' She looked at him; he was hiding behind a bush again, he'd been crying. She put her arm around him. 'Dickon, please don't cry. Please. Look – oh, Pattie, hallo.'

'Hallo,' said Pattie. 'Dickon, what is it?'

'He's a bit upset,' said Poppy. 'I think you'd better . . .' Her voice tailed away.

'Of course,' said Pattie. 'Look, you go and get on with the game. I'll see you in a minute.' She sat down on the grass, took Dickon on her knee. 'Come on, sweetheart. Tell me what the matter is. Please?'

A few minutes later, Dickon rushed up to Gideon. 'Can I play in your team?'

'Yes. You can help Megan be wicketkeeper. Go on, quick, we're going to start.'

'What did you say to him?' Megan said to Poppy later.

'Nothing. It was your mum. She was brilliant.'

'She is brilliant,' said Megan, 'except when it comes to clothes.'

Lucilla looked on approvingly. This was really a very nice gathering. Charming people, well-behaved children, a genuine sense of community. And Mrs Duncan was a delight. The only flaw in the day had been Nora, who'd suddenly said she was hot and taken off her cardigan, to reveal a ghastly see-through nylon blouse that, she told Mrs Duncan proudly, had come from her catalogue. Still, Mrs Duncan's eyes and her own had met over Nora's head; she could see they were going to be allies. How very good life was going to be. And that charming Mr Madison, volunteering to help with fundraising . . . She realised that the other two guests from Bartles House were fast asleep in their chairs, both with their mouths hanging open. How very unattractive old people were at times. Maybe they should get back; she wasn't tired herself, but Mrs Spencer would be snoring in a minute, and she really couldn't face that. She signalled to Bert Brand, who had driven them to the party in the minibus, and was now hovering on the edge of the party.

'Time to go, Bert,' she said, and then turning to Charles, whom she had been regaling with a long story about how she had once danced the tango with Nehru at the Calcutta High Commissioner's residence, said, 'I'm afraid we shall have to go. Those poor old souls over there are clearly ready for their beds. They get so tired, you know.'

'I expect they do,' said Charles. He smiled at her. Pattie David had told him Lucilla was at least eighty-six, probably older. He loved old people and the living history they represented, never found them in the least boring. He was going to enjoy his new enterprise: enjoy it a lot.

'Marianne! How lovely! And Nico.' Octavia kissed them both. 'Come on in and have a drink.'

'We've both had much too much to drink already,' said Marianne. 'A cup of tea would be nice though.'

'Speak for yourself,' said Nico. 'A glass of nice chilled white wine would be delightful, Octavia.'

'I'll get it for you. It's so nice you came. How was the house?'

'Beautiful,' said Marianne, 'absolutely beautiful.'

'Glorious,' said Nico.

'Are you going to buy it, Nico?'

'I am indeed. You'll love it. I shall throw lots of parties in it, and you will always be guest of honour.'

Marianne took the cup of tea she was being offered, waved away a plate of sandwiches. Octavia stared at her left hand; at an extremely pretty sapphire and diamond deco ring on its third finger.

'Marianne,' said Octavia, 'you're not – well, are you – I mean . . .'

'She means are you going to marry me,' said Nico. 'I think.' He smiled at Octavia. 'No, she isn't.'

'Oh,' said Octavia. She flushed. 'Oh – I'm sorry. I feel awful now.'

'But are we betrothed,' said Nico. 'Officially betrothed. That is our new joint status. Does that make you feel better?'

'Much better,' said Octavia. She kissed them both. 'I don't quite understand, but I hope you'll be very happy. Betrothed.'

'I'm confident that we will,' said Nico Cadogan.

'I don't know how I'm going to get home,' said Melanie, 'I'm as drunk as a – a Lady.'

'I'll drive you home,' said Gabriel. 'I'm as sober as a judge.'

'You can't. I live in London.'

'I meant to my home. You can stay with me, pick your car up in the morning.'

'Angel Gabriel, are you trying to compromise me?'

'No, of course not. I have an extremely nice spare room. But I might say that any woman who can bowl a cricket ball like you do has an instant place in my heart.'

'You're on,' said Melanie. She leaned rather unsteadily on his arm as they made their way across the lawn to say goodbye to everyone. ''Bye, Fleming,' she said, kissing Octavia, rather feebly. 'The Angel Gabriel is taking me home with him. To his earthly residence, I trust.'

Octavia watched them go with amusement. As a match, it suddenly seemed rather suitable.

She called the twins, went to fetch Minty who was asleep in Pattie's old playpen in the corner of the garden.

''Bye, Pattie, it's been a lovely day. So lucky with the weather. Well done. What a success. Goodness, we're the last. I'm so sorry.'

'Don't be sorry,' said Pattie. 'I'm sorry it's over.' She went down to the gate, waved them off.

Dickon rushed after them, shouting, 'See you soon,' and then rushed back to Megan. They were working their way through the leftovers.

'He seems quite different,' said Sandy to Pattie. 'I saw you talking to him, whatever did you say?'

'Oh,' she said quickly, 'just cuddled him and talked to him for a bit. He's very afraid of people dying, isn't he? Thinks if they're ill, they're going to die.'

'Yes, I'm afraid so. He's observed that happening rather a lot lately. But what else can I say about – about Louise? It's better than he should think she's a criminal.'

'Of course. Anyway, I said – oh, it's all so silly. You don't want to hear.'

'Yes, I do. He was so upset earlier, I can't imagine how you could have done that.'

'Well, I said there was different sorts of illness. And that his mummy was ill in her mind, that nobody ever died of that. I hope that's all right. It seemed to – make sense to him.'

'I'm very grateful,' said Sandy. 'I hadn't thought of trying to explain that. It's quite a difficult concept. For someone of five.'

'I know. But I've always talked to Megan as if she was much older than she is. They do seem to be able to cope with it.'

'Yes. I can't thank you enough, Pattie, really.'

'Don't try,' she said quickly. There was a rather strained silence.

Then, 'Well, I'd better go and retrieve what's left of that wine,' said Sandy. 'Not a lot, I think: Gabriel Bingham and that partner of Octavia's were making huge inroads into it. Not to mention my father-in-law. I hope he'll get home safely.'

'He's gone back to Bartles House,' said Pattie. 'Lucilla's invited him to look at her Indian scrapbooks.'

'Oh, how nice,' said Sandy. 'Well, if you'll excuse me a moment, I'll just get the wine.'

Pattie suddenly felt very bleak. The lovely day was over: turned from warm Indian summer to chilly autumn. Clouds were filling the clear sky, a dramatic sunset heralded a stormy night. The party was over; and the house would now return to its quiet, half-empty self. No more campaign, no more Bartles House; she would miss it. Of course there was still Foothold, she'd been neglecting that lately, but—

'I'll give you a hand with the clearing up,' said Sandy.

'No, it's all right,' she said quickly. 'You have a long way to go.'

'But I'd like to,' he said.

'No, really. I'll do it in my own time. I wouldn't want to keep you.'

'You're not keeping me,' said Sandy. 'Well, not from anything important.'

She was silent. Then she said, 'You must let me know what I owe you for that wine.'

'Pattie, you don't owe me anything.'

'Of course I do. I can't accept that.'

'Well – Pattie, is anything the matter?'

'No. No, of course not. Why should there be?'

'You seem – upset.'

'I'm not in the least upset,' she said. 'Just a bit tired. Obviously.'

'Yes. Of course. Well, if you'd really rather I went . . .'

'I would. Yes. And thank you for all your help.'

'My pleasure.' He called Dickon. 'Come on. Time to go home.'

'Oh, Daddy. Megan wants us to stay for a bit.'

'Well, we can't,' said Sandy, 'it's getting late. Come on. Say goodbye to Megan and Pattie.'

'It isn't late, it isn't even dark.'

'No, but we want to get home before it's dark.'

'But why?'

'Come on, Dickon. 'Bye, Megan, 'bye, Pattie. See you soon.'

No suggestion they might meet again; no further conversation of any kind. The car disappeared down the lane. She'd been right; she must have embarrassed him dreadfully. He obviously couldn't wait to get away.

At that moment, the rain began: heavy, unrelenting, dashing down on the garden, the tables, filling the empty glasses, melting into the paper tablecloths. Sandwich crusts, crisps, half-eaten sausages floated dismally on plates; Pattie looked at it all and started to cry; sat down at the kitchen table and buried her head in her arms.

'Mum,' said Megan, easing her chair closer to her, putting her own arms round her, 'Mum, what is it? What's the matter? Please, don't cry . . . Oh, hallo, Sandy. I thought you'd gone.'

'We had,' said Sandy, 'but we couldn't let you try and clear up in this.' He looked at Pattie. She was turned away from him, blowing her nose.

Megan backed quietly out of the kitchen.

'What is it?' he said gently.

'Nothing. I . . .'

'Yes, there is something. Come on, tell me. I'm not going to give up until you do.'

'I'm – I'm sorry I embarrassed you earlier,' she said stiffly.

'Embarrassed me? What are you talking about?'

'When I – that is, when I . . .'

'When you kissed me, do you mean?'

'Yes,' said Pattie abruptly. 'Stupid of me. Too much wine.'

'In that case,' said Sandy gently, 'I'd like you to have some more. Immediately. I wasn't embarrassed, Pattie. I was overwhelmed. That's all. I've wanted to – well, to tell you how much I want to see more of you. For weeks. But with the circumstances . . . Oh, damn! now the children are coming back.'

Dickon and Megan came into the kitchen. Dickon went up to Pattie, gave her a hug. 'Next to my mummy, you're the loveliest lady in the world,' he said. 'Isn't she, Daddy?'

'Yes,' said Sandy firmly. 'Yes, she is.' His eyes met Pattie's. He grinned. 'Will that do for now?' he said.

'Yes,' she said, smiling back at him. 'Of course it will. For now and for a long, long time.'

Octavia drove very carefully and slowly towards the cottage. This had been one of the good days. They weren't all good; rather like someone convalescing from a long illness, there were times when she still felt dreadful. Still hurt, still bewildered, still afraid.

But it was getting better. And she knew it was going to go on getting better.

Tom had refused to tell her what it was. What he had done or said that had made her father change his mind so dramatically.

'Let's just say it impressed him,' he had said, 'which was not, I might say, the idea. Rather the reverse. Actually. But I'm not going to tell you. Ever.'

'But Tom, why not?'

'Because,' he had said, 'it would do none of us any good. Any good at all. And it would change your father's opinion again, if I did. He'd be back, like an avenging angel.'

'So – I just have to go on wondering,' she said.

'Yes, you do. But he was right. Absolutely right. I do—'

'Don't,' she had said gently, 'don't. Please. Not now.'

She wasn't ready for it yet: not to hear him say it. And it stood between them: a still-dark shadow.

She just couldn't let him say it. That he loved her. She didn't quite know why, she supposed she was afraid of it: that she would hear it and not believe it. But everything else was becoming all right.

She found it hard to explain, even to herself, how everything had changed for her; how her father's acceptance and forgiveness of Tom had made her own possible. But it had. If he could do it, from his position of fierce hatred, then so surely could she. He couldn't have been wrong, her father; he never was. Her trust in him, in death even as in life, was total; if he said Tom loved her, then Tom must love her. Whatever he had done.

She could accept it. And having accepted it, she could do other things. She could talk to him, smile at him, laugh when he was being funny. She had stood with him, holding his hand at her father's funeral, had wanted him there, had drawn strength from him.

She could make plans with him again, discuss work, the children, the house; they were all going on holiday, skiing, to Aspen at Christmas.

She could look at him across a room or a dinner table, and be pleased at how he was being charming and amusing, instead of angry and outraged, feel indulgently amused at the absurd attention he gave to his clothes, admire his business sense and skills, recognise how good a father he was.

And above all, she could see for herself now that Louise had indeed been mad, that Tom had been most horribly and swiftly trapped by that madness; and that although it would be a long time before she properly forgave him, the betrayal had not been as dreadful as at first it had seemed.

But she couldn't hear him saying he loved her. Not yet. And she couldn't tell him she loved him.

The rain was awful; flooding down.

The main roads were all right, although slippery after the long dry spell, but the side roads were flooding, mud sliding across them. She had the windscreen wipers going at double rate, the lights on full beam. Summer was certainly over now.

The twins were arguing about the cricket match, whether it had been fair: 'We got all the girls,' Gideon said sulkily.

'What's wrong with that? What about Melanie? She was *brilliant.*'

'She couldn't bat.'

'She could. Anyway, she could certainly bowl.'

'It's not batting.'

'I never said it was.'

'You did.'

'I didn't.'

'Twins,' said Octavia in exasperation, 'please, please stop it. It's difficult enough driving through this, without that going on behind me.'

By the time they reached the cottage, she was exhausted. She sat there, hooting the horn.

Tom finally appeared. He looked irritable. 'What was all that about?'

'I thought you might have noticed that it was raining. That we might need help getting in.'

'Sorry. I was reading.'

'Well – and oh, God, Tom, you haven't even lit the fire. It's freezing.'

'Of course it's not freezing. Here, give me Minty. I'll take her upstairs.'

'What's for supper?'

'What?'

'I said what's for supper?'

'Nothing. What should there be?'

'Tom! You said you'd get supper ready.'

'Did I?'

'Yes, you bloody well did. It's not much to ask.'

'And I suppose you've had a really hard day,' he said.

'Well, yes, I have actually. I nearly got stopped for speeding. Pattie was in a fearful state about the food, I had to make a speech, we played an endless game of cricket, the rain driving over here was frightful . . .'

'It all sounds terribly hard,' he said. 'I've actually been working, Octavia, I've—'

'Oh, you're so bloody wonderful,' she said. 'Coming today, joining in, would have been far more like work, I can tell you. Writing a few memos, making a few marketing documents . . .'

'Damn,' he said, looking down, 'bloody child's put chocolate on my shirt.'

'How terrible for you!'

'This is new,' he said, 'I only got it yesterday, cost me a fortune from Paul Smith, it's—'

'And don't start going on about your wretched clothes,' she said. 'I am so tired of hearing about them. I don't go on about my clothes half as much as you do.'

'Oh, shut up,' he said, 'just shut up, will you? You're so bloody sanctimonious, Octavia, you really are—'

And then he stopped. Stopped dead and stared at her.

'Good God,' he said.

'Now what?'

'We're having a row.'

'What do you mean?'

'We're having a row, an ordinary row, like we used to have, a proper married people's row.'

'So?'

'So don't you think that's rather good?'

'No,' she said sulkily. 'What's good about it?'

'It means we're back to normal.'

'Oh, great!' she said. 'We're having a row and you think that's good. Tom . . .'

He put Minty down on the floor, came forward, pushed her hair back, took her face in his. 'I'm sorry I didn't get the supper ready,' he said. 'Sorry I didn't light the fire. Sorry I didn't come out to help you in from the rain. Now, then. Isn't that nice?'

'Tom, what is this? What's nice?'

'That I'm having to apologise for such ordinary things. It makes me feel really good. Like a normal bad husband.' He grinned at her.

Reluctantly, very reluctantly, she grinned back. 'I'm sorry I was so cross about it,' she said. She reached up and kissed him. She suddenly felt very happy.

'That's all right. Now I'll go and light the fire.'

'Thank you,' she said and turned to go upstairs. She could hear Minty wailing, the twins arguing furiously about what video they were going to watch. She turned; he was staring up at her, his face very serious.

'Octavia,' he said.

'Yes?'

'Am I – am I allowed to say it now?'

'Yes,' she said finally, after quite a long silence, 'yes, Tom, you're allowed to say it now.'